BOOK ONE

Uncertainties

The horse that comes from the road,
The rider, the birds that range
From cloud to tumbling cloud,
Minute by minute they change;
A shadow of cloud on the stream
Changes minute by minute;
A horse hoof slides on the brim,
And a horse plashes within it.

W. B. Yeats: *Easter 1916*

CHAPTER ONE

September 1931

It was a soft autumn day, the golden air luminous with floating silken seeds and spider threads. The harvest fields were every shade of tawny from amber to flaxen; the flaming woods burned without being consumed, like Moses' bush, as if it would be autumn now for ever.

In the hedges, swollen with hips and scarlet haws, the birds stuffed themselves, too frantic with greed to fly up as the ridden horse passed. Solly sneezed in the dust raised by his rhythmic tread. A golden horse in a golden land: the chestnut's name was Roi Soleil, but the grooms could not get their tongues round it, and Polly had bowed to the inevitable. She was golden too: hatless, with the sun bright on her gilt hair, slim and flexible in the saddle, at one with her steed.

It was dinner-time when she rode into the yard at Huntsham Farm. She had not long been the owner of the Morland Place estate, but she had grown up here, so she knew it was the best time to find the farmer at home. She also knew she would be invited to 'tek a bit o' dinner', and that Yorkshire folk did not like to be refused. They did not like to be hurried, either, so she had come prepared to eat and to wait.

Over the normal farmyard odours of manure and straw she caught a sweeter whiff of boiling ham from the open kitchen door. Solly pricked his ears and let out a ripping whinny, as was his way. He was only a youngster, in the process of finding out about life. The whinny announced her arrival and Mrs Walton appeared at the kitchen door, a cloth in her hands, frowning at the interruption. Seeing who it was, she called over her shoulder, 'It's the mistress,' and ducked back in, to be replaced a moment later by her husband, an enormous, bony man, who filled the doorway and had to lower his head under the lintel.

'Now then, Miss Polly,' he hailed her. 'Fine day.' The greeting was cordial, though his face, brown and rigid as wood from long exposure to brutal weathers, could not smile. It was frosted with grey stubble: like most of his kind, he shaved only on a Saturday night.

'It is indeed, Mr Walton. Good drying weather,' Polly offered.

'Aye,' he nodded. 'We've been turnin' this morning, and we s'l cart tomorrow. An' they're cuttin' oats over to Thickpenny.'

He made to come forward to take her rein, but she forestalled him. 'I see you're in your stockinged feet. Don't come out.'

'Ah'd nobbut just tekken me boots off for dinner. You'll coom in and tek a bit wi' us?'

'I'd be glad to,' Polly said. She slipped down from the saddle, and had run up the stirrups and loosened the girth by the time the younger Walton boy, Tom, had got his boots back on and come running out to take him.

He gave her a shy smile. 'I'll put him in the old stable for you and give him a bit o' hay.'

Inside the farmhouse kitchen – the big room that ran the width of the house, in which almost all of the Waltons' living took place – the wooden table took up the central space, flanked by wooden benches, with a high-backed chair at either end. The range under the chimney provided the hot water to the house as well as the cooking, and was never let go out. But despite the warm day outside, it was not unbearably hot in the kitchen: the stone walls were two feet thick, and the wide stone flags on the floor were laid directly on earth.

Mrs Walton – Ruth – hurried over as Polly came in. She was little and thin – farmer's wives rarely ran to fat – but gave the impression of wiry strength; her grey hair was secured out of the way in a tight bun behind and her sleeves were rolled up for action at all times, except at church on Sunday.

'Now then, Miss Polly, what a grand surprise. Sit in, won't you? Dinner's ready.'

Polly took the end place on the nearest bench. The men, who had stood for her in native politeness, sat again. Ernie and Ted, the two labourers, kept their eyes modestly to themselves. This was not just 'Miss Polly from up the Big House', which would have been overpowering enough, but the new owner, who held all their fates in her hands. And she was young and beautiful to boot – inexplicably, frighteningly beautiful. They couldn't begin to think how to address her.

Ancient Walter, the cowman, didn't hold with females, and looked away on general principle.

As Farmer Walton – Isaac – took his place in the big chair at the foot of the table, the only one to meet Polly's eye was his elder son Joe, who gave her a nod and a smile. He had lost an eye and half a leg in France in 1918, but despite his disability, he was a cheerful soul. He nipped about on his tin leg and threw himself into his work with gusto. He counted himself lucky, not only for having survived – the eldest Walton boy, Matt, had been killed at Passchendaele – but for having found a girl, May Gatson, willing to marry him, missin' bits an' all.

May was bringing bowls of steaming potatoes to the table: a red-faced, solid girl whose early beauty had flowered and set, like a wild rose turning to hip. She was the only other female in this overwhelmingly masculine household. The two children she had so far presented to Joe were boys, aged five and three. They were sitting at the end of the table, opposite Polly, where they would be bracketed between their mother and grandmother. The elder boy was too shy to look at her, but the younger gazed in wonder, a crust clutched in his fist ready to do service as a 'pusher', his eyes round and brown under his tow-coloured hair.

Tom returned, hauled off his boots, went to his place, and Ruth Walton took the baked ham out of the oven and brought it to the table. The smell of it was glorious, and Polly, who had been up and about since first light, found her mouth running with anticipation. There were potatoes and a great dish of runner beans, which smelt heavenly too. The men's hands twitched helplessly towards the victuals, and were halted by Ruth's stern look and the words, 'Grace, Father!'

Isaac, a little red from the consciousness of who was listening, spoke the words: 'Bless this food to our use, O Lord, and us to Thy service. An' fill our hearts with grateful praise, an' keep us always mindful of others, for Christ Jesus' sake. Amen.'

And then Ruth started carving and the plates started going round, and the bowls of vegetables were passed, and the jug of gravy, and six men hunched over their plates with the desperate urgency of those who have been up since before dawn doing physical labour. The women minded their manners and made the children mind theirs, but there was no time for talking until the agonising pangs of hunger were assuaged, and Polly knew better than to try to engage anyone in social chit-chat.

Afterwards, May cleared the plates while Ruth went to the oven and brought out an enormous apple pie, baked in a tin two feet square, and fetched it to the table along with a tall enamel jug of custard. After that a vast pot of tea was brewed and brought to the table, along with – in honour of the guest – a plate of oat biscuits. Isaac and Walter filled their pipes and the younger men lit cigarettes.

'Well, now, Miss Polly,' Ruth said, signalling that the social part of the meal was to begin, 'how are you finding it, being back? I reckon it'd seem a bit strange, like, after all them years you were away.'

6

'I'm getting used to it slowly,' Polly said. 'It's not the place – I *was* brought up here.' She felt it did no harm to remind them. 'It's the new responsibilities.'

'Aye, it's ower much for a bit of a lass,' Isaac said.

Walter piped up in his querulous voice, like a creaky gate that always complained and wouldn't be oiled. 'If Master'd wanted th'estate to go to a lass, he wouldn't have left it to Mr James.'

Ruth thought that was plain rude. 'It's not for us to question Master's ways, God rest his soul. And you know right well it were them wicked death duties as changed everything,' she said sharply.

'That's right, Mother,' Joe said, giving Walter a quelling glare. 'If Miss Polly hadn't bought the estate from Mr James, everything'd've had to be sold to a stranger, an' likely we'd've all been out on our ears. So think on, Walter, and don't talk so far back.'

But Walter used the privilege of age to refuse to be quelled. ''At's as may be, but Mr James is the eldest son, and right's right. There he is, living up at th'Place as ever is, and you're tellin' me he's not Master? Well, Ah don't understand it, plain an' simple. If he's not Master, what's he doin' there?'

'You don't understand anything, Wally, so keep a still tongue in your head,' Isaac said. 'Folks as 'ave nowt to say should say nowt.'

But Polly thought, half humorously, that Walter had a very good question. What *was* James doing? When she had bought the estate from him, to save it from being broken up to pay the death duties, he had said he wanted to go off and travel round the world; that he loved Morland Place but didn't want the responsibility of it; that he might come back one day, but only when the gypsy urge had left him and his longing to roam had been quelled.

But since the papers had been signed and Polly had parted with a large chunk of her fortune and shouldered the work and worry, James had seemed able to resist the urge to wander very well. He was apparently quite content to go on living at Morland Place, riding the horses, pottering about on his motor-bicycle, seeing his friends and having them over, just as he had done when Papa was alive and he was heir apparent.

Still, this was not the place to discuss the phenomenon.

'Morland Place has had a mistress instead of a master before now,' she said mildly, 'and flourished all right. And in any case, that's the way things are, so we must all get on with it as best we can.'

'True for you, Miss Polly,' Ruth said firmly. 'Pay no mind to the awd fool. We're right glad and grateful that you came home and rescued us all, and that's the truth, and there's no-one under *this* roof 'at won't give you any help you need to get job done.'

'Hear hear, Mother,' said Joe.

'Ah were on'y sayin' it were a big task, for a lass on her own,' Isaac said belatedly.

'But we're behind you all right, Miss Polly,' Joe insisted.

'I'm very glad to hear it,' Polly said, taking the opening, 'because I want to put a plan to you.'

'Oh, aye?' Isaac said warily.

'I'd like to start a bull club,' said Polly.

It didn't take much explaining – the men had heard of such things – but there was a deal of persuading needed, of which Polly was aware this visit could mark only the beginning. It had always been the habit of dairy farmers to put any male bovine they could get the use of to their cows, just to get them pregnant. They were not interested in the calves: in the nature of things, half would be useless males; the better of the females might be kept as replacements, the rest sold for what they'd fetch. It was the lactation that mattered, and scrub bulls did the work all right, so why bother with anything fancier? 'If it's got 'orns an' balls it's good enough for me,' was the saying.

The bull-club system was one whereby a number of farmers clubbed together to buy a pedigreed bull to serve all their cows, paying a fee per service to cover expenses, with the aim of improving the stock and therefore the quality and quantity of the milk. The Ministry of Agriculture would make a grant of a quarter of the cost of the bull towards this end.

'Of course,' Polly explained, 'I would put up the rest of the initial cost. You know Sir Bertie Parke has a herd of pedigreed shorthorns, and he has agreed to sell me a suitable animal.'

They knew Sir Bertie: he had run tame about Morland Place in his youth, and had married 'their' Miss Jessie – Polly's cousin who had been brought up with her like an older sister. The Parkes now bred horses at Twelvetrees, and Sir Bertie also had a farm at Bishop Winthorpe, where he kept his dairy herd.

'So the bull would belong to me,' Polly went on, 'and the idea would be that all the Morland estate farmers would belong to the club and have the use of it.'

'Ah don't doubt there'd be a sharpish charge,' Isaac said suspiciously. 'You don't get owt for nowt in this world.'

'Yes, there would be a fee – just enough to cover the running expenses. But it would improve the quality of your herd no end. What I want to see is all of you moving towards getting attested, and producing graded milk.'

Isaac scowled. 'More ministry interference,' he grunted. 'Ah don't hold wi' it. We've farmed on this land since the year dot, wi'out any ministry feller tellin' us how.'

'But Grade-A milk sells for at least a penny a gallon more. And your cows will produce more of it, too. They'll milk better, and for longer, and they'll be less susceptible to sickness. Wouldn't you like a herd free of tuberculosis?'

The latest report from the ministry had calculated that the average working life of dairy cows in England was less than half what it should be, because of tuberculosis deaths, and that replacing the losses put an extra threepence a gallon on the cost of milk production. She tried to explain this to Isaac, though it was a tricky concept for a man of no formal education. 'True enough it costs a bit to get to an attested herd and clean milk, but it pays handsomely in the end,' she concluded.

Isaac was setting his jaw. 'Handsomely, is it? Aye, an' Ah don't doubt when Ah get this fancy-work herd all set up, you'll be putting ma rent up.'

'Yes,' said Polly, 'but only by a fair amount. That's the point – to improve all the Morland land, to get the most possible out of it. I'll be better off, certainly, but you will too. It's good for you, good for me, good for the land – good for the whole country.'

'Aye, well, Ah've enough on me hands tekkin' care of me own family. Ah've nowt to do wi' the rest o' th' country. Let it tek care of itself.'

'By all means,' Polly agreed. 'But I'd like to see my estate become a model for estates everywhere. I want to see strong, healthy cows giving rich, grade-A milk. And I've other plans.' She could see she was getting nowhere, but she expected to have to make the argument many times before it was accepted. 'Milking machines, for one thing.'

Isaac looked startled. 'Nay, Miss Polly. Them things are unnatural – downright dangerous. I heerd of a feller got his arm pulled right off wi' one.' Such stories always circulated when any new machinery was proposed.

Joe spoke up. 'I seen one once, when I were at training camp down in Devon, on the farm we were billeted at. It were always breaking down. And the cows didn't like it.'

'Downright cruel, I heard,' said Isaac.

'Those old pre-war machines were crude, but the new ones they're making now are quite different – worlds better,' Polly said. 'I've seen them used on Sir Bertie's farm. The cows don't mind them at all. And the best thing is, the milk goes straight into a closed container, so there's less chance of contamination. And they're so quick, compared with hand-milking.' She had got carried away with her enthusiasm now. 'With one machine and six steadings, a man and a boy can handle sixty cows. Just think!'

Walter scowled. 'Aye, Ah'm thinkin', and Ah can see where that goes: machines tekkin' over men's work. What'll become of the likes o' me? Thrown out on't scrap-heap! Tha s'd be ashamed, Miss Polly, to talk of puttin' men out o' work at a time like this.' He jutted out the wispy white beard that decorated his jaw. 'An' pullin' cows to pieces wi metal fandangoes, wrenchin' their ewers about – unnatural, Ah call it! Tha'd have 'em down wi' felon in no time. And all for t'sake of a bit o' profit! It's not the way thy father would have gone, God rest his soul – the best Master we ever had, and a true gentleman. Understood the land like it were his own child.'

Polly knew it was no use going on. Like water on a stone, she must work away over time. She knew from Bertie that while good hand-milkers were worth their weight in gold, there were plenty of hard-handed, clumsy milkers (she suspected Walter was one), who wrenched the teats so roughly that mastitis – which local farmers called 'felon' – was a common occurrence. Milking machines, Bertie said, had completely eliminated traumatic mastitis from his herd.

When later she rode away again, her mood was slightly less buoyant. Solly, on the contrary, was refreshed by his rest and snack in the stable, and pranced about, shying at birds, falling leaves and sinister gateposts, so she went back a different way, and gave him a good gallop over the stubble to settle him.

The movement and pleasure of it restored her natural optimism. After all, she told herself, she had not expected it to be simple. She had been an innovator before. In New York she had set up a fashion business from scratch, had built it up until at the end she had been a well-known figure in top society, invited everywhere. She had sold gowns to Manhattan's best families – Whitneys and Vanderbilts, Paynes and Duers, Morgans and Rothschilds. And none of that had been easy.

Of course, New York was a place that valued enterprise, and was accustomed to powerful matriarchs, so being female had been no barrier to success. Yorkshire farmers, on the other hand, didn't like change, and they liked women to know their place. She had sold her business when she had married Ren Alexander, an immensely rich and well-connected man, and dedicated herself to his political career, becoming an influential hostess. The Crash had brought that world tumbling down like a house of cards; and though Ren had seen it coming, and safeguarded most of his fortune, he had been killed in an aeroplane accident soon afterwards, leaving her a rich widow with a posthumous son to bring up.

Absorbed with her own sorrows, she had not realised that her father back in England was fading away until it was too late. Then Jessie had written in desperation, to say that death duties combined with the terrible cost of borrowing since the Crash meant the estate would have to be sold. James could not cope at all; could Polly help? So she had come home at last, to a Morland Place without Papa.

He had died without the comfort of seeing her one last time, something that still haunted her conscience. She should have come home earlier, to tell him that she loved him, to tell him she was sorry . . . She missed him every day. She had been his most precious jewel, and he had been her stay and comfort. He had been her home.

Well, she told herself, shaking away weakness, all she could do now was to be the best mistress Morland Place had ever had. From the depth of imminent destruction, the estate should rise like a phoenix to become the pattern of England. And she was not going to let any stubborn, backward-looking farmers stand in her way. She was not Polly Morland, her father's daughter, for nothing! She was going to—

She found she had stopped, her hand checking Solly at some subconscious signal. He blew vibrato from his velvet nostrils in protest, curving his neck and fidgeting his feet, but she held him, looking about her like one waking from sleep. What? What was it?

She was looking at a dry-stone wall, neatly made, holding up the bank where the field was higher than the track. Memory flooded her, and suddenly her throat was rigid with pain. She saw him there, as he had been all those years ago, bare-headed in the sun, his sleeves rolled up to show the brown, lean strength of his arms, his hands white with stone dust, his hair bleached flaxen at the front, his eyes narrowed against the glare as he looked up at her, smiling . . .

Erich, her first love, her forbidden love – for he was a German prisoner of war, and it was her duty to hate him. But gentle, erudite, country-bred, he had taken her untried heart, as he worked about her father's land that long summer, when she was still a girl and the war seemed far away. This wall he had repaired with his skilled, unhurried hands. All around her land there were examples of his work, which had the power to ambush her with memories when she was least expecting them.

He had been taken away to be deported to his own country, and she had been told he had been killed in a riot at the docks. For so very long she had grieved for him, Erich, her lost love, unable even to admit why she was so unhappy, until years later she had met him again in New York and learned that the story had been a lie. But by then she was married to Ren; and Erich was married too, having believed he would never see her again.

She jerked her head away from contemplation of that neat wall, baking in the sun, laid her legs to Solly's sides and sent him on. She must not think of him; he belonged to someone else, and their lives now lay apart. She had promised herself she would not think of him, though there was a hollow place inside her that could never be filled.

Solly settled into his swinging stride as she berated herself. She had enough to do without mourning over the past: a house full of cousins and orphans whom her father had taken in and who now depended on her; the farms to mould in her own way; the factories in Manchester, the shops and the rest of the estate, properties and little businesses, stocks and shares she hadn't even had time to get to the end of yet. It was a huge burden for anyone, but for a woman on her own . . .

Yes, a woman alone: it came to her in that moment that she was lonely, and it seemed an odd thing to say when Morland Place was stuffed full of relatives and servants, and when invitations came from neighbours every day to this or that social gathering. But of all that crowd, the only person who was really hers, and hers alone, was her baby, little Alec up in the nursery; and he depended on her, too. There was no-one to whom she could say, 'Hold this burden for me, just for a moment, while I take a breath.'

Her mind turned, as it so often had, to Lennie, her dear cousin and friend, whom she had left behind in America. He had always been there, ready to help; he would have shouldered the burden, given her advice, help, warmth and support, and never asked for anything in return. He loved her, not as a cousin, but in that way she could not love him, but he had never let it be a trouble to her. She wished suddenly that he were here, now, so that she could talk to him; talking to Lennie was often all she needed to solve a problem.

'When I get home, I'll write to him,' she said aloud. Solly turned back an ear; and even to Polly it sounded good. Yes, she would write to Lennie . . . And wouldn't it be a fine thing if he decided to take a vacation, and make a visit to

14

the old country? Her heart warmed at the idea. She wouldn't depend on it, of course – he would probably be too busy – but it was a fine thought. Anyway, she would definitely write.

It was just a routine flight – but, then, no pilot enters his cockpit believing it will be anything but routine. Not in peacetime, anyway. And Jack Compton had been flying the Imperial Airways Silver Wing service from Croydon to Paris (and the extended Croydon–Paris–Basel–Zürich route in summer) since its inception.

The Handley Page HP42 was an ungainly-looking craft – an unequal-span biplane, with an enormous three-finned tailplane, and four engines, two mounted close to the centre of the upper wing and one on each side of the fuselage on the lower wing. But despite its odd appearance, it was strong, reliable and comfortable. It was the first commercial aircraft to have the pilot's compartment enclosed inside the aircraft, for which Jack and his flight crew were grateful. There were two passenger cabins, one in front of the wings and one aft, with substantial space for baggage and mail amidships, where the engine noise was greatest. The passengers had padded armchairs and large windows from which to enjoy the view, and there was a galley for the serving of food and fine wines by a uniformed steward. It was the most modern way to travel.

Jack was not far from Croydon, with sixteen passengers on board and three crew, when the port lower engine failed. He smelt the smoke first, but had barely time to mention it when he heard the splintery crack, and felt the jar as something inside the housing broke away. A piece of debris, spun out at high speed, crossed his line of sight like a hurtling missile, making him flinch instinctively; his body knew about dodging the hazards of Archie – anti-aircraft fire – even though he tried not to remember the war.

He heard Tony, his young navigator, exclaim, 'Christ, what was that?' The debris struck the propeller of the port upper engine with a terrible screech of abused metal. At once the engine began to labour and chop, vibrating so violently that he did not even wait to see if it would even out. That sort of vibration could rip the wing in half. He shut it down, feeling sweat break out under his hair line, as the old under-fire tension gripped him.

Two engines down. 'How far are we from Croydon?' he shouted over the roar as the remaining engines laboured to keep the heavy craft aloft. With two of them out of action on the same side it was a struggle to keep her level. She pulled like a wounded whale, trying to turn, wanting to dive.

Tony answered. 'Thirty miles, sir.'

'Too far,' Jack said.

'Can we make it to Biggin Hill?'

Jack glanced at the altimeter. Between them and Biggin Hill was the western end of the North Downs. He shook his head. 'I can't get enough height. I'm going to have to put her down somewhere. Better let 'em know at home.'

He heard Guy, his engineer, radio in as he concentrated grimly on staying level, while he and Tony looked out on either side for a suitable piece of clear ground. Kent was not called the Garden of England for nothing: it was heavily cultivated for fruit and vegetables – hop country too. Empty fields were in short supply. Ahead he saw the glitter of the Medway, a silver snake in the afternoon sunshine, to his left the roofs and chimneys of Tonbridge, and beyond them the ground rising towards Sevenoaks, green and wooded hills they could not clear.

The engines laboured; the vibration passing up his arms was making his neck and jaw ache. 'Anything?' he asked Tony. 'Can't be too fussy. We're still losing height.'

'There, sir!' Tony cried, his young voice high with tension. 'What about that?'

Jack saw it. A strip of grass-greenness amid the cultivation – a field recently cleared but not yet planted, he guessed. Rough-looking green; a hedge at the end, but no tall trees; a little village beyond; scattered woods beyond that. Not as flat as he'd have liked, but wide enough and long enough. Probably.

'It'll have to do,' he said. The HP42 was known for handling well at low speeds, and with those vast wings she was a good glider, but the imbalance of the redundant engines was an incalculable factor. But the hills were coming closer. They had no choice. 'I'm going in,' he said.

The earth speeded up, came up towards them greedily, wanting them back: gravity, which had turned a blind eye to them for the past couple of hours, now glanced again in their direction, wondering what they were doing up there. *Wait*, he urged it inwardly. *Just give me a few more minutes.* Lower, lower, the aircraft feeling impossibly heavy in his hands now. They passed over a lane between lines of hedges, sending a cloud of sparrows darting frantically in every direction. For an instant he saw how uneven the ground really was, hummocks and hollows, shallow trenches where some kind of machinery had been dragged along, deep ruts with the distinctive lug marks of tractor wheels. Then it became just a blur. 'Hold on!' he shouted.

The wheels touched down, and the HP42 jolted and bounced, leaping like a flea as one wheel or another went over a hump. He throttled back, the engines whined – his arms were being wrenched out of their sockets. Tony said, 'Christ!' as they hit a bump and leaped ten feet, and Guy said, 'Ow!' They were being flung against the hard surfaces of the cabin.

The vast, long wings that had given her lift were now a handicap. As they hit another bump she tilted violently and the starboard wingtip hit the ground with a horrible splintering sound, leaving a brown gouge in the rough green.

Only her weight kept her from flipping right over. But the impact snapped off another propeller – he saw it fly like a child's rubber-band toy, up and over the wing surface, whirling end over end – and swung her hard round. With a noise like the end of the world, her tail met some unseen object and was ripped away. The craft juddered to a halt, almost flinging them through the windscreen, and from somewhere above Jack's head a gauge in a metal box tore from its housing and fell, hitting his shoulder a sharp blow.

But in his relief he did not notice the pain. He shut off the engines. For an instant the three men sat motionless, staring ahead in silence, drawing carefully those precious first breaths of life miraculously continuing. The earth had claimed them, but kindly this time. Sounds filtered in from the outside, the relentless chirping of birds, some far-off shouts of men hurrying to see what had happened, a dog barking. Smells of hot oil, bruised grass, man sweat. Jack felt his arms trembling, and a great wave of gratitude flooded him that they were safely down and there was no fire – most of all, that there was no fire.

'Better check on the passengers,' he said, and was amazed to hear his voice come out so steady.

Wonderfully, no-one was hurt. The passengers were shaken and there were some bruises and minor abrasions but they were taking it very well, chattering and laughing among themselves in the relief of peril past, insisting on shaking Jack's hand to thank him for getting them down safely. It would be something to talk about at cocktails for weeks to come. The only person making a fuss was a very fashionably dressed lady who had torn her stockings – and they were not art silk at 1s. 11d the pair from Gamages, but the real thing, she would have them know, and from Paris.

After that, it was just a matter of waiting while transport was sent from Croydon for the passengers and their luggage, a separate van for the mail sacks, and a lorry bringing ground crew and an inspector to look at the damage. The HP could not fly, and would have to be dismantled and taken by road to Croydon to be rebuilt.

Jack discussed the incident with the inspector, Anstruther, as they walked round his poor old bus, piecing together what must have happened. It turned out to have been a tree stump that had ripped off her tail. The ground had recently been cleared of an old orchard, the trees grubbed out or felled, the stumps pulled out and dragged off with chains – except for the one the farmer had missed and Jack had not.

'You couldn't have chosen a rougher place to put her down,' Anstruther said.

'Didn't have a lot of choice, sir,' Jack said, unsure whether the inspector was admiring his skill or chastising his careless- ness. The passengers and the cabin steward had gone now, but there was a crowd of onlookers from the village, including a number of small boys who were trying to edge closer in the hope of snaffling souvenirs. A hot and bothered young man had arrived from Tonbridge, representing the press, accompanied by a photographer who was trying to set up a camera and being impeded by the rough terrain and the Croydon ground crew, who would not stop their work to give him a clear view.

Guy and Tony were sitting on the grass on the side away from the crowd, smoking in philosophical silence, and a longing for a cigarette came over Jack. The sun was declining and cool shadows were easing out from the trees to join up with the smoke-blue dusk of autumn. He was suddenly very tired – reaction to the strain of the incident, he supposed. The tussocky grass dragged annoyingly at his weary feet as he tramped after Anstruther. He felt that even one more question would break his heart.

At last, another vehicle was arriving – he could see its

upper part above the hedge, trundling along the road towards the gate.

'Looks as though your limousine's here,' Anstruther said whimsically. 'You and your boys can go on back. I'll stay with the ground crew. We'll talk again later.'

Jack was glad to go, feeling that if he didn't sit down soon he might fall down. He was amused to see that the vehicle they had sent for him, Guy and Tony was an old Crossley, the transport every RAF pilot knew intimately from wartime, after the hundreds of jolting miles they had travelled in them, criss-crossing northern France from station to base and base to station. It was somehow rather comforting to see one again.

It seemed a very long time afterwards – weeks, even months – that he pulled into his own front drive. It was late, dark, and the lights of the house glowed welcomingly from behind drawn curtains. Helen came out of the front door and went to open the garage for him. The dogs, Stalky and Captain Midnight, sat on the doorstep with the lighted hall behind them. Stalky's whole mien was alert, ears pricked and stump tail switching under him, but the Captain was overcome with an enormous yawn, then hoisted a hind leg for a leisurely scratch under his chin.

Jack drove into the little timber-and-tarpaper garage they had had built last autumn, set the handbrake, turned off the engine. He climbed out, aware that stiffness had set in during the drive home, and tried hard not to limp. Changing position brought the bruise on his shoulder jangling to life. He and Helen closed the doors together, which left him standing right next to her, close enough to read everything in her face. It was an old story and he knew all the words.

'I'm sorry,' he said.

'You must be hungry.' She was trying to sound normal.

'Starving,' he agreed.

'I've kept supper warm in the oven for you.' She continued to examine his face with a searing look. 'You're not hurt?'

'Only bruises,' he said. 'And wrenched muscles.'

She relaxed a little. 'Come on, then,' she said. 'Supper first, then arnica.'

'I suppose a large whisky-and-soda doesn't feature in your programme?'

'You can get that yourself while I dish up,' she said.

The dogs stood to let them pass. Stalky went up on his hind legs just as Jack stooped his hand towards him, so that hand and hard curly head met halfway in a practised movement. Helen shut the door behind them, and the familiar warmth and smell of home closed around Jack as he headed for the dining room and the drinks tray while Helen went to the kitchen.

Helen watched him across the dining-room table as he consumed steak-and-kidney pie and whisky-and-soda, her own drink untouched before her. She would ask him no questions while he ate, but his tired mind ticked and jumped anyway over the memories of the incident, like a roulette ball bouncing from number to number on the wheel but not fully engaging with any of them. Her expression was brooding. He knew it was hard for her. All through the war she had waited, never knowing if she would see him again. But this was different, surely. It had turned out all right, after all.

He laid down his knife and fork. In the quietness the click of metal on porcelain was too loud. 'You're not going to nag me, are you? I'm too tired.'

'I'm not going to nag, but we are going to talk about it,' she said implacably.

'I wasn't hurt. Everything's all right,' he tried pointing out.

'It *isn't* all right.' She examined his face across the table, seeing him in clear and minute detail in the way that doesn't often happen when you've been married for a long time. Jack Compton, DSO, DFC, Air Ace, hero of the war, the man she loved, father of her children; not so young and dashing now, but always her love, her dear husband. His hair was greying and receding from the temples, and he looked tired to death, but they had to have it out. She had been a flyer herself: she knew too much.

'It's always something. Last year it was the R101—'

'I wasn't even on board,' he said, trying to sound reasonable.

'But you should have been.' He had been prevented at the very last moment from taking the doomed flight. 'They burned, Jack! They burned up! Don't you think I replay that in my mind over and over? In the war, it was the thing I dreaded—'

He stopped her by putting his hand over hers across the table. 'It was what we all dreaded.' He had seen men – friends – jump to their death from thousands of feet up rather than burn. 'Today, when we came down, all I could think was, would she catch fire? But she didn't. I'm all right, darling, truly I am.'

'Well, you may be, but I'm not,' Helen said.

Under the table, Stalky, sitting pressed against Jack's legs, sensed his mistress's distress and whimpered.

'You're forty-five,' she went on. 'I know that's not so old, but flying's a young man's game. It always has been. I think it's time you took a ground job.' It had been hard for her to say it, and she tried not to see the hurt in his eyes. She knew what flying meant to him. 'You enjoy the design and engineering side too. You've so much experience and talent to contribute. And it doesn't mean you can't fly any more,' she added pleadingly. 'We can fly at the weekends, for fun. We might even buy a little two-seater of our own. Wouldn't it be better to fly for pleasure, instead of this commercial grind of back-and-forth every day?'

'You don't understand,' he said bleakly. But she did. His youth, his pride, all he valued in himself, his very identity were bound up with flying – the first and perhaps greatest love of his life. To give up flying was like an admission that the best part of his life was ended, that he was over the hill, on the downward slope towards death.

Now she took his hand. 'It's time, Jack. For me. And the children. Don't think of it as the end. There will still be fun and challenge and adventure. But not this. I can't bear to see you drive off to work one more morning, not knowing if you'll come back.'

He sighed deeply. 'I know it's hard on you,' he said. And when she drew breath to speak again he said, 'I was offered a job recently, as it happens. A ground job.'

She was surprised. 'When?'

'Last week.'

He finished his drink, and she took the hint and went to refresh his glass. Then she sat again and said, 'Tell me.'

Airships had had a chequered history in Britain, and had never been successfully developed for commercial use, but the Germans had managed to run reliable passenger services with them. Rivalry was not the only thing on the government's mind, however, when it had put the R100 and R101 schemes into action. Britain had an enormous and far-flung empire, and needed quicker means of communication than the sea. Aeroplanes hadn't the capacity: airships seemed to offer the solution.

The R100 was to be built by a private firm and the R101 by a publicly owned consortium: that way, it was thought, there would be healthy competition that would produce innovations. The Capitalist Ship and the Socialist Ship, they had been dubbed. Jack Compton had been hired by the air ministry to liaise between the two. As a reward he had been booked on the inaugural flight of the R101 in October 1930, but had slipped from a ladder during a last-minute check of the engine-rotation mechanism and cracked his head on the concrete. He had been taken to hospital with a concussion, while the R101 took off without him to meet her fate outside Beauvais.

The loss of the airship, and particularly the death in the inferno of all but a handful on board, so shocked the nation that in December 1930 the government had cancelled the whole airship project for good. It was particularly hard on the private company, the Airship Guarantee Company of Howden in Yorkshire – a subsidiary of Vickers – whose R100 had safely carried passengers and cargo across the Atlantic to Canada and back. But airships were out of fashion. The company was closed down, and its staff faced unemployment.

Two of them, Arthur Hessell Tiltman, a designer, and Nevil Shute Norway, stress engineer, had refused to accept their fate and had started up their own aircraft-building company, using as many of the old employees as possible. They persuaded the Yorkshire banker and racehorse breeder Lord Grimthorpe, the wealthy solicitor A. E. Hewitt, and air ace Sir Alan Cobham to put up enough money to make a start. In February 1931 they rented half a bus garage in Piccadilly, York – six thousand square feet – for their works, and in March they officially set up the company as Airspeed Limited.

Jack had heard about it from his old friend Geoffrey de Havilland, who had been taking a fatherly interest in the fledgling company. Tiltman and Norway were former employees of the De Havilland Aircraft Company, which they had left to join the Airship Guarantee Company; Cobham had been one of its test pilots.

'I sent them a telegram with my good wishes on the founding of their company,' he wrote to Jack in April. 'They haven't managed to get together a great deal of money yet, so they're going to start on a glider until they're more settled.'

When they met in July at an Aero Club get-together, however, things were looking up. 'Cobham's put in an order with Airspeed for three ten-seater ferries for his National Aviation Day company,' de Havilland told Jack. 'It's an excellent start for a small concern. In fact, I rather think they might start taking on more staff. I have my doubts whether Tiltman can do everything himself. Norway's an excellent calculator and stress engineer, but he's never been much involved in engines.'

At that point he had looked at Jack rather penetratingly, but Jack had not made anything in particular of it. Interested though he was in anything aeronautical, it happened that he had domestic problems on his mind: his son Basil was in trouble, not for the first time, at his school on the Sussex Downs. At the end of the summer term, a letter had come requesting that Basil should not return to the school in the autumn. He had, in fact, been 'sacked' for persistent smoking, not only in the dorm but in the chapel vestry, which was by way of being the final straw after all his previous misdemeanours. The headmaster said he was a bad example to the younger boys. Basil seemed to find the situation amusing, and Jack was forced to take a strong line with him, which he did not at all like doing. Then there was the question of finding another school, and – more urgently – of how to keep him out of trouble over the summer.

The latter problem was solved by a fortunate invitation from the parents of a school-fellow to spend six weeks with them at their estate in the Highlands, shooting, fishing and stalking. Evidently they had not heard about the sacking.

'They can't know what they're taking on,' Helen said.

'I've hardened my heart against them,' said Jack. 'I'm accepting right away before anything happens to put them off.'

'He may not want to go. You know he's not a great one for the outdoors.'

'I shall take a firm line,' Jack said.

And he did. 'Basil, I want no argument from you. And if you do anything to get yourself sent home before the summer's over, I'll lock you in the attic on bread and water until school starts again.'

But, oddly, Basil was keen to go. 'And you needn't worry about Mr and Mrs Stokesby, Mum,' he told Helen later, when she was looking out clean linen to pack for him. 'Stoky's every bit as bad as I am. Worse. In fact, I fancy they want me to exert a calming influence on him. He's a shocking one for getting into scrapes at school.'

Helen shuddered. 'My consolation is that there can't be much you can damage in Kinlochleven.'

Basil lounged against the doorpost, hands in pockets. His mother thought how annoyingly handsome he looked, and older than his fifteen years. How could Jack and I have given birth to this charming reprobate? she wondered.

'I thought damaging things was the whole point – salmon, red deer and whatever wretched birds they pot away at up there. But don't worry, Mumsy. I intend to use the time quite virtuously, learning to shoot.'

'Why?' Helen asked, arrested with suspicion.

He grinned. 'Oh, because I've learned enough to know a man must be a good shot to get invited to the best houses, and I intend to be invited nowhere but the best when the time comes. I mean to be comfortable.'

'Well, just don't shoot anything you're not supposed to,' Helen said, laying folded shirts into the trunk with 'G. E. B. COMPTON' stencilled on the lid. Basil was his third name, but somehow he had never been called anything else. 'And don't set fire to anything.'

With Basil safely out of the way, the younger two, Barbara and Michael, were no trouble at all. Barbara, fourteen, went on bicycle rides and to picnics and tennis parties; eleven-year-old Michael disappeared into the woods with the dogs, his village friends and a sandwich in the morning and came home grimy, tired and happy at tea-time. So Helen felt she had nothing more to worry about.

Until Jack's accident.

'What *is* this job?' she asked him.

'It's with Airspeed,' he said. 'Design engineer. They're expanding and the board asked Geoffrey de Havilland for advice and he recommended me. I had a letter from them last week. It'd be interesting work, all right, and it's always fun to be in at the beginning of something.'

'Then why didn't you tell me?' Helen asked.

'Because I wasn't going to take it,' Jack said. He looked uneasy. He had never kept secrets from her and should at least have shown her the letter. The truth was he hadn't even wanted to think about it. 'I have a job, a good one, and I'm happy with it. Why should I change?'

'Because aeroplanes crash. There are stories every week. And one day perhaps your luck will run out. Jack, this could be your chance to start a new career, one that won't keep my heart in my mouth half the time. And you love designing!'

'It isn't as straightforward as that,' he said. 'They're a new company, still finding their way, so they can't pay a great deal. I have a good salary with Imperial Airways – it would be a lot less with Airspeed.'

'How much less?' Helen demanded. He told her. It was a bit of a shock. She rallied. 'We'd manage,' she said. 'We've managed on a lot less than that in the past. We don't need a big house like this one, and we could get by with fewer servants.'

'And the other thing is, we'd have to move,' Jack said. 'Airspeed is in York.'

Helen began to laugh. 'Darling!' she protested.

'But I thought you liked this house, and the area,' he said.

'I do! But York? It's your home! We'd be near Morland Place. Best of all, we'd be near Jessie and Bertie.' Jessie had always been Jack's favourite sibling, and now she was the only one left: Frank had been killed and Robbie had died in the war. 'And the children will be able to see their cousins. And there are good schools in Yorkshire.'

Now Jack began to smile. 'Schools where Basil is entirely unknown,' he suggested. He reached across the table for her hand. 'Would you really be willing to move, have a smaller house, live on a lot less money?'

'You know I've never cared about luxury. The thing is, would you be happy doing this job?'

'It would be fun working with the old Howden team, and getting something going from scratch,' he said, with perhaps the gleam of a light in his tired eyes. 'But I'd miss flying.'

'You could still fly. There are lots of airfields around York.' She gave a mischievous smile. '*I* might even get a job – you know, delivering aeroplanes, like I did in the war.'

They talked on, going over the pros and cons, while the dogs dozed at their feet. Helen saw Jack grow animated, despite his weariness, and knew it would be all right. It would be an upheaval to pack up and move, to find a new place and settle in, but most of that burden would fall on her shoulders. And at the end of the turbulence they would be in a good place. Though his surname was Compton, Jack's mother had been a Morland, and he was a Morland at heart. And what all Morlands really wanted was somehow to get back to Morland Place.

CHAPTER TWO

'Mummy, did you see this piece in the paper?' Robert said, as he came in, bringing with him the smell of buses on warm days – cigarette smoke, a hint of diesel oil, and that curious undertone of dusty upholstery. Violet, Dowager Countess of Holkam, had grown used to buses, since taxis had become an unaffordable luxury, though she had never yet managed to venture down into the tube. Robert worked in Holborn – it still hurt her to think of her son, the earl, having a *job* – and their little house was in Lancaster Gate, just across the road from Hyde Park, where the great old trees were sporting their September colours. The tube was more direct, but buses were pleasanter when the weather was fine.

'What piece is that, dear?' she asked, noting that his hair needed cutting. She supposed it was because he was mixing with 'artistic types' in the world of publishing.

'On the obituaries page,' Robert said, folding open *The Times* and slapping it into a manageable quarter-size.

'I haven't read it yet,' Violet said, taking it with faint reluctance. The fact was that she hardly read the newspaper, these days. The news was so depressing. And since her husband's bankruptcy and sudden death two years ago, she had become almost nervous of seeing which of her acquaintances had encountered bad luck or the Grim Reaper.

'It's about our friend Fellowes,' Robert said, poking the page with a helpful finger.

'Lord Tunstead,' Violet corrected automatically. Avis Fellowes had assumed the cadet title of the earldom last November when his elder brother had died childless in a motor accident.

'Well, he's not Lord Tunstead any more,' Robert said. 'His father's died, so he's the Earl of Belmont now.'

Violet stared at the page without seeing the words. She had no need to read any of the details. Lord Belmont had been very old, and had been frail for some time, and the last time she had seen Avis he had said he was afraid the old fellow would not last much longer. Her thoughts were, first, sadness for Avis, who had been fond of his father; but second, a wonder, which she was slightly ashamed of, about how this would affect her.

Robert's voice continued with cheerful unconcern: 'I don't suppose we'll be seeing much of him for a while. He'll be so busy sorting out the estate, he'll hardly have time for anything else. Of course, we have no idea what condition the estate's in, have we? Or how those wretched death duties will affect him.'

Violet made vague sounds of agreement but she was not really listening. She was thinking of Avis, his cheerfulness, his warm interest in her. When she had first met him, he had been only a younger son, while she had been a countess, a leader of society, dispenser of valued invitations, so there was every reason for him to be attentive. But she had felt even then that it was more than that.

After the shame of bankruptcy had hurled her and her family into obscurity (it was only thanks to her brother, Oliver, who had lent her the little house and provided a small pension, that they were not destitute), Avis had not deserted her. He had sought her out, and shown her and her four children friendship and consideration that had done much to ease their exile.

Now he had come into the earldom, and what would that

mean? As Robert said, he would be horribly busy for a long time – winding up estates of that sort could take a year or more. And, of course, his life would change: he would have new duties, concerns and occupations, and it would not be surprising if Violet slipped out of his mind.

This realisation brought home how important he had become to her. It was many years since she and Holkam had had more than a polite relationship; her lover, the painter Laidislaw, had died on the Somme; her lifelong friend and confidant Sir Freddie Copthall, who had squired her when Holkam was otherwise engaged, had married six years ago and disappeared from London life. It had been years now since she had had any man to talk to; even longer since she had known anything like love.

She was forty, and perhaps ought to be resigning herself to old age, but she was painfully aware – now, when it was too late – that Avis had been coaxing into life feelings she had thought long dead. From lifelong habit she kept an impassive face and showed nothing to her son, but inwardly she was quivering with dismay and longing. She didn't *want* to be alone, always alone. She wanted Avis to be near, and smile at her, and look at her in the way that made her feel alive again.

'I'm sorry, dear, what did you say?' she said faintly, aware Robert was still talking.

He sat down opposite her in an impatient movement. 'Oh, Mummy, please do listen! It's important.'

'Yes, dear. I'm listening now. Carry on.'

'I was saying that I had a long talk with Lord Oldham at the House last night about how I'm not really happy in publishing.'

'Aren't you?' she said in surprise. Oliver had got Robert what he called 'a comfortable billet' as a junior editor at John Gaunt and Staveley. Though it was a job, publishing was at least a gentlemanly business, and it was something that someone with no training or qualification could enter. 'Of course,' she said, trying to pin down his objection, 'it doesn't pay very much—'

'It's not that – though of course salary matters,' Robert said. 'Not immediately, perhaps, but sooner or later I shall want to marry, and as far as I can see, I'm never going to be pulling down enough at Gaunt's to support a wife.'

'But other people must do,' Violet began doubtfully, aware that Robert had not found it easy to be suddenly poor.

Robert waved that away. 'More to the point, it's not what I want to do for the rest of my life,' he went on. 'The work isn't really interesting to me.'

'I didn't know you had any particular interests,' Violet said. 'What do you *want* to do?'

'I want to be in politics – that's the only thing that matters, these days. Lord Oldham said I was the sort of chap they wanted. And the thing is, Mummy, that his son, Malcolm Failsworth, is an MP, and he needs a political secretary. It wouldn't carry a very good salary to begin with – hardly more than I'm getting now – but it would be the perfect way for me to learn the ropes, and make useful contacts.'

'But, darling,' Violet said, perplexed, 'you're already in the House of Lords.'

'Yes, but not in the government. Oldham says that in a couple of years I could get a junior ministry, and then – well, there's no knowing how far I might go. I might be prime minister one day.'

'Do you *want* to be prime minister?'

'Perhaps. But if not, there are other things – a governorship, you know, would be very comfortable. And all sorts of business opportunities would become open to one – directorships and so on,' he added vaguely. 'At any rate, politics is the place to be, not mouldering away in a backwater, nothing more than a wage-slave.'

'*Wage-slave?* Where did you learn such an expression?'

'Oh, that's what people call nine-to-fivers, wretched chaps who go back and forth on the trains every day to a job that will never lead anywhere. I don't want to be like that. I'm the Earl of Holkam! I know it's just an empty title now, without money or land, but it needn't always be. I want to make it count again – for Papa's memory, if nothing else.' He gave her an intense, worried look, and she was touched by his earnestness. 'And, Mummy, the world's becoming a more dangerous place. Communism, socialism, Fascism, anarchism. War. I want to have my hand on the levers of power so that I can *do* something about it.'

'Bravo! What a speech! Is that what you mean to give on the hustings?' said a new voice from the doorway. Violet's second son, Richard, stood there, looking handsome and a little ruffled from whatever motor-car he had just been driving, his gloves in his hand and a rather wilted rosebud in his lapel.

Robert frowned. 'How long have you been listening?'

'Just long enough, not a minute longer,' Richard assured him, grinning. 'Communism and Fascism and so forth. "My Country, 'Tis of Thee." Brought tears to the eyes.'

'Oh, you never take anything seriously,' Robert said crossly.

'On the contrary, brother dear. I just show it in different ways. So you're going into politics?'

'I've been offered an opportunity,' Robert said, trying for dignity. 'The thing is, Mummy, what do you think Uncle Oliver will say? I don't want to offend him, after he went to so much trouble to get me a place.'

'He won't care a bit,' Richard answered for his mother. 'You know Uncle Olly – he's all for people doing what they want to in life. Besides, we might need someone with inside knowledge when the revolution comes.'

'Darling, don't talk like that,' Violet said. 'There isn't going to be a revolution.'

'What? With all these "isms" stalking the streets? It'll be "*À la lanterne!*" before you know it. Being stony broke won't save us. We'll need Robert to guide us poor aristos to the secret dug-out under the Houses of Parliament before the Red mob catches us.'

'You can laugh all you like,' Robert said loftily, 'but I'd like to know what *you*'ll be doing to protect our way of life.'

'Haven't decided yet,' Richard said easily. 'I'll have to keep an eye open for where my talents are best suited.'

'What talents might those be?'

'Being able to drive isn't a bad start,' Richard said. He had secured himself a job demonstrating and selling expensive motor cars for a firm in Mayfair. They had recently added motor-hire to their business, so he was called upon a couple of times a week to drive a party in one of the larger models. 'In any revolution, they always need drivers. The first thing Stalin did was requisition a motor-car, and he didn't drive himself, you know. What time is dinner?'

'Any moment now,' Violet said. 'Are you going up to change?'

'It's just us, isn't it?' Richard asked. 'Then I don't think I'll bother. I say, I got an enormous tip today.'

'A *tip*?' Robert said, injecting the largest amount of scorn he could into the short word. 'A gentleman doesn't accept tips.'

'I don't think that particular old buffer saw me as a gentleman, more like a sort of favourite nevvy. I drove him about and let him jaw me about the war, and by the time I dropped him at home, I think he thought he'd been visiting me at school, you know, so an avuncular tip was just about *de rigueur*. He patted me on the shoulder, called me "my boy", and thrust a five-pound note into my hand before he tottered off.' He displayed it with a cheery wave.

Robert stared at it, feeling a little sick. Five pounds was a week's wages at Gaunt's. Richard always had all the luck. 'What are you going to do with it?' he asked.

'I thought I'd give four pounds to Mum for my keep,'

Richard said, 'and keep a quid for myself, for those little extras that make life worth living. I intend to blow a couple of bob this very evening, taking a pretty girl to the pictures.'

'Another of your young women?' Robert said, trying to sound withering. As a matter of fact, he was jealous of the way Richard's devil-may-careity – not to mention always having a fine motor-car at his disposal – attracted females.

'Can I help it if they throw themselves at me?' Richard said airily.

'They're always rich girls, I notice,' Robert complained.

'Of course. If *they* have money, I don't need to have it – that's just common sense.'

'And you seem to have a different one every week.'

'Well, as a matter of fact, I've had this one for a long time,' Richard said. 'I thought poor old Charley was looking awfully glum this morning. Greta Garbo's on at Marble Arch, and there's nothing more cheering than watching Garbo being moody and mysterious.'

Violet smiled at that. No matter how flippant he pretended to be, Richard had a warm heart. 'You're a good brother,' she said. It was true, Charlotte had been rather downhearted lately. It was hard at nineteen to find yourself shut out from the pleasures enjoyed by all the other young women you had come out with.

'I'll take you, too, Mum, if you like,' Richard offered, with a grin.

'No, thank you, dear,' Violet said. She was still too much the Countess of Holkam to queue up outside a picture palace, or sit in the crowded dark next to Heaven-knew-who. If truth were told, she had only the haziest idea who Greta Garbo was.

Charlotte was grateful to her brother for breaking the monotony of her life, but she didn't understand his insistence that she 'dress up a bit'.

'For the cinema?' she queried.

35

'And put on a spot of lipstick,' he added firmly. 'I really can't be seen in public with a dowdy, my dear girl – I have a reputation to keep up.'

She went to change, and her reward was the approving squeeze he gave her arm as they went out of the front door.

The sight of Greta Garbo coming from a poor home, struggling against adversity, running away to a circus, becoming a fallen woman and ending up with the man she loved was very cheering, and Charlotte managed to lose herself completely in the slightly improbable story, and even fell half in love with the leading man, played by Clark Gable.

'He's MGM's new man,' Richard told her, as they left the cinema. 'They're going to make a big thing of him – he's just done something with Joan Crawford, which ought to make his name. They only give Crawford to their special pets.'

'How do you know such things?' Charlotte asked wonderingly.

'Uncle Oliver tells me, of course. He knows all the "movie" news. I bumped into him the other day. I was waiting in the motor on Wigmore Street for my client, and he came out of Harley Street on his way to feed, and stopped for a jaw.'

Oliver had consulting rooms on Queen Anne Street. He was a noted plastic surgeon with an important clientele among film stars.

Richard grinned. 'He said he was hoping Mr Gable would come through his door one day and ask to have something done about his ears.'

'I didn't notice anything wrong with them,' Charlotte protested.

'They stick out. According to Uncle, the head of the studio said they made him look like an ape. But I suppose you women must like something else about him.'

Charlotte thought it was rather cheering to be called a woman by her older brother, and so did not argue with him. He had, after all, taken her to the pictures, and not the cheapest seats either; and now he had hailed a taxi. She stepped in, feeling instantly smarter, and inhaled the wonderful fragrance of leather (ignoring the hint of stale cigar in the background), which reminded her, more poignantly than any other scent, of better days.

'Where are we going?'

'I thought you might like to dance a little, even if it is only with your brother, so I'm taking you to the Kit-Cat.'

'Oh, Richard, really? You are a darling! And I don't mind dancing with my brother, not a bit, as long as I dance.'

He smiled. 'I might even be able to do better for you, if we bump into some people I know.'

She examined his face. 'You know we will! You've planned it all, haven't you? You're such a sport to do that for me.'

He patted her hand, and said, 'I'm dashed fond of you, old thing. You're not half bad for a sister, dear old Charley. And as a fond brother,' he went on in a different tone, 'there's something I ought to tell you. I did think of holding back on the bad news until later, but there's a chance someone at the Kit-Cat might say something, and I don't want you to be surprised. So, at the risk of spoiling the evening . . .'

She looked alarmed. 'What is it? Come on, you have to tell me now.'

'All right. I've noticed you looking rather blue the last couple of weeks, and I sort of gathered you hadn't heard anything from Amesbury lately. Were the two phenomena connected, by any chance?'

Charlotte looked down at her gloved hands. Rupert Amesbury had been the most promising young man from her come-out, and though she had lost sight of him after her father's bankruptcy, Avis Fellowes had reintroduced him to the family at Lancaster Gate that spring. She had thought they were getting on rather well, and had allowed herself to dream that he might become more than a friend. She had been disappointed that he had disappeared so completely over the summer season, but so many people went out of Town it was perhaps not surprising. She had pinned her hopes on seeing him again in the autumn.

'Has something happened to him?' she asked, in a quiet voice.

Richard noted her hands clasping themselves together as though for comfort, and felt a pang. It was beastly being a girl, he thought, always having to wait for the man to make the move. At least he, Richard, could go out and *do* something about his situation.

'Yes, something has,' he said, 'but nothing bad – or not bad for him, at any rate. The thing is, Charley, that he's gone to Hong Kong.'

'Hong Kong?' She sounded bewildered. It was not what she had expected him to say. She had thought he was going to say he was ill – or married.

'A new posting. And Hong Kong's one of the popular ones, like New York or Paris, so it's good for him. Means the Foreign Office values him. His career's going up.'

'How long for?' she asked.

In the dim light of the taxi-cab he thought her large eyes looked like those of a doomed animal, a cornered deer perhaps. 'Three years,' he said gently. 'And if he didn't tell you – or say goodbye – or anything . . .'

'No,' Charlotte said sadly. 'Not anything.' She sighed, a very small sigh that Richard could hardly hear. 'If his career's going up, he won't want to be pulled down by someone like me, with a bankrupt father in the background.'

Richard took her hand and squeezed it. 'You did care for him, then?' She didn't answer. 'I must say I thought better of him, but if he can drop you just like that for the sake of a—'

'There was nothing between us, nothing – declared. You mustn't blame him,' Charlotte said. 'I expect I read too much into it. One does, you know, when there's only the one. My

38

fault.' She freed her hand and gave her shoulders a little shake. 'Well, that's that. Thank you for telling me. It's best to know the truth.'

'I'm sorry, Charley,' Richard said. 'But you'll meet someone else one day.'

She managed a fairly convincing smile. 'Oh, goodness, don't worry about *me*. I'm in love with someone new now, anyway. What do you think of my chances with Clark Gable?'

'We can't have you marrying a monkey man. I'll find someone better for you.'

'Don't bother. And don't feel sorry for me, Dickie. Let's just have fun tonight and dance. I really, really want to dance.'

'Then dance you shall,' he said. 'We're here.'

'Oh, golly, look at those people going in! All the furs and the jewels! Richard, are you sure you can afford it?'

'I know the manager – we'll get in free. So long as you don't order champagne . . .'

'I just want to dance,' Charlotte said eagerly, her feet twitching in anticipation.

Richard came round to let her out and pay the driver, and was hailed by a shriek from a gaggle of smart young women just arriving with a mixed group.

'Richard! Coo-ee! You came after all! You'll never guess who's here. Teddy Blythe! Sonia says you know him. I couldn't be more thrilled, could you? Oh, you'll die when I tell you . . .'

The coloured lights blinked and the traffic crawled past, the pavements thronged with the young, rich and beautiful, uniformed doormen flung open doors, and the warm night air throbbed with anticipation. The cream of society might still be out of Town, Charlotte thought, but this was lively enough for her, after Lancaster Gate.

It would have been easy for Helen to linger at Twelvetrees, delay looking for a new house. It was supremely comfortable having everything done for her, not having so much as to decide if it should be beef or mutton for dinner. Besides that, it was wonderful to spend time with Jessie and have the leisure to talk all they wanted; and she knew Jack enjoyed Bertie's company, too. It was like a delightful holiday, and Jessie said many times there was no need for them to be in any hurry about finding a place.

But she knew she mustn't get too comfortable; and once she made the effort, it didn't take her long to find a suitable house to rent. It was on the Shipton road, out past the Clifton Hospital. There was a tram stop practically outside, which was handy for Jack for getting into work. She told herself she would soon come to like the sound of the trams running by; though she would have to be careful to keep the dogs from running out.

It was a newish house, semi-detached, built just before the war, and it had electricity – she really hadn't wanted to go back to gas lighting. There were three bedrooms and a servant's room in the attic, and downstairs a dining room and a drawing room that threw into one by means of folding doors. The rooms seemed very small after what they had been used to, and she wasn't sure what Basil would think about having to share a bedroom with Michael when he was home from school; but she reasoned to herself that they could always move again when Jack's position was more assured. At the moment it was comfortably within their budget, and that was what mattered. Once their furniture was in, it would feel more like home.

Michael and Barbara were young enough to be excited simply by the novelty of a new house; and Jack was already absorbed in the job.

'He's loving it,' she told Jessie, when she took her to look round the place. 'It's wonderful to see a spring in his step and a light in his eyes again. That R101 business gave him quite a knock, you know.'

40

'The concussion?' Jessie said in surprise. Surely he must be over that by now.

'No, I meant a mental knock. The fact that they all burned, and he should have been one of them.'

'God, yes!' Jessie said.

'I could see that he'd been quite depressed for a while,' Helen went on, 'so a complete change of scene, and a new, challenging job is just what he needed. I think wallpaper in here will do, don't you? It's quite clean.'

'Yes, if you have the skirtings repainted. They're very scuffed.'

'They'll get even more scuffed with three men in the house,' Helen said cheerfully, 'to say nothing of a new servant. I shan't bother. He's enjoying the company, too.'

Jessie caught up. 'Jack, at work, you mean?'

'It's rather a solitary life, flying a commercial liner back and forth. In his new job he'll be working with lots of other chaps, solving problems together. One of them writes books, you know.'

'Books about aircraft design, you mean?'

'No, actual novels! Nevil Norway's had two published by Cassell as Nevil Shute – Molly told me.' Molly, her sister, was a writer and married to a publisher. 'The first one, *Marazan*, was about a war pilot. It had smuggling and escaped convicts and such jolly stuff in it. It did rather well, and Molly said Vivian wished he'd managed to get it for Dorcas Overstreet. But the second one's terribly political, about the threat of Communism, apparently – quite a different tack.'

'There seems to be all too much politics, these days, without having it in novels, too,' Jessie said. 'How is Molly? I did enjoy *Death's Acres* and *Stone Angels* and – what was her third called? I love a detective yarn.'

'*Black Moss*,' Helen supplied. 'And the new one, *Granite Roses*, is about to come out any time, I understand. I thought it might slow her down, having another baby, but not a bit of it. Angelica was born in the middle of February, and she was back at her typewriter by the end of March. She said she had a deadline to keep. *Granite Roses* had to be delivered on time and that was that.'

'I hope Angelica knew who she was dealing with and kept *her* deadline,' Jessie said.

'Oh, she did!' Helen laughed. 'Nine months to the day. Molly's so efficient, she'd never brook a late delivery. All those years as a secretary during the war. Mind you, she has an absolute marvel of a nanny.'

'Speaking of which,' Jessie said, 'I think you'll have trouble finding the right kind of servants. There's not much unemployment in and around York. And the girls mostly want to go into the factories anyway.'

Domestic service was not covered by the unemployment insurance scheme, so a servant would not be able to claim benefit if she lost her job, as a factory girl would. That was part of the reason; but there were also the long hours and the lack of personal liberty. A factory girl might have to find her own food and lodgings out of her wages and be less well off, but she could do as she pleased when the whistle blew at the end of the day.

'Terry's and Rowntree's probably take up most of the women and girls,' Jessie went on, 'and, of course, the men find plenty of work on the railways, and in the printing works and small factories. And in the building industry, what with the council putting up all these new houses and building new roads.'

'Well, I shan't want any men, anyway,' Helen said. 'These french windows are stuck. Can you push that side while I push this?'

'They only need rubbing down a little,' Jessie said, when they had forced them open. The dogs – Helen's two and Jessie's big Morland hound, Glee – came surging up to greet them, all wags and wet noses and dripping tongues, then ran off again. 'The garden's not a bad size, considering. And

42

I think that's a vegetable bed over there. You'll probably want a gardener.'

'One day a week, at most,' Helen said firmly. 'And I'm going to manage with a cook-general, and a live-out girl, part time, for the heavy cleaning.'

'A cleaner's easy enough, but a good cook-general . . .' Jessie shook her head. 'Still, I don't mean to depress you.'

'You won't,' Helen said. 'I shall take my time and find the right one. It won't kill me to do my own cooking and dusting for a while. I've done it before.'

'You must come and dine with us often. That will ease the strain. Oh, and I can recommend a very good laundry.'

'Thanks. And once the children are back at school, there won't be so much to do. I must say I felt a bit guilty about Barbara, taking her away from her school and all her friends, just at the age when it's hardest to change. I'm not worried about Michael – he's such a happy soul he'll fit in anywhere.'

'But what about Basil?'

'Ah, yes, Basil,' Helen sighed. 'I really must have something decided for him before he gets home. If he's not presented with a *fait accompli* he'll argue, and there's nothing more exhausting than Basil arguing.'

Michael was soon settled at St Edward's, the local grammar school originally founded by the Morlands; and through a recommendation from Lady Chubb they secured a place for Barbara at St Anne's in Scarborough, where Julia Chubb was already enrolled. Barbara had met Julia at a tennis party at the Chubbs' and the two had struck up an instant rapport.

Bertie, urged by Jessie to exert himself and not liking to see Helen worried – for she had been very kind to both of them during the war – came up with a school for Basil in Felixkirk, near Thirsk: a small and very old foundation where a number of boys of good family were boarded in a former abbey. It was not highly academic but it was set in nearly fifty acres, with hunting, shooting and fishing on their own grounds, suitable sports in season, and a programme of cultural activities aimed at turning out a rounded man. It was more expensive than Helen and Jack felt they could afford, but Bertie said he could negotiate a lower fee as he and the headmaster were old friends, and had been at Oxford together.

He drove Jack and Helen down to look at the place, and they liked it, and thought Basil might do well there. The discipline was not so harsh or the regime so hearty as at his previous school on the Sussex Downs. 'I think Basil's too much of a sybarite to settle down to rugger, cold baths and bad food,' Helen said apologetically. 'And he never respected his old headmaster. But Mr Cockburn seems a very intelligent, cultured man.'

'Yes, but with a core of steel,' Bertie added. 'I don't think he'll take any nonsense.'

'God, I hope not,' Jack said. 'The last thing my son needs is a soft place where he thinks he can do as he pleases.'

'Dearest, he did as he pleased at the last place, and you chose it specifically for *not* being soft,' Helen said. 'Perhaps it will work better to go with the grain instead of against it. Music and drama and painting might rub off some of Basil's rough edges and—'

'Soothe the savage beast?' Jack finished for her. He looked at Bertie. 'We're most enormously grateful to you, old man, and I only hope our young savage doesn't ruin your fine old friendship.'

'Oh, Cockburn likes a challenge,' Bertie said. 'And he's a wonderfully civilising influence. He had that young tough of Lord Grey's for two years, and had him eating out of his hand at the end of it.'

'Well, if Basil doesn't settle down at Felixkirk, there's nothing left but the lunatic asylum,' Jack said moodily.

Helen was optimistic. 'We haven't heard a peep all summer,

44

so he must have been behaving himself with the Stokesbys. I think he's reformed.'

Polly sat at the desk in the steward's room, going over the estate books. Outside, the October weather had turned cold and wet, and rain was teeming down from a leaden sky, stripping the leaves, blattering on the window every now and then when the wind gusted. But the steward's room was a haven of peace, with a good fire reflecting a glow from the well-polished furniture and glinting off the brass fitments of her father's desk: the lamp and the vast old inkwell, and the pencil holder made out of an old shell case brought back from the Boer War as a souvenir.

In front of the fire, her father's dogs, the terrier Bigelot and the spaniel Blossom, were spread out luxuriously. Since she had come home, they seemed to have adopted her – probably because, feeling sorry for them, she had taken the time to be kind to them. They followed her about devotedly when she was in the house or out walking, but they couldn't keep up when she was on horseback, and if she headed for the stables they would sit down on their tails in the yard and watch her with expressions of acute disappointment and the occasional blackmailing whimper. They were completely happy at the moment, however, and the only sounds in the room were the ticking of the clock on the mantelshelf, the scratching of her pen, and the occasional moan of pleasure from a toasting dog.

All this harmony was disturbed by a knocking at the door, which opened before she could call, 'Come in,' to admit Maltby, the bailiff – someone else she had inherited from her late father. His job was to oversee the lands and buildings of the estate, collect rents, and to liaise between the master and the tenants, issuing the orders of the one and fielding the complaints of the other.

He was a big man, in his sixties but hale and strong still,

with a square, weather-reddened face topped by wiry grey hair, and strong, old-man's hands, all knuckles and ridged, chalky nails. He wore moleskin breeches and gaiters in every season, and a hefty tweed jacket, which, when brought into a warm place, as now, emitted a strong smell of wet sheep. He always carried a long staff, and was accompanied everywhere by a wall-eyed collie whose cowed demeanour made Polly think that he sometimes hit her with it. As he came in now, Bigelot and Blossom heaved themselves up to approach her with friendly interest, but he nipped her response in the bud with a jerk of his foot and a growled 'Down!' which made the home dogs think better of coming any closer.

It was not precisely wrong of him to come in without invitation, if the servants had told him she was alone in the steward's room, but Polly did not like him – at least partly on account of the collie – so today it annoyed her. Also he had not found it necessary to remove his cap, so instead of smiling or asking him what he wanted, she confined herself to staring at it pointedly.

Maltby was immune to stares. 'Now then, miss,' he said, giving her a sour look in return.

'What is it?' she responded unwelcomingly.

He wasted no time. 'I've had the tenants on at me about this daft scheme o' yourn. Bull clubs and milking machines an' I don't know what.'

'What do you mean?' she asked quellingly. She disliked his grim face, which seemed to want to suck all the pleasure out of life. If ever there were a living example of what it meant to be a 'kill-joy', he was it. He was the sort to water petunias with little children's tears, as the saying was. 'Which tenants?'

'All on 'em. Banks o' Woodhouse, Walton o' Huntsham, Hackett o' Prospect, Jack Pike from Eastfield. All coom to me, radged as 'ell about it.'

'Bellerby?' she asked quickly. The Bellerbys at White House had been particular friends of hers in childhood.

46

'Nay, Seb Bellerby's hauding his hand back, but he don't like it any more'n the others. Fair stalled they are, wi' all this mellin' an' changin'. They want namore of it.'

'And what did you say to them?'

'Say to 'em? What d'you think I said?' He was reddening. 'Told 'em I'd come to you, o' course, and sort it out.'

'Sort it out,' Polly said coldly, 'as in, tell me to drop it?'

'Aye.' He had not seen the danger approaching. 'We've enough on our plates gettin' by these days, leave out muckin' about wi' schemes like this.'

Polly's voice was low and controlled, but she was quivering with anger now. 'So you told them you'd fix me. You sided with them against me. Your job is to explain what I want and help them understand it, then see it is put through. You seem to forget who employs you.'

'Ah've been bailey here thirty year,' he said angrily, his accent thickening, 'an' Ah don't need tellin' ma job by a bit of a lass as knows nowt about owt.'

'I think you do need telling. You would not have dared to talk to my father like this.'

'Tha's not thy faither! He'd'a' known better'n to set fowks about like thee, mellin' wi' their livelihoods like it were a game o' taws.'

'Don't you dare to "thee" me. You forget I am mistress here.'

'Just cos tha's got a bit o' gold to chuck about doosn't change facts. Mr James is Master, now the old master's gone, else why's he still here? Tha's not mistress nor never will be, not while Ah'm bailey.'

'Then it's soon settled,' Polly said, her eyes flashing blue ice. 'You are no longer bailiff. You are dismissed.'

He stared at her, his eyes bulging in his congested face. 'You can't sack me!'

'I just have.' She could see his fist snatching in anger and, just in case, she reached behind her and rang the bell. 'Leave now, please, and never come to this house again.'

'You can't do that. There's laws in this land. Ah'll speak to Mr James about it.' Polly stood up and resumed the silent stare she had begun with. She would not deign to argue with him. 'Ah'll have the law on you!' he cried.

The door opened, and she was glad to see it was the footman, Frederick, who was young and strong, not the elderly butler, Sawry.

'Maltby is leaving now,' she said to him, past the bailiff's shoulder. 'See him out, please. And he is never to be allowed into this house again on any pretext whatsoever, do you understand?'

'Yes, madam,' Frederick said, in his best impassive manner, though Polly thought she saw a gleam of something in his eyes.

Maltby clenched his fists, and grounded his staff with a bang of fury. 'We'll see about this!' he shouted, swung on his heel, and went out, his collie slinking behind him. Frederick followed him and closed the door softly, leaving Polly to savour her triumph and quell her trembling. And when she had, to think with pleasure of getting in a new bailiff, a younger man, perhaps, one with forward-looking ideas. Oh, and she must go and see Seb Bellerby and see what he really thought, and whether the others were as against change as Maltby had said. She wouldn't put it past him to have talked them into resistance himself.

The next day the rain had gone and a hazy, autumnal sunshine returned. The sky was like faded felt; the sliding clouds glided across it like skaters. By the afternoon the paths had dried enough for Polly to take a walk, to clear her head and to comfort her two canine shadows. As soon as they were outside, Bigelot rushed importantly ahead, saying, 'Come along, hurry up, everyone follow me! Where was it we were going?' Blossom couldn't wait to bury her nose, followed by her whole head, in the nearest clump of long grass, and emerged spangled with raindrops and fragments of dead leaf.

I should get a dog of my own, she thought vaguely. 'Big' and 'Bloss' – as James called them – were sweet, but they didn't really count. She had always had a dog, since she was eight years old, until she went to New York, leaving Silka behind. You couldn't have a big dog in a city like that. She hadn't had time to look into the kennels yet, with so much else to do. She must ask James about them – she knew he had kept an eye on them.

She had been walking for about an hour, and the dogs had stopped frisking and settled down into plain travelling, when she heard the sound of a horse approaching, and in a moment round the bend of the path James appeared on Firefly. She was a dark red chestnut, four years old and still full of flightiness, hating to walk if she could trot or trot if she could canter. At this moment she was walking as fast as she could and throwing a high foreleg every few steps. As soon as she saw Polly, her hind end started dancing all on its own in sheer high spirits. Polly stopped in the middle of the path and Firefly almost knocked her over in her eagerness to be sociable.

'I'd only just got her to walk,' James complained.

'You call *that* a walk?' said Polly, caressing Firefly's long silken ears, while the filly nudged and bumped her with her nose.

'After jogging every step of the last ten miles, it's near enough a walk for me,' James said.

'Going home?' Polly asked, looking up at him past Firefly's shoulder. Cut out against the sky, with the low sunshine in his golden hair, she thought he looked very handsome; every inch the young squire in his hacking jacket, breeches and highly polished boots, his hands brown and capable on the reins. He had been away for the night, staying with the Chubbs – Tony, the eldest son, was a particular friend. 'I was just about to turn round.'

'I'll walk with you,' he said, freed his feet from the stirrups and swung down with a quick, lithe movement. It was no wonder all the local girls were mad for him, Polly thought, and felt an odd little stirring of pride that he was her brother. *Half*-brother.

He slipped his arm through hers and they started walking, with Firefly nodding along behind and the dogs, glad to be heading homewards, out ahead. 'I want to talk to you, Pol,' he said, turning on her blue eyes that Polly knew, from looking in the mirror, were very like her own. Polly Blue, that colour was called – her father had had a dress dye made up in the exact shade to sell at his haberdashery store. 'What's all this I hear about you sacking old Maltby?'

'How on earth do you know about that?' she asked.

'Oh, news travels fast in these parts – especially anything to do with Morland Place. It was brought to me with my early tea this morning. And when I passed Twelvetrees coming home, Jessie came out and asked me if I'd heard, so it's got to them as well. What's it all about?'

Polly told him; and James was gratifyingly prompt to her defence.

'Well, no wonder you sacked him. He deserved it. How dared he talk to you like that? I should black his eyes for him. You're a lady, apart from "the boss".'

'Ah, but he doesn't think I *am* the boss,' Polly said lightly.

'What on earth do you mean?' James said.

'He thinks because you're living at Morland Place, that makes you Master.' Firefly inserted her nose between them, and her long lips tested Polly's ear for edibility. She put her hand up to fend her off and the filly mumbled at her fingers instead. 'Old Walter, the cowman at Huntsham, said the same thing. I suppose it *is* confusing for them. And of course they'd always rather have a man for a boss than a female.'

'I see,' said James, frowning in thought. The light wind stirred the loose hair over his brow. 'I never thought about

50

it before, but – is my being here making things awkward for you?' Polly didn't immediately answer, and he said, 'It's been so marvellous, like a holiday, and there didn't seem to be any particular reason . . . But I never meant to make trouble for you.'

'You mustn't think like that,' Polly said. '*I* don't want you to go. Though, out of interest, why didn't you? You said you were longing to travel the world.'

'I was. I am,' James said, perplexed by his own feelings. He was not much given to introspection. 'I suppose it's because – as soon as you took over, all the problems sort of disappeared, and it was, well, as if Dad was alive again, and I could just enjoy being here without the worries.'

She nodded. She understood perfectly. But she had to ask. 'Jamie, do you regret selling the Place to me?'

He shrugged. 'I didn't have any choice, did I?'

'But would you want it back? If you could have it?'

'God, no!' he said promptly. 'What – be Master and have all those people depending on me? I've seen how you work – never a moment to yourself. I never realised while the Old Man was alive how much there was to do. But he was a natural at it, and you're a brainbox, Pol. I know you can cope. You proved that in New York, didn't you? No, I don't regret it for a minute, except that . . .' He paused, frowning again.

'Yes?' she encouraged him.

He looked at her. 'I realise now I've been a cad. Lazing about enjoying myself while you break your heart keeping things going. And, on top of that, now the beastly tenants are telling you you're not mistress. I'm just making your life more difficult for you.'

'No, it's not that,' Polly began.

'It is,' he said forcefully. 'And I'm sorry, Pol, I really am. I never meant to do you harm. But I see now that as long as I'm here there's going to be this problem. Can't expect

51

the lower orders to understand. I've got to go away, and let you settle in and make your mark.'

'I didn't ask you to go,' Polly said.

'I know.' He smiled. 'Don't worry, old girl. It's only bringing my plans forward a bit. I would have gone eventually. And I'll come back in a year or two – if you'll let me?'

'This is your home, Jamie,' she said firmly. 'Now and always.'

'Thanks.' They walked on in silence for a bit as he thought things out.

'Where will you go?' she asked at last, finding the silence awkward.

'Well, I wanted to visit my old pal Pennyfather, down in Wiltshire. I might go and see him first, maybe get work in that racing stables for a few weeks. He's sure to be able to fix it. Then abroad somewhere. I've always wanted to see Italy. I could work my way there, just pottering along, stopping when I felt like it, doing a day's work here and there for my keep.' His voice had taken on enthusiasm as he spoke.

She felt comforted. Yes, there was a genuine dream there – she was not forcing him out. 'You take your time, and make your plans properly. No need to dash off in a hurry before you're ready.'

'Maybe after Christmas, then,' he said. 'I'd like to get some hunting in before I go. And I'll have to think hard about Black Beauty.'

That was what he called his motor-bicycle. 'What about her?' Polly asked.

'I'm not sure if she's up to the job. She's getting to be a bit of a veteran now, you know, and a long trek might just finish her off – especially with the bad roads abroad.'

'What makes you think Abroad roads will be bad?'

'Bound to be, shouldn't you think? I'd hate her to die out there and have to be abandoned. Perhaps I should look at part-exchanging her for something newer and bigger.'

They talked about it a little more – or James talked, and Polly nodded and agreed every now and then, knowing nothing about motorbikes. It was clear to her, if not to him, that she would have to fund the purchase of any new machine, since James had no money of his own, which would be rather like paying to have him go away, and made her feel bad. Her father would not have wanted her to send him away. Perhaps it was up to her to force the people to accept her, whether James was here or not – wasn't that what her father would have said? But if he really *wanted* to go – and he sounded now as if he did – it would certainly make things easier for her in the short run. And he could always come back.

She decided she would not say anything, not press him in any way, and see what happened. If he really did leave after Christmas, well and good. If not, she would have to find a way round it. She sighed inwardly. It was hard to be a woman on her own. Perhaps if James stayed she could make him take some of the responsibility – like a sort of partner. But she knew even as she thought it that it would never work. Morland Place was hers, and only she should decide how it was run. The thought of having anyone go to James for instructions made her set her teeth and stiffen her neck.

'I say, what's the matter?' James asked, interrupting his monologue on camshafts and cylinders. 'You looked so grim just for a moment. Like indigestion.'

'It's getting chilly,' she said. 'Let's walk faster.'

'Better still, why don't we ride? You can get up behind me all right, can't you?'

'We'll be too much for her.'

'Oh, it won't hurt her, for that little distance. And you're only a slip of a thing.'

CHAPTER THREE

Violet had an arrangement to meet Sarah Vibart, her cousin Eddie's wife, for luncheon at the Ritz, and at the last moment Charlotte said she would travel up to Town with her to do some shopping.

'Why don't you join us for luncheon?' Violet asked. 'I'm sure Sarah would be delighted.'

'I'm sure she wouldn't,' Charlotte said firmly. 'It's you she wants to talk to.'

'She'll like to talk to you, too. And then we could shop together, afterwards,' Violet said.

'I thought I might go to the cinema.'

'Alone?' Violet was a little shocked.

'I might or I might not,' Charlotte said. 'Don't fuss, Mummy, please. I'm quite old enough to go about on my own.'

They parted at Marble Arch, where Charlotte walked off down Oxford Street and Violet changed buses for Piccadilly. The trouble with travelling on buses, she found, rather than in one's own motor-car or even in a taxi, was not being able to control the journey time. She arrived early at the Ritz, and since Sarah, unusually, was a little late, it meant Violet was sitting at the table on her own for quite ten minutes.

In the old days she wouldn't have minded – she adored this lovely pink and gold room, with the Italianate frescos, the mirrors, the tall windows onto the park – but since the bankruptcy she felt self-conscious in places like this, where once she had been queen. Fortunately she was shown to a corner table, and sitting with her back to the room, looking out onto the terrace, she hoped no-one would recognise her.

She had been sitting for five minutes and was deep in her own thoughts when two ladies were shown to the table behind her. Just from the noises they made, she knew the type: bird-thin, fashionable women who somehow always reminded her of monkeys, all quick movements and inquisitive, chattering voices, nervously puffing cigarettes and drinking endless cocktails.

She gave a quick, careful glance in the wall mirror over her shoulder and saw it was Veronica Glenforth-Williams and her constant satellite, Nancy Wherring. Her heart sank a little, and she hoped they would not notice her. Both were part of the lively society circle and 'went everywhere'. They were not particular friends of hers – though she had met them at some of Oliver's parties – but she feared their probing eyes and scathing tongues. Fortunately she was sitting right by one of the marble wall columns that divided the mirrors, so unless they recognised the back of her head she hoped she might escape unnoticed.

They seemed, indeed, completely absorbed in their own conversation, and once they had their heads in the menus she began to relax and stopped listening to them, until the mention of a name that meant something to her brought her attention back.

'. . . Avis Fellowes? One never sees him anywhere, these days.' That was Nancy, asking a question.

'Oh, didn't you know?' That was Veronica. 'His father died.'

'Don't tell me! Old Belmont? I thought he was going to live for ever. He was up at Trinity with my grandpa – he must be a hundred and five, that's all!'

'Not nearly so old, darling, but he died, anyway. Popped off – oh – a month ago. It must have been in the paper.'

'I never read the obituaries. Too gloom-making. One's always afraid it'll be someone one knows.'

'Bobby Sutcliffe is such a stitch – he says he never reads the obituaries in case he sees himself in there and finds out he's died without realising it.'

'Scream! I die for Bobby!'

'Me too. Anyway, I don't read the obits either, but I had it from Diana Cooper, who had it from Johnny Rutland, so I know it's true. It's too sick-making!'

'I didn't know you knew Belmont.'

'No, I mean for poor Avis, stuck in the country sorting things out. Derbyshire, I think. Somewhere utterly bogus like that, anyway.'

'What a bore! Poor pet. So he's Earl of Belmont now? I suppose he'll be looking for a wife.'

'He'll have to, that's all. Death duties are too utterly ruinous.'

'Wasn't he sweet on someone last Season? I'm sure I heard he was courting some widow from Kensington.'

'I heard Bayswater. Too shame-making! But a widow's no good for Avis anyway, darling. He needs a young wife – he was the only son, so he'll have to be thinking about breeding an heir.'

'Darling, how frightfully agricultural! Oh, well, I suppose he'll marry one of those American heiresses, then. There's bound to be a new batch when the Season starts properly, so he'll be able to take his pick, and they're always so young and healthy, they give one a frightful pain.'

'Talking of American girls, have you heard the latest about Starr Faithfull?'

'The girl who jumped off the *Mauretania*?'

'Ah, but did she? I was talking to Batchworth last night and he knows someone who knows the doctor who did the autopsy.'

'Too thrilling! What did he say?'

The voices were lowered, but Violet had stopped listening anyway. She reflected bitterly on the adage that eavesdroppers never hear good of themselves. How could she have been so stupid? She had wondered what old Lord Belmont's death would mean when it should have been obvious. Of *course* Avis would have to look for a young wife – and in all probability a rich young wife. She had no idea what state his father's affairs had been in, but death duties were taking their toll of all the great estates. Violet's absolute poverty alone should have told her that she could not now be anything to him; but how much more bitter was it to realise that she would also be considered by everyone to be too old for him, even though they were the same age?

It was fortunate that her thoughts were interrupted by the arrival of Sarah, being shown to the table by the *maître d'hôtel*. 'I'm so sorry I'm late! Have you been waiting an age? There was a domestic crisis that I shan't bore you with.'

Violet managed to smile. 'You're hardly late at all.'

'Bless you for that,' Sarah said, sitting down. She had accorded the females on the next table no more than a nod as she passed. Her husband, Lord Vibart, was an equerry to the Prince of Wales; she was the daughter of the Marquess of Talybont and her mother had been a lady-in-waiting to the Queen. She no more than 'knew' the Glenforth-Williamses of this world, and sometimes deplored Oliver's somewhat catholic tastes. She moved to different music, and Lord Holkam's bankruptcy would never have led her to 'cut' Violet. Blood was everything.

Violet's brother Oliver Winchmore had followed their mother into the medical profession, serving in the RMC during the war. He had become interested in the new discipline of plastics, which had had a rocky start in the twenties: it had been barely acknowledged by the medical fraternity as a legitimate field at all, and none of the great hospitals had plastics departments. Even now, the pejorative 'face doctor' or 'beauty doctor' was still used by the older and stuffier consultants, along with worse insults: Oliver had been called a mountebank and a music-hall illusionist among other things.

But he had seen what a difference reconstructive surgery to the face and hands could make to the lives of terribly burned RAF pilots. Even without the war, there were enough domestic and industrial accidents, not to mention birth defects, to keep him busy; and he saw no reason to apologise to anyone if he amused himself outside that in dealing with oversized noses, disfiguring moles, drooping eyelids and such other features as made people feel uncomfortable about themselves.

He had a thriving practice among movie stars, who came all the way from Hollywood to consult him – a fact that did not endear him to the old guard in the hospital senior common rooms. It annoyed them more than a little that, after the loss of his brother in Russia during the revolution, Oliver had become Earl of Overton and Chelmsford; he had a seat in the House of Lords and the opportunity to influence all manner of things they felt should be left to themselves alone.

The fact of the matter was that he was too young, too wealthy, too high-spirited, too cheerful, too well liked, and far too well versed in the ways of the modern world to be one of that august body of consultants. They ran the medical establishment along nineteenth-century lines, looking down on ordinary mortals in the manner of the great ducal landlords dealing with meek and deferential tenants. It annoyed them almost to apoplexy when they were obliged to send patients to Oliver because there simply was no-one else. Anderson of St Thomas's was an ex-army doctor and Scottish to boot, which put him beyond the pale to begin with; and there had been that string of tonsillectomy children who had all died, which didn't look good. And Nugent of Bart's might be a gentleman, but he was hardly more than an ear-nose-and-throat man who had branched out into a little reconstruction.

Of course, they would always have preferred to send to Nugent rather than to Winchmore, but he only had one pair of hands, and not very gifted hands at that. He might sew together a cleft palate or separate webbed fingers, but the more elaborate reconstructions were beyond him, and he knew nothing about skin grafting, which that damned showman Winchmore tackled with the dedication and delicacy of an eighteenth-century French nun creating a tapestry.

Oliver didn't help matters by persisting in finding the establishment's attitude towards him hilarious, enjoying his work and life enormously, and consorting with famous film stars and other such unworthy people whenever the opportunity arose.

He was in his consulting rooms in Queen Anne Street that morning, signing some letters, and was about to go off to the Winchmore Hospital where he had a list. The John Winchmore Hospital had been founded by his mother so that he would have somewhere to operate, in the days when plastics beds were non-existent. She had named it after his father, which he had always thought a fine and private joke, since his father's nickname had been Beauty, which made it the Beauty Hospital. He referred to it that way in conversation with the stuffed-shirt consultants, which they took to be flippancy, and endeared him to them even less.

He was surprised when his secretary came in to tell him that his niece had called and was asking to see him.

'Alone?'

'Yes, sir.'

He took out his watch. He had five minutes in hand, and if it took longer, so be it. Charlotte had never called here before. Perhaps it was just a social visit, but if she was in some kind of trouble . . .

When Lord Holkam had died, it had been put down as accidental death. Oliver hoped and believed that Violet had accepted the verdict, but he had his own reasons for thinking it was probably suicide. He had never liked Violet's husband, and his plunging his family into bankruptcy had given him a contempt for the man; but he knew other things about him, horrible secrets about his sexual life that he would take to his grave, and he couldn't help feeling Violet was better off without him.

It had not needed a second thought for him to take responsibility for Holkam's family. Now his brother Thomas was gone, and both their parents, there was only him and Violet left, and family was family. He had found her a house, paid her a pension, and he and Sarah made a point of arranging something of a social life for Violet, who otherwise would have mouldered away at home, too conscious of the shame of Holkam's end.

He put away his watch and looked up at his secretary. 'Show her in.'

Charlotte came through the door with a mixture of shyness and determination that he thought adorable – but, then, he was her uncle. He dismissed that from his mind and tried to look her over with a professional eye. In the current taste, which liked little, skinny, boyish women, he could see that Charlotte was too tall and too big-boned for fashion, but she had learned to carry herself as if she liked being tall, not to stoop apologetically as she once had. Her dress – navy blue, with round white collar and cuffs – he recognised with a surgeon's eye as an old one made over, but it had been done with skill. Violet was very good with a needle, and there was nothing that looked 'home-made' about it. Hems were longer this year, down to mid-calf, which was a relief – few women, in his view, could advantageously expose their knees – and the length suited her better. The new shape was close-fitting, with the waist in its natural place, and a slight flaring of the skirt at the hemline, which suited a tall, well-made girl better than the skimpy, shapeless flapper dresses of the twenties. Hats were being worn much higher up, off the face, with an asymmetrical brim and the decoration to the back, and it was usually of a contrasting colour to the dress. Charlotte's was boldly red, with iridescent cockerel feathers at the back. She looked attractive, smart and modern – for which he felt a curious little relief.

'Charlotte, my dear,' he said, getting up and coming round the desk. 'What a pleasant surprise.' He kissed her cheek and stepped back. 'You look very smart. Especially the hat. You're turning into a good-looking woman.'

She blushed a little, but she said, with some self-possession, 'You mustn't flatter me, Uncle Olly. When one grows up with a beautiful mother, one is under no illusion.'

'I wasn't flattering,' he said. 'I meant it. Your mother has one sort of looks; you have quite another.' It was true. Violet was like a porcelain shepherdess, delicate, exquisite. But Charlotte, now she had grown into her features, was becoming distinctly handsome. Her eyes were blue and well shaped, and she had inherited her mother's thick black hair, which curled attractively from under the brim of her hat. 'You have to believe me,' he added, with a smile, 'since I'm an expert. Come and sit down, and tell me to what I owe this pleasure.'

Charlotte sat – he recognised her mother's training in the way she moved – and he perched on the edge of the desk beside her to put her at ease. 'There's no trouble, I hope?' he invited, studying her expression.

'Not really – not exactly,' she said. She folded her hands in her lap and took a breath. 'I wanted to ask you a favour. Really quite a big one, so I hope you don't think it's an awful cheek.' She looked at him seriously, part hopeful, part fearful.

'I suppose I'd better get my cheque book out,' he said lightly. 'How much is it this time?'

He was joking, to put her at her ease, but she blushed again and said, 'It will cost some money, but it isn't that, really. It's persuading Mummy – you see, I know she has some money put away for me, but she might not like it to be spent this way, though of course I'd hope to be able to pay it back eventually. Oh dear, and she always says it's terribly vulgar to talk about money!'

'My sensibilities have been coarsened by my profession,' he said cheerfully. 'They resemble pumice stone by now, so you can say anything to me. Just tell me what it is you want, and we'll go from there. Come on, Charley, old thing – how bad can it be? No niece of mine would want to do anything really shocking.'

She gave a small smile. 'I sort of hoped *you* wouldn't think it was, but I'm afraid Mummy will. You see— Well, I'd better come to the point.'

'That would seem like a good idea, if you want me to understand what you're talking about.'

'Uncle, don't tease! I want to take a secretarial course.'

It wasn't what he had been expecting. He sat up straighter. 'Good God! Well, I can see why you'd think your mother won't approve. What's behind it?'

He half thought she might confess to some crush on a man who ran a secretarial school, but was shamed out of his flippancy when she said seriously, 'I can't stand doing nothing any more. I'm at home all day, and I help out a bit, dusting and so on, but it's not enough; and frankly, I can't see that it even matters whether I dust the drawing room or not. It doesn't alter the fate of nations, does it? And in the long run, what's going to happen to me? Mummy's still thinking the way she did when Papa was alive, that I've only got to sit around looking well brought-up, and an earl's son is going to come and ask for my hand. But things have changed.'

'I'm sure your mother knows that.'

'But she *doesn't*, Uncle. Oh, yes, she half knows it may

62

not be an earl's son any more, but she still thinks *someone*'s going to come and rescue me. She can't see any further than me being married and provided for.'

'It's what most girls do,' Oliver said, but he was looking at her with sympathy. He was realising at last – *really* realising – what an awful bind a girl like her would find herself in when the name and the money disappeared.

She looked up at him seriously. 'There aren't enough men to go round any more, since the war, and the sort of husbands Mummy would approve of aren't going to ask for me. They can have their pick. And I can't just wait around for ever – I *can't*! Watching myself get older all the time and being quite, quite useless. So I want to take a secretarial course, and then get a job. And I know Mummy will hate the idea, but I thought you might approve. And that if you did, you might speak to Mummy for me, and make her let me do it. Because I really think I shall go mad if this goes on much longer.'

'I see,' Oliver said. 'Yes, I do see. And you're right – your mother will hate the idea.'

She was still gazing up at him. 'But I know I could do it. You think I could, don't you, Uncle Olly? I'm not stupid, and I'd work very hard.'

'You're not stupid at all. Of course you could do the course and get the certificate, and I'm sure you'd be capable of holding down a job. What sort would you want – had you thought?'

'Not really. I don't care much, though it would be nice if it were interesting in itself. But I'd do anything. And I'd save every penny out of my salary and pay back whatever it cost for the course.'

'Well, don't worry about that at this stage,' Oliver said absently, for ideas were running through his mind. 'Look here, are you sure you wouldn't sooner wait for the right man to come along?'

'No-one's coming along, Uncle,' she said seriously. 'No-one ever has yet. And if someone did, well, secretaries get married, don't they?'

'All the time.' He smiled ruefully, from experience. 'Otherwise, where do all the little secretaries come from? But if you took a job, you'd be mixing with a different set, and the other sort of right man probably wouldn't come into your circle.'

'I don't care,' Charlotte said. 'I don't even *want* to be married. I want to be useful and independent and not have to rely on someone else, and have them let me down, like—'

'Like your father did your mother?' he suggested, and she looked down and didn't answer. He studied her bent head, and suspected she had been crossed in love, and that it was a particular disappointment that was prompting this ambition. And yet he couldn't fault her logic. The chances of her securing the sort of husband Violet would want for her were small; and a life of useless spinsterhood as the daughter-at-home would be torture to any girl who had a little something about her, as Charlotte did. No, a job would be better in the long run, and might lead to marriage eventually, though to an ordinary mister, not a lord. Violet would just have to put up with that.

He would help, of course he would. His own mother, a duke's daughter, had become a doctor in the face of immense opposition, from her own family as well as society. And he hated oppression of any sort. Poor Charlotte's bent head looked so meek and unhappy. She might hate a secretarial course and loathe having a job, but at least she deserved the chance to try it and find out.

But Violet would hate the idea. She didn't even like her boys going out to work, and he knew she was secretly hoping for something better for Henry when his turn came. And for a *daughter* – for Lady Charlotte Fitzjames Howard to take a job!

'I'll talk to her,' he said.

She looked up, her eyes wide and damp – she had been trying not to cry. 'Will you? Really? Oh, *thank* you, Uncle Olly! I know you can persuade her if you try.' She jumped up, flung her arms round him and pressed a passionate kiss to his cheek.

'Oh, I will try,' he smiled, 'but your mother can be very stubborn. It may take a while.'

'I don't care,' she said, looking very gay. 'I can wait. I've waited this long. It's what I'm good at – waiting and dusting.'

He was horribly moved by these words. He gently wiped a trace of moisture from her cheek with the back of a forefinger and said, 'We'll see you get to do a bit more than that with your life. And now I must chuck you out – I have a list.'

'You are so *lucky*,' she said. And he knew she was right.

Polly caught up with Seb Bellerby at last, drilling one of his upper fields for winter wheat. The drill was an old one, from which all the original parrot-bright paint of green and red and yellow had long been worn, but the horses, Sampson and Duke, were healthy, glossy, groomed almost to show standard, their forelocks and tails tied up with red ribbon. Like his father before him, Seb loved his horses. When he got into a friendly argument with Bob Wheldrake down at the Rose and Crown in Askham Richard about machinery, and tractors in particular, he always said, 'You can't grow rhubarb on what tractors leave behind.' But the lightness didn't disguise his passion: horses went deep into his soul. Wheldrake, the publican at the Rose and Crown (who was an honorary farmer by virtue of the two breeding sows and dozen weaners he kept out at the back), said it accounted for why Seb had not yet married. 'No lass'll ever get nigher Seb Bellerby's 'eart than 'is 'osses.'

But he was a good-looking enough man and, at twenty-eight, just coming into his prime. Since his parents had died, he had farmed White House with the help of his younger sister Rosie, who also kept house for him. Two older brothers, Joe and Tom, had been killed in the war, and when Seb's younger brother Stephen had died in an accident with a thresher at the age of fourteen, it had taken the heart out of the old people: they had gone into a decline and died within a month of each other in 1926.

When Polly rode up on Solly, Seb was at the top of the field, but saw her as he turned and raised a hand in greeting. Solly sent out one of his deafening, side-shaking whinnies to the two heavy horses, but they were too well mannered to answer, though their ears pricked. Polly dismounted, tied Solly to the gate and hitched herself up onto the wall to watch as Seb and the horses came down the field. It was a lovely sight, three creatures in tune with the job and the place, working in lovely quietness, no tractor noise or stink, followed by a drifting cloud of birds as a ship is followed by seagulls.

When they reached the bottom, Seb halted them, and Polly jumped off the wall and walked along to meet him.

He doffed his cap politely. 'Good morning, Miss Polly,' he said, and then blushed. 'I mean Miss Morland – ma'am – Mrs . . . ? I don't know what to call you,' he confessed.

'Miss Polly is just fine,' she said. 'Good morning, Seb.' She noted that he did not greet her with the usual gruff 'Now then!' There was a 'bit o' summat' about Seb Bellerby. He had been to grammar school; and after the war his parents had paid for him to go to a summer school on agriculture at Oxford University, so he had seen a little of the wide world. Perhaps, Polly reflected, that was why he had not yet married one of the local girls: he was different from other farmers.

'Have you a moment to talk?' she asked him.

'Of course,' he said. 'It won't hurt 'em to take a break. I'll just put their nosebags on, and they'll stand for a bit.'

Polly helped him, for the chance to stroke and pet the great gentle animals. Soon they were happily shoving their noses down into the bags and chomping the chaff with great grinding toothy noises that made Polly feel hungry. Seb asked politely if he might smoke. He lit up and leaned comfortably against the wall, surveying his half-drilled field, and as Polly settled herself beside him, he said, 'Well, you've certainly stirred things up, sacking old Maltby like that.'

'He deserved it,' Polly said.

'I don't doubt it,' said Seb, evenly.

'I can't have my orders disputed. I can't have my own man going behind my back.'

'Fair enough,' Seb said. 'And from what I heard, your ideas are good – the bull club, milking machines, improving the soil. Anyroad, it's your land to do what you like with. I'm only telling you. The older lot are up in arms.'

He gave her a frank sideways glance, inviting her questions.

'What are they saying?' she asked, giving in weakly to curiosity.

He imitated a stronger accent to take the sting out of it. 'A bit of a lass tellin' us how to farm our land? Th'old maister wouldn't 'a' done such a thing.'

'Much they know! Daddy was always interested in new things.'

'A lot of it's Maltby, making trouble. But you could have a rebellion on your hands, Miss Polly. At the moment they're looking on you as the enemy.'

'I only want to improve things – for everybody,' she cried in frustration. 'What's the *matter* with them?'

He drew on his cigarette and exhaled smoke, staring up the field at the circling rooks, blowing like scraps of burned paper from a bonfire caught on the wind. 'They're scared,' he said quietly. 'Everyone's scared, these days. The whole world seems to be going to the bad.'

Polly thought about it. She'd had her head deep in her own local concerns lately, but even a glance at the newspaper in the morning, which was all she had time for, told the story. In America the financial crisis she had left behind continued, with poverty and unemployment still rising, exacerbated now by a severe drought that had killed all the crops in the Midwestern and southern plains, America's bread-basket, bankrupting small farmers and driving up food prices.

In Austria and Germany there had been a run on gold, which had led to widespread bank failures; and in the near collapse that followed, the leading German industrialists had given financial backing to the authoritarian Nazi – National Socialist – Party, which had made a lot of commentators uneasy. The nation looked likely to be torn between the forces of socialism and Fascism.

In Spain, with poverty, unemployment and unrest in the streets, recent elections had given an overwhelming victory to republican parties. A republic had been declared and King Alfonso (whose wife was England's Princess Ena) had gone into exile; and though it was announced as a voluntary exile, there was a strong monarchist party in the country, and the situation, far from being resolved, promised trouble further down the line.

And in England, still struggling under recession, the Austrian and German breakdown had led to a renewed financial crisis. Bickering in cabinet over what to do next had brought the government down and forced the nation to abandon the Gold Standard. There was to be a general election later this month and no-one seemed able to predict what would happen. Unemployment had reached record levels, the cost of unemployment benefit was pushing up taxes, and increasingly shrill political movements seemed to have the country – indeed, the whole world – teetering on the brink of revolution.

Into these thoughts, Seb Bellerby's quiet voice intruded.

'Things keep changing too fast, and no-one knows what's ahead, and when you're scared you want to cling on to what you know. That's the long and short of it. They're scared of anything new, Miss Polly, and – begging your pardon – you're very new.'

'I was *born* here.'

'Aye, I know, but you've been away. And you're a female.'

'Well, I can't do anything about that,' Polly said bitterly. A little breeze fingered the back of her neck, and she shivered. The sky was mute, grey, but heavier towards the north, where the weather was coming from. It was going to turn colder, and rain later. She smiled inwardly as she caught this automatic thought, remembering New York, where you couldn't see the sky or feel the wind, and never knew about the weather until you stepped outside into it. What a country girl she was becoming!

She felt the comforting, solid presence of Seb beside her; she felt he was on her side. 'What should I do?' she asked.

'You could take Maltby back,' he said, so promptly that she knew he had been thinking about it; and when she stirred to protest he forestalled her. 'Nay, hear me out. Maltby's got his faults, but he knows the land and he knows the people and, more important, they know him. They're comfortable with him.'

'But he'd have to do as I told him,' Polly said.

'Aye, and that's a problem, because he thinks nothing to females. So what I think, Miss Polly, is you should have someone over him, a manager between you and him.' He turned to look at her. 'An agent for the whole estate – not just the land, but all your father's businesses.'

'So that all these bone-headed men can deal with a man instead of a woman?' she said angrily.

His voice was always the opposite of passionate. 'Aye, if you like. Changing the nature of people takes time. But it's not only that. You shouldn't have to do everything yourself.

You're the owner, the boss. You're like the general in the army. General Haig decided the overall strategy, and then he told his staff to see it got done. He didn't go and do everything himself, and nor should you. You should have your adjutant, like he did.' She was silent, thinking about it. He said more softly, 'You're looking tired, begging your pardon, Miss Polly. When did you last have a bit o' fun? People've been saying there's no entertainment at Morland Place any more.'

'I don't have time for entertainment,' Polly began automatically, then stopped. She saw her days since she had bought the estate, head down in paperwork, interviewing people, going over accounts, planning and worrying. Of course these things needed doing: she had to find out what she had and how it worked. But there ought to be more to life than that. And she knew that the Big House, as well as providing employment, had always been looked to to provide jollity to the people, a chance to meet each other in merriment. Her father would have said so, if she had asked him.

And the thought of being able to pass the implementation on to someone else and just decide the direction, like a king issuing decrees – yes, it was very attractive.

Seb waited as though he could actually see the thought process pass through her head, and seemed to know the exact moment she reached that point because he said, out of his silence, 'The tenants would respect you more for it, as well.'

She had a brief struggle with pride. They should respect her anyway, and on her own terms, damnit! But she knew he was right. In her fashion business, it would not have gone down well with her employees if she had swept the floor or cleaned the bathroom basin. The sailors wanted the captain to look like a captain.

Still, she had to retrieve something. 'He'll have to *ask* me for his job back,' she said. 'I'm not going to ask him.'

'Quite right.'

'And he'll have to apologise.'

Seb gave a small smile. 'Those are things your estate manager can arrange.'

'Yes, and that's another thing. How do I find a suitable man?'

He gave that some thought. 'Maybe there's someone you could ask. Mr Pobgee, perhaps. Or Sir Bertie – there's a gentleman as knows everybody.'

Mr Pobgee, the lawyer: she would probably have consulted him, anyway. He had been her father's man of business and knew the estate as well as anyone. And, yes, Bertie was the sort of person who knew people. Between them they ought to be able to help her. Perhaps she had been foolish and stubborn in not asking for their help before now. But in New York she had been used to running her own affairs.

Ah, but there she had had Lennie always within call. Lennie! He had not replied to her letter, though there had been time for it to get there and a reply to get back. But perhaps hers had got lost in the post. Such things happened.

Seb finished his cigarette and ground it out carefully on the top of the wall, slipping the butt into his waistcoat pocket.

Polly took the hint. 'Well, I mustn't keep you. You'll want to get on.'

He straightened up, looking round at the horizon. 'Going to rain later,' he said.

'That's just what I was thinking,' she said, and laughed.

He smiled. 'Aye, you're a real countrywoman now.'

'I always was,' she said.

If the reversals her parents had suffered had taught Charlotte anything, it was patience. But now she had spoken to Uncle Oliver and had something to hope for, she found the waiting desperately hard, and never had she been so aware of having nothing to do to keep her mind off things. Her mother had come back from Town that day seeming distracted. Violet had had a lifetime's practice in hiding her feelings, but Charlotte had been her daughter for long enough to have learned to read the smallest signs. And she saw it was an unhappy distractedness, which did not bode well for her.

When would her uncle speak? What would her mother say? She tried to make herself useful, did her dusting and sewing, took her mother's dog Fifi for walks, helped her brother Henry with his homework, read aloud to her mother in the evenings. And as days passed and Uncle Olly did not appear, and her mother seemed to sink further into whatever unhappiness was afflicting her, Charlotte's hope died. I shall live here for ever, she thought, looking round the small, dull drawing room. I shall never know anything beyond these four walls.

Oliver had been researching the matter so as to have all the facts at his fingertips before he tackled Violet, and had no idea of the pain he was causing his niece. He was, in any case, a busy man, and knew of no particular reason to hurry, so it was two weeks before he found the opportunity to address his sister. It was at a bridge party given by him and Verena at their London home, Chelmsford House in Pall Mall. There was a lively group there, but all close friends: Eddie and Sarah Vibart, a fellow equerry 'Fruity' Metcalfe and his wife Baba, the Mosleys – Oswald and his wife Cimmie, who was Baba's sister – and the Mountbattens, Dickie and Edwina. And for Violet, to make the numbers even, the painter Valentine Wilton, whom Oliver had first met in the Sidcup hospital during the war where he had been the plastics unit's artist.

There was dinner first, and the talk was partly about King Alfonso and his queen, because Metcalfe had been in Paris and had seen them. Oliver had played with Princess Ena as a child (she was the daughter of Queen Victoria's youngest child Beatrice, or 'Baby' as she had always been known) and was interested in her welfare, and they discussed the suggestion that had been aired in the press that the exiles might be allowed to retire in England. The general consensus was that it was unlikely, since governments and royal families always seemed to feel that revolution was somehow contagious. And the Mosleys talked about the new political party they had formed and their hopes of the general election. Mosley was an amusing rogue whom Oliver encouraged for his entertainment value, and because of Cimmie, who was a sweet, generous and warm person whom he truly liked and felt rather sorry for. She adored her husband but he was notoriously unfaithful.

Violet was quiet during dinner. She did not really like parties very much any more. Once, they had been the main constituent of her life – planning them, dressing for them, talking about them afterwards: dinner parties and card parties and soirées, tea parties and dances in the Season, dinners for balls and balls themselves. She had dressed for and attended something almost every day of her life, desired guest and envied hostess: opening nights and the opening of galleries, military reviews and hospital charities, birthdays and weddings and royal gatherings of all sorts. Now, from the other end, it seemed a strange way to occupy a life, and she watched the faces around the table and thought how odd it was, all those mouths opening and shutting, taking in food and putting out words, as though it were the most important thing in the world to be doing.

But Wilton, on one side of her, did his best to engage her, and seeing she did not care for political talk, spoke to her of the arts, to which she could listen with a degree of pleasure; and on her other side Dickie Mountbatten, whenever the company turned that way, was longing to talk to her about her lost brother's experiences with the Romanov family. He had visited the Romanovs in childhood, and developed a crush on Grand Duchess Marie, which still seemed to persist despite his marriage. He told her he had a framed picture of Marie on his bedside table – a confession that embarrassed her.

But she was glad, at any rate, not to be seated near Mosley, about whom there was something hard and glittering and obsidian. He talked non-stop, and his rapid, staccato delivery was like machine-gun fire, rattling out his ideas in hard little relentless bullets, regardless of anyone else's interest or opinions.

When the bridge tables were made up, Violet was able to relax a little. She was a good, well-taught player, and concentrating on the cards meant she did not have to think, or talk, about anything else. After a few hands, she found herself dummy and, glancing round, saw that Oliver was also out, and was standing near the fireplace, beckoning to her. She excused herself and went to join him.

'I wanted to speak to you. Having a nice evening?' he asked.

'Yes, thank you,' she said dutifully.

'Are you really?' He scrutinised her more closely. 'You're looking peaked. Are you quite well?'

She avoided this. 'What did you want to speak to me about?'

He still looked at her closely, but he said, 'About Charlotte. She came to see me last week.' Violet looked surprised, then, frowning, guessed it must have been when she was at lunch with Sarah, and was annoyed at the secrecy. When Oliver explained Charlotte's mission, she looked even more annoyed.

'No. It's out of the question. My daughter, to take a *job*?'

'Don't dismiss it out of hand, Vi,' Oliver said. 'The poor girl has nothing to do all day, and she's too bright to bear that for the rest of her life.'

'Rest of her life? What nonsense! She'll get married.'

'Will she? Has she had any offers lately?' He saw that go home, painfully, and was sorry, but there was no sense in sugaring matters. 'Or ever?'

Violet thought briefly, guiltily, of Avis, and said nothing. Their cases were not comparable. But that nice young man Charlotte had liked had not come calling in a long while. Was that to be the way of it? Charlotte left on the shelf for her father's sins? It was the way of the world, as she knew only too well.

'I've done what I can to make a social life for her,' Oliver was saying. 'For you, too. But you know how things stand. And, look here, Vi, it can't do her any harm to take a course, as she wants. I've looked into it, and there's a very decent school in Oxford Street, not five minutes from my rooms, where really quite nice girls go. The new term starts after Christmas. I'd be happy to pay for it, and I could keep a distant eye on her, take her out for luncheon now and then. And afterwards, when she has the diploma, if she still wants a job, I promise to find her something respectable. A lot of nice girls go into publishing, you know, or work in galleries, or other branches of the arts. Law secretaries are highly prized and get to meet eminent barristers and so on. Good opportunities for marriage there. Or I've even thought about taking her in with me.'

'With you?'

'Yes, I can always use an extra hand. And if she likes it, well, there will always be a need for medical secretaries, and it's a field where I can use my influence.'

Violet thought of her daughter being connected, even so remotely, with sickness and operations and hospitals, and was repelled. But, of course, Oliver didn't really deal in sick people, did he? And his fee-paying patients were generally out of the top drawer. Perhaps she might meet someone that way. But no: how could she marry them, knowing intimate details of their medical history? It was preposterous. It was out of the question.

Oliver was smiling. 'In my rooms she might even meet a great actor or film star and take his eye. She would be quite a catch for a Hollywood star – they love titles, and they don't care about a little thing like bankruptcy. What do you say?'

The party went on late, and when it finally broke up, Oliver sent for his car to take Violet home – a kindness she appreciated, but which sadly brought her to reflecting on the days when she had had motors of her own, and a chauffeur at her beck and call. And, she thought, as she struggled to extricate her door key from her purse, always someone to open the door for her, and see that there were refreshments waiting in her private sitting room.

Just as she finally got the key into the lock, the door was opened from the inside, and she stepped in to find Charlotte in pyjamas, dressing-gown and slippers, holding it for her.

'I heard the car pull up and guessed it was you. Did you have a nice time?'

'What are you doing up?' Violet countered. Charlotte seemed to be scrutinising her closely, and she averted her face.

'I was reading in bed, and I was suddenly thirsty, so I thought I'd come down and make a cup of tea. I was just crossing the hall when I heard the car. Would you like one?'

'No, thank you,' Violet said discouragingly. She went to move past her. 'I'm tired. I'm going to bed.'

Charlotte felt a stab of disappointment. *Surely* he would have taken the opportunity . . . 'Mummy,' she said desperately, 'did Uncle Olly say anything to you about me?'

Violet paused, and turned unwillingly to her daughter. 'I was going to talk to you about it in the morning.'

And leave me another night in suspense? Charlotte thought. It was unbearable. 'It's "no", then?' she said bleakly. She wasn't to be allowed. She was to moulder away her life in this prison.

Violet was arrested by her daughter's expression. 'Does it mean so much to you?' she said wonderingly.

76

Charlotte didn't want to cry, but tears spurted to her eye corners at the very thought of how much. 'I must *do* something!' she cried.

To Violet it was like the cry of something caught in a trap. This was the wrong solution, she thought; but, then, the problem was the wrong problem. Charlotte had been brought up to be an earl's daughter, just as she, Violet, had. To be something else entirely involved a metamorphosis so fundamental that she felt it might break something in her. But perhaps Charlotte, being younger, could manage it.

In the motor, coming home, she had suddenly seen herself very clearly: a penniless widow, living on charity, trying to pretend she was still a countess. What a pitiful, ridiculous creature! She despised it. Her boys had adjusted to the new world, were making a different kind of life for themselves. She admired, but could not emulate them. Because she simply had no idea *what she was supposed to do.*

'You really want to do this?' she asked, and her voice sounded faint and unattached to her. 'Take a course and get a job as a secretary?'

Charlotte nodded. 'But what's the use? I knew you'd say no,' she cried resentfully.

Violet felt tired. 'I said yes. And now, if you don't mind, may I go to bed?'

'No, Mummy, wait! What do you mean? You said "yes"?'

'To your uncle Oliver,' Violet answered. 'He has found a course that starts after Christmas. He's going to pay for it. And afterwards, if you get the diploma, he'll help you find a position. I said I would agree to it, if it was what you really wanted. That was what I meant to talk to you about in the morning. But I suppose I have my answer. You seem really intent on it and so – so be it.'

'*Mummy!*' Charlotte cried, lifted from despair *aux anges* in one moment.

'Very well, darling,' Violet said, patting Charlotte's shoulder and detaching herself from the embrace. 'Now I really *am* going to bed.' But at the foot of the stairs she paused and turned back to look at her daughter, frozen with joy in the middle of the hall. Her own heart was so heavy she felt it might fall out with a leaden thud onto the parquet. She had to have *something*. 'What your uncle will help you find is a "position",' she said, one foot on the first stair. 'You are *not* to call it a "job".' And she went upstairs to seek her solitary bed, and the vertiginous dark spaces of a sleepless night in which to contemplate the pointlessness of her life.

Charlotte watched her mother mount the stairs with the consummate grace that made her look as if she was floating upwards without effort. There was no-one did stairs like Mummy. And she hugged herself, thinking that while she would never be able to move as beautifully as her mother, with any luck that would never now matter.

CHAPTER FOUR

It was Mr Pobgee who found Polly her agent. He had been wholly supportive of the idea that she should have a factotum and not do everything herself. But, of course, she told herself, he was of the generation and background to think a woman should not be in charge anyway. He told her he would make enquiries immediately for a suitable person, and offered to undertake the unpleasant task of addressing Maltby, and impressing on him that if he apologised and asked humbly – and only then – he might have his job back.

Bertie and Jessie were also sympathetic, and Bertie said that he would ask around, adding, 'I'm sure it won't be too hard to find someone. A lot of good men are out of work through no fault of their own.'

In the event, Mr Pobgee got there first. He 'took the liberty of proposing to call' on her one day, and arrived with the news that he had found and interviewed on her behalf what sounded like a suitable person.

'His name is John Burton,' Pobgee said, 'and I found him a pleasant and conversable man, with an able mind, and a great many useful and modern ideas about estate management.'

'What's his background?' Polly asked.

'He has been employed for some years in the East Riding, though he is from this area originally – born in Wetherby, I believe. He has been assistant estate manager at Long Riston Hall, the seat of Sir Arnold Catwick.'

'Assistant?'

'I understand from enquiries that his senior was old and quite inactive – kept on by favour of Sir Arnold – and it is Mr Burton who has effectively been doing the work and taking the decisions. So, though he is comparatively a young man, I would judge him to be quite capable.'

'Why is he leaving Long Riston?' Polly asked.

Pobgee sighed. 'The usual story, I'm afraid. Sir Arnold died, and the death duties are such that the estate must be sold to pay them. His son was killed at Passchendaele, and his heir, a second cousin, I believe, is in any case a town dweller and does not care to take on the responsibility. It is the greatest pity to see our old estates disappearing in that way. I know Long Riston a little – fine farming land on the Holderness Plain, and a beautiful early-Georgian house. The style is not so much admired, these days, but its purity of line and proportion . . . I suppose it will become a school or a nursing-home. If I may say so, ma'am, I am more grateful to you than I can express for preventing the loss of Morland Place in the same manner. My family has served it for many generations and I feel, if I may be permitted, a quite *personal* interest in it.'

Polly nodded permission for him to feel as he pleased, and said, 'You really think this Mr Burton will do? You say he's young?'

'But experienced,' Pobgee said. 'I have obtained good reports of him from one or two other people in the Long Riston area – people of substance. And I believe that he would prove quick of learning. The land I feel sure he understands, and the property. As to the rest of your father's business, the factories and the shops—'

'The shops *I* understand, Mr Pobgee,' Polly said firmly. 'However, the factories in Manchester are new to me. How will it be if they are new to Mr Burton as well?'

'I doubt whether it will be possible to find someone expert in both fields,' he said. 'Unless you wish to take on two agents—'

'That would defeat the object,' Polly said.

'Then a person of good intelligence and readiness to learn would seem to be the best option. If in the longer term the double role does not work out well, we can think again. At all events, you would not be worse off.'

Polly discussed the matter with Bertie, who agreed the man sounded suitable, so she agreed to see him and an appointment was arranged by Mr Pobgee. As some emphasis had been laid on Burton's youth, she was amused at the appointed hour to have a man shown into the steward's room who looked to be around forty years old. Seeing Polly's expression, he raised his eyebrows in enquiry.

'I was expecting someone younger,' she said. 'Mr Pobgee gave me to understand . . .'

'I beg your pardon, ma'am. I'm getting older as fast as I can,' he said solemnly.

For an instant she was surprised, and then laughed, pleased at this evidence of a sense of humour. He laughed too, and any tension in the atmosphere dissolved.

He was a man of medium height, with a weather-tanned face, blue eyes and barley-coloured hair that seemed a trifle unruly: he had slicked it down for the interview, but little wisps were already defying the oil. She thought he would look nicer with his hair ruffled up by the wind: it was outdoor hair, not made for parlours and weddings. His figure was neat, with strong shoulders and large, capable hands, and he had an air of quietness about him that she knew would make animals trust him. Indeed, Bigelot and Blossom had come straight to him, smiling and wagging, and as he sat opposite her across the desk they had settled one either side of him to make a thorough examination of his trousers and shoes. You would not have called him precisely handsome, but there was something attractive and altogether very *nice* about him. He reminded her vaguely of someone, but she could not think who.

They talked first about his background and experience and, from what she could gather, he knew his business. He seemed confident about taking over the Morland estate, but she was glad to see he also seemed excited about it. 'I grew up in these parts,' he told her, 'so I've known about Morland Place all my life. In fact, my mother brought me here once, to look over the house on a sixpenny visit.' He smiled. 'I never thought I would be back here one day, hoping to help run it.'

She was glad he had put it that way – not 'run it' but 'help run it'. She mentioned a few of her ideas for improvements, and he seized on them eagerly. A vigorous discussion followed. He had more ideas of his own, and she felt a thrill of excitement about implementing everything they were talking about and making Morland Place a model modern property.

She left the subject reluctantly, but it was necessary to talk about the rest of the estate. The various houses and buildings and small businesses he accepted with the same confidence. 'At Long Riston estate management included property management. Sir Arnold owned buildings in the village and surroundings, and commercial properties in Hornsea. And I imagine you can tell me anything I need to know about the management of shops.'

'But the factories, Mr Burton, I know nothing about spinning and weaving.'

'I have to confess complete ignorance myself,' he said, giving her an anxious look. He was afraid this would scupper his chances. 'But I would say that business is business everywhere – that is, it runs on certain universal principles, whether it's milk and cheese or bales of cloth.' Polly nodded slightly. Lennie had always said that. 'I presume that you have local managers in place, and that what you want is someone to liaise between them and you. I'm sure I could learn enough within a few weeks to be able to do that. As time went on, I would build up more understanding of the business, so that if you wanted to make changes, I could advise you on their feasibility and help you implement them.'

At that point they were disturbed by Sawry, who knocked and entered to say that Sir Bertie Parke had called and wished to see her. Polly smiled inwardly. He had known the date and time of her interview of Burton, and was obviously presenting himself in a friendly way to 'look the blighter over' for her and give his opinion.

'Show him in, will you?' she said, and in a moment Bertie appeared, dressed in riding clothes, with Ellie and Wolf running ahead of him to greet everyone with much frisking and sloshing of tongues.

Burton stood, Polly performed the introduction, the two men shook hands with a frank examination of each other's faces, and at once plunged into a discussion of pedigree cattle breeding, milk yields, feeding, and the weaning of calves, which made them sound as if they'd known each other for years. Polly knew then that she had the right man, though she felt so comfortable with Burton she hardly needed the endorsement.

Bertie extricated himself, saying he had just been passing and hadn't meant to stay. He gave Polly a little nod over Burton's head as he left. When they were alone, Polly offered Burton the position, which he accepted with evident delight – and a little relief, natural in these times.

'As this is a new position, there isn't an estate manager's house to go with it,' Polly concluded, 'but there is a small cottage you could have. It's quite sound, and conveniently positioned, but it's not very palatial. I'm not sure what your wife would think of it. And only two bedrooms. If you have a numerous family . . . ?'

'I'm not married, ma'am,' he said. 'I haven't seemed to have the time to go looking for a wife. And living, as I was, on the estate at Long Riston meant that ladies did not often come in my way. It's a long way from anywhere. You are so close to York here, you can't imagine how isolated we were.'

'I hope York won't prove too distracting to you,' Polly said.

'I promise you all my efforts will be concentrated on your needs,' he said, and their eyes met for an instant. Suddenly she realised who he was reminding her of – it was Lennie, nice, ordinary, kind Lennie.

She pulled her mind away from that thought and asked when he could start.

'Next week, if it suits you, ma'am. I am already on notice at Long Riston and they have agreed to let me go at once if I find another position. I have only to finish one or two things and pack up my belongings.'

'Very well, on Monday, then,' Polly said.

She stood, and so did he, but he was hesitating, looking at her enquiringly. 'I have taken the whole day off to come here,' he said. 'If you like – if it would not inconvenience you – I could spend the rest of it here, making a start on going through the books and learning what's what. I don't have to catch a train until five o'clock.'

That, Polly thought, was enthusiasm. 'You can have the run of the steward's room,' she said. 'And every record is at your disposal.'

Having settled him at the desk, she left him to it, and stepped out into the staircase hall with a feeling of lightness. For the first time since she had come home, she felt she had nothing to do. She would go up and see Alec, then out for a ride – not a stolen ride, but a leisurely one that she was completely entitled to. What a thought! She walked towards the stairs, felt that something was not right, looked round, and realised that Bigelot and Blossom had not followed her

84

out of the steward's room. They had stayed with John Burton. Oh, fickleness! Polly laughed, and went on up.

Robert was shocked. 'My sister, Lady Charlotte Fitzjames Howard, to become a wage-slave?'

'Oh, Robert, don't talk like that,' Charlotte said. 'I'm so happy about it. Don't take away the pleasure.'

'There's nothing wrong with earning a screw,' Richard said. 'If there's any slavery, it's having no money. Having a wage sets one free. Charley can't do anything now, but once she has her little pay packet in her pocket – I say, that's very nearly poetry—'

'It's different for females,' Robert interrupted.

'Not any more, old chum,' Richard said. 'Well,' honesty forced him to add, 'not as much, anyway. I say, Charley, it'll be a whole new life for you.'

'I know. I'm nervous. What if everyone hates me?'

'Oh, Lord, why should they? You're a nice girl.'

'They'll treat you with the respect your rank commands,' said Robert, but it was a threat rather than a prediction.

'If I were you,' Richard said, 'I'd drop the ladyship stuff and introduce yourself as plain Miss Charlotte Howard. No sense in setting yourself apart from the very beginning. It's much better to get on with the people you'll be working with.'

Charlotte thought this was good advice. Robert was shaking his head, and said, 'Well, thank God, at least you'll be living at home. The next thing,' to Richard, 'you'll be telling her to go into lodgings.'

'Oh, no,' Richard said. 'We've tried those – most uncomfortable. No, no, while you've got Uncle Olly providing the creature comforts here at home and a job to put a little rhino in your pocket, you've got the best of both worlds.'

Robert was willing to let the matter drop. His disapproval was automatic, but he had other things on his mind

85

that were more important to him. He had started his position as political secretary to Malcolm Failsworth and was finding it not only absorbing but challenging. His previous experience of working had been in the benign and leisurely world of publishing. Politics moved much faster, and Failsworth was much more demanding, and made no allowances for the fact that Robert was an earl. Robert had to 'hustle', in the American jargon, be on his toes the whole time, and ready with information when questions were asked. He came home exhausted every day, and Richard, observing the pleat of anxiety between his brows, smilingly opined that this job would either be the making of him or destroy him completely.

Fifteen-year-old Henry was the most pleased of all for Charlotte. He was very fond of old Charley, who was pretty decent as sisters went, and it was jolly tough old boots that the man who'd seemed to be fond of her – Amesbury – had disappeared from the scene. Girls, he had found, set a lot of store on romance and soppy things like that.

'You're bound to meet a lot of new chaps when you've got a job,' he assured her, 'and one of them will take a fancy to you. I know a lot of fellows whose sisters aren't half as pretty as you, and *they*'ve got boyfriends.'

'Oh, Henry, really!' Charlotte protested.

But Richard said, 'He's right, you know. Remember, I go about Town all the time, and there are plenty of men to be seen. Not titled, but perfectly decent middle-class chaps. It was mostly our sort who got killed in the war, you know.'

Charlotte smiled. 'Can you imagine Mummy welcoming a middle-class chap as a suitor for me? Anyway, I'm not doing this for romance – please note, Henry – but to be useful and have something to do.'

'Fate will find a way,' Richard said mysteriously, hoping to make her blush.

Henry said, 'Well, it was jolly decent of Uncle Olly to take

86

your part. I must say, he's the best uncle a fellow could have, and while he's in the giving mood, I'm thinking of asking him for something for myself.'

'He's already let you stay on at school,' Robert pointed out.

'I know, but it's not my sort of school. Grammar and history and French! I want to study engineering. I want to go to a technical college.'

Robert rolled his eyes. 'Oh, my God!'

Richard grinned. 'Good for you, nipper. What do you want to study engineering for?'

'I want to design aeroplanes, like Uncle Jack. He was a hero in the war, you know. A real Air Ace.'

'He's not an uncle, he's a cousin,' Richard said. 'We only called him "uncle" when we were little. Aeroplanes, eh? Want to fly 'em as well?'

'Of course,' Henry said. 'You can't design them if you don't know how they fly.'

'Mummy thinks you're going to be an artist,' Charlotte said.

Henry blushed with vexation. He hated the old story that his father wasn't really his father and that his mother had had an affair with a famous artist. She had taken him all the way to New York to see an exhibition of the artist's paintings; but as far as Henry was concerned, Lord Holkam was the man he had called Papa and that was that. And the fact that he was pretty good at drawing and painting had nothing to do with anything. 'You have to do drawing to be a designer,' he pointed out. 'That's all the art work I'm going to do. Or maybe I'll paint pictures of the aeroplanes I design to hang on the walls of my office when I'm famous.'

Richard slapped his shoulder. 'Go it, young 'un! Someone's got to make this family famous, so why shouldn't it be you?'

'You seem to forget,' Robert said, abandoning his dignity to join in the silliness, 'that I'm going to be prime minister.'

'Just being a secretary doesn't sound like much to hold up against that,' Charlotte said.

'That's only the beginning,' Richard assured her. 'Once you have the basic skills, there's no limit to how far you can take them. You only have to decide what you want to do.'

'That's rather the problem,' Charlotte smiled.

'You're one to talk,' said Robert to Richard. 'Look at you idling away your days driving cars. *You* haven't decided what you want to do.'

'That *is* what I want to do,' Richard said airily. 'Unlike all of you, I'm perfectly content with my life.'

During the war, the great shipyards on the Clyde had known good times, as orders for battleships had flooded in. They had expanded capacity and workforce and injected capital; and when the war ended, they believed the boom would continue as the thousands of merchant vessels lost in the hostilities were replaced.

But it didn't happen. World trade was declining throughout the twenties. The switch from steam to oil meant faster, more efficient ships carrying more cargo, so fewer of them were needed; and overseas shipbuilders, starting from scratch, had more modern facilities and working practices than the old British yards, and scooped the new orders. By 1930 almost no new business was coming in, and the big yards were in serious trouble.

The one light in the gloom was the announcement in May 1930 from Cunard that they were to commission a new ocean-going liner to challenge the great ocean racers for the luxury Atlantic trade. The contract was awarded to John Brown & Co. of Clydebank, and on the 1st of December 1930, on a nasty, raw, foggy winter's day, the plate was laid and named Job No. 534, to a general rejoicing that did not reflect the weather. Hull 534 was to be John Brown's salvation, and Clydeside's: three or four years' work for thousands of men, and at the end of it, a new and superlative ship to carry their pride into the world and show it that British shipbuilders were still the best.

Everyone involved with the project was determined to work as never before to make it a success, and the initial progress was remarkable. By the end of January 1931 the whole keel had been laid and the lower part of the ribs and frame was in place. By late spring the frame was completed and plating could begin, and by November 1931 most of that had been finished, and the ship was really looking like a ship, looming huge over the yard and dwarfing the riveters, who clung to her sides like barnacles. She was so massive she made the great cranes that served her look frail, yet her design was graceful and her lines elegant. Like a swan, she would be superlatively beautiful in her element. She was, as sailors said, 'a lady'.

Hull 534 was Polly's concern because one of her father's last commercial acts had been to negotiate the contract for linens and other soft furnishings with Cunard. It was a very good contract to have secured, especially at a time when other work was hard to find, India had put up tariffs against imported cotton goods, and most of the Manchester mills were on short-time working. It had meant the Morland mills had an enviable degree of security.

But on Friday, the 11th of December 1931, Polly received a telegram to say that the directors of Cunard had decided in a meeting the previous day to cancel the order for Hull 534. All work on her was to cease forthwith, and at seven that Friday morning a notice was nailed up in John Brown's shipyard terminating the employment of all workmen as from noon that day.

The shock hit the whole nation. It was reported in all the newspapers in terms of dismay. The directors blamed 'world conditions' for the cancellation. The great days of the Atlantic racers had already been over when 534's keel was laid. After

1926 the bottom had dropped out of the market. Fewer people were making the crossing, and the Crash had only exacerbated matters, so that by 1931 trade had halved. And those who did travel had less money to spend: income from passenger liners had dropped from £9 million in 1928 to £4 million in 1931. The wonder was more that Cunard had put in the order in the first place than that it was cancelling now.

But there was no doubt it was a catastrophe: not only the three thousand men directly involved in building the ship had lost their jobs, but an estimated ten thousand employed on subsidiary contracts for completing and fitting out would be sacked or go on short time – and this at a time of severe national unemployment.

Fervid articles were penned in the newspapers and questions were asked in the House. Given the amount the nation was spending on unemployment benefit, was there not a case for direct government subsidy to complete the ship? The government, struggling to keep the national head above water, regretted that it was impossible. The MP for Clydebank and the general secretary of the shipbuilders' union begged and pleaded, and private individuals even sent donations to Cunard, but all to no avail. Hull 534 lay like a dead thing in her dock. Behind the chained gates of a ghostly shipyard, nothing moved but cats and watchmen, while the indifferent gulls perched on the silent cranes, shuffling their wings in the cold west wind and contemplating man's folly.

The telegram to Morland Place announcing the cancellation of the contract was soon followed by a heartfelt plea from the general manager of the mills, Kenneth Pullar, for instructions. It would be the first test of Burton's grasp of the factories and their business, but Polly felt it personally as well. It would be easy enough to shrug and leave it to someone else, but that would be to play into the hands of those, like Maltby, who thought women couldn't be bosses.

'I think,' Polly said to Burton, when he arrived that morning from his cottage for instructions, 'that we should go there and see for ourselves.'

'I believe you're right,' he said. 'I've been reading all I can find on the Lancashire cotton industry, so I'm not completely ignorant now, but as to the immediate and local conditions, there's nothing to beat actually being there and asking questions. I'm ready to go at a moment's notice. But do you feel you need to go as well, ma'am?'

'Yes,' said Polly, decisively. 'I always meant to, at some point – I want to see everything I own at first hand. Now it's urgent. I don't know if you were aware that Cunard intended to build a sister ship after 534: the work would have kept the mills busy for years. It's not a blow we'll easily get over, so, yes, I think I do need to go.'

'Very well, ma'am. When do you want to leave?'

'First thing tomorrow,' she said.

Kenneth Pullar turned out to be an old man, perhaps in his late sixties, though as he was also evidently not a well man, he might have looked older than he actually was. He was tall, stooped and unnaturally thin, with hollow cheeks and sparse grey hair; his nose and lips had a bluish tint, and he seemed sometimes to have difficulty breathing, at others muffling a slow, careful cough with his handkerchief.

He received Polly and Burton in his large corner office at No. 2 Mill, handsome with panelled walls, a chandelier, mahogany fire surround, solid old furniture and a thick carpet. Both the chandelier and the fire were lit. Beyond the two windows, two equally dismal streets were suffering under a beast of a December day, cold, raw, the lowering sky making twilight of midday, the rain lashing sideways and threatening at any moment to turn to sleet.

Pullar introduced his assistant, Edward Mawson, a man in his early fifties with a careworn face and an even more careworn suit; he looked as though he could do with a square meal, but his eyes were alert and noticing. Tea was offered and accepted, and Polly drew near the fire to thaw out her fingers and legs, while the men exchanged commonplaces about the weather. She had forgotten how grim parts of Manchester could be: soot-streaked, unloved, with cracked pavings, broken kerbs, water-filled holes in the road, rubbish blowing along the gutter, and thin, shabby people hurrying along with their collars turned up or huddled hopelessly in doorways. And in the taxi on the way there they had passed the ends of streets and courts down which she had a glimpsed a life even more grim.

The tea came, Mawson poured, and they got down to business. Pullar was nervous of Polly, glancing at her every few words even though he addressed his remarks to Burton, as though he could not calculate what she might do: scream, faint, burst into tears or dance across the room kicking her legs like a Tiller Girl.

But if anyone seemed likely to burst into tears it was Pullar. His faded voice, with its faint Ayrshire accent, quavered as he told again the story they already knew, of the cancellation of the contract for Hull 534. 'It's a disaster – a catastrophe,' he said. 'The ship was to be launched in May or June, so we've started work already. We've got goods waiting in the warehouse, and what's to become of them? We're tooled up, and now no work to come in. We'll have to lay off. And even then I can't see what can save us from closing altogether. In all my years – never seen such a – don't know what to do – Mr Morland, always so kind—'

His words became broken, and disintegrated into a coughing fit, which prevented any further talk for some minutes. Mawson fetched a glass of water in what seemed to Polly a practised routine.

'Beg your pardon – so very sorry,' Pullar was gasping between paroxysms.

'Please don't apologise,' Polly said. 'And don't try to speak.'

At last the coughing stopped and Pullar was leaning back in his chair, dabbing his forehead, his cheeks flushed and his eyes shiny, his breathing audible in the quiet room.

'I'm afraid you aren't well, Mr Pullar,' Polly said quietly.

'This setback has been a shock,' he confessed. 'It has taken a great deal out of me.'

'Perhaps you should think about retiring,' she said. She meant it kindly, but alarm immediately overspread his face.

'Oh, no, certainly not! I am quite well, quite well. It is nothing, I assure you, just a tickle in the throat. I could not think of retiring now. I am needed more than ever in a crisis such as this.'

Polly did not press the matter, though she was sure the situation was beyond him and was quietly determined he should go. But another time would do for that.

The talk went on for hours; books and schedules were brought out; Pullar looked more and more alarmingly exhausted. Still he addressed everything to Burton, but Mawson seemed to have a better grasp both of who Polly was and what she was capable of. When he spoke, it was to her he looked, and as Pullar tired and he took over more of the conversation, it became almost equally balanced between the other three. Polly felt a distant triumph; but more immediate was the real problem of the cancelled work and the mills' future.

'I can't make any decisions now,' she said. 'This is going to take days of going over everything and considering possibilities. I hope—'

'Possibilities?' Pullar keened. 'I wish there were any!'

But Mawson said, quietly but firmly, 'There is a solution to every problem. It only takes finding.'

Polly was impressed by him. Though he looked frayed and worn, there was nothing wrong with his mind, and he evidently had a complete grasp of everything to do with the business. She suspected, in fact, that it was he who had really been running things for some time; and it was at him she looked when she finished her interrupted question. 'I hope I can call on you for information as I require it.'

Pullar answered, looking at Burton, 'Of course, of course. Anything you need. Though how it can help . . . But certainly, I shall be at your complete service for your entire visit.'

And Mawson, looking at Polly, said, 'It may help if I were to show you over the mills. I'd be happy to escort you whenever it's convenient to you.'

'Thank you. That's a very good idea,' Polly said. She stood up. She felt drained after all the talk, and the strain of being only half visible. 'That's enough for today. We'll take these books and plans away with us, if you don't mind. And tomorrow morning, first thing, I must visit Makepeace's. Will you hold yourselves ready for me in the afternoon?'

'At any hour, ma'am,' Mawson answered for both.

Polly took her time, not only looking around the mills but around Manchester as a whole, and she visited Makepeace's department store several times. There she was more readily accepted as the proprietor, perhaps because, in the nature of things, most of the customers were female and the elderly and wealthy ones would have been quite autocratic. She found trade down, the displays lacklustre, the staff depressed and alarmed for their jobs, and the manager, Mabbott, with no suggestion but to lay off staff.

Polly set to work with relish: this was something she knew how to do. She had changed the York Makepeace's to make it more modern and cheerful, had introduced there the idea that the displays should entice and not just inform; and, of course, she had run her own fashion house in New York, where the competition was fierce. She set the simple things in train. She ordered a redecoration: just applying a coat of fresh, light paint, restaining the floorboards, and cleaning the light fitments so they were not clogged with ancient dust gave the place a look of being open for business. She ordered new carpet, chairs and curtains for the fitting area of the ladies' modes department – 'Wealthy people want to feel they are being taken seriously,' she told Mabbott – and told him to re-hire the experienced staff he had laid off. 'In difficult times, people like to see familiar faces, and to know people understand their jobs,' she said. Seb Bellerby had been right about that, and she was not ashamed to learn as she went along.

'But, madam,' Mabbott demurred, swallowing hard, 'the expense! I laid off staff because we hadn't the trade to justify them.'

'Don't worry about that,' Polly said. 'You can't make money without spending money.' It was a maxim she had learned in America. 'And you can't attract customers by looking as though you don't expect them.'

She went through each department, finding the most lively and likely person in each, and discussed with them what could be done with the displays. She gave each of them a free hand and said she would come back in a week and see what they had done, and if she liked it, they would have the job as a permanency.

When they left, Burton said to her, 'That was impressive, ma'am, if I may say so. You obviously knew exactly what you were about. I've learned a lot.'

'I'm on my own ground there,' she said. 'It's good to feel comfortable about knowing how to fix something. I feel very much at sea with the mills, though.'

'I'm sure solutions will present themselves,' he said.

'Are you? I'm not. This is not just a problem for the Morland mills. It's Manchester-wide. How should we succeed where everyone else is failing?' She turned to look back critically at the façade of the store. 'I wonder if having the sign illuminated would help,' she mused. 'Or would it strike the wrong note?'

'It depends whom you're hoping to attract,' Burton said.

'You're right,' she said, and then sighed. 'I hate the sight of that empty shop right next door. It's so depressing – makes the street look shabby. I want people to go to Makepeace's because it makes them feel happy. I want them to go there just for the pleasure of it, whether they want to buy something or not. Because as often as not, if they're in there and feeling happy, they will buy something.'

An idea was planted in her mind at that moment, but she hadn't a chance to pursue it, because they were on their way back to the mills, where the problems were more urgent. As they drove in the taxi, she noted the number of obviously unemployed people, mostly men, huddling on street corners, queuing patiently outside the labour exchange, waiting for soup kitchens to open; and others, mostly women, queuing outside mean-looking food shops, carrying newspaper-wrapped treasures into the pawn shops, trudging home with heavy shopping bags to save the penny on the bus fare. It made her feel angry in her frustration that she could not help all these people.

'But surely,' she said aloud, 'I can help *some* of them. My own people, anyway. But how do you conjure trade out of the empty air?'

'If I knew that . . .' Burton said.

By the time they reached the mills, she had come to one determination.

'The canteen,' she said, as soon as she arrived in Pullar's office, where Mawson was also in attendance. 'The one my father built during the war to feed the employees, to make sure they had the energy to do their job.'

'We closed it down,' Pullar said. 'Economies had to be made.' Seeing her look, he added in self-justification, 'Before the Cunard contract started, things were difficult, trade was slow, and it was a case of cutting costs where we could. I – I was meaning to open it again once we started working full time.'

From Mawson's small but telling glance, Polly guessed that this was not true. He did not see the point of wasting money on giving the employees a hot meal – that was what they were paid wages for, to find for themselves.

She said, 'We will open it again, if you please. One hot meal for each employee each working day. Starting tomorrow.'

'Tomorrow! But that will take—'

'Tomorrow,' Polly interrupted firmly. She was gratified to see Mawson making a note on his pad. 'You can use the menus and recipes laid down by my father. I'll inspect it later during my visit and make any adjustments needed. The important thing is to get it up and running. And now, if you please, I would like to inspect the warehouses, and see the finished work you have for Cunard.'

In the sitting room of her hotel suite, Polly and Burton worked and talked every evening, discussing possibilities and their drawbacks.

'All those sheets in the warehouse,' she said one evening. 'I can't bear for them to go to waste.'

'Other people must need sheets,' Burton said. 'What about the big hotels?'

'They'll already be supplied – they'll only need occasional replacements, nothing on such a scale. Unless it was a newly built hotel – but who is building new hotels at a time like this?'

'I suppose the army won't want them?' Burton said. 'I know your father had a lot of army contracts – uniforms, shirts . . .'

'And shrouds,' she added, with a rueful smile. 'Lots of shrouds.'

Burton raised his eyebrows. 'Well, why not sell the sheets

97

as shrouds? Undertakers still need them – people still die, even in a recession. Perhaps especially during a recession.'

'What – sheets of that quality? They're far too good.'

'No good at all if we can't sell them.'

'You'd have to undercut the existing supplier.'

'We could do that – sell them at cost, if need be.' And, to her shocked look, 'Better to get something for them than nothing.'

'Hmm. You may be right. But it doesn't solve the problem of forward orders. We've got to find some work for the factories to do.'

'That might require someone to go and look for it,' Burton said. 'A travelling representative to go out and get orders.'

'Yes,' Polly said, 'but in the mean time, the mills lie idle and the workers— What *does* happen to the workers when they've no money coming in? Who stops them starving?'

'They get unemployment benefit,' Burton said. 'Or most of them do.'

'And is it enough?'

'I sincerely doubt it,' he said.

She was silent, brooding a while. Then she said, 'Tomorrow I want to find out about the unemployed – how they live. If I'm going to be laying off our people, I have to know what's going to happen to them.'

Burton looked doubtful. 'That would require going into some pretty rough places.'

'You needn't come if you're afraid,' she said.

Polly had known that there was hardship for the unemployed, but she had always assumed that those in employment could get by. She was to learn that there were degrees: those in work whose wages met their needs; those in work whose wages did not; those in short or part-time work – and there were many ways of putting hands on short time, like 'playing the warps', which meant giving a weaver less than the full

98

complement of looms to work and paying him correspondingly less; and those with no work at all. And the latter were further divided into those who qualified for the unemployment benefit, and those who didn't.

Even in work, it was rarely possible for a woman to stay at home on her husband's wages: a weaver made only a little over two pounds a week. Everyone had to work, and bring home what they could. Couples with small children were the worst off, so much so that Polly wondered why they had children at all – except that she supposed they couldn't help it. But on the dole, a man got 18s. 6d for his wife. How could anyone live on that?

Things had recently got worse because, concerned with the continuous rise in the bill for unemployment benefits, the government had brought in an Act subjecting benefits to the Means Test. This meant an inspection of the household by the dreaded Means Test Man, who would take a tally of all household income, including pensions or savings, and counting anything earned by a son or daughter still living at home. The allowable income was 15s. 3d a week; after that, the man would lose his entitlement to benefit.

The rule had led to much bitterness, and sometimes family break-up, as young people were forced to leave home so that their parents could get benefit. Sometimes they might go and live with a relative, or sleep in an outhouse, or, if they had a way to get wind of the inspector's call, go into lodgings until the inspection was over. But the Means Test Man tried to call when he was least expected.

Polly heard a story about a son who was not supposed to be living at home. He was in the bathtub in front of the kitchen fire one evening when the inspector knocked at the door. The lad jumped out and hid, naked and shivering, in the pantry while his mother resourcefully threw the dog into the bath and pretended to be washing him when the inspector was let in.

Perhaps the most resented element of the Means Test was that it was not just income that was counted but possessions as well. So, if an unemployed man had a decently furnished home, paid for out of the fruits of his labours over the years, perhaps with a few much-loved items handed down from a father or grandmother, the inspector would make a list of everything he had. Then he'd be told to sell a wardrobe this week, some chairs next week, a picture or vase the week after, until all he'd got left was a bed, two chairs and a table. It was humiliating, and it struck at a man's pride in his small achievements, to see all he had worked for come to nothing, for the sake of a few shillings' dole. When he had saved hard week after week to buy some modest addition to the household's comfort, to see it taken away in the Means Test van was not losing furniture, it was losing part of himself.

One evening when she was alone in her room, Polly took a piece of paper and made some calculations. If a man with a wife and two children aged eleven and nine received £1 7s. a week, and his rent for the worst kind of slum cottage was 4s. 8d, that left £1 2s. 4d. Sixpence for gas, two shillings for coal, and that left 2s. 10d a day for everything else: food, laundry, cigarettes, soap, razor blades, essential replacements and repairs to clothes and boots.

Milk, seven pence a pint. Five Woodbines, two pence. Now she understood why they lived mostly on bread, margarine, tea and potatoes, occasionally a few scraps of bacon, or sausages made of gristle and stale bread, hardly any meat in them. For a rare treat, perhaps twopenn'orth from the fried-fish shop, a penn'orth of fish and a penn'orth of chips – but shared among how many?

Sit in the dark to save the penny in the gas. Trudge for hours looking for the cheapest food, the stale bread and the damaged vegetables. Scour jumble sales for old clothes. It was down to the pawnbroker on a Monday to pop the wedding ring and wear the sixpenny brass one from Woolworth's until

Friday. And if, come Friday, there wasn't enough to redeem it, or you had to sell the pawn ticket in the mean time, that was another thing lost, another step down that couldn't be climbed up again, sinking bit by bit further into misery.

She heard one story that nearly broke her heart. A woman told of her sister having a baby. The sister and her husband put it to bed in a drawer, and made nappies out of newspaper because they could afford no better. But when the husband went before the Public Assistance Committee to have his dole assessed, they asked him if the baby was breast-fed; and when he said it was, they reduced the child allowance because he needn't buy it milk.

It seemed like an omen that the bitter, sleety wind from the north had gone round a few points easterly, bringing something a touch more tolerable: still cold, but drier, and with a blink of weak sunshine between the clouds that seemed worth its weight in gold. In the panelled office, which Polly had come to know fairly well, the fire was still welcome. Poor scrawny Mawson was flushed with enthusiasm, and old Pullar was simply flushed – Polly suspected his lungs.

The first part of her plan had been germinating in her head since the original visit to Makepeace's. That empty shop next door . . . Burton had made enquiries. Property prices were very much depressed; the bank, who had repossessed it, would be glad to get it off their hands, and it could be had for a very reasonable price. Burton even managed to argue the price lower by reminding them of lost interest on their capital all the time it was empty. Refitting would be cheap enough, with so many men out of work, and it was the easiest thing in the world to knock a doorway through and make the new shop a department of the old one.

'People need clothes,' she had explained to Burton. 'Not the unemployed – they're beyond my help – but the employed, the clerks and shop workers, the lower middle classes: good-quality cottons that are easy to wash, at a reasonable price, and in nice styles and cheerful colours. Everyone needs to be cheered up, these dark days.'

But she did not want to mix her clients, for the sake of saving both sorts any embarrassment. A new department to the old store: a bright, smart look, an air of fashionableness, a new name. 'I'll call it Polly's Modes,' she told Burton.

'But, forgive me, what does this have to do with us?' Pullar asked, when she had explained her plan.

'All those sheets you have in the warehouse. We could try to sell them, but it would take a long time and we need to keep the business moving. It's good, durable cotton that will launder well.'

Mawson caught up. 'You want to make clothes out of them?'

Pullar looked shocked. 'Cut them up? All those finished sheets?'

'Why not? Better than wasting them.'

'But we're not set up for that sort of finishing work,' Pullar objected.

Burton took over. 'That's true. But there's that old weaving shed in number three mill that's not being used for anything.'

'The machines were obsolete. We pulled them out years ago and sold them for scrap. Since then, we haven't needed the room,' Pullar explained falteringly.

'Quite so,' said Burton. 'No criticism of you intended. But it's an empty space, and putting in cutting-out tables and sewing-machines couldn't be easier. And as to the dyeing – your next-door neighbour, Corson's mill, is having a very hard time. They've been on short-time working for months. I've spoken to the manager and the proprietor, and I think we can work out a useful agreement with them, on very advantageous terms.'

'You see,' Polly said, 'this isn't just to use up the sheets.

I want to make it a permanent part of the business. We weave the cloth, Corson's dye and print it, we cut out and finish, and sell not only to my Makepeace shops but to stores everywhere.'

'But – but we've never done that sort of work,' Pullar said. He was almost tearful.

'No reason not to start now,' Burton said. '*Tempora mutantur, nos et mutamur in illis.*'

'I beg your pardon?'

'Times have changed. We have to change with them,' Mawson said, earning himself an approving look from Burton and a raised eyebrow from Polly. There was something *to* this man. 'But I have another query,' he went on. 'The shops in question must already be buying from somewhere. What will make them change to us? What do we offer that's better?'

'In the first place,' Burton said, 'we have a secure market in the Makepeace shops. We have control over their purchasing. So we will have a margin of time and income where we can perfect our processes. And second—'

'Second,' Polly said, 'shops don't only buy women's clothes from just one source. That's the beauty of it. Fashion changes all the time, and new suppliers come into the market all the time. I have worked in the business, Mr Mawson. I understand it.'

Burton smiled. 'That was going to be my second point.'

'Do you really think we can do this?' Mawson said, but he was looking interested, eager to start.

'Yes, we can,' Polly said. 'If we get it right, we can sell to shops all over the country.'

'But who will design the clothes?' Mawson asked.

'I'll start it off myself. But it won't be hard to find the right people. We shan't be trying to create new *haute couture*, you know, just copying the best designs from elsewhere. It's a matter of going through magazines and collections and translating what we decide to copy into patterns. Pattern-making, cutting out, finishing – these are all basic skills.'

Pullar had been listening in silence, and was now shaking his head slowly, his face a mask of misery. 'I don't like it,' he said. 'I don't like it at all.' And he was seized with another of those coughing fits.

When it was over, Polly said again, quite kindly, 'Mr Pullar, I think you really ought to consider retiring. You're not well, and no-one would think any the worse of you for—'

He had been red; now he paled. 'I can't. Please – don't – I really can't. What would I live on? My wife – oh dear, oh dear. Please, you have no idea what it would mean! I'll try the new way, I'll do anything you want, only please don't dismiss me!'

Polly was stricken. 'I hadn't thought of dismissing you,' she said. 'I thought you would enjoy the chance to take your leisure.'

'We've nothing saved,' he said, a small, stark cry that made Polly ashamed of hearing it, as though he had exposed something too personal that she ought not to have witnessed. 'My wife – not a well woman. The medical expenses . . .'

Polly held up a hand to stop him. She felt partly sad for him, partly annoyed at having her hands tied. She couldn't leave him in charge of the new business when she went away, with his muddled thinking and lack of enthusiasm. Neither could she stay; nor would she spare John Burton. But he did know the mills and the workforce. 'Very well,' she said at last. 'This is my decision. You and Mawson will exchange jobs. He will be manager, you will be his assistant.'

'But—' said Mawson.

'But—' said Pullar.

Burton smiled to himself.

'That's my decision,' Polly said. 'There's no more to say. Tomorrow we must have a meeting with the manager of Corson's, then look at the weaving shed and work out what's to be done there.'

'I know where we can lay our hands on sewing-machines at a very good price,' Mawson said. 'Lintott's is closing down. We may get some skilled hands from there as well. And there may be other machinery and fittings we could use.'

Polly felt a sense of relief that Mawson seemed ready and able to take on the job; that she was not going to have to do it all herself. They talked a little more, and then she took her leave. 'Oh, and by the way,' she added, ' I see that the canteen is open again.'

'Yes,' said Mawson, 'though as we're only running one shift, it's doing just one meal a day.'

'So I gathered,' said Polly. 'There are a lot of hungry people in the streets near here. While we're on short time, have the canteen stay open in the evening, and let it give the meals to the unemployed that it would have made for the night shift.'

'*Give?*' Pullar moaned. 'Like a soup kitchen?'

'Do you think they'd feel better about it if they paid? Very well, a penny for the dinner, twopence with pudding. And children under ten free. But if anyone's in a really bad way, tell them to waive the penny. I don't want anyone to starve outside my factory gates.

'And now,' she said to Burton, as they walked down the stairs, 'I can look forward to my dinner with a little more pleasure.'

Outside, darkness had come, and with it a dead cold that seemed to still all sound and movement in the street. She lifted her nose to smell if snow was coming, and then remembered that this was Manchester where, as in New York, you could not smell the weather. A slash of homesickness struck her, but she did not know which home it was she was sick for.

'It must be nearly Christmas,' she said aloud, a not unrelated thought.

'It's the twenty-second,' said John Burton.

'Then we had better conclude our immediate business tomorrow, so we can be home on Christmas Eve.' She had not communicated with them at home. She supposed they would have made all the preparations for Christmas without her. She didn't know if that made her feel relieved or sad. 'What will you do?' she asked Burton, as they climbed into the taxi. Just at the moment, he felt like the closest person to her on earth. She hoped he wouldn't be alone in his cottage.

In the half-darkness she saw the white of his face turn towards her enquiringly. Then he said, 'My parents still live at Wetherby – Sandbeck Wood. I shall go and see them. It's easier from Morland Place than it was from Long Riston.'

She was silent a moment. Then she said, 'Good.'

CHAPTER FIVE

Oliver had taken a house at Hampden in Buckinghamshire for four weeks around Christmas, for himself, Verena and their three young children. He had not scheduled any operations for the period, and the House was, of course, in recess, but it was close enough to London for him to go up in an emergency, or to keep an eye on long-term patients.

He invited Violet and her family to stay for the whole season, with Robert coming down at weekends and Richard as his employment dictated. Oliver was worried about Violet. She had never been one to show her feelings so it had been hard to tell, at various difficult times in her life, what she felt about the things that were happening to her. In any case, he thought her quite a resolute little person. Just lately, though, he had felt that her quietness was less to do with stoicism than unhappiness. But when he asked her, 'Is everything all right, old thing?' she would only smile and tell him how grateful she was for all he did for her, which was not what he wanted to hear.

He hoped, at least, that getting away, and having Verena to talk to, would help; and he assembled a large and varied guest list, which, he reasoned, ought to cheer her up. As well as Eddie and Sarah and their children, he asked the Westhovens: Emma was another, though more distant, cousin; and Kit had served with Oliver in the RMC during the war, though he had since given up medicine. They brought with them their small baby Alethea. Normally at that time of year they would have been at their own place in Leicestershire for the hunting, but Emma was expecting another child, and Kit, who could be surprisingly uxorious for such a frivolous man, wanted her to be careful. Emma was lively company, and she and Violet had always been close. Perhaps she would be able to get to the bottom of that blank staring-out-of-the-window that had so disturbed him.

He had also asked a selection of friends for the various Saturday-to-Mondays, saving the most cheerful and interesting for the Christmas weekend itself – and since Christmas Day fell conveniently on a Friday that year, it made a nice long break.

He could see from the first that Emma was doing Violet good, giving her something other than herself to think about. Charlotte was practically hero-worshipping her: Emma, with her cheerful, healthy face and strong curly hair, could never be a sparrow-like Glenforth-Williams smart and, gloriously, she didn't care, which made Charlotte feel much better about not being flat-chested and waif-like. Emma had been a FANY during the war, and had tales to tell of her adventures and the dangers faced, none of which involved being passively ladylike and marriage-worthy. Of course, Emma was a huge heiress, which made a difference, but even though she was now married to an earl and a mother into the bargain, she was not confining herself to luncheons and genteel committees but dedicating a large part of her fortune to building decent housing for the working classes in London, while decorating interiors for rich people for fun in between whiles.

At the moment she was full of her new scheme, and was telling Violet and Charlotte about it at tea one day, perching eagerly on the edge of the sofa opposite them and not stinting on the muffins – 'Being pregnant always makes me so hungry!' Charlotte could only look on in envy: she would never dare to take more than one with her mother present.

Emma also had two darling dogs, rough-and-tumble mongrels called Alfie and Buster, while Kit had an elegant saluki called Sulfi and a black greyhound, Eos. All four were eagerly tussling with Violet's Fifi, who was a different dog when she had company. Charlotte wished she could have a dog – and, oh, how she wished she had not been too young to drive a lorry in France during the war!

'Of course, Oliver and Verena already know about it, so they'll have to forgive me for repeating myself,' Emma said, licking butter from her fingers, 'but I'm very excited. Some little slum courts and yards near Covent Garden – on the corner of Drury Lane and Tavistock Street – have come on the market, and they're perfectly suited for clearing. In fact, they're practically falling down already and, of course, dreadfully crowded and insanitary. So I'm going to buy them and put up another Weston Trust building. It will be my biggest project so far.'

'A hundred model flats, five storeys, ten to a storey,' Kit interjected, standing before the fire, cup in hand. He was extremely handsome – even Charlotte, to whom anyone of her mother's generation ought to be beyond being attractive, thought he looked like a film star – and was very popular, being a great raconteur, dancer and merry-maker, with seemingly no ambition beyond having an exceedingly good time.

'But here's the new thing.' Emma took the story back. 'There's so much rehousing needed in the area that the London County Council has hinted they'd be willing to put in some money.'

'That's very good,' Violet said – and then added, doubtfully, because she didn't really understand the ins and outs of it, 'isn't it?'

'Oh, very good,' Emma said, 'as long as they don't want to dictate the design or anything of that sort. But if they do, well, I may have another string to my bow.'

109

'Beaverbrook,' Kit said. 'He's quite the philanthropist, you know, and he likes getting in on schemes like this. I think we could get him to stump up, all right. And he could make a splash about it in his newspapers, which would be good for him and for the Weston Trust.'

'So if the LCC gets too bumptious,' Emma finished, with satisfaction, 'I can play them off against each other.'

Charlotte was full of questions, which Emma was happy to answer, about the design of the flats, which allowed Violet to drift a little. *Perhaps if I had something like that to do . . .* she thought. But, of course, Emma had money. And she had lived a different sort of life, orphaned young, her own woman from the age of twenty-one, and a FANY, when Violet was only sitting on committees to find clothing for Belgian refugees. There was only five years between them in age – as a young matron Violet had chaperoned Emma in her come-out, and enjoyed it all as much as her – but now Emma might have been of a different generation. It helped being married to someone like Kit, who never had a serious thought in his head and used to run with a very fast set. Violet had been married young to stuffy Holkam.

A footman came in, murmured something to Verena, then approached Violet. 'Telephone for you, my lady,' he said. Violet was as surprised as everyone else in the room, though they politely tried to conceal their curiosity. She rose and followed him out. The instrument was in the passage that led to the kitchen quarters, in a strange sort of narrow wooden cupboard, like the sentry-boxes outside Buckingham Palace. Violet had not spoken to anyone on the telephone since her husband died, and felt awkward about it, taking up the receiver as if it might turn into an asp and bite her, and saying, 'Hello?' in a voice so uncertain it was barely audible. And a vagrant thought crossed her mind – something she remembered Oliver saying years ago – that when the first telephones came into existence, no-one had known what

110

to say when answering them, and the first fashion had been for 'Ahoy!'

A voice at the other end said, 'Hello? Is someone there?'

Violet cleared her throat and said, more firmly, 'This is Lady Holkam. Who is it?'

'Lady Holkam! I'm so glad!'

Violet felt her cheeks grow warm. It was a voice she had not expected to hear again. 'Lord Belmont,' she said faintly.

'I hope you don't think it impertinent of me to telephone you there.' He sounded nervous. 'Please excuse me to Lady Overton, if you would. I've been trying for some days to track you down. I called at Lancaster Gate, but the servant couldn't – or wouldn't – tell me where you were.'

'It isn't my usual woman,' Violet heard herself say – how calm her voice sounded!

'So I gathered.'

'As we were going away, I gave Mrs Drayton leave to visit her family, and took on a temporary girl.'

'Well, she was admirably discreet. May I be permitted to ask, how are you?'

'I'm quite well, thank you. I heard about your father – my condolences.'

'It was expected, but still a shock. But now I— Oh, hang! It's hopeless on the telephone. There's so much I would like to talk to you about, but not at arm's length like this. May I call on you? Do you think it would be acceptable to Lady Overton?'

'Call on me? Here?' Violet said, in surprise.

'I shall be in the area tomorrow. I could call in the fore-noon, if that is agreeable to you. I wouldn't ask, except that as you are with family, a degree of informality might be excused.'

Her heart seemed to be pounding in several of the wrong places. To see him again! What on earth could he have to say to her? He sounded so stiff and formal – but people

111

often were, on the telephone. Oliver and Verena would not mind, she was sure; and she wanted very badly to know why he had abandoned her so completely, without a word. Only – what if he were engaged to be married already? She didn't want to hear that, to be obliged to force congratulations out from her unwilling lips. But, no, why would he want to announce that to her in person when a card would do just as well? On the whole, she thought it could not be that. Probably he was just being polite. He had said he would be in the area.

'You are very welcome to call,' she said, and her voice sounded faint again. 'I am sure my sister-in-law will have no objection.'

'Thank you. Until tomorrow, then,' he said. And was gone.

She took her time walking back to the drawing room, and by the time she entered, she had got control of herself again. Emma, who was talking, looked up but did not pause. Violet went over to Verena and explained. 'I hope you don't mind.'

'Not at all,' Verena said quickly. 'I understand he has been a good friend to you and the children. I hope he will stay to luncheon.'

Violet murmured her thanks, returned to her seat, and was glad when shortly afterwards a nursery maid came in with baby Alethea in her arms.

'Ah, there's my little princess! Give her to me – I haven't seen her all day.' It was Kit who held out his arms for his daughter, while Emma looked on indulgently. The maid was followed by Oliver's three children, John, Amabel and Venetia, who were seven, four and two, and who created a pleasant disturbance that allowed Violet to escape any attention or possible questions.

It was a cold day, but sunny: the wind, having swung round to the east, had blown away the damp clouds and brought icy air across the dry lands of East Anglia from the continent, gripped in its usual winter freeze. Violet had no idea at what time Avis would present himself, and she wouldn't wait indoors and be seen to be waiting, so after breakfast she put on her warmest things and went out into the grounds with the excuse of taking Fifi for a walk. Kit and Oliver had already gone off somewhere with Sulfi and Eos, and Emma was not down yet – pregnancy made her sleepy as well as hungry – so Alfie and Benson insisted on joining her, claiming that Fifi was their new best friend and they couldn't possibly be parted from her.

It was so cold that Violet was obliged to walk briskly. The dogs romped ahead, their breath clouding upwards in puffs as if their barks had become visible. A parlement of rooks called back and forth from the tall elms that sheltered the churchyard next door. The bare rose beds were like frozen brown seas; every blade of grass was as stiff and silver as a spear head. Beyond the grounds, the Chilterns rose in handsome, rolling folds of green, patched with winter woods in shades of brown and violet.

The sky was an acid, wintry blue, but it was good to be out and to see the sun, however heatless. From childhood stays at Morland Place she found a memory that told her it was not good hunting weather – too cold for scent. She wondered if they were hunting there now. Jessie would always go out if at all possible. Oliver had asked Jessie and Bertie for Christmas, for Violet's sake, but they had Helen and Jack and their family so could not come. She was so glad that Jessie was happy. They had come out together, had both fallen in love with Holkam – Lord Brancaster as he was then – but he had chosen Violet. How different their lives would have been if Jessie had married him! It was hard to imagine what might have happened to them both.

Despite the sunshine and the walking, she was getting cold and thinking about going in when the dogs came bounding past her, giving tongue, and she turned to see what they were barking at. Someone was coming towards her along the gravel path. Her heart jumped. Even bundled up in a greatcoat and hat he was instantly known to her. He took off the hat, and advanced bare-headed, fended off the dogs with a laugh, came towards her with an eager look that she almost could not bear, not knowing what it portended. She forced her feelings down with iron control: she would *not* make a fool of herself before a man who had already shown his indifference.

'Lord Belmont,' she said in cool greeting.

His smile faltered, he stopped a step further away than he otherwise might, and regarded her with a faintly questioning look. 'Lady Holkam,' he said. And then, as if he could not repress it, 'It's so *good* to see you after so long!'

'Yes, it *has* been a long time,' she said, keeping valiantly to the cold and formal, when just the sight of his face was making her feel crazily happy. She had not realised she would mind as much as this. But what was he *doing* here? 'I read about your father's sad death in the newspaper, so I understood you would be kept too busy to call as you once used to.'

He looked frankly puzzled. 'I'm sorry, I don't understand. I wrote to you – my letter explained— Have I offended you in some way?'

She stared. 'I received no letter,' she said.

'Oh dear, now I think I understand,' he said. 'My letter must have gone astray, and you have been thinking I had so little regard for our friendship that I left you to find out through the newspapers.' He cocked his head a little. 'Have I that right?' She nodded stiffly, feeling an absurd urge to burst into tears. 'I'm so sorry,' he said gently. 'But please believe that was not the case. I wrote to you after my father died – a long letter, explaining how much there would be to do that would keep me in Derbyshire for many, many weeks, begging you to forgive me, asking if I might call on you the first moment I could.'

'Oh,' said Violet. Despite the cold, she could feel warmth running under her skin.

'You do believe me?'

'Yes,' she said. She knew perfectly well how much work was involved in the death of an earl and the orderly passing over of his estate. Letters did go astray And she knew he would not tell an untruth.

'Your friendship has been the most important thing in my life, these past two years,' he said. He seemed to have come that step closer, though she was not aware either of them had moved. 'If I thought I'd lost that – caused you any pain—'

'I—' said Violet. It seemed to be all she could manage.

He was looking into her face searchingly. 'I had thought, before my father died, that you had begun to feel something rather warmer for me than just friendship. I know how impertinent that was of me, and you've every right to be offended if—'

'No,' Violet interrupted and, for an instant, saw his face collapse as if she had slapped him. She hurried on. 'I mean, no, you weren't mistaken, but *I* thought you could never—'

He smiled, and took her hands, and though they were prevented by two sets of gloves from any intimate contact, the thrill of it shot through her more piercingly than any touch she had known since Laidislaw had died on the Somme. 'I think,' he said gently, 'we had better have some plain talking. Please may I tell you that I love you, that I've loved you since that day at the races in New York, when I came upon you standing all alone and looking as though you needed to be rescued but didn't think anyone would come. And you let me give you my arm and amuse you, though I was nobody and nothing; you entrusted yourself to me, and all I wanted then and afterwards was to dedicate my life to making you happy. But you were married and – and were surrounded by other people with the same idea. So I knew

I wasn't needed. But still I loved you. I couldn't help it. I love you so much, Violet. Is it possible that you—'

'Yes,' she said. It didn't seem like much of a response to such a pretty speech, and she had to give him a little more. 'I love you, too,' she said, feeling absurdly shy about it, but it was a very long time since she had said those words, and the emotions fermenting inside her were making her feel like a seventeen-year-old at her first ball. Not just love, but requited love! She had forgotten how very, very wonderful that felt.

He pressed her hands, gazing at her in urgent delight, and she longed to be taken in his arms and kissed, but they could not do that, two middle-aged people in someone else's garden. All things in their time, perhaps . . . and that thought made her feel a little faint.

'Violet,' he said, looking at her so hard his eyes were almost consuming her face, 'will you – will you marry me?'

'Oh, yes,' she said gladly. 'Yes, please.'

He squeezed his eyes shut. 'Thank God,' he said. He looked around wildly. 'I wish there was somewhere we could go. I long to kiss you. It will have to wait, I suppose.' Instead, he drew her arm through his and they started walking again. During this long stationary period the dogs had wandered off and gone indoors again. The rooks had stopped calling, and a great stillness seemed to have fallen. It was even colder, but Violet didn't feel it any more, with the warm, male, protective bulk of his body close to her. Oh, God, she loved that feeling!

'I ought to tell you something about my circumstances before you agree to marry me,' he said.

'I don't care,' Violet said, and she laughed, more at the sound of her own voice than anything. It suddenly occurred to her that with Avis, married to Avis, she could be someone else, not the strictly governed, formal, well-regulated person she had been all her life with Holkam, but that other Violet, the inner one rarely seen, the spontaneous, wild and passionate Violet she had been for those few weeks with Laidislaw. But this time it would be better, because then she had been a child and a pupil and he the teacher; now she would able to give and take as an equal. And say whatever she wanted – oh, to speak her thoughts, not repress them! What freedom! 'I don't care! You know *I* have nothing. What does it matter? I love *you*, that's all. If I have you, what else do I need?'

'A noble and, if I may say so, remarkable speech for Lady Holkam,' he said, laughing at her, but in a way that caressed, not ridiculed. 'If you are willing to sacrifice the world for love, I had better see to it we have a crust to live on and a roof over our heads. *One* of us has to be practical – and, fortunately, I have money.'

'Oh, that's nice,' she said gaily, and was simply amazed at hearing herself. She had *never* talked like this. 'Did you escape the death duties, then?'

'*No-one* escapes the death duties,' he corrected her sternly, 'but my father left things in good heart, no debts or mortgages, and by selling one or two outlying properties and the London house, I can keep the central part of the estate together, and still have a decent income. Enough to invite the most beautiful woman in England to be my wife and not be afraid I won't be able to keep her in new dresses.'

'I don't care about new dresses,' Violet said happily.

'Well, you ought to,' he said. 'I intend for us to entertain, and while the new Countess of Belmont is lovely enough to dazzle even when dressed in sacking, I would rather see her elegantly clad.'

They went on talking pleasant nonsense for a while, until they reached the end of the walk and the turn gave a new direction to her thoughts.

'You know that I have four children,' she said.

'It did catch my attention at some point,' he answered. 'I had the impression they quite liked me.'

'They did – they do. Henry so admires you. Robert and Richard are quite grown-up so they won't be in the way. And Charlotte . . .' It occurred to her at that moment that now Charlotte would not have to do the secretarial course and take a job. She would be able to take her place in Society again. Marry the right sort of man.

And then she thought of something else. He saw her expression change, and squeezed her hand against his side in concern.

'What is it? You've thought of something bad. What is it about Charlotte?'

'Not about Charlotte,' she said. She shook her head. She didn't want to talk about this, and yet she must – *they* must. It was too important to leave undiscussed. But how to put it? What words to choose? 'I heard,' she began falteringly.

'What did you hear?' he asked, when she had paused too long. 'Something about me? I will answer any question you want to ask, I promise you.'

She shook her head again. 'I heard some people talking. They said you would need a rich wife because of death duties.'

'Well, I've scotched that one, at least. I've told you I shall be comfortably off.'

'They also said you would need a young wife. Because there's only you left now. And you will need an heir.'

She couldn't believe she had just said that. Her cheeks were so hot the cold air stung them. He looked at her with such tenderness it made her want to cry again. 'Oh, my dear,' he said.

'I'm forty years old,' she went on bravely. 'You need to take that into consideration.'

'I know how old you are,' he said. 'I'm forty, as well.'

'It's different for men,' she said.

He didn't try to deny it. He was thinking – in a flash of sympathy she knew he was selecting words with care, too.

It was possible for two people in love to hurt each other much more than strangers could.

'I would like a child,' he said. 'Of course I have family feeling. I won't deny that. I would like to pass the estate on to my own flesh and blood. But much more than that, I would like *your* child. I know that's easy for me to say. If *you* would like a child, we will make it part of our future plans. If you don't want one, so be it. It makes no difference to my love for you, or my desire to marry you, and we'll be happy together whatever happens.' He looked at her anxiously. 'Have I said it right? I want you to feel comfortable about it.'

She smiled at him. 'You said it beautifully. And – and I would like a child.' She hadn't known she was going to say that, but when she did, she knew it was true. She had looked at Emma yesterday, taking baby Alethea from Kit and holding her, and had felt the ache of empty arms. They called it 'grandmother love', didn't they? And her children were old enough now to make her a grandmother. But it was as Avis had said – she wanted *his* child. She was not too old yet.

'Are you sure? You don't have to say it to please me. Look, we won't talk about it now. There's no need. I want to marry you – *you*, as you are. Whatever happens, let it happen.'

'Very well,' she said, but there was a small seed of excitement deep inside her, where perhaps one day soon she might grow a child of his. She thought they'd have very pretty children.

She saw a face at the drawing-room window, quickly withdrawn. 'We should go in.'

'Tell everyone the good news,' he said.

'Do you want to?' She felt shy again.

'I want to tell the world, but I don't think they'd all be terribly interested. Your family and friends, however . . .'

'Let's tell them, then,' Violet said comfortably. The sky

was clouding over, a thin, high veil of grey that was creeping almost imperceptibly towards the sun. She wondered if it was going to snow. She became aware that her feet were very cold.

When they went inside, they discovered that Eddie and Sarah and their children had arrived; and Robert and Richard, coming down on the same train; so there was an even larger audience for their good news. It was gratifyingly well received, especially by Oliver, who felt he now understood what had been ailing his sister.

After Christmas, Polly felt things were at last on a steady keel. With John Burton overseeing the estate, and keeping in touch with Mawson at the mills, she was able to give all her attention to the Makepeace shops. Those in York and Leeds were holding up, but she wanted more from them than that. She went into each in turn, reorganised the staff, redecorated, changed the displays and some of the merchandise, and introduced her new line of good, cheap, nice-looking women's clothes. In the York store they had a separate department that sold servants' uniforms, and with the recession and the reluctance of girls to go into domestic service, people were taking on fewer servants and the department was not pulling its weight. She found a niche for it next to ladies' underwear, and turned the department into a Polly's Modes.

In Leeds there was no department suitable for annexation, and no empty premises she could take over. The shop next door was a seed merchant's, Gale's, and flourishing with new lines of bagged chicken feed and caged-bird seed to add to the old bulk orders from farmers. It was Burton – the admirable, growing-to-be-indispensable John Burton – who found the solution. There was an empty shop on the corner diagonally opposite Makepeace's. He took on the lease, then started working on George Gale, the seedsman, pointing out to him how much better placed the corner property was, with windows on two streets and a yard behind with much better access than he presently had.

'And it's bigger,' he said. 'You've already branched out into bird seed and so on, and look how crowded it's making your shop. I've no doubt you've other good ideas you want to bring forward, but how are you going to accommodate them?'

'I s'l manage,' Gale said, tight-lipped with suspicion. Yorkshiremen didn't like other folk telling them their business.

'I'm sure you would, but there's managing and then there's getting on. With the corner shop you could branch out into, say, garden tools and flower seeds and potting soil and so on, put all that with the bird seed and domestic stuff into one side, and have the bulk feeds in the other, each with its own shop window, so the farmers aren't kept waiting while Mrs Featherstone buys a small bag of canary mix. And Mrs Featherstone in her best coat and hat won't be jostled by a man with muddy gaiters.'

He could see Gale was imagining the picture he had painted, and finding it a good one. But suspicion was still rife. 'An' what's it to you, yoong man? How coom you're so keen on ma business, with your Mrs Featherstones and gaiters and nonsense? I don't see how it matters to you whether I flourish or perish.'

'I like to see all men getting on,' Burton said calmly, 'and empty shops in a street don't help anyone. But I make no bones about it, I want this shop. It's right next door, it's the right size, and it'll improve my trade. The other shop's better suited to you. You need a bigger premises, and your farmers'll prefer being further away from windows full of women's doo-dads when they're buying oats and corn.' He spread his hands. 'So it suits everybody. I take over your shop, you take over the corner shop. Everyone benefits.'

Eventually Gale was convinced, but he had to make one

last protest, for pride's sake. 'Aye, *you* benefit, I make no doubt. But I'll have a bigger rent to pay, an' all the fuss o' moving.'

'I've spoken to the agent and to the owner of the property. Persuaded them that an empty shop does no-one any good, and it's better to rent at a lower rate than not to rent at all. So I've got it on very favourable terms, and you can have it on the same. I've already booked my men to go in and redecorate, and I'll still do that at my expense – and you can choose the paint colour, if you like. That ought to offset the bother of moving. In any case, business *is* bother. You can't make brass without making an effort.'

This last chimed so well with Gale's own philosophy (and his disappointment with his son, who took no interest in the business and preferred lounging around smoking and going to the cinema with a different girl every week) that he began to look very favourably on John Burton and almost to wish for his advice about one or two things – not least how to make his own son more like him. It didn't take much more to persuade him to the swap, and a date was fixed for a month ahead, when Gale's would move to the corner, and Burton could get his men in to strip out the old seed merchant's and transform it into a Polly's Modes.

Polly was working on dress designs, which involved ordering a copy of every lady's magazine on the market to be delivered each week – something that pleased the young females of the house greatly. It was the part of the business she had always enjoyed most, and she not only copied but added some originals as well, and mixed new colours using water paints.

But this did not use up all of her time, and with Burton taking so much of the burden from her, she found herself with time on her hands. The household, to which she had been a distant and rather frowning power who had made them feel nervous about their futures, found her suddenly descending among them, fresh and full of energy, ready to take charge of the house and all that was in it. They had not realised before that she could make fun for them, that she could make them laugh.

'It's rather like waking up Sleeping Beauty,' she told Jessie. 'Oh, Jessie, I feel as if I haven't been to a party in years!'

'That's easily remedied,' Jessie said.

'Yes, but I want to entertain at home, make people think of Morland Place that way again. And before that – everything's so drab and old-fashioned-looking.'

'Your father was an man, remember, and since he died no-one's cared for the house, not really.'

'I know. Well, I'm here now, and I'm going to make it shine.'

But first there were departures. James, to Polly's private surprise, really was going – she had thought he would continue putting it off. And though to begin with he was only riding his motorcycle down to Wiltshire to stay with David Pennyfather for a few weeks, it felt more like Ulysses going off to war.

From James's point of view this was because of his new motorcycle, an almost new Triumph 500cc NT, which had replaced his old Sunbeam model 90. It had a 494cc twin-port overhead valve engine and three-speed hand change, was the fastest machine in the Triumph range, and was so much more exciting than Black Beauty (though he had felt almost tearful at parting with her) that the whole journey took on an epic tinge.

From the servants' point of view it was the young master going away, and who knew when he would be back again? Time for ceremonial farewells and many tears.

Hardly had they been mopped up when the butler, Sawry, asked Polly for a private interview, and when she stepped out of the drawing room into the great hall, he faced her with distinctly moist eyes and told her he wanted to retire.

'Oh, no!' Polly cried, genuinely taken aback. Morland

Place without Sawry was hard to imagine. 'But *why*, Sawry? Aren't you happy here?' It crossed her mind that it might be because he saw James as the rightful heir and couldn't accept her as mistress.

But he only blinked faster, and said, 'Oh, madam, Morland Place means the world to me. I should never want to leave. But it's my back, madam. It pains me all the time, and I can't do the work as I should like to do it. I feel I'm letting the place down.'

'But – where would you go?' Polly asked. He had been at Morland Place all her life.

'Well, madam, you see, Mrs Stark and I had an agreement that one day we would buy a little place and set up together – when we got too old to work any more. We have some money put aside. Enough, we think.'

So she was to lose the cook as well? This was even more of a blow – good cooks were hard to find.

'I had no idea,' she said.

'Well, madam, we kept it a secret, for fear of the other servants gossiping.' Something occurred to him. 'We mean to get married, you know – everything respectable.'

Polly took his hand. 'I'm sure. But we shall miss you most dreadfully. *I* shall miss you. It won't seem like Morland Place without you both.'

Sawry abandoned the effort to be proper. 'Oh, Miss Polly,' he said, a tear escaping and rolling down his seamed old cheek, 'it's terrible to leave. This is like my home to me. But it's time, it really is. I can't do the work properly any more, and Mary – Mrs Stark – she wants us to have a bit o' life together before it's too late.'

Polly nodded. 'You must do whatever's best for you. But I can't think how we shall manage without you.'

He hesitated. 'If it wouldn't be impertinent to say so . . .'

'You couldn't be impertinent if you tried. What is it? Speak out.'

124

'Well, Miss Polly, Frederick's a good man, and I've trained him in my ways. He was a bit rough and ambitious when he first came, but he's matured, and though he's a bit on the young side, I think you could do worse than trust him. I know he'd like the job, and – well, he might not settle down under a new man.'

Polly smiled inwardly at the thought of Frederick being too young. He must be in his mid or late thirties. 'If you think he's the right man for the job,' she said.

'Oh, he can do the work. To tell the truth, Miss Polly, he does most on it already, me being so poorly this long time past.'

'Then you may send him to me – if you're quite sure you want to leave?'

'I'm sure I must,' he said sadly. 'Oh, and as to a cook, Mrs Stark didn't want to leave you in the lurch, so to speak, and she wouldn't agree to leave with me until she was sure she'd found someone to replace her. If you would be so kind as to consider her, there's a Mrs Starling, who is Mrs Stark's own niece. She's been cooking for a big house down south, but there's been a change of mistress, which has upset her, and she wants to come back north to her own country. So she'd be available on the giving of notice, madam, if you thought it right to enquire about her.'

With the 'madam' he had recovered his butlerly poise, and Polly stepped back into mistress to make it easier for him. 'Tell Mrs Stark I'll interview her with pleasure. Do you wish me to keep this secret still?'

'If you wouldn't mind, madam, until you're sure of our replacements. Then we'll fix the day to suit, and tell the rest of the servants' hall.'

The third departure was even more unexpected. One afternoon when Polly came back from a ride, she found Amy waiting for her in the stableyard – not the place she had ever expected to see her father's widow since Amy was a town person, who regarded horses only as creatures that were dangerous at both ends.

'Hello!' Polly greeted her cheerfully, as one of the boys ran up to take Solly's head. 'Is the house on fire?'

Amy looked up at her with an even more hesitant air than usual. 'I was waiting for you. I hoped I might have a private word with you. About – something private.'

Polly swung down from the saddle and said to the boy, 'I'll take him. You can hop off now.' When he had gone, she said to Amy, 'Come with me while I untack him and rub him down. We'll be private in the stable.'

She led the horse with a great satisfying clopping of hoofs into the warm twilight of the stables, with the smell of straw and sweet equine breath, and the flicker of sparrows up in the rafters, slipped off his bridle and put on his head collar. Released from the bit, he took a step forward and shoved his nose into the manger to see if there was by any chance a stray bit of breakfast he had missed. Amy hovered in the stable doorway, keeping well back from the big shiny rump and those unpredictable, iron-shod feet. Polly took off the saddle and came out with it, heaved it onto the half-door, took up the bucket of feed left waiting for her, and said, 'You'll have to come closer if you want not to be overheard. Come into his stall with me. I promise you he won't kick or bite. Haven't you seen me in here with Alec? Do you think I'd have him around Solly if he were dangerous?'

Amy thought that people who weren't afraid of horses never saw the danger, but as Polly went up past one side of the chestnut and dumped the feed into his manger, she bit her lip and eased herself past Solly on the other side. Certainly she felt safer at the top end, especially as the horse had his nose in the manger and was eating as though he hadn't been fed in a week, chomping and grinding with a sound like the chaff-cutter at work.

Polly took a brush from the shelf above the manger and

started on Solly's neck. Across it, she said, 'So, what did you want to talk about?'

Now it had come to the point, Amy had difficulty finding the words. 'I've been – seeing someone,' she said awkwardly.

'*Seeing* someone?' Polly was mystified. 'You mean, a ghost?'

'No, I mean, meeting someone. In York. Going to meet them. Him. Meeting him.' Why was there no phrase for it, when you were past the first flush of youth? 'Walking out.'

'Oh!' Polly was enlightened at last. 'Well, that's – wonderful. I'm very glad for you.'

'Are you? You don't mind?'

'Mind? Good God, Amy, how could I mind? You don't have to answer to me.'

'But I live in your house. You pay me my widow's portion. You didn't have to do any of that, and I'm grateful, truly grateful, and I didn't want you to think—'

Polly reddened. 'Oh, bosh! This is your home as much as mine – more, really, all the years I was away in America. And my father would have wanted me to see you got what he meant you to have. So there's no need to be grateful or – or anything, really.'

'You're very kind,' Amy said, and hesitated. For an awful moment Polly thought she was going to bring up again the fact that Polly had been against Amy's marriage to her father at the beginning, and had behaved very badly, for which she was now ashamed. But she said at last, 'Should I tell you about him?'

'If you want. I mean, you don't have to, but I'd like to hear.'

Amy nodded. 'I met him at a friend's house – Lucy Tibbett's. His name's George Unwin, he's a widower, and he owns Unwin's the florist's, at the top of Goodramgate. So, of course, we had something in common, me having worked in a florist's in London. He was very interested in that, and we got talking, and then he asked me if I would like to meet him one day. So I did. We had tea at Brown's, and another day we went to the cinema, and somehow it came to be a regular thing.'

'I understand perfectly,' Polly said. 'Is he nice?'

'I think so. All his customers trust him and ask his advice, and he's very good to me. I think your father would have liked him.'

'I think he did like him,' Polly said, screwing up her face in the effort to remember. 'Wasn't it from Unwin's that he got his buttonholes, and flowers for special occasions? I seem to remember him saying something about trusting Mr Unwin to get anything he asked for.'

Amy blushed a little. 'That was his father – George's father.'

'Oh, of course. Silly of me.'

'George is my age, just a year older.'

'I see.' Polly stopped brushing Solly's saddle patch and leaned on his back to look at Amy. 'I'm pleased you've found a nice gentleman friend, but you didn't need to—'

'He's not just a friend,' Amy said, with an air of taking the plunge. 'He's asked me to marry him. And I've said yes,' she went on boldly. 'But I thought you should be the first to know, so I haven't told anyone else yet, and he won't say a word until I tell him it's all right.'

'All right? It's wonderful news,' Polly said. 'I'm so happy for you.' And then the thought crossed her mind that Amy might want to bring her new husband to live at Morland Place.

A moment later she felt ashamed of it, as Amy said, 'George has a house just a little way out on the Malton road where we're going to live, and of course it's fully furnished, so we won't need anything. I wanted you to know that I know the pension you pay me will stop when I remarry, which is as it should be, and that it's quite all right, because George can support me very well. We'd like to marry in Holy

Trinity, Goodramgate, which is the church he goes to, and hope that you would honour us by coming to the wedding.'

'Wouldn't you like to get married here, in the chapel?' Polly offered.

Amy smiled, and looked younger, and for the first time really happy. 'Thank you, you're very kind, but we'd rather do it our way. I'm not really a Morland, and the chapel's for family. And we'd like all our friends to come to the wedding, which wouldn't be fair on you, being people you don't really know. So, if you don't mind, we'll arrange the wedding ourselves, and just be very glad if you and everyone else at Morland Place will come.'

'I'll come with the greatest pleasure. We all will. And you must let me know what you'd like for a wedding present. I know you said you didn't need anything, but there's bound to be something, and whatever it is, it's yours.'

'Oh, no, really, there's no need.'

'It's what my father would have wanted,' Polly said sternly, 'and you know it. So don't fob me off with some little thing. He'd want me to buy you something really nice, expense no object. Just let me know.'

'Thank you. I will,' Amy said shyly. And she smiled again. 'Now we can tell everyone. George will be so pleased. He hates secrets.'

'I look forward to meeting him. I hope you will bring him to dinner,' said Polly.

'Well, that's as nice an ending to a story as I've ever heard,' Jessie said, walking with Polly in the garden at Twelvetrees. 'Uncle Teddy rescued that poor woman from destitution, and now she's settled comfortably and happily with a man her own age.' She stopped herself. 'Goodness, I'm not usually so tactless! Forgive me, Polly dear. I meant—'

'I know what you meant and there's no need to apologise. Daddy loved her and I think she loved him, but he's gone now, and it's right she should have a fresh start and a new life. And George Unwin is just right for her. He's a perfect poppet. I hope meeting everyone at dinner next week won't be too much of a challenge for the poor man.'

'I'll keep an eye on him,' Jessie promised. 'But if he runs a shop, he must be used to dealing with people. So, Polly, now that one of your dependants is being taken off your shoulders, it might be a good moment to review the rest.'

These were Polly's orphaned cousins, whom her father had taken in, and Polly seemed to have 'inherited' with the estate.

'Review them? How?' Polly asked.

'I haven't bothered you about it, because you've been so busy getting the estate on a firm footing, but now you have that wonderful John Burton running everything for you . . . By the way, I like him *very* much. I can't believe he's a bachelor. We must look out for a nice wife for him.'

'He doesn't need one,' Polly said quickly. 'Leave him alone – he can find a woman for himself if that's what he wants.'

'Sorry,' Jessie said, with a smile. 'It's wedding fever taking hold. I was saying, now you seem to have more time to spare, and James and Amy are gone, perhaps you should sort things out for the other children. Jeremy, for example. He'll be twenty this year, and he's earning a decent salary at the bank. It's time he paid you something for his keep.'

'But I don't need the money,' Polly said.

'Perhaps not, but it would be good for him to learn that you have to pay your way in life. He tends to think everything grows on trees, and I've noticed he's spending a lot on neckties and hats and that horrible hair oil he uses. And isn't that a new cigarette case he's been flaunting lately?'

Polly was amused. 'I can't say I've noticed.'

'Well, I have. He needs to learn the value of money before it's too late. Make him pay for his keep. If you don't want the money you can always put it aside without telling him, and give it to him when he gets married one day. He'll need it then.'

'All right,' Polly said. 'I'll do that, if you think I should. What else?'

'Roberta. She's twenty-one this year.'

'Yes, I suppose she is. I wonder, will her mother have a party for her?'

'I doubt it. I don't think she has two farthings to rub together. Donald's not been well, you know, and the doctor's bills are a constant drain. Between you and me, I don't think he's much longer for this world, poor old fellow. But it wasn't a birthday party for Roberta I was talking about. She needs a job.'

'I thought she helped you around the stables.'

'She does, but she needs a proper job, with regular hours and discipline and responsibility. And wages. I'd hate to see her living at Morland Place on your penny for the whole of her life. And, yes,' she forestalled Polly, 'I know you don't mind. But I do. She's a bright girl and she ought to get out into the world and find out what she's good for.'

'What do you suggest?'

'I think she'd like a job in a racing stables. There are plenty of them around the area, and they all take on girls nowadays. And the only way she'll ever get married is if she finds a nice man who's as interested in horses as she is.'

'You want everyone to get married!'

'It is the most natural state,' Jessie said.

'All right. I'll look into a stable for Roberta, if you're sure that's what she'd like. What about the others?'

'Martin would like to stay on at school and go to university afterwards. If you're willing to have him be a charge on you for that long, I think he'd appreciate being told he can. I know he worries about it.'

'It's what my father would have wanted, I suppose,' Polly said. 'I'll tell him.'

'And Harriet would like to stay on at school, then train to be a teacher. That would get her off your hands, at least, once she's qualified,' Jessie offered temptingly.

Polly laughed. 'And what about John?'

'All John wants is to leave school and go to work in Hanbury's garage,' Jessie said, 'and if I were you I'd let him. The boy is a dim bulb, but he does understand engines. And, of course, Laura's only eleven so you won't have to worry about her for a few years yet. I've no idea what makes that child tick, despite the fact that she's over here more than she's at Morland Place. She's a queer one, always watching and never speaking. I suppose she'll reveal herself one day.'

'At least she'll have a little money when she grows up,' Polly said, 'from her father's book.' It was a memoir of the war and had proved immensely popular.

'Yes, and perhaps she'll show a literary turn herself. For now, all she wants is to be around the horses and play with the dogs.'

'Well, then, let her. It's all I wanted at her age.'

'Hm,' said Jessie. 'You were in rather a different situation.'

CHAPTER SIX

When Violet and Avis had come in from the garden and told their news, it had caused surprise – politely concealed – and a great deal of pleasure. As Avis became the centre of a crowd and told his story, Violet had retreated to a corner where she could sit quietly and enjoy the luxury of looking at him and thinking, *He's mine!*

Oliver said, 'As Violet and I are orphans, I shall have to take you into the business room, Belmont, and subject you to an elder-brotherly interview.'

'I'd expect nothing less. I'm prepared to be grilled,' Avis said, with equanimity. 'My intentions are honourable and my circumstances respectable.'

'That about covers it,' said Eddie, with a grin.

'Oh, how men do go off after the trivial!' Emma said. 'The important thing, Violet, is when is the wedding to be?'

Across the room Violet met Avis's eyes for a second that was like a lance of white fire to the pit of her stomach. 'As soon as possible,' she said. And she laughed.

Robert and Richard exchanged a glance with raised eyebrows. They couldn't remember ever hearing their mother laugh. She had always been even-tempered and smiled the proper amount, but she did not laugh.

Later, Avis came over to them in the course of circulation and said, 'I hope you don't mind my marrying your mother.'

'Of course not, sir,' Richard said. 'I can see you've made her very happy.'

'It seems a respectable and appropriate match,' Robert said, trying to sound like the head of the family.

Avis tactfully mirrored his solemnity. 'Thank you. I assure you I have her honour most deeply at heart. And if there is anything I can do to help advance your interests . . .'

'Oh, I'm very well placed, thank you,' Robert said. 'My mentor, Lord Oldham—'

Richard interrupted before his brother could entirely deflate the joy of the moment. 'We shan't be a burden on you, sir, don't worry. We're out in the world and can take care of ourselves. I suppose you and Mum will live in the country?'

'Some of the time,' Avis said. 'I've had to sell the ancestral London house but, frankly, it was too big, too cold and too ugly anyway. We'll rent a suitable place for the Season. I wouldn't want to separate your mother from the world she knows. She's a Town person at heart.'

'She and Uncle Oliver were brought up there,' said Richard, relieved he understood.

Henry's gladness was straightforward. He had got to know Avis on the boat going to New York and thought him a good egg; and after his father had died and they had become poor, Avis had shown up with a spiffing motor-car, taken them all out and generally made life less dreary.

Avis said, 'I don't want my marrying your mother to change your life too much. If you're happy at your school, I'm sure we can work out a way for you to stay on there.'

'Well, actually, sir . . .' Henry said, and told him about his desire for technical college. 'Do you think there's a chance I could go?' he concluded, wide-eyed with hope.

'It's a very decent ambition,' Avis said. 'We need good men to design aeroplanes. Our country deserves to have the best in the world. Have you any idea which college you'd like to go to?'

'No, but now I know I can go, I'm going to find out.'

The wedding day was set for the end of January, which was further away than Violet wanted, but Avis was still much occupied with estate and legal business. Violet had wanted a quick register-office wedding, but Avis was determined they should marry 'properly' in church. 'I shall begin to think you're ashamed of me,' he complained.

It was arranged that she should be married from Oliver's house and that he would give her away. The ceremony would take place in the church of St James, Piccadilly, and there would be a wedding-breakfast afterwards at Chelmsford House.

Henry, whose ideas about weddings were formed by newspaper reports, assumed his mother would wear a white dress with a long train and a floating veil, and worried considerably that she might be too old for this and make them all look foolish. When at last he confided his fears to Charlotte, she told him that she had heard about the outfit and that it was to be quite seemly: ivory crêpe-de-Chine, calf length, fitted, with a matching jacket and a small hat. Violet was going to Verena's dressmaker, Loiret, who had trained with Madeleine Vionnet and made simple, elegant gowns of beautiful cut.

'And no bridesmaids,' Charlotte reassured him; then added wickedly, 'but I did put in a good word for you to be a page-boy in a Gainsborough suit. You'll look so sweet . . . No, *pax*, *pax*! No pinching!'

All the children were to stay at Chelmsford House for the wedding, and Charlotte and Henry were to remain there afterwards while Violet and Avis had their honeymoon (they were sailing on the *Mauretania* to New York). It had not yet been decided what would happen to the house in Lancaster Gate that Oliver had provided for them after Holkam's death. For the time being Robert and Richard would stay there; arrangements for the boys would have to be discussed after the honeymoon.

Everything was progressing merrily when Charlotte came to her mother one day to say happily, 'Mummy, Uncle Oliver says if the boys decide to go into lodgings or take a flat instead of staying on at Lancaster Gate, I can stay with him for as long as I like. Isn't he marvellous?'

Violet looked surprised. 'But, darling, you'll be with me and Avis. Don't worry about missing the Season. We'll be going straight down to Derbyshire when we come back from America, but we'll come up for a few weeks in May and June.'

'But, Mummy, I can't go down to Derbyshire! My course lasts for eight weeks. And then I'll have to be in London to look for a job – position, I mean.'

'Don't be silly, darling. You won't need to do the course now. I meant to tell Oliver to cancel it, but I forgot.'

'Cancel it?' Charlotte said, with a waver in her voice.

'You'll have a proper position in society as Lord Belmont's step-daughter. We're going to entertain, and you'll move in the best circles, so you'll soon meet someone—'

'*Meet* someone?'

Violet frowned. 'Don't be deliberately obtuse, Charlotte. We can put your father's bankruptcy behind us now. It will be completely forgotten, I promise you, and you shall go to all the right places and meet the right people. You've grown up into a very nice-looking girl and you'll have plenty of proposals – you'll be able to pick and choose.'

'You don't understand, Mummy,' Charlotte said, with despairing calmness. 'I wasn't doing the course because I had to. It was because I *wanted* to. And I still do. I want to learn to be a secretary, then get a position and live in the real world.'

'The *real* world?'

'Things have changed, Mummy,' Charlotte said. 'You still think things should be the way they were when you were a girl. But the war changed everything, and we can't go back.

136

I don't *want* to go back. I belong to the new world, like Richard does. I can't be a simpering debutante waiting for a nice young man to rescue me. It's too late. You must see that.'

'I don't see it at all. It's out of the question for you to take a job. I'll hear no more about it.'

But she did hear more. Robert was on her side, especially as, now she was to be Lady Belmont and comfortably off again, he meant to start using his own title more: he agreed it was unseemly for his sister to take a job. Richard, however, said that Charlotte would be twenty in May and would be humiliated by having to parade herself alongside seventeen-year-olds in the hope of catching a husband. Henry, of course, thought getting a job (oh, all right, a *position*) would be much more fun than just going to parties all the time. Oliver simply felt people should be allowed to follow their own path, as long as it was legal and hurt no-one: forcing people into the wrong mould seldom worked out well.

Verena, who entered more fully into Violet's feelings than any of them, said, 'Richard's right, Vi – Charlotte's too old to go back to being a debutante. Lots of nice girls are working in shops and galleries, these days – there's nothing at all *off* about it. And the young men like it that way. They like wives who have seen something of the world outside the school-room. Look at how they snap up the American girls as soon as they arrive.'

'That's because they're heiresses,' Violet said.

'It isn't only that. They have a different outlook, a freer way of talking and thinking. They're more amusing companions. Let Charlotte do her course, and let Oliver steer her into a suitable job, and before you know it she'll have met a delightful man and everyone will be happy.'

Violet was not convinced, and there were several days of painful uncertainty for Charlotte, who moped miserably and could take no interest in the wedding. She spent her time taking Fifi for long, exhausting walks or reading in her room until her eyes gave out. Richard and Verena continued to work on Violet, but in the end it was her daughter's unhappiness that persuaded her. She herself was so happy, longing for life with Avis as a caged bird might long for freedom and the wide sky, that it hurt her to see Charlotte pining in what Violet had to come to realise was a real cage to her.

So one evening she went up to Charlotte's room, and when her daughter looked up from the book she was reading, she noted the puffy eyes and said, 'Does it really mean so much to you to do this silly course? Would you really rather have a job than live at home and go about with me?'

Charlotte nodded, without hope. 'Yes, Mummy. I'm sorry.'

Violet sighed. 'I think you'll find it isn't nearly as nice as you expect. But if it's what you want, I'll agree to it. As long as you follow your uncle Oliver's advice.'

Transformation. 'Oh, Mummy, I will! Oh, thank you, thank you!'

'And if you change your mind at any time, you can always come home to us. Don't be too proud to admit it.'

'I won't. But I won't – if you see what I mean. Oh, *thank* you, Mummy!'

'It seems an odd thing to be thanked for,' Violet said. 'But now we had better go through your wardrobe. I don't know who you'll be mixing with, but I think you'll need some new outfits for your life of commerce.'

Lennie Manning led a nomadic sort of life, travelling regularly between New York, Washington and Los Angeles, though these days it was the latter that he regarded as his home – in so far as any place could be home without Polly. In Los Angeles there was his young cousin Rose Morland, whose Hollywood career he was overseeing: at twenty-two she had three movies under her belt, and was making a fourth. Her third picture, *Hearts of Courage*, had given her her first starring role, opposite Robert Montgomery, who had played the part of an Englishman for the third consecutive time. It had opened in the fall of 1931 to rapturous reviews, and had brought in so many offers that Lennie was wondering whether it would be possible for her to get out of her contract with ABO.

He was a large ABO shareholder, and it had seemed a good deal when she had signed it in 1929, but five years is a long time in Hollywood. ABO was a smaller company than Universal or MGM, or even Warner Brothers and Paramount-Publix – though Warner's didn't seem to be able to make anything but musicals, these days, and Paramount were expanding so fast there were rumours of financial troubles and looming bankruptcy. The answer, of course, was for ABO to take over some smaller film companies and get bigger, become the studio that sent out poaching offers to big and up-and-coming stars. He should talk to Joe Kennedy, his fellow investor, about that – Kennedy had bought up quite a few small companies in the twenties and had a knack of getting them for very low prices.

As an ABO director and stockholder, Lennie naturally wanted to keep Rose, and hoped that the movie she was currently making, *The Veil*, would be as big a hit as *Hearts of Courage*. On the other hand, as Rose's honorary uncle, he wanted the best for her. One of the offers was from MGM, to lead in a romantic comedy called *Mother and Daughter*, about a young woman in New York who, through a series of misunderstandings, is saddled with a precocious little girl whom everybody believes to be her daughter. The child part was to go to juvenile star Peach McGinty, she of the round cheeks and golden curls, famous for such smasheroos as *Little Daisy Sunshine*, *Lollipop Girl* and *All-American Miss*. Child stars were all the rage at the moment; and there was a cute dog in it as well (it got hit by a car, so that Peach could hug it with large glycerine tears shining on her cheeks, but recovered in the end), so the film was bound to be a big hit.

And it had to be considered that MGM had Clark Gable under contract, and he was so popular that crowds had broken the barriers around the Montmartre restaurant's entrance just to get his autograph. Lennie dreamed of Rose starring opposite Clark Gable and shooting straight to the top.

On the negative side, Peach McGinty was always the star of anything she played in, and it was possible that the grown-up playing opposite her might be completely overshadowed and barely register on the public's notice, despite billing right under Peach – which Lennie would insist on. And, of course, getting out of a contract could be costly and generate bad blood. It was a tricky conundrum.

Rose's mother Lizzie was another reason for being in Los Angeles. She and her husband Ashley had uprooted themselves from New York to bring Rose to Hollywood for her career, leaving behind on the east coast their two married sons and their families. And this winter, an unusually damp one for the City of Angels, Ashley, who was a lot older than Lizzie, had taken bronchitis and died. So Lennie needed to be on hand to comfort Lizzie and help her through the first difficult period. For himself, he had less reason now to go back to New York, since his father, his only close family, had died just before Christmas at the age of seventy. Lennie had thought of keeping on his father's apartment to use on his visits to New York, but one stay there, to sort out his father's effects, had changed his mind. It was too big, too empty, too full of memories. He had decided right away to sell it, and stay at his club or in an hotel when business took him to New York.

Business was his radio-manufacturing company – Manning's radios could be found in every home, and he was working to put one in every motor-vehicle, too – and his radio-broadcasting company. He kept abreast of the financial news while he was in New York, and dined with the influential people in Wall Street, top financiers and journalists.

In Washington his business was at the White House: he was a founder member of the Federal Radio Commission, and President Hoover had appointed him to chair a special White House committee on how radio and television could and should be used by the executive. He and Hoover had a good relationship from way back, and discussed many matters on which Lennie understood he acted as a sounding-board for new ideas.

The economy was naturally foremost in everyone's minds in Washington – which made it a very different place from Hollywood, where studio news beat the economy not just into second place but entirely out of the running. Hollywood, people said, was not so much a place as a state of mind: Lennie thought it was very definitely a place, but a place on a different planet. Hoover liked to hear his more outrageous tales, and Lennie made sure to bring him some when he visited. It gave the President relief, for a few moments, from the pressing problems that seemed to be all but insoluble.

The depression rolled on; unemployment was still rising; credit was so hard to get that good businesses failed for the want of it. It was thought that a quarter of working-age men were now unemployed; companies went broke and houses were repossessed; families went on the road with all their possessions packed into the family car or the back of a truck, hopelessly searching for work. Travelling on the train across the country, you would see them trundling along, all kids and dogs, cooking pots and flapping tarpaulins, each an anonymous cloud of dust in the great central emptiness of America, looking for what could not be found.

Malnourishment was becoming a widespread problem, and on its back, tuberculosis had made a comeback and was spreading; deaths in childbirth were increasing, and children were getting rickets. It was painful to the President that the

141

shanty towns that had sprung up on the edges of cities, built by the homeless out of packing cases, cardboard, corrugated iron or any other rubbish that came to hand, were beginning to be called Hoovervilles. Of all things, to be remembered for that . . .

What to do about any of it? Taxes would certainly have to go up that year, and considerably: the top rate was to rise from 25 per cent to 63 per cent in that year's Revenue Act. A Federal tax of one cent per gallon was to be put on gasoline – the blood in America's veins. It was the first time it had ever been taxed. That was something that had to be kept a great secret until the time, as was a slated 30 per cent cut in public-employee wages. And in an effort to get the economy moving and more people into employment, the government was working on an Emergency Relief and Construction Act, to fund public works such as roads, bridges, airports, dams, post offices and courthouses. Taking money out of one set of pockets to put it in another – but what else was there to do? Until private enterprise picked up enough to take up the slack, the public purse had to.

It was a relief for Lennie to get back to the town where the important questions of the day were whether Cagney would really retire or Garbo really come back, where the most urgent topic of conversation was MGM's new movie, *Tarzan the Ape Man*, with Johnny Weissmuller, the Olympic gold-medal swimmer, playing the jungle hero and dialogue by Ivor Novello.

There was comfort there, too, in his 'Mediterranean-style' house in Whitley Heights, his devoted housekeeper Wilma, and his pleasantly undemanding and intermittent relationship with the film starlet Evelyn Evans. She was a svelte, pretty young woman, with marcelled golden hair and a Cupid's bow mouth, and was gay and amusing company. The difficulty was that she reminded him too much of Polly, while falling well short. Her eyes were blue, but not the imperishable blue of summer skies like Polly's; her blonde hair came out of a bottle, unlike Polly's pure gold threads; she was the same height and build, but did not move with the athletic grace that had made watching Polly, for him, like hearing music.

Still, he would not burden Polly with emotions she had made it clear she didn't want, so he wrote cheerful letters to her in England, and she wrote cheerful, sadly brief letters back to him. But in his busy life, surrounded always by people who knew his name and wanted (for various reasons) to be with him, there was an empty space inside him that ached like an old wound when rain was coming. He managed to put it out of his mind for most of the time, but it made its voice heard when he was alone and the whirl of activity died down. In the cavern of night, when he couldn't sleep, it ached and ached, and he rubbed absently at his chest as though that might ease it, and thought of Polly in England, and wondered what she was doing.

There was one thing for which he envied his colleague Joe Kennedy. Kennedy was a rogue and pretty much of a scoundrel, too – he had made no attempt to conceal his affair with Gloria Swanson, even from his wife – and many of his business dealings would not bear the strong light of scrutiny. But when Lennie visited Boston to see his cousins there, he would generally be invited to take a family dinner with the Kennedys, and there would be the comfortable home filled with a wife and a fine brood of sons and daughters. All Lennie had, despite his wealth, position and influence, was a maid, a gardener and a chauffeur.

'You should get married,' Joe would say boisterously, slapping him on the back. 'Nothing like it! Find some nice girl and tie the knot. Don't tell me you haven't got 'em chasing after you in droves, a fine feller like you. Marry Evvie Evans, why don't ya?'

But that would only be to swap one kind of loneliness for another. And his chest would still ache in the night.

He arrived back in Los Angeles from DC one day in February 1932, glad to see the sunshine again: Washington had been grey and dank and shivery, wreathed in fog and with snow turning to mush underfoot, everyone in the street huddled in mufflers, their collars turned up, and the lights indoors on at one thirty in the afternoon. It was hard to believe he was in the same world when he stepped out to the high blue sky, palm trees and bougainvillaea, and white houses that weren't streaked with sooty rain.

His chauffeur Beanie was waiting for him, with the big, comfortable limousine, to waft him home. 'How are things?' Lennie asked him, as he settled back on the leather upholstery.

Beanie considered, as he edged them out into the traffic. 'Well, sir,' he concluded, 'Miss Garbo say she lost two-thirds of her fortune in Sweden in the Crash. An' Mr Gable, he's mad cos summun put pencil shavings in his tobacca jar in his dressin' room at MGM fo' a joke, but he don' think it funny *at* all. Mr Zanuck's s'coored Ginger Rogers fo' his new musical at Warner's – she's a honey, that Miss Rogers, pretty as a picture. An' dey say Olympic Pictures is goin' bust, an' Paramount lookin' to buy 'em.'

The important news last, Lennie thought. Olympic might be a good purchase for ABO. He must look into it. 'What about at home?' he asked, amused as always that Beanie put the studio news first.

'Icebox broke,' he offered. 'Wilma got a man in t' fix it, and he trample dirty footmarks all over the kitchen flaw. That Wilma madder'n a wet cat. She flang a pan at him, and she din' even take the taters out first.' He chuckled. 'He ended up cleanin' the whole flaw on his han's an' knees, taters an' all. That Wilma, she's a piece o' work, Mr Lennie.'

'She's a wonderful woman,' Lennie said. 'Anything else?'

'Well, sir,' Beanie said, and paused. Then, 'I don' like to gossip, Mr Lennie. No, sir. I cayn tell you.'

'Go on, or I'll make you get out and walk home,' Lennie threatened pleasantly.

'Well, sir,' Beanie said reluctantly, 'dey sayin' Miss Evans been hittin' the town wid Napier Coles. That's what dey sayin'. I don't know if it true.'

Lennie merely nodded. He and Evelyn had never made any vows to each other, but he was disappointed that she would fall into such an obvious trap as Napier Coles. He was a rogue Englishman who claimed to be a baron and called himself Lord Coles when it suited him, though Lennie had never found him in any stud book. He was a playboy and lived by his wits, financing himself with gambling – he was very lucky – and gifts of money from rich lovers, male and female. He was handsome and charming and gave the impression of knowing everyone – and, indeed, he was such good company that he was at least acknowledged by almost everyone in Hollywood – and Evvie would not be the first hopeful to be seduced by his promise of advancing her career. But she would not interest Coles for long: he dropped hopefuls quickly if they didn't make enough money to support him. Sadly for Lennie, he didn't think he could keep seeing her now, not when she had been handled by Coles's promiscuous paws.

They arrived at his gates, which were opened by Dawes, the gardener, who saluted with his rake and grinned a wide welcome as Lennie went by, and then they were home. Wilma was at the door waiting for him. 'Welcome home, Mr Lennie,' she said, picking up the portmanteau as if it weighed nothing. She had arms like legs and hands like hams, and Lennie reflected that the icebox man had done well to obey her meekly upon his knees, because a clout from her could have sent him sailing through the window. She had once performed an A&C on a press man who'd climbed over the wall that had sent him halfway down the drive in one perfect arc of flight.

'How is everything, Wilma?' Lennie asked.

She gave an expressive backward roll of the eyes. 'Miz Morland is here to see you. Been waiting an hour.'

Lennie's heart jumped for just the instant before he remembered that Wilma called all females 'miz', a word that did not distinguish married from unmarried, and that, while Polly had reverted to her maiden name in widowhood, Lizzie's surname was also Morland. 'Did you give her coffee?' he asked – the first thing that came into his head while he recalibrated.

Wilma knew it for what it was. 'What kind of question is that?' she protested. 'You going straight in, Mr Lennie, or you want me to stall her some more while you freshen up?'

'Straight in,' he said meekly. 'But I could do with some of your coffee. Strong.'

'Coming right up. You go on – she's on the porch.'

The porch – which Lennie, from his years in Europe, sometimes called a verandah – was one of the nicest parts of the house, he always thought: shady, hung with bougainvillaea and roses, and with a magnificent view down the steeply terraced garden, past the sapphire swimming-pool, which sat at the top of a short cliff, and across the lush ravine to the hills, pleasantly green at this time of year. Here he found Lizzie sitting in one of the comfortable porch chairs but not looking comfortable, staring out at nothing and so deep in her thoughts that she started when Lennie came out from the house.

'In a brown study?' he said, stooping over her to kiss her cheek. She was Polly's first cousin – her aunt Henrietta's elder daughter – and, though much older than her, bore just a faint family resemblance that tugged at Lennie's heart. 'Or is it more of a blue one?' He sat down in the next chair, hitching it round to face her, and said, 'What's the matter?'

'Oh, Lennie, I didn't mean to worry you the minute you arrived. I got it into my head you were coming back yesterday so I came over today thinking you'd be—'

'Spit it out,' Lennie invited. 'If it's serious enough for you

146

to wait an hour for me . . . Anyway, that's what I'm here for, to be worried.' She was looking careworn, he thought, and so she might, having lost her husband of thirty-four years; but she was a person of great fortitude (he remembered that in her youth she had been a suffragette and had gone to prison for it) and had not given way to sorrow.

'It's Rose,' she said. 'I hate to be a tattle-tale, and I know she's supposed to be practically grown-up, but she's not twenty-one yet—'

'Not for another week,' Lennie said drily. He and the studio were planning a big party for her on the eve of her birthday, which should be good publicity, and there would be a private luncheon on the day itself, with him and Lizzie and a few close friends, when they would give her their presents. 'What's she done?'

'I don't know,' Lizzie said. 'That's the trouble. The night before last she didn't come in and, Lennie, she *lied* about it.'

'That's not like my Rosie.'

'She turned up at breakfast with her makeup smudged and pretended she'd just got up, but she *never* goes to sleep without taking it off. Then she wouldn't eat, just took a cup of coffee back to her room. And when she'd gone, Dola told me she'd just that minute come in, walked up through the backyard so as not to be seen, and quickly changed her clothes. So I went straight to her room to have it out with her, and she admitted she'd been out all night but she wouldn't tell me where or who with.'

Lennie nodded gravely. That was bad, all right. It was such a problem with young movie starlets (see under Evvie Evans *et seq.*) that every rogue in town was after them, and they hadn't the experience to tell friendship from flattery. Being so important to the studio, they started to get big ideas about themselves and believe everyone had to step aside for them. He had thought Rose happily free of the taint, but if she wouldn't say whom she had been with that night, it had to be something she wanted to keep from her mother. 'Where was she that evening, do you know?'

'She'd gone out with Rula Packer and her brother and Tory Del Orio. They said they were going to a party in Angelino Heights, and Bobby Packer is such a sensible young man, I thought it would be all right. Lennie, what am I to do? She's never lied to me like that before. Is this the start of something?'

'I'll have a word with her,' Lennie said. 'Sometimes girls will tell a male relative things they wouldn't tell their mothers. Is she at home now?'

'Sleeping,' said Lizzie.

'Why don't you invite me to lunch, then, and after lunch I'll go for a walk with her and try and get to the bottom of it? Try not to worry yet.'

'I can't help it,' Lizzie said. 'She's lost her father, and girls can go astray when that happens.'

'Well, she's got me – and so have you. Run on home, now, and get something in for my lunch. Got to make it look good.'

Lizzie gave a watery smile. 'When Dola knows you're coming she'll want to pull all the stops out. You know how she adores you. She'll scold me for not giving her notice so she can do her pot roast.'

'Tell her I dream about her pork chops too,' Lennie said.

Later, feeling uncomfortably full of pork and mashed potatoes, Lennie suggested a stroll to shake it down. Lizzie said she had letters to write, and Rose rather sulkily agreed to accompany him.

'I know Mom's been telling you things about me,' she said, when they were alone, strolling along the shaded street beside the small, bright front yards. 'You two are as subtle as a dose of measles.'

'All right, no subtlety, then,' Lennie agreed. 'Why won't you tell her where you were on Thursday night?'

148

'I don't have to tell anyone where I've been. I'm a grown woman.'

'Not for another week,' Lennie said. 'And I hate to break it to you, but part of being under contract is that the studio has a say in your private life as well as on screen.' He looked at the mulish scowl and said, 'You know that perfectly well, because it was explained to you at the time. And I've explained it to you more than once since.'

She muttered something that included the word 'ridiculous'.

Lennie softened. 'Come on, Rosie,' he said, 'you can tell me. What have you done? I promise I won't be shocked.'

She looked startled. 'What *do* you mean? Oh, but it's no use! You don't want me to have a proper life, any more than the others.'

'My dear girl,' he said, 'it doesn't matter to me if you're a movie star or not. If you don't like it, give it up. But if you want to go on with it, you have to follow the rules. It's a straight choice.'

'I *do* want to be a star,' she said. 'It's what I've always wanted. But does that mean I can't have love as well?'

'Oh, love, is it?' he said, gently teasing. 'Well, that's serious. Who is it?'

'He's wonderful,' she said, suddenly glowing. 'He's handsome, and smart, and he makes me laugh, and he knows *everything*, and he's so sophisticated, miles better than Bobby Packer and his set, who are just such *boys*, you can't take them seriously. I know he's a bit older than me –' Lennie didn't like the sound of that '– but what does that matter? Age is just a number.' She said that as though someone had recently put the words into her mind. 'A man ought to be older than the girl, so he can know what to do in an emergency. Anyway, I like older men. They just – know heaps of stuff, and how to order in a restaurant and things.'

'All right, so who is this paragon of all the virtues?' Lennie asked, still keeping it light.

'*You* ought to like him,' she said, switching her earnest gaze on Lennie. 'He's English. He's got the most delicious accent. *And* he's a lord, though he doesn't make a big thing of it.'

Lennie felt cold inside. 'Name?' he demanded.

She heard the change in his voice and looked anxiously at him. 'His name's Napier, Napier Coles, but his friends call him Napes. Why? What's the matter? Do you know him?'

He caught her by the upper arms. 'How far has this gone?'

'Lennie, don't – you're hurting me. What do you mean?'

'Have you kissed him? Has he made love to you?'

She was trying not to cry now. 'We've been out to lunch a few times. Why are you so mad? Stop it! I hate you!'

'Why did you stay out all night? Were you with him?'

'We were at a party, and he came, and we danced a lot, and then he said would I like to see the sun rise over Beverly Hills? So I left Rula and the others and he drove me and we parked and waited for the sun and—'

He shook her. 'And what?'

'We kissed a bit. He's a marvellous kisser. And—'

'*What?*'

She was crying now, though being an actress she was able to do it without crumpling up her face. 'He said he loved me,' she whimpered. 'You're hurting my arms.'

He released her. 'Is that all?'

'What d'you mean *all*? He loves me!'

'I mean, you just kissed? You didn't do anything else?'

'We just kissed. What's wrong with kissing? Why are you being so mean about it? Is it because he's older than me? If that's all—'

Lennie gave her a rueful shake of the head. 'If only that were all.' He drew her hand through his arm – against a certain resistance – and resumed walking. 'I'm sorry I was rough with you. But, yes, I do know Napier Coles. He's English, but that's probably the only true thing he's told you. He's a *lot* older than you, he's not a lord, and he certainly doesn't love you. He makes a habit of picking up pretty young actresses and breaking their hearts.' He left out the bit about the actors. She was still innocent, thank God.

'You're just being mean about him,' she said, with a wobble in her voice. 'You don't know him like I do.'

'Oh, honey, I do know him. I wish I didn't. I've known him for years. He has dozens of mistresses and borrows money from them all that he'll never pay back. He lives on gambling and his looks.'

'But he said he loved me,' came the last weak protest.

'You must never judge a man by what he says but by what he does,' Lennie said. 'This man who says he loves you has been seeing Evvie while I've been away.' He was sorry to sacrifice Evvie, but it was in a good cause. He wondered now if Beanie had been trying to warn him about Rose. Beanie cared about the family.

Now Rose was shocked. 'Your Evvie? Evelyn Evans?'

'Well, not mine any more, it seems.' He pressed her hand against his side. 'So you see, we've both had our hearts broken.'

They walked in silence a few moments, then she said, in a small voice, 'Not mine, not really *broken*. I'm just—'

'Mad?' Lennie supplied.

'Kind of. And disappointed. What about you?'

'About the same. Not really heartbroken.'

Now she squeezed his arm. 'Poor Lennie. You ought to have someone nice. You deserve it. You're such a nice person.'

'Thank you. And so are you.' She looked up at him, arrested. 'You deserve someone nice. Someone you'd be proud to bring home to meet your mother. Someone you know I'd like. Not someone you feel you have to lie about.'

'I didn't really—'

'Do you understand me?'

She looked troubled. 'I think so.'

'You're in a dangerous profession, Rosie. There are sharks and shoals all about you, and I'm sorry to say the press like nothing more than to see a nice young woman stumble and disgrace herself. It makes good headlines. But your mother's here and I'm here, and we'll watch over you, if you'll let us. And the most important person who has to watch over you is . . . ?'

'Me,' she said. 'I get it.' She sighed heavily, but he saw she was resigning Napier Coles to the past. 'Lecture over?'

'Lecture over.'

'I'll be more careful in the future,' she said, after a minute. 'I don't want to be the sort of star who has smutty stories told about her. I want to be the sort everyone admires, the sort they say, "She's a big star but she's a real nice person, too."'

Lennie bent and kissed the top of her head. 'Good for you.'

'I suppose I have to apologise to Mom?'

'I think you do, for lying. And then that will be that.'

'Let's go home,' she said. 'I feel better now.'

'Do you think Dola would make us some of her popovers?'

'I bet you she already has,' said Rose.

Later, when Rose had gone to take a telephone call and Lizzie and Lennie were alone, Lizzie said, 'Is it all right? What's going to happen? Do I have to worry about her for the rest of my life?'

'You'll do that anyway,' he said.

'True. But you know what I mean.'

'I told her today she's in a dangerous profession. Men, drink, drugs, flattery and deception all around her, fuss made of her, people telling her she can do as she likes and the money to do it.'

'If this is meant to be reassuring me—'

'But she's a smart kid, Lizzie. It's your Rose we're talking about. She's got more brains in her little finger than most movie actors have in their whole bodies. And she's a good kid. I think she'll come through. We'll keep an eye on her and make sure she does.'

'I feel better about it all when you're here,' Lizzie confessed.

'I'll always be here,' Lennie said, and there was sadness in it, because where he wanted to be was with Polly. 'Apropos of which, I have an idea.'

'What is it?'

'I think you and Rose should move in with me. You ought to have a man around the house, and this place really isn't suitable for a movie star. Too easy for people to get up to the door.'

'Don't,' Lizzie said, and shuddered.

'So move in with me – there's plenty of space.'

'I'd hate to have to turn Dola off after all these years. Could we bring her?'

'I'm counting on it. Wilma doesn't really like cooking. Laundry is her great passion.'

'But will they get on?'

'Like a house a-fire. They can talk about Rose's career to their hearts' content – it's all Wilma wants to do anyway. Beanie can drive Rose to the studio so you won't have to. And I'll feel better about you when I'm travelling.'

Lizzie smiled, and looked five years younger. 'It would be such a load off my mind. If Rose agrees to it—'

'She will.'

She did. Lennie was prepared to use the weight of the studio to force her if she resisted, but she loved the idea, so it wasn't necessary. 'Your pool is miles better than ours, and I love the view from your porch. And it'll be fun seeing you when you're home. Oh, and can I have a dog? There wasn't room in our house, but you've got loads.'

'Yes, you can have a dog. But you have to look after it. No leaving it to Dola because you're tired after a day on set.'

'I won't. The first thing Queen Victoria did after her coronation was rush upstairs and give her dog a bath,' Rose said. 'I read that. I'll be that sort of mistress.'

So it was decided, and at the same time Lennie decided not to encourage Rose to switch studios. Instead he would negotiate a release for the one movie with Peach McGinty. It would be a good stepping-stone for her, with Peach taking most of the spotlight. Rose was very young for her age in many ways. Better she work her way up, gain the maturity she needed for a long career, than be rushed into big roles too early and suffer the crash that so often came afterwards. Clark Gable would just have to wait.

And he would continue to build up ABO. Olympic Studios first. And there were others struggling and ripe for take-over – K-Bel and Americana to name but two. He wasn't going to leave it to the big boys, the Warners and Paramounts of this world, to make all the running. But he'd need more finance. He should talk to Joe Kennedy. Wonder when he was coming out this way next?

He'd make ABO as big a player as MGM, and Rose would be the jewel in its crown. And then they'd be the studio all the big names wanted to work for.

He'd have to find someone else to squire to Rose's studio party. And that meant he'd have to talk to Evvie and break it off with her. That was something he didn't relish. He headed for the telephone and, as so often when he was facing the bits of his life that made him unhappy, his mind turned for escape to Polly and little Alec, so far away in a milder, greener land, that England for which he had risked his life against the Germans, and which still held more than half his heart.

CHAPTER SEVEN

The wedding was over, the wedding-breakfast was over. The car drive to the station, the boat train to Southampton, over. Southampton itself – the great sheds, the uniformed officials, the cranes scratching the sky, the sound of gulls, the salty, oily smell of the sea – seemed far in the past, like a dream. *Mauretania* was the most dreamlike of all: an artificial world, a construct of money and bustle and unnatural activities, a smell of carpets and wax polish and starched linen. All the ants'-nest activity of first night, people milling, complaining about journeys, cabins, lost luggage; meeting and parting, greeting old friends, making plans; dinner a hum of voices, a thrill of excitement, ripples of laughter coming and going like waves on a flat shore, the clink of silver on china, the lance-like sparkle of crystal glasses raised and of diamonds on the hands that raised them.

All that was over; part of the immutable, forgettable past. Now, here, in the low-lit cabin, which was anywhere and nowhere, was the point at which time began. Violet came out of the bathroom, acutely aware of her body underneath the new chiffon négligée in a way she had forgotten; tense, yet not afraid, knowing pleasure was hers to give as to receive. Avis was sitting on the bed in unfamiliar pyjamas. He had become dear and known, but now she was pierced with the excitement of the strange. Then unbearable longing: she wanted, she *needed* touch – lips, hands, the sweetness of flesh against flesh. A sixteen-year-long famine was to end here.

His look as he gazed at her was almost troubled. Words she did not know she knew tumbled from her lips as she went to him.

Si tu veux nous nous aimerons
Avec tes lèvres, sans le dire

Wisely he did not ask where she had learned them. This was the Violet he had loved without ever having seen her, trusting only an instinct that knew her without meeting: this unloosed creature of lips and eyes and tumbled hair, holding out hands that trembled slightly, but not with fear – not fear.

He took her into his arms, and in a moment they were naked together in a newness that was like the first day of creation: passionate, innocent, wise and wordless.

In this anonymous place that was nowhere and everywhere, Violet held at last what she had longed for. She went to her fate joyfully, meeting flame with flame, plunging into the fire, and, like the phoenix, was both consumed and renewed.

At the beginning Charlotte had found the course harder than she had expected. It was a long time since she had been at school, and she had lost the habit of concentration. Much as she tried, she found her mind wandering, as it did in the long, dull days at home when there was little to do and no expectation of anything different. She would find herself drifting on a sea of words and come to with a jerk, not knowing how long she had been away or how much she had missed. She had, shamefacedly, to ask someone at the break, and some, from competitive schools and not used to sharing their notes, did not want to help her.

Mostly they were younger than her, girls coming straight from the schoolroom, sleek with the advantage that that bestowed, but suspicious of anyone who was in any way different, seeking out anything that might be 'unfair', ready to resent anyone who got ahead of them. The first day she also went hungry, not having realised that she had to provide her own midday meal – something that had never happened in her whole life. From home to school and back to home, it had always just arrived at the right moment. Many of the girls – the poorer ones, she guessed – brought sandwiches from home; others went off, arm in arm, to nearby cafés. She had brought nothing with her but her tube fare. As she sat stupidly, looking blank, realising her predicament, one of the other girls – one of the older ones – stopped in front of her on her way out and said, 'I say, is something wrong? You look as though you've got a pain.'

'Oh – no – thank you. I'm fine.'

'Are you sure?'

'I've just realised I forgot to bring any money for lunch, that's all,' Charlotte admitted, reddening.

'If that's all, I can lend you two bob, if you can give it back tomorrow,' said the girl, kindly.

But Charlotte could not bear to accept, not from a stranger, not when she didn't know if the girl could afford it. Probably not, if she had to have it back the next day. She said, 'That's frightfully nice of you, but really, I'm fine. Please don't bother.' The girl shrugged and went away, and to the pangs of hunger Charlotte had to add the worry that she had offended her. For the rest of the week she persuaded Mrs Drayton to give her sandwiches, and crept out alone to eat them on a bench in Hyde Park, to avoid what she thought were hostile eyes.

She found the days long and lonely and, that first week, was exhausted all the time from the sheer effort of paying attention. The second night she fell asleep on the tube going home, not waking until the train terminated at White City and the guard came to eject her. It was lucky, she reflected, that it was turning round there – she might have gone all the way to Ealing. After that, when she felt herself nodding off, as she did every night in the stuffy warmth of the carriage, she did her best to jerk herself awake. But on the Friday she failed again, and woke to find her head had slipped gently over and was nestled on the shoulder of the man beside her. He did not seem to mind, and smiled and said, 'Not at all,' but she was mortified.

A weekend at home with no work refreshed her, and restored her sense of proportion. At least she was able to report truthfully to her family that, exhausted or not, she was loving it. Exercising her brain, learning new things and, above all, knowing that she was working towards usefulness and independence, gave her a huge sense of satisfaction. She started back on the Monday with renewed energy, a much better sense of how to grapple with the course, the deter- mination to make friends, and sufficient money for lunch in her pocket.

The girl who had spoken to her on the first day nodded a greeting as she passed on arrival, and Charlotte nodded back. She looked to be about Charlotte's age, a small, neatly made girl with cropped black hair, a dancer's gait and a wide mouth that seemed made for smiles. Charlotte liked the look of her and resolved to talk to her. When the class ended for the lunch-hour, she packed her things quickly and stood up as the girl approached. She said, 'I'm tired of sandwiches and I've brought lunch money with me today. I was wondering if you'd mind showing me some places to eat?'

The girl looked flatteringly pleased. 'I'm having lunch with Betty,' she said, 'but you're welcome to join us.'

'Oh, no, really, if you're—'

'Come on! I've been wanting to talk to you since the first day.' She looked around with an amused shake of the head. 'You and me and Betty are the only old ones among all these infants. We have to stick together.' She thrust out a small, thin hand. 'I'm Myra, by the way – Myra Fox.'

Charlotte shook it. 'I'm Charlotte Howard.'

Myra grinned. 'I know who you are. My mother loves reading *Tatler* – I've seen your picture. Coming-out ball.' She tapped her brow. 'I never forget a face. But don't worry, I won't say anything if you're trying to go incog. Good idea, really. Some of these girls are seething masses of jealousy. Ah, here's Betty.'

The other older girl Charlotte had noticed was very different from Myra: tall, solid, square-built, with a heavy jaw, a high colour, and marcelled hair of an indeterminate shade. She walked heavily, but her dark eyes, under thick, straight brows, were intelligent.'

'Betty Harris, Charlotte Howard.' Myra performed the introduction. 'Betty's a tremendous brain-box. She's going to be a legal secretary. Gosh, I'm starving. Let's go to the Corner House.'

Charlotte was not long in learning that it would always be that way – Myra was the one who decided what they did and where they went. There was a Lyons Corner House on the corner of Oxford Street and Tottenham Court Road: she had passed it in a car or taxi many times but had never been in. Her mother, if she was in Oxford Street, used the Selfridges restaurant, but Charlotte sailed past that on the bus they had hopped on without a pang. She was looking forward to a new experience.

On the ground floor there was a food hall, selling hams, pies, cakes, pastries, hand-made chocolates, fruit from the Empire, wines, cheeses, flowers and much more. The smell was delectable, but with only an hour there was no time to explore. They went up the stairs, past the Mountview Café, which had white tablecloths and flowers on the tables, marble pillars and an orchestra playing a Gilbert and Sullivan selection, and on up to the Brasserie, which was less formal and more cheerful, with checked tablecloths and a small group playing dance music. The place was already busy and they had to thread through the tables to find a space. They were lucky enough to reach one near the band's dais just as a party of early lunchers was leaving. They hastened to sit down, and a Nippy came up with a tray to clear the table and give them menus.

'That's the only trouble with Lyons – so busy.' Myra sighed, resting her elbows on the table. 'Trying to get fed and back in an hour is such a pain. But I do like this music.' She jiggled her head to the rhythm and flicked her fingers in a curious way.

'Don't mind her,' Betty said stolidly. 'She used to do ballet. It made her rather flamboyant.'

Myra was sitting facing the dais, on which were a pianist, a bass player and a violinist, the leader; he smiled at her and nodded a greeting, and she smiled back. When she really smiled, her mouth seemed to make a complete semi-circle.

'Do you know them?' Charlotte asked.

'I come here quite often,' Myra said lightly.

'The violinist is her uncle,' Betty said.

Myra pouted. 'I was going to make it a surprise. Now you've spoiled it.' Then she beamed at Charlotte. 'If you have a request, I'll get them to play it.'

'A request?'

'A tune you'd like to hear.'

'Oh. I don't know many songs, really.' She saw incredulity on Myra's face, and thought back to her coming-out days. '"Painting The Clouds With Sunshine",' she suggested. She remembered dancing to that one with— Well, she wouldn't think about him any more.

Myra caught the leader's eye, mouthed the title, along with a rather graphic mime from her expressive fingers, and he nodded. When the current tune came to an end, it slid almost seamlessly into the very song Charlotte had requested. She blushed with pleasure. 'That's amazing,' she whispered.

'Nothing to it,' Myra said airily, but she was obviously pleased. 'We'd better get on and order or we won't be back in time. Have you decided? Where's that girl?'

For Charlotte everything was a new experience. She only had poached eggs on toast and a cup of coffee, but here she was, without any chaperone, sitting in this gay café with two nice girls, ordering whatever she wanted and paying for it out of her own purse. She found herself thinking, 'Bliss was it in that dawn to be alive, but to be young was very heaven'! And then a sense of proportion reasserted itself and she laughed at being so bowled over by so little. All the same, it was a fine day for her, and she felt it marked the beginning of a new life.

When she had been two weeks at the course, there came the weekend of her mother's wedding. On the Friday night after school all her belongings, which she had been packing by instalments during the evenings, were loaded into Uncle Oliver's motor-car and taken over to Chelmsford House. Henry was already packed and gone. Robert and Richard were staying on for a week or two more, but Robert was to move into a flat nearer to Westminster with two other parly secs, and Richard was going into lodgings when he had completed everything to do with the move. So Charlotte was leaving Lancaster Gate for the last time. It was sad to say goodbye to Mrs Drayton, but otherwise she found she had no feelings for the house at all. It was where they had gone in sadness and despair, and it had taken care of them, and ushered in a new life for them all, but it had never really been home. Uncle Oliver had tenants waiting to move into it, who would love it far more.

The wedding was lovely, as was the wedding-breakfast at Chelmsford House – the feast, as she thought of it to herself because it was extremely lavish – and then the couple departed (her mother and Avis, a couple! How strange that sounded!). Sunday felt rather flat. But on Monday morning she went back to her course with a feeling of rightness, like going home. The journey was different (not as straightforward as from Lancaster Gate, but sometimes Uncle Oliver took her in his motor and dropped her off) and it was strange at first, living in an earl's household again, with servants and large spaces around her. She had to get up earlier to take Fifi for a walk in St James's Park before school – for her mother had left the dog with her. But none of that mattered. The only thing that was real to her was the course, the work, the girls and their cheerful lunches. Part of her wished that it could last for ever, because at the end was an uncharted sea, and the probability of not seeing Betty and Myra again.

It was John Burton – the invaluable Burton – who found Roberta a place in a racing stables. Polly had taken to discussing matters with him first thing in the morning, when he walked up to the house for the day's instructions. The ritual had grown quite naturally and developed its own customs. One morning she had been late at breakfast and had taken her cup of coffee to the steward's room to finish, and had naturally offered him some when he arrived. After that, there was always a pot of coffee to accompany their discussions.

They began by talking about the farms and land management, went on to the other York businesses, then the mills and the Makepeace's. They discussed first what Burton had to do that day, then made their longer plans. Finally one day, when the weather had improved, he confessed that he thought better while walking about, and she said it was a shame to be indoors, so after that, having discussed the immediate matters and drunk their coffee, they took to going out with the dogs and walking round the moat while they talked.

From there it seemed quite natural to confide in him

about anything and everything else that was worrying her. It was he who was keeping an eye on John at Hanbury's garage, to which John now bicycled every morning: he seemed to be settling in well, Burton reported, which was more than Polly would ever have got out of John when they passed in the house, the lad being naturally inarticulate.

She discussed with him the question of a place for Roberta, and told him that Bertie was looking into it. But some weeks later Burton visited Bertie's place in Bishop Winthorpe to look at his pedigreed cattle, and in the course of a long talk learned that Bertie was so busy at that period he was having difficulty finding time to research the matter – indeed, he had pretty much forgotten about it.

'But I'm happy to look around for you, if you'd like me to,' he told Polly, as they walked round the moat, throwing a stick for Rex, the kitchen dog, who had joined them and adored the fetching game. Bigelot would only fetch rarely, and as a great favour, and Blossom looked at you with incomprehension: 'If you wanted the stick, why did you throw it away in the first place?'

'I'm sure you have far too much to do already,' Polly said, frowning in thought. 'I can't load any more onto your shoulders. It's a family matter, not estate business.'

'I can always find time to do anything that will help you,' he said, with a smile. She looked up, caught it, and felt absurdly warmed by it. 'And family and estate are inextricably linked to me, as they must be to you.'

'Why do you say that?'

'Well, the family couldn't thrive if the estate didn't thrive. And there'd be no point in the estate thriving if the family didn't.'

Polly laughed – a little nervously, because she seemed to be staring at Burton and not able to remove her gaze. 'I'm not sure my father would have agreed. He always talked about the estate as if it was a person in its own right.'

'I can see that,' Burton said. Her staring didn't seem to bother him. He seemed, as always, completely comfortable in her presence. 'And I should hate anything to happen to the estate, even if it wasn't part of you. But people come before land. It has to be so.'

'Perhaps you're right,' Polly said. Then, feeling foolish, 'I've forgotten what we were talking about.'

'Roberta,' he said. 'I have an idea of somewhere that might suit her, if you'd license me to look into it.'

'I'd be glad if you would. What is it?'

'There's a racing stables at Stillington – not too far away. About ten or twelve miles. It belongs to a woman, Hilary Maddox. I expect you've heard of her?'

'I haven't had time to catch up with the racing world yet,' Polly admitted.

'Well, she's new to the scene – she's had the stables five years – but she's already a successful trainer and I happen to know she's just bought another parcel of land with a view to expanding.'

'How do you know that?' Polly wondered.

'I follow all land sales in the area. It's part of my job to know who owns what.'

Polly laughed. 'When do you sleep?'

He gave her that smile again. 'Oh, I don't sleep very much. My father always used to say, "You can sleep when you're dead." My thought was that, being a woman, Mrs Maddox might be willing to take Roberta on more as a trainee than merely a groom. It would be better for her to have a proper career than a job that led nowhere.'

'Mrs Maddox? She's married, then?'

'I don't think so. I've never heard of a Mr Maddox. She may be widowed or divorced. Or it may be a courtesy title.'

'Like a cook,' Polly concluded.

He nodded. 'So would you like me to go and see Mrs Maddox and sound her out?'

164

'Oughtn't I to do it?'

'You'd need to meet her at some point, but better let me make the ground first.'

'You don't trust me,' Polly said with feigned indignation.

He looked at her seriously. 'I'm afraid you'd intimidate her.'

'What can you mean? I'm a very nice person.'

'Oh, I know. But you're too beautiful for most women to cope with until they get to know you.'

Polly turned her head away, feeling her cheeks grow warm. 'Very well,' she said, rather shortly. 'You do it.' And then, feeling she had been ungracious, 'Thank you.'

'No need to thank me,' he said in a perfectly normal, everyday way. 'I'm here to serve the estate.' And then he spoiled it by adding, 'And you.' He said it still matter-of-factly, but at that moment Polly found it difficult to hear the word 'you' coming from his mouth.

He changed the subject. 'By the way, you were talking about getting a dog of your own. I heard from Hatkill that Juno had had a litter.' Hatkill was the kennel man. 'I wondered if you knew. I had a look and they're very fine pups. It might be an idea for you to choose one, if you really wanted a dog, before Hatkill has them all promised. He won't be short of customers for them.'

Burton's testing of the water was so effective that only a few days later Polly drove herself and Roberta over to Stillington to meet Mrs Maddox. Stillington was a pretty place on the edge of the hills, with a village green and fine old trees. The Maddox stables were at the far end, and Roberta sat up straighter as she saw paddocks divided by white fences, full of glossy thoroughbred horses. They turned up a long drive between the paddocks and arrived at the stables – a range of new buildings – behind which was the house. It was much older: a typical plain stone Hambleton farmhouse, not very large, and square with four windows

165

and a door in its face, like a child's drawing. Behind that again there was an old stable yard and barn, beyond which an enormous new manège had been built.

'They do seem to have all the facilities,' Polly agreed.

'It's *gorgeous!*' Roberta cried. 'Oh, I *do* hope she'll have me. I'd even be a groom if she didn't want a trainee.'

'You can be a groom at Twelvetrees,' Polly pointed out.

'But this isn't Twelvetrees,' Roberta said, as if there was no comparison.

They knocked at the farmhouse door, and Polly wasn't very surprised that there was no reply. At a stables there was hardly ever anyone at home – they'd all be out working. Still, they did have an appointment. 'We'll try round the back,' Polly said. Here they had better luck. The back of the house, which opened onto the old yard, housed the kitchen; the door was open, and inside there was a middle-aged woman in a flowered overall, grey hair pulled back into a practical bun, chopping something at the kitchen table. Polly knocked on the open door, the woman turned, and Polly said, 'Mrs Maddox?'

The woman smiled and said, 'Eh, now, you must be Mrs Morland. You've caught me out. Ah'm all be'ind this morning.'

Polly looked at the clock on the overmantel. 'We're right on time. I did ring the front-door bell—'

'Eh, miss, that's not worked in a long time. You didn't stand there long, Ah hope?'

'Is Mrs Maddox in?' Polly asked, revising the initial thought that this was her. It must be the housekeeper, or the cook. There was a fine smell in the air of a meat pie baking.

'She told me you were coming, so Ah dare say she'll be back any minute. She's out wi' the vitnery over some horse wi' a bad foot. Now, I'll put you in't parlour and bring you a cup o' summat, and she'll be back dreckly, Ah shouldn't wonder.'

She bustled them through the kitchen, along a narrow hall with a stone-flagged floor, at the other end of which was the front door that had denied them entry, and into a parlour. It had a small brick fireplace with last night's ashes in it, two chintz-covered armchairs the worse for wear, a sagging sofa covered with a brown chenille cloth, and a table under the window heaped with old copies of *Horse & Hound*, stock reports and sales catalogues. Because the window was small, it was quite dark, and cold; there was a smell of dog and of leather, a bridle hung from a hook on the back of the door, and instead of pictures on the walls there were framed photographs of horses. To Polly it all seemed very comfortless, but Roberta looked about her as if it were Eldorado, and went at once to the table and started reading the first *Horse & Hound* she picked up.

Polly waited impatiently. The clock on the mantel had stopped, and apart from the sound of pages being turned by Roberta, it was very quiet. She wondered if Mrs Maddox had forgotten they were coming. After a bit she sighed heavily, and Roberta looked up, divined her thoughts, and said, 'If she's with the vet, she won't be able to hurry. It must be something that's come up suddenly.'

Polly relaxed. 'You're right. Throw me one of those magazines. I wonder what happened to the promised tea.'

It seemed a long time later that there was the sound of voices from the kitchen region, and in a moment they were disturbed, first by a Jack Russell terrier, which bustled in to inspect them, then by the housekeeper carefully edging through the door with an enormous tray of tea and cake, and finally by what would have to be Mrs Maddox, who was not at all what Polly had been expecting.

For one thing, she was no older than Polly herself – possibly a year or two younger. Polly had been expecting someone much older. For another, she was extremely attractive: tall, with a graceful, upright carriage, straight features, beautiful dark eyes and thick, glossy black hair. She had an air of health and vigour, and as she strode across the room to shake Polly's hand, Polly couldn't help seeing her as a fine thoroughbred mare in peak condition.

'Sorry I kept you waiting,' she said briskly. 'Case of laminitis – poor animal was in agony.'

'I quite understand,' Polly said. 'Mrs Maddox, I presume?'

She laughed, showing strong white teeth. 'The "Mrs" is a courtesy title. I'm not married, but it seems to gain me more respect. Mrs Morland, isn't it?'

'Mine's courtesy too, in a way,' said Polly. 'Everyone expects the owner of an estate to be a Mrs at least.'

'I've never felt the need to have a man to sponsor me, but it's the world we live in,' she said, with easy acceptance. This was not a woman, Polly felt, who would waste her substance fighting pointless battles. She looked across at Roberta. 'And this must be your ward – Miss Compton, wasn't it? You needn't keep scratching Billy's ears – he'll keep you at it all day unless you're firm with him.'

'He's a darling,' Roberta said, coming forward to shake hands.

'Best ratter in the Riding,' Mrs Maddox said. 'How do you do, my dear?'

Roberta was gazing in frank hero-worship. Mrs Maddox was not only tall – taller than Roberta – and beautiful, and dressed in well-cut breeches and tweed riding jacket, which was how Roberta would have liked to be dressed every hour of the day, but she owned her own stables and didn't feel the need to be married.

'Do sit down, and let's have some tea. A slice of cake? Mrs Robins makes a superb fruit cake. She's a wonderful cook altogether, and fusses over me like a hen with one chick, so I'm very comfortable, for the little time I'm indoors.'

They sat, and she poured, and cut large slices of the cake. She attacked hers immediately with the appetite of one who had breakfasted early and worked hard since. Roberta followed suit, glad that dainty manners didn't seem to be required.

'Now,' said Mrs Maddox, when she had swallowed the first mouthful, 'let's get down to business. That man of yours put the whole thing to me very clearly. Good fellow that – I'd like to poach him.'

'Please don't,' said Polly.

'No, I can see you wouldn't want to lose him. Anyway, I hadn't thought about taking on an apprentice, but I can see it makes a good deal of sense, and if Miss Roberta here is as good as he says she is, she'll be very useful to me. And here's what I thought: a trial first for, say, a month, to see if we get on. That's fair on both sides.'

'I agree,' Polly said.

'After that, I'll give her full training for, say, two years. At the end of that time, she ought to know enough to go on and get a job as a trainer anywhere.' She had been watching Roberta's face, and saw the look of consternation pass across it. '*Or*,' she continued, now looking at Polly, 'she might stay on here. I've an idea about that, but I won't go into it now. We'll have to see how she works out. Now, Roberta, what do they call you? Roberta's a mouthful. Is it Bobby?'

It was now. Roberta nodded eagerly.

'Right, Bobby it is. Tell me what you can do.'

Roberta began, but Mrs Maddox soon found her modesty was slowing things down too much, and initiated a catechism. Could she quarter, strap, pull and plait? What weight did she ride? Could she ride both across and sidesaddle? Did she hunt? Point to point? Could she mouth, back and lunge? What did she know about shoeing? What were the causes and symptoms of colic? Of thrush? Of laminitis? How would she treat cribbing, saddle galls, overreach? How many pounds of oats would she give a working horse of sixteen hands?

At the end of it she nodded briskly, said, 'You seem to

be well taught. Now I must see you ride,' and got straight to her feet.

Polly smiled inwardly, abandoning her tea and the half of the cake she had not managed to eat yet, thinking, This is a woman of action.

Mrs Maddox led the way out into the old yard, where a nice-looking bay gelding was tacked and tied up to a ring. 'Up you get, Bobby, and ride into the field there at the back.'

Dry-mouthed with nerves, Roberta could hardly remember which end of the horse was which. But as she approached and the bay cocked his ears at her and all but smiled, long instinct took over. She managed to mount neatly, not forgetting to check the girths first, and rode him into the field. Mrs Maddox and Polly followed, and stood in the middle while Mrs Maddox snapped out instructions and had Roberta trotting and cantering, changing rein, halting and backing, and finally taking the bay over a couple of small jumps. Then she called her across.

'You ride very well,' she said, catching the bay's rein and rubbing his nose. 'I'm willing to give you a trial. No pay for the trial month, of course. If I like you, and you want to stay, you'll get your full training and thirty shillings a week, plus your keep and laundry.'

Roberta was too enraptured to speak, but Polly said, 'She can live at home and bicycle in.'

'No, no, that would never do. Can't have her wasting her energy cycling up and down. We start early and she'll need her sleep. The hours here are long and, besides, you never know when you might be called out. If she's to learn from me, I must have her at my side all the time. She'll live in or not at all. Mrs Robins will take care of her along with me, and she can have Sunday afternoons to visit home, if we're not otherwise engaged.' She raised her eyebrows in an imperious way, and Polly saw that she would get her own way more often than not through sheer force of character.

170

She looked at Roberta. 'It's up to you.' She thought thirty shillings was meagre – a housemaid got almost twice that – and wondered whether Roberta was going to end up as cheap labour for the very canny Mrs Maddox. Though, of course, if she did get proper training, that could be invaluable.

'Oh, please, I want to – very much!' Roberta said breathlessly. 'May I?'

'You'll be on a month's trial to begin with, so if you don't like it, you can come home after that,' Polly reminded her.

Mrs Maddox was smiling into the distance, as if she knew exactly what was going through Roberta's mind.

'I shan't want to,' Roberta said hastily, as if afraid of offending her new heroine. 'I know I'm going to love it here.'

'I think you will,' said Mrs Maddox. 'Now, I've just time to show you your room, and then I must get back to the stables. Be here tomorrow at half past eight with your luggage. You can have half an hour to settle in, and at nine I'll come over and fetch you and show you round the stables. Can you drive, by the way? No? That's a pity. But you'll soon learn. I'll need you to be able to drive the car and the horsebox.'

It was like being sucked along by a whirlwind. The bedroom was small but adequate, with a narrow wooden bed, a wardrobe and chest of drawers, a washbasin on a stand, a bare wooden floor, and a small window that looked out over paddocks towards the rise of the hills – a view, Polly thought, that might make up for many deficiencies in comfort. Having been given the minimum time to look at it, they were swept out, shaken hands with and dismissed, and Mrs Maddox was striding away towards the stables with Billy running to keep up, and they were getting into the car to go home.

'Are you really sure you want to do this?' Polly asked, as she started the engine.

'Oh *yes*!' said Roberta. 'To be a racehorse trainer!'

'But Mrs Maddox . . .' Polly began, wondering how to phrase it. Overwhelming? A martinet?

'Isn't she *wonderful*?' said Roberta, her eyes shining.

So that seemed to be that. Polly said no more, but resolved to drive Roberta herself the next day, and to make sure she had a few creature comforts for that bedroom – a rug for the floor, a comfortable chair and some books at least.

It was while Roberta was still on her first month's trial that her mother's husband, Donald Broadbent, finally succumbed to old age and ill health, and died quietly in his sleep. Ethel immediately called for Roberta to hurry to her side to support her, but Polly did not want her to jeopardise her new career from the beginning and, besides, in recent years Roberta had shown little patience with her mother or desire to dance attendance on her. Ethel had likewise lost interest in Roberta when she realised she liked horses better than men and would never be a credit to her mother at a dance.

Quiet, sensible Harriet stepped into the breach and said she could more easily miss school than Roberta could miss work, and that she was better at calming her mother. Jessie drove her over there, saw what needed to be done and attended to the official parts of the business, then left Harriet to keep her mother company for the time being.

There was a funeral, of course, and Roberta was allowed a day off for that, came home the evening before and travelled with her siblings to Knaresborough the next day. Jessie and Bertie went, as did Polly, mostly for Ethel's sake, for none of them had ever had anything much to do with Donald. It was a sad little funeral, with only a handful of friends outside the family: Donald and Ethel had been retreating from social life for some years as Donald's health failed. Afterwards, back at River House, there were sandwiches and cake, sherry and tea, all put together by the efficient Harriet; she and Roberta served everyone, while John and Jeremy sat either side of their mother, who clung to their hands and shed tears and said, 'Now I'm all alone! But my boys will comfort me.'

Jessie and Polly, across the other side of the room, watched and wondered.

'What will happen now?' Polly said aloud.

'She'll try to get one of them to come and live with her,' Jessie said.

'They won't want to do that.'

'She *is* their mother.'

'But she's never been very motherly. When they were little she always foisted them onto my mother or the servants. She never wanted to bother with them, except to show them off when her friends came to tea.'

'I'm wondering what she'll do for money,' Jessie said. 'I don't think Donald had anything except his pension, and apparently that dies with him.'

'Perhaps they had something saved,' Polly said. She had a suspicion of where this was going to end.

Jessie sniffed. 'Doesn't it smell damp to you?' she said. 'As if they haven't had the fire lit often enough. I don't think there's any money. Ethel never had to housekeep before she married Donald, so I don't suppose she had much idea of economy. And Harriet said that when she went to get the ham for the sandwiches, the butcher told her there was a big bill. He only let her have the ham because it was a funeral.'

'Oh dear! What now, then?' said Polly.

Jessie met her eyes. 'It would make it easier all round . . .' she began hesitantly.

'She's not *family*,' Polly objected.

'She was my brother's wife,' Jessie said. 'I suppose that makes her my responsibility, really. I can't abandon Robbie's wife, can I? I'll have to ask her to come and live with us.'

Polly sighed, but not very much. She had already accepted

her fate. 'No, you haven't enough room. I'll ask her to come to Morland Place.'

'I have a spare bedroom,' Jessie said.

'Yes, but she'd drive you mad. I think you need a lot of space for Ethel. Anyway, it's what my father would have wanted. He kept her and her children after Robbie died, and I know he wouldn't have left her to rot in Knaresborough now she's all alone. She can come to Morland Place.'

'You're a good soul,' Jessie said.

'It's a big house. I probably won't even notice her,' Polly said, to avert the praise, which she didn't feel she deserved. If she really had been a 'good soul' she'd have found something to like in Ethel, wouldn't she?

So, having reduced the household by James, Amy and Roberta, she increased it again by Ethel, who was easily equal to three when it came to the upheaval she could cause.

Ethel accepted the offer with a flicker of relief in her eyes that reconciled Polly, just for that moment.

'I'll be able to help you around the house,' Ethel said. 'Take lots of tasks off your hands. I won't be a burden.'

But as soon as she arrived she complained about the number of dogs (she wasn't fond of dogs), disliked the way the hall table had been placed, remarked that it was very cold and she had felt the cold so much since Donald had died and could the fire be made up and, before that was done, retired to her room with a headache. After that she divided her time between her bed and the drawing-room sofa, saying she felt too distraught to do anything but lie down.

'I'm a poor wretched widow, good for nothing. When I'm stronger, I'll help you, Polly dear,' she said.

Polly didn't suppose she'd be feeling stronger for a very long time, if ever.

At the knock on his study door, Mr Cockburn called out, 'Enter,' and the door opened to reveal Basil Compton.

'You sent for me, sir?'

'Ah, yes, Compton. Come in. Come in.'

Basil lounged in, trying to look as couldn't-care-less as possible in the circumstances, but he couldn't help wondering which of his sins had found him out. There was nothing to be told from Cockburn's face. The Old Man was famously impassive: could have made a fortune at poker, if he hadn't had such a 'down' on cards.

Cockburn studied the handsome, slightly sulky face before him, and sighed inwardly. He had known Compton was going to be a handful from the beginning. He prided himself on his way with handfuls, but there was something about this boy that he hadn't yet fathomed. Every boy had a key; it was Cockburn's job to find it.

Compton was studying him back, not precisely with insolence but with an interest that was not quite respectful.

Cockburn struck. 'Stand up straight, please. Take your hands out of your pockets.' Basil obeyed, in a way that managed to convey that he was doing it because he wanted to, not because he had to. 'I've been observing you, Compton,' Cockburn said pleasantly, to put him off balance.

Basil eyed him cautiously. This didn't sound like the firecracker that had broken the glass in the greenhouse, or the carp in the san's bathtub. Something more long-term. Smoking in the dorm? Probably. The Old Man didn't approve of smokes and he'd been warned last week. What was it to be – whops, deten, lines? He was looking moderately civilised so far – maybe it would be lines. Basil had a fourth-form boy who did them for him at sixpence the hundred; could copy his fist so Basil himself couldn't tell the difference. That boy would be a master forger one day: probably end up in Wandsworth – or the Civil Service.

'This term is only four weeks old but you've been up before me three times already,' Cockburn went on. 'You were punished four times last term.' He paused. 'What's the matter with you, Compton?' Basil looked taken aback, which was what Cockburn had wanted. He liked to keep his lads off balance, particularly the miscreants. 'You're a bright boy. You have quite a following with the juniors. But you seem to *want* to be an unwholesome influence. *Is* that what you want?'

Basil didn't answer. He kept his own face impassive now, wondering where the Old Man was tending.

'Dumb insolence?' Compton queried.

'No, sir. Can't think of anything to say, sir.'

Cockburn looked down at Basil's file before him. 'I see your father was a war hero. DSO, DFC. A genuine Air Ace.' He looked up quickly, and Basil's eyes shifted away from him minutely. 'Is that the trouble? Can't live up to your father's reputation, no point in trying?'

Basil didn't answer, but there was a spot of vexation in each cheek. Ah, that was it, Cockburn thought. And he didn't like having his sore place touched.

'The war changed things,' he went on conversationally. 'It unsettled everyone. Left a generation out of its place and wondering what it was all for. And your generation tends to think it has missed out. The old order swept away and nothing put in its stead. Your fathers had all the fun, and there's nothing left for you.'

Basil didn't answer.

Cockburn picked up his pen and ran it through his fingers absently. He spoke quietly. 'You'll have your chance. There's going to be another war, you know.' The eyes shifted back to him in surprise. 'I shouldn't be saying this to you, and I hope you won't repeat it, but the way things are going in Germany . . .' He paused. 'We shouldn't have let them march home under arms, you see. It means they don't think they were really beaten.'

'I've heard my uncle say the same thing,' Basil said, reluctant to respond and yet too interested not to.

'Sir Bertie Parke? Yes, well, he should know. He was there

176

at the end. One of the few who fought right through from Mons to the Armistice. A VC, too. It's a lot for you to live up to, Compton. So much courage. So much achievement. A lot riding on your shoulders. It could crush a lesser character.'

Basil's eyes slid away again. He didn't like the way this was going. The Old Man was as cunning as a fox, everybody said so, and the more he smiled the faster he bit. *Reculer pour mieux sauter*, was what Harrison of the sixth had said, and Basil had had to look it up, but it was right. He was unpredictable, which was a bad thing in a beak, and the reason everybody in the school respected and feared him. He didn't even have a nickname, though his name lent itself to ridicule – he was just the Old Man.

'I have something I want you to do,' Cockburn said suddenly, out of a lengthy silence.

Here it comes, thought Basil, bracing himself.

'I want you to take over editorship of the school magazine.'

Basil was so surprised his voice squeaked. 'Who, sir, me, sir?'

'Yes, sir, you sir,' Cockburn said, imitating him. 'You are to take over forthwith and you will be completely responsible for the end-of-term edition.'

'But—' Basil began.

'Why so surprised? Your essays are the best thing about your work. You have an enterprising mind – too enterprising, some might say. Time it had something to occupy it.'

'But, sir . . .' Basil began again. The magisterial brows drew together, but he had to go on. 'I'm not even in the sixth form.'

'Oddly enough, I am aware of that,' said Cockburn.

'All the others on the mag are sixth-formers, sir. Mostly pre's.' The editorial staff of the school magazine were a clique, a self-perpetuating élite, and they took themselves very seriously. And sixth-formers always stuck together. He'd have the whole lot against him. 'They won't like it, sir, me barging in.'

'I'm sure they won't. But that's for you to cope with. You will have full powers, and may sack anyone you don't want to work with, and take on any other boy from any part of the school to help you. You may go about your editorship in any way you please. The one requirement is that the issue will be out, complete, and on time. Oh, and that it will be the best issue of the magazine ever seen in the school's history.'

Basil was staring at him in something like horror, his mind racing, visualising all the problems, the arguments, the responsibilities, the hostilities it would stir up. The pre's would pick on him for everything they could. They'd grind him. And write a magazine? He hadn't the earthliest how you did that – and the old bunch wouldn't lift a finger to help him.

Cockburn gave him a grim sort of smile. 'I have gained the impression, Compton,' he said genially, 'that you have been trying to goad me into expelling you. Oh, yes, you needn't look surprised. I've heard the whispers around the junior school about your reputation. Well, you may put that out of your mind. I assure you I am not going to sack you, no matter what you do. You have my word on that.'

Basil met the grim eyes reluctantly; his mouth was dry. 'Sir, I—'

'You are going to produce the best school magazine ever. You may put what you like in it, take it in any direction you please: political, humorous, literary, or a mixture of many things. Put your satellites out to work as press hounds, get the brain-boxes in the school and the live wires and the expert hobbyists on board. I want it to be lively, engrossing, superbly written and presented – anything but dull. I have to read that damned magazine from cover to cover every term, Compton, and every term I dread it. *Felix Culpa* indeed!' The magazine's title was the *Felix Dies*, but the boys

178

all called it the *Felix Culpa*, or sometimes the *Unfelix Culpa*. 'This term I shall be able to look forward to it for the first time. You will not disappoint me. That is all.'

For once in his life, Basil was lost for words. He bowed his head in a sort of submission and left the study in silence. Outside he stood still, staring at the wall, took a deep breath, and said softly, 'Well, that's a hell of a thing!'

Inside the study, Cockburn smiled gently, uncapped his fountain pen and went back to work. Perhaps if Compton had the entire sixth form against him and the rest of the school at his back, he might find it in himself to be a hero. At any event, he ought to be kept too busy for the rest of the term to get into mischief.

CHAPTER EIGHT

New York had been a good choice for the honeymoon. American society loved a title, the Belmonts were already known separately, and together they made a handsome couple. And in London Lady Belmont had moved in the *very highest circles*, which made her an object for every hostess with pretensions to fashion – though it turned out to be bafflingly difficult to get her to talk about the Prince of Wales. It wasn't that she refused, exactly – you just found yourself treading gently down a different conversational path without knowing quite how you had got there. But even that very English reserve was delicious in its own way, and she was pronounced 'charming'. The little matter of her first husband's bankruptcy was nothing. It could happen to anyone, especially these days, and was quite forgotten.

New York was particularly lively that season. Everyone believed that Prohibition would go for good next year, and the law was so widely ignored it was hard sometimes to remember it existed. Broadway was sparkling with new productions, from musicals and romantic comedies to thrillers and Shakespeare. There were exhibitions at the Museum of Modern Art and the Whitney. Horowitz was playing Liszt at the Carnegie and Milstein was playing Brahms. There was ballet, there was opera, there were restaurants and nightclubs, dancing, and parties, parties, parties.

Violet shone through it all, like a bright star, illuminated from within. Duty, position, marriage to a stern and unsympathetic man, long years of guarding propriety: all had made her grave. Now the past was wiped away. Love made her happy, requited passion made her gay. She was suddenly light-hearted, something she had not felt since her coming-out ball when life had seemed so happily uncomplicated. Loving Avis seemed just such a simple joy.

Hostesses declared it was 'darling' the way Lady Belmont looked at her husband. She was such a success that in no time it became fashionable to be in love with your husband. The press followed and photographed her wherever she went; even the *New Yorker* mentioned her as a phenomenon, while *Vogue* and *Vanity Fair* raved about her 'English fashion', and copies of her gowns were rushed out to the stores.

She did not notice her success, and wouldn't have cared had she done so. It was enough simply to be with Avis.

After four weeks in New York, they travelled up-state for a change of scene; then visited Boston, Philadelphia and Washington. The terrible effects of the Crash were plain to see if you turned off the main streets into the side streets, or went outside the fashionable areas, and there was plenty about it in the newspapers. But, everyone said, there was no sense in letting it get you down. Restaurants and theatres and all these entertainments provided employment for people, didn't they? For the rest, it was the government's business.

As Easter approached, Avis said it seemed a shame to hurry home when America was such a big place and there was so much to see.

'We don't have to go back, do we?' Violet said. 'I'm having such a nice time.'

'I'm sure they'll manage at home without us,' Avis said. In Washington the cherry blossom was just coming into full bloom, and a whole new round of celebrations and parties was being planned to celebrate it. Blossom time was big in

Washington. 'We ought to stay for that,' he said. 'And then – how about California? I've never been, but I understand it's quite different over there. Summer all year round, and oranges and lemons growing right beside the road.'

Violet was entranced. 'How would we get there?'

'On the train. It takes several days – like being back on *Mauretania*, I expect. A little world apart.'

'I should like to sleep with you on a train,' she said, her eyes full of messages. 'And Lizzie is in California – I'd like to see her again. Perhaps we'll catch up with Lennie there, too.' They had missed him, being in New York when he was in Washington, and not reaching Washington until he had gone back west.

'Then it's decided: we'll go to Los Angeles. The City of Angels.'

'How pretty!'

'We could ask Lennie to show us round a film studio.'

'I didn't know you cared about the cinema,' Violet said.

'I don't, especially, but Hollywood is such a phenomenon, from all I've read, one can't help being interested. Shall we cable Lizzie and see if she'll have us to stay?'

Oliver was not particularly surprised that Violet and Avis didn't come back at Easter. For two people in love, and with sufficient money, America would be a wonderful place, too full of wonders to hurry over. 'It will eat them up,' he said to Verena, when they read the latest cable putting off their return.

'You sound very American sometimes,' Verena objected mildly.

'It must be the company I keep,' said Oliver. 'Carleena Day came in yesterday. She wants her face lifted.'

'Where to?' Verena asked. 'She can't be more than thirty-two.'

'Darling, she's well over forty-five. Proof that the face-lift she's already had was worth it. But I told her, no. I might do a little trimming round her jaw for her, but another lift, no. She'll end up with a snout like a pig and Chinese eyes.'

'I think your job is very unethical,' Verena scolded him.

'Unfair, when I've just said I refused!' Oliver objected, hurt. 'And when I've a child with a club foot tomorrow, and a young woman with a benign facial tumour the size of a tennis ball.' He sighed theatrically. 'A prophet is never understood in his own country.'

'I think you understand profit all too well, my love,' said Verena. 'All the same, I'd love to go to America some day.'

'We will, when the children are older,' he promised.

'Talking of children, Violet doesn't mention hers. Do you think she's forgotten them?'

'I think she may have, just for the moment. But let's not blame her. She had a very dull sort of life with Holkam, and then all the misery of the past few years. She deserves to have a frolic, now she's happy. Henry and Charlotte are no bother to us.'

'I wasn't thinking about us. I was thinking about them.'

Henry was not particularly worried about his mother's extended absence. He was settled in school until the end of the summer term, and was sure they'd be back before then to arrange his move to technical college. And if they weren't, Uncle Oliver would fix it. Uncle Oliver was a trump and could fix anything, he firmly believed.

Charlotte, however, was not happy. Her course had finished the week before Easter, and she was now the proud possessor of a diploma and a whole set of new skills that she died to try out.

She had parted sadly from Myra and Betty, exchanging addresses and promising to write. 'Once we're all settled in our new jobs in London,' Myra had said, 'we'll be able to meet very often.'

Charlotte was happy enough to have a week's holiday, to enjoy family fun and look forward to Easter and her mother's return. There would be parties at Chelmsford House and elsewhere, and she had worked hard enough to feel she deserved some dancing. But after that she wanted to be getting on with her life, not waiting around, slipping back into the old do-nothing routine. She had a nervous notion that her newly acquired accomplishments would seep away like water into sand if she didn't start using them at once.

One day in April, about a week after Easter, Emma called. She and Kit had been entertaining at Walcote, and as the guests had departed she had decided on a quick trip to London to visit her friend Molly (Helen's sister), and do some shopping for the new baby.

'May I beg a bedroom for tonight? I'm going straight back tomorrow – or perhaps the day after,' she told Verena. 'I'm too gruesomely big to enjoy any of the Season.' She looked down at herself with a mixture of dismay and pride. 'Honestly, were you ever as big as this with any of yours?'

'Never,' said Verena, loyally.

'Kit's sure it must mean that it's a boy,' Emma said hopefully. 'We do so want a son to inherit the title – though if it weren't for that, I'm sure Kit would prefer another girl. He dotes on Alethea. He's gone to look at some pigs today, and taken her with him. I think he prefers her company to mine. But it would be a shame for the title to be lost, so I do need it to be a boy.'

'Come to think of it,' Verena said, putting on a thoughtful look, 'I'm sure I was bigger with John than with either of the girls.'

'You're sweet,' said Emma, 'and I'm an idiot, but I still like to hear you say it.'

'Where do you mean to have it?'

'At Walcote,' Emma said. 'I'd really rather have it in London, but it will be July and Kit thinks London will be impossible. I suppose he's right. And I do enjoy the green and fresh air now I'm so whale-like. But we'll come back to

Town as soon as possible afterwards. I want the children to be Londoners, as I was. I like the idea of them growing up in the same nursery as Oliver and Violet.'

She and Kit had taken over the house in Manchester Square from Oliver's mother Venetia when she had moved to Chelmsford House for the last few months of her life.

'How is Violet, by the way?'

Verena told her about the extended honeymoon.

'Sounds as if they're having fun. Good! She deserves it. And I really like Avis.'

'Everything's good about it, except poor Charlotte, pining at home.'

'Surely she doesn't need to wait for her mother to get herself a job.'

'She's afraid Violet might object if she isn't consulted about its suitability.'

'Oh, bosh! If she's having such a topping honeymoon she won't mind about anything,' Emma said. 'Look here, why don't I take her with me to see Molly? She might be able to find her something. She found a billet for Charlotte's brother, all right, and Charlotte's much brighter.'

'*And* armed with a diploma and seventy-five words a minute,' Verena added.

'There we are, then. And if Violet felt publishing was respectable enough for her son and heir, she can't object to it for Charlotte, can she?'

'I'm sure she could, but perhaps she won't,' said Verena. 'And it would be so good to do something for poor Charlotte. Are there any nice young men in the publishing world?'

Emma laughed. 'You mothers! You all have the same mind – get your daughters married!'

'Wait till Alethea comes out,' Verena said, unabashed.

Charlotte was relieved, and grateful to Emma for taking her problem seriously, and after Emma had put in a telephone call, she went with her to Molly's flat for luncheon in excitement and hope.

Molly and her husband Vivian Blake, the publisher, lived in a large flat in a smart new block in Arlington Street. It had been built on the site of a peer's grand house, which, like so many others recently, had been pulled down when the owner fell on hard times and had to sell. Kit had mourned at the time that soon there would not be any of these old houses left; Emma had mourned that she had not managed to get in first and convert rather than demolish the building; but at the time, June 1924, she had been busy buying Turnberry House in Piccadilly for that purpose and couldn't have managed two.

However, she did like what had been done, and found Molly's flat light and airy and very practical. Charlotte loved everything about it, beginning with the uniformed porter at the street door and the modern automatic lift, and going on to the flat itself, its wide, metal-framed windows, the parquet floors, the bathrooms (with almost as many fitments as she had seen in American ones), the delightful décor, all in shades of cream and beige, and the light, stylish furniture.

Molly was pleasantly amused by her admiration, and happily showed her round, demonstrating some of the modern conveniences, like the electric carpet-sweeper, the electric plate-warmer in the little service pantry next to the dining room, and the magnificent walnut radiogram that rivalled Uncle Oliver's in beauty, and surpassed it in having an automatic stylus arm that lifted itself on and off the gramophone record with balletic delicacy.

Vivian Blake was managing editor at Dorcas Overstreet, a most respected publisher, and was the nephew of the chairman. He and his cousin jointly were expected to inherit it one day. Molly went into the office for a few days a month, but mostly worked at home, editing manuscripts and writing reports.

'But Vivian says I'm most useful to the firm when I'm holding the hand of fragile novelists and poets. I take them out to lunch and tell them they're marvellous, or give them tea here and let them cry and tell me that no-one understands them. You're lucky, really, to find me at home without some pale, flop-haired boy curled up on my sofa looking pensive.'

Emma laughed. 'I can't imagine you having so much patience! You never had any truck with emotions.'

'I've developed a knack for nodding in the right place while my mind is actually engaged elsewhere.'

'While they're pouring their hearts out to you? Cruel!'

'I sit them in front of the fire and get them to make toast, and they end up perfectly happy,' Molly said serenely.

She performed these functions for Dorcas Overstreet when she wasn't working on her own detective novels, which she did in a small bedroom that had been converted into an office for her, complete with desk and very fine Remington Noiseless typewriter.

'If only I had noiseless children as well,' she said, 'everything would be perfect.'

'But you do have a wonderful nurse,' Emma said.

'True. Nana is marvellous. And she has almost a religious belief that children must be out of the house between ten and twelve, whatever the weather, so I'm assured of two hours' quiet a day. It's surprising what you can get done in two hours when you have to. And talking of children, you'd better come along and see them before lunch, or I'll never hear the end of it.'

Esmond, nearly three, and Angelica, fifteen months, were duly visited and admired, and under the stern eye of their nurse they demonstrated their charms until the maid came in to say that luncheon was ready. The flat was so modern and 'labour-saving', in the American phrase, that Molly managed with only a cook and a housemaid, apart from the nurse, though the building did have a house valet, who looked after Vivian's clothes. 'And we hire extra staff if we give a dinner or a party.'

Having said this, Molly suddenly laughed, and when Emma raised an enquiring eyebrow, she said, 'I was just watching you wondering how I managed on such a small staff, while I was busy being amazed that four years ago I was living in lodgings and had never had a servant in my life.' She smiled at Charlotte. 'It must be very different for you, living at Chelmsford House. Are you sure you want to "rough it" in the world of commerce?'

'Oh, yes,' said Charlotte, passionately. 'And I'd love most of all to live in lodgings one day, with my own door key, and do my own cooking.'

'It isn't as exciting as you might think,' Molly said. 'I much prefer Mrs Monday's elegant meals to burned sausages and cocoa every evening. But I understand what you mean. Squalor has a sort of attraction, if it doesn't go on for too long. What do you say, Emma?'

Emma shook her head. 'You haven't the first notion of squalor. You should have lived in a hut behind the dunes at Étaples during the war.'

'There you are, making me feel inadequate again,' Molly complained. 'You know I was too young to do anything in the war. And my mother would never have let me. She almost had a fit when Helen said she was going to get a job delivering aeroplanes. After that she was determined to keep me pure.'

Charlotte could see that it was a well-worn routine between them, and that they were really fast friends. 'My mother wouldn't have let me do anything either, if I'd been old enough,' she said. 'She doesn't really want me to have a job now.'

'Ah, yes, the job,' Molly said.

Charlotte blushed. 'I hope it wasn't cheek to ask, especially after you found my brother a position at Gaunt's, and then he gave it up.'

'Oh, don't worry about that. I never expected him to stick it out, and neither did anyone at Gaunt's. Young men like him come and go all the time. They're decorative, and sometimes they'll contribute something novel and unexpected, which is why we bother with them, but they rarely last. But you, with your diploma and your determination – you're much more useful. A workhorse. If you're willing to work hard?'

'Oh, I am!'

'That's the ticket. Now, I'll have to talk to Vivian about it, but there is a clerical and typing job becoming vacant at Dorcas Overstreet. You can file, I suppose, and answer the telephone? Then I'm sure you'd suit perfectly. The salary won't be much to begin with, but if you fit in, which I'm sure you will, there will be plenty of scope for you to improve your position. And when Vivian and I set up our own publishing company, you can come with us.'

'Have you done anything about that yet?' Emma said. 'You've been talking about it for years.'

'We're still working towards it. The time hasn't been right – the depression has hit the trade hard – and there are lots of difficulties in the way, not least Vivian's relationship with the firm. But we're still determined to go our own way eventually. In a year, or two years, I'd be willing to bet we'll be up and running. Vivian Blake Publishers. Sounds nice, doesn't it?'

Emma said, 'I'm only surprised to hear you say "in a year or two". The old Molly would have wanted everything *now*, if not sooner.'

'Having babies changes that,' Molly said. 'When you've twice had to wait nine months to see what sort of little monster you'll be getting . . .' She looked at Charlotte. 'Be wise, and know when you're well off. Stick to single blessedness. Don't get mixed up in all this marriage-and-baby business.'

She was joking, of course, Charlotte could see that, but she couldn't help saying, a little sadly, 'I don't suppose I'll have the choice.'

Violet loved California: the warmth, the amazing light, the tropical vegetation – palms and jacarandas, hibiscus and blazing bougainvillaea; the orange and lemon groves, dark leaves a setting for the glinting gold of the fruit – and always the astonishing mountains to one side and the vast ocean to the other. The days were brilliant, and the nights were as warm as milk, singing with cicadas and tree frogs, canopied with stars, so that you never wanted to go to bed.

She loved the wide roads and the huge, bright-coloured motor-cars. She loved the food – so fresh and varied. And she loved the people – so relaxed, so kind, so overwhelmingly polite. She had been brought up always to mind her manners, but these people of the perpetual sunshine seemed to have taken courtesy to a new level. It was a very different place from the frenetic New York of 1929, before the Crash. Everything seemed to be done here at a slower pace, with larger gestures and bigger, whiter smiles.

She loved Lennie's house, with its big, slow-moving ceiling fans and its wonderful view. She and Avis were made comfortable in a guest room that had its own bathroom; Wilma brought them tall glasses of chilled fruit juice to refresh them; dinner was fresh shrimp and crab with a spicy sauce and a beefsteak of epic proportions, accompanied by a salad in which she didn't recognise half the ingredients. And then such a profusion of fruit – at this time of year!

The next day Lizzie persuaded her to go out and buy a bathing-costume so that she could make use of Lennie's private swimming-pool. Violet was hesitant, not having swum since she was a child, but the experience was so delightful, she and Avis were soon in the habit of getting up early to swim together in the luminous light of dawn; and by the end of the first week she even felt equal to taking part in a 'pool party', though she did not get into the water in front of strangers.

It was good to see Lizzie again, for the first time in three years. Lizzie wanted to know most of all about Polly, how she was settling in, and whether she was happy. Violet was sorry she couldn't give more detailed news. She hadn't seen Polly since she came back, though she had heard of her from Jessie, in letters. Lennie listened intently to her answers, but they seemed to disappoint him. He wanted particulars she couldn't give him.

If Violet loved California, California loved her, too. Her beauty, her elegance were admired much more vocally than would be considered polite in England, but it was impossible to be offended when it was obviously so kindly meant. Her 'wonderful English skin', they cried – so fresh, so dewy! How did she manage it? Violet, at a loss to answer, was glad when Lizzie stepped in to say with a laugh that it was the 'wonderful English fog' that did it. Violet found Californians quite restful since they seemed willing, agreeably, to do all the talking, and she would always rather listen than speak. They did insist on calling her Lady Violet instead of Lady Belmont and she was too polite to correct them, but it was a small enough thing to accept.

She found that Rose had grown into a beautiful young woman since she had last seen her, and a pleasant, sensible one, too, with plenty to say for herself but nice, old-fashioned manners, despite the fuss that was made of her wherever she went. Both she and Lennie were very busy and it was mostly Lizzie who showed them around, and since Lennie left his motor-car and chauffeur Beanie for their use, they did it in comfort.

When they had been there ten days, Violet and Avis went to their first big Hollywood party, given by the ABO studios and held at the home of Al Feinstein, the president. Lizzie referred to it as a 'mansion', and when Violet first set eyes on it, she saw that it couldn't possibly be called anything less. It was a vast pale pink edifice set in acres of landscaped grounds full of tropical trees and shrubs, with an enormous pillared and pedimented porte-cochère dominating the front, under which a long, long caravan of huge motor-cars was disgorging smart guests.

Inside, the ceilings were so high as to be practically out of sight. Violet was an earl's daughter and was used to grand houses back home, but even she opened her eyes a little at this palace. The hall beyond the vestibule was the size of a ballroom, with a curving marble staircase fifteen feet wide, and beyond that they were shown into the 'Louis Drawing Room' where the party was being held, which seemed the size of an aircraft hangar. It was all done out in rose and gold, with French furniture, and mirrors and chandeliers rivalling those of Versailles, 'in the style of some Louis or other, I can never remember which', as she heard from the owner himself later. Everything, however, was brand new: in England, Baron Ferdinand de Rothschild had imported entire interiors, right down to the panelling, from defunct French châteaux to furnish his new manor at Waddesdon; but the sturdy American belief was that anything they made was better than anything foreign-made, and that new was better than old.

The far wall of the room was almost entirely made of french windows, which opened onto a terrace with an enormous fountain (it looked oddly familiar to Violet, until she realised it was copied from the one at Castle Howard) and beyond that an extensive lawn, so that the party could spill out in an agreeable way, and people could go into the sunshine and back into the cool interior as it suited them. An army of uniformed black servants moved about like benign ghosts, silent and smiling, offering glasses of champagne and silver trays of delicious hors d'oeuvres, while out on the lawn long, white-clothed tables were being spread with a more substantial buffet.

And everywhere, eating, drinking, and most of all talking, were the glamorous and glittering people, the guests of the studio. 'A lot of film stars and actors,' Lennie explained, 'and other people associated with films – agents, managers, investors, writers, directors and producers. Journalists, newspaper proprietors – everyone wants publicity in this world. Movie critics. And then the leading people of Los Angeles, the society people and financiers and politicians – everyone it's important to know.' He looked down at Violet. 'And some friends, of course. It would be an even duller party without some friends.'

'Do you think it dull?' Violet marvelled. She had given and been to thousands of parties in her life. She had been to the garden party held by King George V at Buckingham Palace in 1922, when there had been ten thousand guests; but though that had been larger, it had not had the overt glitter, the sheer self-confident swagger of a studio party in Hollywood – some of the jewellery rivalled what you would see at a Court reception.

'Very dull,' Lennie asserted. 'Most of the people here just come to be seen, and they're only interested in advancing their own careers. Watch them looking over their shoulders while they're talking, in case there's somebody more important they're missing.'

'Don't spoil it for us,' Avis laughed.

'I didn't mean to. It's fun if you don't have anything to lose, or any business to perform. Which I have, I'm afraid – I'll leave you with Lizzie and be back shortly.'

He did come back quite soon, with a short, very round, bald man, with thick glasses and an unlit cigar between his teeth, and a taller, black-haired man, with a dark, melancholy face and eyes full of tragedy. These he introduced to

Violet and Avis as Al Feinstein, their host and head of ABO Studios, and David B. Reznick, the director.

Feinstein grasped Violet's hand in both of his, wriggled his cigar to the side of his mouth, stared fixedly at her face and said, 'You are a very beautiful woman, Lady Violet. Have you ever had a screen test?'

'I don't believe so,' Violet said faintly. 'What is it?'

'A test to see if you're suitable to be in movies,' Lennie said, with a hint of impatience. 'And of course she hasn't, Al. She's an English lady.'

Feinstein released her hands and removed the cigar, the better to speak emphatically. 'That's the point. That's exactly the point. She's got a quality we don't grow at home. We could use that. You can see it, Reznick? It's all over her. That script we had the other week, the Scarlet Pimple thing – she'd be perfect for the brave and beautiful Lady Margaret.'

'That script was a stinker,' said Reznick, in a tone that suggested the horror of it had blighted his whole life. Violet almost expect to see great tears well up in those dark, tormented eyes.

'Sure, sure, we gotta change it. And the title's no good – Scarlet Pimple, what is that? Who thinks up a title like that?' He shook his head in disgust. 'But we can fix it up all right.'

'Lady Margaret, as you call her, was a Frenchwoman,' Lennie said.

'French, English, who cares?' Feinstein said robustly. 'How long you been in the movie business, Manning? You fix up the script to fit your assets. If I want Lady Margaret English, she's English.'

'Well, Lady Belmont is not one of your assets,' Lennie said. 'She has no ambition to be an actress.' He glanced at Avis, afraid he might have taken offence, but saw that he was trying valiantly not to laugh.

'Wouldn't hurt her to take a screen test,' Feinstein said stubbornly. 'Whaddaya say, Lady Violet? Back me up here,

Reznick. She's got a quality, I dunno what it is – wouldn't you like to see it up on the screen?'

'She has beauty. Pure, serene beauty,' said Reznick, in tragic tones. And then, briskly, 'But it wouldn't translate. Leave it alone, Al. You're embarrassing your guest. She doesn't want to be in pictures, okay?'

'Everybody wants to be in pictures,' Feinstein said. 'Swear t' God, I woke up one morning with a girl climbing over the balcony rail outside my bedroom! She climbed right up the creeper to make me give her a test for the jungle movie we were making.'

'And did you?' Avis asked, interested.

'Sure – gotta reward spunk like that. But she was lousy. She works in the commissary down at the studios now. But at least she got a job out of it.'

'You're obviously a warm-hearted man,' Avis said.

Feinstein brightened, considering this, and smiled. 'Yeah, you're right. I am. I'm a generous guy. A whaddayacall—'

'Philanthropist?'

'Yeah, one a those. Hey, I like you! Anything I can do for you?'

'Thank you,' Avis said, slipping Violet's hand through his arm, 'but I have everything I want.'

'Yeah, I can see that,' Feinstein said. 'You're a lucky man. Manning, I can see Rose talking to that crook Eberhart. We gotta go rescue her. She's a nice kid but too trusting. Enjoy the party, folks – nice meeting you.'

Feinstein and Reznick went away, taking Lennie with them, and leaving Avis and Lizzie to burst into laughter. 'What an introduction to Hollywood!' Avis said. He pressed Violet's hand. 'You could have been a movie star, darling, if you'd seized your chance.'

Violet was smiling. 'From what Rose says, it's very hard work, and involves a great deal of standing around doing nothing.'

'That's true,' Lizzie said. 'But most people think it's worth it to be famous.'

Violet shuddered. 'I can't think of anything worse than being famous.'

'That's a very nice, old-fashioned view,' Lizzie said.

Violet and Avis did enjoy the party, strolling about together and listening to conversations, noting the movie stars that Avis recognised from the screen, and that Violet had heard of and sometimes seen in magazines. Lizzie had been taken away by her own acquaintance and was lost to them, when one of the actresses, Claudine Ramona, came up to them and said, 'I must introduce myself. You're Lady Violet, aren't you? Someone said you're the sister of Lord Oliver, the plastic surgeon, is that right?' Violet admitted it, and Miss Ramona seized her hand and wrung it and said, 'That man is just the cat's pajamas!'

'He is?' Violet said, a little surprised.

'He truly is. He's the bee's knees. Look what he did for me!' She drew away the hair from her ears and turned her head back and forth, showing either side of her face to Violet, who was merely bewildered. Miss Ramona saw the look, and said triumphantly, 'Forceps marks!'

'I – I don't see any,' Violet said.

'Exactly!' said Miss Ramona, in triumph. 'That's what he did for me! Gone! As if they never were. That man's a genius! I tell everyone the same. He's the antelope's elbow, and I wish you'd tell him that when you see him. Tell him Claudine Ramona says he's the tops.'

'I will,' Violet promised gravely.

'Bless you,' Miss Ramona beamed, and was gone in a whirl of spangled scarves.

Avis burst out laughing. 'This place is mad!'

'What's so wonderful about an antelope's elbow?' Violet puzzled.

Someone else had come up to them, a tall, handsome,

196

fair man with very blue eyes, and she looked at him warily, wondering what new assault was to be made on her reason. But he said, in a quiet voice, 'I beg your pardon, it's Lady Holkam, isn't it?' His accent was pure English, so pure that in contrast to the American voices all around it sounded crystalline and almost artificial.

'It's Lady Belmont now,' she said, with a touch of reserve. 'Lord Holkam died. This is my husband, the Earl of Belmont.'

'My apologies,' he said, with a slight bow that was somehow not quite English. 'We have actually met, but you were Lady Holkam then. I am Eric Chapel, the artist. We met at an exhibition of my work in New York. Mrs Holland introduced us.'

Violet's reserve melted. She had met Mrs Holland, an arts patron, on her previous trip to New York. He was not being impertinent; and it was good to meet another Englishman after so long. She remembered that his paintings had been very good. At least, she couldn't now recall what they had looked like, but she knew there had been very good reviews at the time.

'Yes, of course,' she said. 'How do you do, Mr Chapel?' They shook hands all round. 'What are you doing here?' she asked. 'It's a long way from New York.'

'I live here now,' he said.

'Is there a good artistic community in Los Angeles?' Avis asked.

'You sound as though you would be surprised if there were, but the city is very cultured. You mustn't judge everything by Hollywood. We have a great many art galleries and – most importantly, perhaps – wealthy patrons.' He smiled deprecatingly. 'Athena must sit down with Mammon. Even an artist must eat.'

'The patron has had a respected role all through the history of art,' Avis said politely.

'I'm glad you think so,' Chapel said, 'because there were

197

some in our community who blamed me for taking a job in the movie business. I came west, Lady Belmont, to work for Aron Brodsky, the head of Olympic Studios. He invited me to paint the scenery for his religious epic pictures.'

'Goodness. That must have been a change,' Violet remarked, feeling something was needed.

'Painting murals – which is what it was in effect – is a very different discipline, but there is something very freeing to the spirit about it. The sheer scale, you understand. And, of course, my studio art makes my other art possible. I have never regretted the move.'

'The climate is certainly more agreeable,' Avis said.

'Indeed. My wife's health was suffering from those New York winters.'

'Your wife? Is she here?' Violet looked round.

'She doesn't come to these parties.' It was not polite to ask why, and while Violet was looking for something else to say, Chapel filled the pause with a question of his own. 'You are related, I believe, to Mrs Renfrew Alexander?'

Violet had to think for a moment. 'Oh, yes, Polly. I'm a distant cousin.'

'Indeed – Polly,' he said. He cleared his throat. 'I was acquainted with her in New York, but since I came west I have heard nothing of her. How is she?'

'She is very well,' Violet said. 'Her husband was killed, you know, in an aeroplane crash.'

'I didn't know. I'm very sorry.'

'She came home – to England. She bought her childhood home and she's busy taking care of it.'

His eyes widened. 'You mean, Morland Place?'

'Yes,' Violet said. 'Do you know it?'

He didn't answer for a moment, seeming to be following thoughts. Then he said, 'Polly spoke about it to me so passionately, I feel as if I know it. So she went home? I'm glad for her. She loved Yorkshire. She belongs there.'

'Were you ever in Yorkshire? I know you are English, by your accent.'

'No, I was never there,' he said, then gave that odd little bow again. 'I have taken up too much of your time. It was a great pleasure to meet you again, Lady Belmont. Lord Belmont.'

He was departing, and Violet called after him, 'Shall I give Polly your regards when I write to her?'

He turned back to say, 'Please not. She won't remember me. But thank you.' And he was gone.

'Strange man,' Avis said. 'Did you really know him in New York?'

'He was one of Freda Holland's *protégés*. I only met him once, but I heard a lot about him. So he came to Hollywood? He seemed rather sad, didn't you think?' she mused.

'Probably feeling bad about betraying his art for financial security,' Avis said. 'Athena must sit down with Mammon, indeed!'

'I expect painting scenery is quite tiring,' Violet said. 'I wonder if Polly would remember him. He's a very good-looking man.'

'Much better not ask,' Avis said. 'He showed too much interest in Polly for a man with a wife. I'm hungry – let's drift over and see what's on that buffet table. I can see people starting to eat.'

Polly woke; and finding no more sleep in her, got up and, barefoot in her nightdress, padded to the window and pushed it wide open. Dawn had not yet broken. The June morning lay soft and damply furled, waiting for the sun, the sky pearly with anticipation, the dew unbroken silver on the fields. The air felt cool, with the clean, grassy smell that promises a fine day.

She dressed in jodhpurs and a shirt and let herself out of the buttery door, into the yard. It was deep in shadow. The kitchen dog in his kennel did not wake, but in the stables her new horse, Zephyr, a black six-year-old from Twelvetrees that she hoped to hunt this winter, whickered to her as she came in with his bridle. She slipped it on and led him out, the hollow clop of his hoofs on the cobbles the only sound in the morning stillness.

She mounted bareback from the block and rode out, alone with the slowly turning world. The pale sky flushed slowly with gold, and the wisps of mist still clinging to the trees dissolved; then the first rim of the sun appeared on the horizon. By the time she reached the fishponds it was up and climbing through a transparent sky. The upper pond was a pool of pure light, like a molten mirror. Zephyr snorted and shook his head with a jingle of bit rings, disturbing two ducks, who broke out of the bulrushes with a frantic slapping of feet, smashing the surface into shivers of gold, until they took the air and beat away. Behind them the concentric ripples of light and dark, gilt and chrome ran and ran to the edges, lapping the rushes, but slower and slower, until the surface only rocked, magically mended, and then was still.

Polly could feel the true summer warmth of the sun on her bare head. There was no breeze; the air was still. The world slipped back into silence, innocent of movement, as it might have been before mankind. It was still enough, as her father used to say, to hear a bird fold its wings.

It would be hot today. She remembered her childhood, here at Morland Place in that long, golden time before the war, when it had seemed that nothing would ever change. In memory it had always been summer: the air full of floating gossamer, the paths white with dust, the heat rising in pure light to strike you under the chin.

She remembered the days when the world lay stunned with heat, where nothing happened and nothing ever would. Pushing through waist-high grass, white scratches on brown arms; sitting on a rise, squint-eyed from sun-dazzle, chewing a grass stem. She remembered the sound of bees dithering in the clover; the smell of horses on hot days, somnolent in the cool of a tree's shadow, grass seeds tangled in their eyelashes, their sweet breath a damp furnace-lick. Days as long as lifetime, easing into violet dusk, earth-smelling, spiked with stocks and jasmine. Then the big, hot moon would rise slowly and float free of the black trees like a soap bubble.

Zephyr eased from one foot to the other and sighed. A moorhen came stalking over the grass, slipped into the water and paddled away, pushing arrowheads of light before it, just as moorhens always had. The past seemed laid over the present, almost visible, like a transparent film. Whatever changed, Morland Place itself was eternal, and it seemed that the Polly she had been, the rough-haired, bare-legged child, was still here, unseen, locked in the amber of unending summer.

The year since she had bought the Morland estate from James had passed in a whirl of confusion, of trying to learn everything at once while answering questions from every side on subjects in which she was still unversed. It was a huge responsibility: she had not realised, at the time she signed the papers, how huge. It had seemed so simple and necessary and right to save the estate that she had not stopped to think what it entailed.

Well, she understood now what she had taken on: a burden she could never put down. On this exquisite summer morning she knew it was worth it, because whatever happened – and in this year of grace 1932, there could not be any thinking person who did not fear what the future might hold – whatever happened, Morland Place was home. It had bred and nourished her and, wherever she went in the world, it held her.

The sun was high enough to have dried the dew, and she felt it must be breakfast time. She must go back. Today was a big day: Alan Cobham's Flying Circus was coming. She

had made fields available for the aeroplanes, for the spectators' cars, for side stalls and roundabouts, beer tent and food
marquee. There would be two days of aviation displays, but
today the setting-up would take place. Some of the aeroplanes
would fly in, others were coming by road with the ground
crews to be rigged on site, and this afternoon the various
traders would take up their pitches.

And she would be receiving visitors: Violet and her new
husband were coming to stay, arriving after luncheon, and
this evening she was hosting a dinner for them. With Jessie
and Bertie, Helen and Jack, Alan Cobham himself, Nevil
Norway and his wife Frances, Lord and Lady Grey, Geoffrey
Howard, the Lord Lieutenant, and his wife Ethel, Colonel
and Mrs Chubb, and Lord and Lady Lambert and their
daughter – oh, and James, of course – they would sit down
twenty at the table; and after dinner a lot more people would
be joining them for dancing.

She turned Zephyr and started back, going round by the
fields to give him a canter. She was walking him the last bit
along the track towards the barbican when she saw a familiar
figure standing by the drawbridge. He took off his hat as
she approached, and when she got close enough to see him
smile, she felt a twinge of pleasure. Working together so
closely, she and John Burton were bound to have grown in
intimacy. She depended so much on him, and he was so
quick to understand what she wanted. Above all, she had
no other man in her life on whom she could depend. He
was the only person who took responsibility from her shoulders and allowed her the freedom to be light when she
wanted. Just the sight of him gave her a feeling of comfort.

'You're out early,' he said, as she reached him. Zephyr
jabbed him in the chest in greeting; he caught the rein in
self-defence, and rubbed the black's nose for him. 'I was just
coming up to the house to see you when I spotted this fellow
on the horizon. Good ride?'

'I wanted a moment to myself,' Polly said. 'It was so peaceful, watching the sun come up. But you're early, too. It's only just about breakfast-time.'

'I wanted to see everything was ready at the fields for the aircraft to land, and then I was going to check that the direction signs were up. But it suddenly occurred to me that you wouldn't want any traffic coming past the house, would you?'

'No, certainly not,' she said.

'In that case, we ought to have someone at the other end of the track, by St Edward's, to make sure no-one comes in this way. I know the signs will direct them round by the Acomb road, but anyone coming from the south who knows the area might try to take the shortcut.'

'That's a good thought – but won't a no-entry sign do?'

'People are good at ignoring signs they don't like,' he said, with a smile. 'Better to have a human being there to reinforce it.'

'We'll need someone there both days, then,' she said.

He nodded. 'Don't worry, I'll see to it.' He released the rein to let her go, but stood looking up at her, with a faint smile, much as if looking gave him pleasure. 'It's going to be a good two days,' he said.

'I'm glad the weather's set fair,' she said.

'Yes. I think practically everyone in Yorkshire's coming.' He laid a hand on Zephyr's neck and ran it slowly down. 'Despite the war, aeroplanes are still a novelty. A lot of people will never have seen one, still less have been in one.'

'I expect the half-crown trips will be very popular,' she said. 'It's a pity Alec's just too young to remember any of this.'

'Ah, yes, that's the other thing I meant to say to you,' Burton said. 'I think I might have found a good pony.'

'Really?' Polly said, pleased. It was Alec's second birthday on the 30th of June and, following the Morland precept that a child should be put on horseback at the age of two, she was planning to teach him to ride as soon as she had a suitable mount. She was about to ask for details, when her stomach growled and she realised how hungry she was. She cocked an eye at Burton. 'Have you had breakfast?'

He gave a rueful smile. 'I forgot,' he said.

'I'm sure you forget all too often. It's living alone. Come in and have breakfast with us, and you can tell me all about the pony.'

'Thank you,' he said. 'Now I come to think of it, I am hungry.'

He walked beside her across the drawbridge and into the yard, sunny now, with sparrows busy in the gutters, the dog out of his kennel, sunning himself, and the kitchen cat sitting on a window-sill delicately licking a paw. He held the rein while Polly jumped down, then handed it to the groom, who had come out at the sound of hoofs. They walked together up the steps to where Frederick, now transformed into Barlow the butler, was waiting at the open great door. Polly did not need to tell him it was one more for breakfast: a nod and a flick of her eyes towards her companion was enough.

BOOK TWO

Ventures

They reach me not, touch me some edge or that,
But reach me not and all my life's become
One flame, that reaches not beyond
My heart's own hearth,
Or hides among the ashes there for thee.

Ezra Pound: *In Durance*

CHAPTER NINE

Polly had not been terribly surprised when James came back to Morland Place. He had visited his friend David, had enjoyed working in the stables and, just when he felt his presence in the Pennyfather household might be creating a financial burden, was luckily invited by Lord Stalbridge to stay as a house guest. But when the Easter party broke up, it was plain that he could not trespass any longer on his lordship's hospitality.

Fortunately, another of the guests, Aubrey Fox-Manners, who had a place near Salisbury, invited James to stay. The Fox-Mannerses had two grown-up daughters as well as a racing stables, and James spent a very agreeable time there, but a month is long enough to be a house guest, even if your hosts are too easy-going to make it plain. Besides, the elder Miss Fox-Manners seemed to be getting rather fond of him, and he didn't think it fair to her. He left, intending to take up his new life of gypsying, wandering where the fancy listed and living on his wits. But it seemed his wits were not yet sharp enough to keep him in boot polish, and his fancy didn't seem to list in any particular direction, so towards the end of May he found himself, almost by chance, back at Morland Place.

Polly had half expected that she would never really be rid of James, but his few months' absence, and the efforts of John Burton, had done the trick, and most people now viewed Polly as lawful mistress of Morland Place. And though he was greeted with great enthusiasm on all sides, he modestly effaced himself and insisted to all that he was nothing but a guest. There would always be those who thought differently, but Polly had more self-confidence now. At least James made the numbers even at the big dinner, and took care of Lord Lambert's rather shy daughter; he would be invaluable during the evening, dancing with the wallflowers and keeping the atmosphere lively.

It was good to see Violet and Avis again, and they spent the whole afternoon talking about America. They were to stay for a week at least, but Jessie could not wait until the evening to see Violet and came over around tea-time for a warm and slightly tearful reunion. They had seen little of each other in late years, but they had always been each other's best friend, as their respective mothers had.

'I'm so glad you're happy at last,' Jessie whispered, as they embraced.

But she needn't have whispered: this was a different Violet. She smiled and said aloud, 'I *am* happy, very happy. As happy as you are with Bertie. It's like a fairy tale, after all that's happened, isn't it?'

'*Two* fairy tales,' Jessie said.

'You and Bertie must come and stay with us often at Tunstead Hall – mustn't they, Avis?'

'I hope so,' Avis said. 'It's very pretty country there – do you know the Peak District?'

'Not at all,' Jessie said. 'I'm sorry to say I've never been there. Will you have a house in London as well?' She wondered as she said it what had happened to Fitzjames House in St James's Square, the Holkams' London house, sold in the bankruptcy.

Violet must have heard the thought. 'We'll hire one for the season each year. We drove past Fitzjames House when we came through London on our way home. It's still empty.

It looked so sad, with the windows boarded up and dead leaves in the corners from last autumn. People simply don't want those big houses any more. I expect it will be turned into flats in the end.'

But Jessie could hear that she didn't mind about it. It was part of her old life, which she seemed to have shrugged off as a snake sheds a skin.

Basil was home for the air show – indeed, Mr Cockburn was so seized with the importance of air-mindedness to the nation that he had encouraged parents to take their sons out for the weekend. Any remaining boys he took himself in a hired charabanc.

Basil was pleased about the Flying Circus as it would make something substantial to put into the *Felix Culpa* – he was very short of material. He was wary when he heard his father was to take part. That sort of thing could bring a boy great credit or great ridicule: the balance could easily tip either way. He prepared his face for either lofty indifference or modest insouciance. His mother caught him practising in the mirror, and wormed it out of him.

'My dear boy,' she said, 'how could it *not* reflect to your credit?'

'You don't know the sixth,' he said darkly. 'They hate me, and they'll jump on anything they can use against me.'

'Why on earth should they hate you?' she asked. He had not told her of the Head's devilish scheme.

'Can't explain – too complicated,' he said. 'I'm *persona non grata*, that's all.'

'You're Latin's improving, at any rate,' Helen said.

He grinned. '*Gratias, mater,*' he said.

Helen thought her handsome boy could not come to too much harm as long as he kept his sense of humour. 'Well, I'm willing to bet when the other boys know what your father is doing, you'll be a hero on his account.'

Basil looked at her carefully, detecting something in her tone. 'He's not doing anything *very* dangerous, is he?'

Basil hadn't used to be so quick to pick up on things. He was growing up, she reflected. She kept her tone light. 'Oh, just some trick flying. Nothing he hasn't done before.'

'He's been working at a desk for a year,' Basil objected.

'You don't forget how to fly in a year. And he's been practising, of course, out at Sherburn.' He was still looking at her suspiciously, so she thought this was a good time to distract him. 'If your sixth form is likely to torment you for having a flying father, what will they think of a flying mother?'

His eyes widened. 'What do you mean? Are you taking part as well? Oh, good Lord, Mother! What are *you* going to do?'

She smiled. 'You'll have to wait and find out.'

It was another fine day, and people started arriving early to get the parking spots under the trees; and also to walk about and look at the aeroplanes on the ground before the flying began. In a separate field a merry go-round, swing-boats and a coconut shy had been set up, along with stalls selling sweets and cakes, all sorts of handicrafts, and souvenirs comprising anything that had remotely to do with flying, including enough different model-aeroplane kits to delight the heart of the most avid collector. And to refresh the inner man there was a beer tent and a luncheon marquee.

The official day began with the Lord Mayor making a speech to introduce Sir Alan Cobham, and then a speech from Cobham himself, introducing his company, National Aviation Day Limited (though everyone always called it Cobham's Flying Circus), and emphasising the importance of flying. He said that there was a move by Geneva to place civil aviation 'under the stranglehold of international control'. That would be disastrous, he boomed. 'It would doom our flourishing industry to stagnation. Our British aircraft constructors would lose the leading place they have won as world leaders, and thousands of skilled workers would lose their jobs.'

The crowd hadn't much idea of who Geneva was and couldn't follow his argument, but they happily applauded his closing slogan, 'Make the skyways Britain's highways!' which sounded rousing enough to be right. And they especially liked the next bit: 'And now, no more talking – let the fun begin!'

It was a wonderful display. Many of the crowd had never seen an aircraft before, and of those who had, few had witnessed the kind of trick flying seen that day. There was upside-down flying and looping the loop, the most spectacular swoops, skimming over the heads of the crowd and making them duck. There were machines that climbed almost vertically to a great height, then plunged towards Earth as if they were going to crash, to the gasps and occasional screams of the spectators. Three aeroplanes flew one after the other through a set of large goalposts set up in the middle of the field, and there was a display of formation flying by nine craft. There was a sort of game where an aircraft fitted with spikes below the wingtips picked up handkerchiefs from the ground. And there was wing-walking, and there were parachute drops.

Alongside all this, there were two aeroplanes providing pleasure flights: ten minutes for half a crown (children a shilling), in an open cockpit. This was enormously popular and there were long queues for the ride, some people even joining the end of the queue again for a second trip. Basil had been strolling about, keeping a sharp look-out for any of his especial tormentors, when he heard two people discussing the pleasure flight.

'I'm not going to try it,' said a woman. 'Maisie did and she said it made her feel frightfully sick.'

'Yes, but she went with the man,' said her companion.

211

'Everyone says the lady flyer in the other aeroplane gives a really smooth ride.'

'Oh, Ronald, I don't think I'd feel safe with a lady flyer. I mean – it *ought* to be a man, oughtn't it? To put one's life in the hands of a *female* . . .' She gave a theatrical little shudder, mostly it seemed for the purpose of clutching Ronald's arm more tightly.

'You little goose!' he said, looking down at her with masculine pride. 'It's the chance of a lifetime. You ought to try it – I know I shall.'

'Oh, Ronald, you're just so much braver than little me . . .'

Basil was glad to stop listening as they walked out of earshot. A horrifying thought had come into his mind. He strolled, trying to look casual, across to where the pleasure flights were starting from. One of the aeroplanes had just arrived back, and he walked carefully round to look up into the cockpit where the flyer was checking gauges. A leather-jacketed flyer, unrecognisable in cap and goggles. It might have been anyone, and either sex. But as he stood looking, the flyer turned and saw him, waved and called, 'Hello, darling! If you want a trip, you'll have to get in the queue.'

Basil felt his ears turn red, and scurried away. He could at least hope no-one would ever find out who she was.

There was no escaping the connection with his father because the loudspeaker introduced his event, not only giving out his name but describing in glowing terms his war exploits. At the very moment the words were booming out all over the field, Basil saw two prefects standing nearby, staring at him. He backed away into the crowd and hoped they would not follow. He found a place among the Circus lorries where he could watch without being disturbed as his father trundled down the field in a sturdy mongoose-engined Avro Tutor and took off. Never before had he been able truly to understand how his mother felt. He watched in enormous pride, but his heart was in his mouth as his father put the nimble craft through its paces, climbing and diving, rolling, looping the loop, and finally performing what the loudspeaker unhelpfully described as a 'death-defying three-hundred-mile-an-hour stall dive', in which the aeroplane seemed to stop dead, then flutter and fall and finally plummet, like a shot bird. He heard himself moan just before the aircraft recovered itself and swooped up again, and was glad there had been no-one nearby to hear. It was clever flying, and he knew his father would be enjoying himself in the cockpit even more than the spectators on the ground, but for the first time in his life he had really appreciated that one tiny miscalculation or mechanical fault could have ended his father's life then and there in a horrific crash and probably a fireball. He had to wait a while until the sick feeling in his stomach subsided before he left the shelter of the lorries.

Almost immediately he found his way blocked by the menacing forms of Carter and Wilkins, the two prefects he had spotted before. He swallowed, looking up at them: they were both very big boys – young men, really. Carter was captain of the school rugger team and a powerful prop forward, Wilkins was captain of both footer and boxing, and both were enthusiastic disciplinarians. They had furiously resented Basil's taking over of the school mag (though it was the preserve of the swotty rather than the sporty sixth) because the sixth had to stick together and crush any uppitiness in the lower school. Wilkins in particular was known to have 'a short way with fags', and though Basil was no longer a fag, Wilkins never minded delicate distinctions of that sort. He was not a delicate sort of person.

He was scowling now at Basil in a particularly ferocious way. 'Compton,' he growled, 'was that your pater in that aeroplane?'

Basil's mouth was dry, but he attempted a casual insouciance all the same. 'My pater? Oh, you mean that last display? Nice little craft, the Avro – very good handling.'

'It really was your father?' Carter said, staring as if Basil was something simply beyond understanding. 'Doing all that trick flying?'

'Yes,' he said, with a shrug, 'but one can't help one's parents, can one? I mean, you don't choose them.'

'It was wizard,' said Carter, seriously. 'Absolutely spiffing.'

'Yes,' said Wilkins, 'and if he was my guv'nor, I'd have told everyone about it, but you didn't say a word.'

Basil flinched as the vast hand on the end of the solid arm shot out, but the palm was open, and he realised, as the fog of fear cleared from his brain, that Wilkins was proposing to shake hands. *Wilkins!* He watched as his own hand disappeared into that vast paw, even now fearing the worst.

'I've always thought you were a little tick—' said Wilkins.

'And a frightful show-off,' Carter added obligingly.

'But you didn't swank a bit about your pater, so good for you.'

'It must be tremendous having a father like that,' Carter said, in hero-worshipping tones. 'Mine's only a solicitor.'

Other boys had gathered around the scene, and now bombarded Basil with questions about his father. Was he frightfully brainy? Did he take Basil up in his 'plane? What did he like for breakfast? Could Basil get them his autograph?

Basil, bemused, found his hand being shaken several times, and the questions came so thick and fast there was no need to answer any of them. And then a younger boy, Phipps, ran up and cried shrilly, 'I say, I've just been up on one of those pleasure flights, and what do you think? The lady flyer is Compton's mater! One of the ground crew told me.'

In a brief silence Basil thought his last moment had come, but then there was uproar: he was surrounded, his hand shaken, his back thumped, and everyone was congratulating him. His mother was an aviatrix! The word had only recently come into the vocabulary of schoolboys, because less than a month ago the American lady, Amelia Earhart, had become the first woman to fly non-stop across the Atlantic. Her fifteen-hour trip from Newfoundland to Ireland had been attended by rain, ice, fog and mechanical problems and she hadn't seen the sea from the time she had taken off, but in interviews afterwards she had said she was 'tired, hungry but cheerful' and that she had never had any doubts of succeeding.

Several more sixth-formers, including some of the ousted *Felix Culpa* team, had joined the throng, and now Tenant, ex-editor and a senior prefect, came up to shake his hand and said, 'You've shown character over this, Compton. Good show. And I don't suppose you could help taking over the mag. Make a decent fist of it, and you're forgiven.'

'Thank you, Tenant,' Basil said.

It was a huge relief but, oddly, even as he registered that his troubles at school must now be over, Tenant being a man of large influence, he also felt a twinge of disappointment. He realised that he had rather enjoyed the battle; and being accepted into the fold because of what his parents did was a bit of a let-down. The Old Man, he thought, had known what he was doing when he had tipped Basil over the precipice.

Now he had no need to fight for his life, he could feel his old laziness seeping back. He could fill the summer-term issue with aviation stuff, and spend his time lounging about, reading the paper and smoking. Next term, if he stayed on, he'd be in the sixth himself and able to do as he liked. But, somehow or other, this golden prospect didn't appeal as much as before. The Old Man, curse him, had managed to take some of the shine off indolence.

The surprise that James was going away again was compounded by the surprise of his destination. 'Bear Island,' he said, and added vaguely, 'I don't know where it is exactly. Somewhere north, I think.'

It came about in consequence of the Flying Circus.

Wandering about early on the first day, being a good host, he had come across a young man of about his own age standing with his hands in his pockets, watching the ground crew doing something to one of the aircraft. Aware of James's approach, the young man turned his head and smiled, then went on watching. It felt to James as if he was inviting him to watch alongside him. So James took up a similar stance.

After a few moments of silence, the man said, 'Marvellous things, aren't they?'

'Are you interested in aeroplanes?' James asked.

The man looked at him. 'Isn't everyone? You can't help but be interested, I'd have thought. The possibilities!'

'One of the flyers is a cousin of mine,' James said.

'Really? Gosh, how fine for you!' He pulled his hands out of his trouser pockets and felt in his jacket. 'Cigarette?'

There was nothing like a cigarette for breaking the ice: in a moment they were chatting away like old friends. Not that there had really been any ice – there was something about the look of him that James immediately liked. Being himself such a colourful character, he had always attracted, and been attracted to, quieter, less flamboyant chaps. All his boyhood friendships had been with boys of duller plumage and more reticent character, like David Pennyfather, who had admired him, and on whom he had depended; and with David gone and settled in his own life, he had a vacancy.

The new friend's name was properly plain – Patrick Brompton – and he was ordinary-looking, not handsome, mouse-haired, but with a pleasant, frank face and trusting eyes. They spent the rest of the day together, without its ever having been stated as an intention, and enjoyed each other's company too well to need to comment on the fact.

Pat Brompton was up at Cambridge, James learned, as a postgraduate, working towards a doctorate in ornithology. James, like his father before him, admired brainy people without in any way wishing to emulate them, or feeling oppressed by them. He had a happy confidence in his own qualities, though not actually knowing what they might be saved him from any taint of conceit or arrogance.

The two young men took a luncheon of bread and cheese and beer together, and afterwards James invited Pat to go and see his motorcycle. He showed off its best features and described the journey he had made on it down to the West Country, the mechanical problems he had encountered and how he had overcome them.

And Pat said, 'I say, you know your way round an engine, don't you?'

'Pretty well have to, if you're out on the road. There's not usually anyone else to ask for help. I've had her to pieces a few times – pretty much know what makes her tick. All engines are the same, in principle, you know.'

'I'm afraid I'm a bit of a fool when it comes to engines,' Pat said. 'Don't know one end from the other.'

'Oh, I could teach you in a minute,' James said. ''Tisn't difficult. That's the nice thing about machines: they have to follow the rules. You can always find out what's wrong if you take the time. Course, my little trip to Wiltshire was nothing. What I really want to do is to take her abroad, and then I'd really have to know how to fix her.'

'Where abroad?' Pat asked, with a more intent look than James felt the question warranted.

'Oh, anywhere,' he said. 'I'm not fussy. I'd like to travel, that's all – and the more far-flung and exotic, the better. I want to see a bit of the world before I settle down.'

Pat did not follow this conversational lead and James was slightly disappointed: he liked talking about his plans for travelling the world, even though he didn't seem to get any closer to carrying them out. Pat was in York for both days of the Flying Circus and had a room booked at the Lamb and Lion for the night. James would have invited him to stay at Morland Place, but both of them had dinner engagements that evening, and agreed to meet the next day instead.

'And that's when he came up with the suggestion,' James told Polly.

Pat Brompton was taking part in an expedition to Bear Island, arranged by his department at Cambridge, to study the abundant bird life there, especially in relation to the ecology and the 'food web', an idea first proposed after a Bear Island expedition in the twenties by Summerhayes and Elton. The four ornithologists would be accompanied by three members of the meteorological department and four geologists, who were to study mineral composition, and explore if there were any deposits worth mining for. The latter commercial consideration was due to their being given funds by a mining company, funds that made the expedition possible.

'But, Jamie, you're not a geologist or an ornithologist,' Polly said.

James struck his forehead. 'Ornithologist! That was the word Pat said for bird-watcher. Been trying to think of it all day.'

Polly persisted: 'Why would you want to go?'

'Of course I want to!' he said. 'You know I want to travel the world, and this is a chance to go somewhere very out-of-the-way. Pat says very few people have ever been to Bear Island. It's much more of an adventure than going round France and Italy, isn't it?'

'I suppose so, but why do they want you along?'

'It was Pat's own idea. They're going to have various vehicles over there and a generator, and someone has to take care of the machines. These academic types aren't very good with their hands,' he said fondly. 'I'll do the driving, too, and various other odd jobs – make myself useful. Pat says just having me along will keep everyone cheerful. Make sure the conversation in the evenings isn't all about work.'

218

Polly considered this, and said, 'I'm afraid you might find it very dull.'

'Oh, no, Pat says they're a very good bunch of chaps, not eggheady at all once they relax and put the books away. And this Bear Island will be interesting. Do you know, at one time of year the sun never goes down? You can see it going round the horizon all night, apparently.'

Polly frowned, not seeing how that could be possible, but she said, 'Well, if it's what you want to do, good luck to it. How long is the trip? And when do you start?'

'It starts at the end of the month – so I'm afraid I'll miss Alec's birthday. It's a shame. I'd have liked to see the little chap's face when you give him his pony.'

'And how long is it for?'

'A year,' James said. 'There must be a lot to see if they need a whole year to study one island. Exotic native customs and strange tribal dances, I expect. Colourful costumes, outlandish rituals, all that sort of thing. Strange animals – tigers and elephants and so on. Mind you, it takes a while to get there, Pat says. He was saying how much easier trips like this would be if you could fly there instead of going by boat. Still, a trip on a liner will be fun. You had a good time on *Mauretania*, didn't you?'

'I wasn't in the mood to have fun at the time,' Polly reminded him, 'but you certainly can if you want to. Well, it will be quiet here without you, but I'm sure you'll have an interesting time.'

'There's just one thing,' James said, a little awkwardly. 'I hate to ask you but, you see, everyone has to put in a bit to cover their food and so on. And I don't have a bean. So I wondered . . .'

'How much do you have to put in?' Polly asked.

'A hundred and fifty pounds, but Pat says I'll probably need some special clothes as well, so if you could manage two hundred, that would be fine.'

Polly had been expecting much more. She was sure she would spend more than that on James's food and drink in a year. 'Yes, of course,' she said. And then, warmly, 'I'm glad to see you getting on with this travel of yours. I was beginning to think it wasn't going to happen.'

'Oh, it just needed the right opportunity to come along,' James said airily. 'Thanks, Polly. You're a brick. And d'you know what? I'm going to keep a diary for the whole trip. Pat suggested it. They all keep diaries, of course, but theirs are dull scientific stuff. I'm going to write a proper travel *mémoire*, and he says he wouldn't be surprised if I shouldn't get it published when I get back. It's bound to be damned interesting.'

James's enthusiasm for the trip was very little dented when, with the aid of an atlas at the public library (the schoolroom one didn't help), he discovered that Bear Island was far to the north of Norway in the Barents Sea, in fact on the edge of the Arctic Ocean.

'I don't think there'll be tigers or elephants,' Polly said doubtfully.

'Well, but there'll be something. Bound to be bears, at least – Bear Island?'

On the map it was a tiny speck in the middle of a great deal of blue; but being so isolated only meant, he said, that it would be different from other places and more worth seeing. He was slightly more concerned when Pat told him what warm clothes he would need, but Pat also said the sea kept temperatures relatively mild in the winter, and that there was very little rain, so there would not be snow: it would not be like going to the South Pole, like Captain Scott. And in the summer, he reasoned, when the sun never went down, it must be very warm.

In any case, he had accepted the invitation, and would not make a fool of himself by saying he didn't want to go if it was going to be cold. Besides, he was beginning to realise what an honour it was to be part of it. When he went to London to assemble his kit and meet the others in the expedition, he was approached by a reporter who wanted to interview him for a piece for *The Times*. When the piece came out, mentioning that he was going to keep a diary, a publisher wrote to him asking to be allowed to see it when he got back with a view to publishing. So he would not now have pulled out for any consideration.

The take-over of Olympic Pictures, and the disruption to the studio schedules caused by the rebuilding project, made it easy for Lennie to negotiate a one-picture release for Rose to make *Mothers and Daughters* with MGM. By the time shooting began on the MGM lot in Culver City in the fall, the title had been changed several times. Peach McGinty had objected that putting 'Mothers' before 'Daughters' made it sound as if she wasn't the star, but though they tried with *Daughters and Mothers* it somehow didn't stick. Besides, Miss McGinty pointed out, there was only one daughter in this movie, or only one that mattered. The others were practically walk-on parts, only appearing in the scene where the unofficial mother had to take Peach to a children's party. After that the studio put up suggestions, which Peach rejected as not making it clear enough that she was in it and was the most important person. Finally she came up with her own suggestion, and the blackboard outside Studio Two on the first day announced that shooting was taking place there for *Broadway Cutie*.

'It's a terrible title,' Rose objected as she sat, caped, in Makeup.

'But it will probably do well at the box office,' Lennie said, perched on a stool out of the way. 'It's memorable, and if it keeps Peach happy . . .'

Keeping her happy, as Rose had already learned, was the main priority if the picture was to be made at all. Peach

McGinty was a monster, Rose said. But she was a box-office-draw monster, Lennie countered.

'I half wish you hadn't talked me into this,' Rose said.

Lennie was robust. 'Nonsense. It's a good chance for you to show what you can do. Mr Mayer is bound to be on set a lot of the time, and if you can impress him, he'll know perfectly well how good you have to be to catch his eye when Peach is around.' Louis B. Mayer was the head of the company, which had now overtaken Universal as the biggest in Hollywood.

'Suppose Peach cuts the legs out from under me?' Rose grumbled.

'Honey, the worst that can happen is that no-one will notice you – but no-one will blame you for that. And you'll have made friends here, and shown you can act, and you'll gain valuable experience, and another title on your curriculum vitae.'

'Tell me again what my billing will be,' Rose said.

'Right under Peach's. It will say *"Broadway Cutie* starring Peach McGinty, with Rose Morland". And underneath that, everybody else in smaller letters.' Rose nodded, but did not seem hugely impressed, so Lennie said, 'That's a big achievement, you know. There's normally no "with" on Peach's bills. You're the first to get one.'

Rose allowed herself to be comforted.

A little later, Lennie walked with her to the floor. The studio lot was like a small town, surrounded by high walls and with a uniformed guard on the gate. Inside the walls, streets criss-crossed the blocks of buildings, offices and workshops and the studios themselves, called floors, vast as cathedrals. The town had its own restaurants, street cleaners, even its own cops and fire brigade. Lennie was taking mental notes for the new spread that ABO was building on the empty lots by Olympic.

Inside Studio Two Lennie sat with Rose while she looked

over the schedule of the day's scenes and the stand-ins did the levels for the first shoot. There were six sets around the floor, each like a room with one wall missing. On the catwalk overhead, the lighting men moved about setting up and adjusting the huge lamps, while down below the cameras, some fixed, some on wheels, were already attended by the cameramen and their assistants. All of the varied personnel for movie-making were assembled: ground electricians, the microphone men, the sound controller in his glass booth, the wardrobe and makeup people and the hairdressers, the stills cameraman, the script editor, the continuity girl and the properties girl, the assistant directors and assistant producers. Other actors appeared, greeting Rose and Lennie and standing about, chatting; and finally the producer and director strolled in together talking, the director waving his hands eloquently, the producer nodding gravely and sometimes shaking his head, as if saying he agreed that whatever it was was bad, but there was nothing to be done about it.

But they were not the last: Peach McGinty's manager walked in after the producer and director, and was followed by her dresser and her secretary, and then Miss McGinty herself, with her black maid scurrying along half beside and half behind, carrying her bag, her wrap and a number of other articles the star felt necessary to a day's filming.

Lennie watched this parade with amusement. To arrive after the director was rude and would lead to most other actors losing their job, but Lennie reckoned Peach had only a couple of years left at most as a juvenile star, and that both she and the director knew it. She was a big money-maker for the studio, so what harm to indulge her a little, when it was a finite thing? It was hard to know what age she was – it was not information that was given out. She had made her stage début at the age of three, and her first movie at five. The character she was playing was supposed to be nine. Lennie reckoned she must be at least twelve, but she was still tiny – rumour had it she had been kept small with gin. However, sooner or later puberty would kick in, and once she grew bosoms she was finished.

She passed quite close to him, and he thought she looked quite grotesque in the heavy makeup that had to counteract the effect of the lights. The top part of her costume seemed strangely bulky. He wondered if the bosoms had started already. Poor old Peach! She was certainly taller than the average nine-year-old: he wondered whether Rose had been offered the role partly because she was tall for an actress and therefore wouldn't show Peach up.

His sympathy for Peach soon evaporated when she began to screech at the assistant producer about her dressing room, which did not meet her exacting requirements. But even she fell silent when Louis B. Mayer walked in. He greeted everyone cheerfully as he passed and received reverent murmurs of 'Good morning, Mr Mayer.' He had a few words with Peach, the producer and one director, then came over to Rose, took her hands and leaned over to kiss her cheek. 'Good to have you with us, sweetheart,' he said. 'You'll be great.'

And then he was gone. Lennie was pleased for Rose – being noticed like that by the great man was a very good start. But looking beyond her he saw Peach scowling horribly, perhaps because the great man had not kissed *her*. He hoped she would not take it out on Rose.

As it happened, someone else was on hand to defuse the rage. One of the assistant floor managers – the lowliest fetchers and carriers – had been sent to get coffee for the director, and as she approached with it, Peach stepped backwards and bumped into her. The coffee slopped over onto the floor, missing Peach's foot by a narrow margin.

The fury was unleashed. None of it had actually been spilled on the diminutive star, but you'd have thought she'd been drenched, and scalded into the bargain. She screamed and hurled abuse as the girl cowered under the storm, then turned on the producer and demanded that the clumsy idiot be sacked right away.

The director spoke up mildly. 'It was an accident, Peach. No harm done.'

'*No harm done?*' Peach screamed, red in the face. 'Do you want me to walk off the set? *Do you?* Because that's what I'll do if you don't get her stupid ugly face out of here right now! I'm the star of this movie! Without me you've *got* no movie!'

A speck of spittle had gathered at the corner of her mouth and there was sweat under her eyes. The assistant floor manager was crying quietly. The director turned his head away, but the producer stepped in to soothe Peach, ordered the girl tersely to get out, put his arm round the star and walked with her, talking her into calmness. The makeup girl stepped forward to dab her face, and the director said wearily, 'Shall we make a start?'

Rose gave Lennie one eloquent look that said, *What have you got me into?* and got up to take off her wrapper and head for her first mark. Lennie had meant to stay and watch the first scene, but the memory of the assistant floor manager was bothering him, and he slipped quietly out of the studio into the sunny street.

The girl was standing just to one side of the door, wiping her eyes on an inadequate-looking handkerchief. Lennie stepped up to her and offered his own: large, clean and manly.

'Thank you,' she said, with a hitch in her voice. She made use of it.

Lennie looked at her bent head and felt a strange interest in her. She had smooth golden hair, much the colour of Polly's, but unlike that of almost every other girl he knew it was not cut and marcelled but plaited and the plait wound round her head like a crown, an old-fashioned style. Her face was a smooth oval, rather pale, not especially pretty, but her eyes, when she had finished mopping up and lifted them to him, were blue, blue as Polly's, and looking directly and frankly into his in a way he did not much see these days. Girls were always either coquettish or playing propriety – another form of coquetry – so that you got the impression they did not see you as a person, just as a man, who had to be impressed in one of a certain number of set ways. But this girl saw him. She looked straight into him as if he were transparent as glass.

'Thank you,' she said again. She glanced at the handkerchief and said, 'I'd better wash this before I give it back to you.'

'There's no need,' he said automatically.

She gave a rueful smile. 'I don't think you'll want it in this condition. It's so stupid of me to cry. I know what she's like. But it was a shock, losing my job like that.'

'You won't lose it,' he said gallantly. 'I'll talk to Mr Gibson. He didn't mean it.'

'He might not have, but Miss McGinty did. She'll make sure I'm dismissed.' She sighed, and the sigh had a quiver in the middle of it that went straight to his heart. 'I liked my job. And I need it. I have to take care of my mother, and she's not well.'

'What's your name?' Lennie asked.

'Beth Andrews,' she said.

'I'm Lennie Manning,' he said, holding out his hand. She shook it, her eyes still on his face, not flirtatiously but simply with interest. 'I'm a large shareholder in ABO Pictures.'

'I know,' she said. 'You're here with Rose Morland. She's lovely.' It was a simple compliment on Rose's beauty, but Lennie, sensitive to this woman for reasons he didn't yet understand, realised from its tone that she had meant something more by 'with' than simply 'accompanying'.

'She's my cousin,' he said, smiling. 'I'm a sort of honorary uncle.'

'Oh,' she said.

'Come and work at ABO,' he said. 'I can get you a job. I have enough influence for that.'

'What sort of job?' A faint wariness.

'The same as you're doing. But you'll like it more. We're a little smaller than MGM so you'll have more to do and be involved in everything.'

'You really mean it?'

'Of course. I wouldn't say it otherwise.'

She did not yet look delighted. 'You're very kind,' she said. 'But why would you do that for me?'

'I hate bullying of any sort,' he said. 'Or oppression. Or injustice.'

Just at that moment he realised what her slight hesitation had been about. He was a powerful and wealthy man, she was a lowly assistant floor manager, and in such cases there was usually only one reason for kindness. He knew the realisation showed in his face: an 'Oh!' followed by confusion – what on earth could one say without sounding like an idiot or a cad?

And she was still reading his face, and must have seen all that: colour came into her cheeks, and her lips rehearsed several words she did not seem to be able to speak.

He recovered first. 'So, will you, then? Come and work at ABO?'

'Yes,' she said. 'Thank you so much.'

There was a moment of silence, in which Lennie became aware of the sounds of the lot around them, and the Californian sunshine pouring down, and the short, black shadows at their feet, and a feeling as if the world had paused and looked round at them in curiosity; as if the question and answer had been about something entirely different.

'I'd better go and collect my things,' she said, after a moment.

'I have to go and watch Rose for a little,' Lennie said.

'Can you give me half an hour? Then I'll drive you over to ABO. Go and have a cup of coffee in the commissary, and I'll meet you there.'

'All right,' she said, a little shyly. And then smiled. 'But not coffee.'

He had forgotten for the moment how the whole thing had started. He smiled too. 'Not coffee,' he agreed.

By the autumn of 1932, unemployment was edging towards three million, with the heavy-industry areas, South Wales, the north-west, the north-east and Scotland, being the hardest hit. In Scotland the closure of the shipyards added to the misery of the closed pits, and nearly one in three men was out of work. Here in particular the National Unemployed Workers' Movement found ready candidates.

The NUWM was a Communist-backed movement set up in 1921 to mobilise unemployed discontent, since the Labour Party largely accepted that the government was doing its best in exceptionally difficult circumstances and had no answers to offer. The NUWM wanted thirty-six shillings a week for an unemployed man and his wife, plus five shillings for each child, rent allowance of up to fifteen shillings and a hundredweight of coal or the equivalent in gas. The reality fell far short of that: many a family of four had to live on little more than £2 8s. all told and buy its own coal. And means testing could reduce that even further.

The NUWM's interests were not wholly focused on the plight of the unemployed. Every member was required to take an oath 'never to cease from active strife until capitalism is abolished', and the unemployed, it reasoned, would provide the foot-soldiers when the revolution came. They had organised and funded several hunger marches, as well as local protests and actions, but without managing to gain much publicity. The Labour Party and the trade unions along with most of the press were hostile to Communism as a threat to the whole country, and contrary to British traditions. The poorest, they said, would suffer the most if there really was a revolution.

The march the NUWM was organising in 1932 was expected to be the largest yet, and was against the Means Test and the Anomalies Act. The latter, which had come into force in the autumn of 1931, was intended to eliminate abuses of the benefit system in an attempt to reduce the national bill, which was climbing out of control. It removed from benefit those whose connection with the workforce was considered to be marginal, such as seasonal workers, agricultural workers and domestic servants.

But the biggest sector to find itself excluded was married women. Previously they had been able to claim benefit by virtue of contributions paid when they were single. Now they were denied benefit unless they had made a minimum of fifteen contributions since they were married. In addition they had also to prove they were normally in 'insurable employment', and were not only actively seeking work but also likely to find it in the local area – which automatically excluded those who needed the money most.

The Act was not just about saving money: there was considerable hostility to the idea of married women working. Their place was in the home raising their children, it was argued, and neglect of children led to criminality and the breakdown of society. Furthermore – an argument often aired in newspaper columns and letters, and even brought up in the House – these women were taking men's jobs. If married women stayed at home, unemployment could be wiped out overnight.

By March 1932 over 80 per cent of married women's benefit claims had been disallowed; and at the lower end, a family could not live on the husband's wage or benefit alone. So the 1932 hunger march was expected to be the biggest ever. Eighteen contingents would set out from various parts of the country and converge on London for a rally in Hyde Park. The NUWM claimed it would have a hundred thousand marchers.

The Glasgow contingent of 250 was the first to leave on the 26th of September – though some of them had already marched eighty miles or more to get to the starting point in Glasgow. The men, mostly in their twenties and thirties, but with some as young as eighteen and a few considerably older, marched twenty or so miles a day, taking a ten-minute break each hour. The cook's lorry would go on ahead, ready to serve a meal in the middle of the day, usually a hearty stew. The stopping place each night was prearranged. In sympathetic towns there would be billets and a meal for everyone, paid for by subscriptions raised in advance, and a rally would be held in some public space.

In St Albans, thirty-eight women marchers were met on the road and escorted into town, accommodated and fed at the Trade Union Club, with a concert laid on to entertain them. A cobbler volunteered to mend any faults in their shoes while another group washed their clothes for them; and they were sent off the next morning with a packet of sandwiches each.

In other places things were not so comfortable, and where nothing else could be found they had to go to the local workhouse for the night and were put on the 'vagrants' ward, and fed the basic 'spike', which was two slices of bread and margarine and a mug of tea. Sometimes they were met with hostility and there were skirmishes in the road; in some towns they were banned from making speeches, and the police tried to move them on.

They carried banners and sang as they marched, and most contingents had something by way of music – a flute or fife at least, and drums, sometimes cymbals or a triangle. But otherwise they travelled light, each carrying his tin plate and mug, knife and fork and blanket, a hand towel, a bit of soap

230

and shaving gear. Some had a change of shirt and socks in their haversack, but most did not bother: many had never owned spares. As to underwear, few from the poorest places wore any in the first place. But a walking-stick was not only useful to help one along, but could be used as a weapon in case of trouble.

Polly saw a north-eastern contingent from Darlington pass by late one day, heading for Leeds. She had driven into Wetherby to look at some feed, and was just about to set off home when a policeman asked her to wait to keep the road clear while the march came through. Perhaps because it was late, and also raining, they were not singing. They trudged along in silence in their shabby jackets and trousers and heavy boots, every man sheltering under a flat cap, one or two wearing a mackintosh or a cycling cape, but most just getting wet with a terrible resignation. Each had his pack on his back. There were a couple of banners – 'Marching Against Starvation' and 'Darlington Men Against the Means Test – Abolish It!' – but she could see others had furled them for now. Perhaps in the rain they became too water-logged and heavy to carry aloft.

The little she had read on the subject condemned the march because it was organised by the Communists, and warned of possible disorder, as if the marchers were dangerous animals on the loose. Polly thought they simply looked very sad. The grey rain streamed unkindly down and they marched in silence, keeping step effortlessly after so long on the road, their eyes fixed on nothing, their faces set not in anger or determination but in a sort of blankness, the tramp of their boots on the road a counterpoint to the gurgling of the rain in gutters and the hoofbeats of the mounted policeman escorting them through.

And the residents of Wetherby who paused to watch them looked on in silence too, not hostile but indifferent, most not having heard of the march, knowing nothing of what they were marching for. Times were hard for everyone. Who were these men? Who cared?

As the leading files passed out of the other side of the town, someone among them struck up a tune on a flute, but no-one sang, and it added little jollity. As the end of the column passed, the policeman turned to Polly to wave her on, and said, 'They'd better have stayed at home. They'll get nothing for their trouble.'

'Don't you think so?' Polly said.

'Nobody's got nowt to give 'em,' he said simply.

Polly drove home thinking that he was probably right. If a hungry man came to your gate, you gave him bread. But when it was a hungry three million, it became the government's problem, and what could they do?

The march attracted little attention from the press on its way to London, but when it arrived there, on Thursday, the 27th of October, it was a different matter. The marchers, numbering only around fifteen hundred, were met in Hyde Park by crowds of a hundred thousand in excitable mood. The commissioner of the police, Lord Trenchard (whom Jack had once taught to fly), had taken extensive precautions and met the marchers with 2,600 policemen including 136 on horseback.

Unfortunately, 750 of the constables were 'specials', who had neither the training nor the discipline for such a volatile occasion. Goaded on by the crowd, they eventually drew batons and attacked the marchers, who retaliated, and general disorder broke out. Railings were torn up and branches broken from trees to use as weapons, for the marchers had been made to leave their walking-sticks behind in the approaches to London, though some had managed to conceal them. By nightfall nineteen policemen and fifty-eight demonstrators had been injured and fourteen people had been arrested.

In the following days there was more disorder in other

parts of London, culminating in the attempt on the Tuesday to present a petition to Parliament for the abolition of the Means Test and repeal of the Anomalies Act, to which they claimed to have a million signatures. But processions were not allowed by law within a mile of the Palace of Westminster, and they were met by three thousand policemen, including two thousand on horseback, and fighting broke out again. There were running battles in the streets that went on through the evening and spread as far north as Edgware Road and south across Westminster Bridge, and led to dozens of injuries and arrests.

The petition was never presented. The next day the marchers started their journeys home, by train; four of the leaders were arrested and given prison sentences; and the home secretary, Sir John Gilmour, had to answer questions in the House. There was some sympathy for the marchers expressed in journals by the intellectual left, but the Labour Party remained hostile to anything organised by the Communists; the government and society in general was nervous about Red revolution; and everybody else had other things on their mind, so nothing changed. Had Polly had the leisure or inclination to think any further about it, she would have concluded the policeman in Wetherby had been right.

CHAPTER TEN

Charlotte found the world of work congenial. She liked being kept busy, the sense of purpose it gave her, the satisfaction of completing a task. The work itself she found interesting: though she was only on the very fringes of the main endeavour, she yet felt she was part of the process of getting books before the public, which was a worthwhile thing. She enjoyed the company of the other employees – hers had been rather a solitary life for some years – and the lunch-hour, when there was chat and laughter and eating in cafés. She sometimes felt she could never get enough of eating in cafés.

And there were her wages, of course: it was very agreeable to have money in one's pocket, especially money one had earned oneself. It was not a great deal, but Oliver and Verena refused to take anything for her keep, so it was all hers. She spent on lunches and necessities, like stockings and shoe repairs and her fares to and from work, but even so she was gradually accumulating a small pot of savings, which also gave her pleasure.

The one thing she didn't like was the restriction placed on her freedom by living, as she saw it, under the supervision of the family. When other girls proposed going to the cinema or to a dance together in the evening, she could not go. She met Myra and Betty sometimes for lunch, and heard their stories of living together in lodgings and thought it sounded wonderful. The girls she envied thought her life – living in a grand mansion with someone to do her washing and cook delicious meals for her, to say nothing of the entertainments and dinner parties – would be very heaven.

But she was biding her time. She was glad to see her mother so obviously happy with Avis, and felt that sooner or later Violet would soften, and the attention would be removed from her long enough for her to escape.

When Violet and Avis came back from America they went on a few wedding visits, then settled down in Derbyshire for the summer. Violet wanted Charlotte to visit, and she did go once for a weekend, but it was a long way to travel for one night, since she would have to leave after luncheon on Sunday to get back for work on Monday. Violet, in fairness, saw that; and since she was, in any case, too wrapped up in her happiness with Avis to need anyone else, she said that Charlotte must come when she could, and not worry otherwise.

The trouble came in the summer. As soon as Henry finished school he went straight down to Tunstead to spend the summer holidays there. It had been arranged that he should go to technical college in Manchester – the same one that his hero, Jack Compton, had attended – in the autumn, and he was glad to have several weeks of 'messing about', with fields and woods to mess about in. Violet therefore thought that Charlotte should do the same: 'London is impossible in August. You must come here for the whole month.'

Charlotte tried to explain that she could not take a month's holiday from work. In fact, she had been told that next year she would be allowed two weeks' annual leave – though she would not be paid for those two weeks, of course – but that she had not worked there long enough to qualify for leave this year.

Violet was impatient. 'I'm sure they'll let you go if you ask,' she said. 'Just explain to them that you need to get out of London, and that your mother wants you to visit. I'm sure they'll understand.'

'They won't, Mummy,' Charlotte said, impatient herself.

'But, darling, Molly gave you the position, and her husband owns the company. Surely that must give you special consideration.'

Charlotte tried to explain that she did not want special consideration, that this was a real job not a 'pretend' one, that she wanted to be treated like the other employees, that she had worked hard to deserve her position and hoped to rise in the firm, which she couldn't do if she were thought to be 'playing at it'.

Violet didn't understand any of that, but she would not argue. She had been brought up to believe that disputing was unladylike. She merely said, 'Verena will close up the house during August, so you'll have to come here.'

That was a problem, and Charlotte fretted over it for some weeks before Henry asked her what was wrong and she told him. Henry quite naturally confided it to Uncle Oliver, who, he firmly believed, could solve all problems. Oliver, knowing perfectly well what Charlotte was trying to achieve – though he didn't necessarily agree with it – went to Molly, who said at once, 'She can come and stay here until you open the house again. We have a spare room. I shall be taking the children to the seaside at first, but Cook and Clara can look after her till I come back.'

Charlotte was a little worried that staying with the boss and his wife might make the other girls suspect favouritism, but neither Molly nor Vivian ever mentioned it at work, so no-one knew. Vivian came home in the evenings, but he went to join Molly and the children at the weekends; she rather enjoyed those few days of having the house to herself. She went for long walks in the Park and listened to the band concerts, visited museums, and on one of the Saturday afternoons met Myra (Betty was visiting her parents), went to the pictures and afterwards had supper at Lyons in the Strand.

236

It was, she felt, just about a perfect afternoon and evening, and she told Myra so.

Myra laughed. 'You're easily pleased, I must say! That picture was awfully soppy, and while this haddock is perfectly nice, it can't be a patch on what you normally feed on.'

'Oh, but I thought the picture was wonderful! My heart was in my mouth when the man told her he didn't want a girl with a past, and she knew she'd had an affair with the other chap, and he mustn't find out!'

'Yes, I was there, you know! I suppose when you haven't seen many films you're more affected by them.'

'As for dinner – Aunt Verena does have a first-rate cook, and Uncle Oliver gives parties all the time—'

'And he knows *everyone*,' said Myra. 'You don't know how lucky you are, meeting so many important people.'

'Oh, but they're so dull – all people their age, *old* people, and talking about the things *they*'re interested in. And there's always one young man invited for me, and he's always the sort my mother would approve of, and I *know* I'm supposed to fall in love with him and try and charm him so he'll ask me to marry him and then everyone will be happy, but I *can't*!'

'Only you could object to being provided with handsome young men to talk to,' Myra said solemnly.

'I didn't say they were handsome. But I suppose you're right. I ought to be grateful for what I have, but it's hard when it isn't what I want.'

'Never mind, the time will come,' said Myra. 'In a few more years they'll decide you're too old to get married and stop worrying about you. Then you can come and live with us and we can be three old maids together.'

'Oh, Mysie, it sounds like bliss,' Charlotte sighed, and made Myra laugh all the more.

When Verena opened the house again, Charlotte went back there, having enjoyed the different style of life at Molly's flat, with their simpler dinners, their less grand and more literary friends. She noticed particularly the difference in reading habits: at Molly's house everyone read books, even the servants; at Chelmsford House Oliver read only medical journals and professional papers, and Verena barely flicked through the *Tatler*. Charlotte felt rather flat and dull being back there, but had she known it, worse was to come. For in October Avis rented a house in Belgrave Square and he and Violet came up for the Little Season and for Avis to attend the House. The first thing Violet did was to send for Charlotte to join them.

'Sent from pillar to post like a parcel,' Charlotte grumbled to herself. In her case the problem was not that she was unwanted but that she was wanted too much. When she first heard her mother was coming to Town, she begged Uncle Oliver to 'explain to Mummy that I have to go to work *every day*. I can't just not go so that I can do things with her.' And he did speak to his sister, fairly sternly it seemed, for when Charlotte arrived with her luggage, Violet only said, 'It's so lovely to see you, darling. Come and have some tea and tell me what you've been up to,' and did not suggest any career-destroying absences.

But the fact was that Charlotte, living in her mother's house, was now exposed to her for evenings and weekends. The Little Season was never as hectic as the real one, but Violet, having been brought up a Londoner, did not make the distinction and, being a new bride, was much in demand. So there were social gatherings of one sort or another most evenings, and theatres, operas and ballets into the bargain. Charlotte enjoyed some of them; might have enjoyed more, but her mother was evidently making a big push to present to Charlotte as many eligible men as she could find. Violet thought it was a Heaven-sent second chance: now she was Countess of Belmont and respectable again, she could give Charlotte the social life her birth had entitled her to, and enable her to marry properly. She found it infinitely frustrating that Charlotte did not seem to want to seize the opportunity.

The conversation went round the same wearying track.

'I don't *want* to get married, Mummy.'

'But you must, darling. What will happen to you otherwise?'

'Lots of women don't get married. They're perfectly happy.'

'Not *lots* – and I'm sure they're not. It isn't natural to be alone.'

'But I shall have women friends.'

'That's not the same thing.'

And so on. Charlotte began to feel nostalgic about Chelmsford House. Her mother told her that she and Avis meant to live in London for six months of the year, so she saw no end in sight except, as Myra had promised her, eventually being too old to be thought marriageable.

But, though she did not know it, relief was on the way.

There was a dinner party at Chelmsford House one evening in early December to which Charlotte was invited, along with Violet and Avis. The food was good, as always, but Charlotte found the talk very boring because it was all political. The Mosleys were there, and Sir Oswald dominated the conversation with his own concerns. His New Party of February 1931 had failed to win any seats at the last election and had disintegrated, and he had recently formed a new one, the British Union of Fascists.

'I've been to Italy,' he said, in his declamatory manner. 'I've met Mussolini and talked to him. I've seen what he's doing. He has the vision and drive our politicians lack. Our parliament is too big, too unwieldy. It's make-do. Magna Carta, the barons – it worked in the old days, but it can't tackle the complex problems of modern society. You need experts, not well-meaning amateurs. You need a plan.'

Oliver laughed. 'Everybody has a plan. It's the most

over-used word in the political vocabulary. The remedy for every ill is a plan. The Soviets are famous for it.'

Mosley looked serious. 'Fascism is the only possible defence against Communism,' he asserted.

'I can't tell the difference between them,' Oliver said.

Verena looked reproachful. 'Darling, don't tease.'

He looked at her, still smiling, but she saw his eyes were serious. 'I wasn't teasing. Government control, using public money to create new industries and revitalise the old ones, a massive programme of public works to end unemployment, education standardised from the centre, discipline and healthy living – have I got it right?'

'Exactly!' Mosley said triumphantly. 'We can't go on as we are. The country is in the hands of old men with old ideas. The clutter of past generations held together with rotten bits of string. Drift and stagnation. We have to mobilise national resources with systematic planning. We can't solve our problems without energy, hard work and discipline. We must have a plan!'

'Quite,' said Oliver. 'But those things I mentioned were part of the Communist plan. You'll find them all in Soviet Russia.'

There was an awkward silence for a heartbeat, and then Fruity Metcalfe spoke up gallantly to ask, 'What's the hunting like around Tunstead, Belmont? Mean to go out at all this season?' and the conversation turned with relief to horses.

Soon afterwards the ladies withdrew, and Charlotte, following at the rear of the procession, became aware of a mild disturbance at the head of it, without knowing the cause. But as she followed the lady in front of her into the drawing room, her arm was taken and she was drawn aside by Sarah Vibart, who whispered, 'Come with me. Your mother is not quite well.'

Upstairs in the bedroom set apart for ladies to refresh their toilette, her mother was reclining on a sofa looking pale, while Verena fanned her.

'Mummy, are you all right?' Charlotte asked in fright. She had never known her mother ail in all her life.

'Hush,' Verena said. 'Just a little fainting fit. Nothing to be alarmed about.'

Charlotte didn't agree, but Sarah placed a steadying hand on her arm and squeezed it reassuringly. Verena's maid came in with a tray on which reposed a decanter and a glass.

'I don't drink spirits,' Violet protested when Verena poured a little and put the glass under her nose.

'This is medicinal. I promise you it will make you feel better. Don't sip, or you'll taste it. Just swallow it in one go.'

Violet did as she was told, gasped a little and closed her eyes. 'Lie back,' Verena commanded.

'Shall I get a cold cloth for her forehead, my lady?' the maid asked.

Violet waved a hand. 'I'm better now. Really, it was nothing. Just dizzy for a moment.'

Verena sat down beside her and chafed her hands. 'They're like ice.'

'My hands are always cold,' Violet said.

'It's true, they are,' Charlotte confirmed. At the sound of her voice, Violet looked across at her and smiled. It was a smile such as she had never seen, and for an instant made the hair rise on her scalp, it was so beautiful and spiritual. A smile, Charlotte thought in a fearful instant, that someone dying might give.

'Don't look so frightened, darling,' Violet said. 'I'm quite all right. Better than all right.' Her eyes went to Verena and then Sarah – eyes too sparkling to be those of a dying woman.

Verena had already guessed. 'Do you mean to tell me—'

'As we're just family here,' Violet said, 'I don't mind saying – yes, it's true.'

'Mummy?' Charlotte protested against all the mystery.

Violet answered her. 'You must keep it secret for a little

while,' she said, 'but I want *you* to know. I just found out for sure this afternoon. I'm going to have a baby.'

The two women were quick with their congratulations and questions, but Charlotte didn't know what to think. Her *mother*, having a baby? Of course, marriage usually *was* followed by babies, but naturally she hadn't applied that to her mother. Surely she was too old. She thought Avis would be a good father for a child to have, but that brought her up against the idea of her mother and Avis. And she had had a crush on him once. It was all rather awkward and uncomfortable, and she turned her mind resolutely from that side of it. Instead she told herself that Avis would be glad to have an heir, and that her mother would be glad to make him glad. She rearranged her face accordingly and went to kiss her mother's cheek and say, 'I'm so pleased for you, Mummy.'

Violet looked at her anxiously. 'Are you really, darling? Because I know this must seem a little strange for you – but I'm so happy about it, I hope you will be too.'

'Of course I am, Mummy.'

She stepped back and let the experts continue with the conversation.

'You'll have to be very careful,' Verena said. 'At our age, it doesn't do to take it for granted. Don't take any chances.'

'I shan't,' Violet said. 'I wouldn't put Avis's son at risk. We'll be going back to Derbyshire for Christmas and then I mean to stay there until the baby's born. It's rather a shame when we'd rented the house for the whole Season, and now I shall miss it all, but the baby comes first.' She glanced at Charlotte. 'I'd meant to give you such a good time, darling. I'm sorry.'

'Doesn't matter, Mummy.'

And Verena said, 'She can stay with us as long as she likes. Don't worry about that.'

Charlotte drew an inner sigh of relief. She would much

sooner live with Uncle Oliver and Aunt Verena, even at the price of political dinner parties. And perhaps when her mother had a new baby to fuss over, she'd forget completely about marrying Charlotte off.

Everything about the Bear Island expedition was completely different from what James had expected – and not different in a good way, either. But once he had set off, there was no way of pulling out of it; and unless he wanted to seem a fool, he could never admit – not even to himself – that he had made a mistake.

It began well enough. The group met up in London, and there was a rather jolly farewell party. The other chaps were, in general, fearfully brainy but, like Brompton, pretty nice with it. Still, he would have felt rather out of things had it not been for the inclusion of Emil Bauer, the son of a Swiss millionaire, who did not at first sight seem any more suited to the expedition than James himself. Bauer had been a high-spirited youth, and a wild undergraduate, but underneath the pose of an idle, pleasure-loving man of the world, he had a first-rate brain, and having got a good degree, he had gone on to do post-graduate research in climate and weather patterns at Cambridge. His father was paying a large sum towards the expenses of the trip, and it was because of him that the farewell party was lavish with champagne. Because he was a natural clown, and talked only about being comfortable and having fun on the trip, James did not realise until later that he *was* clever.

They set off straight from the party, and the first leg, taking the night train to Edinburgh, was well enough, since, thanks to Bauer, they went by first-class sleeper. They did seem to be turfed out awfully early in the morning, James thought – too early for him to take much interest in the city, strangely ethereal in the early mist, as they drove through it to Leith docks. But now came the first shock. It was no

Mauretania that waited for them, no huge, graceful liner full of white-coated stewards ready to see to their every need. He thought there must have been a terrible mistake when they were directed towards the gangplank of a dirty-looking coaster with surely worrying amounts of rust showing through the paint, and attended by rough-looking men in coarse dungarees, pea jackets and oily caps, who stared flat-eyed at the arrivals and didn't even seem inclined to carry their luggage for them.

He soon discovered that there had indeed been a mistake, but on his part. *Sjøfugl* – he couldn't even attempt to pronounce the boat's name, there seeming to be both too few letters and all the wrong ones in it – was to be his home for the next few weeks. His bed was one bunk out of four in a small, windowless metal room that managed to be both stifling and freezing cold at the same time. Meals were taken together in another small and oppressive room where the metal walls sweated what seemed to be pure fish oil, and they were crowded so closely together at the one table that a new way of eating without the use of elbows had to be learned.

Not that eating featured in James's plans for the first few days. Once they had steamed out of the Firth of Forth they met the North Sea in playful mood, and the further north they sailed the more vigorously the waves objected to their presence. James very quickly discovered that when you are seasick, the only thing you want is to die – really truly to die – so that the terrible misery would end. Once he had thrown up all he had to lose, he lay on his bunk moaning pitifully, dry-heaving with hideous regularity, and feeling as though his head were filled with some malign substance that was swelling and swelling with the intention of splitting his skull open from the inside. He was beyond protest and beyond hope. Just let him die as soon as possible, he prayed, so it would be over.

Pat Brompton, himself rather pale, came to see him and murmured in concern, feeling guilty since it was he who had recruited James in the first place. He told him that the crew said he would soon adjust to the motion. He said that several other fellows were ill in the same way.

Neither statement helped. James only moaned, 'When will this storm end? We should never have set out in it.'

'There's no storm, old fellow,' Pat said gently. 'It's a fine June day out there. This is just ordinary up-and-down motion. It'll get much rougher later on.'

Oddly, this did not give James any comfort either. Every breath he drew was tainted with oil; the motion tried to tip him out of his hard bunk one second and flung him against the metal wall the next. He felt cold and clammy and had lost all sense of time.

Several years later, Bauer came in, looking brisk and cheerful. 'Time to get up,' he said. 'It's a lovely morning out there.' James made a sound that did not even approximate speech. 'Come on, show a leg,' Bauer said. 'Drag on some clothes and come on deck. I promise you'll feel much better up there.'

James knew he would never feel better, but Bauer insisted, dragged him to a sitting position, helped him on with some clothes and, holding him in a tight embrace, walked him, weaving and stumbling, along a metal corridor and up some metal stairs and finally out through a metal door onto the, thank God, wooden deck. The sunshine was dazzling, the air so bright it hurt to breathe; purblind and bewildered, James groped forward, with Bauer's arm round him holding him up, until he could grasp the taffrail and there was nothing in front of him but the sea. The green waves ran up to and under the ship, breaking into whiteness. James thought his stomach was going to force its way out of the top of his head.

'Don't look down,' Bauer commanded. 'Look out, towards the horizon.'

Further off the green waves were dark, dark blue, with little white caps on them here and there, and the sky was milky blue, and there was nothing else to be seen anywhere but sea and sky. The air was fresh and keen and smelt faintly of salt and not at all of oil, which was a blessing. He took a cautious breath, and then a deeper one. The colour of the sea, he noticed, was quite lovely.

'Better?' Bauer asked.

'A little,' James said doubtfully.

'Good. Stay there, keep looking out to sea, and I'll be back in a moment.'

James did as he was told, watching the waves and the horizon. Quite soon he was taking his weight on his feet, instead of merely dangling from the railings, and adjusting his balance as the ship moved. Now he could see what was causing it, he could anticipate the rocking, and discovered that it was not chaotic but understandable. By the time Bauer came back, the awful sense of oppression had lightened, and he felt only queasy and apprehensive.

'Here we are,' Bauer said cheerfully. James turned his head and saw that he was carrying a bottle of champagne and two tin mugs. 'Sorry about the mugs, but daren't risk a glass when your hands are so feeble.' He started pouring.

'I couldn't,' James protested feebly.

'Finest thing for *mal-de-mer*,' Bauer said. 'Trust me, I know about these things. First rule, get out on deck. You see, when you're below, your eyes are telling you nothing's moving but the rest of your body knows differently. Get the two working together and the sickness goes away. Rule two, get some champagne inside you. Drink it up, my dear boy. Why do you suppose I'm so jolly and bright? Relaxes the muscles, soothes the stomach and settles the nerves. Don't argue, don't think, just drink.'

James thought the sensation of anything at all going down his throat would make him vomit, but the champagne was cool and light and easy to swallow. And in a few minutes he was draining his mug with something approaching pleasure.

'It seems to be working,' he said cautiously to Bauer, who was watching him closely.

'Didn't I tell you? Have some more. Ah, my God, this air smells good!'

'Those clouds are pretty,' James remarked, as his body relaxed under the influence of the wine. The raging disorder inside him was being calmed, like a storm dying away and the sun coming out again. He realised, with some astonishment, that he was actually hungry.

Bauer topped up his mug again. As a meteorologist, he knew that those pretty clouds were the sign of an approaching front, and that the sea was likely to get rougher in a few hours' time, but he didn't tell James that. Sufficient unto the day . . .

Following Bauer's rules, James managed to survive the sea voyage, never again feeling as bad as he had at first, though he had further bouts of sickness, especially when the weather was too rough for him to get out on deck. After the sickness, boredom was his worst problem: there was nothing to see and nothing to do, reading made him feel queasy, and he had little in common with most of his companions. Again, it was Bauer who saved him. He made up a bridge four with James, Pat Brompton and Bryant, a geologist, and they played for hour after hour, giving them all just enough mental exercise. And in conversation they told each other their life stories. Bauer's was the most interesting. James felt he'd done very little by comparison, but when he threw in tales of other members of his family, he came off quite well.

Still, he was looking forward ever more keenly to arriving at Bear Island and getting dry land under his feet. He was used, by now, to things not being the way he had expected, but still his natural buoyancy and optimism kept telling him that perhaps it would be *almost* the way he had imagined, with only unimportant differences. But he deliberately didn't ask anyone what it was like, just in case. There was no going back now until the whole expedition returned in a year's time, and he would rather keep his illusions as long as possible.

They did not survive the first sight of the island. It rose out of the sea fog, a thing of stark grey cliffs and wheeling seabirds, whose haunting cries sounded like a warning. The island was roughly triangular, he learned, and about twelve miles by ten at its largest, mountainous at the southern end, the highest peak being about fifteen hundred feet. The northern end was a lowland plain that covered about two-thirds of the island.

It was no tropical paradise, either. There were no trees at all, and the vegetation consisted of mosses, lichens, low-growing salt-marsh plants, like saxifrages and scurvy-grass, and a few dwarf shrubs. On the lowland plain there were numerous freshwater lakes and streams running into the sea, but that was the extent of the excitement. There were a lot of birds, but no mammals apart from a few Arctic foxes – no bears, despite the name. There were some sandy coves, but the water was far too cold for bathing.

As to beautiful maidens, exotic customs, colourful costumes and the like, there was hardly anyone living there. There were a few fishing settlements, a meteorological station with a small staff, and the small harbour at Herwighamna in the north, which provided facilities for expeditions like theirs, and for the occasional yacht and the regular ships plying between Norway and the large inhabited island of Spitsbergen, 150 miles to the north.

There was not, James noted within hours of arriving, a restaurant in the place.

They lived in several large wooden huts, three of which were dormitories, each with four wood-framed beds. James shared one with Pat Brompton, Bryant and Bauer, since they had struck up a friendship on the boat. The fourth was their living hut, with a big wood-stove, a galley at one end and a wash-house at the other. The huts had been occupied by other expeditions before them, so they were not without comforts: some armchairs and sofas, bright Norwegian rugs on the floor, novels and magazines that had been left behind, some packs of cards and a chess-set. They had plenty of hot water from a boiler and, as long as James kept the generator in good health, electricity.

A local couple came in by day, the woman, Alvrun, to sweep the floors and take away their laundry, and the man, Agdar, to tend the stove and hot-water boiler and to cook for them when they did not want to cook for themselves. The food was plain and rather monotonous: bread and jam for breakfast, cheese for lunch, fish or fish stew for dinner, supported by potatoes, carrots, onions and cabbage that were brought in by the regular boat. Fortunately the excellent Bauer had taken the precaution of bringing several cases of tinned goods with him to supplement the diet and relieve the monotony. James had not thought there would ever come a time when a tin of bully-beef would seem like a luxury. The fish was fresh and varied but, as he said to Pat, if God had meant him to eat fish every day He'd have made him a dolphin.

Agdar had two bushy-haired grey dogs similar to huskies that followed him everywhere, and when James admired them, he said something in Norwegian that was accompanied by wide smiles and gestures, so James thought he had made a friend, even if he didn't understand a word he said. James was especially pleased to see the dogs every day – they seemed a link with home and normality. He made a ball out of screwed-up paper wrapped in surgical tape to throw for them, and encouraged them to accompany him on walks.

As on the boat, boredom seemed likely to be his biggest

problem, trapped for a year on a small island with a very small circle of people. At least he had his job to do, and he threw himself into the unloading, the unpacking and the settling in with a frustrated energy that got him a good reputation among his colleagues, who had been privately wondering what he was doing there and looking askance at Pat Brompton for having brought him. He tended the various motors – two touring cars and a small truck – and the generator, with a concentration born of desperation that had them the cleanest and most loved machines in the northern hemisphere. He drove anyone who wanted driving and fetched loads up from the harbour. He helped with the domestic chores. He even started to learn to cook, and when Agdar had shown him all he knew – which was not much, it had to be said – he began experimenting. A hash of bully-beef, potatoes and onions was his first success, and he had more pleasure in the praise of his companions for that than for anything else he had achieved in his life so far. It had certainly been harder won.

The island was not without interest, even to a non-scientist. They had arrived in the middle of the period of the Midnight Sun, which lasted from the 2nd of May to the 11th of August, a phenomenon that intrigued him. The long hours of sunshine brought the temperature up to a balmy 42° Fahrenheit; in the winter, when he now learned the sun would not rise from the 8th of November until the 3rd of February, it would be below freezing for most of the time, though he was assured earnestly that the maritime climate meant it never got much below 15°.

In exploring the island he visited the coal-mining settlement of Tunheim, which had been abandoned six or seven years before, and found there a steam locomotive that had been left behind. It gave him hours of pleasure, stripping it and putting it back together, finding out how it worked. He fished in the freshwater lakes for Arctic char, which was similar to salmon and trout and made a welcome change from the sea fish that was most of their diet. He pretty much had to become interested in birds, since they were about the only living things apart from humans on the island, and they were so much talked about by Pat. There were ptarmigan and snow bunting and migratory ducks and geese on land; and among the seabirds, puffins, which he found charming, guillemots, kittiwakes and gulls of all sorts; around the coast there were colonies of seal and walrus. Never since childhood had he spent so much time watching wild creatures, but as his mind slowed from the normal speed of civilisation to a pace more suited to this sparsely inhabited island, he found he could sit and watch their comings and goings for hours at a time.

Gradually he settled in, and in sheer self-defence found things to do. He kept his diary every day. Agdar taught him a little carpentry and he began making small repairs and improvements around the huts. Bauer had an ingenious mind and was always drawing plans for labour-saving devices and cunning contrivances, and he and James tried to make them real. The results were more often entertaining than useful.

The best thing he discovered was drawing. Again, he had never done any since he had left the schoolroom, but when McGuinness, one of the bird-men – as he called them from a reluctance to keep pronouncing the word 'ornithologist' – kindly offered him a sketching pad and pencil one day to take with him when he went to see the puffins, he discovered a new pleasure. Gradually he got better at it, until Pat, looking over his shoulder one evening as he worked on a sketch of a guillemot colony, said, 'I say, you *are* a dab!' James silently turned over some pages and showed him some other drawings, and he gave a whistle. 'These are very good. I've seen worse illustrations in proper bird books, you know. Perhaps you've found yourself a new career.'

James laughed. 'I don't flatter myself. But I enjoy doing it. I never knew before what a pleasure it could be.'

From drawing he moved on to watercolour painting, and found the ultimate solitary pleasure, of which he felt he could never tire. McGuinness very kindly provided him with paper and paints out of his own stock, until fresh supplies could be sent out on the regular boat from Tromsø. He painted the island, the birds, the seals, landscapes and seascapes, the harbour and the boats. He painted his companions about their daily tasks. He painted Agdar's dogs, usually asleep, since that was the only time they stayed still for long enough.

One day Agdar arrived with a fat grey puppy, which he handed to him with many nods and a broad grin, and James realised what Agdar had meant all those weeks ago when James had admired the dogs and he had talked and waved his hands: that he should have one of his own by and by. James took the warm, wriggling bundle and had his face washed for him, and Agdar said, 'Helmy. Helmy.' James didn't know if this was the pup's name or some other comment, but it was good enough for him, and he called it Helmy from then on. He had fun training the little thing, and in a few weeks, when he had taught it not to chase birds, he had the perfect companion for his expeditions. Helmy liked most of all to travel in the truck, and would sit on the passenger seat with his front paws on the dashboard and bark a greeting at everyone they passed. At night he slept curled on the end of James's bed.

On one of his trips to Tunheim, James found under stacks of old boxes and other rubbish an abandoned upright piano. With the help of some of the others, he got it onto the truck and back to the living hut. The air of Bear Island was so dry that it was in fairly good condition, though several keys did not sound, which gave anything played an odd, syncopated rhythm. But it was a great novelty, and James was a good pianist and could play popular tunes by ear, which he felt made another justification for his presence.

'You'll be a boon and a blessing come the winter,' said Bryant, 'when we have to spend more time indoors.'

James did not like to think of that time in November when the sun would set for three long months; but at least there was the whole winter and the return of the sun to come before he would have to get on that boat again. Time seemed to work differently on Bear Island: as he slowed to fit the rhythm of his new life there seemed to be more of it, just as there was more sky and space all around him. England, green and lush and crowded by comparison, seemed like a strange and distant dream, as did the other James who had lived there. And with his tasks, his painting, his cooking and his carpentry, and his very own dog at his heels, he was able to reflect almost every night, just before he fell into a dreamless sleep, that, oddly, he was happy.

Jack had also never been happier. In 1932 Airspeed successfully launched the AS 4 Ferry, a three-engined bi-plane capable of carrying ten passengers; the third engine was mounted at the centre of the upper wing, rather than on the nose as was usual, and this gave the pilot a better view and improved stability. And for the rest of the year he had been working with Hessell Tiltman on the AS 5 Courier, a low-winged, six-seater cabin monoplane. The exciting innovation in the Courier was that they were designing the wheels to retract into the body, which would give it a far better aerodynamic profile and improve fuel efficiency. This was important because the Courier had been commissioned by Alan Cobham to use in his attempt to fly non-stop to India. The other novelty was that Sir Alan was going to try mid-air refuelling, to avoid having to carry a large weight of fuel on board. Obviously if this could be perfected, the value to commercial flight would be enormous, and the Courier had to be designed with that in mind.

The trouble was that there simply wasn't enough room

in the bus garage in York, especially as in September 1932 Airspeed won the contract to build the Shackleton-Murray SM 1, a parasol-winged pusher monoplane, whose wings could be folded back along the sides. So, early in 1933, Jack broke it to Helen that they would have to move.

'I'm sorry – I know you like it here, being near Jessie and so on,' he said.

'Break it to me gently,' Helen said. 'Where are we going?'

'Nevil's looking at some premises in Portsmouth,' said Jack.

'Portsmouth! I know nothing about Portsmouth. I've never even been there.'

'But you've been to Southampton, which isn't very far from Portsmouth,' Jack said beguilingly. Southampton was where he had had started out, working for Rankin Marine; it was where he had first met Tom Sopwith, who had been so important in his career. 'I took you and Molly down one day to see my speedboat being demonstrated, if you remember – years ago, before we were married.'

'I remember the occasion very well,' Helen said, with affected grimness. 'I wore a new hat to try to get you to notice me, but you were in love with the asinine Miss Fairbrother at the time.'

Jack put his head into his hands and groaned. 'Don't remind me! When I think of the years I wasted, not realising you were the most wonderful woman in the world . . .'

'Yes, it does beggar belief,' she said. 'As does the idea that I might be reconciled to Portsmouth because it's not very far from Southampton!'

Jack emerged from his hands. 'It's the only thing I could think of to say,' he admitted sheepishly. 'I believe it's quite a nice town, though. Historical, you know.'

Helen gave him a straight look. 'None of that matters, does it? You will go, so we'll have to go with you.'

'What choice do I have?' Jack said.

The choice was for him to find another job, but she knew she couldn't ask him to do that. He was so involved in the new designs that it would be sheer cruelty to pull him away. But she sighed, thinking of the upheaval, when she had just got nicely settled in.

'I suppose we can find a new school down there for Michael, poor little gypsy,' she began.

'He'll love it,' Jack said. 'The sea, and all the boats. I can teach him to sail, and perhaps he can have a little sailing dinghy of his own.'

'And Barbara would have been finishing school this summer – we'd have to decide what to do next with her anyway. But, Jack, what about Basil?'

'He can stay on at Felixkirk, surely,' Jack said. 'That's the beauty of a boarding-school.' Basil was in the sixth, and had another year to go after the current one.

'Yes, but I don't like the idea of being so far away.'

'Dearest, I can't see that it makes any difference. We can't watch him through a telescope from here, can we? And he seems to be doing all right. At least, he hasn't been sacked – the head hasn't even complained about him. I think he's settled down. And he'll come home for holidays just the same. I don't understand what you're worried about.'

Helen found it hard to articulate, but the further Basil was from her, the more she anticipated mischief. As to coming for holidays, what would he think of Portsmouth? York was enough of a backwater to him. And to get to Portsmouth he would have to travel through London. She couldn't help fearing that he would somehow go astray on the journey. But there was no point in saying any of this, because Jack's job was moving and Jack with it, and she would have to go too. And she didn't want to make him unhappy.

So she said, 'I'm just being silly. Pay no attention. It will be fun moving to a new place: new things to see, new people to meet.'

He looked at her gratefully. 'You'll miss Jessie, though,' he offered in return.

She would. There was no point in saying perhaps they would visit, because she and Jack wouldn't be able to afford a house big enough to receive five visitors; and, besides, Jessie had her home and family and business in the stables and was reluctant to leave it all even for a day, let alone longer.

'When do you think we'll be moving?' she asked.

'Soon,' Jack said. 'March or April at the latest. We've got to get on with the Courier as quickly as possible.'

'I'd better start thinking about packing, then,' Helen said.

In the summer of 1932 the state of Germany had given cause for unease, with six million unemployed, a collapsing economy and widespread hunger. Troops of Fascists marching the streets with cudgels, chanting, 'Blood must flow! Blood must flow! Smash the Jewish Republic!' had met gangs of Communists equally ready for a fight. Shop windows had been smashed, property damaged, bystanders injured; the situation had escalated into gun-battles, in the worst of which, near Hamburg, nineteen people had been killed and three hundred wounded. The Chancellor, Papen, had proclaimed martial law and used the emergency to name himself Reich Commissioner with extensive powers.

The autumn brought strikes and disorder and no end to the hunger. Unable to form a workable coalition in Berlin, even with his extended powers, Papen resigned. Schleicher became the new Chancellor: he had the backing of the aristocracy, who wanted a return to the old days, with aristocratic rule enforced by the army. But the National Socialists – their name abbreviated to the Nazis – were the largest party and had the backing of industrialists and businessmen, whose priority was to restore order so that they could put Germany back on its economic feet.

In January 1933, the elderly President, von Hindenburg,

tired of all the government intrigue, backstabbing and disorder, decided that only the Nazis had the influence to sort out the dire situation. Public life had come to a standstill and the people were hungry and desperate. He called the Nazi leader, Adolf Hitler, to the presidential palace and had him sworn in as chancellor, though with aristocrat-backed Papen as vice-chancellor to keep him in check. Hitler was received with huge public acclamation as the man who would save the nation. Only the former General Ludendorff dissented, sending a telegram to von Hindenburg warning, 'This evil man will plunge our Reich into the abyss and will inflict immeasurable woe on our nation.' It was brushed aside as jealousy – Hitler, who had never risen higher than corporal in the war, was not well regarded in the generally aristocratic army circles.

By March 1933 the new Chancellor had replaced most holders of public office with his own supporters, and had issued an emergency decree to restore order by restricting personal liberty. Free speech, free press and freedom of association were suppressed; the privacy of postal and telegraphic communications was ended; and house searches, confiscations of property and summary internment were introduced.

Thousands of Communists and social democrats were rounded up and imprisoned. The local states' governments throughout Germany were taken over, and anyone politically opposed to the Nazi Party was interned; a decree making it a crime to criticise the Party or its leader made this easy. Disused army barracks and factories became prisons, and barbed-wire compounds sprang up all round the country.

Chancellor Hitler promised an end to unemployment and pledged to promote peace with France, Great Britain and Soviet Russia, but to do this, he said, he needed absolute power. Longing for an end to disorder, the German parliament agreed, voted by a huge majority to make him supreme leader, and effectively dissolved itself.

The new regime was greeted with huge relief and joy all over the country: at last someone was going to do something, and the loss of democracy seemed a small price to pay when you were starving and the streets were unsafe to walk in.

But there was a steady and increasing trickle of people who did not agree with dictatorship, even in a good cause – intellectuals, artists, writers, musicians, philosophers, scientists – and who quietly left the country to head for England or the USA. They brought with them reports of the street violence and repression behind the new order; and the even more disturbing news that the new Chancellor had privately repudiated the peace accord of the League of Nations and had started to rearm.

John Burton sometimes mentioned things he had read in the paper about Germany to Polly. She was, like most people, disinclined to feel much sympathy for the nation that had caused so much misery, and to think that a bit of starvation and misery was no more than it deserved. In any case, she was much more interested in the establishment that year of the Milk Marketing Board, to control the production and distribution of milk in the United Kingdom, driving up standards and, by acting as a buyer of last resort, guaranteeing a minimum price. With a guaranteed price, it was easier to explain the benefits of improvement to her tenants. She was seeing the first fruits of her bull club now, and though a couple of tenants were still holding out, the others were embracing record-keeping and tuberculin testing, and working towards getting segregated-herd status and certified milk.

On the other side of the business, she had made a couple of visits to Manchester to see for herself how things were going. The mills were still not making a profit, but Mawson expressed himself confident that by the end of the year they would have broken even, and that they should make a small profit the following year if everything went to plan. In the Makepeace shops the new line of Polly's Modes was starting to sell, and she had found herself back in the old routine of working on 'spring lines' and 'autumn lines'. She was employing a small team of designers now, who worked in York, but she enjoyed taking part herself, sketching ideas and fabric patterns.

And while talking to them one day she had a new idea, which she explained to Burton as they were driving out to visit Thickpenny, one of her farms. 'It isn't everybody who can afford to buy ready-made dresses, even at my good prices,' she said, 'and a lot of women do home-sewing. So I was thinking, why not sell the fabric by the length and the paper patterns as well? I ought to double the returns on a single design that way.'

'Yes, I see,' said Burton. 'I'm in a foreign area here, but wouldn't it mean that no-one would buy the new fashions, that they'd just buy the pattern and have someone make it up for them?'

'No, because you wouldn't put a new design straight into pattern form. There would be a time lag, and the patterns would be simplified, without any *very* modish details, because they'd have to be saleable over a period of at least a couple of years. The question is, how do we get the patterns manufactured?'

'Oh, that's the easiest part,' Burton said. 'We have a great many printing firms here in York, all hungry for work. If you can tell me exactly what's involved, and what price would be viable, I'll go round them and see who'll suit us best.'

Polly smiled. 'I knew I could depend on you to solve the problem.' She liked the way he had said 'suit us' and not 'suit you', but she didn't say that aloud. They talked about it a little more, and then he changed the subject.

'I heard something when I was in York yesterday. There's a small farm beyond Overton Wood called Moon's Rush—'

'Oh, yes, I know it. I think my father used to own it once, a long time ago. But it's been abandoned now for quite a while.'

'That's right. But I heard it's going on the market. The house is more or less derelict, but there are some useful outbuildings and ten or twelve acres of pasture.'

'You want me to buy it?' Polly asked, surprised. 'What use would it be?'

'You know Underwood of Thickpenny's eldest son, Carr?'

'Of course,' said Polly. He had been christened Carrington, after his godfather, and rather than submit to being called Carrie all his life, had made up his own abbreviation and forced the grown-ups to use it by refusing to answer to anything else. A certain amount of fisticuffs had been required to make his peers follow suit; Polly thought it had shown character to tackle the problem head-on in that way.

'Well, Carr is mad about pigs, and he wants to set up on his own – not with a mixed farm, just pigs. I've talked to him, and he knows his stuff. But, of course, he doesn't have the funds to get started, and you know the banks won't loan anything to anyone, these days.'

'So now you want me to make myself into a bank?' Polly said.

'I thought that if you bought Moon's Rush Farm, Carr could do any work needed to convert the buildings himself – I expect his brothers would help him, too – and then if you could advance him a loan to buy the stock, he could rent the place from you and pay you back out of the profits.'

'If any,' Polly said.

'There's a big market for bacon and pork products in York and Leeds,' Burton said. 'Demand for pig meat goes up when times are hard, just as demand for beef and lamb goes down.'

Polly considered. 'Where would Carr live? The house isn't fit for habitation. I know it's only a mile or so from Thickpenny as the crow flies, but there's no crossing the river there, so it would be a long journey every day if he lived at home.'

'Moon's Rush is only a stone's throw from Wood Farm and I happen to know the Harrises would be happy to take in a lodger.'

'"Happen to know"?' Polly said. 'I wonder how. Did you *happen* to ask them?'

He gave a rueful smile. 'You've smoked me out. I confess I have such a liking for Carr Underwood I did a little research on my own behalf, just to see if it could be done.'

Polly studied his face. 'You really want me to do this,' she said.

He met her eyes seriously. 'Not only for his sake. It's good farming. These days, the trend is all for specialising, and that's good, but as a landowner you won't want all your eggs in the one basket by having nothing but dairy farms.'

'Mixed metaphor,' she said, with a faint smile.

He returned it. 'I don't think you could lose by it. Even if Carr couldn't make a go of it – and I'm convinced he will – you'd still have the land, which you'd have bought at the bottom of the market, so it's bound to improve in value.'

'Well,' Polly said, 'you make an eloquent case. And I do like pigs. We'll have to put some figures down on paper and see how it works out. And talk to Pobgee and Pickering.'

'Of course,' Burton said, 'but if we can get in quickly with an offer before it actually goes on the market, I think we'd get a better price, so speed is of the essence.'

'You've already spoken to Pickering,' she discovered. 'All right, I'll think quickly, but I must think.' In the back of her mind she could hear her father's spirit urging her towards the idea. He had always believed in acquiring land whenever he could: land was something you could be sure of, when all else failed. You could never have too much. And what had been Morland land once ought to be so again. It would please her father, she knew, if she brought Moon's Rush back into the estate.

They turned into Thickpenny yard, and her new dog, Fand, shoved his head out of the window of the car to challenge the farm dogs, while Blossom and Bigelot jumped about wanting to see.

Burton got out of the car and came round to let her out. She liked the courtesy – however much she wanted to be master of Morland Place, she still liked to be recognised as a woman. She climbed out and the dogs surged past her to coalesce into a furry mass with the welcoming committee.

'Don't say anything to Carr yet,' she said to Burton.

'No, of course not,' he replied.

'I wouldn't want to get his hopes up. But if you can work the conversation round to pigs in a natural way, I'd like to hear about his dream in his own words.'

Burton smiled, the particular smile that she felt was only for her – she never saw him offer it to anyone else. 'I can do that. He'll pour his heart out, but he won't know what's happening to him. I can be very insidious when I try.'

'I know that,' said Polly.

CHAPTER ELEVEN

Jessie had everything she wanted or needed at home, and had no particular desire ever to leave it, even for a holiday. Bertie, too, had done all his travelling, living in India in his youth, fighting in South Africa and all over France, and was now content to stay at home with his wife, his children and his estate. Occasionally they liked to go to a horse sale together, or for a long ride, or for a drive out into the North York moors and a lunch of bread and cheese at a village pub, but that was enough change to refresh them. They had both seen enough of war to want to hold on to what they had. Events in Germany did not inspire confidence. They were both afraid that the war had not, after all, been the one to end all wars. It was something they did not discuss, but it was there between them unspoken, and when they lay in bed at night, it made them hold each other the tighter.

But when Violet wrote to Jessie to say that she was nervous about the upcoming birth, and asking if she would come and be with her when the time came, Jessie could not refuse. 'It's a long time since she had Henry, and it's a more serious matter when you get to our age,' she said to Bertie, when the letter came. 'If Cousin Venetia had still been alive she'd have gone, and I wouldn't have worried.'

'You don't need to excuse yourself to me,' Bertie said. 'Of course you must go. I shall miss you, but I quite understand.'

'You could come too,' Jessie said hesitantly. 'It could be a sort of holiday.'

Bertie smiled his protest. 'Darling! In June? Far too much to do. And if we both go, who's to do your work? And the children still in school – if Violet had waited a little, you could have taken them with you for a romp around the Peaks.'

'I expect they'd sooner be at home with their own friends,' said Jessie.

The baby was due in the middle of June, and Jessie travelled to Tunstead with the intention of being there a week before it came. She found Violet large and uncomfortable, with very swollen ankles, but otherwise in good health, only very bored.

'The doctor here is in a tremendous fuss about me, and wants me to lie on the sofa all day,' she confided. 'I think he's afraid if something goes wrong he'll lose all his patients.'

'Why should anything go wrong?' Jessie said robustly.

'Oh, I'm sure it won't. But the new countess, you know . . . and the family needing an heir, with Avis's brother dying childless. To tell the truth, he fusses me to death and I wish I could just not see him, but Avis worries so, and he'd worry even more if I didn't. But now you're here perhaps you can keep him away.'

'I'll do my best,' Jessie said.

But the doctor was elderly and steeped in family loyalty, and since he had not been in the war he had an old-fashioned view of nurses, so Jessie's experience did not count for anything with him. But Jessie made a point of going into the village and meeting the midwife, who turned out to be about her own age and a veteran of the conflict, so they got on well and Jessie had faith in her.

She spent all her time with Violet, keeping her amused – playing the piano, sometimes, or playing cards, but mostly just talking. They had so much to say to each other, so many memories to go over, and they'd had little time together of late years. Jessie got up early in the morning to take a vigorous walk to set her up for the day. She got Violet out of doors later in the day, pushing her in a wheeled chair Avis had borrowed from a neighbour, and encouraging her to walk a little when the ground was level; but the baby was low and walking was not comfortable, so they were only brief totters between chair and a suitable bench.

'Dr Ramsay says the baby being low means it will be a girl,' Violet said wistfully.

'Old wives' tales,' Jessie said briskly. 'There's no way to tell until it comes.'

The fresh air and sunshine did Violet good. The grounds of Tunstead Hall were lovely and the views well worth going outside for.

Avis was away a good part of the day, having a great deal to do about the estate and the village, which he had been putting off to stay beside Violet. He was grateful to be released by Jessie, but still would not go far, ready to dash back as soon as a message or a telephone call summoned him. Of the two, Jessie thought he was the more nervous. But then, of course, Violet had had babies before; and she supposed he had more to lose. He was a good host, sought out the best from his cellar for her each evening, chatted lightly and amusingly at table, and begged her to make free of the telephone to call home as often as she wanted. Jessie rang once or twice, just to hear Bertie's voice, and each time had to report: 'Nothing happening yet.'

She had left behind a pregnant mare, Angelus, who was nearing her time, and in response Bertie would say, 'Nothing happening here, either.'

She was there ten days before Violet's pains started. The butler and housekeeper, who had been with Avis's father, went into a tailspin of anxiety. Jessie steadied them, told the butler to send a boy to find his lordship, to telephone to the doctor's house, and to follow his instructions for summoning the midwife. She told the housekeeper to put water on to boil, to fetch out the clean sheets and towels that had been assembled ready, and to send two housemaids up to make the bed. With someone else taking responsibility, they immediately became calm – so calm, indeed, that she had to hurry them up.

In the event, the birth was so quick that, of the trio sent for, only the midwife had arrived before things entered the second stage. Now that she was actually engaged in the business, Violet ceased to be nervous, though she held Jessie's hand and said several times, 'I'm so glad you're here.'

Jessie was glad the doctor had been at an outlying house without a telephone, for he would only have got in the way. The three women managed the business in a quiet and seemly manner, which was how Jessie felt all children should be received into the world. Ramsay arrived in time to cut the cord, examine the child, and place it in the mother's arms, saying, 'A boy, my lady. A fine boy, little Lord Tunstead.' It was the only part of the business he would have enjoyed, anyway, and was enough to secure him his fee.

Jessie felt she would never forget Violet's expression as she looked at the baby, and the smile she gave her when she said, 'It really, really is a boy! I did it, didn't I?'

'You really did,' Jessie said.

But later, when Avis was allowed in, and Violet held out his child to him, she realised that that smile had been only a rehearsal: the real thing was almost too much to bear.

Avis held Violet's hand so tight her fingers went white. He whispered, 'If anything had happened to you . . .' Then his son was settled into his arms and he had no more words.

Dozens of telegrams were sent off, dozens of congratulation came back, including one from the Duke and Duchess of York, and one from the Prince of Wales, who sent a teddy bear. The tenants came up to the house with a tribute of flowers. The church bells were rung and healths were drunk in the two village pubs. Violet's children were to come and visit at the weekend. Oliver and Verena sent a silver cup: they would visit in a couple of weeks, when Violet was stronger, for the christening.

By the time Henry arrived late on Friday from his college in Manchester, the baby had been given his names, Edward John Halley Fellowes – Edward and John after his two grandfathers, Halley for Avis's mother's maiden name.

Henry, who would be seventeen in August, had grown tall and rather lanky with a flop of dark hair over his forehead and blue eyes like his mother's. He kissed her and asked after her health, then examined the baby gravely and minutely as if it were an engine of unusual construction – which Jessie supposed, in a way, it was.

'Well,' he said at last, 'he looks like a good one. Sturdy enough, wouldn't you say? I don't know about these things, but he doesn't look as though he's likely to break.'

'Don't you try,' Avis said, with a smile.

'Lord, no! Quick, take him, before I do something wrong.'

'You won't,' said Avis, but he took him anyway. He couldn't have enough of holding his son. The baby slept on, indifferent to the change.

'I must say, though,' Henry said, 'he doesn't look like an Edward or a John.'

'What do they look like?' Avis asked, amused.

'I don't know, but I know he doesn't look like 'em. He'll have to be Halley. Or Hal. That's a jolly sort of name. He looks as though he's going to be a jolly chap.'

That evening, just before dinner, Bertie rang to say that Angelus had foaled. 'A filly,' he said. 'All's well. No complications, and the mare's feeding her all right. You can think about a name for her and we'll have a celebration when you come home.'

Later she relayed the news to Violet, who had known she

was waiting to hear. Violet said, 'A filly! I'm glad I had the boy. God got it right.'

Charlotte was the last to arrive, since she had to work on Saturday morning, while her brothers had been able to get away. She was met at Buxton by a car, arrived at around tea-time, and found everyone but Jessie assembled on the terrace around the tea-table. Avis took one look at her travel-pale face and said, 'Have a cup of tea and a sandwich at least before you go up and see your mother.' Charlotte hesitated, and he added, 'Jessie's with her. Another half-hour won't make any difference. Did you have lunch?'

'No, I missed it. I *am* hungry.' She was glad to put off the moment a little longer, not being sure what she was going to feel. The boys were scoffing, she noticed – scones and cucumber sandwiches and slices of Victoria sponge following each other in rapid succession down their throats – so all must be well upstairs.

But when she did go up – with instructions to take Jessie's place for a while and send her down to get some tea – and saw her mother propped up on a pile of pillows, wearing a pink satin lace-trimmed bed-jacket, her hair softly loose around her face, the one thing she felt was overwhelming relief, and it was only then that she realised how worried she had been for her. Violet's face lit at the sight of her daughter and she held out her arms. 'Darling, how *lovely* to see you!' Charlotte went and kissed her, and Violet laughed and said, 'Don't look so solemn, darling. Everything's all right. Go and have a look at your little brother.'

There was a wheeled crib in the corner of the room, draped in white voile and blue ribbons: Violet liked to have the baby with her as much as possible. Jessie, perhaps understanding something of Charlotte's uncertainty, went with her and lifted the baby out of the crib.

'Oh, don't wake him,' Charlotte said in alarm.

But Jessie put the baby in her arms. 'It's all right. He's a good sleeper.'

So she had no choice. He was tiny, like a doll, she thought, but warm and living, softly breathing, not to be dropped or put aside when something more interesting beckoned. She had never been very good to her dolls as a little girl. She had been afraid of what she might feel – or even not feel – about her new brother, but when she held him, she was simply enchanted. He was so exquisite, such a miracle of craftsmanship, so helpless and yet infinitely precious, that she loved him at once. She felt like laughing that she could ever have feared she wouldn't.

She looked up at her mother. 'He's beautiful,' she said.

'Yes, he is,' Violet said, and for once mother and daughter exchanged a look of perfect accord.

In July 1933 James returned to Morland Place. Polly hardly knew him. To begin with, instead of announcing his return and asking to be met, so he could roll up to the door in a motor in style, he gave no notice, walked up from the station, and was discovered by Barlow standing in the yard staring up at the house as if he had never seen it before. Barlow was only alerted to his presence by the furious barking of the yard dog at Helmy, who sat firmly on his tail, half hidden behind his master's legs. Barlow was on the point of telling the vagrant to be off when he realised who it was. He managed to change the sentence on his lips to 'Good to have you back, sir,' and sent a boy scurrying to fetch the mistress, who was working in the steward's room with John Burton.

So Polly's first sight of the returning wanderer, as she reached the great door, was of a burly, bearded and weather-stained stranger. It was not possible, she supposed, that he could have grown taller, but he looked so much bigger she couldn't help feeling he had. He had certainly filled out with muscle, and no longer had the slender boy's figure he had gone away with. His hair was weather-bleached at the front, and unruly, not having enjoyed the kiss of oil, it appeared, for some time – perhaps not even of a comb. The beard was a shock; under it the face was weather-browned, with lines around the eyes like a sailor's. But the biggest change she saw in that first moment was a new stillness in him. James stood where he had stopped, looking around him, as if he had swallowed a great cold ball of patience and now had all the time in the world to be still and do nothing.

He changed his focus from the façade to her face and, in lieu of greeting, said, 'I wonder why I never noticed how glorious this house is. The way the light picks out the texture of the bricks.'

It was not at all a James thing to say. Polly went forward hesitantly. 'James! It's – it's good to see you. Are you well?'

He smiled, as if he could read her thoughts. It was unnerving. 'You find me changed?' he said.

She waved an uncertain hand. 'All this hair,' she said, trying for lightness. 'I know it was called Bear Island, but I didn't know it would change you into a bear.'

She was close enough now to be looking up at him – surely he *had* got taller – and to smell the salt and a faint tang of sweat from him. She ought to embrace him but somehow she dared not. He put up a hand to scratch his chin, and the hand looked big and hard, like a workman's, not like the manicured hand of a gentleman.

'The beard comes off,' he reassured her, 'and I'll have a haircut. Don't worry, when I've cleaned up I'll look fitter for your drawing room. I'd kiss you, but I'm still covered in journey and I don't suppose I smell like a rose.'

Polly was aware, without looking, that John Burton had come to the door behind her, and felt stronger for his presence. 'You shall have a bath just as soon as you like, and a change. Though, from the look of you, you won't fit into any of your old clothes. Where did you get all these muscles?'

'I've some clean things in my dunnage,' he said, 'that will do until I can see a tailor.'

Faces were appearing at windows as the news dashed about the house, and servants jostled for a glimpse of the new arrival. Mouths opened and shut excitedly in the pale ovals.

'Where is your luggage?' Polly asked.

'I left it at the station. Can you have it fetched, Barlow?' he said, over Polly's shoulder. 'I wanted to walk home, make the pleasure last, see it appear bit by bit as I got closer.' He grinned, something like the old James grin. 'You can't think how it's taught me to make pleasures last, living on Bear Island for a year.'

'Oh dear, poor James, wasn't there much to do?' Polly sympathised.

'I got by,' he said. 'I'll tell you all about it. But first—'

He was interrupted by a muted yip from Helmy behind him. Fand had come past Polly to investigate the newcomer, and Bigelot had shoved him out of the way to put the big hairy intruder in its place. Polly quieted him with a sharp word and stooped to offer Helmy a hand.

'He's a Norwegian Elghund, which is a moose-hound. I was given him as a puppy last year. They're tremendously loyal, and very clever,' James said. 'He won't be any trouble.'

'He's a handsome fellow,' Polly said. 'Is that all you brought back?'

'Pretty much. There wasn't much to buy on Bear Island, you know. But I made one or two things for the children, and there are my paintings—'

'Paintings?' Polly exclaimed.

'I've got a lot to tell you,' James said.

'I can see you must have. Well, come in, let's have some tea at least – or would you prefer something stronger?' she wondered suddenly.

A wide grin now. 'No, English tea for me. How I've dreamed

of it!' They turned towards the door, Helmy and Fand, friends already, following, Bigelot rushing importantly ahead.

Burton stepped aside for him, and said, 'Good to have you back, sir.'

'Thanks,' James said, and wondered why that sounded slightly odd. Perhaps it was just being in a place so strange, after thirteen months, and yet so familiar. As they went into the hall, little Alec came running in from the other side, having escaped the hand of his nurse. He got almost as far as Uncle James when he saw him properly, and evidently found him very changed, for he skidded to a halt, stared, then backed a step.

'Hello, Alec,' James said. 'Yes, it is me – don't mind the face fungus. I say, you have grown, old chap.'

But Alec, all eyes, would not approach; instead he sidled across to John Burton and slipped a hand upwards into his for security.

'He'll come round,' Burton said. 'A year is a long time at his age.'

James nodded agreement; Polly scooped Alec up onto her hip and he buried his face shyly in her neck; they walked past Burton towards the drawing room. That was what he had found odd, James realised: when Burton had said, 'Good to have you back,' it had not sounded like Barlow saying it, but somehow as though he had a special right to do the welcoming.

Bathed, shaved, trimmed and changed – though it was only into flannel trousers and a clean shirt – James looked more like his old self. He had done something about his hands, too, so they looked less rough. But he was not the James who had gone away. That stillness seemed now part of him. He listened more and spoke less, though as the returning traveller he had the best right to be speaking. He seemed more observant, looking around him all the time, studying people's faces; and sometimes in the middle of an exchange he fell silent, just thinking.

He had brought back one or two presents for his older cousins from Tromsø, and had carved some little animals for Alec and a horse for Laura. She was delighted with it: she had been struck with wonder when she first saw him, and since then had hung about him every minute she could, drinking in his words, luxuriating in his simple presence. She had never known the like of him: he was her Ulysses, her almost mythical hero returned from lands so strange she almost expected stories of dragons and unicorns. She had made friends with Helmy and often sat at James's feet in the evening with the Elghund half across her lap, both of them content just to be as close to him as was physically possible. Polly noticed that where it might have amused or annoyed the old James always to be tripping over a child, now he treated her with a careful gentleness.

Roberta, who had had a crush on James in younger days, found him less handsome when she came home for a visit from Stillington, and concluded briskly that she was over him. He was rather intimidating, in fact, with his silence and his staring, and his just not being like the James she remembered; but by the time she had to go back to the stables, she had discovered what a good listener he was, and had told him more of her hopes and dreams about the stables and her life there than she would have thought possible twenty-four hours earlier.

Polly was most impressed with his paintings, which he showed her over the first few days, starting with his earliest, shaky efforts and going through the evolution of his ability into a style of his own. The latest pictures she thought beautiful and a little disturbing: he had not produced images that were like photographs of the place he had been, but yet they seemed to evoke it better than a photograph could have. She looked at his watercolours and experienced the open

273

space, the great sky, the emptiness and bleakness; she smelt the air, felt the wind, heard the sea birds' cries.

She could not express all this, but she said, 'They're *beautiful*, Jamie,' and he seemed content with that. He asked her to choose her favourites, as her present from him, and she picked out four – a seascape with cliffs and wheeling gulls, the mountains viewed from the plain, the little harbour, and a view of ducks on one of the lakes – and said she would have them framed and hung in the drawing room.

She took him riding several times. 'How green everything is!' he exclaimed. 'The trees are so tall. Cows and sheep – and, look, rabbits! I didn't realise how I missed animals. After Bear Island I think I could rave about a chicken.'

She took him to see the tenants, and to show him her improvements, and he listened quietly to her plans. He seemed to have learned to be interested in many more things than before.

'You've really changed,' she said one day, as they walked, he on Firefly and she on Solly, across Marston Moor, with Fand and Helmy inseparable behind them. 'I really feel I can talk to you now.'

'I think I was a frightful tick before I went away,' he said.

'No, not that, but—'

'Oh, I was. But that place changed me. Everything moves so much more slowly there that you find yourself thinking an awful lot. And if what you're doing most of the time is thinking, you have to start doing it in a different way or you'd just go mad.' He looked down at her. 'Do you mind me being here?'

'No, why should I?' she said, with honesty, though she knew what he was really asking.

'When I sold the place to you I said I'd go away, but even though I half meant to, I didn't really understand how important it was that I *did*. I think I put you through a kind of hell, and I can only apologise. I didn't mean to, but that's no excuse.'

'It was difficult at first,' she admitted. 'But everything's all right now.'

'All the same, you must promise to tell me honestly if my being here makes it difficult for you. If you'd prefer me to go away.'

'Honestly, I'm enjoying having you back,' she said. 'You and I – we ought to stick together. We never had mothers, and now Daddy's gone, and Aunt Hen, we don't have anyone but each other.'

'And little Alec,' James said. 'I'm glad he's got over the fright of me.'

'So I don't want you to go,' Polly concluded.

'Thank you,' James said. 'But if I stay, I have to make myself useful to you.'

'All right, if you like.' She saw that he was looking about him in that new way he had, and she guessed it was something to do with his painting. Already he had made a lovely pencil sketch of Laura and Helmy curled up asleep together on the sofa. 'But aren't you longing to get your paints out?'

He looked at her and laughed. 'Very sharp of you! Yes, everything is so different from Bear Island, and I have a crazy urge to get it down on paper, as though it might escape me if I don't.'

'Not crazy. You're good at it, so you should do it. Spend all day painting, if you like.'

'I'll help you, too,' he said firmly. 'But I would like to paint. I'll have to go into York and get one or two things, though,' he added. 'Some of my paints are running low and I really need some new brushes.'

'I know – you've run out of money and want me to give you some,' Polly said, with a grin. 'I'm amazed you managed to last all that time on just two hundred pounds.'

'There wasn't anything to spend it on,' he said. 'And I actually have a few pounds left, so don't be too clever, Miss.'

'You need some new clothes as well,' Polly said. 'Better let me give you some.'

'Lend me some,' he corrected. 'I'll work for you to pay it off.'

'You don't have to,' she said.

'But I want to,' he answered.

Miss Husthwaite and John Julian, her father's former secretary and chaplain, visited not long after James's return. They had worked together to edit and publish Laura's father's posthumous *mémoires*, *A Voice from the Trenches*, and had enjoyed the experience so much – and encountered such success with it – that they had undertaken another task, to put the Morland Place Household Book into publishable form. It was in fact not just one book but a series of ledgers in which the mistresses of the house through the ages had put down recipes, sovereign remedies, hints on housekeeping and the directing of servants, accounts of great occasions, feasts and dinner parties, and various fragments of history, both domestic and of a wider nature.

It was such a formidable task that they had been working on it for four years now without coming near to an ending. Miss Husthwaite was now Mrs Julian and they lived in a cottage in Fulford and came over to Morland Place about once a month to bring back some documents, borrow others and browse through the house's archives and books. Polly usually asked them to stay for dinner – they were amusing company, and always had something new to tell her about her house that they had discovered during the last month's poking about. She suspected they might never finish the task; and further suspected that they did not really want to. In this matter it was a case of being better to travel than to arrive.

They were delighted to see James again, and Polly, watching their faces as they talked to him, saw that they found him changed, too – and approved of the change. They were very impressed with his drawings and paintings. Miss Husthwaite particularly liked one of the scene outside the living hut, which he had painted that May on an unusually warm day. One of the geologists was sitting on the verandah reading; Bauer was leaning back against an upright, smoking, with Helmy dozing beside him; one of the touring cars was off to one side, up on bricks with its front wheels off, and Agdar's dog had curled up on top of one of the tyres to sleep; and in front of it Agdar had his saw-horse out and was working on a piece of carpentry.

'It's delightful,' Mrs Julian said. 'It shows me so much of what your life was like there. And the light – you've captured the light and the sky so well, I can imagine what living under the midnight sun was like from this. You have a wonderful talent, James.'

James's reaction was to give her the picture, at which she demurred. 'I'd love to have it,' she said, 'but it's an important part of the record of your visit. You must have kept a diary – tell me you kept a diary!'

'Yes, I did,' James admitted. 'Of course, I'm not very good at writing. I never was a scholar, and somehow I find it easier to paint, now, than to use words. But I stuck at it, and I think I managed to put down something just about every day. Except when I was really sick on the boat,' he added, with a mischievous grin.

The Julians exchanged a swift glance – they were so attuned to each other they often communicated without words.

He spoke for both of them. 'Would you allow us to read it?' he asked. 'We would consider it a great honour, especially now you've shown us the pictures.'

'You can read it and welcome,' he said, 'but you'll find it isn't very good.'

They took it away with them, and on their next visit they told James that they thought his diary ought to be made into a book, with his drawings to illustrate it. 'Travel *mémoires* can tell us so much about places we will never see,' said Mrs Julian, 'and Bear Island is *so* remote – I looked for it in the atlas, James, and I was astonished. Very few people will ever have a chance to go there, and I really think you owe it to the world to publish.'

James said, 'I was approached by a publisher before I went, but I don't think my writing is good enough. I know it isn't, really.'

'But that's where we can help you,' Julian said. 'If you would allow us, we could transcribe your words, and amplify them by talking to you and adding what you say; perhaps put in some context – the history and geography of the island, if we can find it out. Shape the book, in fact, and ready it for publishing. As you know, we did something similar with Palgrave's book, with some modest success.'

'Modest?' James laughed. 'That book is famous – everyone's heard of it.'

'You're good to say so. But what do you think? I promise you, you shall have the final say over every word. Nothing, not a single comma, shall be added or omitted if you don't like it. It shall be your book, first and last.'

'Better for it if it wasn't,' James said, 'but if it pleases you, go ahead with my blessing! What about the Household Book?'

'That can wait,' Mrs Julian said. 'It's waited long enough already. Thank you, James dear. Oh, I'm excited about this!'

'Meanwhile,' James said, seeming more amused than excited, 'if you won't accept the painting of our living hut, perhaps I'd better go out and paint something else for you. What would you like? I'm better at landscapes than buildings, but I could try to paint Morland Place if you liked.'

'I should be honoured to have a painting of yours,' Mrs

Julian said, 'and of anything you chose to paint. But you will let me pay you for it?'

'Pay me? No, nonsense.'

'My dear boy, you could sell your paintings in York, or indeed London, for a respectable sum. And the labourer is worthy of his hire.'

James refused, insisting that he wanted to make a present of it, and she accepted gracefully. But it did give him an idea. He didn't like to 'sponge' on Polly and keep asking her for money, and if he could sell his paintings for enough to cover his paints, his baccy and other small expenses, he would feel better about things. The next time he went into York he would take one or two pictures to that fine art shop in Low Petergate and see what they said.

The presidential election campaign of 1932 had been a bitter one. Hoover had been reluctant to face another term of having to deal with the intractable problems of the depression. He resented the opposition of the Democrats, whom he believed were blocking his measures for purely party reasons, risking the economy of the country for the sake of winning political points. But when the time came, he put himself forward from the fear that things would get worse under any other candidate. He at least had a solid understanding of business: there were too many career politicians and lawyers in both houses, to his mind.

He meant at first to make only one or two major speeches and leave the rest of the campaign to his team. But the opinion polls were not looking favourable, and on one of his increasingly frequent visits to Washington, Lennie warned his long-term patron that, unless he got more involved, the Republicans were facing a resounding defeat. So Hoover expanded his programme to include a large number of public addresses all over the country and, with Lennie's help, made nine major radio addresses to the nation.

But campaigning in such difficult times was particularly hard for the incumbent, who was bound to be blamed for everything that was wrong. Hoover faced hostile crowds, was not only wearyingly heckled at meetings but had his train and his motor-car pelted with eggs and rotten fruit, and even had attempts on his life. The secret service arrested one man trying to get near to him with sticks of dynamite under his coat, and on another occasion arrested a man who had loosened the railway lines over which the presidential train was to travel.

In his radio addresses Hoover defended his administration and explained the philosophy behind his method of tackling the depression, but the Democrats portrayed this as an apology, and their candidate, Franklin Roosevelt, was thus able to charge Hoover with being personally responsible for the dire state of the economy.

Yet perhaps none of this mattered as much as a suffering and fearful nation's longing for a change of government. What had already been tried was not helping, they believed, so someone else must have a go. Hoover suffered a heavy defeat: Roosevelt took 57 per cent of the popular vote against his 39 per cent, and the Democrats took control of the Senate and increased their hold in Congress.

After a stay in New York, the Hoovers returned to California in the spring of 1933, where they had a house in Palo Alto. President Roosevelt had promised the American people a 'new deal', and the words were on everyone's lips after he took the oath of office in March 1933. Certainly action of some kind was desperately needed: banks were still failing, unemployment was at 25 per cent overall and higher in heavy industry and mining. Almost a million farms had had their mortgages foreclosed, farm income had fallen by 50 per cent, and the terrible droughts of the past two years were turning the centre of America into a dust-bowl.

Perhaps the most dangerous aspect was the loss of trust

in the banks, which could lead at any moment to panic withdrawals and wholesale collapse of the financial system. If that happened, there could be anarchy, riot and revolution. It was a pervasive fear. Lennie's colleague, Joseph Kennedy, visiting ABO in which he was also a shareholder, said to him, 'I'm a rich man, as you know, but I'd be happy to part with half of everything I own if I could be sure of keeping the other half under law and order.'

During the electoral campaign Roosevelt had attacked Hoover for reckless and extravagant spending, for taxing and spending too much, for trying to control everything from Washington, and for putting too many people on the government dole. Others in the campaign had declared that all these were the tools of the hated creed of socialism.

However, when details of the New Deal emerged, it turned out closely to resemble the action taken under Hoover. Taxes were to go up, public employees were to have a pay cut, and an extensive programme of public works was to be undertaken – hospitals, schools, parks, roads, bridges and airfields – to create employment.

'Some of those public works are schemes I recognise,' Hoover said to Lennie, when he visited him at Palo Alto. 'Things we'd planned but hadn't put into action yet. Damnit, he accused me of taxing and spending too much, and now he's just working out of my book.'

Lennie nodded in sympathy. The trouble was, he thought, that the economy had reached its worst point that winter and was just beginning to turn. If there was, as he and most other businessmen believed, a recovery starting, history would credit the new President with it, and blame the old one for the previous depression. But there was nothing to be done about that.

'He's even rushing through my Emergency Banking Act,' Hoover grumbled. Under this, which had been largely drafted by Hoover's advisers, the Treasury was to undertake supervision of the banks, and deposits were to be guaranteed with the funds of the Federal Reserve.

But, though angry, Hoover declined to speak out or form the focus of discontent for the opposition. 'I've done my stint. Now I'm finished with it. I just want to go fishing.'

One of the new President's first acts was to put in train the ending of Prohibition. The temperance movements and some of the religious groups might object, but it would definitely add to the gaiety of the nation, and bring a welcome new source of revenue to the various states.

'People are going to drink anyway,' Lennie said to Beth. 'You might as well make it legal and put a tax on it. All banning alcohol has achieved is to make the criminal gangs more powerful.'

She frowned. 'But you can't make law based on what you think people will obey.'

'That's just what you have to do,' Lennie said. 'The government has no God-given right to make laws: the people have to consent to be legislated over. And the vast majority have to agree to keep the law voluntarily because you can't watch every person all the time.'

They were sitting in Delamitri's restaurant on Vine Street, eating Del's famous meatballs and spaghetti. Lennie was taking his courting of Beth Andrews very slowly. She was suspicious of him because he was rich and an influential person in the world of movies, and he had to get her used to that gradually. She found it hard to believe he had any legitimate interest in her, since she was not, in her own eyes, in any way special enough to warrant his looking at her twice. The first few times he had asked her out, she had refused, saying he could have any glamorous movie star or society girl he liked on his arm, so why should he want a plain, poor nobody like her? He had admired her refusal, since she clearly thought he had only got her the job at ABO in order to have access to her, and believed refusal would lead to dismissal.

One day, when it was obvious she was not going to lose her job, she looked puzzled and said, 'But *why*? Why me?'

He said, 'I like you. Isn't that reason enough?'

'But why do you like me?'

'There's no reason about these things. I just do.'

Eventually he overcame the initial hurdle by sheer persistence and she allowed him to take her out. Since then his good behaviour was gradually building up trust. But he had to be careful not to take her to glamorous places or spend large amounts of money. A modest restaurant in a quiet location, a simple meal and conversation, that was what she liked. Rock crabs and cold beer at the Beach Shack at Santa Monica; pizza pie at Felice's in Wilshire; a Reuben sandwich at Katz's in Fairfax. He had taken her to a show twice, though only to local, neighbourhood theatres, and to the movies a few times, and they had been for walks along the beach once or twice.

But he could not take her to a club, or dancing, and so far he had not touched her, except to cradle her elbow as he escorted her across the road, or shake her hand when they said good night. His patience was beginning to intrigue her, he could see: she was starting to think he really did like her and had no ulterior motive. He was even a little surprised at himself: he had never run after any woman so persistently with so little encouragement.

Except Polly, of course. His first attraction to Beth had been her slight resemblance to Polly. But it was a long time since he had thought about that. She was not really like Polly at all. She was better educated, to begin with – a solid, middle-class education at a school that taught academic subjects – and was quieter and more thoughtful. Their conversations were informed on both sides, and she had views on subjects that had never interested Polly.

She hadn't Polly's vivacity and drive, but she had a quiet determination that carried her through her difficulties. Her father was dead, and her mother was an invalid – another check on the progress of their relationship, since she could only go out when she could arrange for a neighbour to watch her, and she could never stay out late because 'Mamma worries.' Lennie had never been inside her house: she would not even let him walk her to the door, but insisted on his staying in the car at the kerb.

And, of course, she had never been to his house. In fact, nobody at home knew about her. Their dates were not so frequent that anyone was obliged to wonder where he was, and since they went to quiet places, the gossip columnists had not yet seen him in her company. And at work he behaved discreetly, careful not to place her in an embarrassing position. But over the winter and early spring he had been away a lot, in Washington and New York, and had thus discovered how much he missed her. Now he felt he had served his apprenticeship and demonstrated his bona fides. He wanted their relationship to go further. He wanted to do something for her financially, so that she could get help for her mother and be freer to see him; and he wanted to see her more often; and he wanted to kiss her. That was becoming quite an urgent concern with him. But he was afraid that if he changed anything in their rules of engagement it would frighten her off, so he hesitated, in a way that would have surprised anyone who knew only Lennie the businessman, Lennie the investor, Lennie the former escort of ambitious starlets – even Lennie the war hero from the trenches.

Meanwhile, he was still supervising Rose's career, and was pleased with the way it was going. *Broadway Cutie* had worked very well for her. The picture had been a box-office success, as everyone had expected: it had premièred in February at the darkest time of the depression when everyone needed a boost to their spirits, and while Peach McGinty might be a monster in real life, on screen she was innocent, pretty, dimpled and as cute as the title of the movie. She sang, she danced, she elicited laughter and sighs of pleasure from the audience, and jerked such cathartic tears from them as made the relief of the happy ending the more effective. They came out from the cinema into the gloom of real life feeling rested and restored, better able to face their problems.

And in all this Rose had come across as charming and warm, managing to carve out a little bit of attention for herself from the spun sugar of Peach's performance. Those inside Hollywood's machine knew how well she had done to be seen at all without fatally provoking Peach's jealousy. She had really *acted*, they said, yet had seemed spontaneous, light. As the reviews of the picture came in, she found herself suddenly all the rage. There were 'Who is Rose Morland?' articles in magazines; hairdressing salons did a brisk trade in dyeing young ladies' hair 'Rose Morland blond'; offers from agents to represent her arrived in every post; MGM, trying to sound casual about it, hinted at a contract for her when she had finished with ABO.

Lennie waited anxiously for Peach to throw a fit, but after a tense silence she came out in the movie press as a Rose Morland admirer. Either she had seen the trap before her, or those around her had, and persuaded her that denigrating Rose would only make her look as if she had something to fear. So she was suddenly Rose's best friend. Working with her on the movie had been a pleasure. They'd had just loads of fun. Rose was modest, Rose was hard-working. Rose was sincere. That was the word Peach used most often: 'sincere'. Quite what was meant by it no-one troubled to ask. It passed through the interviews and into the minds of the public, and it was attached to her name at almost every mention.

At home, Lennie and Lizzie teased her with the sobriquet 'Sincerity Rose' and any question – such as 'What would you like for supper?' or 'Do you like this hat?' – was followed by, 'Sincerely, now!' Rose took it in good part. She knew they were trying to make sure she did not get above herself with all the praise that was being heaped on her, but she could have told them that shooting a picture with Peach McGinty was all the lesson in humility anyone would ever need.

ABO, of course, was delighted. Aware that she would probably move on when her contract ended in 1934, they determined to get the most out of her in the time left. The take-over of Olympic had been concluded and the new studios were half built; both Lennie and Joe Kennedy had shown faith by putting in more money. ABO looked set for success, with Rose a rising star, and a new leading man, a very handsome newcomer called Dean Cornwell, who was a competent actor but, more importantly, had a very compelling screen presence, especially when he was making love. So in the late spring and early summer they had Rose and Dean making two movies back to back, using more or less the same sets, one a romantic comedy called *Love of a Woman*, involving that old staple mistaken identity, and one a romantic weepy called *Live Tomorrow*, about a young woman dying of some unspecified disease who could not tell her beloved, and had to make him believe she no longer loved him.

Lennie was pleased with the exposure but felt Rose ought to be able to show her range, and brought Al Feinstein the script of a serious drama about a female medical graduate trying to make her way in a man's world. Feinstein took it on, but insisted there had to be a love interest in it, so the elderly doctor who blocked the 'doctorette' (as Feinstein called her) out of misogyny, and almost drove her to suicide, became a young and handsome doctor, played by Dean Cornwell, who blocked her out of jealousy but eventually fell in love with her. And he changed the title from *The Hard Road* to *Doctor Lady*.

Lennie felt Rose needed a full-time agent now that her star was rising, and while he would always take a close interest in her career, he told her she needed someone there all the time, which he could not be. She would need a hawk-like agent to negotiate her contract with whichever studio she went to after ABO. While *Doctor Lady* was being shot in the fall, she signed on with Michael Rosecrantz, a very clever and successful agent, who agreed with Lennie that Rose needed to make a serious film before she was hopelessly typecast for romantic comedies.

'Nothing wrong with romantic comedies,' he added. 'Don't get me wrong. You can make a very nice living that way. But they don't get you Oscars. Rose can act. I saw her in *Broadway Cutie* and, believe me, that was a tough call, to get seen past McGinty. If she makes a big, heavyweight picture now, she'll be able to choose her roles in future, do all the romantic comedies she likes and still be taken seriously.' He took a draw on his cigar and eyed Lennie gravely. 'Question is, can ABO do a heavyweight movie? David Resnick I like, I've no doubts about him, he needs this like Rose does, but Al Feinstein – is he serious? Will he take on a big project and see it through, without putting in dancing girls and talking dogs and I don't know what else?'

Lennie thought this a little unfair, but he knew what Rosecrantz meant. 'If he gets the right script, he will. I know he fiddled with *Doctor Lady*, but his instincts tell him you can't get people into the theatre by concentrating on women's careers – and I don't know that he isn't right. But tragic love – that's something he can relate to, and tragic love can be as big and heavyweight as you like.'

Rosecrantz nodded. 'I'll look around. But it'll need to happen quickly, if she's to do it before her ABO contract finishes, and I'd sooner she had something like that under her belt before I go to the other studios for a new contract.'

As it happened, everything fell out perfectly, because within days of that conversation, Rosecrantz was brought a script by an aspiring and talented writer about the life of Anne Boleyn. 'Tragic love in spades!' Rosecrantz exclaimed. There had already been a very successful film that year, *The Private Life of Henry VIII*, starring Charles Laughton and Merle Oberon, but it had shown Henry as an unattractive, fat old man, and it had been played for laughs. This script had Henry as young and vigorous, Anne beautiful and doomed, and was entirely serious: Henry loving Anne but forced to sacrifice her for the sake of an heir; Anne loving Henry but assenting to her fate for the good of the country.

'And historical is good – historical is great!' said Rosecrantz. 'Sets, costumes, storylines – everything to make Rose look good and show her Shakespearean credentials. If Feinstein makes this and makes it straight, there could be Oscars in it for everybody.'

Rose loved the script and was very excited about it; and Lennie and Rosecrantz decided they should approach Feinstein together – 'give him both barrels', as Rosecrantz put it.

It turned out not to be hard to sell: Feinstein had long been thinking about what might be Rose's last picture for him, and he wanted something with stature. The subject was good and the script was good and, boy, oh, boy, it was more than a tear-jerker – the audiences would drown in their own saltwater! They'd show United Artists how it was done! They'd got Eric Chapel, inherited from Olympic, still under contract, to make the sets and make 'em fabulous. He'd try and get Edith Head from Paramount to do the costumes – all that velvet, gold and fur! Rose would look gorgeous! What were those halo things women wore in those days? *Coifs?* Whatever, they were perfect! Like sexy nuns! And those tights the men wore would suit Dean Cornwell down to the ground because that boy just had fabulous legs.

David Resnick was so thrilled with the script he almost smiled; and when Al told him he could make it straight with no tampering and no light comedy additions, he actually did smile.

Lennie was delighted with the outcome, and left Rose to

Mike Rosecrantz with confidence, keeping no more than a substitute-fatherly eye on things. Business was picking up rapidly all through 1933, and he had plenty to do about his own empire to keep him busy and happy; but what made him happiest of all was that his relationship with Beth was moving forward. His patience and restraint were bearing fruit. She had allowed him at last to enter her humble home and meet her mother, Marion, a tragic figure if ever a movie-maker wanted one, a woman with a fine mind trapped in a failing body. Lennie could see where Beth had got her brains, her looks and her fortitude. And when she had seen him to the door, Beth had at last allowed him to kiss her goodnight. It was a wonderful kiss, and Beth's response told him that when they finally did cross the last barrier, it would be well worth waiting for.

Now he hoped that by stages he could bring her to allow him to help her by making her mother more comfortable, providing her with a full-time nurse so that Beth could have more freedom, and moving them to a better part of town. And then, when the moment was right, he would propose to her. He had been pursued on both seaboards by a variety of the handsomest and richest women in the country, but he had never seen any woman since Polly that he had wanted to marry, until he had found Beth. When she yielded her warm lips to him, he knew that she loved him, too; and he didn't care that the courtship had taken so many months and would take many more. He was relishing every moment of it.

CHAPTER TWELVE

Violet and Avis took the same house in Belgrave Square for the 1934 Season, and came up at the beginning of February, bringing the young heir and his nursery staff. Charlotte was summoned to come and stay.

'We'll have a lovely time, darling,' Violet promised her.

'But, Mummy, I'm very busy at the moment. Big things are afoot at Dorcas Overstreet.'

'What big things might they be?' Violet asked.

'I can't tell you,' Charlotte said. 'It's all rather secret at the moment.'

A scheme dear to Molly and Vivian's heart was beginning to take shape. He had long wanted to set up a list of sixpenny books, which would have paper covers rather than card, and would be available to a wider public than the usual book-buying élite.

Sixpenny books were not new: they were the staple of twopenny libraries, in the cheap, bright and sensational form. Many British publishers had toyed with the idea of reprinting out-of-copyright titles from their backlists as cheap editions, and Ernest Benn had produced a library of non-fiction works in drab brown-paper covers.

Furthermore, there was the example of Albatross Books in Hamburg, which for two years had been issuing English-language reprints on the continent in smart paper covers. Vivian wanted to take Albatross's example and expand on it. He wanted to bring the best of modern literature within the reach of everyone. The works themselves must be of the highest quality, and the books must look clean, smart and bright, the covers modern enough to attract the sophisticated, while not offending the dedicated reader.

Charlotte took the notes of the 'Albatross meetings', as they were called for convenience. She was to be involved in the whole process.

Molly had told her that she seemed to have a feel for publishing. 'Not everyone has. You've chosen the right field to make your career.'

Charlotte was delighted. 'I never thought to hear anyone use the word "career" in relation to me.'

Reading voraciously over the past two years, she had discovered in herself an unexpected critical faculty. Molly often gave her manuscripts to read, for her opinion on whether or not they should be published, and why.

'I nearly always agree with you,' Molly had told her. 'I think you could go far. When Vivian and I set up our own imprint, we had better make sure we take you with us – we don't want a rival company to snatch you up!'

She had said it as a joke, but Charlotte felt that she had meant it.

At the Albatross meetings, Charlotte did not often speak, but she had made one really important contribution. At a meeting that January in Vivian's office at Dorcas Overstreet, she had been taking shorthand notes for some time, and making the shape for 'Albatross' so frequently brought her to say aloud, 'Shouldn't the list have a name by now?' The others looked at her enquiringly. 'It's just that I've written the word Albatross down so often it's beginning to annoy me.'

Vivian shrugged. 'Yes, why don't we settle on a name now? It might focus our thoughts.' He looked at Charlotte. 'Have you anything in mind?'

'Oh, no – not really. But I think it ought to be something

you can visualise – perhaps as a simple picture that you have on each jacket.'

'Like a trade mark,' said Derek Hammond, another of the team, who was in the sales department. 'Good idea.'

'So should we adopt another bird – or perhaps an animal – as our mascot?' said Pip Armstrong, a young editor.

Molly said, 'I like that idea.'

'You'd want something with a distinctive shape,' said Joan Colefax, who was from the design department of Dorcas Overstreet. 'What about a camel? Can't mistake that outline.'

'Camel Books?' Vivian said. 'No, I don't like that. Camels don't come across as very literary creatures.'

'Not very attractive, either,' said Armstrong. 'People don't feel fond of camels.'

'What about an elephant? Everyone likes them,' said Molly. 'And they're regarded as wise.'

'For wisdom you want an owl,' said Joan. 'An owl with spectacles, perhaps.'

But Elephant Books and Owl Books did not sound right to any of them. 'I think it's the vowel at the beginning that's not right,' Molly said, after some discussion. 'We want a bird or animal beginning with a consonant. And it has to be something friendly and clever.'

'And with a shape that makes a good outline,' Joan added.

After a long discussion, and the fetching of a book on birds and mammals from Joan's studio, they had created a shortlist, against which Charlotte had written the objections.

- Bison Books: nice alliteration but too American.
- Badger Books: English enough, but negative connotations of 'badgering' someone.
- Robin Books: outline of a robin looks much like any other bird.
- Jackdaw Books: see above. And don't they steal? Or is that magpies?

- Salamander Books: connotations of burning unhelpful.
- Centaur Books: no-one would know whether to pronounce it Kentaur or Sentaur.

'I think Badger Books is best,' Molly said, in dissatisfied tones.

'You sound like an advertisement,' her husband noted, amused.

'At least I *like* badgers. We need an animal people automatically like.'

And without knowing she was going to say it, Charlotte said, 'What about dolphins?'

There was a short electric silence. Then Armstrong said, 'I like dolphins.'

Joan said, 'Perfect for an outline. Instantly recognisable.'

'And it sounds good,' said Hammond. 'Dolphin Books. Yes, I can see myself saying that to the customers.'

'Dolphins are clever,' Molly said. 'They save people's lives.'

They all looked at Vivian, who thought for a moment, smiled, and said, 'Dolphin Books it is. Well done, Charlotte!'

Charlotte longed to tell her mother this, because she was proud of her contribution. And without being able to tell her, it was impossible to make her understand that this was a proper job, that she was not there on tolerance, amusing herself as a favour to the family.

But she did not mind moving into Belgrave Square so much this time. She had more self-confidence now that she was doing well at her job. It was nice to be able to see little Lord Tunstead – who was usually known as Halley – whenever she wanted. She also saw more of her older brothers, who often called in there.

Almost to her surprise, she enjoyed the parties and dances and dinners of the Season. At twenty-two she had grown into both her looks and her character, and could hold her own in company, and consequently found herself liked, and in a small way popular. She was even amused, rather than annoyed, that her mother constantly invited a young man called Jocelyn Barber to escort her.

He was a perfectly pleasant young man, but whenever Charlotte saw him she had a terrible urge to giggle, for he proved how far down the scale her mother had felt it necessary to look. Jocelyn was not heir to a title; he was not even a peer's younger son. He was only the son of an MP, and the grandson of an earl. His father was an Honourable, and a minister, and his mother was country gentry, but in the old days, before Papa's bankruptcy, he would only have been on the list of diners to be called at the last minute when someone 'chucked'. Charlotte liked him and they chatted comfortably together, but she could not tell if he saw himself as a suitor.

In early March she went with her mother and Avis to a cocktail party given by the Duchess of Westminster. Oliver and Verena, Eddie and Sarah were also there. Loelia Westminster, née Ponsonby, was the daughter of Frederick Ponsonby who had been secretary to Queen Victoria and a particular friend of Oliver and Violet's mother, so they had known her all their lives.

Among the other guests were Benny Thaw, secretary to the US Embassy, and his wife Connie, who was the sister of Thelma, Lady Furness, the current paramour of the Prince of Wales. Charlotte was not supposed to know about Lady Furness and the Prince, but she had overheard too much at Chelmsford House for Oliver not to tell her the rest, though he begged her never to mention it in front of her mother.

'I know,' Charlotte had said, when first warned about this. 'Mummy never talks about the Prince, but I remember him being around a lot when I was younger. She was his mistress, wasn't she?'

294

'She says not,' Oliver said firmly, 'and you know your mother never lies. She was his close friend, and what any outsider wants to make of that is neither here nor there. But when you came back from America he'd transferred his affections to Lady Furness, and that was that.' He shrugged. 'He does seem to get on better with Americans than English people.'

Jocelyn Barber, who was going into Parliament himself very soon, had political things he wanted to talk about to Secretary Thaw, and eased himself and Charlotte into the fringes of his group. But Benny and Connie were not talking politics: they were more interested in the situation of Connie's sisters.

Thelma had gone to New York to support her twin Gloria through a very unpleasant court case she was involved in. Gloria had been married young to a much older man, the fabulously rich Reggie Vanderbilt, and had borne him a daughter, also called Gloria. Reggie had died only two years later, leaving his young widow in charge of his baby daughter and the $2.5 million fortune left in trust to her.

For years Gloria had lived a gay life in New York, Paris and London, usually taking the child with her, to the disapproval of her Vanderbilt in-laws, who finally challenged her fitness to be a mother. Her sister-in-law Gertrude Vanderbilt Whitney argued that the child would be better off in Long Island, with a stable home, regular hours and a nurse, than gadding about in Paris with a mayfly of a mother.

Benny and Connie Thaw talked about the case, which made for livelier listening than the League of Nations and Germany's rearmament plans. 'They've got the child's nurse to testify against Gloria,' Thaw said. 'She's making terrible allegations.'

'She's in Ger Whitney's pay, I'm sure of it,' Connie cried. The three Morgan sisters had always been very close. 'It's not a fair trial at all.'

'Drink, men *and* women,' said Thaw. 'Hints about Nada Milford Haven.' He nodded significantly, and Charlotte, on the edge of the group, held her breath, but he did not amplify.

'The press coverage of the trial has been an utter disgrace,' said Connie. 'Nothing but sensationalism and prurience.'

'Well, I'm afraid it's all over for poor Gloria,' said Benny. 'She'll lose now for sure, and they'll take the kid away from her. The only comfort is that it means Thelma will soon be home. And then perhaps HRH can stop pining.'

Jocelyn managed to break in at that moment with a question about the Gold Standard, and the group split as the new topic took hold among some of the men and others drifted away. Charlotte abandoned him, exasperated, then saw that Kit and Emma had just arrived and were standing talking to a group around Oliver. She went over to them.

'. . . annoying, because Kit and I have been invited to the Fort this weekend,' Emma was saying.

Fort Belvedere was a house in Windsor Great Park built in 1750 and remodelled in 1828, looking like a miniature castle with crenellations and a tower. It had been rather dilapidated and with overgrown grounds when the King had given it to the Prince of Wales as a country retreat in 1929; he had been occupied in modernising it, while clearing and replanting the gardens, ever since. It was where he liked to spend his weekends, surrounded by his own friends rather than courtiers.

'Sooner you than me,' Eddie said. 'Last time I was there, HRH had me out with a billhook cutting down rhododendrons all day. He's like a madman when he gets out in the garden.'

'Who's hostessing, with Thelma Furness away?' Verena asked.

Emma made a face. 'Mrs Simpson. Apparently, when Lady

Furness went to New York she asked her specifically to look after her "little man". Both Simpsons will be there, of course. I can't think what HRH sees in them. *He*'s just a bore, but *she*'s so brash and pushy.'

Kit said, 'Oh, I don't mind him – he's harmless enough, can even be interesting if you get him on the right subject. Emma thinks he's hard-done-by, but he's mad about royalty, loves having the Prince drop in. Says it's the greatest honour he can imagine that His Royal Highness is "just like one of the family".'

'*Is* he?' Verena said in surprise. 'He drops in? At their house?'

'At their flat,' Kit corrected. 'In Bryanston Court.'

'Where on earth is that?'

Eddie, who equerried for the Prince, answered disapprovingly, 'In a dull street somewhere north of Marble Arch. A place that can never before have seen the like of the heir to the throne being dropped off for cockers and cosy suppers.'

'Don't I remember that she wanted you to redecorate that flat for her?' Sarah asked Emma.

'She found out I'd done Mipsy Oglander's,' said Emma. 'They grew up together in Baltimore, apparently. Mipsy introduced her to me, but it turned out she thought I'd do it for nothing, so I had to disabuse her.'

'They're not poor, are they?' Verena asked. 'I think I've met his sister.'

'No, but I suspect Ernest's ambitions are a tiny bit above his income,' Emma said. 'So the flat stays as it was.'

'Except that now, apparently,' Kit said, 'there are *three* armchairs drawn up in front of the fire.'

'It's true,' said Eddie. 'HRH walks in unannounced, heads straight for the drinks tray, as if he's lived there all his life, and mixes everyone's favourite without asking. If Thelma's not careful she'll find herself ousted when she comes back.'

'I don't believe it,' Sarah said. 'Wales is devoted to her.'

'It happened before, didn't it?' Oliver said. 'He has a record in that respect. It's what the police call a *modus operandi*.'

Verena thought he had gone far enough, likening the Prince of Wales to a criminal, gave him a reproachful look, and changed the subject.

Charlotte was thrilled to have been privy to such important gossip. Her mother did not approve of gossiping, which was very proper and noble – but, it had to be said, it led to much more interesting conversations.

Emma had not been impressed with Mrs Simpson when she first met her. There was something hard and masculine about her: insistent eyes and a harsh voice, quite different from Mrs Oglander's soft, southern tones. She hadn't expected to see her again, the Simpsons not being in the same circle, but somehow or other the name kept coming up, and they kept appearing at social gatherings, so she had learned more about the couple than she had ever intended.

Mrs Simpson, according to Mipsy, had been born Bessie Wallis Warfield, but had dropped the Bessie part as being suitable only for a cow. They had come out together and, the Warfields being poor, Wallis had borrowed from rich, easy-going Mipsy a lot of the things needed to make an impression: clothes, jewels, lifts in motor-cars – escorts. While not pretty, she had a lively manner and a line in witty banter that attracted the men.

'So she did okay,' said Mipsy, 'but it was always a strain, poor Wally. She had a kind of hungry look, and the other girls didn't like her – not that she ever cared what *females* thought about her.'

Wallis had married young to a handsome and dashing naval officer, but he had turned out to be a drunk and a wife-beater. She had divorced him, and a few months later married Ernest Simpson, who had divorced his first wife for her. Simpson was in the shipping business, was half English and half American. He had served in the Coldstream Guards during the war and, being enamoured of all things English, had taken British citizenship. On his second marriage he took up residence in England, where he had an older sister, Maud, who was married to Peter Kerr-Smiley. Kerr-Smiley, a former MP, was thoroughly pukka, a member of the Carlton Club, the Marlborough Club and the Cavalry Club, and lived at 31 Belgrave Square, a few doors from Violet and Avis's rented place.

The Simpsons then seemed to settle themselves to the task of conquering the heights of London society. Though they had an 'in' through Simpson's sister, it would be no mean feat if they accomplished it. Divorce was more common, these days, but it was still not entirely acceptable. In Court circles the divorced were not admitted, and some of the more punctilious hostesses would not receive them either. Nevertheless, there could be few people in society who had not sat down at a table at some point with a divorced person. It was not, however, something to be spoken of or taken lightly. Mrs Simpson had divorced her husband to marry a divorced man, whose first wife, moreover, was herself divorced before she married him. It was all rather too messy for good taste.

And then, Emma thought, with a sigh, there was the loudness and pushiness of Mrs Simpson, who was one of those people you kept tripping over in unexpected places, who claimed you as a friend when you were just an acquaintance, and who dominated the conversation with her rather foghorn voice. Wherever she was, she had to be the centre of attention, and she was completely unsnubbable.

Kit thought it all very funny, and encouraged the Simpsons whenever he met them, in a perfectly devilish way, egging them on to expose themselves for his amusement. He had a soft spot for Thelma Furness, whom he thought pretty and good-natured, though lamentably ignorant. 'But that makes her a perfect match for HRH,' he said to Emma, when they were packing to go to the Fort, 'who hasn't a thought in his head. So I hope this Simpson female isn't meaning to oust poor Thelma. It would be too bad!'

'Darling, I can't see it,' Emma said. 'Thelma's pretty. The Simpson's very plain – no figure at all, bad skin, and that nose! She's not even young.'

'If you'd been paying attention *at all* over the last I-don't-know-how-many years,' Kit said severely, 'you'd have noticed that he's not particularly interested in "young". His loves, apart from Thelma, have all been older than him. Notably matronly.'

Emma paused and looked up at him. 'What are you saying?'

'I don't think the Little Man wants a lover. He wants a mother. You know he and Thelma don't *do* anything?' he said significantly.

Emma caught his drift, and raised sceptical eyebrows. 'She told you that?'

He gave a smug smile. 'Ladies tell me all sorts of things they wouldn't tell other chaps. You do yourself.'

'I'm your wife.'

'And a very lovely one,' he agreed. 'Are you going to put in your taffeta?'

'Isn't it too formal for the Fort?'

'But we might get asked over to the Royal Lodge. The Yorks will be there,' he reminded her.

'With the little princesses, lucky them,' Emma said. 'The bad thing about the Fort is not being able to have the children with us.' Alethea and Electra, aged almost four and two, were the delight of their lives.

'But the good thing is being able to take the doggies,' Kit comforted her.

Apart from the Simpsons, the guests at the Fort that weekend were Fruity and Baba Metcalfe, another American couple,

Taylor and Poppy Lamarque, and Humphrey and Poots Butler (he was an occasional equerry to Prince George, and his Dutch-born wife was an old friend of the Prince of Wales).

Over drinks before dinner, Emma talked to Baba Metcalfe, whose sister, Cimmie, had died suddenly of peritonitis the year before. Her husband, Oswald Mosley (whom those close to him called Tom), had long been having an affair with Diana Guinness, who had taken the extreme step of leaving her husband Bryan and setting up alone in a flat in London as Mosley's acknowledged mistress. It was, even for those easy-going times, a shocking thing to do.

Cimmie's death had seemed to leave the way open for Tom to marry Diana; but instead he had turned his attentions to Baba, with whom he had previously had an affair. 'He's toying with me,' she said bitterly, 'playing me off against Diana, the way he used to play Diana off against Cimmie.'

'But surely,' Emma said, perplexed, 'you can't *want* a man like that, who would be so wantonly cruel?'

'Oh, Emma, you're such an innocent!' Baba said despairingly. 'It's all right for you, married to a man who adores you and whom you adore. You don't understand. Of course I'm *fond* of Fruity, but all he cares about are horses and getting drunk. Tom's so vibrant, so full of life! He always says passion and conviction can't be separated. Love and politics go together for him, and now Diana's been to Germany and heard Herr Hitler speak, she'll talk Fascism to him and take him away from me. She's in Munich now with her sister, and I'm here with . . .' she waved a dismissive arm around the company '. . . so many stuffed dummies.'

During dinner the conversation turned, as it did so often these days, to Germany and its intentions on leaving the League of Nations and the Disarmament Conference.

Humphrey Butler said, 'The Germans feel they've been punished quite enough. It's fifteen years since the war ended. Sooner or later the world has to move on and let bygones be bygones. It has to be remembered that Germany lost a great deal more through the war than we did.'

'Chancellor Hitler has sworn to promote peace with us, France and Russia,' Poots said. 'It was the first thing he did.'

'But I wonder if Herr Hitler's intentions are quite as peaceable as he pretends,' said Taylor Lamarque, quietly. 'Speeches are all very well, but actions speak louder than words.'

'I understand Herr Hitler is a *wonderful* speaker,' Mrs Simpson said emphatically. 'So full of passion and fire he simply carries everyone along with him.'

'He's certainly carried Diana Guinness,' Kit said, with a straight face. 'And her sister Unity can't be prised away. I hear she sits in Hitler's favourite café in Munich for hours on end, hoping he'll come in. Then when he does, she stares at him like a schoolgirl with a crush.'

Emma was too far away to kick him under the table, but she gave him a glare for bringing up Diana Guinness. He knew as well as she did how things stood between her and Baba Metcalfe. He always knew how things stood with everyone: it was true, people told him things.

Mrs Simpson leaned across the table to say to the Prince, 'What do *you* think, sir? What are Mr Hitler's *real* intentions?'

The flattering implication was that he alone could know the truth about the delicate international situation. The Prince looked pleased to be asked, and said, 'I don't think we need to be too worried about Fascism. It's Communism that's the real danger. If there's another war, it'll be the Reds we have to fight, so if it comes to a showdown we'd better line ourselves up with the Germans, because no-one else seems to be willing to take the Reds on.'

'I do so agree,' Mrs Simpson said. 'Sometimes you have to prepare for war in order to keep the peace.'

'How very true,' the Prince said, seeming quite struck by the phrase.

As well he might, for Fruity sidled up to Emma afterwards and said that those words had been spoken by the Prince himself at a dinner a few days before, and reported in a newspaper. Mrs Simpson, Emma said to Kit afterwards, certainly did her homework.

In the morning, it was as Eddie had warned. The Prince and Fruity Metcalfe appeared in old tweeds and chivvied the menfolk out of doors with billhooks and axes to clear an overgrown area where HRH fancied a rock garden. 'Bushwhacking', he called it, in jovial mood.

Kit extracted himself delicately from the activity, saying he had to walk the dogs, and Emma hurried to include herself and get out of a morning spent with Mrs Simpson, Mrs Lamarque and Poots Butler – Baba Metcalfe had claimed a twisted ankle and was sitting with her foot up on a stool, reading moodily, in a manner meant to repel boarders.

It was a cool and breezy morning, with a very liquid feeling about it, and after a while it started to spit a little rain. Emma said they should turn back.

'Not yet,' Kit said. 'The dogs haven't had nearly enough.'

Emma looked at them. Buster and Alfie were still darting about, nose-deep in tussocks, but Sulfi was keeping close to Kit's legs and the greyhound, Eos, was shivering reproachfully. They both hated getting wet. 'They have,' she asserted.

He rolled his eyes. 'The rain won't stop Sir. If we go back too soon I'll get roped in.'

'Not you. I'm sure you can talk your way out of it.'

'But it won't be much better inside. I didn't think Simpson looked very keen on bushwhacking. I wouldn't be surprised if he hadn't sprained something by now and gone indoors, spoiling for a chat.'

'I thought you liked him.'

'In small doses. A whole weekend is not small enough. I'll take my chances with the rain.'

She shook her head. 'You'll just have to find a way of refusing next time you're invited to the Fort.'

'You can't refuse a royal command,' he said, pretending to look shocked.

'Well, I'm going back,' she said. 'Don't keep those poor dogs out too long.'

When she got back she found that it was as Kit had predicted: Ernest Simpson had got out of gardening and wandered indoors, where he had ensconced himself in the sitting room with the newspaper, thereby driving Baba Metcalfe out of the room with a miraculously cured ankle. She was lurking in the hall and seized Emma's arm as soon as she appeared, saying, in a low, shocked voice, 'You'll never guess what they're doing!'

'Who?' said Emma, hoping she could go and change her damp stockings soon.

'That Simpson woman's taken Poppy Lamarque and Poots into the kitchen. They're making sandwiches!'

It was a shocking breach of protocol. In anyone's house, you had to be as close as family to make use of their kitchen, and with the Prince of Wales, it was self-evidently impossible for a commoner – let alone a foreign divorcée – to be that intimate. It was taking liberties.

'The servants are furious – the butler's beside himself,' Baba whispered. 'The impertinence of it!'

'I expect she just doesn't understand the way things are done here,' Emma said. 'Americans don't set the same store by protocol. She probably doesn't mean any harm.'

'I shall make Fruity say something to Simpson,' she hissed.

'Oh, I wouldn't,' Emma said. 'Really, you know, it will just make for bad feeling.'

Just then they were interrupted by the appearance of the villainess herself, dusting her fingers, very pleased with herself, and followed by a sulky-looking servant carrying a vast silver platter of sandwiches.

'Hello! Secrets?' she said gaily, but giving them a sharp look. 'We'd better call the men in. I've made us all club sandwiches for luncheon. David does so *love* my club sandwiches. I couldn't find any dill pickles, though – it seems they don't have them here, can you imagine? We'll have to make do with olives.'

She paraded past them, with Poots and Mrs Lamarque bringing up the rear. Emma and Baba Metcalfe exchanged a look. *David?* That was what his family called him. Now what was this? Baba gave a furious glare at Mrs Simpson's back and stalked away.

Dinner was caviar, followed by roast lamb, marmalade tart and angels on horseback for a savoury. The Prince carved the roast and they served themselves, passing dishes up and down the table, which induced a kind of informality, and conversation was lively. Mrs Simpson – Emma was fair-minded enough to allow – showed at her best, keeping things going with amusing anecdotes and apposite questions. She was sitting next to Fruity, and was happy enough talking about horses when the conversation was not general; down the table, Kit was being fascinating to Poppy Lamarque. The Prince, she thought, was not the only one who liked Americans.

After the savoury there was no withdrawing of the ladies. The Prince entertained them by playing his bagpipes, walking round the table as he said they did at Balmoral. Emma could not tell whether he played well or not. She had spent time in Scotland in her young days and had been courted by Scots gentry and nobility, and had been exposed to bagpipes then. She had come to the conclusion that expertise probably wouldn't make much difference to the outcome. At least, she thought, they were spared the sight of him dressed in the kilt that she knew he affected sometimes. She didn't think God had designed men's knees to be seen.

When the bagpipes had been put away, they sat talking round the table until Emma became uncomfortable, thinking about the servants waiting to clear; but there could be no moving before the Prince did, and he seemed quite happy to stay. Eventually they transferred to the drawing room, and Poots Butler suggested bridge, but Mrs Simpson objected, saying that the Prince did not care for it. There was an awkward silence – it was not for her, the newcomer, to claim a better acquaintance with his tastes than anyone else present. After a moment she broke it herself, suggesting Casino instead. Halfway through the evening Prince George arrived, having walked over from the Royal Lodge where he was staying with the Yorks, and they changed the game to Tactics, which went on until midnight.

On Sunday it rained solidly, which made the company rather dull. There was no church-going at the Fort, so after a late breakfast there was nothing to do but read the papers until lunchtime. Emma found a pack of cards and laid out patience on a table in the morning room, with the dogs keeping her feet warm. Kit was in a corner with Baba, heads together – Emma guessed he was getting more details about the Tom–Diana axis.

After luncheon everyone was even duller, and Ernest Simpson actually slipped into a post-prandial sleep in an armchair in the drawing room. Everyone tactfully left him and wandered into the morning room, where Poppy Lamarque was tentatively suggesting a game of some sort to pass the time, when it was suddenly realised that the Prince and Mrs Simpson were missing.

'Someone must know where they are,' Baba said, her nostrils flaring at the scent of a scandal.

'I expect Mrs S is in the kitchen, baking cakes for tea,' Kit murmured provokingly.

'Why not ask Mr Simpson? He might know,' Emma suggested.

'No, he's still asleep. It'd be a shame to wake him,' said Taylor Lamarque, who had had enough of talking about shipping with him already that day.

'I expect they're looking round the garden,' Poots Butler said. 'You know how fond Wallis is of gardening.'

'They're not looking round gardens in this,' her husband said, waving a hand at the torrents falling past the window. He looked worried. Although it was Fruity who was equerrying and therefore responsible, it would make everyone uncomfortable if there were a breach of protocol.

Fruity, who had gone out of the room, came back in to say, 'They've taken a car, apparently, and gone up to the castle.'

'Without telling anyone?' said Butler. 'And why?'

'I hope they haven't dropped in at Royal Lodge uninvited,' Baba said. 'The Yorks would have a fit. You know how strict they are.'

Fruity shrugged. 'Nothing we can do about it now. I can't very well ring them and ask, can I?'

The dressing bell went and the missing pair were still not back. Everyone hesitated, not knowing what was going to happen. Would dinner be put back? But then there was the bustle of arrival at the front door, voices, the unmistakable sound of Mrs Simpson laughing. Everyone hurried, trying not to appear to do so, into the hall to see what had happened. The major-domo was looking pained, receiving wet umbrellas and overcoats and passing them on to a waiting footman. Mrs Simpson was radiant, all smiles and liveliness; the Prince was saying nothing, just smiling complacently.

'You'll never guess where we've been!' Mrs Simpson said, emerging from her overcoat and removing her rain-beaded hat. 'We went to St George's Chapel up at the castle to hear evensong. It was heavenly! Those boys sing just exactly like angels. It does one good to hear music of that sort now and then, especially on a Sunday. Don't you find Sundays terribly *worldly* otherwise? All that stuffing and sitting around, one needs something to lift up the soul, make one aware there is a spiritual dimension to life.'

As she prattled, Emma tried not to catch Kit's eye, in case it drove him into some naughtiness, and in avoiding him she looked at Fruity, who rolled his eyes expressively.

'The dressing bell has gone, sir,' Fruity said, in the hope of ending the embarrassing outflow.

Mrs Simpson was stopped. She said, 'We'd better go up.' But then she glanced down at herself and said, 'Oh, would you just look at the state of my shoes! They're covered in mud. David, take them off for me, would you?'

In the horrified silence that followed, the Prince of Wales knelt down and began to untie her shoelaces. The major-domo was too frozen with shock to move; everyone in the hall stared at the floor or the wall in rigid embarrassment. In her stockinged feet, Mrs Simpson pattered off upstairs in gay indifference, the Prince handed the shoes to the servant and followed, and the rest of the company, released, found an intense desire in themselves not to meet the eyes of or speak to anyone else, and made their separate ways silently upstairs.

In their room, Emma said to Kit, 'I feel as if I've just witnessed a horrid road accident. If it weren't so dreadfully embarrassing, I'd almost feel sorry for her.'

'Or for him – poor Ernest,' Kit said. 'So much for his ambition to be best pals with the future king.'

'I don't suppose they'll ever be asked again,' Emma said. 'I can't say I shall be sorry not to have to meet her again. All these alarms and excursions are bad for one's heart.'

'Never mind, darling – home tomorrow and our dear little girls,' said Kit.

'Yes, but we've got to get through tonight first, and dinner's bound to be uncomfortable.'

It was, but in a different way from how Emma had

expected. The two protagonists, Mrs Simpson and the Prince of Wales, were all smiles and jolliness – it was the rest of the company who were perplexed and anxious. Emma wondered if perhaps the Prince was going along with her out of politeness, so as not to show up his American guest who had crossed the line out of ignorance; yet there was something glittering and knowing in Mrs Simpson's look, something satisfied about the way she chatted and laughed, and leaned across the table to speak to the Prince with so much ease she might have been his older sister. Emma had the oddest feeling that the shoe episode had not been a *faux-pas* at all, but that she had known exactly what she was doing. Yet how could it have been a design? What could this strange, ladder-climbing woman hope to gain by being so shockingly rude to the heir to the throne?

The next morning there seemed an unusual air of relief about the bustle of packing and leaving. Baba Metcalfe came up to Emma after breakfast and whispered, 'There was a telephone call last night, just after we all went up. Fruity told me. From Thelma in New York. She'll be home in a week. Then perhaps things will settle down. I don't think we'll be seeing the Simpsons any more.'

Jocelyn Barber proposed at the Desboroughs' ball, and Charlotte did not immediately hear what he said because she was thinking deeply about the Dolphin list.

'I beg your pardon?' she said, when it was clear he had not just made a comment on the excellence of the band.

'I said, will you marry me?' He looked put out. It was not something you felt you ought to have to repeat.

Charlotte laughed. 'No, of course not!' she said. Then, seeing his hurt, 'You weren't serious, were you? Oh dear, Joss, I'm sorry, but – goodness!'

'I don't see why it's such a silly question,' he said, a little sulkily.

'I didn't mean to hurt your feelings. And I do like you, awfully, but not in that way. I thought you knew that.' She studied his face as they revolved among the other dancers. 'You're not *really* upset, are you?'

'It takes a lot of courage for a chap to ask a girl. And then to be laughed at . . .' But he said it lightly.

'I acknowledge and admire the courage,' she said. 'But come on! You can't *really* have thought . . . I say, did my mother put you up to this?'

He looked away. 'She might have mentioned something about it, in a general way – encouraging, you know. Said you liked me and so on.'

'Well, I do. But now, be honest, you don't truly want to marry me, do you? Aren't you really rather relieved I said no?'

He grinned suddenly. 'You are a devilish girl, looking into a chap's head like that! And how can I possibly say I'm relieved without insulting you? Can't be done, you know – especially on a dance-floor.'

'Never mind. Let's just be friends and vow always to tell each other the truth. And it isn't you, really it isn't. I mean never to marry at all. I'm going to have a career instead. But if I *were* going to marry, you'd be just the sort of person I'd like to ask me. Honest Injun!'

He shook his head. 'You may think that now, but it won't last, I promise you. You're a splendid girl, Charley, and one day some chap will come along and make you fall head-and-ears for him, and that'll be that. But if he breaks your heart, you can always come and cry on my shoulder.'

'Thank you, Joss dear. And vice versa, I'm sure.'

When she got back to Belgrave Square she found her mother waiting up for her.

'There are sandwiches and coffee in the small sitting room,' she said.

'Oh, good,' said Charlotte. 'I'm starving.'

Her mother followed her in. 'Didn't you have any supper?'

'Yes, but it seems ages ago.'

'Jocelyn took you in?'

'Yes.' Charlotte took a sandwich. 'Are you having anything? Shall I pour you some coffee?'

'No, thank you,' Violet said distractedly. She sat down. 'Didn't he bring you home?'

'Who? Jocelyn? Yes, in the taxi.'

Violet watched her eat a second sandwich as she poured herself a cup of coffee. 'Didn't he want to come in?'

'I didn't ask him. Rather late,' Charlotte said. She knew what her mother wanted to know but she didn't feel up to having a row and would rather postpone it until the morning. 'These are rather good,' she said. 'Better than we used to have at home.'

'Charlotte, don't be annoying. I'm not interested in the sandwiches. Did you dance with Jocelyn?'

'Yes, some of the time. And with Timmy Everedge and John St Aubyn and that nice Guards officer whose name I can never remember. And some others. I can't remember all the names.'

Violet waved that away. 'Did Jocelyn have anything in particular to say to you?'

Charlotte swallowed and turned to face her mother. She couldn't put it off any longer. 'He asked me to marry him – as obviously you know very well, since you put him up to it.'

'I did no such thing,' Violet said with dignity. 'I simply encouraged him. He's rather a shy boy. You mustn't hold that against him.'

'I don't.'

Violet's face lit. 'Then you accepted him?'

'No, Mummy, I turned him down. Now, don't look like that—'

'I don't understand. I thought you were fond of him. And it's a very good offer.'

'I am fond of him, but I don't want to marry him. I'm

311

sorry if it upsets you, but I can't help it. I'm not going to marry Joss Barber simply to please you.'

Violet got up and walked across to the other side of the room, where she stood with her back to Charlotte. Charlotte was horribly afraid she was trying not to cry. To make your mother cry would be a most terrible thing.

'Please, Mummy,' she said, in a small voice. 'Don't be upset. I hate to disappoint you. But I don't want the things you want. I don't want to get married and have a house and children and all that sort of thing.'

'Then what *do* you want?' Violet said, turning round.

Oh, good, there was no sign of tears. She seemed merely tired and bewildered, which was bad enough.

'Avis and I have done everything we can to put you in your right place in society, to make up for what happened with your father. And you seem to want to throw it all away – for what?'

'I know it's hard to understand,' Charlotte said, with an effort keeping her voice from shaking. 'I just want to be myself. To be free.'

'Free!' It was both an exclamation and a question.

'I love my job,' Charlotte said. 'I'm good at it. Molly and Vivian will have their own company one day and they'll take me with them, and I'll have a career with them and rise to the top. On my own efforts, not because I'm Lady Charlotte Fitzjames Howard.'

'You wouldn't even have the job without your uncle and cousin putting in a word for you.'

Charlotte blushed with vexation, and Violet was sorry she had said it.

'I know,' Charlotte said quietly, 'but I believe I could have got a job on my own merits, if I'd been allowed.' She made a gesture as if to reach out to her mother, but let her hand drop. 'The world has changed, Mummy. I want to live my own life, earn my own living, choose my own friends. I want to share a flat with some other girls, and go to the pictures with them, and mend my own stockings, and cook sausages at the end of the month when the money's low, and sit by the gas fire and talk about books and poetry until the early hours. I *have* enjoyed this Season with you, the parties and dances and everything, but to me it's like a holiday, not real life. I want to get on with my real life.'

Violet walked back across the room, pausing at the table with the tray to pour herself a cup of coffee. Perhaps her hand was not quite steady, for a single drop fell on the white tray cloth and made a small brown circle. She carried her cup to the sofa and sat down again, sipped, then raised her eyes to her daughter's anxious face.

'Very well,' she said.

Charlotte waited nervously for more, and finally said, 'Very well – what?'

'You can do as you want,' Violet said. 'I've tried my best for you, but if you won't be helped—'

'Oh, Mummy, please don't be angry.'

'I'm not angry,' Violet said, 'only tired. Go and live in a flat and have a job, if that's what you want. I suspect you'll find in the end it isn't as romantic as you think it will be. But I can see I can't change your mind by reason, so – I give up. I can't fight you any more.'

Charlotte bit her lip. 'I never wanted to fight you. I never wanted to make you unhappy. But, Mummy, you have a new life now. With Avis and Halley. You don't need me.'

'Is that what you think?' Violet said, and she looked sad.

'I didn't mean it in a bad way,' Charlotte said helplessly.

Violet shook her head 'No, you're right. Things are different nowadays. The war changed everything, and I suppose you can't change it back again. I just want you to be happy, Charlotte, that's all. You can go your way, I won't make a fuss. But you'll stay with me until the end of the Season, won't you? I enjoy having you around.'

'Yes, of course, Mummy. I've enjoyed it too.'

'Good. I shall be going back to Tunstead probably at the beginning of June, so it's only a few weeks more.'

'That's early,' Charlotte said, and she examined her mother's face more carefully. She *did* look tired. 'You – you aren't ill, are you?'

Violet smiled, a smile to wash away any fear. 'No, far from it,' she said. 'I'm going to have another baby.'

CHAPTER THIRTEEN

By the end of May, Charlotte, Myra and Betty had found a flat to their liking. It was in Ridgmount Gardens, a quiet road in Bloomsbury that ran parallel to Gower Street, a hop-skip-and-jump from the British Museum. Dorcas Overstreet's office was in Russell Square, Betty was working for a solicitor in Theobald's Road, and Myra for a shipping agent in Holborn, so it was convenient for all of them.

Ridgmount Gardens was a terrace of tall, red-brick houses with white trim, built before the war, which had been divided into flats. The girls had the top floor, which was quiet and airy with wonderful views over the treetops. There were three bedrooms, a sitting room, a kitchen, a bathroom, and a small box room. Charlotte's bedroom was tiny compared with the ones she occupied in Chelmsford House or Belgrave Square, but she was enchanted with it.

'A room in Bloomsbury,' Oliver teased. 'How euphonious!' But he was the first to come to see it and give his approval. 'Three little birds in a nest. You'll have a wonderful time,' he said. He was enormously helpful, offering Charlotte all the linens she needed from Chelmsford House ('We have far more than we'll ever use') and any pieces of furniture she might require to supplement the deficiencies of a furnished flat.

'Honestly, I don't think we could get much more furniture into it,' she said, 'but thanks awfully, Uncle Olly.' In the end she did ask for the bedside cabinet from her bedroom, and a standard lamp from one of the small sitting rooms. He made her a present of the small oil painting in her room, which she had always liked, and supplied her with his chauffeur and motor to take her things over when she moved in.

Emma, who was next to inspect and approve the flat, exclaimed, 'Goodness, you'll have such fun!' and said the first thing they must do was to have the chimney swept. 'It's something that's always forgotten by landlords. I'll send my usual man round to do it.' She also sent round one of her decorators to repaint the woodwork and the kitchen and bathroom walls, which made it all look much fresher.

Violet and Avis came to see it just before they left for Derbyshire. Violet looked round the flat in a silence.

Charlotte was afraid it was a disapproving one. 'It's a lot of stairs, I'm afraid,' she said nervously. 'And I suppose the rooms must look awfully small to you.'

Violet walked over to the window and looked out. 'It will be nice and quiet, and the air is better higher up,' she said pleasantly. She thought it a horrid, poky little place, and was sure, once the novelty had worn off, that Charlotte would feel the same and want to come home. Meanwhile, she would go along with it. 'Once you've got your own things arranged, I'm sure it will be charming.'

Charlotte almost sagged with relief. 'Oh, *thank* you, Mummy!'

Avis gave her the box he was carrying. 'We weren't sure what you would need, so we decided in the end to please ourselves. A present, with our love.'

It was a set of elegant crystal wine glasses. 'Oh, they're beautiful! Thank you!' Charlotte cried, and kissed his cheek.

'And on a more practical note, I'm sure you'll have a lot of extra expenses to begin with, things you don't discover you need until after you've moved in, so here's a little cheque to tide you over.'

Charlotte looked at the amount and gasped. 'Oh, you are so kind!'

'It was your mother's idea,' Avis protested.

Charlotte was stricken. 'Oh, Mummy!'

'We're both happy for you to be doing what you want,' Violet said.

'And now we've seen your new home,' Avis concluded, 'we're going to take you to the Grill for dinner.'

There were other house-warming presents. Molly and Vivian gave them a modern bookcase from Heal's because 'nowhere is a home without some books in it'. Richard gave Charlotte a fat velvet cushion because he said she would have to stake her claim on the communal sofa. It was embroidered with the words 'Don't pinch my seat'. She threw it at him in mock outrage. Robert sent her a nice note, reminding her not to forget to sign on to the electoral register. He was expecting to become a junior minister after the recess and was very busy with his career. Henry sent her a drawing of an engine, which he said was the best he had ever done, and included some improvements of his own over the original, 'though I don't know yet whether they would work'. Charlotte was touched, and said she would have it framed as soon as she could afford it, and hang it in her bedroom.

And Uncle Oliver, always practical, sent the three of them an enormous hamper from Fortnum's, 'so that you don't have to cook for the first few days'.

'Your uncle is a poppet,' said Myra, when they had moved all their things in and arranged them, at least temporarily, to their satisfaction, 'and this is a splendid hamper, but, girls, I've been looking forward to this day for weeks, and my plan was always that we should go out to supper tonight to celebrate.'

'Oh, yes, we must!' Betty said. 'And I know just where. There's a nice little Italian restaurant in Goodge Street where you can get a super meal for half a crown, with wine.'

'Look here,' Charlotte said, 'we can't go laying out half-crowns on meals like that.'

'Oh, Charley,' Myra said, with affectionate exasperation, 'we shan't! It's just this one special-occasion meal.'

'With wine,' Betty reminded her.

'Come on, old thing,' Myra said. 'Your freedom was hard enough won. That's worth celebrating, isn't it?'

Charlotte agreed.

Things weren't progressing quite as quickly with Dolphin Books as she had expected. She had thought they would only have to compile the list of books they wanted and all doors would fly open. But acquiring the titles was proving to be a formidable task. To begin with, publishers always moved at a glacial pace, especially when they had to decide on something important. And to her surprise she had discovered that they were not at all inclined to be helpful. Some, like Gollancz, had not even replied. Others sent very damning comments with their refusals.

Putting these cheap editions into the bookshops would cause the sales of other editions to suffer very severely.

Unless we are considerably underestimating possible sales from this venture, I can't see that enough profit would accrue once we had paid the author his share and you yours, even to cover the setting-up of the scheme and its administration.

It is a great mistake to imagine that cheap books are good for the book trade. If a man has five shillings to spend and books are half a crown each, he may well buy two. But if books are sixpence each he won't buy ten of them. He's more likely to buy three and spend the rest of the five shillings on going to the cinema. So the cheaper books are, the less is spent on books. It spells disaster for publishers, and those booksellers who clamour for discounts need to be saved from themselves.

It was disappointing, but Vivian was not defeated. 'We must keep trying, that's all. Somewhere or other we'll break through, and find a publisher with vision. I know Dolphin Books *will* succeed.'

Charlotte was always uplifted in his and Molly's presence; away from them she felt downcast, and even wondered if her marvellous new job would peter out into nothing, and send her back to her mother with her tail between her legs. But that was silly, she told herself stoutly. She could get another job. Secretarial skills were infinitely portable, that was the beauty of them. Businesses would always need someone to type their letters.

The three young women had a splendid evening, and came home replete with food, wine and conversation. As she opened her own front door with her own key, Charlotte thought how wonderful it was not to have a butler letting her in and a footman waiting to take her coat. She was free at last to live her own life, make her own decisions, stand on her own two feet.

It was only in bed later, in the dark and silence before sleep, that she felt afraid. It was such a huge step, so much responsibility. The world seemed very big and unknowable and she very small and ignorant. How would she manage? What had she done?

But the alternative – staying at home to moulder away arranging flowers and dusting the dining room – was unthinkable. She turned over, trying to find a good position on the mattress (which, like all mattresses in furnished lets, had seen better days). She eased herself into a comma around and between the unpadded springs, smiled and went to sleep.

Emma arrived home at her tall, narrow house in Manchester Square feeling hot and tired. As she trod up the steps, Wilson the butler opened the door with perfect timing, and she thought how nice it was not to have to open it herself, and to have someone help her out of her coat.

'His lordship is up in the nursery, my lady,' Wilson said.

'Oh, good. I'll go straight up,' Emma said.

Her secretary, Miss Ames, had come into the hall, and proffered several letters and a fountain pen. Emma glanced through them quickly, signed them, handed them back, and said, 'Thanks. You can go now. I shan't need you again tonight.'

She gave her hat directly to her maid, Spencer, who said, 'Lady Cunard's tonight, my lady. I've put out the beaded emerald taffeta, and what jewels would you like to wear?'

'I'll choose later, when I have my bath,' Emma said. 'I must go upstairs now.'

She had, she thought, as she climbed the stairs, the perfect life. Up on the top floor (the nursery floor where Oliver and Violet had grown up, along with their brother Thomas, now dead, and their orphaned cousin Eddie Vibart), her darling children were waiting for her, and there was time to spend with them and still have a cocktail before the evening's engagement. She had work that interested her, and the most understanding husband in the world. He had insisted, when she presented him with a second daughter, that he would far rather have a girl than a boy.

'What would I do with a boy?' he said. 'They're knobbly, uncomfortable things. I was a boy myself, so I know.'

'But you need an heir,' she had cried.

'Oh, bother the silly old title!' he had said. '*Après moi le déluge.* As long as we have enough of a fortune between us to see the girls set up, nothing else matters. There's a cousin somewhere who can be earl when I'm gone. If there *are* still earls by then. The Red revolution may sweep them all away, you know.'

Emma was comforted by his assurance, even though she hadn't wholly believed it. Any man must want a son, and an earl even more so. Though the entail ended with him, a daughter could not take the title and it would irk, surely, to see it go away to some obscure relative. But in the twenty-two months since Electra had been born, he had never changed his tune, and she had come to believe he really did not mind.

Her only regret was that he had moved out of her bed before she had lain-in with Electra, and now slept in his own room. Having had two children, she was no longer interested in the sexual act, but she had enjoyed his presence in bed and missed their long talks in the darkness with their arms round each other. He did still occasionally get into bed with her for a chat but did not stay, excusing himself with 'I'll let you get your sleep,' to go to his own room. So most nights she went to sleep alone, just as she always woke alone. But he was still her best friend and dear companion, and she couldn't think of another thing in her life she wanted to change.

Buster and Alfie must have heard her coming, for they scampered down the last two flights from the top to meet her with ecstatic wags and licks, then raced ahead of her up to the nursery floor, looking over their shoulders to tell her to hurry up and join the fun.

She could hear the children's giggles long before she reached the door. The day nursery was a long, light room, with three windows and a wooden window-seat running the whole length of the wall. Here she found her husband on his hands and knees, crawling about with the hearthrug pinned round his shoulders. He was growling, so she supposed he was meant to be a bear, but his hair was stuck with coloured spills, which put her more in mind of the banderillas in a bull-fight. The object of the game was quickly evident: the girls were armed with fistfuls of spills, and their job was to dart in and plant them in their father's luxuriant hair without getting caught; his job was to catch them and tickle them into submission. Eos and Sulfi were lying well out of the way, watching with puzzled goodwill, but Alfie and Buster plunged into the game with energy, playing to their own rules.

Emma's arrival distracted Alethea just enough for her to be caught, twisted flat onto her back, and both licked and tickled simultaneously. She shrieked with laughter; Electra dropped her spills and ran to her mother, arms out. The bear turned its head, spotted the newcomer, and rose majestically onto its hind legs to greet her.

Alethea jumped up too, and tugged at her father's hand. 'Oh, don't stop, Daddy! Play some more!'

The nurse had come out from the night-nursery, and was looking disapproving and shaking her head minutely, which gave Emma the hint that she thought there was too much excitement. The words *there'll be tears later* might as well have been floating above her head in a balloon.

'No, let's have some quiet time now,' Emma said. 'Let's all sit down and have a story.'

Kit made a comical face at her and said, *sotto voce*, 'Sensible beast!' Then, aloud, 'Whose turn is it to choose?'

'Me! Me!' said Electra, and ran to the bookshelves that filled the alcove beside the fireplace. They knew what it would be: she always chose *The Gingerbread Man*. Alethea pouted: she wanted *The Little Mermaid*. She would choose tomorrow, but tomorrow, when you are only three-nearly-four, is a long way off, lost in the clouds of myth.

The nurse brought milk and biscuits, Electra sat on Emma's lap and Alethea on Kit's, and Kit read the story while they absorbed their supper. He read very well, and always added extra bits, which Alethea loved, though Electra sometimes objected that he'd got it wrong, and there *wasn't* a elephant in it, Daddy.

Miraculously, the story finished just when the milk did, and then there were hugs and kisses goodnight, and the little Westhovens went away with Nanny to their bath and bed.

On the way downstairs, with the dogs surging ahead of them, Emma tucked her hand through Kit's arm. 'It's wonderful how the children restore me. I was tired when I came home.'

'They've exhausted *me*,' he said. 'I need a drink.' In the drawing room the tray had been laid out and he mixed the cocktail. 'How was the Glenforth-Williams?' he asked.

'Surprisingly biddable,' Emma said, kicking off her shoes and tucking her feet under her in the corner of the sofa. She had been asked to redecorate Veronica Glenforth-Williams's flat in Park Lane. 'She has a large collection of carved elephants – mostly ivory – which have to be accommodated, but otherwise she left it to me, as long as I made it "simply too marvellous".' She imitated Veronica's husky voice. 'I'm thinking of grey and scarlet. Pale grey walls, polished floorboards, scarlet cloth curtains and cushions. Those carved iroko settles that Lady Bellamy ordered and changed her mind about, and I know where I can get some Indian cabinets to match, for the elephants. And as a final touch, an enormous red painting for the wall, in an aluminium frame. Something really avant-garde so she won't know if it's good or not.'

Kit looked up at that. 'Have you got something in mind?' He was interested in all modern arts.

Emma smiled. 'As a matter of fact, I met a young man at Molly's last week who paints rather in the style of Paul Klee. I called in at his studio on the way home, and commissioned him to do a six-feet-by-eight-feet canvas of pure colour fields. He'll be glad of the work, and she'll think she's a leading patron of the arts. Best of all, it will look marvellous against my grey wall.'

Kit laughed. 'You are completely unscrupulous!'

'Not at all. He'll get a commission, she'll get what she wants, and everyone will be happy.' She received her cocktail glass from him and, as if it reminded her, said, 'The only drawback to the whole operation was that Mrs Simpson was there.' She sighed. 'Honestly, I can't seem to get away from that woman. Everywhere I go, I meet her, and she claims me for a friend. Wants me to call her Wallis, but I can't bring myself to reciprocate, so I'm "dear Lady Westhoven". But she calls *you* Kit,' she added, with a reproachful look.

Kit only smiled, topping up her glass with the dregs of the shaker. 'I'm a friendly sort of chap,' he said.

'You encourage her. I don't know why.'

'It amuses me. I want to see how far she'll go.'

'She's gone quite far enough without encouragement, from what I've seen. Everyone's talking about her and Wales. Your friend Thelma is completely ousted. Not only that, but Sarah Vibart learned from Eddie that the switchboard at York House has been given instructions not to put through any calls from Freda Dudley Ward. Now that's just spiteful.'

Mrs Dudley Ward, though many years retired from the post of royal mistress, had always remained on very warm terms with the Prince of Wales, and he had always been an honorary uncle to her children.

'It was HRH who gave the instruction.'

'Do you tell me Mrs Simpson didn't instigate it?'

'Perhaps.' Kit shrugged. 'But Freda should have taken a leaf from Violet's book and made a clean cut. It doesn't do to depend on Wales's loyalty.'

'Well, it seems Mrs Simpson's the top dog now. Apparently a car is sent to Bryanston Court at all sorts of strange times, even late at night, to take her to York House. *Only* her – the husband stays at home.'

'HRH wants his apartments redecorated and modernised, and she's advising him,' Kit said blandly.

'Oh, yes, I know she sees herself as a decorator – she tells me so every time she meets me,' said Emma. 'I could see she was furious today that Veronica had called me in instead of her.'

'Did she say so?'

'No, she wouldn't offend someone with influence like mine, but I could tell. Every time I suggested something to Veronica, she said, "Just what I was thinking myself. You have such good taste, dear Lady Westhoven – it exactly coincides with mine."'

'She didn't!' Kit said, exploding in laughter.

'Well, almost.'

'Don't you think she has taste?'

'She certainly dresses very well,' Emma allowed. 'I've no idea if she knows anything about interiors – she may do. But that's not the point. There's going to be an awful stink if someone doesn't persuade Wales to be more discreet. Taking her to a dinner given by the German ambassador last week! That sort of thing can't be kept secret. Alex Hardinge told Eddie that the King's starting to hear rumours.'

Alex Hardinge was assistant private secretary to the King.

Kit was sitting on the opposite sofa, very relaxed, his legs crossed, Sulfi half across his lap as usual and Eos leaning against his legs. 'He didn't "take her" to the embassy dinner. He only ordered her to be invited,' he said.

'Darling, you know it's the same thing. It's one thing for him to have a mistress – that's forgivable – but quite another to take her to official engagements, and be seen with her so blatantly. I don't know what he sees in her. She's smart and has a certain vivacity, but she's as plain as a post and terribly vulgar.'

Kit sipped his drink and said, 'I've told you before, it's not a lover he's interested in.'

'I know you said he wanted a mother, but what does that *mean*?' Emma cried in frustration.

'I'll tell you,' he said comfortably. 'Wales hates sex. He never wants to have to do it. That's why he likes older women, especially married ones, and why he keeps refusing to get married.'

'I heard the Palace is urging him to look at Frederica of

Hanover,' said Emma. 'Sarah said Alex Hardinge said the King is quite insistent Wales addresses her.'

'But he won't,' said Kit. 'She's young, and if he married her he'd be expected to do his duty and produce an heir. As long as he doesn't marry, he can be Prince Charming and have all the women in the world swooning after him, but he'll never have to do anything about it.'

Emma looked sceptical. 'Surely all men like sex. It's what we're taught from the schoolroom up.'

'Not *all* men,' he said. 'Just most of them. There are a few – just as there are some women – who find the whole business distasteful. Wallis is perfect for him because she hates it too.'

'Oh, how can you know that?' Emma exclaimed.

'Mipsy told me. Wallis told her long ago.' He smiled. 'As I said to you, ladies tell me all sorts of things. Once I get them in the mood, they forget I'm a man. So Wales is safe with the Simpson because he'll never have to do the horrid deed. And besides that, she's very quickly worked out what makes him happy. You remember that business over the muddy shoes?'

'Yes, I never understood why that didn't cause a ruction,' said Emma, frowning.

'She treats him like a stern nanny, and he loves it,' Kit said. 'He likes to be told what to do and be kept under discipline. Something to do with his childhood, I suppose, if we're to believe what Mr Freud tells us. But the sterner she is with him, the better he likes it.'

Emma shook her head. 'And I thought you were being serious!'

'I am, quite serious,' Kit said, but he was smiling as he said it, and she didn't believe him.

'Well, I suppose we'd better go up and dress,' she said, looking at the clock on the mantel. 'What's this dinner for? I've forgotten.'

'We're to meet the new German special envoy, fellow

326

called Ribbentrop. He lived in Canada for a long time, and in London and Paris when he was a boy, so he's fluent in French and English, and altogether quite civilised.'

'Thank goodness for that,' Emma said, standing up. 'Those dinners where the guest of honour has to be translated for are deadly.'

'And we're also meeting a very amusing Frenchman, Charles Bedaux, and his wife. He's about to depart on an expedition across Canada, so I suppose Lady Cunard thought he and Ribbentrop would have lots to say to each other.'

'Well, I hope I have someone amusing to talk to at the table. I suppose Mrs Simpson will be there?'

'Of course. She and Emerald are the best of friends.'

Emma groaned. 'She'll buttonhole me and talk about decorating again.'

'She may not. I hear that HRH may drop in. You know he has a ranch in Canada, so it's the perfect excuse for him. He and Ribbentrop can tell Bedaux all he needs to know. And Mrs S being American, she'll be practically on her own turf. She won't bother with you.'

'All the same, I'm not looking forward to tonight. Why did we accept?'

'You'll enjoy it when you get there. And it's Ascot next week. You know how you love the horses.'

The dinner turned out to be more enjoyable than she had expected. Ribbentrop was fair, blue-eyed and classically handsome, and though he didn't seem very bright, he certainly had social manners and fitted in without difficulty. Charles Bedaux turned out to be an interesting and very intelligent man – probably something of a rogue, Emma guessed, but amusing with it.

In addition there was an English actor turned film star, Edward Oxenford, who was very charming and funny. He immediately set up such a rapport with Kit that they had everyone in fits of laughter, until Lady Cunard said they should go on the stage together. Wallis Simpson said – rather acidly, Emma thought – didn't she mean vaudeville?

But she cheered up when the Prince of Wales arrived after dinner. She had a loud conversation with Ribbentrop about America and Canada. Emma thought there was some considerable flirting going on between them, which kept the Prince rather silent.

When HRH and Mrs Simpson left (together, which caused some eyebrows to rise), normal conversation was resumed, and Emma found herself talking with Charles Bedaux and his wife Fern. The expedition he was about to lead, she learned, would cross the wilderness of British Columbia, and make a movie about it at the same time. She found him very interesting, when she could hear him above the laughter being provoked by Kit and Edward Oxenford.

The Julians had James's book ready by the autumn of 1933, and it was accepted at once by the publisher who had approached him before he went to Bear Island, along with a dozen of his sketches as illustrations. They were very excited about it, and foretold large sales.

James was suitably grateful to the Julians for their work, but they said it had been a pleasure, that James had a clear and simple way of writing so there had been little to do beyond interpolating a little background geographical and biological information.

The book came out in the spring of 1934. He had letters from several of the Bear Island set, and from a number of strangers, praising it, and there was much excitement about it locally. Dozens of people brought copies for James to sign and he was stopped in the street to discuss it. But he took his new celebrity very quietly, and shrugged off the praise onto the Julians who, he said, had done the real work.

His illustrations were much admired. The owner of the shop in Low Petergate had sold all his stock of James's watercolours, and asked for more. James was pleased to go off with his painting equipment, Helmy, and some sandwiches in a satchel, to seek a little solitude and paint.

At the end of April he received a letter from a man called Charles Bedaux, who was to lead an expedition across the wilds of sub-Arctic Canada, beginning that summer. It seemed Bedaux knew Emil Bauer – all these millionaires knew each other – and Bauer had sent him a copy of James's book and suggested he was just the sort of man he'd like to have along. Bedaux had read the book and agreed. He would like to offer James an official role in the adventure. There was to be a moving picture made of the whole expedition from beginning to end, but how would James like to record it all in drawings and paintings?

'The best thing,' James told Polly, 'is that, this Bedaux fellow being a millionaire, not only will my expenses be paid but he'll pay me a fee as well. And, of course, if I keep a diary, there could be another book afterwards, like my Bear Island book. It could be a way for me to earn a living and pay you for my keep so that I'm not a burden on you.'

Polly was delighted for him. 'James Morland, Explorer! It sounds very well! But what sort of place will you be exploring?'

'It starts in Edmonton in Alberta, which is a city. I believe it's quite civilised – it has a railway, at any rate, and it's the centre of a mining area. After that, we set out into the wilds. I think it will be quite different from Bear Island – lots of forests and rushing rivers, bears and wolves and reindeer and so on. The object is to get to a place called Telegraph Creek, which I think is in the mountains, and then down to the Pacific coast. There are going to be so many wonderful subjects for painting.'

'Do you have to walk all the way?'

'Oh, no, there'll be vehicles. Part of the reason for going is to test some new cars that a friend of Mr Bedaux has invented – halfway between a car and a truck, with wheels on the front and caterpillar tracks on the back. The friend is the head of the Citroën car company so he's putting up some of the money for the expedition.'

'So you'll travel in these trucks?'

'Well, perhaps. But there'll also be a troop of Alberta cowboys going along, so I may go on horseback. I imagine if the way is very rough it'll be more comfortable on a horse than bumping about in a truck.'

'And what's this about a moving picture?'

'There's a big film crew going along. Floyd Crosby is in charge. He won an Academy Award a few years back. When the expedition's over, the film will be shown in cinemas all over the world and make a fortune.'

'I suppose that will cover some of the expenses, then,' Polly said.

'Yes, and the Canadian government's putting some money in, because where we'll be going is genuine wilderness, where man has never trodden before, so they're sending two geographers along to make maps as we go.'

Polly laughed. 'It sounds as though there'll be quite a crowd of you!'

'Oh, yes, about a hundred altogether,' said James. He looked concerned for a moment. 'It won't be very quiet with so many people along. I hope we don't scare off all the wild animals.'

But Polly was reassured by the numbers. 'There won't be any chance of you getting lost in the wilderness, anyway. I was rather dreading that you'd disappear and not come back.'

'Would you mind?' James said, almost shyly.

'Of course I would. You're my brother. I want you to come back safely to Morland Place and tell me all about it.' She touched his hand. 'This is your home, you know.'

He was pleased. 'If I do become an explorer, at least I'll be away a lot and not wear out my welcome,' he offered.

The expedition was to start in July, and hoped to reach

the Pacific Ocean in October; but Charles Bedaux insisted that everyone should assemble in Alberta in June, for special training before they set off. The trip would be long and arduous, and everyone must be as fit as possible, learn about living under canvas, and be trained in hiking, rafting and mountain climbing.

Before the departure date James went up to London to purchase suitable clothes and boots and other equipment, and a portable medical kit. Polly offered to advance him money for anything he needed, but he told her he had sold several paintings lately and still had money left from the advance paid on his Bear Island book, so he would be quite all right.

Everyone turned out to see him off when the day came. Polly was glad he was so happy and confident in his new role. James Morland, Explorer, Author and Painter, was a much more satisfactory person than James Morland the sophisticate and cocktail drinker had been. Though he no longer had an estate or a fortune, he seemed to her a much more desirable *parti*, and she hoped that one day soon he would meet a very nice girl who would realise that, and marry him.

Perhaps he'd meet an American millionaire's daughter, or whatever the Canadian equivalent was. Did they have millionaires in Canada? She had a vague idea that Canada was full of wild forests, but that meant logging and furs, didn't it – and had she heard there was mining, too? So there was no reason why there shouldn't be millionaires. And what could be more attractive for a millionaire's daughter than a handsome young Englishman from a fine old family on an exciting expedition into the wilderness? Although since his return from Bear Island he had been living quite frugally, it would be good for James to end up with money.

At the end of June 1934 Basil finished with school, having got through the sixth form without too much trouble, though equally without any great distinction. After the visit of the Flying Circus he had had quite a following in the lower school, and he had come to an understanding with the headmaster, whom he held in some respect. He was made a prefect, and he continued to edit the school magazine (which got him out of sports, which he loathed). Writing was supposed to be his strong suit and, with Mr Cockburn's encouragement, he built up connections with local and county newspapers, which the head thought might stand him in good stead later. It was plain to Basil that Mr Cockburn was gently nudging him in the direction of journalism as a career, and he did write one or two pieces that were published.

But Basil's object was to get through school life with the appearance of working and fitting in rather than its reality, and he hoped that life after school could be similarly negotiated. When asked by grown-ups what he meant to do when he left, it saved trouble to say, 'I'm interested in journalism, sir,' because it always elicited approval and rarely led to any further questions. But he was no more committed to the idea than to anything else.

What he did build up through the two sixth-form years was a network of good fellows, at his own school and at others, with whom he could while away his leisure hours in smoking, drinking and playing cards, and with whose people he could stay during school holidays. He wanted to avoid Portsmouth at all costs. The few weeks he had spent there had been deadly. The end of school life threatened a return not only to Portsmouth but to the parental home, with all its boredom and unwelcome scrutiny of his activities, and the growing pressure on him to do something to earn a living. Three years at university would have offered a respite and a chance to extend his idleness, but he had not shown any academic ability or bent, and his mother had said firmly that there was no point in wasting money on sending him there.

The Comptons were not rich. Airspeed had run into financial trouble the year before, and had had to be saved temporarily by a capital injection from four wealthy shareholders. Now it was in talks with Swan Hunter about a possible take-over, which would put it onto a firmer financial footing. Things were looking more hopeful for the future; but even so, it provided Jack with a comfortable rather than an easy living. And there was Michael to settle.

From the moment they had arrived in Portsmouth he had become fascinated by boats and ships. Jack had bought a small second-hand sailing dinghy, and taught him to sail, and after that there was no holding him back. He soon made friends with other lads and spent every free hour on the water in a variety of craft; he haunted the dockyard, went out with the fishing-boats, and offered himself as crew for races and at regattas.

Helen and Jack were happy to encourage such an innocent and healthy interest, though Helen was rather bemused: 'You'd think that, with a famous aviator for a father, he'd have a passion for flying instead of sailing.'

But Jack said, 'It's natural enough. The sea is in every Englishman's blood. And I started with boats, if you remember. I worked for Rankin Marine long before I got into the aero business.'

'Yes, but that's because aeroplanes hadn't been invented then,' Helen pointed out. 'If they had, you wouldn't have given boats a second glance.'

'I'd have gone wherever I could get a job,' Jack said. 'I had a living to earn.'

'Well, I hope Michael will be able to make a living out of boats one day, because he doesn't seem to be interested in anything else.'

In the spring of 1934, Michael came to his parents and said that he had decided what he wanted to do when he was grown-up.

'I want to be in the navy,' he said.

Helen and Jack looked at each other. 'Well, that's a facer!' Jack said.

Michael looked anxious. 'It is all right, isn't it, Dad?'

It was Helen who answered: a variety of thoughts and images had flashed through her mind, largely focusing on the hazards involved, particularly if there should ever be another war, and what it would be like to be waiting for news of her youngest boy as she had waited for news of his father. She concluded, for no very tangible reason, that he would at least be safer in the navy than in either of the other services.

The thought process was so rapid that she answered without a discernible pause: 'As long as you mean to be an officer, and not serve before the mast.'

'Oh, yes, Mum, if I can. I've been talking to Willans at school – he wants to be a sea officer as well, and his uncle's one, so he knows a bit about it. You have to go to the Royal Naval College, and if you said I could, we could go in together, Willans and me, which would be fun. But it would have to be this year because I'm practically too old.' He looked at them anxiously, his hands gripped into fists with the urgency of wanting it to come out all right. 'But the thing is, you see, it's sort of like a boarding-school, so you have to pay.'

'Ah,' said Jack.

Helen couldn't bear the anxious, pleading eyes. 'I'm sure we can manage something,' she said. 'After all, Basil finishes school this year, so we won't have his school fees to find. We'll look into it, Michael. Don't look so worried. It will be all right.'

When they were alone, Jack said to her, 'I'm not sure Basil finishing school is going to make him any less expensive to keep. And we already have Barbara at home.'

'We'll have to economise on them somehow,' Helen said firmly. 'We've got one son with a decent, respectable ambition that will take him off our hands for good. We can't jeopardise that.'

So it was looked into, the finances worked out, and the application made. Michael had an interview with the college commander, Captain Norman Wodehouse, whom he impressed favourably, especially with his good mathematics, but also with his cheerful nature and common sense. When the letter came saying he had been accepted at the handsome red-and-white college at Dartmouth in Devon – which, as a shore-based naval establishment, also had the ship name HMS *Britannia* – Michael was so overjoyed he turned three cartwheels, the last of which almost broke a window and sent the dogs into a frenzy of barking. He would enter in the new term in September, and spend four years there before starting sea training.

There was also a special summer camp on the Isle of Wight to get the new boys into the right frame of mind, and Michael and his friend Willans were both signed up for that. Helen thought her boy already looked older, and felt rather wistful – and that was before taking him to the approved outfitters in Portsmouth for his long-trousered uniform, which made him suddenly a stranger.

'You'll have to make a go of it now,' she said sternly, pushing the hair from his forehead and letting the hand linger an instant on his warm head. 'We've spent a fortune on your school kit, so you can't change your mind. It's the navy for you, my lad, willy-nilly.'

'I shan't change my mind,' he said contentedly, which convinced her more than a passionate assertion would have.

Helen had been wondering what to do with Barbara, who had turned seventeen in February. Finishing-school was the usual way of occupying a girl's time between the schoolroom and coming out, but they could not afford that now, not even one of the cheaper ones abroad. Nor was there any question of a formal coming-out, since they were no longer in that bracket in society. So Barbara stayed at home and helped her mother, and Helen tried to make sure she went to as many parties and dances as possible to give her a chance at meeting people. Barbara was not academically inclined, which was fortunate in the circumstances. It was also fortunate that she was a pleasant and reasonably popular girl, the sort who neither turned heads nor set up backs, an acceptable tennis partner and a good dancer.

There were a lot of settled naval families in the area, but also quite a lot in the aeronautical interest, retired RAF officers and the like. Jack's job gave him a wide circle of acquaintance among engineers and business people; and then there were the county people. So there was a large pool for Barbara to fish in, when the time came.

It came much more quickly than Helen had expected. The dances and parties of winter and spring gave way to the tennis and boating, cycling clubs and garden fêtes of early summer. Barbara was invited to most things, and seemed to enjoy them all in a calm way. She was good with a needle, and made a lot of her own clothes, which allowed her to look smart without straining family finances. She seemed to have a lot of girl friends – she was one of those middle-of-the-road girls whom everyone liked, and was known as a 'good sport' – but had not expressed, at least not to her parents, a preference for any particular boy.

One May day in 1934 she had been given permission to go out motoring into the country with a group of young people in three cars, with the object of having a picnic on Buster Hill, and stopping somewhere nice on the way back for tea. When the cars arrived, one of them was a fast little sports model being driven by an acquaintance of Jack's, an ex-RAF officer called Freddie Hampden. Helen was surprised: though he was one of those tall, fair, blue-eyed men who look much younger than their age, he was still a lot older than any of the rest of the group. She felt rather sorry for Barbara that the only spare seat left was in Hampden's car.

Barbara came home that day pink-cheeked and happy, and said that after the picnic they had all driven to Freddie Hampden's place in Petersfield, played cricket on his lawn and had tea there, which had been the greatest fun. After that, his name seemed to come up quite often in conversation. He had partnered Barbara at tennis at the Scott-Jacksons'; had rowed her on the river at the Bedhamptons'; had sat by her at tea at the Gadsbys' garden fête in aid of the hospital.

Helen mentioned it to Jack in bed one night, and said, 'I think I know what it must be. Barbara's not as pretty and lively as some of the other girls, and I suppose he takes pity on her if she looks like being left out.'

'That would be like him,' Jack said. 'He's a very decent fellow.'

'I'm sure,' Helen said. 'But what I don't understand is why he's at so many of these young people's affairs in the first place.'

'Oh, he knows everyone,' Jack said. 'I expect they ask him along as a make-weight. Anyway, he's not exactly an ancient stiff, you know. He can't be more than twenty-eight or thirty.'

'Darling, I think he must be older than that. Didn't you say he was in the RAF in the war?'

Jack yawned, and spoke indistinctly through it: 'Hmm, but only at the end. He joined in 1918.'

He fell asleep while Helen was still trying to work out how old that made him.

One Saturday towards the end of June, Barbara asked if she might go out in the car with Freddie Hampden alone. He wanted to drive her to Winchester to see the cathedral, and visit his great-aunt, who lived there, for lunch.

'Yes, darling, I suppose you may,' Helen said, mystified. 'But won't it be rather dull for you, without any of the others?'

'Oh, no, Mummy. I do want to see the cathedral. Freddie's talked so much about it.'

'Very well,' Helen said. She had no doubts about propriety: if Freddie Hampden couldn't be trusted to behave himself, no-one could.

When Barbara returned late that afternoon, Hampden did not just walk her to the door, but stood hat in hand waiting to be invited in. The brightness of Barbara's eyes ought to have warned Helen what was coming, had she been thinking in those terms. Jack was at home, and looked out into the hall at the sound of voices, and said cheerily, 'Hampden! Come in and have a drink!' And when they all went into the drawing room he shook Hampden's hand heartily and said, 'Good of you to chauffeur this child of mine around. What will you have? Whisky-and-soda?'

'Um,' said Hampden, looking embarrassed; and at the same moment, Helen noticed that he was holding Barbara's hand, and felt her scalp shift backwards in astonished realisation.

'Jack,' she warned.

Jack turned back the step he had taken towards the drinks tray and looked at her enquiringly, then at Hampden. 'Eh? What's the joke?' he said. From where he stood he could not see the linked hands. 'What have I missed?'

'Almost everything,' Helen said. 'We both have.'

'Bit awkward, this,' said Hampden, 'but to plug on: sir, I'd like to ask for your daughter's hand in marriage.'

Later, in bed, Jack said, 'She's awfully young.'

'Yes,' Helen said, 'but it's what she wants. I had a long talk with her in the kitchen while you were jawing with Freddie. All she wants is to get married and have a nice home and babies, and I don't think she's going to change her mind about that. Somehow or other, we seem to have raised a very dull daughter.'

'Hampden's a good sort of fellow,' Jack said, 'but so much older than her.'

'Not long ago you were telling me he wasn't so old.'

'He's thirty-five, apparently, and she's seventeen.'

'It is a big difference,' Helen admitted. 'But that's not to say it won't work. He adores her, *that*'s plain to see. And what will we do with her if we don't get her off our hands in this way?'

'That ought not to be the deciding factor.'

'It isn't. But just imagine her moping about broken-hearted month after month, just because she fell in love with a man older than herself. It would be very hard to refuse her permission to marry on those grounds alone. He's an awfully good match for her.'

Freddie Hampden had inherited from his father a factory on the outskirts of Portsmouth making aircraft-engine components, which provided him with a comfortable living, as well as a competence from his mother, and the house at Petersfield with pleasure grounds and about eight acres.

'And the best of it is, she won't be far away,' Helen concluded.

Jack noted that she said 'won't' and not 'wouldn't': she had made up her mind. He supposed he had, too: it was not an easy thing to contemplate, breaking your daughter's heart, and he had nothing against Freddie but his age. Indeed, he liked him very much, thought him steady and reliable, and was sure that he was no philanderer, and would take good care of his girl.

'I suppose the wedding will cost us a bob or two,' he said. 'We'd better start saving up.'

Helen moved against him in the dark, kissed his cheek in gratitude, and laid her arm across him. 'I knew you'd come to the right decision. And I've a little bit put away for the wedding.'

'How come?' Jack said in surprise. 'You didn't know about this, did you?'

'Simpleton,' Helen said. 'I've always known she'd marry somebody some time.' She sighed. 'Two down, and one to go. Now we only have to settle Basil.'

'Only!' Jack said.

Basil got off the train, his portmanteau in his hand, his hat on the back of his head, a cigarette in his mouth, and looked about the grey industrial spaces of King's Cross station as though it were a cathedral. The great locomotives sighed and huffed their way in and out. The vaulted roof was obscured with steam and smoke, the air was bitter with the smell of sulphur, every surface was begrimed with soot, and even the pigeons looked grubby, but to him it seemed the finest place on earth.

All around people were hurrying about their business, their faces mostly set in frowns of concentration, every one of them a stranger. Not a single soul knew that George Edward Basil Compton had just arrived in London, nor would care if they did. He was free – free at last! He looked at the people rushing around and past him, like a stream around a rock; he saw them weighed down with responsibility, with jobs and families, taxes to pay, bosses to suck up to and career ladders to climb, and thought he never wanted to grow that old.

He ought now to be making his way across London to Waterloo, but going back to Portsmouth had never been on his agenda. In Portsmouth lay post-mortems on his school life, recriminations, awkward questions about his future. Above all, Portsmouth was not London. Portsmouth was slow-moving, dull and provincial. It was Respectable. He would have to face it one day, he supposed, but not yet, not before he had had some fun.

He had a plan. At York station, while waiting for his

connecting train, he had sent a telegram to say that, as he was passing through London, he thought it only polite to call in and make his number with Aunt Molly and Uncle Vivian. Aunt Molly had always been fond of him and would probably ask him to stay a few days, which would give him the breathing-space to accumulate some more invitations. He thought sending the telegram while he was *en route* was a touch of genius: they would not be able to contact him to tell him not to.

He found a porter and had his trunk put into a taxi, then gave the address in Arlington Street. He thoroughly approved of the fact that Aunt Molly lived so centrally. The only possible awkwardness might be that he hadn't enough to pay for the taxi, but he was assuming someone would be in. As the taxi eased out into the street, he settled back against the leather to watch the sights of London pass the window, like a parade of entertainments arranged specially for him, stuffing his hands into his pockets and whistling 'Forty-second Street'.

The porter in Arlington Street recognised him, and cheerfully advanced the taxicab fare to save him keeping the driver waiting while he went upstairs. Moreover, he helped the driver bring the trunk into the hall, and said he would have it sent up later when the boy came back from an errand for Lady Daintry in 4B.

'Thanks, Webb,' Basil said cheerfully. 'I'll see you all right later.'

'Course you will, sir,' the porter said. 'Come to stay for long, have you?'

'Oh, I'm in no hurry!' said Basil, with a grin.

Upstairs in the flat he encountered a bit of luck. Neither Molly nor Vivian was in, but Charlotte was there, having been doing some work for the Dolphin Books scheme, typing letters and reports on Molly's machine. Her brother Richard had called in to see her, and she had just rung for tea. It was all much jollier than if the elders had been around. They were both pleased to see him and unsurprised by his presence: what was more natural, after all, than a nephew calling on his aunt?

The tea was excellent and ample, to Basil's relief – he was starving, having had to miss luncheon on the way down for lack of funds. The children were allowed to come in, and Basil, who was good with children, proved himself a dab at entertaining them, winning himself some useful credit with their nurse.

When they had gone, the atmosphere was so relaxed that Basil found himself, without intending to, explaining his situation and his problem. Charlotte, having only just gained her own freedom, was sympathetic, though rather puzzled that there was nothing in particular that Basil wanted to do. She knew the pain of being prevented from doing what you wanted to, but struggled a little to understand the pain of being prevented from doing nothing.

Richard, however, understood perfectly the lack of any ambition, and the faint amusement one felt when contemplating someone full of it, like his brother Robert. He sympathised with Basil, though he did suggest, mildly, that he would eventually have to find something to do. 'I don't suppose your people are terribly well off, not enough to keep you in idleness,' he said.

'You suppose right,' Basil said. 'Dad's a brilliant engineer, but that sort of thing doesn't pay.'

Richard nodded. 'The thing to do,' he said, 'is to find something agreeable by way of a job yourself, before they find something for you that you might not like half as much.'

That seemed good sense to Basil. 'At all events, I must avoid getting stuck in Portsmouth. I thought Aunt Molly would be good for a few days' board and lodging while I look around.'

'I expect she'll play along for a couple of days,' Richard

said. 'But if you like, I think I can probably get you in on my racket. You can drive, can't you?'

'Oh, yes,' said Basil. There was nothing to it, was there? He'd watched his father often enough. 'But is it fun?'

'I think so,' Richard said.

At that moment Molly arrived home, and looked at her increased household with a wry smile. 'Goodness, how people multiply when you turn your head! Richard, dear. And Basil – what a lovely surprise. What are you doing here?'

Basil stood up, smiled his most winning smile, and said, 'End of term, Aunty. I've just come down from Felixkirk, and as I had to pass through London, I thought I should call in on you. Mum sends her love,' he added.

'Are you staying to dinner?' Molly asked cordially.

Basil smoothed down his hair with one hand. 'Well, Aunty,' he said ingratiatingly, 'as to that . . .'

CHAPTER FOURTEEN

Helen put in a telephone call to Molly.

'I've just received a most peculiar letter from Basil. I understand he's with you?'

'Yes, he turned up quite suddenly. Do you want him back?'

'I don't want him to be a nuisance to you,' Helen said, which Molly thought somewhat equivocal.

'Oh, he isn't. He amuses me, and the children adore him.'

'He amuses you?'

'I think he's on his best behaviour so that I won't send him back to Portsmouth. He seems to have an unholy dread of the place.'

'Oh dear. I do wonder what we're going to do with him. But he says in the letter that Violet's Richard has said he can get him a job in the company he works for. Is that true?'

'Yes, apparently. He seems to have taken a fancy to him – Richard to Basil, I mean. Do you object?'

'I hardly know,' Helen said. 'It ought to be good for Basil to have a job of any sort, but the thought of him running loose and unsupervised around London makes me shudder. And where's he going to live? He can't impose on you.'

'Richard says there's a room becoming vacant at his lodgings at the end of the week. He can stay here until then – I told you, he's no trouble.' There was an expensive silence, and Molly prompted, 'You sound worried. I'll send him back to you if you don't think this is a good idea.'

Helen was torn. On the one hand, Basil had to start standing on his own feet at some point, and if he came home they would have to find him a job, which, given his lack of interest in any sort of career, would be difficult. On the other hand, experience had shown her that, with Basil, out of sight was rarely out of mind. 'What do *you* think?'

'I think he might as well try his wings, since he's keen to do so,' Molly said. 'Richard's trustworthy enough, and I can keep a distant eye on him for you. It might be just the thing to steady him. Having to earn it is the best way to learn the value of money.'

The deciding factor for Helen was the thought of Barbara's wedding, which was set for August and would involve a lot of work for her. It would be good to have Basil out of the way for a bit. She didn't suppose this 'job' would settle him down for long, but as a breathing-space it couldn't have come at a better time.

'Tell him I'll send him a cheque for his usual allowance, to get him started. But that will be the last. He'll have to use it sensibly.'

'I'll tell him,' said Molly.

'And don't let him be a nuisance.'

'I won't.'

Samuel Nevinson, proprietor of Mayfair Motors, was a businessman with no time for sentiment. He had surprised himself, four years previously, by allowing himself to be charmed into employing young Richard Howard to demonstrate and sell his expensive motor-cars, when everyone else in the business took salesmen on a commission-only basis. But he had not yet learned to regret it. Richard was good at his job, and brought in customers, and was a pleasant person to have around.

Nevinson was aware that it had been Richard's idea to expand into the hire business, though Richard, tactfully, always allowed it to have been Nevinson's own thought. When times were difficult and people hesitated to lash out on a new car, they still seemed ready to hire one, with elegant chauffeur, for a special occasion. Instead of standing useless in the showroom, the motors earned their keep; and when trade picked up he could sell them as well.

He had come to think of Richard almost as a son; and after he had invited the young man to his home in Earl's Court a few times to partake of family dinner, Mrs Nevinson began to entertain a hope that he would become their son indeed by marrying their daughter Cynthia.

So far Nevinson had not done more than hint in a general way that Richard might aspire to being more than an employee. 'I've no son to leave my business to,' he had said wistfully, once or twice. And, 'I'm getting to the age when I'd like to have a partner to share the burden with.'

Richard had seemed not to understand the hints, so things had moved no further along. Nevinson thought him too modest to understand his own worth.

The fact of the matter was that Richard understood well enough what he was thinking, but he was not yet ready to marry the boss's daughter, become a partner in the business and settle down. He liked Cynthia well enough, thought her a very nice girl, but he didn't want to marry. He didn't want a home, responsibility – scrutiny. He liked the anonymity of his shabby lodgings. He liked having his money to spend on himself, and his leisure hours to roam London, free as a cat, seeking pleasure on his own terms.

Even so, he had discovered in himself a good business sense, which had led to his making suggestions to Nevinson for expanding the enterprise. A new idea had come to him lately, as the nation's financial situation seemed to be slowly improving after the low of 1933. With a little more money and less anxiety, people were beginning to think about holidays, and to wonder about Abroad. There were men who had fought in the war and wanted to visit France in happier circumstances, parents who had never yet visited their son's grave, widows with children growing up whom they wanted to take to see their father's last resting-place. And there were others who simply wanted to have a good time in a foreign country but were a little nervous of taking the first step.

Richard gradually put into Nevinson's mind the idea of hiring out the car, with a chauffeur who would act as courier, and in addition making all the bookings so that the customer had nothing to do but pack and go. Offering the whole service would allow them to charge handsomely. The hotels would be glad of the business and probably pay a commission, too. All that was needed was a fleet of sturdy second-hand cars, and a cadre of bright young men to be the couriers.

Nevinson liked the idea. He discussed it with his wife, Hannah, who was always the cautious and level-headed one, and she thought it good. Second-hand cars were cheap enough to buy, and well-spoken young men from good families looking for a job were all too common. They would need an office with a telephone and a girl to do the bookings, but she and Cynthia could do the work to begin with, until they saw if it would take off.

'Yes, I think it's a good idea of yours, Samuel my dear,' she said to her husband. 'Not too much outlay to begin with, but something that can easily be expanded if and when necessary. What a clever husband I have! My mother always said you would prove so.'

She had a shrewd notion where the idea had come from, but her mother had also always said that it was a wife's duty to bolster her husband's confidence, and she always did.

So in the midst of all this glow of approval, when Richard asked about a job for a young cousin of his, Nevinson was only too glad to say, 'Sure, sure. Send him along to see me. A cousin of yours is bound to be a fine young man. And we'll need more drivers when we start to get bookings for Nevinson's Motor Holidays.'

Basil was peeved to learn that he would have to present a driving licence to Richard's boss before he could get a job. They could be obtained easily enough at the post office – he knew that – but they cost five shillings. He could think of a lot of more agreeable things to do with five bob. On the other hand, his whole scheme for staying in London depended on his getting some kind of temporary employment, until he had found his feet, so there was nothing for it. Fortunately he had borrowed a couple of quid from Richard, on the strength of the cheque his mother was sending him, so he had funds.

Aunt Molly's maid cleaned his shoes, sponged his suit and steamed his hat. He extracted a fresh razor blade from Uncle Vivian's bathroom – fortunately he used a safety-razor too. He borrowed a tie from Richard – all he had was his school tie, which took the description of 'the worse for wear' into new dimensions. He laid out a bob on a haircut at a little barber's in Stafford Street. And thus he presented himself at old man Nevinson's flat in Bramham Gardens looking like a smart young go-getter a man would be foolish not to hire.

Nevinson was already predisposed to like him, and Basil knew how to be winning when he wanted. It was second nature to him to charm the distaff side, and though Mrs N had disconcertingly sharp eyes, the daughter, he thought, was putty in his hands. He made her laugh, always the way to a women's heart, he believed; was just a little pathetic for Mrs Nevinson, to arouse her motherly instincts; and addressed Mr Nevinson with such respect and admiration that he was soon thinking Richard's judgement as sound as ever, and that this really *was* a nice young man. Before long sherry had been brought out and they were all chatting like old friends, and at the end of an hour Basil trotted down into the street with the promise of a month's trial at a wage that, though Nevinson had warned him was small, seemed to him princely, used as he was to pocket-money. It did not occur to him just then that it would have to pay for board, lodging, laundry and bus fares as well. Those things had come free to him in his life so far.

His first day at work was nearly his last. He was sent to fetch a Daimler that had been out on approval from a garage under a block of flats in the Marylebone Road. The garage attendant directed him to the numbered parking bay. He opened the door and got in, settled himself comfortably, breathing in the delicious aroma of new car – and realised he hadn't the faintest idea how to proceed. He had watched his father driving, yes, but not with any great attention. And this was a much more complicated machine, with dials and switches all over the place.

Fortunately, after he had been sitting there a while, growing more and more desperate, the attendant came over to him, and said, 'Anything wrong, sir?'

Basil liked the 'sir'. He bucked up considerably. 'Haven't seen one *exactly* like this before,' he said, as though his vast experience had unaccountably missed out just this one model.

'Beauty, isn't she,' the attendant said, admiringly, 'the Straight Eight?'

'Just what I was thinking,' Basil said.

'Three-point-seven-litre engine. Hundred-and-forty-two-inch wheelbase. Fluid Flywheel transmission,' the attendant crooned.

'Um,' said Basil. 'How do you start it?'

The attendant gave him the look of a man being woken from a dream. He became brisk, leaning in at the window. 'That switch there – that's your solenoid, see? Then your starter button's on the floor – there. That's your choke. Give her a spot of juice. Press the button, all the way down, and – up she comes! Lovely, ain't she? Purrs like a pussy cat.'

'Thanks,' said Basil. He really didn't want to have to drive off with an audience, so he smiled dismissingly at the man and took a long time over getting out his cigarettes and lighting one. The man took the hint and went away.

The drive back was a lively one, but Basil was a quick learner. He had difficulty getting out of the garage, almost ran into another car as he emerged onto the Marylebone Road, and misjudged a turn into a side street, resulting in an unfortunate meeting between the nearside of the bumper and a lamp-post. Fortunately he was going slowly at the time, and the Daimler was built like an armoured tank. He pulled up a little down the street to inspect the damage and found only a small dimple that he hoped would not be noticed. If it was, he was prepared to say the car had been like that when he collected it.

He did realise, though, that he needed a little more practice at this driving game. Having brought the Daimler home he was sent out on an errand to collect a cheque and the signed papers on a Rolls-Royce from the purchaser in Datchet, and was given a two-year-old Austin Twelve light tourer in which to do the journey. This was exactly what he needed. He took his time, and a roundabout route, and 'drove himself in', as he thought of it, coming to the conclusion, by the time he motored back to the main garage in South Kensington, that he had been right all along, and there *was* nothing to this driving business. In his confidence, cruising along, one hand on the wheel and the wind ruffling his hair, he whipped through a village rather too fast, misjudged a bend on the far side, rode up a grassy bank, and stalled. This gave the village bobby just enough time to catch him up on his bicycle, and give him a fierce lecture on speed and dangerous driving.

Basil had to use all his charm, tact and acting ability to persuade the bobby not to summons him. 'It's my first day in the job,' he said. 'I daren't get the sack. I really need this job.' He hinted at a widowed and dependent mother back home and made his lip tremble to enforce the pathos.

The policeman let him off with a warning; and then, impassively watching Basil trying to restart the car, gave him some useful advice about not flooding the engine.

At the weekend came two exciting events in his life. Moving into the rented room at the top of the house where Richard lived was the first. It was an attic room with an iron bedstead, a spluttering gas fire, one ancient armchair with broken springs, a small chest of drawers and a wardrobe wedged under the sloping ceiling with a door that kept swinging open. The curtains did not meet across the window, from which the view was of roofs and chimneys; the room had the peculiar acid smell of cheap furniture about it, and the shared bathroom was two flights down.

But Basil, fresh out of public school, had no high standards of domestic comfort. It was bigger than his study at Felixkirk, and it had a single gas ring in the hearth on which he could heat up baked beans, fry sausages and make coffee. Best of all, it was his! To him it was a palace.

And Richard was just downstairs and disposed to be friendly. On Saturday night he took Basil out to a club where they got chatting to some girls, danced, and were invited on to a party in a basement in Fulham. The basement was crowded and airless, there was only beer to drink and jam jars to drink it out of, and the man giving the party was a poet so they had to listen to a great deal of his poetry, accompanied by his earnest friend on a penny-whistle, but to Basil it was a taste of the sophisticated life he had craved.

And on Sunday – the second big excitement of the weekend – Richard took him to Brooklands and let him drive the four-and-a-half-litre supercharged Bentley he was buying by instalments round the track. 'Get it out of your system,' he advised.

'Get what out?' Basil asked.

'Any desire for speed and excitement. I've put my name on the line to get you a job, Basil old chap, and I don't want you throwing the firm's motors around and getting into trouble. When you drive a Nevinson motor or a Nevinson customer you are to be steady, sober and careful, and treat the goods like the most fragile of fine crystal.' Basil wondered if he had spotted the dimple in the Daimler's bumper, and tried to look innocently receptive of advice. 'So I thought I'd let you let off steam today. You can have three circuits, and then it's my turn. And if you harm a hair of her head, I will personally chop you into small pieces and stamp on them.'

'Thanks,' said Basil, heartfelt. 'I'll be careful.'

So he went into his second week of employment in a better frame of mind, gave satisfaction to his employer, and earned his crust. But by the end of the second week he found himself wondering whether it wasn't rather dull work. Boredom had always been his worst enemy. Was this all that life held? He thought he might look up some of his old boon companions, see if any of them had settled in or near London and might be up for a jolly. Richard was a good sort, but at twenty-three he was rather an aged stiff and set in his ways. Basil was convinced London ought to be more fun.

For Polly the most joyful evidence of the financial upturn was the resumption of work on Hull 534. In Saint-Nazaire the French were pushing on with building their SS *Normandie*, to a revolutionary design, which it was hoped would secure the Blue Riband for years to come, and to a degree of luxury they claimed had never been seen before. So national prestige was at stake: if the French could do it, why couldn't the British build a luxurious new liner? Besides, the levels of unemployment in the shipbuilding industry were the worst of any sector in the country. Clydebank had become almost a ghost town. The formerly proud workers, thin and shabby, sat around on walls kicking their feet, lounged on street corners, scavenged for coal and wood, picked up discarded dog-ends for a smoke. 'The dead on leave' was how one commentator described them. And behind the chained gates of the shipyard the gaunt skeleton of the unfinished ship emphasised the hopeless stagnation.

Under renewed pleading from the Clydebank MP, and with green financial shoots just beginning to sprout, the government agreed to lend the three million pounds needed to finish the ship, together with provision for a further five million if a sister ship were later to be built. The loan was made on condition that Cunard should merge with White Star: such 'rationalisation', as it was called, was the idea of the day, leading, it was believed, to greater resilience and efficiency. At any rate the companies preferred it to *nation-alisation*, which seemed to be the only alternative.

Polly's father, who had done work for both companies, would have approved. She was called to a meeting at Cunard headquarters in Liverpool, which she attended with John Burton, about the renewal of her contract. The chairman, Sir Percy Bates, said the ship was to be called *Victoria*, which fitted with the Cunard tradition of ship names ending in *ia*. White Star ships had always had names ending in *ic*, but since Cunard owned two thirds of the stock of Cunard White Star Ltd, they had little say in the matter.

Polly and Burton went from there to Manchester to give the good news to Mawson at the mills. Work resumed on 534 on the 3rd of April 1934, when three hundred workers, their faces almost bewildered with renewed hope, marched through the gates, accompanied by pipers playing triumphant tunes of glory, to face the task of cleaning off the hundreds of tons of accumulated rust and bird guano from the hulk, and restart the building. The ship was expected to be launched in September, when fitting-out would begin, and to make her maiden voyage in the spring of 1936. Carrying at least two thousand passengers, with two indoor swimming-pools, barbers and beauty salons, three dining rooms and an exclusive *à la carte* restaurant, the eighty-thousand-ton ship would require such large quantities of sheets, towels, tablecloths, napkins and other fabrics as to make the heart of a mill-owner rejoice.

Polly's shops were also doing better, her milk scheme was showing results and – a personal pleasure – Carr Underwood had finished his rebuilding at Moon's Rush, bought his first in-pig sows, had his first litters, sold his first porkers and was proudly paying back his loan. She often rode up that way when she had time. It gave her pleasure to see a man so happy about his work; to see trim pigsties and a neatly swept yard where there had been crumbling decay and weeds; to sense the hope and purpose about the place. And she had always liked pigs. She liked the way the sows would come and stand to have their backs scratched with a stick, grunting softly in pleasure, hedonists to their souls; she liked the way the little pigs minced about on tiptoe like fat ladies in over-tight high-heeled shoes.

One day in August, she and Carr were standing by the fence looking at the latest batch of porkers, happily grubbing in one of the fields.

'Better than a plough, that lot,' he said proudly. 'Jim Hackett, over to Prospect, he reckons to borrow a couple to clear an old orchard he wants to replant. I reckon I could hire 'em out, Miss Polly – what do you say?' He grinned. 'A lot o' them new houses going up need their plots cleared before the ladies and gentlemen can plant their gardens.'

'I'd stick to farmers,' Polly said. 'This lot look about ready – when are they going off?'

'Oh, a week or two. It were a good litter, that – Marigold's. I've picked out a couple o' prime gilts to keep. And Rosemary's given me a nice little pig I'm going to keep for me own boar.'

'That's a new departure,' Polly remarked.

'Aye, and it'll be a bit o' work, because I'll have to build a proper boar house for him, but it'll save money in the end. Folks hereabout with pigs all have Large Whites, so it costs a bit in travel to get a stud in.'

Carr, to everyone's surprise, had gone in for Saddlebacks. Polly thought they were even more delightful, especially when they were young: with their black faces, pricked ears and bright eyes, they seemed to her like playful dogs.

'A boar house?' Polly said. 'You haven't any more outbuildings to convert, have you?'

'No, but I've a heap of old stone and tile left over round the back, and some timber, and concrete's cheap enough. I'll build it myself. 'Twon't take long.'

'You're a good builder,' Polly said. 'You've made a nice job of that pig yard.'

He smiled shyly. 'I've another plan, but it'd take a bit o' time. I was going to talk to you about it, Miss Polly, see what you think. It's about th' old house.'

He took her back to the farmyard to explain. The old house had been L-shaped, and the main part, the longer side, was a ruin. The shorter leg was outwardly sound, except for a few missing tiles on the roof, but it was an empty shell.

'What I thought was, if I was to do up the inside, it'd make a right cosy little house. It'd need a chimney built, and a lean-to out the back for a kitchen, but I could build those meself all right. I could take timbers, bricks and tiles and anything I needed from the ruined part – sort of demolish it as I went along, if you see what I mean. It'd take a few years before it was all cleared away, but I reckon I could have the little house ready to live in in about a year. What do you think, Miss Polly?' He looked at her hopefully.

'It's a lot of work,' Polly said. And the work would be on top of what he already did, taking care of his pigs, which was a full day's work seven days a week.

'I'm not afraid o' work,' Carr said. 'What else is a man for? But the thing is, Miss Polly, there'd be some expenses. I can get most of what I want from the old house, but there might be some new timber wanted, and nails, and then there's plaster, and the plumbing and such. Some things'd have to be bought new.'

'Is that what you want from me?' Polly said. 'Another loan?'

'Well, miss, and permission. It's your house, after all. You might not want me messing with it.'

She smiled. 'When you'd finished "messing", I'd own a proper house instead of a ruin. I can see why I'd want it done, but why would you want to do it?'

He looked down at his feet and his ears went pink. 'I were thinking o' getting hitched.'

'Congratulations,' Polly said. 'I'm delighted for you. Who's the lucky girl, and when's the wedding to be?'

'I'm the lucky one, Miss Polly, for it's May Harris,' Carr said. She was the eldest daughter at Wood Farm, where he was lodging. Polly didn't know her, but had seen her once or twice – a tall, calm girl with pink cheeks and curly brown hair. 'As to when – that'd be when I'd a home to offer her.'

'Ah,' said Polly. 'Now I understand. You already have a tenant in mind for the rebuilt Moon's Rush.'

He looked up eagerly. 'I can make a go of it, Miss Polly, me pigs. When that lot o' porkers go off, and the baconers in the other field, I can near to pay off the first loan. I'll have me own gilts in pig by the end o' the year. I can charge stud fees for me boar when he's ready. There's a lot o' smallholders'll buy a weaner or two for their own back yard. And the price o' pig meat is going up. With eight acres here, I can run a hundred pigs, 'llowing for field rotation. I'd make enough to rent the cottage and the land and keep a wife. And if I were wed, she could keep chickens and tend a bit o'garden. We'd be right comfortable.'

Polly was smiling, considering the life and wondering at what another person could regard as comfortable. It would be endless, back-breaking work for both of them, and when the children came along any little luxuries they did enjoy would have to be forgone. Yet she remembered the poor in Manchester in their hopelessness, longing only for a job that would put the minimum for life on the table. Carr Underwood and his wife would be rich in comparison. Work was not an alien thing, or an imposition, to the likes of them. It was the root and basis of existence.

She could not possibly stand in the way of true love. 'I think it's an excellent plan,' she said, 'and I'm sure you and May will be very happy. As for the cottage, I shall pay for any materials you need to restore it, and considering the capital value you'll be adding to it, and the labour you'll be putting into it, as long as you farm here the rent will be a peppercorn.'

She discussed it with John Burton when she got home, and he agreed that she had said the right thing. 'It does nothing but improve the land,' he said. 'I just hope the extra work doesn't break Underwood's back.'

'I'm considering offering him a labourer to help him – otherwise I'm afraid poor May might be waiting a long time to be wed,' Polly said. 'I think he underestimates the time it will take to make that house habitable, given that he has a full day's labour with the pigs and can only work on it in the evenings.'

'That's a good idea,' Burton said. 'I know a family with a boy looking for a job – a nice lad, only fourteen, but strong and biddable. I'll arrange it for you, if you like.'

'As long as it doesn't upset Carr. I wouldn't want him to think I didn't trust him to do the work. I rather think he wants to build May a house with his own hands – a labour of love.'

'It's wonderfully chivalric, isn't it?' Burton said. 'Bringing a tribute to place in your lady's lap. The gauge of your love. For some men it's all the treasures of Araby, for others—'

'A cottage,' Polly concluded. 'And considering that I'm pretty sure the knights went off to the Crusades entirely for their own entertainment, the cottage seems to suggest a lot more devotion.'

'That's very romantic, Mrs Morland,' Burton said, laughing. 'I must remember to take bricks instead of gold when I go courting.'

Polly felt her face grow warm at the mention of courting, and at the use of her name. They were together so much that it was rare for either of them to use the other's name, which did away with any awkwardness, for she felt too close to him to call him 'Burton', though it would not be appropriate for her to call him 'John'. Equally, for him to call her 'Polly' would be quite wrong, yet nothing else really seemed to fit the bill. Sometimes he called her 'ma'am', but on his lips, she thought, the repellent little word sounded like an endearment.

She wanted to ask if he was thinking of going courting, but that would not be appropriate either, between mistress and man. And yet . . . would it be so very bad? He was an educated man, a gentleman. In the almost three years he had been with her, he had never spoken of there being any woman in his life. They got on well together, in an easy and companionable way, not like boss and employee but like two people with the same purpose, the same interest, the same end in view. She was sure he liked her – and was sure he must also know that she liked him. Would it be so shocking for her to provide Morland Place with a master? It needed a master; and she needed – oh, she needed to be loved! Sometimes she felt quite hollow inside for want of the warmth that came with that particular relationship. Nothing else replaced it. She had good, loyal servants and family around her, and her darling boy; she had horses and dogs, tenants who looked up to her, neighbours who wanted to be her friends. But she didn't have a husband. She had had one once; and she had had a lover. She could see quite well that the best of all would be to have the two in one person.

Little Alec loved Burton. She had had to stop him calling him 'Uncle John'.

She came back from her train of thought with a jerk, to realise Burton was looking at her quizzically, and had asked her a question.

'I'm sorry, I was miles away,' she said.

'I could see that,' he said, with a look that made her feel warm all over, it was so affectionate and understanding – almost, she might say, tender. 'I hope I didn't spoil a delicious daydream.'

'What was it you asked me?' she said, giving herself an inward shake.

'It was about the fête next week.'

Polly had reinstated the annual fête that Morland Place had given in August in her father's time – and, indeed, for generations before that. She and Burton had been planning it for months, urged on by the enormous local enthusiasm that had followed the visit of Cobham's Flying Circus two years ago. People were always asking her when she meant to do something like that again, so she had given in at last, and was now simply hoping the weather would be kind.

There were to be all the usual stalls, of local produce and crafts, and of food for sale – sweets, cakes, lemonade and so on; side-shows, like roll-a-penny, hoop-la, a coconut shy, a shooting booth, bowling for a pig, a merry go-round and swing-boats; and, of course, a beer tent and a refreshments tent. The Women's Institute was arranging a flower show in a large marquee; several brass bands were to take it in turn to provide music. For entertainment there was to be a children's pony show in the morning; a cricket match, farmers versus gentlemen, in the afternoon; and dancing in the evening, on an outdoor floor if the weather held out.

The day started off warm but overcast, and there were a few spits of rain first thing, which did not bode well. At breakfast everyone kept saying, 'Rain before seven, fine before eleven,' in tones of varying hopefulness. Polly had been out early with the dogs, checking on the stall-holders, who had started to set up at six o'clock, and were casting anxious glances at the sky as they worked. John Burton arrived as she was about to go back to breakfast, and she invited him along.

'Thanks, I've had mine. I'll keep an eye on things here.'

'The weather can't seem to make up its mind,' Polly said, as two raindrops struck her bare arm, and then no more.

'As long as it stays mainly dry, we'll be all right,' he said. 'A shower or two is bearable, but if it came on to rain properly . . .'

'Don't say it,' Polly shuddered. 'Oh, what's that big van?' She started towards it, but he caught her arm. His hand was very warm on her cool skin.

'That will be the swing-boats arriving. I'll go and see to them. You have your breakfast.'

'I really ought to—' she began.

'I'm here. And I'll have lots of help in a minute. You must be hungry. Go home.'

For a wonder, the adage worked: by half past eight the intermittent spits of rain had ceased and the clouds were higher; by half past nine they were breaking up, and by ten the sun was peeking through. The grounds were already crowded, the first of the bands was playing, and everyone was prepared to have a very good time.

Polly, in a short-sleeved cream linen dress embroidered with yellow and white daisies and green leaves around the hem and neckline, was relieved to be without coat or umbrella: she had planned what she would wear a long time

360

ago. Her hair was freshly waved and she wore a small round straw hat wreathed with artificial daisies to match her dress, and felt she looked at her best.

Just before eleven she was leading four-year-old Alec on his skewbald pony – which he had named Mr Pickles when he first got it, despite the fact that it was a mare – towards the marked-out ring for the pony show. He was looking smart, too, in jodhpurs, a little tweed jacket and velvet cap; he sat up proudly and rather wished his mother would not hold the rein because he could manage Mr Pickles perfectly well himself, even though she was a little peeky because of all the crowds and noise and coloured tents, to say nothing of the brass band. He had only recently come off the leading rein, and felt it was ignominious to be led, particularly in public.

As they walked across the field, neighbours stopped them every few paces to greet Polly, compliment her on the occasion and the weather, and to admire Alec. 'Is this your little boy? My, my, he has grown up into a fine young man. He does look a picture.' He did. He was a handsome little boy, with his mother's fair hair and blue eyes, and Mr Pickles, with her bold markings of cocoa and cream, her long mane and tail, was striking.

Mr Pickles didn't like all the interruptions. People kept stroking her, but they did not produce anything to eat, and in her view endearments without food were pointless. She began to wrinkle her nose at people in a way that Alec knew – and Polly would have, had she seen it – meant she was contemplating biting someone.

Fortunately the person she bit was Polly – a quick sideways nip of the bare arm, not meant to hurt but to warn. Polly flinched, and took the hint, extracted them and hurried on towards the ring at a quick walk.

There were three classes – under sevens, sevens to tens, and elevens to fourteens. Most of the under-sevens couldn't ride at all, and were to be led round the ring, clinging to the saddle, by a parent or groom; but there were a few five-and six-year-olds who could manage their mounts, and one or two cool-eyed tots who rode with frightening efficiency. At the collecting ring Alec begged his mother to let him go into the ring alone.

'I can handle her. *Please*, Mummy. Look, she's being ever so good now. Let me do it.'

He looked at her with such urgency – and he was so different from those baby clingers, some of whom were already crying – that she felt proud of him and nodded. He was a Morland, after all. Morlands were born in the saddle. It would not do to shame young Alec Morland, future Master of Morland Place, by leading him at his first show. When the entrants started to go in, she checked his girth, straightened his cap, made him shorten his reins, and sent Mr Pickles after the pony in front.

She heard the loudspeaker say, 'Ah, and next in is young Master Alexander Morland on Mr Pickles. Master Morland, just four years old, is the son of our generous hostess here at Morland Place.'

There was a burst of applause, and Mr Pickles gave a little frisk. Polly wondered if she'd done the right thing. Alec's cap had slipped, though he seemed otherwise undisturbed, still had his stirrups and the reins and was sitting up nicely. But Mr Pickles had her ears back, not a good sign. She—

'Mrs Morland, is it?' said a voice behind her.

She turned to see a tall, good-looking man in a light grey suit raising his hat to her. His hair was thick and dark, his eyes very blue – an alluring contrast – and his smile was very pleasant. He seemed to be in his early forties. By his side was a young man who looked too much like him not to be his son – he seemed to be about nineteen or twenty – and on his arm was a girl about two years younger, whom Polly took to be his daughter.

'May I introduce myself?' the man said. 'I would not take

the liberty except that we are neighbours. My name is Eastlake – Charles Eastlake – and these are my children, Mary and Roger. We are the new tenants of Shawes.'

Polly shook his hand, which was dry and firm. The girl smiled shyly but did not offer her hand. The boy was staring at Polly intently, unsmiling, but at a meaning cough from his father he whipped off his hat and gave her hand the briefest shake.

'I had no idea Shawes had been let,' she said, 'though I know they were looking for a tenant.'

'We only moved in yesterday,' said Eastlake. 'What a lovely place it is! An architectural gem.'

'It is, but I hope it's comfortable as well,' Polly said. 'These old houses need a lot of attention, and landlords are not the same as owners. If there's anything I can do to help you settle in . . .'

'You are very kind,' he said. 'And as soon as we have everything arranged, I hope you will do us the honour of dining with us.'

'It would be a pleasure,' Polly said. 'But you must come to Morland Place first. Is Mrs Eastlake here?'

'I'm afraid my wife is no longer with us.'

'Oh, I'm sorry,' Polly said.

'Please don't be. It was a long time ago – Mary was only two when she died.' It was said without pathos. 'They don't really remember her.'

'It must be hard to bring up two children alone,' Polly said.

'I'm sure you know how hard.' His eyes were full of sympathy. 'I believe you are widowed too. Forgive me, but the house agent told me a little about our nearest neighbours.'

At that moment there was a commotion in the ring, and Polly, her mother's instincts on the alert, turned in time to see Alec part company with Mr Pickles, who dodged out of line and cantered round the ring, giving one or two flirty bucks and upsetting several other ponies. Mr Pickles got to the exit but there were too many outstretched hands there for her liking so she carried on round to where she had deposited her rider. Meanwhile two other bodies had hit the ground, several ponies had started grazing, and a number of children were crying. Polly had already started to run, pushing her way through the crowds, but by the time she got to the ring someone else had reached Alec – already on his feet – and had caught Mr Pickles, who had come back to him in the hope of starting the game again.

As Polly hurried towards them, she saw, to her surprise, that it was Roberta, looking very smart in a fawn skirt, white blouse and navy-blue beret.

'I'm all right, Mummy,' Alec cried, pale with anguish. 'She bucked and I fell off but I'm all right. Let me get on again.' He couldn't bear the idea that everyone was watching and believing he couldn't ride. He *had* to get back on. Josh, his groom, said only a little piker made a fuss when he took a tumble. He would die of shame to be thought a little piker. '*Please*, Mummy.'

Mr Pickles, annoyed at having been caught so soon, thought to exploit the situation by flashing one of her patented sideways nips at Roberta, and was surprised to get a sound slap on the muzzle for her trouble. She looked instantly chastened.

'He'll be all right,' Roberta said, across the pony's neck to Polly, and added, *sotto voce*, 'Don't show him up.'

Polly nodded, though her agreement was hardly needed, for Roberta was already grasping Alec's leg to toss him into the saddle. She found his stirrups, shortened his reins, and, gripping Mr Pickles by the bit ring, gave her a little shake and an eye-to-eye glare that warned terrible retribution if there were any more playing-up. Then she grasped Polly by the arm and escorted her away.

The loudspeaker said, 'And our brave little girls and boys are all aboard again, so we can resume the class.'

The line moved off. Roberta said, 'I was right opposite so I saw what happened. The sun flashed on something – I think it might have been the band's tuba – and that naughty pony took the excuse to buck. He's a good little rider. If he'd been paying attention he wouldn't have come off. It's a good lesson for him. Look how he's riding now.'

Polly laughed. 'Determination personified!' They ducked under the rope, out of the ring, and she said, 'I didn't know you were coming. It's lovely to see you.'

'I'm here with Hilary,' Roberta said. 'Oh, here she is.'

Mrs Maddox came up to them at that point, and shook hands with Polly. 'I've brought my young nephew and niece and their ponies for your eleven-to-fourteen class. I thought it was time Bobby and I had a little fun. The unbent bow, you know.'

'We've two horses running at York next week,' Roberta said eagerly. 'Our filly Zarina is going to win the Yorkshire Oaks. You should put something on her.'

'I will,' Polly said. 'And I'll come and watch her run, as well. So, are you still enjoying your job?'

'Oh, yes! And I've learned *so* much. Hilary is wonderful – lets me do everything,' she said adoringly.

'I couldn't manage without her,' Mrs Maddox said.

Roberta looked at the ground and went a little pink. Polly was glad that one of her charges seemed to be so happily and permanently settled.

'Oh, they're giving out the rosettes,' Mrs Maddox noticed.

Polly turned to look. Alec was being called into the middle, but Mr Pickles had seen some of the other ponies heading for the exit and obviously felt that was the direction for her. Alec couldn't turn her, so Polly had to dash in to the rescue. Alec, with three other children, was given a white 'highly commended', and was as delighted with it as if it had been the King George V Gold Cup.

Polly watched proudly as he joined in the lap of honour, rising nicely as Mr Pickles trotted in line, and caught the mare deftly when they came round again just before she made an inelegant dash for freedom. Alec, happily patting Mr Pickles's neck and admiring the rosette, had no objection to being led now it was all over.

As they came out of the collecting ring and Josh appeared to take the bridle, Polly's attention was distracted by someone else waiting off to the side to talk to her. 'Take them back to the house,' she told Josh. And to Alec, 'Let Nanny change you and wash your hands, and then Doris can bring you back to look at everything.'

'Yes, Mummy. Wasn't Mr Pickles smashing? And, Josh, I fell off when she bucked but I still got a sustificate, and I didn't blub. Lots of them blubbed, didn't they, Mummy?'

'That's right, son,' Josh said. 'A real horseman never blubs, and he always gets back on.' He knuckled his forehead to Polly and led the pony away, the boy chattering eagerly to him.

Polly turned and went towards John Burton, looking very handsome in a suit she hadn't seen before and a new tie; he was waiting for her, smiling. There was a young woman beside him, with her hand through his arm. Polly frowned. She didn't think she had ever seen her before. A cousin? She knew Burton had no sister.

'Mrs Morland, may I present someone to you?' he said. Polly looked at the young woman. Probably about twenty-five, not as tall as Polly, slender, with light brown hair under a small, round navy hat, ready-made navy linen two-piece with a sailor collar, and white gloves. She had a sprinkling of golden freckles across her nose, and there were sparks of red in her hair where the sun caught them; her eyes were greenish-brown. Nothing about her would have attracted a second glance from Polly, had she not had her gloved hand on Burton's forearm. Polly gave a polite smile; the young woman looked at Polly with admiration.

'This is Joan Formby,' Burton said.

Hands were extended and Polly saw the state of her own glove just too late. 'Oh, I'm sorry! I've been holding my son's pony.'

'That's quite all right,' Miss Formby said eagerly. 'I saw you in the ring. Your son is a fine little rider – John pointed him out to me.'

John? thought Polly. She must be a relative, then. She gave Burton a look of enquiry.

'Joan has done me the honour of agreeing to marry me,' Burton said, smiling down at the young woman, who gave him a quick glance upwards that would have melted any man.

Through the thunder in her ears, Polly heard herself say, 'I had no idea – that is, congratulations. And felicitations to you, Miss Formby. Have you – have you known each other long?'

'We knew each other at Long Riston,' Burton said. 'Her father is the curate there.'

'But Daddy was transferred to Wetherby last year,' Miss Formby went on, 'and I met John again when he went to visit his parents there. And – well . . .'

'We've been walking out ever since,' said Burton. He looked at Polly, smiling, his eyes meeting hers with the same frank warmth as always. His friendly openness evidently expected her to be as pleased for him as he would have been pleased for her in the same circumstances.

My mistake! her mind cried. *All my stupid, ridiculous mistake!*

Now it was only important that she cover her shame, retreat with honour, *never* let anyone know the foolish ideas she had been harbouring.

'When will the wedding be?' she asked, with a bright smile that she felt almost damaged her face to assume. 'And where?

In Wetherby, I suppose. A bride marries from her father's house, does she not, Miss Formby? Oh, but you will need a new house, Burton. Your cottage won't do for a married man.'

It hurt her to call him Burton, but what else could she do? She was his employer, after all.

He didn't seem to have noticed. 'It's quite adequate for us to begin with,' he said, 'but thank you for your concern. I dare say we will need something a little larger if – when – our family increases.' Miss Formby's cheeks reddened at the suggestion, but her eyes did not leave Burton's face.

Polly felt she could bear no more. 'We'll see about that when the time comes,' she said. 'I must go – I see Mrs Chubb calling me. My heartiest good wishes, once again.' And she hurried away, blindly, into the crowd.

It seemed a long day. Polly went through it with a fixed smile, saying the right thing to everybody. Despite the crowds Burton and his fiancée seemed to be everywhere she looked – or was it that he just always drew her eye? That ordinary girl on his arm – how had she managed to capture his heart? Perhaps he was an ordinary person, and she had invested him with qualities he didn't have because she had needed to. She felt embarrassed and ashamed, and prayed hard that he had never noticed her foolishness. She thought he hadn't: he had not shown any awkwardness when introducing Miss Formby.

The weather held and the open-air dancing went ahead. Polly opened the dance with Lord Lambert, as had been arranged, and thought after that to escape, but as she came off the floor she was accosted by Charles Eastlake, and was not ready enough with an excuse to get out of it. But he was a good dancer, and looked at her with admiration, which was balm to her hurt pride. He complimented her on the day, said it had been a splendid affair, and thanked her for letting him partner her.

'I was astonished at my luck,' he said. 'I'm sure every man in the Riding must be glaring daggers at me right this minute.'

Polly smiled a little at the exaggeration, and said, 'Every man in the Riding isn't here, Mr Eastlake.'

'Then they are very foolish to miss the chance of dancing with the lovely Mrs Morland.' Unconsciously she made a weary movement of the head away from the compliment, and he said, in a different tone, 'I'm sorry. You must be sick of flattery, even when it's sincerely meant.'

'It's been a long day,' was what she said in reply. His quickness of observation had comforted her a little.

'Shall we just dance, and not talk, then?' he said kindly.

'If you wouldn't mind,' Polly said gratefully. So they did just that. When the dance ended, he gave a little half-humorous bow, said, 'I hope we meet again very soon,' and took himself off.

When it was all over, and Polly trudged back to Morland Place, Barlow met her at the door and said, 'A very successful day, madam, from all I heard. Will you take supper? The rest of the family is in the drawing room.'

'I'll have a tray in my room,' Polly said. 'I can't face any more talk tonight.'

'Very good, madam. And the post is here.'

'I'll read it upstairs,' Polly said.

In the haven of her room, her maid, Rogers, helped her into her dressing-gown, took away her clothes, and returned with a tray of supper, which she arranged on the small table in front of the fireplace.

'Thank you, Rogers. I won't need you any more tonight,' Polly said. Rogers poured her a glass of wine and left. The kitchen had sent up cold chicken and potato salad, and an apricot tart, and Polly found herself quite hungry. As she sipped the wine she leafed through the letters and found one with an American stamp and handwriting on the envelope she recognised. It was from Lennie – dear Lennie! She put the glass down and eagerly opened it.

A moment later she was staring at the firm black strokes of his writing, trying to make them mean something else: '. . . known her for almost two years, but never felt able to tell you, simply because I could never be sure of her, right up to the moment she said yes . . . so modest, she does not know her own worth . . . think you'd like her, Polly – at least, I hope you will . . . visit England one day, but she does not like to leave her invalid mother . . . simple ceremony before the Justice, no guests, was what she wanted . . . write again when we are back from honeymoon . . .'

He was married. Lennie was married. Her Lennie, who had always loved her and sworn he always would, who had never cared for another woman since he had first met her, when she had been still too young to marry – Lennie had fallen in love with someone else and wedded her.

And now she was alone. She had lost Ren, she had lost Erich, she had lost her father; she had lost John Burton (though she was too ashamed to say those words even inside her own mind, but the knowledge was there); and now the one man she had always been able to count on had abandoned her too. She felt utterly bereft. Who cared for her now? She saw her life stretching away before her, like a bare and dusty road to be travelled, carrying the great burden of Morland Place, with no-one to help her.

Supper forgotten, she put her head down on her arms and wept. Fand made unhappy sounds and pushed his head onto her lap, licking her fingers.

I miss James, she thought.

BOOK THREE

Resolutions

Love can tell, and love alone,
Whence the million stars were strewn,
Why each atom knows its own,
How, in spite of woe and death,
Gay is life, and sweet is breath.

Robert Bridges: *My Delight and Thy Delight*

CHAPTER FIVE

CHAPTER FIFTEEN

James was discovering that his trip to Bear Island had been no preparation for an expedition with Charlie Bedaux. The millionaire was fond of his comfort, which meant those around him benefited too. From the beginning, when James boarded a proper liner and was shown to a proper cabin – second class, but still – he realised this was going to be a very different experience. Bedaux had brought along not just his wife, but his mistress, an Italian countess: it was clear he did not mean to forgo any luxury.

The training camp, based in the town of Jasper, Alberta, was meant to give them their first taste of the wilderness and get them all fit for the adventure; but the people of Jasper were so excited by their presence they had laid on a full programme of entertainments and banquets, so no training ever got done. James discovered that Charlie's under-lying reason for the expedition was to gain publicity for himself and his business, in pursuit of which he was just as happy to attend receptions, drink champagne and give inter-views to journalists as to fell trees and erect tents.

It was no better when they moved to Edmonton, a town perhaps even more excited to be having them, if only because it was larger and contained more people. James got the impression that nothing very much ever happened in Canada, so any distraction was prized. There were more parties, more banquets, more receptions, more – much more! – champagne.

And the young ladies of Edmonton were so excited by James, who was as handsome as a film star, and English ('Say something! I love that accent!'), that he was in severe danger of finding himself engaged if he didn't pay attention and remain at least relatively sober.

The person who kept him on the straight and narrow was a very cool young American woman called Meredith McLean, who was secretary to the expedition and probably the only person who knew exactly what was happening. She knew the names of everyone who was going and pretty much where they were at any time; she liaised with the locals over accommodation and the purchase of supplies, dealt with currency, kept track of bills, and answered all the questions that Charlie could not be bothered with. She had short, thick dark hair and a rather boyish figure, and since she – rather sensationally to James – dressed in khaki trousers and shirt and strong boots, she could be taken from the back for a boy as she strode about the streets in the course of her duties. But she had packed a few dresses, and at the banquets and receptions proved herself all woman, particularly in the deep red silk one that James quickly came to like so much.

It was under Meredith's guidance that James bought himself a wide-brimmed 'cowboy' hat and a deer-hide jacket, more practical than the good English wool he had brought. And with her help he acquired a horse, which the expedition paid for. It was a dark chestnut gelding with a white star, a pleasant-natured animal that James soon grew fond of. Canadian horses, he learned, had Arab and Barb in their blood: they were supposed to have first been sent to Canada by King Louis XIV in the seventeenth century, the best of the French royal stable. In his honour James called his gelding Sun King, but quickly shortened it to Sunny.

Once he was thus attired and mounted, Floyd Crosby, the film director, thought he looked so picturesque that he expended many feet on James, under the tutelage of the

Alberta cowboys, learning to ride cowboy-style and throw a rope, and schooling Sunny, jumping over tree trunks and fording streams. 'This'll give a very good idea of our training schedule,' he told James, and had him finish up by pitching a tent and sitting down cross-legged to a campfire meal with Sunny tethered conspicuously nearby.

James also had time to become acquainted with the five Citroën half-track trucks that were to go with them on the expedition. His time on Bear Island had taught him a lot more about the maintenance of motor-vehicles, and Charlie Bedaux encouraged him to 'get under their hoods', and to try them out over some rough terrain. James enjoyed himself, bouncing them about and prodding their innards, but he was glad he had decided to do the trip on horseback.

They finally started out on the 6th of July, after a champagne breakfast with the great and good of Edmonton, and were led out of the city by the lieutenant governor, in a parade down Jasper Avenue between cheering banks of what seemed to be the entire population of the city. Weeping young women waved handkerchiefs, and James, mounted on Sunny, waved back, winked, and smiled extravagantly, knowing he was safe now.

No sooner were they out of the city and on their own than it started to rain. But spirits – and the level of champagne in the blood – were too high for this to dampen enthusiasm, and the mighty convoy started off north-westerly towards Grande Prairie and the border with British Columbia.

James rode up and down the line to get an idea of where everyone was and how they were settling in, for he meant to keep a diary and write it up every night for the book that was to come afterwards. He found the car where Meredith was riding, her shiny bronze head bent, still doing paperwork.

'Shouldn't you be enjoying the scenery?' he asked her.

'There'll be plenty more scenery before we're done,' she

said calmly. 'Someone's got to keep everything in order.' She gave him a clear look that James hoped was admiring, but she was very good at not giving away what she felt, which was part of her power. Even Charlie was a little scared of her; James was utterly enslaved. 'You enjoy it for me,' she said. 'You look the part in that hat. Go be a cowboy.'

Progress was slow because the movie team had to get ahead and film them coming towards them, then get ahead again, so there were lots of stops; and when they stopped, the chuck wagon had to produce coffee, and people spilled out of their vehicles to chatter to each other about their impression of the journey so far. James used the stops to make sketches. He thought at this rate they would never get to the Pacific. But the roads were good and level, so in spite of everything they made reasonable time.

When they stopped for a meal in the middle of the day, Meredith came and found him.

'Admiring the scenery at last?' he teased.

'Just stretching my legs,' she countered. She sat by him while they ate fried steak and potatoes, and amused him by telling him the background stories of the various people she pointed out. James asked her for her own, and she told him only that she was the daughter of a Wyoming rancher before deftly turning the conversation to him. When they started off again, he realised he still knew almost nothing about her. She spoke like an educated person, so he was sure there must have been more in her past than simply raising cattle. But the trip had only just started, so there was plenty of time ahead, and he looked forward to finding out what it was.

Basil went home in August for Barbara's wedding, and for once was glad that attention was on someone other than him. Not that he had been doing anything very bad lately, but he worked on the principle that whatever he wanted to do, his parents would probably want the opposite, so it was best to keep them from discussing the question.

His mother had no time to do more than ask if he was well, push his hair back and tell him he needed a haircut. Besides the wedding, Michael was just home from the cadets' camp, looking taller already, very brown, and full of stories about what they had done and the various splendid fellows he had met who would be his new friends when he went to Dartmouth. So Basil was free to lurk in the background, tease the dogs and escape into the garden to smoke.

On the wedding morning all he had to do was to keep out of the way, and answer the door to the telegraph boy, the postman, several messengers and the florist bringing the bride's bouquet (white roses and lucky white heather) and the buttonholes. Upstairs, his mother, Barbara and the two bridesmaids had been closeted together since – it seemed to him – dawn. Michael had wisely 'popped out' to the dockyard to see what ships had come in, and his father was reading the paper in the sitting room and looking nervous.

This was such a remarkable thing to Basil, who had never known his father afraid of anything, that he actually went in and asked him if anything was the matter. There was a strained look on Jack's face and his lips kept moving silently.

Jack looked up at Basil's question, hesitated, and then admitted, 'I *am* a little nervous. Never given away a daughter before. And there's this damned speech I've got to give. Your mother wrote it down for me and I've memorised it, but I have to keep practising it inside my head or I'll forget it, so if you don't mind, old chap, I'd rather not talk.'

'Have a quick one,' Basil recommended. 'That'll settle the nerves.'

'I can't have alcohol on my breath,' Jack objected.

'Sherry, then,' Basil said. 'No-one will notice that.'

So he persuaded Jack into a small sherry, and took the opportunity for a large whisky-and-soda for himself. Not that he had nerves, but he suspected he might need it before the day was out. Things could get very boring, he thought.

When Barbara came downstairs he went out into the hall to see her. Her wedding gown was of bias-cut white silk, close-fitting with long sleeves, the skirt flaring below the knee, and she wore a little round white cap covered with lace, from which hung the full-length veil. Basil thought white was not really her colour, especially as she was pale with nerves. 'You look as though you're about to be sick,' he greeted her.

'Beast,' she said.

He handed her her bouquet. 'Too much white,' he said, waving a hand at the ensemble. 'The dress, your face and the flowers – I'm afraid I'll get snow blindness.'

'Double beast,' Barbara said, and her lip began to tremble.

He took her free hand – it was like ice – and squeezed it. 'You don't look half bad, though,' he said, smiling. 'I'm damned jealous of this fellow taking you away from me. You swore you'd always love me best.'

'That was when I was ten,' said Barbara. 'But I do love you. I always will. This won't change anything.'

'I love you too,' he said, kissing her cheek. 'Even if you do look like a gigantic ice-cream.'

Helen came down the stairs. 'Stop teasing your sister, and go and see if the cars are here,' she commanded.

Basil caught sight of the bridesmaids carefully descending behind his mother, and was happy to comply.

The wedding was at St Thomas's, with the reception afterwards at the Keppel's Head. Basil thought the whole thing a frightful palaver, and the bridegroom a dull stick. He'd obviously had a last-minute haircut and the shortness of his hair made him look older than he was; his necktie seemed to be choking him and he hardly had a thing to say. He looked at Barbara as though she was a goddess descended to earth – *Barbara!* – which proved he was simple-minded.

Still, if he did the right thing by her . . . And he seemed very eager to please, which made Basil think he'd be an easy touch for the odd fiver or so at some time. It was good that Babsy had chosen a man of comfortable means. He hoped they would entertain lavishly: he didn't know Petersfield, but it was not too far from London and he'd go down there if they did the thing right.

The reception seemed pretty lavish, and Basil wondered how the Aged Ps had afforded it. He tucked away as much food and drink as possible, thinking he'd better get their money's worth for them, endured the speeches, and during the dancing afterwards did his duty by both bridesmaids before slipping out at the back to fortify himself with his flask, which he had filled before he left home with his father's whisky. This wedding business seemed quite bizarre, a custom from another planet almost, after his recent life in London. He had had a brief talk with his mother the evening before, when she had asked him how he liked his job, and he was able to say truthfully that he enjoyed it, on the whole.

'But it's not a career, darling, is it?' she had said anxiously. 'You can't want to be a chauffeur all your life.'

'It's just something to do while I look round, Mumsy,' he said. 'I'll find something eventually. I don't want to rush into anything too quickly and get stuck with it.'

And his mother had sighed. 'I wish you knew what you wanted, like Michael.'

'Well, I'm not going to be a powder monkey or a drummer boy, or whatever he is, even to please you, Mother dear. Not my style at all.'

'But what *is* your style?' Helen had asked and, looking at him quizzically, had added, 'You look different, somehow. I suppose getting a job has changed you.'

Fortunately she'd had too much to do to pursue the thought. Actually, it *was* the job that had changed him, but not in the way she meant. A new factor had recently entered into it. He had been directed to drive a lady twice a week to a health spa out in the country, where she was taking a 'slimming cure', involving, he understood, steaming and massage. He didn't know how old she was, not being very good at ages, but certainly older than him. She was also extremely handsome (he didn't think she needed a cure of any sort), rich, amusing, and had taken a distinct fancy to him.

It had started with her lighting his cigarettes while he drove – she liked to ride in front with him. She would put the cigarette in her own lips, light it, then pass it directly to his, an act of sensuality that had come as a surprise to him. The second time he drove her, she had invited him up to her flat in Park Street for a drink. The third time had ended with him in her bed.

He had a mistress! He liked the sound of those words inside his head. It was not something he could tell his mother, of course – indeed, he would be horrified if she came near to guessing – but he was pleased to think it had made its mark on him. Mrs Rampling was much more interesting to make love to than the pub and farm girls he had practised on before. She was teaching him a lot, as well as providing pleasure enough to keep him going all day long, just thinking about it. And though his mother might think he needed a haircut, Mrs Rampling – Gloria – liked his hair just as it was, thick enough to run her hands through.

In August, Emma and Kit had been invited to Biarritz to join a party hosted by the Prince of Wales, who had taken a villa for the whole month. Mrs Simpson would be there, but for the first time Ernest Simpson would be absent, which seemed to mark a change in the relationship that Emma thought rather ominous. Jack Aird, who was equerrying, was outraged about it.

Kit had accepted the invitation without consulting Emma,

and she was annoyed. 'I thought we were going to Walcote for the whole of August. I have things planned.'

'You don't say no to the heir to the throne,' Kit said.

'*You* don't,' Emma retorted crossly.

'Besides, Teddy Oxenford's going. You know you like him.'

'Yes, but not half as much as you do. And every time you fall in with HRH's plans you expose me to the Simpson woman. She already believes we're the best of friends, and while you're playing the giddy goat with Teddy, I'll be stuck listening to her lectures on politics and art.'

'Well, it's done now,' Kit said. 'You can enjoy the things one enjoys at Biarritz and rise above Mrs Simpson. She'll probably be fully occupied with the Prince, anyway. And the Perry Brownlows are going at the same time as us. You like them.' Lord Brownlow was an occasional equerry but also a close friend of the Prince. He was a thoroughly good-hearted man, and his wife, Katherine, known as Kitsie, was lively company.

There was no fighting it, anyway, as Emma knew. She said goodbye to her peaceful August plans, had a quick trip to Walcote for Electra's birthday (she held a 'children's party' in fancy dress, which was a great success), shopped for bathing suits, sandals and books, and on the 13th she, Kit and Teddy took the afternoon boat train to Paris. They dined splendidly at the Hôtel du Nord, listened to some jazz, and caught the sleeper to Biarritz.

They reached the villa the next morning before the company was up, having been out late at the casino the night before. Only Jack Aird was about, moodily walking the dogs, which he didn't regard as an equerry's duty. The villa was modern, of pink stucco draped with purple bougainvillaea, set above the point with glorious views of the sea, shaded with umbrella pine, juniper, bay and trumpet vine. It had several terraces, one with a tennis court, another containing a swimming-pool of startling azure. The steps between them wound between aromatic shrubs, and the hot air pulsed with thyme, rosemary and resin. Lizards sunned themselves on the walls, and disappeared like water down the cracks when disturbed, and the cicadas sang so constantly that their sound became a silence in the endless dazzle of the day.

It should have been the perfect place, and in other circumstances Emma would have given herself up to the languor and hedonism of it, but there was no getting away from Wallis and David. Their relationship and their moods dominated everything. *She* was restless and irritable; *he* was extraordinarily, unnaturally besotted with her. He would not let her out of his sight, would not leave the house if she did not, could not be persuaded to play tennis or fish or see the sights unless she went too. And when he was with her he would not leave her alone, had always to be touching her, holding her hand even during meals, running his finger along her arm, tickling her neck with a leaf. He watched her all the time with a doglike expression of devotion, attended to her every whim, lighting her cigarettes, fussing about with cushions and umbrellas and tables and towels, fetching and carrying for her with eager smiles. He even copied her American accent, which, mingling with his usual awkward half-Cockney, made him hard to listen to.

Perhaps *her* irritability was not unconnected with all this: she could not get away from him. He clung to her like a lost child, and the more she snapped and pushed him away, the more devoted he became. The only way, it seemed to Emma, that she could avoid being hung over and touched and gazed at and asked a hundred times an hour if she was all right was to fill her days with activity, at least some of which – like appointments with hairdressers, manicurists, masseurs and seawater therapists – she had an excuse to do alone. Almost, Emma began to feel sorry for her. But her restlessness was not comfortable to live with: she organised trips, guests, and visits to other villas, hectored and bullied everyone to fall in with her plans and, when all else failed, reorganised the villa, moving the furniture around and badgering the servants.

Emma could see why Jack Aird was scandalised: not only by Ernest Simpson's absence but because this was not the way royal affairs were conducted. There was something embarrassingly *wrong* about the Prince's manner towards her. He *fawned*. Emma began to wonder, guiltily – and only secretly inside her own head – if he were actually mentally unbalanced.

She managed to enjoy some parts of the holiday – the swimming, the glorious views, the splendid food. She even embarked, very tentatively, on a programme of 'bronzing'. It was the latest fad, and quite startling when, for the whole of history, ladies had prided themselves on their white skin; but there was no doubt that there was something attractive about a glowing golden skin, if it were not overdone. Kit encouraged her; otherwise, even having seen some bronzed ladies at the casino, she would not have risked it.

He was not much help in keeping Wallis from latching on (whenever she was not being latched on to by David) because he and Teddy seemed to look on the holiday as having been arranged entirely for their benefit. They went swimming together in the sea, hired small boats from the harbour to go fishing, went 'antiques hunting' in the town – a new craze of Kit's – and disappeared to rather louche bars to drink *pastis* and listen to jazz all afternoon. Wallis tried to encourage David to go with them but he wouldn't leave her; and, given how they'd rolled their eyes behind his back when it was suggested, it was probably a good thing.

But in the evenings they earned their keep, inventing silly games, singing musical comedy numbers together, arranging charades, writing and acting little plays, playing madcap pranks on anyone and everyone, and generally keeping the company cheerful, if slightly manic. Kit brought back queer objects from his antiques hunts and made everyone guess what they were, bought ludicrous presents, which he pressed on the Prince and Wallis with the appearance of sincerity, gambled like a madman at the casino – and with galling good luck – and when there was dancing, he made sure every woman in the company was fox-trotted to exhaustion.

On the 16th the Brownlows arrived and diluted the company a little, which made it more comfortable. Perry even managed to persuade the Prince to a game of golf. He tried to get Kit and Teddy to go along, but they simply stared at him for a moment, then burst out laughing. '*Golf?*' As they watched the Prince and Perry go off, the Prince casting lingering looks over his shoulder as long as he was in sight, Wallis gave a little sigh of relief, and said to Kitsie, 'I love the sun, but I believe one can have too much heir.'

For a moment, Emma rather liked her.

The Brownlows had brought news from home: HRH's brother, Prince George, was to marry Princess Marina of Greece. She was, according to Kitsie, a steady and sensible girl who was likely to prove a good influence on Prince George, whose wild antics had caused the King and Queen much anxiety. They were to marry in November or December. Wallis seemed quite excited by the news, and talked of going to Paris when they left the villa to order gowns for the wedding.

She got up to go and fetch a shawl from the other side of the pool, and Kitsie said to Emma, 'Someone ought to tell her that she won't be invited to the royal wedding. The King knows about her, and he doesn't approve, not a bit. The sooner Sir gets married, the better.'

'Do you think he *wants* to get married?' Emma said.

'Doesn't matter,' said Kitsie. 'He's not getting any younger. He ought to grab the first princess he can find and get her pregnant. No-one will mind him having a mistress when he's done his duty.'

Suddenly Wallis was back with them. She could do that

when she thought she was being discussed – move with lethal speed and silence.

'What are you talking about?' she demanded, giving them both an acid look.

'Nothing,' said Kitsie, and heaved herself to her feet. 'I've got too hot – I think I'll have a dip. Coming, Emma?'

But Wallis had clamped her large, strong hand round Emma's wrist. 'She doesn't want to swim,' she decreed. She lay down on the steamer chair next to Emma and arranged the silk shawl over her legs. 'I know what you were talking about,' she said. 'You were talking about the wedding. Wondering when it will be David's turn.' Emma didn't deny it. 'The sooner the better, as far as I'm concerned.' She turned her head to stare at Emma challengingly. 'You think it's easy, keeping David and Ernest both happy?'

'I hadn't thought about it,' Emma murmured.

'Well, it isn't. Take it from me, it requires great tact. And the last thing I want to do is upset Ernest. He's my husband and I love him.' She put on her sunglasses, which had heart-shaped white frames, so that Emma could not see her eyes any more, and leaned back in her chair, tilting her head up as if looking at the sky.

'Do you think he minds?' Emma asked, sensing a rare chance to ask such personal questions.

'Ernest? Not a bit. He thinks it's an honour to be the close personal friend of the heir to the throne. He knows I'm working for the two of us, anyway. This thing with David will run its course one day, and then Ernest will be waiting for me. I just need another year, that's all, and I'll have our futures secured for ever.' She sighed. 'If only David would get married, he'd have something else to think about. He'd be busy, I'd be in the background, everyone would be happy.' She sat up suddenly and whipped off the glasses. Her eyes were angry. 'The King and Queen have no idea how to manage him, no idea at all! If they'd only consult me, I'd tell them how to do it, and we could have him happily married off in no time.'

Emma boggled a little at the thought of the King of England consulting Mrs Simpson about how to handle the Prince of Wales. 'I don't think they could do that,' she murmured.

'In a sane world they would,' Wallis snapped. 'But this is not a sane world. All the protocol and fusty old rules get in the way. Ridiculous! A mightn't talk to B and C has to bow to D or the world comes to an end! My God, I'm not surprised David gets so sick of Court life! What nonsense it all is.'

'It's been around a long time,' Emma said. 'Traditions that go back a thousand years are hard to break.'

'That's the trouble with you British,' Wallis said indignantly. 'You're so stuck in the past, you haven't the faintest idea how to live in the present.' She glared at Emma as if it was all her fault, got up, spilling the shawl onto the ground, and stalked away.

On the 23rd, an old friend of the Prince's, Lord Moyne, arrived at Biarritz in his yacht, *Rosaura*, which had once been a Southern Railway passenger ferry, SS *Dieppe*, so was not very glamorous in appearance. But it gave rise to a change of plan: Prince George and Princess Marina were to stay in Cannes on their way to England, and the Prince decided it would be nice to call in on them there. It was not a long hop by aeroplane, but Wallis was afraid of flying, so the Prince commandeered *Rosaura* for a sea cruise down the coast of Portugal and round Spain to Cannes. As the weather looked like breaking, they decided to leave the villa a few days early and set sail on the 28th.

Emma was glad to be released early, and had to try hard not to show it. Wallis suddenly became affectionate as the time approached to separate. 'I wish you were coming with us. I shall miss you. Are you sure you won't change your minds?'

'Quite sure. We have long-held plans, I'm afraid.'

'Break them,' Wallis demanded. Emma arched her eyebrows. Wallis had developed a way of acting as though she was queen and, when it was pointed out to her, excused it by saying she was acting on behalf of the Prince of Wales – which, to Emma's mind, was not much better.

'I can't,' Emma said coolly.

Wallis didn't seem to heed the snub. She frowned and said imperiously, 'But I need you. You and Kit are *my* friends, and Teddy is so amusing. When you're gone I'll have no-one to talk to.' *No-one but David* – the words were unspoken but hung on the air.

'Perry and Kitsie are nice,' Emma said, reluctantly feeling sorry for her. On a ship it would be so much harder to get away from the lover who grew all over her, like convolvulus. And Jack Aird's disapproval would fill the small space like a cloud of noxious gas.

'They're David's friends, not mine. Or, I'm not so sure, they may be spies for the King and Queen. They may be reporting everything back to them. There's something sharp about Kitsie I don't quite like. And can Perry *really* be as nice as he seems?'

She was beyond being comforted, Emma could see.

When they said goodbye to the Brownlows, Kit shook Perry's hand and said, 'Something of a surprise, this. Shouldn't HRH be somewhere else?'

'I know *I* should be,' Perry said, 'but I'll have to stay as far as Cannes for decency's sake.'

'And to stop Jack exploding,' Kit suggested. 'He's in combustible mood.'

'Can't blame him for being upset about all this,' said Perry. 'It's really not the thing. But it can't last much longer, surely? The hotter the fire, the quicker it burns out.'

'One can only hope so,' Emma said. 'With the Silver Jubilee next year . . .'

'Ah, well, I've heard something about that,' Perry said, leaning in confidentially. 'Of course there will be all sorts of celebrations, and the King has hinted to me that there'll be a royal wedding to round it off. Highlight of the whole thing. So, as I said to Jack, let HRH have his fun – a last fling, if you will. Once he's safely married, there'll be no harm done.'

In the train going back to Paris, Teddy slept, his head rolling over onto Kit's shoulder. Emma said, 'I can't wait to get home.'

'Me too. I miss the doggies,' said Kit.

'Not the children?'

'Them too.' He yawned. 'I think you were right – on the whole it was rather a bore. But it's fun to see Wales go his length. Wondering what he'll do next.'

'Get married, one hopes,' Emma said.

Kit gave her a sidelong look. 'Hope away.'

'Perry seems quite sure.'

'Perry doesn't know everything. I've told you why it won't happen.'

'Hmm-hmm, Mr Freud and so on, I know,' Emma said, tired of the subject. 'Why do trains always make one so drowsy? Either we must get up and trot along to the restaurant car or I shall fall asleep.'

Kit patted his shoulder. 'Avail yourself,' he said. 'I have two.'

'Darling, you're so nice,' said Emma, and settled her head on his pearl-grey shoulder. The familiar smell of him was so comforting.

'Ditto ditto, Lady Westhoven,' Kit said. He put his feet up on the seat opposite, and settled himself. 'I love you, Emma dear,' she heard him say, before she drifted off.

Lennie had rented a cabin near the town of Mount Shasta for a month for the honeymoon. It was stone-built in traditional style, and did not run to any great luxury, but it had a large, hand-carved bed covered with Indian blankets, a wood-stove for chilly evenings, a verandah for warm ones, and incomparable views of the mountains and the wilderness. There was a well of good water with a pump run by a wind-mill, a melon house cool enough to keep food fresh for days, and Lennie loaded the rented station-wagon with delicacies and drink to supplement the simple life.

Beth's mother was staying in a very expensive nursing-home for the duration, and Lennie hoped she would like it enough not to want to come out again, though he said nothing of that to Beth, naturally. He would do whatever was needed to please her, including having her mother to live with them. But he could see how being free of the voluntary burden changed her. She seemed to straighten up like a stem of grass when a foot is lifted from it. At Pinetree Cottage she became light-hearted, gay, almost childlike in contrast.

There was plenty to do. There was the wilderness to trek through – Lennie hired a couple of horses and a guide, and Beth soon got the hang of riding. It had some of the most spectacular waterfalls in the country, hundreds of trails to follow and wonderful views. There were streams to fish in and lakes where they could boat. A local woman came in daily to clean for them and cook their dinner – they fended for themselves the rest of the time – and in the evenings after dinner they sat together on the verandah to talk, or just listen to the silence of the wild.

Lennie had brought a wind-up gramophone, so when they felt livelier they could listen to music, or roll back the rug and dance, and sometimes they played cards together – piquet, crib or two-handed canasta. Beth was a demon for math and usually won: Lennie looked forward to partnering her at bridge when they got home. But mostly they just talked. He felt he could never have enough of it. She was the perfect companion: good-humoured, intelligent, inter-ested in everything. He was not used to women with anything in their heads, and she charmed and thrilled him. He liked women's company better than men's, but enjoyed men's conversation. In Beth he could have both at once, with the additional benefit of affection, warmth and love, and the incomparable delight of going to bed together afterwards. He had had many lovers in his life, but discovered now the age-old truth, always suspected but never truly *known* until it was experienced, that sex is quite different when love runs in harness with desire.

At the end of the first week he drove them down to the town to stock up on provisions. They had lunch at a restaurant on the main boulevard, then walked about the shops. Noticing how Beth was enjoying looking into every window, he asked, 'Have you had enough of the wilderness? Would you prefer to go somewhere else? If you're pining for civilisation and the Grand Hotel somewhere, you've only to say, and we can be gone at once.'

She looked at him quickly. 'Is that what you'd like?'

He smiled and shook his head. 'Nice try. But I want to know what *you*'d like.'

'Well, I want the cabin and just you, and the silence and the space and no-one around us. But I'll fall in with whatever you say.'

He took her hand. 'I'm so glad you feel like that. I just want to be with you, too.'

'Let's hurry and finish the marketing and get back, then,' she said, looking into his eyes with an expression that made him go hot all over.

He did think about Polly once, one night when the wind had got up and the sound of it under the eaves kept him awake. Beth was slumbering peacefully beside him. He lay and stared into the dark, listening to the sounds the cabin made as the wind worked it like great hands, the creaks and moans, the sudden cracks, the rattling of a shutter somewhere, and the urgent whispering of the trees. Suddenly, for no reason, Polly came into his mind, as clear and close as if she had been transported there by some magic. For a moment his heart hurt with a great twinge as if it had been squeezed too hard in a tender place. How could he have forgotten her? He had loved her for so long, for most of his life, her cool beauty, her unfathomable eyes.

But even as he thought it, he realised that she had become a dream to him, a vision of perfection, unattainable as a goddess, a creature of air and fire. There was something of the silver screen about it, something that ought to be accompanied by soaring music. Beth was real and warm and human and close; she was earth and water, essential and good. They touched each other, gave and took, had life as it was meant to be lived, growing like a plant nurtured between them, putting out leaves and the buds of coming fruit.

The vision of Polly faded, and he felt only a faint, nostalgic regret. He hoped that one day she would find what he had with Beth – he hated to think of her alone and lonely. But Polly was so lovely she would surely never be alone. Men would always flock to be chosen by her. He said goodbye in his mind, and turned away with a sadness that soon melted into joy as he put his arm over his sleeping wife. She grunted – a small, contented, absurd sound – and moved closer to him, without waking.

Violet's baby was born on Tuesday, the 2nd of October. She had a very hard time of it, and lost a lot of blood. Afterwards the doctor said she must never have another. 'If you do, it might kill you.'

Avis concurred. Sitting by her bed, clutching her hand like a man who has only narrowly avoided falling over a precipice, he said, 'I should never have let you do it. Well, never again.'

'I don't care,' Violet murmured weakly. 'I've given you another son.' She had shown those women. An heir and a spare. And she was only forty-three: if she wanted another – a little girl for Avis to pet – well, they'd see. Doctors didn't know everything.

'Even if we didn't have a son at all,' Avis said, 'I wouldn't risk your life again. I'd let the title go hang, sooner. As it is . . .' He pressed her cold little hand to his cheek.

But I'd like you to have a daughter, too, Violet thought. She was too tired to say it out loud. So very tired, she felt as if she never wanted to move again. She knew how lucky she was. Two boys in two years. She could hear the new baby crying in the distance; somewhere little Halley was being told he had a brother, and not understanding what that meant. And Avis was right there beside her. She let his love warm her, and drifted into sleep.

On the Friday Charlotte and Richard travelled down together after work, and Avis sent the motor to meet them at the station. It was a long and tedious journey – not a good train, stopping after Market Harborough – so they did not arrive until nearly ten.

'Your mother's asleep,' Avis greeted them. 'I'd rather you didn't disturb her. You can see her tomorrow.'

'How is she?' Charlotte asked anxiously.

'She's still weak, but not in any danger. The doctor says it's just a matter of time now – rest and good food to rebuild her strength.'

'Thank God,' Richard said. 'And the baby?'

'All's well with him,' Avis said. 'Would you like to see him?'

They glanced at each other, both feeling that the baby might as well keep for the morning, if their mother could, but Avis seemed touchingly eager to show him off, so they trudged upstairs to the nursery where the earldom's insurance lay in his crib. He was wakeful, but not crying – a scrawny, frog-eyed little thing, Charlotte thought, not much to show for having almost killed her mother. He lay staring upwards, his brow seemingly furrowed in thought, as if wondering what he was doing here.

'Fine boy,' Richard said, in a tone that suggested he was groping for something to say. 'Have you chosen a name yet?'

'We used up all the important names on the first one – grandparents and so on,' Avis admitted. 'I didn't want him called after me – I've always hated my name – so we plumped for great-grandparents. He's to be Frederick Guy Oliver Peregrine.'

'Given what's happened to Halley,' Richard warned, 'he'll end up being called Peregrine.'

Avis shrugged. 'I can't help it. He'll have to work it out for himself. If you knew how long it took to pick those names . . . Anyway, everyone has to have some hurdle to overcome in life. It builds character.'

As they walked downstairs, Avis said, 'Henry's coming tomorrow. He couldn't get a train tonight.' Henry, eighteen, had finished his engineering course and had been accepted as a trainee by Hawker's, which had just taken over the Gloster Aircraft Company at Hucclecote, where he was now working. His journey from Gloucestershire was shorter in miles than Richard and Charlotte's, but more complicated by train.

'Any word from Robert?' Avis went on.

'I did speak to him on Thursday,' Richard said, 'but he didn't think he could get away. He sends his love, of course, and says he'll come down as soon as possible.' This part was fiction, Robert being too caught up with his own affairs to think a visit necessary, but Richard meant to make it true when he could corner Robert for long enough. 'His news is that the Party seems likely to give him a junior ministry the next time they reshuffle the cards.'

'A ministry in what?' Avis asked

'Oh, he doesn't mind. It's just a step in his career. He means to be prime minister, one day.'

'Well, it's good to have ambition,' Avis said doubtfully, 'but I don't think the people will stand for a prime minister in the Lords, these days. There hasn't been one since Lord Salisbury.'

'He says there isn't any rule about it, it's just a convention,' said Richard. 'Anyway, at twenty-five he's got plenty of time. Perhaps he'll change the face of the whole constitution. You never know. If there's another war, anything could happen.'

'Oh, don't talk about another war,' Charlotte said. 'Everyone seemed to be worrying about it at Molly and Vivian's dinner.'

The news coming out of Germany did not encourage hope. Though the financial situation was stabilising, unemployment was down and there was order in the streets, the cost, to outsiders, had been high. The new Chancellor, Mr Hitler, had his own private army of 'brownshirt' storm troopers, who harassed and beat up anyone not wholly supportive of the new order; and there were rumours now of a secret police force, called the Geheime Staatspolizei, answerable only to the Chancellor and spoken of in hushed terror.

In May 1933 there had been a shocking incident when students from German universities gathered in Berlin, under encouragement from the government, to burn books containing 'unGerman' ideas, which turned out to include most of Germany's literary heritage, and some notable foreigners, like H. G. Wells, Jack London, Marcel Proust and Ernest Hemingway. The official speeches during the event stated that the new German man was not an intellectual but a man of character and action, ready to build a new Germany by force of arms. Intellectualism and the old forms of learning and culture were Jewish-dominated and therefore suspect.

Since then, Jewish teachers and lecturers, and any others not supportive of the new order, had been sacked, and many had fled to England and the United States. Charlotte had heard Vivian say it was obvious that Hitler was starting by getting control of the youth of the nation, who would be easier to train than adults. She had not forgotten the worried look on his face when he had said it.

Then, on the 2nd of August 1934, the old President, Paul Hindenburg, had died at last, and the government had immediately enacted a new law that stated that in future the office of Reich President would be combined with that of Reich Chancellor, in the person of Adolf Hitler. This odd-looking little man, the unknown Austrian who had fought in the war as a corporal in the German Army, now held absolute power in the country, and styled himself 'Führer of the German Reich and People and Supreme Commander of the Armed Forces'. What he would do with that power remained to be seen, but the book-burning, the ejection of the intellectuals and, above all, the rearming in contravention of the Treaty of Versailles were not reassuring signs.

Charlotte had less global anxieties on her mind as well. Dolphin Books had still to achieve any support in the publishing business. Slowly answers were coming in from other publishers, all of them negative. Typical of the comments was this, from one publisher: 'In my view the steady cheapening of books is a great danger in the trade at present. The clamour of booksellers for publishers to "meet depression with depression" by lowering prices is one of the chief reasons why our trade is finding it so hard to recover from the slump.'

But there was another, more immediate, threat. The financial state of Dorcas Overstreet had never been particularly sound, and at the end of 1933 the accountants had written to Vivian's uncle: 'The situation is desperate and demands that you take most drastic steps to deal with the position. Otherwise on the present volume of sales it is only a matter of time before the business will have to cease trading.'

Vivian had not known about the letter. Unfortunately, most of the power in the company lay with his uncle, James Dorcas, and Jonathon Overstreet, grandson of one of the founders. They had, in Vivian's view, very old-fashioned ideas about publishing – for instance, they would not publish Vivian's own favourite form of literature, the detective novel, not allowing it to be literature at all. Only weighty volumes of Edwardian gravitas and serious scholarship were worthy of the imprint. The rest of the board, and most of the share-holders, were in agreement. Dorcas Overstreet was a grand old firm in the Johnsonian tradition and they weren't going to change their ways just because the world had changed. Standards had to be maintained; the pass must be held against the vulgarity of the modern age.

It had taken positive floods of eloquence and passion on Vivian's part to get them to allow him to try to set up Dolphin Books within the bosom of Dorcas Overstreet, and he was quite well aware that they had only agreed in the end because they were sure nothing would come of it, that he would fall at the first hurdle – which, gallingly, seemed to be proving the case. Vivian stuck to the belief that he would succeed in the end, and he was not deterred by their attitude, or that of the rest of the trade. But in September, when everyone came back after the doldrums of August and the holiday season, his uncle had summoned him to a meeting and put before him the accountants' letter, together with a new warning, just arrived, which said that the company was hopelessly insolvent, and that in the accountants' view a receiver ought to be called in.

Charlotte had been with Molly in Arlington Street when he came home and told them about it. He had said to Charlotte, 'You are intimately involved in all this, so it's right that you should know as well. But I must warn you to say nothing about it to anyone.'

'Of course I won't,' Charlotte had said.

'Because if we are to save anything from the wreck, we must proceed in absolute secrecy for the time being.'

But what means were being considered, or indeed what means might actually be possible, Charlotte did not know. She only knew that her lovely job and hopeful future were in jeopardy. She started, tentatively, to look around for a new job, just in case; but she felt that Dolphin Books was in part her own baby, and she could not forget about it easily.

The next morning she went up to see her mother, and was relieved to find her sitting up in bed, though looking very tired. She had a tray across her lap and was sipping coffee and eating toast and strawberry jam, with a pile of post beside her.

'Oh, good, darling – you can open these for me. I don't seem to have any strength in my hands,' she said, when Charlotte came in. The doctor had decreed, according to Avis (though Charlotte suspected it was his own idea), that she was to have only one visitor at a time, and the boys had said Charlotte had better go first.

'Mummy, are you really all right?' Charlotte asked, taking the seat by the bed. 'I hear the doctor was really worried.'

'I'm quite all right,' Violet said firmly. She was of the generation that never spoke of being ill, so Charlotte was not entirely convinced, but she felt better about it when Violet smiled and said, 'Have you seen your little brother? Isn't he beautiful?'

'He's very small,' Charlotte said, the only thing she could think of that was honest. 'And not as handsome as Halley.'

'He will be,' Violet said. 'Give him time. And, darling, we're determined that he shall be called by his proper name, Frederick.'

'All right, Mummy.'

'Avis is afraid that he'll get called Peregrine, because of Halley.'

'I know, Mummy,' Charlotte said, and didn't tell her that Richard was already referring to the baby as 'Little Peregrine Fellowes'. He was only doing it as a tease, but that was how things got started, and sometimes stuck. 'Frederick's a nice name. I'm sure he'll grow up to be a fine boy.'

Violet was satisfied, and turned her enquiry instead on her daughter's life. 'Just open those while you talk. Tell me who they're from and if there's anything interesting, apart from congratulations. I'll read them later. And tell me about you. What are you doing, these days?'

Charlotte could not relate the trouble at Dorcas Overstreet, so she said she was enjoying her job, spoke of a few shows and films she had been to with Betty and Myra, and then told about a young poet Molly was cultivating, who seemed more or less camped in the Blakes' drawing room, sprawling on the floor like a schoolboy and strewing sheets of paper covered with scrawl like gigantic snowflakes all over the room. 'He's there every time I go,' she said. 'He's awfully funny – terribly Byronic, you know, all burning eyes and sulky lips, and takes himself very seriously. Molly says he really has talent, but I'm afraid he just makes me want to laugh. I was trying not to giggle the other day when he was declaiming, and I suppose the struggle showed on my face because he said he could tell from my expression I had suffered artistic agonies like him! Honestly, I had to run from the room or I'd have burst out laughing. I suppose he thought I was running away to cry.'

This story had gone down very well when she told it to Myra and Betty, but her mother didn't laugh. She looked Charlotte over with close scrutiny and sighed. 'I suppose he wouldn't do for you – poets are too much trouble, and never have any money – but do tell me there's *someone* in your life? You're such a nice-looking girl, but you're twenty-two.'

'Oh, Mummy, don't start all that again,' Charlotte said,

but mildly given her mother's condition. 'I'm quite happy as I am. I don't want to get married.'

'But you will do one day, and if you leave it too late there won't be anyone left. Don't look at me like that. It isn't natural for a woman to live without a man. Now, darling, please, let me know best on this subject. A job is all very well, but it doesn't replace the security of a husband and a home.'

Charlotte was about to argue, when she remembered the plight of Dorcas Overstreet, and the possibility that she might soon be out of a job. If she didn't find another straight away, how would she pay for her rent and food? The uncertainty of the future – not just in her own immediate life but in the greater sphere, of the country and the world, with depression, unemployment and the threat of war – seemed suddenly to hang over her like a cloud, blotting out the warmth of the sun. She thought of Avis's love for and care of her mother, and felt suddenly that that was something worth having, something warm and bright to keep the darkness at bay. Perhaps her mother wasn't entirely wrong.

So she said, 'It's all very well to talk, but what can one do? Husbands don't just come along.'

'Suitable ones do, if you go about it in the right way,' Violet said. 'Next Season, Avis and I will come to Town again, and I shall make a point of entertaining, and putting you in the way of meeting some nice, suitable young men.'

'Like Jocelyn Barber,' Charlotte suggested ironically.

'Jocelyn Barber is marrying the Spenser-Courtfield girl. You've missed your chance with him,' Violet said. 'But I'll make it my business to find some others. Now, darling, do say you'll let me help you. Meet them and be nice to them, and see what happens. That's all I ask.'

Charlotte was painfully aware that she was not supposed to be upsetting her mother; and she told herself it couldn't do any harm just to go to some dances and dinners and pretend to play along. Nobody could make her marry anyone she didn't want to. Why not just make Mummy happy and enjoy the Season?

'Of course, Mummy, I'll meet anyone you want me to,' she said.

'And be nice to them? Not drive them away before you even know what they're like?' Violet said suspiciously.

'I will be a perfect angel, I promise you,' Charlotte said, and said it pleasantly enough to allay her mother's fears. And then she got on with opening the post, to avoid any more discussion.

CHAPTER SIXTEEN

The presence of the camera crew seemed to assume more and more importance as they went along, with the result that the Bedaux Expedition developed in strange ways that had nothing to do with mapping the wilderness.

On the 17th of July they reached Fort St John in British Columbia where they halted for several days, ostensibly to replenish stores and carry out repairs to the half-trucks but, it seemed to James, in reality rather more to taste the luxuries of civilisation again: soft beds, hot baths, electric lights, roofs rather than canvas overhead. St John was as delirious with excitement as Edmonton had been at the arrival of the party, and there were the same banquets, speeches and receptions. Any member of the expedition walking down the street could expect to be accosted by a resident, have his hand shaken, and be cordially invited home to family dinner.

It was all very pleasant, but after the second day James found himself growing restless. He hadn't come all the way to Canada to attend parties. He worked on the Citroëns, inspected his kit, groomed his horse to show standard, and then, in desperation for something to do, presented himself to Meredith and begged her to let him help.

'Feeling bored?' she asked him, with an amused look. 'Don't worry, the terrain will get wilder from here on. You may come to look back on Fort St John with longing.'

'Not me,' James said stoutly. 'I'm a Yorkshireman. We're not made of sugar, you know.'

'Is it a wild place, this Yorkshire of yours?'

'You should come and visit,' James said. 'Come and stay at my house – well, it's my sister's house now, but it's still my home.' And, under subtle questioning, he told the story of Morland Place and how he had sold it to save it.

'It sounds marvellous,' she said. 'Fancy having all that history under one roof – five hundred years! Nothing in America is that ancient. My grandfather built our ranch on virgin ground fifty years ago, and we think that's old. It must make you feel very different.'

'One's terribly proud of the tradition and so on, but it ties you down as well. You're so much freer over here.'

'I suppose that's why you've come,' she said.

'Men always want adventure,' he said. 'But what about you? Why are you here?'

'You think women don't want adventure too? That they don't want to get away from everything and be free? And it's worse for girls. My brothers can get on a horse and be gone all day, but parents watch their daughters all the time.'

'Even in Wyoming?' James asked.

'Especially in Wyoming.' Meredith laughed, and changed the subject. 'But if you're aching for something to do, you can go through these receipts for me, make sure they've all been signed and add them up.'

James would have felled trees for her or fought wild Indians, but even his best friend wouldn't have called him a mathematician. 'I'm not terribly good at sums,' he confessed, blushing with annoyance at having to confess it to her.

'Don't worry, I'll check your total,' she said and, without looking at him, added, 'Business practice. When it comes to money, you always have at least two people doing the numbers.'

So James toiled happily in her office – a shed at the end of the railway-station platform, loaned by the town and handy for the telegraph office – doing whatever little task she could think up for him, and happily unaware that she didn't actually need any help at all. They were in St John until the 22nd, and in that time Meredith discovered a great deal about James Morland and Morland Place, and he thought he discovered a lot about Meredith McLean and the McLean ranch, but in fact, had he thought about it, he would have realised it added up to almost nothing. Fortunately, he never did think about it, happy just to be in her company.

During this stop, he learned that Bedaux had decided the expedition was not nearly newsworthy enough, and that the sensation it was causing in the press would soon peter out unless more exciting things happened.

'So we're going to stage some accidents,' he said. 'We're going to risk our lives facing terrible perils.'

'I thought that was going to happen anyway,' James said. 'Isn't that what the wilderness means?'

'It might do, but then it might not. Nature is too unreliable. We'll have to give it a helping hand. And I want you, James my boy, to make sure your diary and your book reflect *my* version of the trip. Can't have you contradicting the movie.'

'Isn't that wrong?' James said tentatively. 'I mean, it won't be true, will it?'

'What is the truth? It will reflect a *greater* truth,' Charlie said energetically. 'An *inner* truth. We all came here to risk our lives, and if the movie shows that, it will be more honest than reporting that nothing much happened. When people go to a movie they don't expect to see life as it really is, but life as they wish it was. And the same with your book. Do you think any publisher will publish it if all you do is eat and sleep and jog along looking at the scenery? No, no, they want *action*, and action we'll give 'em! Are you with me?'

James had only to reflect that his whole trip was being paid for by Mr Bedaux, and that he was, in effect, doing a job of work. He nodded. 'What had you in mind?' he asked.

After that, James lived a kind of dual life on the trail: the real one, and the one he wrote about in his diary every evening, which reflected the world being created by the camera crew. Charlie decided that the Citroën half-trucks were not very camera-worthy, trundling slowly along, and that they could very well do without them. He concocted a higher destiny for them. Two of them were filmed falling over a ninety-foot cliff near Halfway River. The third was to meet the most spectacular end of all: it was put on a raft and floated down the river with a stick of dynamite under it that was supposed to explode it into a ball of fire in mid-river. Sadly the dynamite failed to go off, and the half-truck floated on serenely until it got stuck on a sandbar. Still, the Canadian and American newspapers carried the news that three of the half-trucks had been lost, members of the party narrowly escaping with their lives, and the expedition was praised for its courage and determination in carrying on despite all setbacks.

But the travelling did get more difficult as they got into the mountains and the weather worsened. In mid-September when they reached the Whitewater Pass, one of the geographers, Frank Swannell, who knew northern British Columbia and understood a bit about the terrain they were facing, told Bedaux that they ought not to continue: the going would be too hard through the mountain passes when the snow came down, as it might any day. But Bedaux could not bear to give up the good newspaper reports yet, and they pressed on, now facing real hardships, picking their way through rough trails in penetrating winds and sleety rain.

This really was the wilderness, and there was no help within reach until they got to the other side. When two of the horses died, it was clear they risked too much by continuing. On the 17th of October, Bedaux, crouched in a tent that gave inadequate shelter from the piercing wind, said they should turn back. James was only sorry he wouldn't get to see the Pacific Ocean. He went to clear the accumulated sleet from Sunny's face and whispered the good news into his warm ear, and the horse pushed his head against James's chest, glad of a moment's shelter.

At the end of the month they reached Hudson's Hope on the Peace River, having been almost four months in the wilderness, and they came in looking a great deal more like explorers than when they had set out: thinner, weather-beaten, bearded and weary. They had not completed the intended route, but the town went wild with excitement anyway. It threw them a party the like of which had never been known in British Columbia, and the telegraphs buzzed with reports heading for all the big newspapers on the continent.

James gave himself up to physical pleasure – bathing, shaving and sleeping coming first and, when he had woken properly, eating, drinking and making merry. In spite of everything, he felt he really had tasted adventure and proved himself. Now he was looking forward to going home. His only regret was at having to part with Sunny, of whom he had grown very fond, his only worry that of never seeing Meredith again.

'What will you do now?' he asked her one day, as they sat in the window of a café in Hudson's Hope, watching the world go by and occasionally waving as townsfolk recognised them through the glass. 'Will you go back to Wyoming?'

She shuddered delicately. 'That's the last thing I want to do. No, I've got out once and I'll never go back, if I can help it. Luckily, Charlie's offered me a job. He's impressed with my work, apparently.'

'He'd be a fool if he wasn't,' James said. 'The whole thing would have fallen to pieces without you. What job has he offered you?'

'Something in his office in Paris. It was pretty vague, but

the important bit is that it's *Paris*! Do you know what a dream that is for an American girl?'

'So you're going to take it?'

'I'd be mad not to, especially as he's paying my fare over there. I'll travel with him and Fern, so it'll be luxury all the way.'

'I thought you despised luxury,' James said.

'Of course I don't. It just isn't the be-all and end-all,' said Meredith.

They were silent a moment, Meredith looking out of the window and James looking at her. Paris was a lot better than Wyoming, he thought – better than anywhere in America – but still a long way from Morland Place.

'At least we'll be on the same continent,' he said at last, a little dolefully. She looked at him questioningly, and he couldn't read any particular encouragement into that. 'Perhaps you'll visit England while you're there,' he tried.

'Having got as far as France,' she said, 'it would be silly not to go the extra few miles. I've always wanted to see London.'

'If you came to London, I could come up and see you,' James said. 'Show you around.'

'That would be nice,' she said. 'And if you came to Paris, I could show you around.'

They looked at each other for a moment, and there seemed to be all sorts of words hanging in the air, but James was not confident enough to speak them. What had he to offer, after all? And she was so self-contained. If she had given him a hint of wanting more from him . . . But she hadn't. He could imagine her in an office in Paris, cool and confident and efficient, living in a Parisian flat, eating in Parisian restaurants. Meeting Parisian men . . .

'Do you speak French?'

'Mm-hm,' she nodded, and there was a gleam of amusement in her eyes as if she had read his thoughts.

James sighed inwardly. But his fortunes might change. He

would not give up so easily – not James Morland, the intrepid explorer of Bear Island and British Columbia. 'If I give you my address,' he said, 'will you write to me when you get to Paris? And I'll write back to you.'

'I know your address,' she reminded him. 'I have everyone's address.'

'Oh, yes,' he said.

'What will you do now?' she asked. 'When you get back to England, I mean.'

'Write the book, I suppose,' he said. 'And then look for another adventure.' He squared his shoulders. 'I'm an explorer now.'

'You are,' she agreed. 'I'm sure something will come up.'

'But you'll write to me?' he urged, with something of a descent into bathos.

'I'll write to you,' she said. 'If nothing else, you could come and explore Paris.'

Hull 534 was launched on the 26th of September by the Queen, accompanied by the King and the Prince of Wales. The latter was fresh back from his holiday trip, which had taken him to Cannes (but not before Prince George and Princess Marina had left for England) and on round the coast to Italy. After that he had left Mrs Simpson most unwillingly in Paris to fly back to England for the annual royal migration to Balmoral.

Polly was invited to the launching in Clydebank, and stood with the directors and other important people as the King made a speech about British expertise, industry and world-beating ingenuity and skills. Then, under an awning on a raised platform, the Queen, a big fur collar on her coat, a diamond brooch in her hat and three rows of pearls at her neck, named the ship, wished her good luck and pressed the buttons that smashed the bottle on her bows and sent her sliding down backwards into the Clyde.

Below the podium, a crowd of two hundred thousand, undaunted by the pouring rain, cheered and waved their hats and handkerchiefs as this hope of their town and the nation, looking like a great white cliff, settled into the specially dredged and widened waterway, where the tugs waited to tow her to the fitting-out basin.

At the reception afterwards Polly was presented to the Prince of Wales who, throughout the ceremony, had seemed restlessly anxious to be somewhere else. He was in naval uniform, so small, thin and slight a figure that he looked like a fourteen-year-old cadet, until you got close enough to see his face. It was very brown from his holiday, and wrinkled, like a walnut. Polly thought he looked like a boy in an elderly man's skin. He spoke in a strange, half-American accent – Polly, who had lost her own American tinge by now, noticed it particularly – but he was very cordial.

'I had a tour of Yorkshire some years ago,' he said, when she told him she was the owner of Morland Place. 'I dined with near neighbours of yours, the Holkams, at Shawes. Very fine old Vanbrugh house. That was in May 1923.'

She was impressed by his memory for such small detail. 'Lady Holkam is a cousin of mine,' she said.

'Ah,' said the Prince, closed his mouth, nodded and moved on. Polly wondered if he had realised that she knew Violet had been his mistress. It had been much talked of in New York when Violet had visited her there; but she had learned that such things were not much known in England, where the press were more deferential. She had no idea, for instance, whom his current mistress might be.

The ship was not, in the end, called *Victoria*, and after the royal party had left, Sir Percy Bates, under the influence of a couple of glasses of champagne and Polly's extreme beauty, told her the story, about which he swore her to secrecy. In courtesy, he said, he had approached the King and asked his permission to name his new liner after

England's greatest queen. The King had beamed and replied that he regarded it as a compliment and that his wife would be only too delighted. So they'd had no alternative but to name 534 RMS *Queen Mary*.

'But I count it a lucky omen,' Bates said. 'Usually only capital ships are named after sovereigns, so we shall stand out in a crowd, m' dear, and that's always a good thing.' He smiled down at her. 'Your father would be very pleased that you are carrying on his relationship with our company. I hope you will keep up his tradition and sail on the maiden voyage?'

'I should like that very much,' Polly said, though with inner reservations. She thought it rather tactless of Bates, since her father had been on the maiden voyage of *Titanic*; but perhaps he had forgotten that. It might be nice to try out the new *Queen Mary*, but it was not a trip she would want to go on alone – where would be the fun in that? And what did she need with a holiday in America anyway, when she had lived there so long? She had closed the book on her American life when she had come home to rescue Morland Place.

Prince George's wedding to Marina of Greece was to be on the 29th of November, and a Court ball was given in their honour at Buckingham Palace on the 27th. Emma and Kit were invited, and Emma decided she really needed a new gown. On the day before the ball she had just come from a final fitting with her dressmaker in Bond Street when she met Verena Overton, who said, 'I'm on my way to lunch with Sarah at the Café Royal. Do come and join us. She's been showing foreign royalties round London for the past three days and needs cheering up. They're so tiring, all so short of money but still terribly on their dignity.'

At the Café Royal, Sarah Vibart was already at the table, and said, 'I vowed to talk about anything but the wedding at lunch today, but something's happened I must tell you about. Eddie met Humphrey Butler last night and came home with such a story.'

She paused while they settled themselves and a third place was laid. 'Well,' she went on, when they were alone, 'apparently Wales added Mrs Simpson's name to the guest list for the ball without telling anyone. When the King saw it, he simply threw a fit. He called in Prince George and demanded to know who'd done it – Humphrey was with him, which is how he knows about it. Anyway, George said it was Wales's doing, and Wales was sent for and torn off the most frightful strip, right in front of George and Humphrey. The King bellowed, "I will not have that woman in my house!" and crossed her name off there and then.'

'I didn't know the King knew who she was,' Verena said.

'Oh, yes,' said Sarah. 'The King and Queen both. They've been ignoring her existence up till now, but if Wales insists on rubbing their noses in her, he'll come a cropper.'

Emma spoke. 'Kit had it from Tommy Lascelles that the King said at least Mrs Dudley Ward was of a better class, and he wished HRH had never broken with Violet Holkam. He said it had been all downhill since then. And he said the Prince hadn't a single friend who was a gentleman.'

'Ouch!' said Sarah. 'How did Kit take that?'

'He couldn't think it funnier. But obviously the King didn't mean *him*.'

'When HM's angry he lashes out indiscriminately,' Verena said.

'Anyway,' said Sarah, 'the King's given strict orders that Mrs Simpson's not to be let into the palace on any account, and that she's never to be allowed in the Royal Enclosure at Ascot, or invited to any Silver Jubilee function. So I'm afraid that's the end of your friend Wallis's pretensions,' she concluded to Emma.

'She's not my friend,' Emma said automatically, but she added thoughtfully, 'I wouldn't write her off quite yet. If

410

you'd seen the way HRH behaves around her, I don't think he'll let her be sidelined. I don't think Their Majesties have quite realised the situation.'

'Well, she can't get round an out-and-out ban,' Verena said.

'No, but the Prince can,' Emma said.

In the event, she proved right. On the night of the ball, she was standing in the vestibule at Buckingham Palace with some other guests, waiting to progress further, when the Prince of Wales came dashing through the crowd to the door, and a moment later returned with a beaming expression of delight and triumph, ushering in Mrs Simpson, in purple lamé and a diamond tiara. He escorted her straight through, leaving those who were not in the know wondering who on earth it was that the Prince had taken the trouble to meet personally, and the rest either shaking their heads in dismay or fuming in resentment.

The Prince didn't leave her side all evening, danced with her several times, introduced her to many of the distinguished guests, and even managed to present her to his mother. The Queen, not realising who she was, nodded politely to the flamboyantly dressed woman, so different from the beige-silk and oyster-satin ladies all around, and the Prince would have followed up this triumph by presenting her to the King, had the King not recognised what was happening and turned sharply away, his nostrils flaring ominously.

The next day the talk in the inner circle was of nothing else. Emma was obliged to learn that Mrs Simpson's gown had been made by the Chicago dressmaker Main Rousseau Bocher, who now practised out of Avenue George V in Paris, that her tiara had been lent by Cartier in Paris, and where she had had her hair and nails done. Speculation was rife over whether the Prince would smuggle her into the actual wedding, though Sarah said Eddie had heard the King say she must be kept out at all costs, if it meant posting Gurkhas at every entrance.

411

In the end, Mrs Simpson did not go to the wedding – though Emma heard she had had a gown made for the occasion – and Prince George was able to walk down the aisle of the Abbey in peace. He was made Duke of Kent for his marriage, and he and his new duchess were taking a house in Belgrave Square, a few doors down from the one Violet and Avis rented for the Season.

Emma and Kit were invited to a post-royal-wedding party at Lady Tunbridge's in the evening of the 29th. Emma was buttonholed by Veronica Glenforth-Williams, who wanted to talk about more alterations to her flat, and in passing told Emma a piece of gossip about someone Emma knew only slightly. An old friend of Veronica's had taken on a new young lover, who was 'practically a schoolboy, darling, too thrilling!' and 'too terribly handsome, and rather *farouche*, Gloria says, but, my dear, what *can* we be coming to, not a day over eighteen years old, too shame-making, young enough to be her son, though she was a child bride, poor pet, and the husband is never home, so what's a girl to do? But I die to see him, don't you? Like a young Bacchus, or that shepherd boy, what was his name?, in the Greek myths, with the curly hair like ram's horns. I simply *die* for the ram's horns . . .'

None of this would have interested Emma a bit, had Veronica not mentioned that the boy's name was Basil Compton.

Mrs Rampling had inherited money from both her parents, who had died when she was seventeen, putting paid to any chance of a come-out. She had been left in the charge of her aunt, her father's sister, who really, really didn't want the responsibility, and showed it. So after living a scant year with her, Gloria had rushed into marriage with Cedric Rampling in order to get away, and to get possession of her inheritance, which came to her only on marriage or at the age of twenty-five.

Cedric Rampling was thirty years her senior, of her aunt's generation – indeed, he was her aunt's bridge partner, which only exacerbated her crime in her aunt's eyes. He lived in the same Surrey village of Oxshott Green, had a pleasant house, The Pines, there, and his own engineering company. He was quite wealthy enough to be free of any taint of marrying Gloria for her money. In fact, it was a case of love, pure and simple. He had been in love with her from the moment she arrived in the village, heavily clad in black, her expression a mixture of abject misery and furious resentment. He had never dreamed she would marry him – indeed, *she*'d had to ask *him*, after his feelings had become plain to her – and was so grateful and bewildered to find himself in possession of this delicate, exotic creature that he hardly asked anything more of her than her existence. She was fond of him, and grateful to him for rescuing her from her aunt, but there had never been any more to it than that on her part.

From her parents, as well as money, she had inherited their large flat in Park Street, filled with antiques and *objets d'art*, and from her father his art-dealing business, and two galleries, one in Ryder Street and one in Kensington. Having grown up with paintings, Gloria had absorbed enough to take over the enterprise rather than sell it, and discovered she had a good business head. Cedric's affairs often took him abroad, sometimes on extended trips, so early in their marriage she took to living in London, going back to Surrey only reluctantly when Cedric was at home. He disliked London, and had a romantic longing for 'the country life' – which Gloria privately thought you would not be likely to find in a suburban village on the electric railway.

She had her son, Anthony, in a London nursing-home, attended by every luxury, but still the experience was so unpleasant she determined never to go through it again. Since then, she and Cedric had lived more or less separate lives. They entertained now and again, sometimes giving a smart dinner in Park Street for the arty and fashionable crowd, sometimes what she thought of as a 'pastel and chintz' one for the Surrey set in Oxshott Green. Until he went away to Eton, Anthony had lived permanently with Nanny at The Pines, where he was supposed to get the benefit of 'country air and food', and Gloria, who was really quite fond of him, made a point of going there for Christmas and Easter, and visiting him at some point during his annual seaside holiday in August. Otherwise, she stayed in London.

Cedric, who adored the child, spent all his time in England at The Pines, only visiting London on business or to see his tailor, and staying at his club, unless Gloria was entertaining and needed him. Despite this separation of spheres, they remained on good terms, much as they had been from the beginning – Gloria affectionate and grateful, Cedric worshipping and wistful – and they were known as good hosts. People always accepted their invitations to dinner.

Gloria was invited everywhere among the smart and the arty sets. She was known as a woman of great style, envied for her dress sense, which trod the delicate line between the new and the acceptable, impressing without shocking. What Gloria Rampling wore today, they said, everyone would be wearing tomorrow. It was also said of her that she had a man's head on a woman's body, because she was reputed to understand finance, to read the serious newspapers, and to have opinions on arcane subjects. Intellect being something most women were slightly nervous of, she inspired admiration among the smart set rather than affection. But she was consulted on matters both of fashion and money; and any hostess in that circle wanting her dinners to be talked of would make sure Mrs Rampling was free before setting the date.

And she was definitely envied her series of lovers, drawn from the ranks of the handsome, the witty and the very truly run-after. The elegant Gloria Rampling, cool and sophisticated, walked alone, but she slept in the best of company.

414

Basil was a departure from the norm, which startled her as much as it did her circle. Her own son was twelve years old: Basil was not much older. On first seeing him she had thought him extremely handsome, but his youth had not attracted her. Yet after a few hours in his company she found herself hopelessly smitten. There was something about him, she sensed, a wildness, a lack of fear or regard for the usual prohibitions, an intellect untrained; a sense of endless possibilities. Suddenly her own life seemed to her hopelessly, horribly constrained: everything neat, precise, done exactly to a rule to the limit of perfection. Her clothes, her appearance, her taste in everything; her flat – the modern juxtaposed so artfully with the antique; her finely balanced dinner parties – the guests so well matched, the food exquisite, neither too rich nor too meagre, the wines chosen to complement; her social calendar – the envy of her circle. Even her lovers: well dressed, well mannered, serving their term so attentively, accepting their dismissal with such wry good humour.

But then Basil: untamed, uncivilised, barely house-broken, indeed, thinking himself so sophisticated, but underneath a creature of untapped passions. Suddenly she was in revolt: how could she have resigned herself to such a staid, grown-up life, as if she were old and past the age of adventure? She might have a son of twelve but she was only thirty-two; her figure and her skin were still perfect; and she had never yet known love. Basil was her Endymion, the beautiful boy glimpsed and desired, but she had no intention of leaving him asleep in a cave. He wanted to frolic, and she was going to frolic with him.

She found him a willing partner. Basil had had no more intention of falling in love with her than she with him, but he could hardly help it. She was his gateway into a world he had wanted since he had first gone to school, a world of silk shirts and fine wines, expensive cars, the best restaurants, the élite of society for company. But there was more to her than that.

She had opinions, knowledge, wisdom, expertise he had never known he wanted. He had a brain, but had never bothered to use it, thinking it much cleverer to be ignorant. Now he wanted to impress her, and he hated his own naïveté. So he opened his mind and absorbed everything she gave him. He thought he was learning from her without her knowledge. Such subtlety of behaviour was beyond his experience.

And from passion – the grateful passion of the adolescent who hardly knows what it is he is craving – he progressed to love. He was proud she had chosen him. He saw that to the world she was the perfectly groomed, elegant, never-ruffled, famous Mrs Rampling. But he had seen her naked, with her hair tumbled, her expression softened, her voice blurred with desire, drawing him to her with those round white arms and the hands he sometimes kissed in devotion. In bed she had taught him, but now he was no longer the acolyte. They were equal. And alone together they talked and laughed like equals and she was as young as him – or perhaps ageless, which in some ways was even younger.

'Darling, it's none of our business,' Kit said.

'Isn't it?' Emma said. 'This is Helen's son, Molly's nephew. I don't think they know about it.'

'I'm sure they don't, and that's all to the good, wouldn't you say? Why upset them? It's not doing him any harm. Better an education at the hands of Mrs Rampling than getting tangled with showgirls or suburban vamps. At least she'll teach him manners, and how to dress. My God, I should think the King and Queen would be grateful to get her for Wales.'

'Wales is in his forties. Basil's hardly more than a boy.'

'Enough *not* a boy to keep Mrs Rampling happy,' Kit observed. 'Leave well alone, that's my advice. She'll tire of him eventually, and he'll come out of it a better person. At least he's not a car salesman any more, thanks to her.'

Gloria Rampling had given him a position in her Ryder Street gallery, where he had to greet the customers and show them around. His purpose was to be decorative and charming; other assistants were there to be knowledgeable.

Gloria also took him with her on buying trips, to country-house sales and breakdowns, to private houses and provincial galleries. The trips were serious in intent – she told him she was training him, and she was – but they were also fun. They took their time, shared the driving, stayed in country inns where they might pass unnoticed, or at least unremarked on, stopped where they fancied, took long walks or sat and looked at views.

Outsiders, like Kit, might guess the 'buying trips' were more a series of honeymoons, but in official terms they stood up to scrutiny and there was nothing scandalous about them.

'But Basil's a kept man,' Emma said unhappily. He now had respectable rooms in Babmaes Street, round the corner from the gallery, which she was sure Mrs Rampling must be paying for.

Kit shrugged over that, but he didn't like to see Emma upset, so he said, 'Would you like me to go round and call on him? Have a talk with him?'

'Would you?' Emma said gratefully. 'Babmaes Street is awfully close to Arlington Street, and anything Molly knows she's bound to pass on to Helen.'

'It may be close geographically,' Kit said, 'but Molly's world is a million miles from Mrs Rampling's. That's the beauty of London,' he added. 'All these different circles that never intersect.'

'But you'll go and see him?' Emma urged.

'Of course, if you want.'

Basil was startled to receive a visit from so illustrious a person as Lord Westhoven, but it certainly raised his stock with the hall porter. It was an old building divided into bachelor sets of varying sizes, rather in the Albany style, some of which were large enough to accommodate a gentleman's servant. Basil had one of the smallest, consisting of a sitting room and bedroom with a tiny modern bathroom inserted into what had once been a closet.

'This is charming,' Kit said. 'You must be very comfortable.' The rooms were oak-panelled, each having a large fireplace with an elaborately carved surround and high mantelpiece, and a sash window looking onto the tall waving plane trees of Apple Tree Yard. The furniture was solidly antique and comfortably shabby, the rugs were old Turkish and probably valuable, and on the walls Kit noted a delicious pair of Sisley canals, a tiny seashore that was probably Monet, and a very witty interior that might have been Bazille. Basil's walls were keeping very distinguished company, he thought.

Basil, looking faintly apprehensive but proud to be host to his first visitor, showed Kit round his tiny domain (there was a pot of flowering cyclamen on the window-sill, the only woman's touch in the place), then offered him sherry, which turned out to be excellent. It seemed a rather elderly choice for someone just about to turn nineteen, but Kit was glad to spot a cocktail tray on a table in the corner as well.

'Can't help noticing your paintings,' Kit said, settling himself in an armchair. Basil perched nervously and offered cigarettes. The case was rather a nice one, plain and heavy gold.

'Oh, they're not mine,' he said. 'Just borrowed. I have to give them up when a customer's found for them. But there's always something else. Rather nice to have the variety.'

'You're enjoying your new job, then?'

Basil shrugged. 'Not much different from the old one,' he said. 'Selling cars, selling paintings.'

'You don't equate the two things, do you?'

'Don't you think a fine motor-car is a work of art?' Basil countered.

Kit grinned. '*Touché.* Seen any shows lately?'

'I don't get to the theatre much,' Basil said, with the puzzlement so plain in his voice that Kit felt guilty. What was he doing there, after all? It was not his business to get Basil to give up Mrs Rampling, nor did he want to. Yes, Basil was a bit young, not yet of age, but from what he had heard, via Molly and Emma, he had been a headache to his parents for years, and was one no longer.

'I go to the pictures now and then,' Basil said, plainly feeling something was required of him by way of conversation. He went to the cinema sometimes when Mrs Rampling was otherwise engaged in the evenings. Though she paid his rent and bought him clothes and gifts, like the cigarette case, she did not give him money, and expensive entertainments, like clubs and gambling, were out for him. Not that he particularly wanted those things, now he had Gloria.

Kit loved the cinema, and knew lots of people from that world, so he could talk films all day if he had the chance. They chatted on the subject, Basil visibly relieved that he was not being grilled, then Kit finished his sherry and stood up. 'Must be toddling,' he said.

Basil stood too. 'Was there something in particular you wanted?' he asked politely.

'No, no, just happened to be passing. Heard you'd got a new billet, thought I'd poke my head down your burrow, see how you were getting on. Well, toodle-oo.'

Basil showed him out, puzzled but relieved. That he had just been inspected, he was quite sure; but it seemed that whatever the test was, he had passed it.

Downstairs the porter, whose job it was to know every notable in London and knew quite well who Kit was, was happy to accept a smoke from the gentleman and discuss the weather and the runners at Cheltenham; and, on the passing of a couple of half-crowns, was likewise happy to answer me lord's questions. So Kit came away with something solid to tell Emma, to soothe her anxieties. The young gentleman, the porter said, had never had a visitor in the rooms, barring himself that day, and no lady had ever called there for him. Mrs Rampling, they might conclude, was being discreet. It was only through the unregulated tongues of the likes of Veronica Glenforth-Williams that the story was being spread, and much of the detail of what was being said was probably imagination. For all they knew, Kit said, he might indeed just be an employee.

With James home from his travels, it was a lively winter at Morland Place, with guests staying for the hunting every weekend, leaving only the three days in the middle of the week to recover and prepare for the next. And since Polly quite often went out with James mid-week as well, she had to pack her work into a very few hours, which meant she was busy all the time and had no leisure to brood. Alec was too young to hunt, but she did take him to a couple of meets, Josh escorting him home as soon as the field set off; and there was a lawn meet at Morland Place in December where he was allowed to follow as far as the first covert.

When the Christmas season started there were guests and parties and dances, both at home and in the neighbourhood. There was a very grand Christmas Eve masked ball given by the Greys at Rawcliffe Manor, and Polly went as the Empress Joséphine, because the Regency style suited her tall, slender figure. James, who was escorting her, absolutely refused to be Napoleon, who, he said, was short, fat and bilious, and went instead as the Duke of Wellington. He looked so delectable in white breeches and hose – he definitely had the legs for them – blue frock coat and white stock that he drew all female eyes, had his pick of partners, and never had to explain who he was supposed to be.

420

On Christmas Day, Jessie, Bertie and the children joined the Morland Place family for the goose and plum pudding, all the cousins were home (Roberta rather wistful that Hilary Maddox had gone to her sister's for the day), and Amy came with her husband George Unwin. To entertain the children there was a dogs' Christmas dinner in the Great Hall, with a low table made out of planks and bricks, which the dogs were meant to sit around while their masters and mistresses served them with dishes of meat and gravy. The reality did not match up to the ideal, however, as the dogs were more interested in playing with each other until the food came in, when certain elements fell to fighting, but the children loved it and it made the adults laugh.

On Boxing Day the servants from Twelvetrees and Shawes joined those of Morland Place for a Servants' Ball, where the employers and other invited guests danced with the staff in an evening of bonhomous egalitarianism. Polly had invited the Shawes family and servants to be part of it because she felt rather sorry for them, celebrating Christmas without a wife and mother in the house. Since the summer she had met them pretty regularly. She'd had the Eastlakes to dinner, had been to dinner there, and had encountered them at Twelvetrees and various other houses in the neighbourhood.

Charles Eastlake had come to Shawes to be sociable. He went out hunting regularly on a hired horse (his daughter did not ride and his son was now away at university) and James had invited him to shoot. On several occasions at dinner parties, Polly and Charles Eastlake had been partnered, for even if she went with James, it was thought to be a waste to put them together when there were so many unattached females in the Riding and James was so young and handsome.

Polly found a friendship growing with Charles Eastlake. He was kind and attentive, with a fund of good conversation, and in the wake of Burton's emotional defection she had been lonely, especially with James away. She had taken an interest in the alterations he wanted to make to Shawes, and had spent some happy hours there walking round the rooms with him and making her own suggestions. He was interested in the history of the house, and she had given him access to Morland Place's archives, and introduced him to the Julians, who were fast becoming the experts on 'Morlandology', as Mrs Julian facetiously put it.

Charles had a fine black Labrador, which he liked to walk in the early morning. His path often crossed with that of Polly, who also liked to be out early, and in the fine weather of the autumn they had taken to meeting unofficially to walk their dogs in the misty first light.

In consequence of so much time spent together, their friendship had grown warm. She had learned a good deal about him. He came from the Yorkshire wolds near Burton Agnes, where his father had been rector, and had also owned a decent estate. As his elder brother was to inherit everything, Charles had turned to the army for a career – there were soldiers in the Eastlake background. He had distinguished himself, early won his commission, and married a colonel's daughter just as the war broke out and changed all lives for ever.

His son had been born in 1915. He had served with distinction, won rapid promotion, and was decorated after the Somme, where he had been injured and invalided home. On his recovery he had been transferred to the War Office. His daughter was born in 1917. His wife had died in 1919 from the Spanish flu, leaving him two small children to bring up. He had remained in the army, at first in the War Office and later as an inspector of training facilities, but he and the children had led a somewhat nomadic life until early in 1933 when his mother had died, leaving him her fortune, and he had decided it was time, for Mary's sake, to find a permanent home. After a search, he had found Shawes, where he meant to settle down, and to bring her out in York the following year.

Much of this history had come out in the course of their

walks and rides together, and under the warmth of his interest, Polly had told him something of her own life. Men were not always sympathetic towards women who ran their own businesses, but Charles Eastlake seemed to admire her for it, and never once said that running a great estate must be such a burden for a mere woman that she must long to hand it over to a man.

Jessie and Bertie liked him, too, and Bertie in particular had long talks with him about the army and the war, and said to Polly that he was a true soldier, which from him was a great compliment. During the autumn, after Roger had gone back up, they often had him and Mary to family dinners, and sometimes Polly joined them. Those evenings were very pleasant, full of sensible talk and quiet humour.

Jessie and Bertie noticed, though apparently Polly did not, that Charles Eastlake was watching her with increasingly wistful eyes.

'It wouldn't be a bad thing for her,' Bertie said, when the subject came up between him and Jessie one evening. 'It isn't natural for a woman to live without a man.'

'I agree,' Jessie said, 'that marriage is the happiest state, but not *any* marriage.'

'He's a fine man,' Bertie said.

'You think that because he was a soldier,' Jessie teased.

'Not only that. He's sensible, educated, good company, and he has a respectable fortune. What more could any woman want?'

'Well, to be in love, I should think. And Polly isn't.'

'She might grow to be,' Bertie said. 'She has to think of Alec. A boy needs a father.'

'But he's a lot older than her.'

'Not so very much. Seven or eight years. That's a good difference between husband and wife.'

'And he has grown-up children. I can't see Polly wanting to be step-mother to people their age.'

'She'd have a lot of fun bringing Mary out, dressing her and giving her parties. And the boy's not in anyone's way at university.'

'All the same,' Jessie said, 'she's still got half the cousins on her hands and I don't think she'd want to add to her dependants. I'd like to see her have some fun.'

'She seems to be having fun all right, with all these week-ends and parties,' said Bertie. 'But she's not a child any more, dearest. She's a grown woman.'

'I suppose so,' Jessie sighed. 'I always forget. She's so beautiful and looks so young, I still think of her as a girl. It's so very sad that her husband died. She oughtn't to be alone. I wish she *would* fall in love with Charles Eastlake, since he seems to be in love with her. But I wouldn't have her marry just to be comfortable. She was made for love. It would be an awful waste of all that beauty if she never had it again.'

'She can have it with an older man,' Bertie said gently. 'You found it with me.'

She smiled at him. 'But I always loved you, right from when I was a little girl. I sometimes thought—' She stopped.

'What, my love?'

'Oh, that Lennie was Polly's true love,' she said. 'But it didn't seem to work out that way.'

CHAPTER SEVENTEEN

Barbara very much wanted to have Christmas at her new home in Petersfield, and Helen was not so devoted to her house in Portsmouth as to argue. So it was at Crossways that the whole family, plus dogs, assembled for the Christmas season. Crossways was a well-built Victorian house, not particularly handsome, but comfortable and spacious. It sat squarely in the middle of its grounds, which were mostly rough grass, pine trees and rhododendron thickets, invaded occasionally by deer and much favoured by rabbits, so the dogs adored it. Barbara said apologetically that the grounds had been rather neglected and that she hoped to start working in spring on planting a flower garden. Jack advised cutting down some of the tall pines to get more light into the house to begin with. Helen thought any attempt at a flower garden would delight the rabbits and deer and break Barbara's heart, but she didn't say so.

She was envious, though she didn't say that either, of so much space, however rough. Jack's job enthralled him, but it didn't pay him much. After the financial troubles of 1933, Airspeed had agreed a take-over in July 1934 by Swan Hunter and Wigham Richardson. The old company had been wound up and a new one, Airspeed (1934) Ltd, created, with a Hunter and two Wigham Richardsons added to the board.

All this had pretty much passed Jack by. He had been far more interested in the first attempt at non-stop air-to-air refuelling in September, and the England to Australia air race in October, in which an AS 5 Courier had come third in the handicap section. He was even more absorbed in the development of the AS 6 long-range aircraft on which he was working, for which they anticipated an illustrious colonial future. They were going to call it the Envoy, and he was working on modifications for the Lynx engine. With other new models also in the pipeline, he was happily and busily occupied, and his domestic surroundings did not impinge on him.

Helen, however, now had too much time on her hands, and noticed the smallness of the house, the shabbiness of the furniture and the threadbareness of the carpets. She berated herself for wasting mental energy thinking of such things, but the alternative was worrying pointlessly about Basil. Jack, she knew, was quite glad to have him out of the house and usefully occupied. As he could not afford to send the boy to university, he was glad he had a respectable job, and was certainly not going to insist he came home for no other reason than that he was very young. 'He has to get out into the world at some point,' he reasoned. 'Don't worry about him.'

'But he's our responsibility until he's twenty-one,' Helen argued. 'I have to worry.'

Jack was unmoved. 'Boys younger than him fought and died in France. Nobody said they were too young.'

The war, Helen found, was always the unanswerable full stop to any argument. She did, however, manage, through some very heavyweight insisting, to get Basil to Crossways for Christmas. Michael came from Dartmouth, brown and fit and happy, having enjoyed his first term enormously. His conversation was full of the names of the 'other chaps', the instructing officers, who were loved or loathed, and impenetrable technical terms, which amounted to a whole new language. Helen listened patiently because she was proud of her boy, and hoped to trade for a few motherly questions about his physical welfare, how they slept and what they ate and so on.

When Basil arrived, she was pleasantly surprised at the change in him. He was smarter, cleaner, better dressed; his manners seemed improved – quieter and more manly; and he had remembered to bring presents. Perhaps she shouldn't have been surprised, given that he now had a salary for the first time, but she had assumed he would forget. She was touched; but the presents were so well chosen she came to suspect the presence of a woman in the background. Even Jack, who loved her dearly, never got it so right. But Basil spoke of no woman. She asked about his new rooms, and he said that he had moved because they were closer to his job. There was no landlady on the premises, and no cooking facilities; he had to eat out or order in, but there were plenty of cheap places in the area, and he was managing all right. From the little he said, the rooms sounded small, so she was relieved of the worry that he was splashing out too much. He also seemed to be drinking and smoking less, which was good. Altogether she was pleased, and though he made some odd remarks she didn't understand and had so little to say about his new job she was afraid he would not last long in it, she felt able to relax and enjoy Christmas.

Basil had come to Crossways because Gloria was going to The Pines to spend Christmas with Cedric and Anthony, so he would not see her for the best part of two weeks. He was surprised to find himself horribly jealous: it was an emotion he had never felt before. It had led him to behave very badly when Gloria had told him she was going away. First he asked her not to, then he wheedled, then he begged, then he sulked and snapped. What was *he* supposed to do? Why, go and be with his family, of course. But he didn't *want* to be with them, he wanted to be with her. That was a shame, but the arrangements were made. She always spent

Christmas at The Pines. So she preferred their company to his, did she? Gloria would not stoop to answer that.

He thought of her with Cedric (her husband!) and Anthony (a kid! She preferred a little kid to him!) and hated them with a grinding passion that burned in his entrails. Discovering that sulking and snapping hurt no-one but himself, he changed tactics and tried to make himself unleavable, but though being nice to Gloria made her and therefore him happier, it did not change her mind. Frenzied kissing and wild lovemaking made her sorry to leave him, but still she went. Having flung himself face down on his bed, pounded the mattress with his fists, and vowed to remain in his rooms all Christmas and starve himself just to punish her, he recovered a little sense of balance and took himself off to Crossways, where at least there would be food and drink and company.

He took with him the presents Gloria had chosen for everyone. That had been the only enjoyable part, going shopping with her, describing his family to her and approving or debating her choice. She had paid for them all as well, which was a help, because his present to her had pretty much cleaned him out. He had bought her a delicate bracelet of turquoises set in silver from a jeweller in the Burlington Arcade, and he could only afford that because it was second-hand. Gloria didn't seem to mind: when he gave it to her on the eve of her departure, she said she loved it, put it on right away and wore it in bed when she thanked him in a practical way later. Her present to him was a pair of gold cufflinks. He knew they were expensive because they were so plain.

So here he was, at The Pines, still smarting with jealousy and already missing Gloria with a hollowness like being hungry, but at any rate determined to get what pleasure he could out of Christmas. He thought the house a joke: the people he had respected at school and those he mixed with now through Gloria did not admire Victorian style or taste, and the Victorian trappings of Christmas they thought laughably 'suburban'. It was a pejorative much on his mental tongue, these days. He managed not to use it out loud, but he could not help the occasional snort as the ludicrously proud Barbara showed off every little feature to him as though it had been wrought to her personal design. But he had always been close to Barbara – in their childhood his firm admirer and biddable lieutenant – and did not want to hurt her feelings, so he admired as much as he could and bit his tongue over the rest.

Freddie seemed a decent old stick, but stolid, middle class and dull. He did not know what Babsy saw in him. He could see her growing as middle class and dull herself by contagion. At one point, when they were walking round the garden together, well bundled up, he was foolish enough to say so. Barbara looked puzzled, and said, 'Well, we *are* middle class. So are you. What's wrong with that?'

He could not explain, not really understanding it himself. He struggled. 'But there's so much more to life,' was what he came up with.

She gave him a canny look. 'Silk shirts and cigars and cocktails? I suppose that's what you have in London.'

'Not just that. There's – there's art. And culture. And – oh, so much more, I can't tell you.'

'But, Basil darling, that's your life. This is what I've always wanted, a house of my own and a nice husband.'

'Nice!' Basil exclaimed. 'That says it all – oh, the *niceness* of suburbia! It's ridiculous. Can't you *see*?'

'No, I can't, and I don't think you can either. You've got in with a different set, and you're bowled over by them, and take up their attitudes, but it won't last. It never does. You'll get tired of them and move on to another set, and then it'll be something else you think is ridiculous.'

'No, I won't, not this time. This is the real thing,' Basil said. 'These are the universal values of all civilised people.'

429

But Barbara only laughed, tucking her hand through his arm and hugging it. 'Dear old Bozzy!' They had been Bozzy and Babsy to each other in the nursery. 'So we're not civilised now? You're so funny when you get all enthusiastic like this.'

'You'll see,' he said. 'It's different this time.' But he could not stay cross with her. 'Did you like your present?'

'It's *lovely*!' she said. It was a satin nightdress case with her initial embroidered on it. He had thought it ghastly, but Gloria had said she'd like it and she did. 'How *clever* of you to choose it, darling.'

He almost told her then; but at the last moment thought better of it. He liked the pleased and slightly surprised tone of her voice when she praised him.

But Christmas went on too long, and his good behaviour wore out. He missed Gloria. He started to drink more, and Freddie was too polite to refuse him when he asked for another bottle to be opened at dinner or reached again for the brandy decanter. There were friends in for cocktails and supper on Boxing Day evening, and Basil made a joke of saying that he was the resident barman, and insisted on mixing, and mixing strong; and since he finished off what was in the shaker each time as well as his own glass, he was soon noticeably drunk.

On the eve of his departure for London he got Freddie to one side and, through a long tale with too many twists and turns to follow, managed to borrow twenty quid from him. He had just come out of Freddie's study and was shoving the notes into his pocket when he saw Michael watching him from the shadows of the passage that led past the staircase to the back door. He had just come in from walking the dogs. It was noticeable that they stayed by his side and did not run to Basil.

Basil scowled at his brother, thinking he was becoming too horribly wholesome in the navy. 'What do you want?'

'Nothing,' Michael said. 'I was just wondering the same about you.' His eyes moved deliberately to the notes in Basil's hand. 'What are you up to? You're being very odd.'

'I'm not. It's this place that's odd.'

'You know it isn't. You're getting too grand for us now you live in London. And where did that money come from?'

'None of your business,' Basil snapped.

Michael was unmoved. 'You might think of Babs, you know. She's very loyal to you, but if you put her in the position of having to choose between you—'

'Choose between us? What rot!' He felt awkward under those clear sailor's eyes. 'I ran a bit short, that's all – Christmas and so on. Having all those presents to buy,' he added, on an inspiration. 'Didn't you like yours?'

It was a very nice small compass on a leather wrist-strap. 'I liked it very much,' Michael said. 'But I bet you didn't choose it. A woman did. Was it Aunt Molly?'

'No, it wasn't, and if you don't shut your trap I'll shut it for you.'

Michael shook his head, unmoved by the threat. Basil had never cared for fisticuffs. 'You're up to something, I know. And sooner or later Mum will find out. You may be able to fool Dad, but you won't get round her.'

For a moment Basil stared, wondering if he had guessed, but then he shook the thought away, and put on a superior look. 'You're such a child,' he said. 'You don't understand anything.' And he strolled away upstairs with as much dignity as he could muster. He was going back to London tomorrow. Gloria would not be back until after the New Year, but he had twenty quid to tide him over, and once he'd filled up his flask and his cigarette case from the dining-room stock, he should manage nicely. He would go to the pictures, maybe see Richard, do a show, find some good fellows – there were always some in London – to while away the time with. At least it would be London, and not the beastly suburbs. How

431

anyone could live in a deadly place like this he couldn't think.

The Falcon and the Rose, the film about Anne Boleyn starring Rose Morland, was a huge box-office success when it opened in America in the fall of 1934. Then, at the 1934 Academy Awards presentation, held on the 27th of February 1935 at the Biltmore Hotel, Los Angeles, it won a fistful of Oscars: Best Picture, Best Actress for Rose Morland, Best Actor for Dean Cornwell, and Best Art Design for Eric Chapel for the sets.

On the back of the success, Al Feinstein wanted to do more big, important pictures. No more dogs and high-kicking legs, he vowed: he wanted to be remembered for epic movies like *Falcon*. With funds from his principal financial backers, including Joe Kennedy and Lennie Manning, he took over a couple more small studios that had been feeling the pinch post-Crash – Forley's Films and Cohen's Circuit Theatres – making ABO a big enough player to stand alongside MGM, Warner and so on. Rose and Dean, who were by now having a much-publicised love affair, signed on again with ABO despite a counter-offer from MGM. Michael Rosecrantz advised Rose that she had plenty of time ahead of her, and just now it was better for her to be the big star at ABO than merely one of many at MGM.

When Lennie had brought his bride home from honeymoon, Rose had moved out from his house to one of her own in Roxbury Drive, which she could now easily afford. Lizzie accompanied her as a sort of companion-housekeeper, though Lennie believed her role was more Rose's chaperone. But not too long afterwards, just when *The Falcon and the Rose* was due to open and the press were beginning to make much of Rose and Dean walking out together, there was some kind of quarrel between Rose and her mother, with the result that Lizzie left her house. She stayed for a while with Lennie and Beth, in the guesthouse in the garden. Neither would talk about it – Lennie could gather only that Lizzie had objected to Rose's social life, and Rose had objected to Lizzie's objections, but what was at the bottom of it he couldn't find out. He tried to reconcile them, but neither would back down. At Christmas Lizzie went back east to visit her son Martial and his family, and from there wrote in the New Year to say that she was staying permanently in New York, where she felt welcome and could be of use to her grandchildren.

The breach upset Lennie, who valued family above all, and hated anything to come between those he loved. But Rose was now growing too grand for him. She refused to discuss it with him and, when he pressed the matter, grew angry. 'You're not my father,' she said once, heatedly. 'You can't tell me how to live my life.'

Al Feinstein, who was something of a puritan, insisted that Rose could not live alone and must have an older woman resident with her. He had behind him the force of the contract she had signed, so Rose, rather sulkily, installed her dresser, Ellie Naumann, in a separate suite within the property. Thus the decencies were preserved for the studio and the press, though Ellie, as everyone close to them knew, was no match for Rose if she was determined on some course.

But Rose at least had the sense to know her reputation was important. She behaved discreetly in public, and she and Dean had a very clean-living, boy-and-girl-next-door affair, leading to a very high-profile Hollywood wedding as soon after the Oscars as could be arranged, in March 1935. The magazines had a field day: everything was 'Rose and Dean'; every detail was lovingly pored over, and there were photographs of everything from Rose's shoes and Dean's boutonnière to the automobile they would go away in. Rosecrantz saw to it that they made a good sum out of granting exclusivity on photographs of the wedding itself and the reception for three hundred held in the ballroom of the Roosevelt Hotel.

They were to live at Rose's house, now renamed Roselands, but Dean was also leasing a 'shack', as the stars called them – a summer home – in the 'colony' at Malibu Beach, where they would spend their honeymoon (privacy was more easily secured at the colony than in any hotel). They would probably live there as much as at Roselands. There were many interviews with the couple on how they would adapt their careers to married life, and speculation on what their next movie together would be.

As well as an agent, Dola to keep house for her, and her dresser Ellie, Rose now had a secretary, a publicist and a very pushy lawyer: 'A staff as big as Peach McGinty's,' Lennie joked with her, but she didn't laugh, only gave him a faintly affronted look. He didn't seem to know how to talk to her, these days. So when she acquired a husband as well, he decided it was time to let her go.

His life was changing shape. With the Democrats in power, he was not wanted nearly so often in Washington, and his trips to New York were now infrequent – his businesses there ran themselves pretty well. He was more interested in ABO, in expanding his radio empire on the west coast, and in opening up another radio station. His life seemed to be settled on the west coast, and now he had a wife, too: enough to keep him occupied.

'The fact is she doesn't need me any more,' he said sadly to Beth, as they sat on a bench at the bottom of their garden, looking over the ravine and the hills opposite.

'But that's good,' Beth coaxed. 'It means she's all grown-up.' Lennie didn't answer, and she said, 'She's twenty-six, Len. She's not a child any more.'

'To me she is,' Lennie mourned. 'She's like my little sister. I've always looked after her.'

'You have me to take care of now,' Beth said.

434

He looked at her and laughed. 'You? You don't need taking care of. You're the original tough kid. I half expect a black eye whenever I try to help you on with your coat.'

'Oh, you'd be surprised how much looking after I'm going to take. And there may be someone else, as well.'

'Your mother? But we *are* taking care of her.'

Mrs Andrews had her own suite in the house and a full-time nurse to take care of her. Seeing her daughter happily married had improved her health, and knowing she was secure had lifted a weight visibly from Beth's shoulders.

'Not Mother,' Beth said patiently. 'Someone else to take care of. Jeepers, I've married a moron!'

He stared in dawning hope. 'You don't mean . . . You aren't . . .'

'I'm not sure yet, so don't get too excited,' she said, her eyes shining. 'But I think I might be.'

Wordlessly, he folded her in his arms.

The Falcon and the Rose came out in London in March 1935, attended by a great deal of excitement and publicity. The Prince of Wales went to the première, and Oliver, who loved a good movie, secured tickets and went with a party of Verena, Emma and Kit, Sarah and Eddie.

The Prince gave a few words of commendation afterwards to the press, then trotted off to the Ham Bone Club in Soho's Ham Yard for dancing with Mrs Simpson, Emerald Cunard and the Ribbentrops.

Oliver's party enjoyed the film hugely, then went to dine at Frascati's where they toasted Rose's career in champagne.

Charlotte also went to see it – not at the premiere but a later performance – in the company of Myra and Betty. They were deeply impressed by her connection to Rose.

'You never said you had a cousin who's a *famous film star*!' Myra exclaimed, at supper afterwards at the Corner House.

'Only a very distant cousin,' Charlotte modified.

'But you *have* met her?' Betty asked.

'Yes, when I went to New York with Mummy. Of course, she wasn't a famous film star then.'

In fact, she reflected, Cousin Polly was the famous one then, *haute couturière* and married to a high financier.

'But she knows you,' Betty pressed. 'I mean, if you met her now, you could go up to her and say hello and she'd know who you were? She'd –'

'– hello you back?' Myra finished.

'I expect so,' Charlotte said. She thought of something else. 'She was on the *Titanic*, you know. She and her parents and brothers.'

'I know – I read about it in the *Tatler*,' Myra said.

'Well, relative or not, I thought she was jolly good,' Betty said. 'She almost had me in tears at the end. A jolly good bit of acting. Wasn't so impressed by *him*. Dean What's-his-name. Rather wooden, I thought. He looks a dull dog.'

'She married him,' Charlotte said. 'In real life, I mean.'

'I know,' said Myra. 'I read it in—'

'The *Tatler*!' the other two chorused.

At Frascati's the conversation had drifted from the pictures to the Prince, natural enough since they had just seen him. Eddie had some new scandal: the Prince had approached Lord Cromer, the Lord Chamberlain, about the ban on Mrs Simpson's appearing at Court, and when Cromer gave him the cold shoulder he went direct to the King and asked that the Simpsons be invited to the Jubilee Court Ball in May.

'He must be infatuated,' Oliver said impatiently. 'The King will never allow it. For Heaven's sake, why can't he just be discreet? No-one would care a fig if he kept his private life private.'

'But wait, I haven't told you all yet,' said Eddie. 'Halsey was actually there, and he told me. Of course, the King said very coldly that he couldn't possibly invite his son's mistress to such an occasion. Then Wales said she was not his mistress! Apparently the King asked if he swore that was true, and the Prince gave his word. So the King said in that case she could come to the ball.'

Oliver protested, 'But everyone *knows* she's his mistress.'

Eddie nodded. 'Halsey was outraged. The Fort servants have seen him going into her room at night, and Aird's seen him coming out in the morning with his upper lip all red.'

'To think he would lie on his oath to the King!' Verena said, shocked.

Kit and Emma looked at each other. Emma thought Kit might repeat his belief to the company, but he only gave her a closed smile and a shake of the head. It seemed hard to Emma, if Wales was telling the literal truth, that everyone believed him a liar. But then, she reasoned, even if Kit was right, it was a mere technicality. Even if they sat up in bed all night playing pinochle and flesh never touched flesh, she was his mistress in intent, and what he had said to the King was a sophism.

'He's just storing up trouble for himself,' Eddie said. 'Even if she goes to the ball, it won't make any difference. The Establishment won't accept her. The Duchess of York has said she won't meet her, and the Duchess of Kent says she's an adventuress and shouldn't be received.'

Kit said, 'Well, I think we're bound to see a lot more of her this year, whether we want to or not. Wales is intent on launching her socially, and he's roped in Sybil Colefax, Emerald Cunard and Margot Asquith to help. They don't mind being seen in her company.'

'They wouldn't,' said Verena, who didn't care for Lady Cunard.

'And Ribbentrop thinks she's the bee's knees,' Kit said naughtily, knowing it would annoy her. 'He sends her flowers, you know – armfuls of red carnations. I don't know what his wife thinks.'

'It's a good job David's got her the invitation to the ball, though,' Emma said. 'She's already ordered a gown for it from Main Bocher in Paris.'

Sarah gave her a grimace. 'You seem to know a lot about Mrs Simpson.'

'Only because everyone keeps talking to me about her,' said Emma.

'Well, let's talk about something else now,' Verena said.

Charlotte had enjoyed the evening at the pictures and the Corner House, a sharp contrast to many of her other evenings lately, attending the Season's dinners and balls with her mother. Not that she wasn't enjoying those, too. She had had to accept some new clothes from her mother, her salary not being up to providing the sort of gowns that wouldn't disgrace her; and she was enough of a girl to enjoy dressing up. She had, she thought, a strangely topsy-turvy world that year, going from her humble room in Ridgmount Gardens to the grand homes of the rich and titled; from her work as a secretary to glittering balls; from struggling through rush-hour on the tube to being wafted along in near silence in a Rolls-Royce. If the essence of happiness was variety, she should have been the happiest girl in London.

Myra teased her about it, but was envious. 'I can't think why you grub away as a typist when you could live in luxury in Belgrave Square.'

Betty was engaged to a young man – a pupil in chambers in Lincoln's Inn, the son of old friends of her parents – and was looking forward to being married in a year or two. She said, 'I can't think why you don't just let your mother find you a suitable man to marry.'

'She's trying to,' Charlotte said. 'But I don't want to marry a suitable man.'

In addition to the stimulating variety of her social life, she was particularly happy at work, because there had been a breakthrough for Dolphin Books. In January there had been a positive reply from the publisher Nathaniel Cope, who had a very good list of top-flight modern authors. Vivian had written to Nathaniel asking for ten titles, offering an advance of twenty-five pounds on account of a royalty of a farthing a copy, payable on publication. Nathaniel had written back at last, saying, 'You can have them for an advance of forty pounds, all payable on signature.'

'Now we really can make a start,' Vivian said.

That evening Charlotte was invited to a celebration family dinner with Molly and Vivian. Molly said, as she raised a glass to Dolphin Books, 'It's wonderful that Nathaniel believes in us, after all the rejections. Everyone else thinks we'll fail.'

Vivian gave her a wry smile. 'So does he. I rang him up this afternoon to thank him for helping us to a good start, and he said, "I'm just helping myself to a bit of your cash. Why do you think I'm insisting on a signature advance?" So I asked him what he meant, and he said – humorously, you know, but he obviously meant it underneath – he said, "Everyone in the trade knows you're bound to go bust. I thought I'd take four hundred quid off you before you do."'

'Never mind,' Molly said. 'We'll show him. We'll show them all.'

Having secured the titles, the next thing was to secure the outlet. The bookshops were happy with the titles on the Dolphin list, but they didn't like the format or the price, and subscriptions into the shops were too low to break even, let alone make a profit.

'We need a different kind of outlet,' Vivian said. 'Something less traditional and stiff-necked.'

'What about Woolworth's?' Molly said. 'They're always taking on new lines. It could be a breakthrough for them as well as for us.'

'But would people go into Woolworth's to buy a book by

our kind of author?' Vivian said worriedly. 'Isn't it a class thing?'

'Darling, everyone in the country goes into Woolworth's every day for something or other. It's the great leveller. And once they're in, and they see the books there, looking so gorgeous, and costing just sixpence, they'll buy them – why not? They won't care that it isn't a bookshop.'

The Woolworth's buyer, when Vivian approached him, had the same concerns; but when he saw the list, and spotted the name of an author he knew his wife read, he said he would take a chance on them. To Dolphin, the order, which in his terms was cautious, was huge, compared with normal bookshop subscriptions, and it was enough to make the launch possible, bringing to the public fine-quality writing for the price of a packet of cigarettes. With Woolworth's under his belt, Vivian had no difficulty in persuading W. H. Smith to take them for their railway-station kiosks, and in getting them into the Finlay's tobacconist chain, now owned by John Menzies.

'Everyone buys cigarettes,' he said. 'Let them start to associate Dolphin Books with their packet of gaspers and we'll have a captive audience.'

The only worry was the continuing financial crisis at Dorcas Overstreet. The company was hanging on by a thread, according to Molly, but Charlotte did not allow herself to think about that. She was sure Vivian would not let Dolphin Books fail now they had got their start: he would ensure that it survived. They would manage somehow. Even if it meant taking a cut in salary – well, she could live on very little.

Outside the Corner House she discovered that she had left her scarf behind. She told the others not to wait for her, that she'd see them at home, and they walked off, while she went back inside. She was running up the stairs when she met a young man coming down with her scarf in his hand.

He obviously recognised her, because he smiled and said, 'I think this is yours, isn't it?'

'Oh, yes, thank you! I was just coming back for it. How did you know?'

'I was sitting at the next table,' he said. 'I noticed it after you'd left.' He did not seem to be in any hurry to give it back to her. He had stepped down to the same stair that she was on, and was leaning against the banister, looking at her with interest. 'I wouldn't want you to think I was eavesdropping, but I thought you seemed to be having such fun with your friends, I was quite envious. I wished I could have joined you.'

'Well, you could have,' she said. 'We weren't talking about anything private.'

He was a lean young man, with dark hair, a little unruly, and bright blue eyes. There was something just a little negligent about him, she thought – the way he was standing, the way he wore his clothes, the very fact that he was talking like this to someone he hadn't been introduced to. He was very different from the 'suitable' men she was having presented to her by her mother: they were all formality, their suits buttoned up, their hair oiled down, their manners impeccable. She had a feeling her mother would not approve of this stranger, which was at least partly why she was lingering, instead of taking her scarf with a frigid, correct thank-you-and-goodbye.

'My name's Milo Tavey, by the way,' he said, holding out a friendly hand.

'Charlotte Howard,' she replied, shaking it. She felt a little jolt at the touch.

Perhaps he felt it too, because he said, 'It seems a shame to waste the moment, when we've met each other so fortuitously. I know you've eaten, but would you care to have a cup of coffee with me?'

'Here?' she said, doubtfully.

'Oh, no. There's a little restaurant near here – Italian, you know – where they serve the most delicious coffee. It's only five minutes away, on the corner of Tottenham Court Road.'

That was actually on her way home. Charlotte took it as a sign.

'I'd like that,' she said. 'I can't stay very long, though.'

'Ah, the tyrant Time,' he said lightly. '"But at my back I always hear—"'

'"Time's winged chariot hurrying near,"' Charlotte concluded, and laughed. 'I'm not sure the rest of that poem is quite proper to the occasion.'

They were walking down the stairs together now. He seemed to think, and then laughed too. 'Oh – perhaps not for a very first meeting. I beg your pardon. But I do like the ending: "Thus, though we cannot make our sun Stand still, yet we will make him run." I've always thought we ought to give him a run for his money. Life is so short.'

'But art is long. Dear me, we could talk all night and never have to say a single original word.'

'The poets have taken them all, I'm afraid. We shall have to descend from the general to the particular.' They emerged onto the street, and he guided her left by a touch on her elbow. He was taller than her, just by a pleasant amount. She liked the sensation of walking along a street with him. She half wished people would look at them and notice. 'Are you particularly fond of literature?'

'I usen't to be, particularly, but now I work in the trade, I love books. I find myself fascinated by words and think about them all the time.'

'You work in the trade? What an intriguing statement, Miss Howard. I took you for a lady of leisure.'

'Goodness, no! I have a job. I'm a secretary.'

'In "the trade" – whatever that might be. A poetry factory? A literature mine?'

'Sort of,' Charlotte laughed. 'I work for Dorcas Overstreet. The publisher.'

'Yes, I have heard of them,' he said. 'I don't know if I should alarm you, but I've heard a rumour that they're in trouble.'

'How did you hear that?'

'I'm in a trade, too – the money trade.'

'You work for the Royal Mint? Or the Bank of England?' She repaid him in his own coin.

'*Touché.* I should have said the finance trade,' he said. 'The talk is that Dorcas Overstreet is in a poor way and might have to call in the receivers.'

'I've heard that, too, but I didn't really know what it meant, except that it was bad.'

He explained it to her, which lasted until they reached the restaurant. Conversation was broken off as they were welcomed and shown to a table by the proprietor, who evidently knew the young man, for he shook his hand and called him 'Meester Milo'. He then bowed to Charlotte and said something about a *bella signorina,* and ushered her with great ceremony, pulling out her chair for her with a flourish. Milo ordered coffee.

The proprietor said, 'You have eaten already? What tragedy! But perhaps some dessert? Yes, yes, you will try my *castagnaccio,* from my own country, the recipe of my grandmother in Liguria. To please me?'

When the proprietor had gone, Milo turned to Charlotte, laughing. 'He's a wonderful character, isn't he? Born not a mile from here, in Seven Dials, as were his father and grandfather before him, not to mention the dear old grandmother from Liguria. They came over in the eighteen sixties. The accent is entirely bogus. He forgets he told me his whole life story one evening after too much sambuca.'

Charlotte laughed too. 'What an interesting life you lead, confidant of all and sundry.'

'I hope to become yours, too,' he said. 'I want to hear all about you, and how you managed to escape the fate of other young ladies, dusting the dining room and arranging flowers for Mama.'

'It wasn't easy,' Charlotte said. 'That was exactly what my mother would have liked for me.'

'Why did she change her mind?'

'I don't know, really. She got married again, and they had children, so I think perhaps she didn't mind so much about me any more.'

A waiter came with the coffee and the *castagnaccio*, which turned out to be a strange, flat cake with a flavour Charlotte couldn't identify.

'Chestnuts,' Milo said. 'The poor man's food in Italy, but Tony flavours his with almonds and brandy, so it's not so poor any more.'

'What a lot of things you know,' Charlotte said.

'I like to find things out. I was born asking questions, according to my mother. Go on about you and your job "in the trade". Tell me everything from the very beginning.'

He was such a good interlocutor that she told him everything without feeling that it was at all an odd thing to do, or that he was a stranger. At least, she didn't tell him *quite* everything – not that her father had been an earl and her mother an earl's daughter. She said that her father had died bankrupt – strangely, it didn't seem to hurt when she told him that – and that they had been very poor for a while but that, even so, her mother had not wanted her to work. She said her uncle had paid for her secretarial course without mentioning that he was an earl, too. And once she got on to Dorcas Overstreet, she had plenty to say. She told him all about Dolphin Books, with a ring of pride in her voice.

'And you think *I* lead an interesting life,' he exclaimed, when she paused. 'My dear girl, bringing literature to the masses! What could be more of a crusade?'

It wasn't really proper of him to call her his dear girl, but she found she really didn't mind. 'But what do you do?' she asked. 'You haven't told me anything yet, and it must be your turn.'

'You really want to know about me?'

'Yes. *All* about you. What are you doing in your "finance trade"?'

'Making my fortune,' he said. 'You see, I intend to be very rich.'

'*Is* that something one can intend?'

'It's the only way,' he said. 'My grandfather had a lot of money but my father lost it all, so here I am, out on my own in the big hostile world—'

'I think it's the big hostile world that needs to beware,' Charlotte said. 'But you still haven't said what you actually *do*.'

'It's very simple, really. There are still people who have money, lots of it, and there are people who need money, to start up businesses, or expand in various ways. I bring them together.' He demonstrated with his two hands, making a movement as though he was going to clap, but clasping them together. She watched them: lean and brown and strong.

'And that's all?' she asked, after a moment, looking up to find him watching her closely. The look made her shiver, it seemed so personal.

'Just about,' he said. 'They pay me a percentage of the finance I find for them so, of course, the larger the amount, the more I get paid. At the moment the amounts are not huge, only agreeable, but when my reputation is made, I shall have customers from all over the world, the sums will be immense, and I shall be very rich. What do you think of that?'

'Hmm. It sounds rather too easy. Why isn't everyone doing it?' she asked.

He grinned. 'First, they're not as clever as me. Second, I

know a great many useful chaps from school and so on – not everyone has my circle of friends. Third, I learn quickly, so I know how things work, what businesses need, where to find things. I *understand* my customers, on both sides – those needing money and those with it.'

'And fourth?' Charlotte asked, when he stopped.

'Fourth?'

'You sounded as though there was going to be a fourth point.'

'Well, if you insist – fourth, I'm handsome and charming and generally irresistible. How many people can say that?'

'I really ought to contradict you, for the sake of your soul,' Charlotte said sternly.

'It's too late. *You* didn't resist me, when you really should have – going to a restaurant with a complete stranger, Miss Howard? Tut tut! – so you have lost all moral authority. You have *endorsed* my irresistibility. I shall now be able to cite you as a reference if anyone ever doubts it.'

She laughed. 'You do talk such piffle! I can't remember ever talking so much of it in my life before.'

'Ah, but I do it so charmingly! More coffee?'

She became aware of the time. 'I can't. Thank you, but I must go. My friends will be wondering where I am – I said I'd follow them straight home.'

'You share a place with them, do you?'

'Yes, just a little flat, not far from here, awfully small, but cosy.'

He called for the bill, and said, 'Then I shall walk you home.'

'Oh, no, really, there's no need,' she said, slightly alarmed. She didn't know how such things went. Would he expect to be asked in?

'I can't just abandon you on the street,' he said. 'Tell you what, I'll take a taxi home, and drop you off on the way. Will that do? Taxis are awfully respectable.'

She blushed, thinking he was laughing at her. 'Thank you,' she said. At least it would get her home sooner. She was afraid the girls might think something bad had happened to her and go to the police.

After effusive goodbyes in Italian from Tony, he ushered her out into the street and summoned a passing taxi with the authority of practice, asked politely for the address, gave it to the driver, and climbed in after her.

'I know where Ridgmount Gardens is,' he said, 'so I'm aware we haven't much time. Most important things first – may I see you again?'

'Oh,' said Charlotte. She found herself taken aback by the discovery that while she had only known this man for one evening, it felt so much longer. It had not occurred to her until that moment that she might not see him again, but she realised that *not* seeing him again had always been the likeliest outcome. But now she had been asked a question she had never been asked before, and she wasn't sure what it entailed, or how to answer.

'An interesting "Oh",' he said, 'but not very enlightening. Was it "Oh, I hoped this taxi ride would be the last I saw of him"? Or, "Oh, should I tell him about my fiancé and the reason I don't wear my engagement ring in public"? Or, "Oh, I'm the English Mata Hari and off on a secret mission tomorrow, which I simply can't tell him about"? On the whole, I like the last one best. You do have something of the look of Greta Garbo about you.'

He had made her laugh again. 'None of those. I just wasn't sure what to say.'

'Yes or no make the shortest answers, and "Brevity is the soul of wit", as the Poet says. I could recommend yes – leads to so many more possibilities than no.'

'When you say "see me again" . . .' she began shyly.

'Ah,' he said, 'I needed to be more specific. Well, now, since you obviously like cinema films—'

'How do you know?'

'I *was* sitting at the next table. I wasn't eavesdropping, but your conversation was so much more interesting than my haddock, I couldn't help knowing that you had all just been to see *The Falcon and the Rose*.'

'Well, then, yes, I do like going to the cinema.'

'Splendid. Then how about going with me on Friday, and for supper afterwards? Would you like to see *It Happened One Night*?' He smiled at her in the lamplit gloom of the taxi. 'Quick, we're turning into Torrington Place. You've only just time to say, "Yes," or the whole adventure will be over and I'll disappear in a puff of smoke.'

'Yes,' she said. She hadn't known she would say it, but afterwards she thought she couldn't possibly have said no, never to have discovered what would happen.

He beamed. 'Good girl. I'll pick you up in a taxi at half past seven.' The cab stopped and he leaned across to open the door for her, and for a moment his slim, muscular body was so close to her she thought she could feel its heat. Then she was out, the door was closed, and the taxi was off, leaving her feeling the world had suddenly lost a lot of its colour.

Foolish, she told herself. The world never had colour at night, in the darkness. She walked to the front door, feeling in her bag for her key. What a strange encounter, she thought. How lucky she had left her scarf behind. And then she thought, I'll see him again. We're going out together. What the Americans call a date. What would Mummy say?

And as she walked upstairs, she thought, *Greta Garbo – what nonsense! As if I look anything like her.* But she smiled none the less.

CHAPTER EIGHTEEN

Polly wasn't quite sure how she came to find herself helping to bring Mary Eastlake out. She decided afterwards that Charles must have hidden powers of persuasion. There was also the fact that in February James had made another of his sudden departures, leaving her feeling lonely.

It happened in consequence of a letter he had received from Paris in January. Polly had noticed that the euphoria of coming home had evaporated when the activities of the Christmas season were over. Her brother seemed to have something on his mind. She had expected him to be working on his book, but it seemed that Charles Bedaux had taken all the notebooks and drawings from him when the expedition was over, intending to have them professionally edited, and James had heard nothing more about them. Since Mr Bedaux had paid him a salary to produce them, he owned them and could do as he liked with them, but James was obviously disappointed about it. Yet Polly didn't think that was all. He still hunted twice a week, and helped her about the estate, but he was clearly not present in spirit. She had almost made up her mind to tackle him about it when a letter was placed before him at breakfast one day and his face lit when he read the return direction. He excused himself hastily and bore it away to read it in private.

Later, when he and Polly were inspecting earths together, he told her about Meredith.

'She promised to write to me when she was settled in Paris, but I wasn't sure she meant it, and then as the weeks went by I decided I'd never hear from her again.'

'You like her, then, this girl?' Polly asked.

'She's splendid,' he said, with simple enthusiasm.

'Pretty?' Polly hazarded.

'Oh, yes, as anything,' James said, 'but it isn't just that. She reminds me a bit of you – not to look at, but because she *does* things. You simply know she could run a business or do anything a man does. She practically ran the whole expedition in Canada – we'd never have got anywhere without her.'

'She sounds terrifying.'

He looked at her uncertainly, then smiled. 'Oh, you're joking! She's not terrifying, any more than you are. She's pretty and nice and tremendous fun.'

'And now she's settled in Paris?'

'Yes, she's taken up the job Charlie Bedaux offered, and she's got rooms in a house near the Place Pigalle.'

'Is that a nice place?'

'I don't know,' James confessed. 'But the thing is, she writes such a friendly letter, and she says Charlie Bedaux is expanding his office and she thinks he might have room for me. She says she'll ask him, if I'm interested.'

'And are you?'

'In going to Paris? Who wouldn't be?' James cried. 'And if Charlie would give me a job, it would make it possible.'

'So then you'd move to Paris permanently?' Polly asked, trying not to sound disappointed.

'Well, for a while, anyway. Who knows what's permanent? In any case, there might not even be a job for me.'

Polly pulled herself together. 'It sounds like a wonderful opportunity. Of course you must try for it.' He looked pleased by her encouragement, and she went on, 'Even if Mr Bedaux can't give you a job, you could surely find something to do over there. It's worth a try, anyway.'

But Bedaux had offered him a job. The details seemed rather vague when transmitted through the filter of Meredith's letter and James's understanding, but it was a job with a salary, and that was all he cared about. No, all he *really* cared about was that Meredith obviously wanted him to go. He spent a frantic couple of weeks brushing up his long-languished schoolroom French, with the help of a primer and some lessons from Mrs Julian – the latter was more help than the former, and Mrs Julian concluded that while book-learning was not his *forte*, he had a quick ear and, once he was exposed to it, would soon have enough conversational French to get by.

Then, early in February, he was gone, with no time fixed for his return. Polly thought if the job suited, and Meredith was of the same mind as him, he might never return. The thought made her feel very low. So Charles Eastlake and his daughter were a useful distraction.

She hadn't found much in Mary up till now to arouse affection – she seemed a timid, beige sort of girl with nothing much to say for herself – but it was fun to design and procure clothes for her, like dressing up a life-size doll. Charles gave her a generous budget and deferred entirely to her taste, and Mary did as she was told and expressed no preferences, so Polly pleased herself. Belted waists, very slim skirt outlines, soft sleeves and round collars were the fashion, with beaded panels and detail at the lower back for evening dresses – all very suitable for a slender young girl. Hems were calf-length, and Polly reflected with a sort of wonder on how quickly fashion changed, remembered the long, naked legs of the previous decade, the bare arms and bare backs. Still, there was more for a dress designer to play with now, in all the extra fabric.

She enjoyed that part of it, but when it came to accompanying Mary to events and being seen to sponsor her, she discovered there were unanticipated consequences. She found herself being talked about. People would ask her about Charles Eastlake in a way that made it clear they thought there was a romantic connection between them; and when, crossly, she told Jessie about it, Jessie looked doubtful and said, 'But, darling, everyone's bound to assume you're interested in each other if you're doing so much for his daughter.'

'Everyone ought to mind their own business,' Polly said. '*You* didn't think that.'

'Well, actually, I did,' Jessie confessed. 'There you are, a beautiful young widow, and he's a very personable widower living next door. People immediately think, "Wouldn't it be nice if . . ." and then you confirm their hopes by launching his daughter into society for him.'

'I'm just helping out,' Polly protested. 'He hasn't anyone else to do it.'

'There are lots of people he could have asked,' Jessie said. 'People older than you, less beautiful and romantic.'

'Romantic!' Polly exploded.

'Your situation, I mean,' Jessie said hastily. 'I don't mean to suggest you're anything but a hard-headed businesswoman with no thoughts beyond your account books.' Polly saw she was teasing, and responded with a tense smile. Jessie took advantage of that and asked gently, '*Do* you like him, dear? At all?'

'Of course I like him, or I wouldn't be helping. He's – kind and pleasant and good company. I enjoy talking to him.'

'And he's completely smitten by you.'

'He is not,' said Polly, indignantly.

'Everyone can see he is,' said Jessie, 'and I think you should take that into consideration before you get any more involved with him and his family. Because it wouldn't be kind to arouse expectations in him. Men are not terribly good at reading the subtle signs, you know, and they don't understand friendship between the sexes. If you show any interest, they think it must be romantic in nature.'

Polly was silent, thinking about it. Then she said, 'I miss James. I'm lonely. I miss having a man about the place, but more than that, I miss having a man of my own. And Charles – well, I know he likes me, and I . . .' Her voice trailed off.

'You're thinking he might do?' Jessie suggested. 'Oh, Polly, be careful. You don't want to tie yourself for life to someone you don't thoroughly love and admire.'

Polly gave a nervous laugh. 'Goodness, how you do jump – from liking to marrying in an instant! Can't a girl just have a little fun?'

'Of course she can,' said Jessie. 'Just be careful, that's all I ask.'

But the result of that conversation, Jessie found, seemed to be a lessening in caution on Polly's part. She began to see Polly and Charles Eastlake together more often: walking along the street together in York, taking tea at Brown's on the corner of St Helen's Square, driving together in Eastlake's motor-car. When they dined together publicly in the restaurant at the Station Hotel, people sighed with relief that the question was at last answered, and began to invite them to the same dinners and parties.

Polly enjoyed his company, and the feeling of having a man around, a man who made it his business to see she was taken care of. She wasn't sure yet how much more she wanted from him. He was too courteous to press attentions on her without her making it clear she wanted them, so he had never attempted so much as to take her hand, except to shake it; but she found herself looking at him when he was not watching and wondering what it would be like to be kissed by him. And it was very soothing to be part of a couple again. She felt her prickles die down and a sort of soporific content take over.

One day when she was driving with him into York they passed John Burton going the other way. Burton gave her a long, curious look. It seemed to her, though she might be mistaken, a disapproving look as well, and she felt both upset, because she still valued his good opinion, and annoyed, because it was *he* who had abandoned ship, after all, by marrying the mousy Formby woman. What right had he to judge her? She turned to Charles and gave him a warm smile by way of contrast, and Charles gave her a slightly startled but extremely glad smile in return.

The collapse of Dorcas Overstreet did not bring disaster to Charlotte: in fact, it ushered in a new era of extreme happiness.

Vivian was engaged in talks with the bank to see if he could raise a loan to purchase the stock, copyrights and goodwill of the company, but the amount required was considered by the bank more than could be serviced by the business, and no loan was forthcoming. Another publisher, Bullock and Cox, made an offer to take it over and submerge its list with their own, and Vivian's uncle and the rest of the board preferred that option. Dorcas Overstreet was no more.

Vivian turned his energies instead to extracting the Dolphin Books operation from any association with the old firm, and in raising seven thousand pounds on his own security to establish it in its own right and its own premises. A tiny office above a grocery shop was rented in Theobald's Road, and the warehousing and distribution were moved to the crypt of Holy Trinity Church, a few yards away in Gray's Inn Road. Molly was delighted to find herself just round the corner from Mecklenburgh Square, where she had first tasted the freedom of flat-dwelling, and where she had been living when she first met Vivian.

'It's like going home,' she said.

She was offered a job at Bullock and Cox, but preferred to dedicate herself full time to Dolphin and to her writing. She and Vivian planned to publish a series of detective novels direct to paperback, and she was to provide at least a title a year, so she would have her hands full.

So that spring and summer Charlotte was engaged in an exciting venture, working with the very small staff of the newly independent Dolphin Books to get the books edited, printed and out to the shops. If the office in Theobald's Road was cramped, conditions in the crypt were primitive: it was dark, dusty and smelt (according to Petey, the young warehouseman) 'like mouldering bones'. Charlotte told him he saw too many films and it was only a bit of damp, but she never liked having to poke about in the darkest corners. Apart from anything else, there were spiders to consider. And mice.

There were no facilities: anyone needing to use the lavatory had to walk round to the office, and tea had to be brought in in a vacuum flask, for there was nowhere to boil a kettle. Working down there made one grateful for sunlight and fresh air, and even on wet days, the warehousemen would carry their sandwiches up to the graveyard at lunchtime rather than eat down in the dark.

But work was so hectic in the first months no-one thought about that sort of thing. Because the staff was small, all had to help with every job; and because conditions were so primitive, everyone had to be devoted to the business, which made for camaraderie. Alf, the senior warehouseman, said it was like being back in the trenches. He dubbed the crypt 'Plug Street', and the name stuck.

Access to Plug Street was via a goods lift at the back of the church. There were also stairs down from the church but it was a long way round, so it was usually more convenient to ring the bell for the lift and ride down that way, though the lift was slow and had a querulous creak that made Charlotte think nervously of fraying ropes and sudden crashes. The books going out were brought up in the lift and loaded into Dolphin's own van for delivery in London, or onto railway vans to be taken to the station for shipping elsewhere in the country. Books arriving from the printers were taken round to the side of the church. There were several windows, at ground level outside but high up on the walls inside, covered with metal grilles. One of the grilles had been removed and a chute built, down which the parcels of books could be slid and caught at the bottom.

At busy times, when there were deliveries from more than one printer arriving, or books were coming in and going out at the same time, everyone had to muck in, and a telephone call would summon the office staff round to help. Charlotte relished the variety this gave to her job, though working in Plug Street was very dirty and often cold, and the parcels coming down the chute sometimes got up such a speed that they'd drive the breath out of you or knock you right over. She had to bath practically every night and spent most of her leisure hours, it seemed to her, mending stockings.

Meanwhile, Vivian had been securing the future of the company by buying up enough works to last it three years. This not only attached a stable of first-class writers and a list of excellent titles to the imprint, it also left little material for any rival publishers to get their teeth into, should they think of setting up their own sixpenny books. By May, they were celebrating (with a bottle of champagne brought down by Vivian and drunk out of the enamel tea mugs) the sale of their millionth Dolphin book.

Charlotte was seeing Milo a couple of times a week. His business, she learned, was going so well he had found it necessary to take a tiny office in Cheapside and hire a secretary. Charlotte had felt a ridiculous pang of jealousy when he told her that, thinking for one unclear moment that if anyone was to be his secretary it should be her. But common sense immediately reasserted itself: she would not exchange her present job for anything, and given what she knew about the way he worked, always out and about meeting people, his secretary would see less of him than anyone else.

One day she was down in Plug Street helping unload a

delivery, and at lunchtime she went up with Petey, his sandwiches and flask of tea, to think about her own lunch. It was May, and a lovely sunny day. It had been clammily cold in the crypt, but the work had got up a glow. She came up glad to get away from the smell, her hands filthy, her hair, she knew, a mess. She had put on the overall she now wore to protect her clothes when she was 'grubbing', as she thought of it – a charwoman's overall of hideous floral design – and her stockings were so much mended they probably wouldn't stand another darn. They were on their last legs, she joked to herself.

She stepped out into the fresh air, stretched, and said to Petey, 'Oh, that's better. Let's go round to the side where the sun's shining. I'm starting to feel like a mushroom – pale and flabby.'

'Wouldn't be surprised if we got mould in the lungs, miss,' Petey said. 'My mum says it's not 'ealthy, working down there. Drackeler's tomb, she calls it.'

Stepping round the side of the church to where the sunlight fell in a grateful golden slice, she noticed two things: that the printer's van was just pulling out into the traffic, and that a man was standing there, hands in his pockets, staring with interest at the open grille and chute. He saw her and grinned, and her heart jumped.

'What are you doing here?' she asked, feeling hot and bothered, knowing what a guy she looked.

'I was passing and thought I'd stop by and see where you work,' Milo said, his grin widening in a way that she felt betokened amusement at her sartorial state. 'Didn't expect to see you emerging from the tomb in quite this way, like the Bride of Dracula.'

'Really!' she said indignantly. 'What a thing to say.' Petey had tactfully moved to one side to give them privacy. Charlotte was wishing the ground would open up beneath her: she toyed with the idea of flinging herself down the chute. But he had seen her now. The image would be burned on his brain. '*How* did you happen to be passing?' she demanded, taking the battle to him. 'From where to where?'

'Well, as a matter of fact, it wasn't *passing* so much as *ending up*. My office is only a ten-minute walk away, you know – so convenient, don't you think? And as I was at a loose end, I thought I'd trickle along and see if you wanted to go out to lunch.' Her feelings might have been soothed by this, but he added, with an innocent look, 'Though you might want to wash your face first. I'm afraid you'd stand out rather at the Russell Hotel. The seaside-minstrel look hasn't really penetrated Bloomsbury yet.'

'You are such a beast!' she exclaimed. 'I've been working hard, and if you want to make fun of me on that account, I shall—'

He raised his hands, laughing. 'Don't hit me! You've built up such muscles in your new job it wouldn't be a fair fight.'

'I've no intention of hitting you – or of having lunch with you.'

'Oh, don't say that! I'm so looking forward to hearing about your new life in the underworld, Proserpina.' As she went to turn away he caught her hand and pulled her back, saying, 'Don't go back into the dark, goddess! Come, now, let me at least feed you – and tell you about the new business that's come my way since we last met.'

She allowed herself to be persuaded. 'But I must go back to the office and tidy myself up first.'

'Of course. I'll wait here for you – I'd like to see more of your operation. It looks as though you've worked things out quite cunningly.'

Petey was evidently near enough to hear that. 'I'll show you around,' he offered. 'Shall I, miss?'

'All right,' Charlotte said, 'but I'll only be five minutes.'

When she came back, without the overall and the smuts, and with her hair tidied, she saw Milo squatting by the chute, staring into its depths, while Petey behind him gave explanations of something that required gestures with both hands. As she approached them, Vivian came round from the back of the building, where presumably he had just come up in the lift, so introductions were required.

'This is my friend, Milo Tavey. Vivian Blake, the boss of Dolphin Books.'

'Ah, yes,' said Vivian, 'I've heard a lot about you lately.'

'I've heard a lot about you, too, sir,' Milo said, appraising him over the handshake. 'Dolphin Books are causing quite a stir. A revolution in the book trade, I've heard it called.'

'I hope it is,' Vivian said, appraising him back, though probably for different reasons. Molly would want to hear what he thought of the young man Charlotte had been mentioning in dispatches recently.

'A piece of genius of yours,' Milo said, 'selling the books in Woolworth's, and the tobacconists, and the village shops. Wherever you can buy cigarettes, you can buy Hemingway or Agatha Christie.'

'Or D. H. Montagu,' Charlotte put in loyally. That was Molly's pen name.

'Quite,' Milo said, but pursued his line of thought. 'What next for Dolphin Books, I wonder?'

'I think we have enough on our plates at the moment,' Vivian said, with an amused look.

'The answer to that, always, is – get a bigger plate,' Milo said.

'What line are you in?' Vivian asked. 'I'm not sure Charlotte said.'

'Finance. Capitalisation,' Milo said, and spirited out of his pocket one of his cards, which he presented to Vivian. Charlotte, aware her lunch-hour was ticking away, gave a small cough. Milo nodded to her, and said to Vivian, 'It's been an honour to meet you, sir. I hope we meet again soon.'

'Yes,' Vivian said thoughtfully. 'I expect we shall.'

Charlotte and Milo had a pleasant lunch – not at the Russell Hotel but at the little Polish-owned restaurant in Coptic Street that the Dolphin office staff liked to use – and he walked her back to the office afterwards and made an arrangement for them to go to the pictures on Friday. A little while later Charlotte had to go over to Plug Street to fetch some invoices that had been delivered there by mistake, and on stepping from the lift into the crypt she saw Milo with his jacket off helping Alf move some boxes.

'What are you doing here still?' she demanded.

'Oh, I came down for a look around and got distracted,' he said innocently.

Charlotte narrowed her eyes. 'You're up to something, I can tell.'

He grinned. 'I just thought how much fun you had down here and wanted some for myself. Don't you have the perfect life, Miss Charlotte Howard, messing about with books all day long?'

'Messing, indeed!' she said.

'Believe me, my young friend,' he said solemnly, 'there is nothing – absolutely nothing – half so much worth doing as simply *messing about with books*.'

She paused a moment, then said, '*The Wind in the Willows*.' It was a game they played, identifying each other's quotations.

He reached for his coat. 'And now you have drawn my attention to the time, I realise I must dash, or I shall be late for a very important appointment.'

'"The Duchess, the Duchess, won't she be savage if I've kept her waiting!"' she mocked him.

'*Alice in Wonderland*,' he retorted. 'Too easy! Come and work the lift for me, won't you?'

The Kents returned from their honeymoon in April and took up residence in Belgrave Square, and in early May Violet and

Avis gave a dinner for them. The Bertie Yorks came, and the Westminsters – Bendor and Loelia – with Oliver and Verena, Eddie and Sarah, Leopold von Hoesch, the German ambassador, Lord and Lady Brownlow, Dickie and Edwina Mountbatten, Kit and Emma, and Charlotte, to make the numbers even. It was therefore a much more glittering and staid occasion than Charlotte was used to. Violet had bought her a suitable gown at the beginning of the Season, but had to lend her jewels so that she wouldn't look underdressed. Charlotte was happy to be partnered by the ambassador, who was a charming man, cultured and urbane, with a mellifluous voice it was a pleasure to listen to.

The talk was mostly about the upcoming Jubilee, which was almost upon them. Monday the 6th of May was Jubilee Day itself, and there would be a carriage procession from Buckingham Palace to St Paul's, a thanksgiving service, and in the evening bonfires and fireworks for the people in Hyde Park. Von Hoesch very kindly asked Charlotte to join a party to watch the procession from the windows of the German Embassy, which, being in Carlton House Terrace, looked over the Mall and would have a splendid view.

From the Jubilee the conversation moved naturally to the happy news that Prince Henry was engaged to be married to the daughter of the Duke of Buccleuch.

'So there will be another royal wedding this year,' Loelia Westminster said, with a nod towards the Kents. 'A happy prospect in Jubilee year. Now all we need is to hear that Wales has settled on some princess. What do you say – has he anyone in mind?'

'Not that I've heard of,' said Kent, genially, 'but, then, I've been out of the country, you know.'

Perry Brownlow had exchanged a look with Kit, and now said, 'Oh, I don't think he's in any great hurry. From what I've heard.'

'High time he settled down,' Bendor Westminster said.

'The whole country's waiting. And Their Majesties expect it – am I not right?' he appealed to the Yorks.

Bertie York didn't say anything – he had a speech impediment and rarely spoke – but his duchess gave a very tight and sparkling look at Lord Brownlow and said, 'He must do his duty, that's all. Many of us have to do things we don't particularly like. If everyone pleased themselves it would be a very strange world.'

There was a moment of silence, which Oliver broke by saying, 'What do you think of this new speed limit for motorcars?' It was something he had been campaigning for in the Lords – as a plastic surgeon he too often had to deal with reconstructions of faces after road accidents. 'Will it make a difference? It's certainly time something was done to stop the young people killing themselves. Charlotte, my dear, you're the youngest among us. Do you share this passion for speed? Do you urge your young men to drive you faster and faster?'

'I don't have any young men, Uncle,' Charlotte said. 'And my passion is for books.'

Violet looked as though she was glad there were no young men present to hear this damning confession, but von Hoesch said, 'I'm glad to hear it. Books are the very bricks with which we build society. Tell me what you are reading at the moment. Do you like this writer Evelyn Waugh?'

'I read *A Handful of Dust* recently,' Charlotte said. 'I enjoyed it but I didn't think the ending was right. I'd have liked the story to be resolved somehow.'

Von Hoesch agreed, and the company settled down to discuss books and thence plays and the London Season in general.

When the ladies withdrew, the men gathered round one end of the table, and the talk turned to Germany. Leo von Hoesch revealed that the King had said to him that if Germany went on the way it was, there would be war within ten years – there would be no avoiding it. Von Hoesch was deeply suspicious of Hitler, and horrified by what the National Socialists were getting up to in his beloved Germany. It troubled him to be the official ambassador of such a regime but, he said, if he resigned, they would send someone much worse. He would hold on as long as possible.

'But we're close to an agreement on the navy,' Mountbatten said. 'Limiting the size of the German navy in relation to ours. That's a real step forward.'

'Maybe so,' Oliver said, 'but even if there's an agreement, can you trust Herr Hitler to keep to it?'

'He walked away from the disarmament treaty,' said Kent.

'I don't understand what the people see in him,' Kit said. 'He looks a frightful tick, like the sort of boys who were always copping it at Eton, eh, Bendor? Now if it was *you*, Leo, I could understand it. Charm personified. It would be a positive pleasure to be overrun and enthralled by *you*.'

There was laughter, but it was uneasy. 'We shouldn't talk about war on the eve of the Jubilee,' Eddie said.

'You're right,' said Westminster. 'Better things to talk about over this fine brandy, eh?'

'Have some more,' Avis said hospitably. 'I don't believe there'll be another war anyway. Every country has too much to lose by it. There'll be posturing and blustering, but in the end there'll be agreement. No-one wants to fight again. That's what the League of Nations is for.'

On Jubilee Day, Charlotte found herself sharing a window of 9 Carlton House Terrace with Verena and her three children, John, Amabel and Venetia, who at eleven, eight and six were just the right age to enjoy the spectacle to the hilt. The procession passed under their review, glorious with its horses, soldiers, plumes, gleaming breastplates, scarlet and bearskins, military bands, and finally the carriage with the King and Queen, drawing cheers from the crowds so shrill they were almost like hysteria. The part Amabel and Venetia

463

liked best was seeing the little York girls, Lilibet and Margaret Rose, in their carriage, because they knew them and had been to play with them in their house, which was next door to Uncle Eddie and Aunt Sarah's.

When it was over, they made their way to Chelmsford House for a luncheon party. Charlotte had enjoyed it, and knew how fortunate she was to have had such a splendid position, but she couldn't help wondering if it would have been more fun to stand by the roadside with Myra and Betty, even though she would not have had anything like as good a view. She was glad she would be meeting up with them later to watch the fireworks. Violet was upset about that. There was to be a dance at Grosvenor House to which 'all their set' would be going, which would have been an excellent opportunity for Charlotte to dance with some 'suitable men'.

Charlotte said, 'It's no use, Mummy. You'll just have to accept that I'm a hopeless case. Much better forget about me.'

Violet looked annoyed. 'I will not do any such thing. You're not a hopeless case. You're just perverse. You could perfectly well fall in love if only you put your mind to it. Instead, all you seem to care about is that silly job of yours.'

'Oh, Mummy, it isn't silly. I'm sorry you don't approve, but I really don't do it to annoy you. It's what makes me happy, that's all.'

Violet softened. 'I know, darling, and I want you to be happy. And I expect your job does matter to you. But why can't you marry as well?'

'Only if I can marry a man who likes me to have a job,' she said, and she thought for an instant of Milo, who approved of her 'doing something' and not simply staying home with Mama. Not that she was thinking of marrying him, of course, but if she did, oh, wouldn't Mummy be mad!

Eventually she made her farewells and, feeling like a prisoner released, hurried across Green Park to Hyde Park

Corner and along Knightsbridge to meet the girls as arranged at the Albert Gate. She spotted Myra's scarlet coat a way off, which was lucky, because the crowds were huge; and when she got up to her, she saw there were three figures waiting for her instead of two.

'Isn't this a nice surprise?' said Myra, as she arrived. 'We found him on our doorstep when we got back to change, so . . .'

'They brought me along,' Milo finished. '*Is* it a nice surprise?'

'Very nice,' Charlotte said, and in case he got conceited, 'It's always good to have a man to force a way through the crowd for you.'

'I'm humbled,' he said. 'But even such a menial role is better than nothing. Ladies, had I but three arms to offer . . .' He offered the two he had. 'And since I was sure you were too unworldly to think how impossible it will be to get into any restaurant tonight, I took the liberty of booking a table at Romero's in Beauchamp Place for after the fireworks.'

'We can't afford that sort of place,' Betty said bluntly.

'Oh, it's not "that sort of place" at all,' Milo said. 'Don't let the address deceive you – it's quite unpretentious. And in any case, it will be my treat.'

'No, really—' Myra protested automatically.

'Yes, really,' Milo countered. 'I did a rather good piece of business today, which I'll tell you about –' The first rocket went up into the sky and shattered into stars. '– later,' he concluded. 'Come on!'

The Simpsons did go to the Court Ball on the 14th of May. Emma saw them arrive, Ernest in knee breeches and silk stockings, Wallis in gold lamé and emeralds – not borrowed this time, but a gift from the Prince, as everyone in the inner circle knew. Kit had it from Eddie, who had it from Halsey, the treasurer, that the Prince had drawn ten thousand pounds from the Duchy accounts to buy her jewellery, and was also making her a very handsome allowance: six thousand a year was the sum mentioned, sourly, by Jack Aird.

But that evening the Prince made an effort to behave well, and danced only once with Mrs Simpson, though that was enough to draw whispers when there were so many other high-ranking women he should have asked before her. And there were many who noticed that for the rest of the time his eyes sought and followed her wherever she was in the room. One of those who noticed, it seemed, was the King: at least, when he left after supper the Prince followed him as far as the private door but got no remark from him, not even 'goodnight'. The King would not look at him.

Later that night the Prince and Mrs Simpson were seen dancing together at the Embassy Club.

Basil had grown bored with the gallery. There was not enough to do to keep him occupied. It had been amusing at first to act the part, charm the customers, bamboozle them into thinking he knew what he was talking about. Most of them knew so little about painting he could say what he liked, and as long as it sounded good, they would be impressed. He invented new words and phrases to describe the paintings: the colour was 'corubulant'; the technique of 'fastoliation' had created the 'abbrative' quality of the composition. He invented incidents in the lives of the artists, made one a hopeless drunk, another a religious maniac given to flagellation. The customers, convinced by his low, reverent tone and earnest look, drank it in.

But it was too easy. Success urged him on to ever greater flights, until one day a wealthy mine owner gave him a narrow look and said, 'Are you making fun o' me, young man?' Sebastian, the other employee, who dealt with the serious art lovers and more important customers, began to give him odd looks. And Basil, having conquered this peak, saw no reason

466

to remain on the mountain. He began to come in late and leave early, on other days not to show up at all. He preferred to rise late, find someone amusing to lunch with (generally it had to be someone who would pay, as well) and wander round his favourite haunts until it was time to present himself to Gloria for whatever entertainment she had planned.

Eventually Sebastian took the brave step of complaining to Gloria about him. It was not his frequent absences that troubled him – he and his assistant Sophie could manage the work perfectly well between them – but his destructive appearances.

In a taxi on the way to the theatre, Gloria said, 'You're not happy working at the gallery?'

Basil paused cautiously, but said, 'It's not very amusing.'

'What would you find amusing?' she asked.

He took her hand and kissed it. 'Being with you. Why can't I see you more often?'

'Because I have a business to run, and other people to see. Basil, don't, not here.' He was nuzzling her neck, which made her feel hot and bothered. 'I can't be with you every moment of the day, much as I'd like to.'

'*Would* you like to? You smell so beautiful. Why do we have to go to this silly play? Let's go home and make love.'

She laughed. 'I can't stay in bed with you every moment of the day, either. No, darling, don't. If we were together all the time, you'd soon grow tired of me, and I don't mean that to happen.'

'I could *never* grow tired of you,' he asserted, but straightened up and left her ear alone. He knew when she was serious, and when he would not be able to wheedle her off the subject. This was one of those times.

'All the same,' she said firmly, 'I must attend to my business, and *you* must have something to do. Let me think. You're interested in journalism, aren't you?'

He had told her he had edited the school paper in one

467

of their long, rambling conversations in bed, and he was so used to answering the question in the positive that he said, 'Yes,' without thinking.

'I have a friend,' she said thoughtfully – he had learned that she had 'friends' in all sorts of places – 'in the newspaper business. I'll ask him about a job for you.'

'A writing job,' Basil insisted. 'Not something to do with ink and machines.'

She laughed. 'No, of course I meant a writing job. I think journalism might suit you very well.'

'But what about the days when you want me with you?'

'I'm sure something can be arranged.'

Basil heard that with relief. If absences from time to time were to be built into the job, it shouldn't be too difficult for him to stretch them to his own requirements 'All right,' he said magnanimously. 'I'll try it.'

Gloria's 'friend' turned out to be the son of the proprietor of the *Daily Bugle*, and also its managing director, so the outcome was never in doubt. Basil left the gallery, and after a gap of several weeks, which he managed to extract because of the Jubilee, the various celebrations, and the disruption to business generally, he started work at the *Bugle* at the beginning of June as a copy writer. He was given a desk and a typewriter in a crowded, noisy office where the telephones rang all the time. Everyone was very friendly, always willing to sit on the edge of someone else's desk and chat; work got done in a haphazard way, it seemed to him, and usually at the last minute.

Hours of work seemed to be flexible, and the best thing, as far as he was concerned, was that no-one ever knew where anyone else was. If you were absent from your desk you might be down in Records or up in Vouchers, looking something up in the Morgue, searching for a reference book that someone had borrowed and not put back in the right place, taking copy to an editor or proofs to the compositors. It was the perfect set-up for him not to have to do too much actual work.

He liked the people he worked with, and there was always someone agreeable to have lunch with or go out with in the evening if Gloria was occupied. Some of them were curious about him and how he had got the job, but he didn't mention her or the intervention of John Mainwaring, guessing that it would not make him popular. Instead he played up the school magazine and hinted that he had worked on a provincial paper and had come to London to start a long and serious career in journalism. That went down very well, and everyone was keen to help him along and explain how things worked. Any surprising ignorance on his part could be explained away with 'Oh, we didn't do it that way at the *Record*.'

The pay was better than at the gallery, and there was a whole raft of new people to borrow from. He could loosen or even remove his tie as soon as he reached his desk, and over-long hair was practically a badge of office. He felt he had found his spiritual home.

His parents were impressed that he had managed to get himself a job on a big newspaper, and were proud and happy that he was entering his proper career of journalism at last. 'I always thought it was the right thing for you,' his mother said.

And his father added, 'You can go all the way in it, that's the good thing. There are no limits for a man of your talents.'

They sent him five pounds because he said he needed some new shirts.

Barbara sent him a letter of congratulation and a small sewing kit so that he could do his own repairs.

'How are you enjoying the new job?' Gloria asked him one evening, when he had been there two weeks.

'Very much,' he said. They were dining at Sharvi's, before going on to the Old Florida Club in Bruton Mews.

'I'm glad you're settled and happy now,' she said. 'I was

worried when you kept saying you didn't want to do anything. It isn't good for a man to be idle.'

'I don't count being with you as idleness,' he said, touching her hand across the table.

'But a man needs a career, or at least an interest, other than a woman,' she said. 'Now you're doing something you like, you can be busy and happy, and that will make me happy.' With the hand that was not occupied by his, she pushed a narrow box across the table towards him. 'A little present, to celebrate your new career,' she said.

It was a gold propelling pencil. He kissed her hand in thanks, and promised to thank her properly later.

The tender moment was broken by a loud voice. 'Gloria, darling! Too divine! I haven't seen you in an age.'

Gloria withdrew her hand from Basil's. 'Hello, Veronica. I didn't know you frequented Sharvi's.'

'I don't usually,' said Veronica Glenforth-Williams, 'but Nancy and Peter came last week with the Oglanders, and Nancy said it was utterly spiffikins, so we're meeting them and going on to the Shim-Sham.' Veronica's shadowy husband, Gray, was standing behind her – she was so rarely seen with him that Gloria hadn't noticed him at first. But Veronica's glinting eyes were fixed on Basil, who had risen, in a way that made Basil feel like a tasty scrap of missionary before a lion. 'And this must be your Mr Compton.' Gloria reluctantly performed the introduction. 'I couldn't be more thrilled! I've heard so much about you, I've been dying to meet you!'

Basil obediently took the scarlet-clawed hand held out to him, and found his own gripped in a vice. He decided not to be eaten without a struggle. He smiled his best seductive smile, looked straight into her eyes, and said, 'I've heard so much about *you*, Mrs Glenforth-Williams. With so much interest on both sides we were bound to meet sooner or later, don't you think?'

Veronica squealed. 'Gloria darling, where did you *get* this man? You must bring him to dinner next week.'

'Oh, I don't think—' Gloria began to murmur.

Veronica steamed on: 'Come on Tuesday. The Oglanders are coming, and the Favels, and the Simpsons before they go down to Ascot.'

Gloria asserted herself: 'I'm so sorry, but I'm already engaged for Tuesday,' she said.

'How sick-making! We must make it another time, that's all. I die to get to know this delicious man of yours. Oh, there's Nancy. Must go. Come along, Gray. 'Bye, darling, I'll be in touch.'

With a whirl of blown kisses she was gone, followed by her husband, leaving a vacuum. Basil sat down. '*Are* you engaged for Tuesday? You didn't ask if I wanted to go.'

'The Oglanders are well-meaning bores and the others are the sort of Americans who give Americans a bad name,' Gloria said.

'I thought Veronica was your friend,' Basil said, a little sulkily.

Gloria gave him a canny look. 'I thought *you* wanted to spend more time alone with me. Now you're hankering after a tedious dinner party?'

He adjusted his face. 'All I want is you,' he said. 'I think Aunt Emma knows Mrs Oglander,' he added. 'I've heard Aunt Molly mention her.'

'You don't want to get mixed up in that set,' Gloria said firmly. 'I was thinking, this weekend we might go away somewhere – would you like that?'

Basil expressed his immediate enthusiasm for the plan, and forgot all about the dinner party. He didn't know those people anyway.

'Are you *sure*?' Lennie asked, for the tenth time. 'We really don't have to go.'

471

'Of course I'm sure,' Beth said, also for the tenth time.

'But it will be noisy and crowded—'

'I know what Hollywood parties are like,' she said.

'Only by repute,' Lennie argued. 'You've never actually *been* to one.'

'I am aware of that fact,' she said drily. 'You've never taken me to one. I'm beginning to think you're ashamed of me, Lennie Manning. Big studio mogul that you are, knowing everyone and being invited everywhere, but married to a mousy Miss Nobody – hmm, let me think.' She pretended to ponder, tapping her chin with a forefinger.

He gathered her in his arms. 'You know it isn't that,' he said. 'I couldn't be more proud of you, and I'd show you off to everyone if it weren't such a waste when I could have you all to myself.'

'Not bad for an improvisation,' she said, 'but I could be more convinced.'

'I just don't want you to strain yourself. You're having a baby.'

'Strange to say, I'm aware of that fact, too,' she said. 'And I'll soon be too big and uncomfortable to go out much, so I would like to see just *one* glittering, star-studded, everyone-who's-anyone Hollywood party while I have the chance.'

'Well, if you really want to go . . .' Lennie said. 'I must say, I'm curious to see Rose in her element, see what sort of a hostess she makes. I've hardly been inside Roselands three times. And there'll be a couple of fellows there I wouldn't mind meeting, business-wise.'

'Which makes it all the more silly of you to try to put me off . . .' she said, and then, in a warmer tone, '. . . but I love you for it. I know you're just watching out for me.'

He kissed her. 'Are you sure you wouldn't rather stay home?' he murmured into her ear, which he then nibbled.

She jerked away. 'Don't do that – it makes me crazy.'

'Exactly my intention.'

'It's no good. You can nibble anything you want but we're going. I've got a dress I want to wear, which I'm not likely to be able to wear again for a long time, thanks to you. I'm going to be the size of a house all through the heat of the summer – we didn't plan this thing right *at all*! So I want one self-indulgent, glittery, terrible-taste, celebrity beanfeast before it's too late. *Entiendes?*'

'Understood. Sorry, honey. I'm being a fuss-budget. Go put on your glad rags, and we'll shimmy the night away and drink Rose's champagne until dawn.'

It was a warm evening, so he sent Beanie away and took the two-seater with the open top, driving himself. He helped Beth in fussily and insisted she take a shawl. 'It might be cold later.'

'Yes, Daddy,' she teased him. The night was full of cicadas and tree frogs, and smelt of warm pine and gum, and the stars in the black sky over their hill looked polished, fat and ripe. 'As if you could squeeze them and get star juice,' Beth said.

'What would it look like?' Lennie asked, easing the car into the first of the long curves that took the road down the hill, snaking back and forth across the steep gradient.

'Like gin,' she decided. 'Very clear, and slightly blue. Thinner than moonlight.' She began to sing. '"Place – park. Scene – dark. Silv'ry moon shining through the trees."' She stopped. 'Wait a minute – where's the moon?'

'No moon tonight,' he said, amused.

'No silvery moon? Call the producer! Call the properties manager! I distinctly ordered a practical moon for this scene.'

'Do you miss the business?' he asked.

'A little. But I won't once the baby's here,' she said contentedly. 'Don't worry about me, Len.'

'I like to worry about you. It makes me feel warm and fuzzy.'

'Oh, well, worry away, then,' she smiled, placing a hand on his knee.

'And I was thinking,' he went on, 'what you said before

about the heat of the summer. How would it be if we went away for a couple of months, maybe to—'

The car came out of nowhere. All down the hill there were gateways to other properties, and most of the driveways were steep, but that was no reason for the vehicle to emerge at such a speed, unless the driver were reckless or drunk. It came out later that the four youngsters in the brand-new Auburn 851 Speedster were all hilarious, roaring drunk from a twenty-first-birthday party. The Auburn shot out from the right just as they were passing the gateway and slammed into the passenger side of Lennie's car, hurling it across the narrow road where, encountering the ditch along the edge, it flipped over, landed upside-down on the bank beyond, then slowly toppled back onto its wheels at an angle, half on the road and half in the ditch.

Lennie heard the noise and felt the impact, but everything else was a confusion in the few seconds it took. His body was violently jolted, he felt a hard pain across his legs and a thin, burning pain down his cheek. His head hit the bank, doubling him over forward, banging his forehead against something hard. When all the movement stopped he was still in the driving seat with the cold wetness of blood on his face, his legs, shoulders and neck a growing thunder of pain.

The only words that had passed his lips were, 'What the—?'

The other car was on its side in the ditch, its headlamps probing the sky in search of answers. There were moaning sounds coming from it, and someone was sobbing.

What the—?

Motor accident, his befuddled brain told him. Something hit us.

Us.

'Beth?' he said. It was agonisingly painful to turn his head. 'Beth, honey?' She wasn't in the seat beside him. Had he dreamed her? No, no, she had been there. *Get a grip on yourself.* He turned his head the other way. There she was, lying on the bank, on her back, looking up at the stars. *No moon tonight.* She looked quite relaxed. She wasn't crying or moaning like the kids in the other car. He felt relief.

She must have been thrown clear. It was the steering-wheel that had kept him in his seat. 'Beth, honey, are you all right?' He remembered the child. *Oh, God, what if she lost the child?* He struggled to get out: his hands felt as if he were wearing boxing gloves, his arms and legs didn't want to obey him, he was one big lump of pain. He fumbled with the door, he was out, the ground heaving under his feet; he staggered the couple of steps towards her, slipping on the bank, his foot going down the ditch with a jolt that sent a bolt of agony through his neck.

'Beth, honey?'

She was lying, quite relaxed, in her evening dress, looking up at the stars . . . except that her head was at a very odd angle. It couldn't really be comfortable like that. He crawled up beside her. 'Are you all right, honey?' he murmured. The stars reflected in her open eyes. There was a little thread of blood coming out of her hairline, and he wiped it away carefully with his fingers so it wouldn't trickle into her eye. There should have been a moon for her. He should have arranged it – a practical moon. He wanted to make it right. He sang to her, his voice husky and uneven, the chorus of the song she had started. 'By the light – of the silvery moon—'

Someone's hand was on his shoulder. A male voice said, 'Sir, is she all right? Are you all right?' It sounded very frightened.

She's all right. She's just resting, he said. But only inside his head. His numb lips were occupied with singing, which seemed just then the most important thing to do, though he didn't remember why, and he couldn't hold the tune.

'Honey moon, keep a-shining in June.'

Beth, honey?

CHAPTER NINETEEN

Polly had wanted to have a Jubilee Ball at Morland Place, but others beat her to it and took all the available dates. There were so many celebrations going on that there was hardly time for her to organise it anyway. On Jubilee Day itself there was the civic parade in York, and street parties in many areas. There was one in the village, which the Morlands helped with, lending trestles, crockery and the big tea urns kept in store for the summer fête, and providing much of the food. Every house flew a flag, there were miles of bunting, and hundreds sat down to sandwiches, cakes, and jelly with cream on the top. Afterwards, in Low Field, which Polly had lent for the occasion, there were sports for the children and a couple of novelty events for adults, three-legged and sack races, and a babies-and-prams race, in which one adult pushed another in a perambulator. It was made even more entertaining by some of them dressing up as infants and nurses – usually the burliest men.

On the following Saturday the Chubbs had their Jubilee Ball at Bootham Park. Polly went in a gown of her own devising, of silver lace over grey satin, with a headdress of silver wires and crystal spars. She went with Charles and Mary, who was now thoroughly launched and beginning to come out of her shell. It was good to see her dancing with confidence, looking very pretty in pale pink georgette and a necklace of pearls, her father's birthday present. It was particularly satisfying to observe the attentions of Alan Stead, son of the owner of Stead's Printing Works, who seemed to be seriously smitten.

'He's a very nice young man,' she told Charles.

'Yes, and just the steady sort I hoped she would meet. He inherits the business, I understand.' Polly said he was the only son. 'And it would be nice to have her settled close to home,' he concluded.

Polly had several dances with Charles, and went to supper with him, but plenty of other men were eager to claim a dance with her, so she did not spend the whole time with him. After supper Bertie whisked her away, and said, 'Your gown is causing a sensation. You put one in mind of the Snow Queen of Hans Andersen.'

'Oh, not so wicked and ruthless, I hope,' Polly said.

Bertie smiled at her fondly. 'No, we know you better than that. This Charles fellow—?'

Polly cut him off. 'Now, don't start on that. I've already been lectured by Jessie. Don't you see how I've danced with other people tonight?'

'I've been observing you, and what I see most is that you're very comfortable with him. When you're together you look like a couple.'

Polly blushed with annoyance, but she didn't answer. After a bit Bertie said, 'I'm sorry if I upset you. I only thought he seems to be a very nice man. And wouldn't it be good if Shawes was joined with Morland Place again?'

Polly couldn't help laughing. 'You men! All you think about is land! He only rents it, you know.'

'Nothing to stop a fellow going after the freehold,' Bertie said blandly. 'It's what your father would have done.'

'Well, I promise you,' Polly said, 'when I marry – if I ever marry again – it won't be for the sake of my suitor's landholding.'

'There are worse criteria,' Bertie said serenely, and she saw he was teasing and pinched his arm in retaliation.

Her Jubilee gown was so much asked after that she rushed out a copy in cheaper materials for her shops. The Jubilee was certainly causing a welcome surge of business in all of them, especially in women's clothing.

There were balls and parties and galas of various sorts in the following weeks, and the earliest free date Polly could get was the 25th of June, so she gave up on tying it to the Jubilee and called it the Midsummer Ball instead. To distinguish it from everyone else's she made it a masked costume ball, and to prevent some of the tired old fancy dresses in the area making yet another appearance, she said it was to be on the theme of *A Midsummer Night's Dream*. That, she thought, should give a wide enough scope, and there would be lots of attractive Titanias and Oberons instead of the well-worn Nelsons and Dutch Dolls.

The week before the date, there was some very happy news: Alan Stead asked for Mary Eastlake's hand, and was accepted. Charles was delighted, and at once invited Alan and his parents to dinner at Shawes. He asked Polly to join them.

She demurred. 'It's a family affair.'

'But you're almost a mother to Mary,' he said, and seeing her draw back a little, hastily amended it to, 'I mean that if you hadn't taken a hand in bringing her out, this wouldn't have happened. She and I are both very grateful to you.' He looked at her earnestly. 'Please do come,' he urged quietly. 'It wouldn't seem complete without you there.'

She accepted; but it gave her something to think about in the run-up to her ball.

Morland Place was *en grande tenue*. The great hall was decorated to represent a forest glade: pots of ferns and tall parlour palms and massive white gardenias with their dark glossy foliage; swags of greenery and trailers of ivy hanging from the banisters of the upper hall and around the cornice; tiny white fairy lights twinkling everywhere. The effect was very pretty and romantic: the servants kept coming to the green baize door between their duties for a peep. Alec was for catching some birds and letting them out in the hall to make it 'even more real'. Polly told him it would be unkind to the birds – they would be frightened. He was so disappointed that she allowed him to position a stuffed pheasant from the Long Gallery behind some foliage on the mantelpiece as a sop to his creative urge.

In the dining room a splendid buffet supper was laid out, which would be entirely candle-lit when the time came; and in the drawing room there were the usual card tables for those too old or disinclined for dancing.

Circling in Charles's arms, Polly noticed that despite her orders there was a Bo-Peep, a Greek god, a very shabby pierrot and at least two pirates, one with a multi-coloured cardboard parrot fixed precariously to his shoulder. But she wasn't going to let it spoil her evening. She was in diaphanous chiffon, a tiara in her golden hair, and delicate gauzy wings behind, which, for convenience on the dance-floor, she had wired to lie half folded. She was amused that Charles had found her at once, despite her mask – though she would have been disappointed if he hadn't. She had recognised him the moment he arrived by his height and figure, and was glad he had come as Oberon. There were a number of asses around, and she wouldn't have liked to see him risk his dignity by sporting ears.

'You look magnificent,' he murmured, bowing over her hand. 'The queen of all the queens of fairies. Will you dance with me, beautiful stranger?'

'With pleasure, unknown gallant,' she answered.

Whether it was the lighting or the setting or something to do with the masks, she felt a strange, dreamlike mood come over her. She danced with him, his warm hand holding hers, his strong shoulder under her hand; the scent of him was familiar; she knew the way his hair grew around his neckline, and the exact conformation of the whorls of his ear. She felt his love for her enveloping her. She felt cherished, safe – that most of all. Since she had left her father's home for New York, she had been out alone in the wide world, and her father had died before she had had a chance to come back to him. Her anchor, her citadel, had vanished. But with Charles she felt she had come home again.

There was magic in play that evening, for no-one burst the bubble that seemed to surround them as they danced only with each other. At other balls she was always besieged by requests, but tonight it was as if the neighbours had made a compact to leave them alone. As the evening progressed Polly became less aware of those around her. They were part of the backdrop, like the ferns and the lights: softly coloured misty shapes that moved and parted and never touched her.

When the music stopped for supper-time, and he released her, they stood, still wrapped in the mood. She swayed a little, a faint, soft smile on her lips. She didn't want anything to disturb this dream. People were in motion towards the supper room. Food and drink seemed too gross and worldly for the moment. He bent towards her, his mouth under his mask moving. 'Will you walk with me, Queen? Take a little air?'

She placed her hand in his without speaking. Even words were too much for her just then. He did not know Morland Place as she did, and would have gone towards the great door, but she led him to the door by the chapel and out into the inner courtyard. There was no moon. The light from the dining-room windows was candlelight, faint, soft, shifting, completely in tune with her mood.

'It used to be the herb garden,' she heard herself say. 'But there was never enough sun for them to thrive.' Now there were a few tubs in the centre around a square of grass in memory of it: bay and rosemary and thyme, and white nicotiana, threading the dark with its delicate scent.

Reaching the green they stopped. She turned to him. It seemed simple and natural to be taken in his arms. She looked again at his mouth. She wanted to be kissed. She wanted it so much! It had been so long since she had been held and kissed by a man. The unused well of love in her had filled to overflowing.

He bent over her, but not to kiss her. His hands went to her face, felt gently for the fastening of her mask, undid it and lifted it away. 'It's a crime to mask so beautiful a face,' he said, and there was a tremor in his voice that made her feel hollow.

'Yours too,' she urged. He took his mask off, dropped them both on the grass. His face, appearing now suddenly in the dim light, seemed strange to her – a stranger's. She looked at it in a sort of delicious fear. To be kissed by a stranger! Excitement thrilled in her. His arms made her feel safe while his mouth promised danger.

'Polly,' he said – his voice was urgent, 'you know that I love you. You must know. I've loved you since the first moment I saw you. Will you marry me?'

'Kiss me,' she said. His mouth descended on hers. Oh, the feeling of a man's lips, the taste of a man! She was melting, falling backwards into the void. Only his strong arms, crushing her tighter as his excitement mounted, held her together. She returned his kiss, hungry for more, eager to end the long famine of the body.

His mouth left hers. *No!* she thought. He lifted his head. 'Will you?' he asked, an urgent murmur. 'Will you marry me?'

'Yes,' she said and, putting a hand behind his neck, tugged his head impatiently back down.

She drifted up slowly from the dark water of sleep, feeling, in the half-thoughts before she broke the surface, that something had happened. It was like waking as a child on Christmas morning, having forgotten the date, but aware that this morning would be different from those before.

481

Eyes still closed, she stretched languorously, and licked her lips.

And woke, remembering everything. Charles, the herb garden, the proposal. He had asked her to marry him. She had said yes.

She opened her eyes and stared up at the tester. What did she feel about that? After the euphoria in the garden, as they had gone back in, she had asked him not to say anything yet, and he had agreed; had said he would call on her this morning to discuss their plans.

Their plans: she liked that. When you were young, marriage tended to be a thing that was done to you, by your family and society in general, and you were the largely passive recipient of a wedding and fine clothes and a settlement, and all the things that came afterwards. She had been married that way to Ren. But now it was *their* plans. She and Charles would do things together, decide things together.

Charles. She felt a frisson of – excitement? Fear? Not fear that he would hurt her, but fear of the unknown. She knew very little about him. She had spent the last six months being courted by him, spent more and more time in his company as the months passed, yet she did not feel she knew him. He was kind and pleasant, educated, good company; she enjoyed being with him. She had certainly enjoyed being kissed by him. And with him she felt so safe. Which was a paradox, was it not? How could you feel safe with the unknown?

She shrugged the problem aside and sat up. He was coming to see her. What should she wear? Something simple, she thought. The bias-cut blue linen that brought out her eyes. And the pale straw with daisies. They would go outside and seek the privacy of the gardens for their talk. Was it going to be a fine day? She rang for Rogers, jumped from the bed and went to open the curtains. Fand, lying on the hearthrug, raised puzzled eyes without lifting his head from his paws, knowing it was too early.

Yes, outside was a pale, clear dawn promising sunshine, the sky lightly fretted with fine cat-tails of cloud. They were just beginning to be tinged with gold from the unseen sun. The wind was light, from the south, perfect for a walk in the garden with—

Her fiancé. The word brought her up short. And, oh, my God, there would be a wedding! She would have a wedding to plan, the place, the ceremony, the flowers, the banquet, the cake. The dress. She would have to design herself a wedding dress. Ideas flooded into her mind, and she itched for a pencil and paper. She must get started!

The door opened, and Rogers came in with her tray. 'Up already, miss? Shall I run your bath?'

'Yes, and put out the embroidered blue linen.' There would not be time to change after breakfast. If she knew anything, he would come at the earliest possible hour.

They walked in the rose garden, in its June glory, with the dogs pottering about in front and behind them in a happy morning pack, snuffing the scents captured in the dew that lingered in the shady places.

'It can be any time you like,' he said. He looked bemused this morning, a man lightly stunned by good luck; more familiar than he had seemed last night, but still on the whole a stranger. Polly felt oddly shy before him. 'I imagine you will want some time to plan the wedding. You'll want a big affair? The mistress of Morland Place should have nothing less, and there are your tenants to consider, not to mention family and friends.'

'Yes, it will be an important event,' she said. 'And, if you would, I'd like it to be kept secret for the moment, until we have the main points settled.'

'Just as you wish,' he said kindly. 'Remembering the summer fête last year and imagining how much organisation went into that, I'm beginning to feel it will be like a military campaign.'

'More pleasurable than that, I hope,' Polly said. 'There's another consideration – Mary's wedding. I think we ought to wait until after that. I shouldn't want to upstage her.'

'How like you to think of it,' he said. 'We've been talking about August for her and Alan, if it suits your plans.'

'My plans?'

'Naturally she hopes you will be involved in it. She has no mother to help her and guide her through it. And,' he added, with a smile, 'you really will be her mother once we are married.'

'Yes,' Polly said thoughtfully. 'And Roger's.'

'Well, I don't suppose Roger will be much of a burden to you,' he said, 'away at university for most of the time, and twenty-one next year. And when Mary's married, it will be just the two of us.'

'You're forgetting *my* family,' she said. 'Harriet's at teacher-training college, and Martin goes to university this autumn, but they'll be home in the holidays; and there's Laura and Alec not grown-up yet, and John still living here, and Jeremy until he can afford to get married. And Ethel. And James, if he comes back from France, which one can never rule out.'

'Yes,' he said, looking slightly taken aback. 'I'd forgotten for the moment how many people call Morland Place their home. But they'll all go away eventually, won't they?'

'Perhaps, but I shan't force them to,' Polly said, without emphasis. 'It isn't what my father would have wanted.'

'No, indeed. Perhaps we shall live at Shawes, then. It's close enough for you to come over to Morland Place whenever you needed to.'

She gave him a surprised look. 'But of course we'll live at Morland Place. How could you think otherwise? Though it might be fun to buy Shawes at some point, if it can be managed. It used to belong to us, you know, centuries ago.'

'I feel as though I'm marrying England,' Charles said. He smiled as he said it, but he looked a little daunted by the idea.

Polly felt a surge of sympathy for him. When a man asked a woman to marry him, it was he who made a home for her, and she came to him with only portable baggage. It must be hard for an ordinary man to adapt to the demands of Morland Place, and to understand what it meant. She belonged to it: that was what he would have to understand. It was not a concept a non-Morland would find easy to grasp, and she would have to help him. It was a good thing, she thought, that they would have a longish engagement.

'I don't think we should tell anyone until after Mary's wedding,' she said. 'Otherwise poor Mary won't get the attention she deserves. And she ought to be thinking of nothing but Alan Stead: a potential step-mother might cloud her thoughts. Can we have a secret engagement until then?'

'Yes, of course. I'm sure you're right. But will you let me buy you a ring, at least?'

'I'd like that, but when would I wear it?'

'When we're alone together.' He stopped walking and turned to her, taking her hands. 'I hope there will be a lot more of that, at least.'

She felt the hollow aching again, in the pit of her stomach. Suddenly she remembered Ren, so big he had blocked out the sun, and his love-making. He had taught her what the love of bodies could mean; Erich had taught her about the love of souls.

What would Charles teach her?

'I hope so too,' she said, rather huskily. 'We'll have to be discreet, though, if we're to keep the engagement secret.'

He smiled. 'I hope you don't want me to be climbing up the ivy after dark. I think I'm too old for that.'

One golden June evening James walked along the right bank of the Seine, feeling extremely pleased with life. He was on his way to meet Meredith. Women gave him covert glances as he passed, and sometimes he tipped his hat to them and smiled. He was wearing a new suit of cream flannel, with brown and white co-respondent shoes, a straw trilby with a brown silk ribbon, and a gardenia in his lapel. He looked both jaunty and elegant. He would have twirled his cane as he walked, had he owned one.

He had loved Paris from the moment he'd arrived: dirty, noisy, chaotic – *exceedingly* smelly – yet it had an energy and slapdash vigour that made him feel cheerful. Of course, the presence in Paris of Meredith McLean did it no harm. He probably would have found the ninth circle of hell fairly congenial if she had been there too.

He loved the cafés, the bars, the jazz clubs, the little shops crammed into the low, dim ground floors of ancient buildings. He loved the ritual of going out in the morning for bread, coming back with it tucked warm under the armpit through streets smelling of coffee. He loved the dark churches with their sad ghosts of incense and the living gladness of candles, and the comfortable habit of Parisians of popping in for a prayer when they passed, not waiting for Sunday. He liked the old women, nut-faced, in black skirts and headscarves, legs bent by age and childbearing, who would rub a hand over St Anthony's sandalled foot to get his attention, so that the paint was all gone and the toes worn smooth. He loved the tawdry glamour of the grand buildings, all meretricious glitter outside, founded on truly terrible plumbing. He loved the Métro with its Toulouse-Lautrec nameplates. He loved the slow river, the bridges, the markets, the booksellers along the Left Bank, the artists around Pigalle and up Montmartre.

His stumbling French had improved by leaps and bounds, as Mrs Julian had guessed it would. Having been a singer all his life, he had a musical ear, and soon acquired a good accent, which was more important than the occasional mistakes of grammar or vocabulary. But in a few weeks he had left those behind as well. The two things Parisians valued above all others were a stylish appearance and proper Parisian French, so he fitted in very well, made friends, and was popular.

He was, in fact, exactly what Charles Bedaux wanted: the qualities he had seen in James in Canada, his likeability, adaptability and lack of any deep convictions about anything – with the possible exception of Miss McLean – fitted him perfectly for the job he had in mind.

When he explained it to James, James thought it was hardly something he ought to be paid for. To meet people, sometimes fetch them from the station or airport and see them into a comfortable hotel, take them to restaurants, shows, sightseeing, generally give them a good time, soften them up for business – how could that be deserving of a salary? But a salary there would be, and an expense account.

Charlie would tell him whom to meet and how to entertain them. It would not always be restaurants and shows. Sometimes he would simply have to meet them at a party or a bar and get them talking. Now and then he might be asked to take a letter or package somewhere, or to collect one and bring it back to Charlie. Or to perform other small errands.

'Whatever you want,' James said eagerly, then felt obliged to add one last caveat. 'But I don't know anything about your business.'

'You'll be taught anything you need to know. But I don't want you to talk business to these people. Others will do that. You simply have to impress upon them that I am a good man to do business with.'

'Oh, I can do that, all right,' James said, with relief. He already thought Charlie the best fellow in the world, and could say so with a shining sincerity, which was another of his qualifications for Mr Bedaux.

James got himself a room at the top of a tall, narrow house in a queer old cobbled lane halfway up Montmartre, not too far from Meredith's lodgings. If he hung far out of the window and twisted sideways he could just see the top of the Sacré

Coeur. He loved his jumbled view through the chimneys even without that. Pigeons fluttered down in the morning to sun themselves on the hot slates. There was an attic opposite that had red geraniums in the window, an exotic contrast, like a flame against the darkness inside. A black cat would step daintily out of the casement in the morning in search of the perfect rooftop place to settle for a wash. The sky over the roofs was never the same, and the plumes of smoke made their own brushstrokes on the azure or grey. He felt he could never have enough of the view from his window, and sketched and painted it again and again.

With an advance in expenses from Charlie, he bought himself some new, smarter suits, had his hair cut in the Parisian style, and settled himself in with relish to his new job. When he was not needed, he set about discovering Paris.

He was an affable fellow, and made friends easily, first of all with the artists in his own neighbourhood. Seeing them painting in the street, he began shyly to follow suit. He had been disappointed that Charlie had never referred to his diary and sketches of the expedition, but he had never mentioned the film, either. The whole thing seemed to have dropped completely from his mind. When James mentioned it to Meredith, she said she gathered Charlie was like that, full of enthusiasms that soon passed, to be replaced by newer ones. 'I don't suppose the film will ever see the light of day,' she said. 'That was last year's fad. Forget it, James – that's my advice.'

So he did, and set about building up a new portfolio of memories. He carried a sketch-book with him for a time, but it was not enough to satisfy him: he wanted colour. He went to one of the many art-shops and got himself a port-able kit: a sort of light wooden suitcase that opened up into an easel and contained a folding canvas stool, box of paints, brushes, water-jars and a supply of paper.

Now he was part of the street landscape, another diligent

dabbler. He was accepted in observant silence at first, until his neighbours found what he was made of. A few silent passes behind him as he worked, a few telegraphed exchanges of eyebrows and pursed lips, and the community was ready to decide he was one of them.

They addressed him: a simple '*Bonjour, voisin,*' to begin with, then a comment on the weather and, more particularly, the quality of the light. James did not pretend to know more than he did, which endeared him to them, as did his fluent Parisian French. His painting was not contemptible. He had something, this *jeune homme*, a *je ne sais quoi*: an energy *bien sûr*, but *au fond* something more, an unspoiled talent. And he was *gentil*. Before long they knew his name and he theirs. He was invited to their studios, then to their homes, and then to parties.

Now a different part of Paris was opened to him, not the public but the private. He got to see behind those mysteriously closed great doors to the courtyards inside, past the gnarled and unmovable concierge planted on a wooden chair to deny access – indeed almost to deny existence itself – and on up crooked stairs and along rackety balconies, which seemed attached to the building by will alone, to the rooms. Sometimes they were meagre, even squalid, a mess of discarded clothes and painting materials, half-eaten food on tin plates, a smell of drains and foul French cigarettes; sometimes lofty, high-ceilinged, with a faded, pathetic grandeur and a chipped marble fireplace; and then there were the attic studios, all window, with a worn velvet chaise longue under a thrown fringed shawl, and a sulky-eyed girl with unkempt hair in the background, model or mistress or both.

At the parties he met other people, the patrons, the dealers, hangers-on of all sorts and degrees, and this led him back to the other Paris, the one inhabited by the Americans and Charlie's clients, the Paris of the rich and cultured: the *appartements* so luxuriously *meublés*, all marble and chandeliers

489

and Louis Quinze mirrors; the great *magasins* of the rue de Rivoli and the 'Boul Hauss', their page-boys in buttons and pill-box hats scurrying round with teetering piles of boxes to the Hôtel Meurice; the plush and gilded Opéra; the enormous motor-cars; the restaurants where, if you were not known, the hooded eyes of the *maître d'* held only one message: *Non*.

He relished the contrast between the two worlds, but they had one thing in common: a knowledge of the great painters. He could not carry on in ignorance. It seemed impossible to be in Paris and not know the galleries. He ventured, tasted, then gulped. There was so much to see, he was like a starveling at a Versailles feast. Best of all, he loved the Impressionists, who spoke to something unsuspected inside him. He began to make proper acquaintance with names that had before been blanks to him: Monet, Cézanne, Pissarro, Manet; Renoir, who loved Parisians, Degas, who loved dancers . . .

So he stepped, smiling and increasingly sure-footed, from Clichy to Châtelet and back, gathering confidence, acquaintances and admiration. He loved Paris, and Paris loved him. It ate him up. It petted him. He was *Le jeune Morland, si gentil!* He was *très charmant*, he was *l'anglais doré*; the ladies thought him *beau comme un ange*. He danced so well. He made one laugh. *Et ses dents! Et ses cuisses! Mon Dieu, c'est un Adonis!* He accepted everything that was given to him with the happy lack of conceit of the young man who has always been loved, and trod safely between the dangerous shoals, because his heart was pure. His heart was given to Meredith.

She kept his feet on the ground. She had the sturdy common sense of a rancher's daughter, a steady suspicion of the overblown and overexcited. She was not easily moved to ecstasies by her surroundings, having grown up with the wild panoramas of Wyoming. The historic buildings of Paris, to her mind, were no better than those of Vassar (now James learned where she had been to school!). New York was a better city than Paris, with more interesting buildings, better shops and theatres, more music, and a proper attention to sanitation, which was the hallmark of real civilisation. James found her quite English on that point.

But underneath the firm refusal to be bowled over, she loved Paris too, with an ache of wonder and the laughter of release. She was not *quite* the same Meredith she had been in Canada. On fine days they sometimes met for breakfast before work, took a *café complet* together, sitting on the pavement outside the Café Nancy on the corner of the rue des Martyrs, savouring the morning air before the traffic fumes took over. It was very clear why Parisians started their working day so early. Sometimes he would meet her at lunchtime and they would wander through Les Halles to look at the flowers and marvel over the fruit. But her days in the office on the rue St Honoré were busy, and mostly they explored by night, when he was not on duty, and on Sundays, when Paris put on her Sabbath quiet, the bells replaced traffic noise, and you could actually *hear* the sparrows chattering in the plane trees.

That evening he met her from work and they went to the cinema. He thought it a waste of such a golden evening to be indoors, but there was a picture she wanted to see, *Les Beaux Jours*, and it was the last day. When they came out, the sun had set, but there was still light in the sky, torn flags of flame behind the purple clouds, and by unspoken consent they walked down towards the river and along the *quais*. He wanted to ask her where she would like to go for supper, but the silence between them was such a warm one he didn't want to break it. He felt for her hand, and it was there, and agreed to be held. His heart jumped. There was a little restaurant he knew on the Boul' Mich'. They would go there, he decided.

Crossing the river, they stopped halfway over the Pont St Michel to gaze, and he was so overcome by the romance of the situation, with the water below reflecting the lights and the twin black towers of Notre Dame rearing against the last of the crimson in the sky, that he kissed her. She kissed him back. It was the first time. He had kissed many girls in his twenty-five years on the planet, but he had never felt anything like this before. He could have gone on for ever.

But she disengaged from him, and pushed him gently back with her hands against his chest. 'That's enough,' she said.

'No, no,' he protested, 'it's not nearly enough. It could *never* be enough.'

'Now, James,' she said sternly, 'you know you're just getting carried away because of Paris and everything.'

'Not at all,' he protested. 'It's you, only you. I love you, Meredith. You're the most marvellous girl in the world and I'm mad about you. Kiss me again.'

'No,' she said, but she did. 'Now this really must stop,' she said at last, breathlessly. 'People are looking.'

They were, but it was with indulgence. After all, if a man could not kiss a pretty girl on a summer evening on the Pont St Michel in the heart of Paris, where could he?

'But you like me, don't you?' James asked.

'Yes, I do, but it doesn't follow that we have to be – spoony.'

'Spoony!' James laughed. 'Where did you get such a word?'

'I'm serious, James.'

'So am I. I love you and I want to marry you. Let's get married.'

'Don't be silly.'

'What's silly about it? You love me, don't you? Say you love me.'

'I might do. I don't know yet. I *like* you.'

'Good enough for a start. Let's get married, then.'

'On what? Have you saved a penny of your wages since you got here? No, I thought not.'

'I've had a lot of expenses,' he said. 'Charlie needs me to look smart. *Et enfin, il faut manger.*' He gave a very Frenchified shrug.

'And drink, and smoke. I'm not blaming you, James, only saying you can't afford to get married, and neither can I.'

'We'll be poor together.'

'Not a good way to start married life. No,' she said firmly, 'you can't ask me to marry you until you have the means to support a wife. And that's my last word.'

James looked crestfallen, but not for long. She had, after all, as good as said she loved him and *would* marry him – eventually. 'All right, then, I'll court you,' he said. 'How would that be? A nice, old-fashioned English word, that – courting.'

She laughed. 'All right, you can court me. Nicely,' she warned, as he looked likely to lunge.

'Oh, I'll be as nice as all-get-out,' he said. 'Now kiss me again. *Embrasse-moi, chérie. Tes lèvres sont comme la soie, comme les cérises . . .*'

'Your French has gotten altogether too good,' she said, but she kissed him. It was really very nice.

James was invited to a party at the apartment of Hélène Gilbert, which was in the rue Auber at the other end from the Opéra. He knew her from both his worlds. She was a wealthy patron of the arts, whom he had met at a studio party a couple of months before, and he had bumped into her since at a gallery, and in a shop in the rue St Honoré where he bought his ties. But because so much of the money to invest in the arts reposed in the Americans, she was very much in with their crowd, too, and James had met her on other occasions with Charlie.

She and Charlie sometimes shared customers: he would send her businessmen with the money to buy paintings, and she would send him art-lovers whose money arose from their businesses. Charlie had recommended her to James as a fount of knowledge and of useful introductions. She had taken a fancy to him, and he liked her brashness, and her lavish entertainments.

They usually started late, and went on through the night, often ending with scrambled eggs and truffles as the sun rose over the chimney pots. There would always be Americans, always artists, and often French politicians, opera singers, ballet girls, and interesting people Hélène had picked up from various walks of life. There would always be high-powered talk and there would always be money. It was said that any American who checked in at the Meurice or the Hôtel de Crillon was bound to end up at one of Hélène's parties sooner or later.

There, he met his old friend Emil Bauer, who was living in Paris now, and involved in something he described vaguely as 'Political – very boring – don't ask, James.' James didn't enquire how Emil knew Hélène, though it seemed to be more than a casual acquaintance. He was delighted to see him again, grateful that it was to Emil's intervention he owed his present good fortune, including Meredith. The two of them renewed their acquaintance and had several splendid nights on the town. It was good, James thought, to go out with a millionaire whom he didn't have to impress.

Sometimes there were rich English at Hélène's parties, too: James met the Marquess of Cholmondeley – 'Rock' – and his wife, who had been the immensely rich Sybil Sassoon; and the Duff Coopers – she was the daughter of the Duke of Rutland and once thought to be a suitable wife for the Prince of Wales; and 'Chips' Channon who, though born in Chicago, had moved to England after the war and was making himself steadily more and more English, buying a country estate, marrying the daughter of Lord Iveagh, and this year even standing for Parliament.

From them James heard the gossip from 'back home', and was given an insight into Court and government circles. It might have turned his head to be mixing with such important people, had he had even the faintest interest in politics or power, but he took life so much as it came that he was equally at home with marquesses, millionaires, railway porters or impoverished artists. Hélène adored this trait in him, and could not get enough of him, inviting him to every gathering and introducing him to everyone. What made it even more delicious, to her, was that he was unaware of how unusual he was in that respect.

'I believe you could tame even Herr Hitler,' she said. 'I'd like to have him here and see you take the stuffing out of him. You'd have him eating out of your hand.' James had no idea what she was talking about. He was aware, however, that Hélène would like to take him as her lover. Although around forty she was a very handsome woman, very rich, and could have done him a great deal of good, but his only regret in not accepting the tacit offer was in possibly hurting her feelings. He liked her, and thought her enormous fun, but it never occurred to him to look at any woman but Meredith.

That evening Hélène's party was given in honour of an English painter, who had made his fame and fortune in America, had been the darling of New York and had later taken his talents to Hollywood, where he had won an Oscar for artistic direction in the motion picture *The Falcon and the Rose*. He had just arrived in Paris, and the papers had made much of the story that he felt he had gone as far as he could in Hollywood; now he wanted to return to his artistic roots and paint.

'*Entre nous*,' Hélène said to James, when she invited him, catching him coming out of a shop on the rue de Rivoli, 'I think there is more to the story than we have heard. Normally someone only abandons 'Ollywood and its great sums of money when 'Ollywood has abandoned them first. But that is not the case here. I understand that the studio did not at all want him to leave. So there is a mystery, *mon cher*. To leave it all to paint again? Pah! And why Paris? He could paint in California just as easily.'

'*Does* he paint well?' James asked.

'*Bien sûr*. He was celebrated in the best circles in New York, where one must be good to be noticed at all. And I've seen some of his work. It is – powerful. It sells for very large sums, when you can get it. But he will face more competition here, and not so big prices. So why leave the United States? *Chéchez la femme, je crois*. Find out for me, James, if you can. I think of taking him up, but not if he is going to waste his talent on some tawdry love affair.'

'You told me thwarted love gives rise to the best art,' James reminded her.

'But it must be *grrreat* love!' She rolled the *r* in emphasis, raising her eyebrows. 'Not the itch *en moyen age* to prove oneself still young.'

'I wouldn't know about that,' James said vaguely.

She laughed, and leaned in to kiss his forehead. 'I know, and I love you for it! Just come to my *soirée* and talk to him in your usual way and I'm sure he will tell you everything. *Au 'voir, chéri*. Until Tuesday.' And she departed in a whirl of subtle scent, a glint of gold, and a swing of fox-tails.

The artist, Eric Chapel, was very tanned compared with Parisians, and the cut of his suit was rather American, wide at the shoulders and draped, but otherwise there was nothing about him to mark him out as either American or an artist. He did not dress with flamboyance, his hair – so fair it was almost white – was cut conservatively, he spoke quietly, with no trace of an American accent. He was a good-looking man, with straight features and blue eyes, probably in his late thirties. James had heard himself called an Adonis often enough to have gone and looked for images of Adonis in the Louvre, and he thought Mr Chapel fitted the description much better than he did. The flawless perfection of a Greek statue must have been his in youth, and he was still very handsome in a chiselled sort of way, which struck James as not being terribly English. The English, being a mongrel race, did not often attain to this perfection: their attractiveness tended to reside in their very flaws.

Not that James thought in those terms. He put him down as a good-looking chap the women would fall for, and vaguely thought him rather 'European' in aspect.

James hovered on the edge of the group to begin with, listening to Chapel speaking rather good French and praising Madame Gilbert's generosity in helping him to settle and establish himself. He had brought a number of paintings with him to show at an exhibition she was arranging in September, along with some new work he hoped to complete before then. 'Show – and sell,' he added, with a smile. 'Even the muse needs to be fed. We are all the children of Mammon, one way or another, aren't we?'

'Did I hear you say Mammon?' said Saffy Erlinger in English, having listened so far with the baffled look of a fly trying to pass through a window-pane. Chapel changed smoothly to English and continued in it, to the evident relief of the non-natives who had been hanging on by their linguistic fingernails.

Sam Muswell, with that admirable colonial frankness, asked, 'But surely, Mr Chapel, working in Hollywood you must have made a fortune. Excuse my asking, but *The Falcon and the Rose* was a box-office smash. Fine movie, by the way. Mrs Muswell and I went to see it last fall when it came out in New York. Deserving of the Oscars in my humble opinion. But didn't it make your fortune?'

'I don't deny that Hollywood has been very good to me,' said Chapel. 'But what is given with one hand is taken away with the other. My wife became ill and required some very expensive treatments.'

'Oh, I'm sorry to hear that,' said Muswell. 'I hope she's fully recovered now?'

'She died six months ago,' Chapel said. There was an awkward silence, followed by murmurings of sympathy, and Chapel went on, 'I felt it was time for a complete break. To return to my European roots, to go back to painting at its simplest, to face the challenge of the bare canvas armed with only the brush and the palette, to measure myself again by human standards. There is something,' he added, with a twinkling smile, 'very *in*human about Hollywood.'

A little laugh marked the relief that the difficult subject had been got over. Conversation moved on to art, the grand subject, and James let his attention drift a little. He had heard enough art talk to recognise the vocabulary and understand something of the concepts being expressed, he could even keep up a conversation when he had to, but it didn't interest him. His liking for paintings was much more visceral. He could tell you whether he liked or disliked a particular picture, but not why, and the idea that there should even *be* a why was alien to him. He watched Chapel charming his interlocutors with the interest of a fellow professional, and thought that Hélène had been right – as usual. There was a woman at the bottom of it.

He moved away and talked to some other people: a man Charlie was interested in, from Philadelphia, with mining interests, and his wife; and some time later, when he was talking to the French interior minister's mistress and Chapel came round again in the general movement of the party, he found himself being introduced to him.

'Morland?' Chapel said, his eyebrows rising as he shook James's hand. 'Not any relation to Rose Morland, the film actress, I suppose?'

'She's a sort of distant cousin,' James said. 'I've never met her, though. I've never been to America. And I haven't seen *The Falcon and the Rose*, I'm sorry to say. It hadn't reached Yorkshire by the time I left. I've been in Paris since February. We're still waiting for it here.'

'Yorkshire? You are from Yorkshire? Do you know Morland Place?'

'I was born there. It was my father's house. It's my sister's now,' James said, faintly puzzled that Chapel should have heard of it. But perhaps Rose had mentioned the connection, or Lennie.

'Your sister – then you are the brother of Polly Morland?' he said eagerly. 'Or, I should say, Polly Alexander?'

'It's Morland again now. She took her old name back. Yes, I'm her brother, or half-brother, really. We had different mothers. How do you know Polly?'

'We met in New York,' he said. 'At various exhibitions. I was under the patronage of Freda Holland, a sort of New York version of Madame Gilbert, and Mrs Alexander – Polly – was in her circle.' He smiled at James, though the smile seemed rather tense, almost troubled. 'I had the honour to count myself a friend. She spoke so warmly of Morland Place that I almost feel I know it.'

'It's a grand place,' James agreed.

'You must miss it,' Chapel said.

'Oh, sometimes,' James allowed. 'But Polly's making a fine job of running everything. It couldn't be in better hands.'

'Forgive me, how does it come to be in her hands? I thought in England sons inherited before daughters.'

James told him the story, of how Ren Alexander had left her a fortune, saved from the Crash – 'I heard that he had died, but not how things had been left,' Chapel said. 'I'm glad she was provided for' – and how death duties had forced James to consider selling Morland Place, and how Polly had come home, like a knight in shining armour, to rescue the estate, pay the death duties and take over Morland Place, with all its responsibilities. 'And she's much the best person for it. My father would never have left it to me if he'd known he was going to die when he did. I'm not responsible at all.

Maybe one day I might be, when I get some grey hairs, but Polly just took to it like a duck to water.'

He paused, thinking he was perhaps being a bore about it, but Chapel was listening with an intense interest that seemed more than polite. How well *had* he known Polly in New York? She had never mentioned him.

Chapel asked a question now. 'I believe there was – did she not have a son?'

'Yes, Alec. A splendid little chap. Put on his first pony at two years old, and rides like a good 'un now. Polly took him to meets last hunting season, and it won't be long before he's following hounds.'

'I have a son, too,' Chapel said. 'At school back in the States.'

'You must miss him,' James hazarded. He obviously had to say something, and it seemed a social sort of comment, though in his experience boys went away to school as a matter of course and if anyone missed them they never said so.

'Of course,' Chapel said, 'but I didn't want to disrupt his education by bringing him with me. He's settled, and happy where he is.'

James was ready to move on to someone else now, but Chapel didn't seem to want to let him go, so he said politely, 'Now you've come this far, you should go over to England, pay a visit to Morland Place – see if it's the way you imagined it.'

'Perhaps I will,' Chapel said, scanning James's face as though for more information than had been given. 'I have longed for many years to see it. There have been – reasons for not going back to England. I won't bore you with them. But now perhaps it would be possible. It might be arranged, somehow.' He was nodding to himself, thinking something through. Then he looked up at James. 'But perhaps I would be intruding.'

'It used to be open to the public for a shilling years ago,'

James said. 'That was before the war, though. It's not open now. But you were obviously acquainted with Polly. I'm sure she'd be happy to show you round.'

'You think – she wouldn't mind if I called on her?' Chapel asked. There was a hungry sort of look in his eyes. James began to get the idea this fellow had been sweet on Polly in New York. He probably oughtn't to encourage it.'

'Why not write? She can always say no,' he suggested lightly.

'Just so. She didn't— Did she marry again?'

Ah, thought James. 'She wrote to me last week to say that she's just got engaged to a fellow. Neighbour of ours. Going to get married some time later this year.'

'I see,' said Chapel. James felt sorry for him just for a moment, he looked so stricken – though the expression was fleeting, and soon covered with a neutral urbanity. 'Well, perhaps I won't intrude. It was just an idle fancy. Tell me, what do you think of the art world in Paris? Has it changed much since the war?'

James couldn't answer that, and was able to use the question gently to shuffle off Mr Chapel on to one of the older art fanciers at his elbow. He ought to find Hélène and tell her about the dead wife. He wouldn't mention the Polly business. After all, he didn't *know* the blighter had fancied his sister, still less that he had come to Europe on her account. Indeed, if that were the case, why hadn't he gone straight to England? No, it was all his fancy. Nothing in it.

He had the residual impression, though, which troubled him slightly as he went the rounds of the party, that the conversation had been somehow odd, and particularly that Chapel had said something a bit queer, though he couldn't remember now what it was. But when the party broke up he went off to have a late supper with Meredith at Chez Jules in the rue du Bac, and by the time he was sitting opposite her at their favourite table and contemplating whether to begin with the *salade mimosa* or to share an *assiette de fruits de mer*, he had forgotten all about Eric Chapel.

Despite deciding to keep her engagement to Charles Eastlake secret for the time being, Polly had written to James about it, knowing he would not tell anyone, as a sort of sounding-board. She hoped he would reply with an immediate cheery encouragement, which would reassure her that she had done the right thing. She had failed to allow for the time it took a letter to get to and from France, and how long it always took James to answer, especially when there were more interesting things to do – which in his present life there always were.

Thinking about postal delays, she thought she ought to write to tell Lennie about the engagement – likewise there was no-one he could tell who would break the news in York and spoil Mary's wedding preparations. And Lennie had been her friend and correspondent for so long he deserved to be told right away. Now he was happily married (it still gave her a pang to think about that, but she mustn't be dog-in-the-manger about it), there was no fear of hurting his feelings. Or perhaps he might feel the same pang, and suppress it for the same reason. Selfishly, she hoped there was just a *little* corner of his heart that would mind.

But before she could act on her resolve, at the beginning of July a letter arrived for her from America. It was not from Lennie, but from Rose, telling the terrible news about the motor accident. Lennie had come out of it with bruises, but Beth had been killed outright, her neck broken; and, worst of all, it had emerged that Beth had been pregnant. Lennie had lost wife and child in one blow.

He was too devastated to write yet, Rose said. He had shut himself into his house and wouldn't see anyone. Beth's mother, Mrs Andrews, had suffered an attack on hearing the news, and had been taken to hospital; it was doubtful, given her frail condition, that she would come out again. Rose had been several times to the house, but Lennie would see her only the once, to tell her what had happened. His maid, Wilma, was looking after him. He left the house only to visit Mrs Andrews. It was all too dreadful, as Rose herself was now expecting a baby, and reading about the accident in all the papers had made her very nervous. She missed her mother very much. Perhaps Polly could write to Lennie – that might comfort him. Nothing else seemed to.

Polly wrote at once, a long letter, pouring out her sympathy. She had lost her husband in an aeroplane accident, but this must be worse, far worse, for Lennie, having actually been there. 'Come home,' she wrote at the end. 'Come home to England, even if only for a holiday. It will do you good to get away for a time, to have a break in scene. Come to Morland Place and let me look after you.'

She posted the letter, but then reflected it would take two weeks at least to reach him. She had left the post office, but turned back to send a cable. Being an outpouring from the heart, it was not the most economical of communications.

JUST HEARD THE TERRIBLE NEWS+ OH LENNIE I'M SO SORRY + DEEPEST DEEPEST SYMPATHY+ LET ME HELP+ COME TO MORLAND PLACE+ COME RIGHT AWAY+ ALL MY LOVE+ POLLY

The telegraph assistant, trying to be helpful, asked, 'Did you really want both "deepests", miss? And that "oh"?'

'Send it just as it is,' Polly said absently. She turned away, deep in thought, and walked the streets of York for some time, unseeing, before going back to find her car.

That evening she walked over to Shawes, through a warm, damp July evening seething with moths and little jigging flies, taking the path beaten through the long grass, which brushed her arms on either side with a dry, whispery rustle.

Bigelot and Blossom ran ahead, snapping at grasshoppers, but Fand, sensing her mood, kept quietly to her heel, pushing his wet nose now and then into her palm for comfort.

At the beautiful old house she asked to see Charles alone and, learning his daughter was with him, said she would wait outside on the terrace. He came hurrying to her, his face tight with the anticipation of bad news. He looked, in the fluky light of the long twilight, suddenly older.

'What is it?' he asked, holding out his hands to her. The dogs surged up to greet him, but she put her own hands behind her back, and looked at him with infinite sadness.

'I'm sorry, Charles. I've come to tell you I can't marry you.'

He was silent a moment, searching her face and finding no hope there. 'Can you tell me why?' he asked quietly.

She shook her head. 'Not really. I should never have said yes. It was – a mistake. I made a mistake. I'm so sorry. It isn't right that you should suffer for it, but I can't help it.'

'Is there someone else?' he asked.

'It isn't that,' she said. 'I realise that I don't love you in the right way. We couldn't be happy together.'

'Perhaps we could. I don't expect perfection,' he began, but she couldn't bear to see him beg.

'I couldn't do that to you. You deserve so much more. And I *do* love you. Just – not in the right way. Please understand, and forgive me.'

'I *don't* understand,' he said. 'But I *do* forgive you. And I shan't give up hope. If you change your mind – I shall always love you.'

How often had Lennie said that to her – 'I shall always love you'? There seemed nothing more she could say to Charles, and with another look of regret, and a sigh for hurting him, she turned away. The dogs, who had been sniffing round the pleasures of a new garden, caught up with her, full of the joys of summer and unexpected outings. They bounced inappropriately around her as she trudged unhappily back through the gathering dusk.

Probably, she thought, she should have told him that there *was* someone else. That might have made it easier for him. And not said she loved him, albeit in the wrong way. She had handled it very badly. But there had been nothing else to do. To marry him would have been impossible for her, and so much worse for him.

She hoped he would not let it spoil Mary's wedding.

CHAPTER TWENTY

Emma and Kit were at the Fort for Ascot. Mrs Simpson was there – though without Mr Simpson, who was away on business – and the Butlers, and the Maxwells. Jack Aird was equerrying, and there was an American couple, the Orvilles, a rather dull businessman and his much younger wife. Emma thought Wallis rather out of sorts. There was talk of their summer plans: David had planned a yachting trip down the coast of Italy and around the Greek islands, but the King had vetoed it because of the tense relations with Italy over Abyssinia. Now the Prince was looking for a suitable villa to borrow. Possibilities were batted back and forth as he sat with his embroidery, jumping up every now and then to adjust Wallis's cushion or light her cigarette. There was much grumbling that the King's veto had been excessive. Why should silly political wranglings spoil a holiday?

Wallis ate very little at dinner – or, rather, even less than usual. Mrs Orville, who seemed to have known her from years back – there were some references to China in their separate conversation – whispered to Emma that 'Her ulcers are playing her up, poor thing.' Emma thought ulcers explained a great deal about Mrs Simpson.

It was a dull evening. Wallis rejected the idea of cards, but seemed too listless for conversation; when David offered to play his ukulele, she snapped, 'For Heaven's sake, no!' Kit and Humphrey Butler talked about the runners for the next

506

day's racing, and since Mrs Maxwell and Mrs Orville seemed to be talking about their respective children, Emma took pity on Jack Aird and engaged him in a conversation about cattle breeding. He was really too choleric for a job that required him to bite his tongue so much.

The next day, Ladies' Day, they met Oliver and Verena in the Royal Enclosure. They were staying at Windsor, the Queen having become interested in the reconstruction work Oliver was doing on children with birth defects. She was a great patron of children's hospitals. Prince Henry was at the castle, with his fiancée Lady Alice, daughter of the Duke of Buccleuch, talking about another November wedding; and the Kents were there, the Duchess already visibly pregnant.

Despite these happy portents, Oliver said there was something of an 'atmosphere'. 'Don't be surprised if Wales is "sent for",' he murmured. 'I think he's suffering by comparison with all the matrimonial bliss. It's a bad show Simpson not being at the Fort.'

'Sir will chalk up a few good points tonight,' Kit replied. 'He's dashing up to Town after the last race to address the British Legion. Nothing could be more wholesome than that.'

The Prince was the patron of the British Legion, and had been invited to address their annual conference. The following day he told the company at the Fort all about it, boyishly excited at how well it had gone. The nine hundred and fifty delegates had given his speech a 'simply tremendous ovation'.

It seemed that the Legion had been invited that spring by four German ex-servicemen's organisations to send a delegation to Germany, to see how veterans were treated over there, to foster closer relations and to promote peace.

'I told them in my speech that I felt that there could be no more suitable body or organisation of men to stretch forth the hand of friendship to the Germans than we ex-servicemen, who fought them in the Great War and have now forgotten about all that,' said the Prince.

Kit and Humphrey Butler exchanged a glance, for the prince had never fought – though, to do him credit, it had not been his decision but the government's to keep him out of the trenches.

'It's a worthy sentiment,' Butler said, 'but aren't you afraid it might be misinterpreted, sir? Those German ex-service organisations have "National Socialist" in their titles. You may be seen as endorsing the current regime.'

'Nonsense! Don't be such a slowcoach, Humphrey! There's a desperate desire among people all over Europe to make sure that the Great War will never be repeated. We veterans in particular have an important role to play in the preservation of peace. We are men apart, you know, we who were there. It's for us to take the lead, and show how the British and German people can understand each other, the way Tommy and Fritz did at the end of the war.'

'Of course, we all want peace . . .' Jack Aird began, stony-faced.

Butler took it up. 'The reports coming out of Germany, some of the things the National Socialists are doing – imprisonments without trial, beatings, the treatment of Jews in particular—'

'Much of that is exaggerated, you know,' the Prince said. 'It's propaganda put out by the Communists. *They* are the real enemy, and we ought to keep that in mind. The Germans are our natural allies in Europe against the Communist menace. No use relying on the French: degenerate and chaotic. The Germans are strong, resurgent, organised. They're doing marvellous things, particularly with respect to unemployment and housing the lower classes. You don't hear so much about *that* from the nay-sayers, do you?'

'It's David's special field of interest,' Mrs Simpson spoke up, 'so of course he's taken the trouble to find out a few facts, unlike most people.'

'Nevertheless,' Butler pursued apologetically, 'you can't

entirely dismiss all the reports of violence and repression as propaganda. For instance—'

The Prince waved an impatient hand; storm clouds were gathering on his brow at being contradicted. 'Of course there are many things that happen in these countries that we can't condone, but their domestic affairs are not our business. *Our* business is to try to create something that will help the peace of the world. Hitler is strong for peace. It's up to the rest of Europe to give up its pinpricks against Germany. Really,' he glowered around the company, 'I begin to think you're all warmongers at heart. Anyone who has seen first-hand what war means would know it must *never* happen again. I think I shall take a turn around the garden. Wallis, would you like to walk?'

He thus made it clear that he didn't want any of the warmongers to accompany them. There was a silence when he and Mrs Simpson had departed. Then Kit said, 'I wouldn't mind betting Ribbentrop is behind this. Sir meets him all too often at Lady Cunard's.'

Aird said, 'Ribbentrop is a dolt, almost entirely without brains.'

'Yes,' said Kit, 'but he's a puppet and Hitler pulls the strings. From Berlin straight to Wales's ear, with only Ribbentrop and Wallis in between. And given how well the National Socialists have learned the value of propaganda from the Reds, I can't imagine their *not* making jam out of this British Legion visit.'

Oliver's prediction that the Prince would be 'sent for' was fulfilled. However, the summons was not concerning Mrs Simpson's presence, but the British Legion speech, which was reported the day after in *The Times*. Aird, who had gone up to the castle with him, told what had happened to Humphrey Butler, who later told Kit and Emma.

'The King was furious. Wales claimed the speech had been cleared beforehand through the Foreign Office, but Vansittart said there had never been any consultation. Anthony Eden said the visit will be a gift to Nazi propaganda. The King said the French are pretty fed up about it, and it's complicated the Anglo-German naval discussions. Wales said he didn't mean to get mixed up in politics, only to express an idea he thought right and useful. So the King said it wasn't his business to *have* ideas. His job was to cut ribbons and keep his bloody mouth shut. Oh,' Humphrey concluded, 'and to stop loitering about with other men's wives and find one of his own.'

'Phew! Pretty strong stuff,' Kit said.

'And on his birthday, too,' Emma mentioned. 'One almost feels sorry for him.'

'We'll have to try to make it up to him tonight,' said Kit. 'I dare say Wallis has something celebratory planned.'

But the atmosphere remained rather subdued, and the Prince and Mrs Simpson went off to bed early, somewhat to the relief of the rest of the company.

There was no reply from Lennie. For a few days Polly looked for a cable, even if it was only an acknowledgement, but none came; and it would take weeks for a letter to arrive, even if he felt like replying, which she did not expect. The torpor of grief generally followed its frenzy.

Things were a little awkward with Charles. He was kind and hopeful at first, then hurt and distant, then kind again, but sad, which was the worst. But he still wanted her to arrange Mary's wedding – and in fairness there was no way she could have withdrawn from that without telling Mary the truth or hurting her feelings. Charles seemed to think his only role was to pay the bills, and that Polly would do everything else, but it was a good way of occupying her hours so that she didn't have time to think.

With constant contact she had found herself growing fonder of Mary. She was a little beige, it was true, but there was no harm in her, and a pleasant lack of conceit or self-promotion. Polly had never met a more modest bride. She really loved plain old Alan Stead, though there had been prettier boys on offer, and her only ambition was to have a husband to take care of, a comfortable house and some children. As for the wedding, she was content to let Polly decide everything, and only hoped that Daddy was not spending too much on it.

White and blue did not suit Mary, so Polly had chosen cream for the wedding dress, with subtle hints of pink, close-fitted, with a wide sash at the waist, and a fullness at the back, created by folds and pleats, to give the effect of a train. For her other outfits Polly had chosen rose-fawn, cream, and soft pale yellows. There were endless fittings, but Mary bore them all patiently. She seemed to have no demands of her own, was silent, or conversed if Polly initiated it.

But one day in the drawing room at Shawes, while Polly turned her and pinned her, she asked suddenly, out of a long silence, 'Are you going to marry my father?'

'No,' said Polly, startled into a plain answer.

Before she could think of how to modify the starkness, Mary said, 'Oh. I'm glad.'

'Really?' Polly said, part relieved, part piqued. 'And why is that?'

Mary blushed. 'Oh, I didn't mean—! I like you awfully, and it's very good of you to do all this for me. But you're so important and busy, and you have so much to do, and so many people to attend to and everything, I don't think you'd have enough time left over for Daddy. I'd like him to marry someone who had nothing to do but look after him.'

'Is that the sort of wife you want to be?' Polly asked.

'I'm not clever like you,' Mary said humbly, 'but I think I can make Alan happy and comfortable. I can do that.'

'I'm sure you can,' Polly said. Mary, she saw, had a heart overflowing with affection and was longing for someone to give it to. Well, she knew what that felt like. For an instant she envied Mary, with her simple desires on the brink of being fulfilled. *I'm lonely*, she thought. She had been lonely for a long time, and for her there was no end in sight. She had almost made a terrible mistake with Charles, attracted by his kindness and the prospect of sharing her life with someone. But he would always have been a stranger to her. And it would have been far worse to be lonely inside a marriage than simply to be alone.

'I'm going to make you the prettiest bride there ever was,' she told Mary, in a surge of affection.

The wedding was at St Stephen's, with the wedding breakfast afterwards at the Station Hotel in York – Polly had balked at organising a reception as well. The Steads were a large clan, and to make sure the Eastlake side of the church was not empty by comparison, Polly made everyone from Morland Place attend. Mary's brother was back from university. He had grown a rather horrid small moustache, and was so preoccupied with trying to catch glimpses of himself in reflective surfaces that he hardly noticed anything else. Polly was glad she was not going to have to be a step-mother to him after all.

After the feasting, the dancing. Bride and groom took the floor, looking suitably blissful, and when other couples joined in, Charles came and asked for Polly's hand. It looked very particular, but it was too late to worry about public expectations being aroused. She went with good grace; and it was surprisingly nice to be in his arms again. For a moment she wondered if she had done the right thing in calling it off.

'I think it's gone well,' she said, after a while. 'Mary looked very pretty.'

'You've done wonders with her,' he said. 'I'm more grateful than I can say. I wish—'

She was afraid he was going to revive his marriage offer. 'Don't,' she said.

'I was only going to say, I wish we could remain friends, good friends, you and I. For Mary's sake, if not for mine.'

'I hope we can, too,' Polly said. And to change the subject, 'That house will seem awfully large when she's gone away.'

'Yes. Too large, really. I shall rattle around in it, all on my own.'

'Well, now you've brought Mary out, there's no need for you to keep it. You could take another house, a smaller one.'

'I had hoped it would be my long home,' he said.

She waited, but he said nothing more. It occurred to her that he might have taken Shawes not only to bring Mary out *from*, but to bring himself a new wife home *to*. If he had come to this part of Yorkshire intending to marry, it meant she was only a random accident, and she needn't feel too bad about him. Perhaps, she considered, with rising spirits, he might soon find someone else. She might make it her mission to put suitable ladies in his way . . .

When the dance ended he kissed her hand, and looked into her face earnestly. 'Friends?' he asked.

'Always,' she said firmly. 'You must come to dinner next week. Things will seem flat after the wedding.' Already she was reviewing a list of unattached females who might do for him, and she didn't notice the little surge of hope in his eyes at the invitation.

That year the world was not a quiet or comfortable place. Everyone wanted peace, but there were hints everywhere that it was drifting once more towards war. The hints even penetrated as far as Portsmouth, where Airspeed entertained a delegation from the Mitsubishi company of Japan, wanting to buy the AS 6 Envoy. Jack and Nevil Norway showed them round the factory, gave them luncheon, and then drove them to the airfield to watch a demonstration flight. The Mitsubishi people ordered two, with a near-promise of a further order later in the year if they performed as well as expected. Then one of the delegates, having drunk more than the usually abstemious Japanese habit, talked about the nation's plans for war with China within the next couple of years, a step towards further conquests thereafter. When they had left, Jack and Norway had an urgent discussion, resulting with the information being passed to the Foreign Office.

Helen was very upset by this overt mention of war.

'But it won't affect us,' Jack tried to comfort her.

'Perhaps not directly, but it's a sign of things to come,' she said. 'Everyone talks of wanting peace, but they're quietly arming themselves for war.'

'It's important to be prepared – surely you must see that?'

'I know that's what we tell ourselves, but the fact is that once all these arms are created, sooner or later they're going to be used. Why do men love war?' she cried.

'*I* don't.'

'I know. But there's a whole new generation now that doesn't remember the war at all, and they'll be the ones eager to rush out and "give Jerry a good hiding", just like last time. Are we doomed to have a new war every twenty years because hotheaded youth can't learn from the past?'

'It wasn't hotheaded youth who started the last lot,' Jack said mildly. 'The statesmen were mostly old men.'

Helen shook her head, not in denial but in helplessness. Jack knew what she was thinking. She had two sons who would be of military age if and when war broke out again. He tried to comfort her. 'There are a lot of people in positions of power now who fought in the war. They won't let it get that far again. That's what the League of Nations is for.'

She raised tragic eyes to him. 'Tell that to Mussolini and Hitler.'

It was a coincidence that, a few days later, Jack received a letter from his old friend Tom Sopwith. He read it quickly over breakfast, then put it away in his pocket to give it some thought. Fortunately Helen was engaged with a letter of her own from Barbara, who thought she might be pregnant, and didn't notice. He mulled it over all day at work, and in the evening, when they were sitting down to dinner, he waited until they were alone and then introduced the subject by saying, 'How would you like to move back to Surrey?'

Helen put down her fork. 'What's happened?'

'Answer the question first.'

'Well, I'm not devoted to this place, but we have just got Barbara settled not too far away.'

'Petersfield isn't so terribly far from Kingston, either,' he said. 'And Kingston's nearer to London.'

'I'm not sure being any nearer to Basil will make any difference. We couldn't do anything with him when he lived under our roof.' She caught up. 'Kingston? You don't mean . . . ?'

He nodded. 'I had a letter this morning from Tom Sopwith. He's asking me to join Hawker Aircraft.' Hawker Aircraft, which had been formed after the original Sopwith company had gone bankrupt, had that year merged with Armstrong Siddeley, which also incorporated Armstrong Whitworth and the Avro company. 'They're starting to build the prototype of their new single-seater fighter, and they want me to join them right away to work on it – particularly the retractable undercarriage design. They think my experience in that field will be invaluable.'

'And you've had more experience than most of flying fighters,' Helen said, in a strangely muted voice.

'That's true – including Sopwiths and Avros, so that makes it nice and friendly. They're like family, really. And it will be wonderful to work with Tom again, and see the chaps at Kingston – if there are any left I used to know. At all events, it will be like going home.' He took a breath as he saw she was less than ecstatic. 'What is it? Are you unhappy about moving again?'

'I don't care about moving,' she said. 'But, oh, Jack, a fighter plane!'

515

'We have to have them,' he said awkwardly. 'If Germany does start something, you can bet they won't ignore air power. Look at the last war – the ebbs and flows were marked by who had air superiority.'

'It's what I was saying the other day. If countries have the weapons, they'll want to use them. It's another step towards war.'

'It doesn't need to be, darling,' he said anxiously. 'Look, let's not talk about it any more now. Let's not spoil our dinner. Just think about it, and we'll talk another time.'

'You said they want you right away.'

'Well, yes – but I can take a day or two to think about it. Tom won't expect an answer by return.'

Helen gathered her courage, thrust down her fears. Nothing she could do or say would change the course of history. The Hawker fighter would be built with or without Jack's help, but his help might just make it a better aeroplane. His contribution might help win the war, if there was one. Besides, she couldn't bear to douse the light of enthusiasm in his eyes. He and Tom had started out in avionics together, and had been very close friends. And, on a selfish note, being so much closer to London, she might get to see more of Molly and her nephew and niece – possibly even of Basil.

'Best not delay,' she said. 'It will take time for me to pack up here, but you could be there on Monday morning making a start, and stay in lodgings until I can find us a house. Does he mention salary? It would be nice if a small rise was involved.'

He looked at her with dawning hope. 'You mean you don't mind? We can go? I can take the job?'

'Far be it from me to stand in the way of history,' she said wryly. 'You were hooked the moment you read the letter, weren't you?'

'I *want* to go,' he said, 'but I also want you to be happy.'

'I'm happy wherever you are,' she said. She picked up her

fork and put it down again. Somehow she didn't feel like eating any more. 'At least,' she said, 'you'll be too old to fight, if there is another war.'

Jack agreed, but looked less than ecstatic at the thought.

In September the news coming out of Germany was of draconian new anti-Jewish measures. They were called the Nuremberg Laws, aimed at codifying the relationship between Jews and 'pure-bred' Germans, who were designated Aryans. Anyone with four Aryan grandparents was deemed to be Aryan. Anyone with three or four Jewish grandparents was classified Jewish, those with two were *mischlings*, or half-breeds. Marriage or sexual intercourse was forbidden between Jews or *mischlings* and Aryans. Aryan women under forty-five could not be employed in Jewish households. Jews would not be full citizens: they would be classified as State Subjects while Aryans were *Reichsbürger*, Citizens of the Reich. State Subjects could not vote, hold public office, or display the national flag. They could not be teachers, doctors, lawyers or journalists. They could not use state hospitals or public libraries or remain in education after the age of fourteen. Even the state lottery was not allowed to award a prize to a Jew. And Jewish passports were to be stamped with a letter 'J'. They could be used to leave Germany, but not to return.

The aim was to purify the race along the lines of 'scientific racism', or eugenics, an idea that had spread widely across Europe and America since the turn of the century. To its adherents, eugenics was 'the self-direction of human evolution', improving mankind by selective breeding, perpetuating the best and eliminating unwanted traits and weaknesses. The First International Congress of Eugenics had been held in 1912 under its president Leonard Darwin, the son of Charles Darwin.

In America an early proponent was Alexander Graham Bell who, studying deafness and concluding that it was largely hereditary, suggested that two deaf people should not marry each other. In England it attracted a wide variety of liberal thinkers, such as William Beveridge, John Maynard Keynes, George Bernard Shaw, Sydney Webb, H. G. Wells, Winston Churchill and the former prime minister Arthur Balfour. But in neither country had there been any leaning towards compulsion; rather, that education in the principles should lead towards a voluntary self-restraint and social discouragement on the one hand, and an informed selection of partners on the other.

Jewish refugees brought the news of the Nuremberg Laws to England and America. There was nothing to be done: it was not possible to interfere in the internal affairs of a sovereign nation; and even if it were permissible, it would surely lead to war. Only invasion could alter the Reich's undesirable direction, and the people of England and America were too anti-war for any government to suggest that.

In March, German troops had reoccupied the Rhineland, a hostile act in clear contravention of the Treaty of Versailles, but there had been no protest from Britain or France. The latter said the only way to get the Germans out was to declare war, which the public wouldn't stand for, and the former said it hadn't the resources to enforce the treaty, and the Dominions wouldn't stand for it anyway.

The British Legion expedition, which had taken place in July, had brought back stories of a friendly reception, with thousands lining the streets to cheer the six delegates as they arrived at the Friedrichstraße station; meetings with Hitler and his deputy Rudolf Hess, and with Hermann Goering, the head of the *Luftwaffe* – the air force. There was a meeting with wheelchair-bound German veterans, the laying of a wreath for the war fallen at the Neue Wache monument in Berlin, and a visit to the Stalmsdorf cemetery to pay their respects to the twelve hundred Commonwealth dead buried there.

The German people did not want war any more than the British, was the message pressed home every day. From Berlin the party was taken on a day-trip to Dachau, one of the recently established 'concentration camps' where criminals and other social undesirables were confined in the hope of improving them with hard work and healthy living. They were 'low types', the delegation was told: the workshy, the professional criminal and the morally perverted. Many were kept in solitary confinement for their own good, as was explained to them by Heinrich Himmler, the head of the German special police, who had set up the camp. He lived nearby, and invited the delegation to a quiet family supper. They found him an unassuming man, anxious to do the best for his country, they reported. Conditions in the camp were tolerable, they said, and the prisoners they saw were well nourished and healthy. (Later, Jewish refugees claimed that SS guards had played the part of prisoners for the duration of the visit, to make sure of giving the right impression.)

And in the background, the trouble in Abyssinia had smouldered all year, demonstrating to the world the vaunting ambitions of Signor Mussolini, and the impotence of the League of Nations. In February Italian troops had begun to build up in Eritrea and Somaliland, the countries bordering Ethiopia. Ethiopia appealed to the League of Nations, which dithered, then applied sanctions but did not enforce them. The French were willing to allow Italian territorial expansion in return for promises of support in the face of any future German aggression. In June the British sent Anthony Eden to broker peace, but the mission failed. Mussolini was determined on invasion, and warned that any attempt to supply arms to Ethiopia would be deemed a hostile act. The British therefore applied an arms embargo to both sides; but by withdrawing warships from the Mediterranean they only made it easier for Italy to get arms and men across to Africa.

In October Italy invaded Ethiopia, and war was declared

between the two very unequal countries. The League of Nations declared Italy the aggressor, but nothing was done except to talk of sanctions. Britain and France did not press for action. It seemed the fear of war was allowing the aggressor nations to take what they pleased without consequence: the desperation for peace, paradoxically, could be making war more likely.

It was a warm and mostly dry summer and the harvests were good and got in early. Polly was feeling a little more cheerful: she had had a reply from Lennie at last, a short letter thanking her for her kindness, and saying he would come and visit, but not yet. He had a great deal to do, and could not leave Marion, his mother-in-law, who was re-installed in his house after her discharge from hospital, but unlikely ever to leave her bed again. 'I long to see the old country, and you most of all, but even if I could leave now, I wouldn't be very good company yet. You will forgive me, given the circumstances.'

After Mary's wedding, the next big event had been Alan Cobham's Flying Circus making another visit to York. Polly offered her fields again and, with Jessie, helped organise the other amusements, stalls and refreshment tents that made it into a first-class entertainment.

Polly was kept busy that summer and autumn. Apart from the harvests and the usual work of the estate, there were the various agricultural shows. Polly and John Burton shared a personal delight when Carr Underwood won first prize at the Yorkshire show with his sow Rosemary; Bertie took a prize at the same show with one of his bulls. Jessie was pleased with a second for 'mare with foal at foot', for in Yorkshire the competition in horses was fierce. Polly and Burton travelled to a few shows further afield to look at stock and implements. He was the same kind, attentive and humorous person she had – briefly – fallen in love with. Now she had got over her agony of embarrassment, she was comfortable with him again – which was fortunate, given how much time they spent in each other's company – though it still gave her a small pang when he mentioned his wife or child.

She took him with her on a trip to Manchester to the mills, where work was picking up even outside the Cunard White Star orders. The depression really seemed to be over. The Jubilee had given a boost to trade, and all the Makepeaces were doing better. She spent a lot of time that autumn designing new lines in women's fashions, looking at fabrics, and employing more women in the workshops.

When the hunting season started, she was busier than ever: she went out twice a week when she could, and had people to stay most weekends, gave a lawn meet in early December, and was planning a ball at Morland Place for later in the season. Jessie and Bertie had a meet at Twelvetrees for the first time, mainly at the urging of the children, who all hunted. The meet itself was a great success, Jessie being a very practised hostess: all enjoyed themselves so much they did not want to leave, so they were very late setting out. It was probably just as well, for the sport was poor, too many blank draws and only one run; but everyone talked of it afterwards as having been a good day, proof of the power of conviviality.

The neighbourhood was very sociable in hunting season, with all the meets, parties, dinners and balls that accompanied it. Polly still met Charles everywhere, for he was a popular guest, and an unattached man was always in demand, but people had stopped asking him 'for' her at last, and at balls she was besieged again by men of all ages wanting to dance with the beautiful – and rich – widow. At Lord Lambert's ball she suddenly realised she was having fun: she was the most beautifully gowned woman in the room, and much the most run-after. She drank champagne and flirted a little, and felt it was rather like being young again.

Her pleasure was increased by the sight of Charles dancing for the third time with Cecily Laxton, whose husband had been killed on the hunting field six years ago and who was surely ripe for remarrying. He seemed to be listening to her with particular attention, and she was gazing up at him with more than the usual politeness. If anything came of it, she thought, she would dance at his wedding with the lightest of hearts.

She danced the last before supper with Bob Russell, who was too young for her by many years but, despite being hopelessly smitten, was very amusing company. In New York, in her salad days, she had encountered too many youths whose ardent first love rendered them mute and awkward. To be sure, Bob wasn't that young – he must be twenty-six or -seven – but he had evidently decided that the best way to win her affection was to make her laugh, which made for a pleasant evening. She allowed him to take her in to supper, where they joined a group of his friends, and the talk soon turned to hunting.

Everyone wanted to describe his own run at the hunt yesterday, which was only interesting up to a point, and despite Bob's efforts to inject some variety and amusement into the serial narratives, her attention began to wander. That was how she came to find herself listening to the conversation of a group just behind her. She did not recognise the voices, and thought they might be friends of Lord Lambert, house guests down from London. At all events, they weren't talking about the hunting or local affairs, but about general topics and, as she began properly listening, London shows.

One man mentioned an art exhibition he had been to. 'Very modern,' he drawled. 'Not sure I went along with all of it.'

'You're such a stick-in-the-mud, Algy,' someone else said teasingly.

'Am not!' Algy protested. 'I don't *only* like country cottages and girls with flowers, you know. A lot of this modern stuff's all right. But I do like it to have a bit of *something* about it, something to get your teeth into – not just a lot of splodges a child could make.'

A woman joined in. 'Oh, I know what you mean. But there was a pair of paintings there, supposed to be views of Paris – you could really *see* what he was getting at.'

'That's exactly what I mean,' Algy said eagerly. 'They were sort of streaky, but wonderful colours, and it just made you think of Parisian streets and rain and so on. Modern, but you could get your *teeth* into it.'

Another woman, with the sort of drawling, smoky voice Polly associated with fashionable parties and hadn't heard for a while, said, 'Darling, I know exactly the pictures you mean, and I happen to know the artist, too.'

'Not really! Sybil, how exciting! How did you come to meet him? I can't remember his name.'

'Eric Chapel,' Sybil replied. 'I adore him, that's all. Met him in Paris when Chuffy was over there for that conference.'

Polly had gone rigid, her ears straining. Erich in Paris? What was he doing there? He had told her he despised the French. But that was just after the war, a long time ago, and feelings could change.

Sybil went on talking. 'He's an Englishman, of course, but not at all like the Englishmen one knows, like darling Chuffy, or Chad, or Reggie – or you, Algy, you dull old sweetie, all buttoned up and frightfully nice.'

'Thanks awf'ly, old thing,' Algy drawled, and everyone laughed.

'This Chapel fellow is simply *divine*. Handsome as a Greek god and smouldering with passion. I suppose it's being an artist, you know. I couldn't fancy him more! I quite decided I'd have an affair with him, but Chuffy got called home again.'

'How come one hasn't heard of him?' asked another man's voice.

'He's been living in America since the war. Frightfully famous over there. He's—'

At that moment Bob addressed a question to Polly directly and she had to stop listening to answer. When she was able to turn her attention to the group behind her again, she was afraid they would have left the topic. But it evidently hadn't been as long as it had seemed to her. The first woman was speaking again, saying something about a hat, and the husky-voiced Sybil interrupted her.

'Darling, it couldn't matter less what she wore! She looks just exactly like a pug-dog whatever she has on. I'm talking about the divine Eric Chapel. Sophie Talbot-Manners and Daisy Fellowes are getting up a one-man show for him next year in London, and he's coming over for it, so I shall have another chance at him, if Daisy doesn't get in first. Chuffy's frightfully busy with the League, these days, and Chapel's not married, and he hasn't been to London since the war, so he'll need someone to hold his wickle hand and take care of him. Now, do admit!'

'Oh, Syb, you are terrible! Anyway, you know you promised to have an affair with me next, when you were finished with Reggie.'

Gales of laughter, followed by more personal anecdotes. Polly stopped listening. Her thoughts were in turmoil. Erich in London next year? He had always said he wouldn't dare to come back to England, in case anyone recognised him. But the war had been over a long time, and surely the likelihood of that was very limited. And Germans weren't hated as they once were. Many people thought it best to let bygones be bygones and hold out the hand of friendship, for the sake of securing peace. Better to forgive and forget, however painful that was, if it could prevent the unspeakable horror of another war.

London. If he braved London, would he come any further? And what had the woman Sybil meant, that he wasn't married? Had something happened to his wife? Or had he divorced her?

Would he write to her? Would he come to Yorkshire?

If he was in London, she could go there, visit the exhibition. She could see him again.

A dull, gnawing ache in the pit of her stomach. And it was half resentful, that her feelings, so long buried they had grown quiescent and slept, had been aroused again.

Sybil might have been mistaken: he might still be married. And if he wasn't – well, he had never contacted her. Perhaps he had moved on, put his memories of her out of his mind. As she had his – until now. She was confused and unhappy, not knowing what to think, what to feel – and only a few minutes before, she had been happy and contented.

Bob touched her hand. 'Are you all right? You looked rather odd just then, as if you didn't feel well.'

'I think it's the heat,' she said. 'I need a breath of fresh air.'

'It'll be *too* fresh outside at this time of year,' Bob said. 'Perhaps a quiet seat somewhere. I think the library's empty. Shall I take you?'

He was eager to help her, she could see. Perhaps letting him escort her to a sofa in an empty library might be construed as encouragement – at least by a man who had been showing the symptoms all evening of wanting to kiss her. Probably it wasn't fair.

But, actually, kissing was what she really needed, to drive the miserable confusion out of her head. And Bob was old enough to take care of himself. In any case, she had to get away from this noise and crowd. She nodded, stood up and walked away, not knowing at first or even caring much if he followed her.

Charlotte dined *chez* Molly and Vivian most Thursdays, when they combined the social occasion with Dolphin talk. Dolphin

Books was doing unexpectedly well. In the first nine months they had sold three million copies, the book stock was turning over every six weeks, and the company had made a net profit of nearly five thousand pounds.

She went to the flat directly from work so as to have a chance of seeing the children before they went to sleep. Esmond, six, and Angelica, four, called her Aunty Charlotte and found her much more exciting, naturally enough, than Nanny or Mummy, whom they could see any time. When the maid let her in she went directly to the drawing room, saying, as she entered, 'Am I in time to see my little angels?'

'Well, you're in time for one of them,' a familiar voice said. 'How nice that you think of me as an angel.'

Charlotte was brought up short at the sight of Milo sitting talking to Molly. He rose to his feet as she came in.

'What are you doing here?' she asked.

'Why do you always ask that?' he countered.

'I don't.'

'Well, quite often.'

'Only when you're somewhere I don't expect you to be. Which is quite often.'

'Now, children, no bickering,' Molly laughed. 'I can see you two spend too much time together.'

'Oh, not nearly enough,' Milo said sinuously.

'I'll talk to Molly,' Charlotte announced. 'What *is* he doing here?'

'Come to talk business with Vivian,' Molly explained. 'And of course I've asked him to stay to dinner. Now, if you want to see the children, we'd better go straight to the nursery because it's nearly bed-time.'

To Charlotte's surprise, Milo came too, and the children seemed to know him. They bounced excitedly and chattered to him.

'You've been here before,' Charlotte said.

'Of course. Why not?' he said, which seemed unanswerable.

Nanny decreed no more bouncing, and the children got into their beds to lie still under promise of a story. '*Two* stories,' Esmond negotiated. 'One from Aunty Charlotte and one from Uncle Milo.' He frowned. 'Mummy, Uncle Milo's not really an uncle, is he? Why do I have to call him that?'

'It's an old Spanish custom,' Molly answered. 'Initiated in the reign of King Carlos the Third and imposed upon little children ever since in the name of courtesy and respect. Now, do you want a story, or do you want to ask questions?'

'Story,' Esmond agreed, since questions were eliciting answers he couldn't understand.

Vivian arrived home just as they were returning to the drawing room. 'Sherry or cocktail?' Molly asked, kissing him.

'Cocktail, I think. How did the writing go?' Vivian answered.

'Ten pages,' Molly said. 'I'd hoped for more, but Cook broke a mixing bowl and cut her hand, and the phone kept ringing.'

'You could just not answer it,' Vivian pointed out.

'But then I'd be wondering who it had been, which is just as disturbing,' said Molly. 'Do you want to mix, or shall I?'

'I'll do it,' Milo said, jumping up. 'I make a particularly good martini.'

When he was busy at the tray, Charlotte said to Vivian, 'What *is* he doing here?'

'Don't you like him to be?' Vivian said in surprise. 'I thought you were fond of his company.'

'Oh, I am, though he's one of the most annoying people I know. Molly says it's business – is it Dolphin business?'

'He's come up with a rather clever new idea,' Vivian said. 'You know that from the beginning we've wanted to sell Dolphin books in a lot more places than just bookshops.'

'Particularly as the bookshops were so hostile to the idea,' Molly put in.

'Yes, of course,' Charlotte said. And the books were now not only in Woolworth's but in all sorts of small shops. The ultimate aim was to have every village shop sell them alongside the cheese, pan-scourers, cigarettes and tinned soup. 'So, what's the new idea?'

'Slot machines,' Vivian said. At the cocktail tray, Milo gave a polite smirk as he poured gin with a liberal hand. 'You see, as Milo pointed out, sixpence is not only a price, it's a coin—'

'And a very widely used one,' Milo added.

'And if you can buy cigarettes and chocolate from a slot machine, there's no reason you can't buy books the same way.'

'But – can it work?' Charlotte asked, frowning. 'Books are rather larger than cigarette packets.'

'They're bigger in surface area,' Milo said, 'but against that, they're thinner. And they don't go stale – or not in the same way. The mechanics of the thing are not actually difficult. I've brought some drawings with me, some ideas of what the machines might look like – how you'd display the different titles, and so on.'

He produced them, and they pored over them, discussing the details while they drank his extremely strong martinis. Charlotte felt her head swimming and didn't finish hers.

'If the mechanics of the thing are not the difficulty, what is?' she asked, in a pause in the conversation.

'How do you know there is one?' Milo asked.

'I know the way your mind works. Come on – spit it out.'

'Not a difficulty that can't be overcome. It's the same as you had with Woolworth's – persuading people to take them. They'll be a little bigger than cigarette machines, and they're a new idea. People are scared of new ideas. My thought would be to try railway stations first. Space isn't a problem for them. Once they're established on the platforms and people have experienced them, and seen they work, the shops will want to follow suit. After all, a slot machine represents very easy profit for a tradesman. No having to take money at the till and make change, no paper bags, and someone else does the maintenance. I think they'll go for them in a big way once they're used to the idea.'

There were neighbours coming to dinner, and once they arrived the talk became general. After dinner, in the drawing room, in one of the general movements, Vivian came to take the place beside Charlotte, and said, 'He's being very useful to me, that young man of yours.'

'He's not really my "young man",' Charlotte said.

Vivian smiled. 'Oh, I think he is. You're seeing quite a lot of him, and he's certainly very attached to you. Don't you like him?'

'Oh, yes,' Charlotte said hastily. 'I just never thought about it like that.'

Vivian gave her a look that told her he suspected she had, but he said, 'Anyway, apart from the slot-machine idea, which is a very good one, I think he may be able to help me in another way. You see, we can't go on using the crypt for ever. It's not a healthy environment. As we expand, I doubt we'll find new people willing to work down there. The lack of facilities will also be a problem with a bigger staff. It's damp, there are mice, and suppose there was a fire? It doesn't bear thinking about.'

'So you have to find another place?'

Vivian lit a cigarette. 'What I'd like to do,' he said, 'is to build somewhere new, to combine the whole operation, office, warehouse, packing, everything. It'll work out cheaper in the long run to build something to order than to muddle through with premises designed for something else. Preferably not in the middle of London, with all the traffic problems for loading and unloading, but not too far out so we can all get there easily.'

'It sounds a good idea,' Charlotte said.

'And for that,' Vivian went on, 'we'll need money. I've already sounded out the bank, of course, but they're not keen. We're an infant enterprise, dealing in a commodity they're not familiar with. They don't know how to calculate whether we'll thrive or turn up our toes. So that's where your – where Milo comes in.'

'Oh, I see!' she said. 'He knows people with money –'

'– and matches them with people who need money.' Vivian smiled. 'A very good sort of business if you have the resources for it.'

Milo joined them at that moment. 'Did I hear my name spoken?'

'No, you didn't,' Charlotte said, 'but we were talking about you.'

'I could tell. My ears were burning.'

'I was saying you were going to find me someone with money to build my new headquarters,' said Vivian.

'As a matter of fact I think I know the very chap. Puffy Elphinstone. Fearfully nice fellow, out of the top drawer, nothing much between his ears, but money coming out of them. And I know he's got a particular fondness for literature, because one of his forebears was Samuel Johnson. Or, in fact,' he corrected himself, frowning, 'it might have been James Boswell, now I come to think of it, because Elphinstone is a Scotch name, isn't it?'

'How do you know him?' Charlotte asked.

'Oh, we were at school together,' Milo said vaguely. 'Important thing is, he's good for the money, and I'm pretty sure he'll like the idea. I'll sound him out first, and if he's for it, I'll get you two together. You'll like him. Everyone likes Puffy. *I* like him, so I'd sooner have a hand in positioning the Elphinstone gold than let someone unscrupulous get hold of him.'

'You're a noble fellow,' Charlotte teased. 'Always thinking of others.'

'Do nothing else, morn till night,' Milo agreed. 'How much do you need?'

'I should think around fifteen thousand for the building,' Vivian said. 'Perhaps two or three for the land.'

'I'll talk to Puffy in terms of twenty, then.' Milo nodded. 'I'll see him next week and get the ball rolling.'

Vivian moved away, leaving Milo alone with Charlotte. 'Another small step closer to your fortune?' she said.

'Oh, I'm just doing this as a favour,' Milo said. 'I've gone rather beyond this sort of level now. International finance and government procurement, that's where the big money is. Didn't you say your brother had got a government appointment?'

The general election had been held on the 14th of November, resulting in a large, though reduced, majority for the coalition, known as the National Government. Stanley Baldwin was the new prime minister – Ramsay MacDonald had resigned due to ill health back in June. The Conservatives had the largest number of MPs, while the Liberal vote had held steady and the Labour vote had collapsed. In the reshuffle of posts, Alfred Duff Cooper had become secretary for war, and Robert had been made a junior minister in his department. It had been in all the newspapers: 'at so young an age'; 'start of a brilliant career'; 'this newspaper confidently predicts', et cetera. One paper had even mentioned Palmerston.

Robert had been so thrilled he was hardly able to show it, and enhanced his 'old head on young shoulders' image by being rather solemn and pompous at first. Violet, of course, had been delighted, feeling that the shadow of Holkam's shame and death was at last lifting from his children. She had been brought up to expect her nearest and dearest to hold government posts, so this was a return to normal for her.

'Yes, he's in the War Office,' Charlotte said.

'I think we could be very useful to each other,' Milo said thoughtfully. 'You must introduce us.'

'I shall do no such thing,' Charlotte said in alarm. If she once introduced him to Robert, there'd be no holding him, and the next thing, her mother would find out. 'You wouldn't like him,' she said, trying to cover up. 'He's awfully stiff-necked.'

'Not like you.' Milo smiled one of his dazzling, sudden sunbursts. Then he added thoughtfully, 'You don't want me to meet any of your family, do you? I wonder why.'

'Because they're not like me,' she said.

CHAPTER TWENTY-ONE

Emma and Kit were invited once more to the Fort for a Saturday-to-Monday on the 21st of December, the last before the Prince of Wales went down to Sandringham for the Christmas season.

'And a good thing too,' Emma grumbled. 'Can't we get out of these weekends next year? I can't believe even you're still finding them amusing. Wales seems to be getting pottier by the minute.'

'We don't get summoned all that often,' Kit said. 'And it's not good form to refuse, unless you have a really good reason. Remember, he'll be king one day.'

'Not for a long time, one hopes.'

'I wouldn't be so sure,' Kit said. 'The King's seventy, you know, and not in the best of health. I doubt he's got many more years left to him.'

Emma shuddered. 'I dread to think what will happen when Sir succeeds.'

'Look on the bright side. Perhaps it will buck him up. Anyway, we have to go, darling, so let's make the best of it. Actually,' he added, 'I feel a bit sorry for him. Christmas at Sandringham's not for the faint-hearted. Jigsaw puzzles and monumental silences. The King looking at his watch and harrumphing if things aren't actually *before* time. Bits of talk so dull they'd turn your face to stone, punctuated by the ticking of clocks.'

'Stop, you're breaking my heart. When does he go?'

'Sunday night, then three weeks without his Wally. So we'll have to do our best to give him a good send-off.'

As it happened, there were other plans afoot. The other guests were the Butlers, the Metcalfes – Fruity was equerrying – Teddy Oxenford, and the actress Elvira Gregory. Kit and Teddy fell on each other's necks like long-lost brothers and began planning who-knew-what mischief. Wallis claimed Emma straight away, wanting to show her what the Prince had given her for Christmas – they had exchanged gifts already as this would be the last time they met before Christmas Day.

'I'm dreading the telephone calls,' Wallis told her, when Emma had admired the gold bracelet in the shape of a snake with ruby eyes. 'He rings practically every hour when he's away, and the calls go on and on. It makes it very hard to have a reasonable conversation with anyone else.'

'Where are you spending Christmas?' Emma asked.

'With friends in Surrey. I suppose I couldn't wangle you down there? I need someone to keep Ernest from fretting when I'm talking to David. One can't blame him for getting upset by the constant interruptions.'

'I'm sorry, there are family plans I couldn't possibly get out of,' Emma said, and then, taking advantage of the desire to confide, she asked, 'Is that *all* Ernest minds?'

Wallis looked impatient. 'Oh, don't *you* ask obvious questions. You should know better, being married to Kit. Ernest is pleased and proud to be on intimate terms with the heir to the throne. But with the phone calls, the constant summonses – I get called away at a moment's notice, in the middle of dinner sometimes – it's hard for us to have any kind of life together, and naturally he starts to feel irritated. And he's afraid they talk about him at his club. Well,' she added frankly, 'not *talk* so much as *laugh*.'

'It's hard to wear horns with any kind of dignity,' Emma murmured.

'Ernest is not a cuckold,' Wallis said sharply.

'Of course not, but that's what people will be saying,' said Emma.

'People should mind their own businesses,' she snapped. And then she sighed. 'Something's going on at the Palace. I think there's going to be another effort over Christmas to make him give me up.'

'Are you worried?' Emma asked.

'They won't succeed,' Wallis said simply. 'David is devoted to me. And I know how to make him happy. No-one else does. All they do is put his back up. If they would work with me I could manage him. But they're terrified of the modern world, the palace set. When David succeeds, he's going to make a new kind of monarchy, modernise the whole bang-shoot, and they're plain-and-simple afraid for their necks.'

'People are always afraid of what they don't understand,' Emma said.

Wallis didn't answer that. She studied Emma's face. 'If Kit hears anything about what's going on, you will tell me, won't you? Come to me, not David. I don't want him any more upset.'

He appeared at that moment. 'Who's upset, darling? Are we going to have drinks before luncheon? Wally's making us her special omelettes,' he added to Emma. 'As a treat, since this is our last Saturday. Oh dear.' The smile vanished, like a rabbit down a hole. 'Three weeks! It's going to be absolutely *bloody*. I *hate* Christmas. I'm going to miss you so much, my darling. Your boy's going to be so lost without you.'

Emma beat a tactful retreat.

It emerged during the afternoon – Emma went for a walk round the garden with Baba Metcalfe, who let her in on the secret – that Admiral Halsey, the Prince's treasurer, and Clive Wigram, his secretary, had drawn up a Grand Remonstrance, which they were proposing to lay before Stanley Baldwin, for him to take to the Prince. They hoped that the government's official weight would make a difference where their repeated urgings and pleadings had not.

'He won't do his duty,' Baba said. 'He turns up sometimes and behaves charmingly, and that's what most people see, so they think he's wonderful. But, of course, Halsey and Wigram see the other side, when he arrives late, or drunk, or improperly dressed, not at all, or simply sits about looking bored, which is so rude, and won't talk to anyone. And the dinners where he sends all the food away and orders them to make him something else. And the way he changes arrangements and forgets he's changed them, and leaves people waiting when he's already gone somewhere else. And how inconsiderate he is to his staff. Godfrey Thomas is one of his oldest friends, and he treats him like dirt, never keeps appointments, loses his temper if he's tackled about anything. Godfrey's in despair – he says if Wales can't run his own little staff, how's he going to cope with a whole country?'

'So it's not Mrs Simpson?' Emma asked.

'Oh, of course, that's what's at the bottom of it. He was always erratic, but it's simply getting worse. He cares about nothing but being with her, thinks about nothing but her. Halsey said to Humphrey that his private life has become his *only* life, and it can't go on. Worrying about him's undermining the King's health, according to Wigram. So they're going to get Baldwin to tell him he's got to change his ways, that the fate of the monarchy and the Empire depend on it. He's got to uphold the old traditions and, most of all, stop frivolling about publicly with his mistress, which is such a bad example to the people – whom he's one day going to have to rule.'

Emma shook her head. 'I can't see Baldwin going along with it. I'm sure he'll think it terribly improper.'

'Frankly, Humphrey agrees, but poor old Halsey's at his wits' end, and so are the rest of the staff. So Humphrey and

Fruity are going to get Sir to one side some time this weekend and give him a good talking-to, man to man.'

'If they can detach him from Wallis,' Emma said. 'He doesn't want to let her out of his sight.'

'We may have to force the issue,' Baba said. 'Take her away by *force majeure*, and tell him we're going to exchange feminine secrets.'

'I'll go along with it, if you like. I don't think it will do any good, though. He's so obsessed with Wallis it's like a sort of madness – and madmen don't respond to reason.'

'There's such a thing as a strait-jacket,' said Baba. 'Enough pressure from the palace, the government and the nation at large might act as a restraint.'

'I'm not sure he'd even notice it, except as an irritant to be batted away, like a bothersome fly. He's forty-one, Baba. I think he's too old to change now, even if he wanted to. And I'm pretty sure he doesn't want to.'

The separation of the lovers took place on Sunday morning, planned and put into action like a military campaign. Wallis went along with it, for the sake of having an hour of peace and quiet away from David, who was always fidgeting about her, asking if she was all right, touching her and trying to hold her hand. She went to church with Baba and Emma while Kit set up a game of indoor croquet with Teddy and the other guests, and Humphrey and Fruity almost frog-marched His Royal Highness out into the garden. He went looking longingly over his shoulder the whole time in case Wallis had changed her mind about church and come back.

'I know what they're up to,' Wallis said to Emma, as they got into the car. 'This is the good talking-to, isn't it? Well, good luck to them. It'll go in one ear and out the other.'

When they got back from church, it was plain from the thunderclouds on Humphrey and Fruity's brows that it had not gone well. The Prince's face lit when his eyes fell on Wallis, and he pranced to her side and began chatting about what they should do after Christmas. 'We ought to get away from this dreary English weather, darling. January's the bloodiest month, I always think. What do you say to a trip to the States? Florida. Lovely sunshine, temperatures in the eighties, couldn't be more different from grey old England.'

'I hate the sun,' Wallis said.

'You could stay in the shade. And there's marvellous shopping at Palm Beach – have you ever been there? We could get a party together . . .'

Emma eased Kit aside. 'No use, obviously.'

'No use,' said Kit. 'Fruity said the worst thing is not that he refuses to do anything about it: the worst thing is that he doesn't even acknowledge there's an "it" to do anything about.'

'Convoluted, but I get your drift,' Emma said.

Oliver was planning a grand family Christmas at Chelmsford House. Violet and Avis were to come, bringing their children; Robert and Richard would be there; Emma and Kit and their two would spend a couple of days before going down to the country to host a house-party at Walcote House. Christmas Day fell on a Wednesday, so Henry had to be back at work on Friday, but by taking the latest trains both ways would be able to have two full days with the family. Eddie was equerrying, and he and Sarah would be at Sandringham, so Oliver and Verena were going to have their boys, too.

Charlotte bumped into Oliver in Oxford Street on the Saturday afternoon before Christmas: she was doing some late shopping, and he was walking to his club, 'To get away from the preparations,' he told her, with a smile. 'It's made clear that I'm only in the way. I was hoping to have a word with you,' he went on, steering her gently out of the flow of pedestrians. 'I wanted to ask you whether you'd like to invite this young man of yours to spend Christmas with us – or even part of it. I meant to speak to you earlier but it slipped my mind – you know how it is.'

Charlotte felt herself reddening. 'What young man is that, Uncle?' she managed to say, but it didn't sound convincing even to her.

He cocked an eyebrow. 'Too soon to be spending Christmas together? I'm sorry if I'm being premature, but I thought things were pretty well along between you two.'

'How—?'

'How did I know? Well, I saw you together in Leicester Square, coming out of the cinema – oh, it must have been some time the week before last. Emma told me even before that that you were walking out with someone. Molly told her it seemed quite serious, and I must say you appeared to be wrapped up in each other. I waved, but you didn't see me – too busy gazing into each other's eyes.'

He beamed genially, but Charlotte looked woebegone. 'You haven't told Mummy anything, have you?'

'No, I haven't spoken to anyone about it. Not a topic likely to come readily to my lips, your *affaire de coeur* – not that I don't have it at heart, you understand, given that you're quite my favourite niece, but I'm rather busy most days thinking about other things.' He examined her unhappy expression, and said, more gently, 'What's the matter? Why don't you want your mother to know?'

'Because she's always trying to make me go out with suitable men, and she'd think he was simply frightfully *un*suitable, and I don't want to have to face a fuss about it.'

'I can see why you wouldn't, but why would she think him unsuitable?'

'Because he's an ordinary person working hard to make his own fortune, and she wants me to marry someone with a title who's inherited one. She'll never be happy unless I end up a countess at least.'

Oliver shook his head. 'I'm afraid you've lost me. If you

don't want to be a countess, why go out with an earl? Or are you meaning to renounce the title and become socialists?'

Now Charlotte was puzzled. 'What title? What do you mean? What earl?'

'My dear child, don't try to bamboozle me. Even if I hadn't recognised the young man, I would only have had to look up his name.'

'His name is Milo Tavey,' Charlotte said, hoping to pin down the misunderstanding.

'Quite so,' said Oliver. 'In full, Milo Giles Deramore Fitzwarren Lytton Tavey, Earl of Launde. A very nice old title, nothing to be ashamed of. Your mother, I assure you, will be very satisfied with it.' Charlotte stared. 'You look as if you've been hit on the head with a large salmon,' Oliver concluded, with interest. 'Don't tell me you didn't know?'

'I didn't know,' Charlotte said in a strangled voice. 'He didn't tell me.'

'Interesting,' said Oliver. 'Well, now you do know, would you like me to invite him for Christmas at Chelmsford House? It would be as good a way as any to break it to your mother.'

Charlotte's lips became grim. 'Thank you, Uncle,' she said politely. 'May I let you know?'

He chuckled. 'Take your time. But do try not to spill any blood, won't you? Makes a mess for the servants.'

'You're very quiet,' Milo said, as they walked down the stairs. He had come to the flat in Ridgmount Gardens to collect Charlotte for their evening out, and Betty and Myra had insisted on inviting him in for a glass of sherry, since it was the last time they'd see him before Christmas. They were both going home to their families. When Milo asked what Charlotte was going to do, she said, 'Haven't decided,' and that was the only time she had opened her lips.

She did not reply to his remark. They walked down towards

Tottenham Court Road to look for a taxi. His business must have been doing well, for he insisted on taxis most of the time now, and he was wearing a new suit. In normal circumstances she would have commented on it, but she was too angry with him to speak at all, lest she explode.

Finally he said, 'Is it something I've done? You seem a little . . . tense.'

That was enough. She turned on him. 'Something you've done? You mean something like lying to me, deceiving me, making a fool of me?'

'My dear girl—' he began to protest.

'Don't "my dear girl" me! Since you started with a lie, I don't know whether *anything* you've told me is true. I thought you liked me, but now I'm wondering what you're really up to.'

'I do like you – well, a lot more than like, really. I thought you knew that. What's this lie I'm supposed to have started with?'

'No "supposed" about it. Do you deny you told me your name was Milo Tavey?'

'So it is. Why should I deny it?'

'Because you're really Milo Giles Deramore Fitzwarren Lytton Tavey, Earl of Launde. You didn't tell me that! You didn't tell me who you really were!'

'Nor did you, Miss Charlotte Howard, *I don't think*!' he retorted. 'Or perhaps I should say Lady Charlotte Augusta Mary Fitzjames Howard?'

The wind was taken from her sails. 'You knew,' she said feebly.

'Of course I did. I knew all along. I recognised you in the Corner House, from your picture in the *Tatler* from when you came out. Didn't do you justice, by the way, the photo – you're *much* prettier in real life.'

She waved that away. 'I don't understand.'

'Oh, it's easy. I recognised you, and I was intrigued about

what you were doing in Lyons dressed like a typist, with two other girls dressed like typists. So I eavesdropped unashamedly – that's the only crime you have to charge me with, by the way. When you got up to leave, your scarf, which was hanging over the back of your chair, slithered gracefully to the floor, and since you hadn't noticed, I saw my chance. Instead of drawing your attention to it, I waited until you'd gone, collared it and followed you. And the rest, my dear little dissembler, is history. I gave you ample chance to tell me who you really were, and since you didn't . . .' He shrugged.

Charlotte rallied. 'But Miss Charlotte Howard *is* who I really am. I *am* a typist. Whereas *you*—'

'Am really Milo Tavey. What do you doubt about that simple statement?'

'You said you were working to make your fortune.'

'So I am. My father inherited a lot of death duties from his father, and by the time he'd paid them, there wasn't enough left to pay the death duties when *he* died. Had to sell the rest of the estate to get clear. So it left me nothing but the title. I *had* to work for a living, but I don't mean to do it all my life. I had to find a way to make a fortune so that I could retire from commerce, buy an estate – preferably the old one – and marry the lovely, charming, sensible and very funny girl whose present mislaying of her sense of humour I hope is strictly temporary.'

There was too much to assimilate for Charlotte to be able to form a reply at once. Milo took advantage of her silence to say, 'Actually, if I hadn't known before, you would have given yourself away when you told me your brother Robert had been given a ministerial post.'

'I only mentioned it because I was proud of him,' she faltered.

'So you should be.'

'And I didn't say who he was, only his first name.'

'My dear child, one only had to look up the names of the

new appointees in *The Times*. They were all listed. And there he was, Robert Fitzjames Howard, Earl of Holkam. After that, Debrett's gave me the rest of your Christian names – charming as they are! Charlotte Mary Augusta: very suitable. Actually, I think we're cousins in some degree. A long way back, though, so it won't be a difficulty.' He waited for a reply, then said, 'Now what's the trouble? You look mournful.'

'I thought I knew you,' she said. 'Now I feel as if I don't know you at all.'

'Everything I ever told you is the truth,' he said, 'and the only omission is the unimportant point about my title, which I never use anyway. Or hardly ever, except when it works to my advantage in business. I must say, the Americans like it. And it opens certain doors.'

'No wonder you knew all those people,' Charlotte said. 'Like Lord Elphinstone.'

'I told you I went to school with him.'

'Eton,' she supposed.

'You really were very incurious. You could easily have found out, you know.'

'Didn't know there was anything *to* find out.'

'Now that just sounds sulky.' He took her in his arms, right there on the corner of Tottenham Court Road and Chenies Street, with the whole world looking on. 'Anything else you want to berate me about?' he asked her. 'It's an awful waste of this rather nice moment. I notice you aren't struggling against having my arms round you.'

'I don't want to make a spectacle of us,' she retorted. 'It's bad enough having you embrace me in public without my—' She stopped. 'Did you say "marry"?'

'An interestingly delayed reaction,' he observed. 'Yes, I said "marry". My fortune is sufficiently repaired for me to enter into an engagement, with the prospect of being rich enough to marry next year. If you would stop worrying about trivial details and concentrate on the main point . . .'

She began to smile. 'Which is?'

'That you are the most delicious girl I have ever met – though a trifle on the schoolmarmy side on occasions, but we'll soon beat that out of you – and that I can't think of going through life without you as anything but hellish. So, if you will allow me to heap the fortune I expect to make at your feet, followed by the riches of the whole world and the stars in the sky if I can get 'em, you'll make me the happiest of men – or should I say of secret noblemen? In other words,' he became serious, looking down tenderly into her face, 'will you marry me, Lady Charlotte?'

'You went a long way round to get to it,' she said.

'I get drunk on words sometimes,' he admitted. 'Well? Simple question.'

'Simple answer,' she said. 'Yes.'

'Thank heaven for that,' he said, and kissed her. After some time, a taxi honked at them and made them break apart, to see the driver hanging out of his window, grinning. They looked at each other, and laughed, linked arms, and began walking down the road, forgetting for the moment where they had originally set out for.

'Will you really have enough money next year?' Charlotte asked, in bliss.

'Yes, though accumulating it will involve me in some travelling. That's why I wanted to make sure of you before I have to leave you temporarily.'

'I thought you only proposed to stop me being angry with you.'

'*Excellent* reason for proposing, wish I'd thought of it. So many people have been angry with me in the past, I could have had as many wives as Solomon. But in fact I was going to "pop", as they say, the question this evening. You just brought the moment forward. I was going to do it in Fratelli's with champagne, but a street corner is much more romantic. I thought you'd be going to your people over Christmas, and I was afraid some bounder would corner you under the mistletoe and steal your heart away.'

'My mother never invites bounders, just very dull young men. And we're all going to Uncle Oliver's this Christmas.'

'Uncle Oliver the Earl of Overton and Chelmsford, I presume?'

She narrowed her eyes. 'You've been looking him up as well?'

'Darling, I know who you are so I know who your mother is and who her brother is. Don't you realise, I'm one of you? I mean, we're two of us. We come from the same bit of the world where everyone knows everyone else. Everyone except you, obviously. But I'm glad you didn't know I was a belted earl, as the twopennies say, before you fell in love with me, because that proves your love is pure and untainted by ambition.'

She roared with laughter. 'Ambition? To marry you, Milo Tavey? Conceit! And who said I was in love with you?'

'Your eyes, my love, and your lips, and the charming little sigh you give when I kiss you. Which I'm going to do again, taxi drivers or no taxi drivers, so if there's anything else you want to say first . . . ?'

'Yes, there is,' she said. 'Would you like to come to Uncle Oliver's for Christmas?'

The telegram arrived at the last minute, but Polly was so glad he was coming, she dropped everything and went to collect him at the station herself in the little two-year-old Hillman Minx she had bought for pottering about. He stepped down from the train and enfolded her in a happy embrace, then stepped back to look at her.

To an outsider's eye they would have been obviously brother and sister – both tall, handsome, golden, and very smartly dressed. He was wearing a fine grey tweed coat with a big fur collar, loose and American in style, and a rather French

Homburg, which he swept off to reveal that his hair had been cut expensively by a foreign barber. She was wearing a grey facecloth suit, a blue-grey wool coat, a sable piece, and a rather saucy hat, tilted over one eye and secured by a diamond pin in the shape of an arrow.

He waved his hand over her. 'You look – splendid! I can't believe all this is for my benefit.'

'No, it's for mine.'

'That's even worse. Is there really no man in the picture? Have all the men in Yorkshire collectively lost their wits?'

She laughed. 'I'm sorry about what's-his-name, by the way,' he added seriously. 'Sorry it didn't come to anything.'

'Don't be.' She slipped a hand through his arm and turned him towards the exit. 'It was my fault entirely. I made a silly mistake. I shall be more careful in future.'

'Not *too* careful, or you won't have any fun.'

'*We*'ll have fun. Oh, Jamie, I'm so *pleased* you came for Christmas. But how come?'

'No Meredith,' he said simply. 'Charlie and Fern went back to the States and took her with them to act as their secretary. That way she gets a chance to see her folks.'

'"Folks"? How American you're becoming!'

'I can speak French to you instead, if you like.'

'Fancy you being fluent in it! Daddy would have been so proud.'

'Daddy would have been so mystified. I'm like him, you know – neither of us had any brains to speak of, not where book-learning is concerned. But it's easy to pick up a language if you're living in a place.'

'*You* may find it so – I'm sure I shouldn't. How long can you stay?'

'A bit more than just Christmas,' he said. 'You see, with Charlie away, there's no job for me in Paris, and I don't know when he's coming back. He said a month, but you never really know where he'll go next. And if he doesn't send

546

for me, if he forgets all about me . . .' He shrugged. 'So I may be out of a job again.'

'Never mind,' she comforted him. 'You can stay here and help me. This is your home, you know.'

'Until you get married,' he said lightly. 'So what have you got planned for me? Hunting, I hope?'

'Of course, if the weather holds. John Burton says Tiddy the shepherd told him there's a cold snap coming.'

'And who told Tiddy the shepherd?'

'The sheep, of course,' Polly said, with an innocent look, and he laughed. They were approaching the car, inside which a forest of waving tails reinforced the message of the grinning hairy faces that were fogging up the glass.

'Good Lord,' James said. 'Don't tell me we're travelling in that!'

'It's roomier than it looks. When did you become so particular?'

'It's working with Charlie – nothing but the best, motor-cars you could hold a ball in. No chauffeur, old girl?'

'I bought this specifically so I could drive myself,' Polly said. 'Don't worry, you can sit in front with me. The dogs can stay in the back.'

When they were settled, he pushed back Helmy, who was breathing lovingly down his neck, and said, 'Go on about the plans.'

'Well, I thought tomorrow a long ride, because I'm sure you haven't been in the saddle for months. Hunting on Saturday – and there's a hunt on Monday with a neighbouring pack, if you want to go out. Firefly's not really fit, and I'll need both mine, but Jessie's got a nice youngster she says you can ride – he's going very well and she wants him to gain experience, but you've to promise not to spoil his mouth.'

'When did I ever?' he scoffed.

'She was joking. She wouldn't lend him if you had heavy hands. And you can take a gun out whenever you like – the

547

pheasants are particularly good this year. I've still got Daddy's Purdeys for you to use. Dinner at Bootham Park on Friday night, and Jessie and Bertie are giving a dinner on Monday night. Christmas Eve at home, Jessie and Bertie and a few friends coming for that. Christmas Day, all the family, and Boxing Day the hunt, and a ball in the evening. I hope you packed your tails?'

'Yes, but my white gloves are a disgrace.'

'They don't seem to last any time, these days. We can go into York tomorrow and buy you some.' She glanced across at him as she waited for the traffic to clear at the junction of Blossom Street. 'It's so good to see you! We're going to have such fun!'

'You've already said that,' James mentioned. It struck him that all was not well with his sister. Had she really loved this Charles fellow? Or was it someone else? It didn't seem natural to him that a beautiful woman like her should not have been snapped up. Probing feelings was not his *forte*, but he was damned fond of her, and he determined to try to get to the bottom of it while he was here. For the moment, however, he couldn't think of a way of asking. So instead he said, 'And how's my little nevvy? Behaving himself?'

'Growing like a weed.' Polly smiled. 'He's so excited you're coming. He wanted to come to the station to meet you, but I said there wouldn't be room, so instead he's drawing you a special picture to put up in your room. It's a picture of Paris – I hope you'll recognise it.'

'I will now,' James promised.

'And he wants to take you out to the stable to see his pony. He said first thing, but I think we can allow you to refresh yourself.'

'I shall pause only to change my bags,' James said solemnly. 'Can't keep a chap waiting when he's got a pony to show one.'

The next day it was clear that Tiddy's sheep knew their

business. Polly had woken to a pewter sky, and now, as she rode home with James beside her, it was pregnant with menace. An iron cold gripped the land, the bare trees stood mute under it, and even the birds had fallen silent. Zephyr turned his long, fine ear back towards her every few moments, in case she should be thinking of giving the order to gallop. Both horses were jogging, and they let them, despite the rule about walking the last half-mile home: Zephyr and James's borrowed Windhover were both clipped for hunting, and it was too cold to dally.

'So, what do you think of him?' Polly asked, after a long silence. Her breath clouded up in front of her as she spoke, as though the words were taking a physical form.

'Hmm?' James came back, from far away. 'Oh, he's fine. A very comfortable ride. Pity the weather's turning – I'd enjoy hunting him, but that sky looks like snow to me.'

'Perhaps there won't be much of it,' she said, without conviction. Then she smiled. 'Perhaps there'll be a regular blizzard, and we'll be snowed in, and you'll have to stay for weeks.'

'You've forgotten – I already am staying.'

'So you are. Jamie, about Meredith. Are you really serious about her?'

'Question is, is she serious about me? I know she likes me, but I think she thinks I'm an awful fool. In any case,' he added sadly, 'now she's gone to the States with Charlie, what if she decides not to come back? I may never see her again. And even if I do, I can't afford to marry.'

'I hope you've saved some of your wages for a rainy day.'

'I always mean to,' he said apologetically, 'but things are so expensive, and one has a certain appearance to keep up and – well, somehow it all goes. I don't know where.' He checked Windhover to keep him level with Zephyr, and said, 'So here I am on your doorstep, old girl, pretty much as I left you.'

He was so handsome and so nice, Polly thought, how

could it be that he had not been snapped up? The Meredith girl was a fool if she let him go.

James wanted to change the subject. He racked his brain, and came up with, 'Oh, by the way, I meant to tell you – I came across someone who knows you, apparently from your New York days. I met him a while back and forgot, but I came across him again the other day at a party given by Daisy Fellowes that I went to with Charlie and Fern. It was quite a do.' He distracted himself. 'The Cholmondeleys were there, and Nada Milford Haven, the Westminsters – I've never seen so many diamonds in one room. And there was—'

'Who was this friend?' Polly said. 'I don't hear from any of the old crowd any more.' But the mention of Daisy Fellowes had given her the hint. She knew what he was going to say.

'Artist chappie,' James said. 'Name of Eric Chapel. Apparently he's the cat's pyjamas in the art world – everyone's raving about his pictures and they're selling for a fortune, if you can get hold of them. Charlie says Daisy's making him hold them back, create a shortage in the market so as to push the price up. Shouldn't think he needed the money, frankly – he was a set designer in Hollywood and won an Oscar for Artistic Direction, so Meredith says. Anyway, he's come to Paris to get away from the silver screen and back to pure art – that's the line one hears. But he really can paint. Hélène knows about these things and says he's absolutely the caterpillar's boots.' He remembered the point of the story. 'Do you know the blighter?'

'I knew him in New York,' she said. Her voice sounded amazingly calm to her ears.

'He asked after you. I forgot to mention before. I told him you were engaged to this Charles fellow.'

'Oh, Jamie, you didn't!'

'I didn't think there was any harm. It was only local people you wanted to keep it from, wasn't it? He sent his best

550

wishes, or something of the sort.' He looked at her curiously. Her face seemed rather strained – though it could just be the cold air. But it might be that this Chapel had meant something to her. Why else would she mind? 'But when I met him last week he said something like, "I suppose your sister is married now?" and I told him the engagement was off again,' he went on. He was not good enough at reading expressions to know whether that piece of information had affected her.

'I wish you wouldn't tell everyone my private business,' Polly said stiffly. She wanted to ask how Erich had reacted, but would not allow herself to.

'I don't,' he defended himself. 'It was just this chap said he knew you, and he seemed interested in your welfare, that's all.'

Polly reached forward and turned a lock of Zephyr's mane back onto the right side. 'I heard someone say he was coming to England to do a show,' she said casually.

'That's right. I had it from Hélène that Daisy Fellowes is putting one up for him in London in March. Do you think you might go up to London for it? If I'm still here we could go together and have a jolly time.'

She smiled what she hoped was a sisterly and affectionate smile, and said, 'I'd like that. I haven't been to London for ages, and it would be fun doing things with you.' *Now I know the date*, she thought. A single fleck of white landed on Zephyr's black mane, and sat there, impudently not melting. 'Was that the first flake of snow?' she asked, glad to change the subject.

James turned his face up, and saw one, and then another, and another, spinning down, looking black against the heavy sky. 'Here it comes,' he said. 'We'd better trot on.'

By the time they reached the gatehouse, there was a fine coating on the horses' manes and the grass to either side of the track was dusted white. The dogs had left them early on in the ride, deciding it was too cold for any decent smells to make the outing worth while, but Helmy and Fand were sitting under the barbican, waiting, and rose, waving their tails gladly, as they came into sight.

'I'm not going to introduce you as the Earl of Launde,' Charlotte said firmly, as the taxi made its way along the Mall. The snow fell prettily past the buildings and lined the branches of the trees in the Park, but hissed into slush under the taxi wheels.

He shook his head in amusement. 'Whatever you like, but they must already know by now.'

'And if you don't mind, I'd like to keep our engagement secret, just for a little while.'

'Too much excitement, with Christmas and everything?' He pretended sympathy. 'You'd never cope. There'd be tears before bedtime.'

She punched him lightly in the arm. 'Don't be facetious. I just don't want to be penned up for days answering questions about the wedding.'

'My darling, you can tell or not tell just as you please. It won't make any difference to the outcome. You're going to marry me, and there's nothing you can do about it.'

'What a caveman you are,' she said.

'You're pretty *farouche* yourself. But we Taveys know how to tame a woman.'

The butler could not be made party to Charlotte's plan: it would have gone against the grain for him to get a title wrong. He announced them with full sonority in the Rose Drawing-room, which had recently been refurbished and was looking magnificent in pink and gold. A huge fire was leaping under the vast marble fireplace, in front of which was an attractive tangle of children and dogs. Verena came forward, kissed Charlotte, and said, 'How cold your cheek is, and your hands. Is it still snowing?'

552

'Yes, and I think it's getting thicker. This is Milo Tavey – my aunt, Lady Overton.'

'You must call me Verena,' she said, as she shook Milo's hand. 'We're so pleased to meet you at last. We've heard so much about you.'

She introduced him to the rest of the company. Oliver shook his hand and offered him a glass of Madeira. Emma and Kit smiled warmly, giving him a keen look-over while trying not to seem to. Henry was shy, Robert a little lofty, as was his wont. Charlotte wasn't worried about any of them. It was her mother she was watching out of the corner of her eye. They got to Avis before her, and he gave Milo's hand a hearty shake and said, 'Launde, my dear fellow. My father knew your father quite well. We did meet once, at Tatton Park, but you were only a boy then – I don't suppose you remember. I haven't seen you in the House. Have you a particular interest? I may be able to put you on to someone if you have.'

Milo was smiling, genial, grateful as the case demanded; reacting, Charlotte saw, in minutely different ways to each person. She narrowed her eyes. It was too polished a performance. She suspected satire. Her mother, seated on a sofa where she had been talking to three-year-old Electra, stood as they approached, gave Milo a very comprehensive once-over, then smiled and held out both hands. 'Delighted to meet you,' she said. 'Charlotte's been very secretive about you, but I hope we shall get to know each other much better from now on. Come and sit by me and tell me all about yourself.'

Charlotte found herself beside Kit, who gave her a wink and said, 'Brave girl, bringing him into this lions' den. I hope you're serious about him.'

'Why should I be?' Charlotte said, trying to hold her ground.

'Because he's been swallowed whole, and you'll never get him back out in one piece. Seriously, though, he seems a nice fellow.'

'He is,' Charlotte said. 'Awfully nice.'

'Then I should grab him while you can. Nice fellows are thin on the ground in these degenerate days. Ask Emma,' he added, as she came up to them, having retrieved Electra from the sofa.

'Ask me what?'

'How hard it is to find and keep a first-rate husband like me. You ladies have to work very hard at it, don't you? You don't deserve us, really you don't.'

'Ignore this reprobate,' Emma said, taking her arm. 'Come and talk to my children.'

It was not possible to avoid talking to her mother about Milo, though she tried hard; but eventually in the course of circulation Violet caught up with her.

'I haven't spoken a word with you yet, darling,' she said. She was looking very beautiful, in a demi-toilette of mauve-blue silk that brought out the colour of her eyes, and pearl clips in her luxuriant dark hair. She was also looking very happy, which Charlotte was glad to see. 'I wanted to tell you how pleased I am.'

'Pleased, Mummy?'

'Don't pretend not to understand. I always knew you would come to your senses at last, and I'm very glad to see you with such an appropriate young man. I don't know how I came to miss him when I was trying to find someone for you.'

'He hasn't any money,' Charlotte said bluntly and, for a moment, was glad to see her mother wince, though she felt ashamed of herself almost immediately afterwards.

'I know about the horrible death duties,' Violet said. 'Avis told me. But Oliver says he's doing very well at making good his position. But that's not important – or not as important as other things. He has his youth and strength and he'll make his way in the world. What matters is that he comes from the right background.'

Charlotte felt obliged to protest. 'Oh, Mummy, that's so snobbish! Nobody cares about that sort of thing nowadays.'

Violet looked surprised. 'It's nothing to do with snobbery. Is that what you think of me? Marriage is a tricky business, Charlotte. Things don't always go smoothly, but if you're from the same background – *whatever* that is – you can get past the difficulties, because you have the same expectations, the same habits and values. You think it doesn't matter, but you'll find out one day that I'm right. People from different backgrounds just can't understand each other, and living intimately with another person is hard enough without *adding* difficulties.'

Charlotte didn't agree, but she did not want to argue with her mother. 'Well, in any case, I don't know why you're talking about marriage. *We* haven't.'

Violet's contentment did not abate a whit. 'But you will do. Now I've seen you together, I can see you're suited.'

Barbara was more exasperated than surprised when Basil turned up on her doorstep on Christmas Eve, carrying a holdall and soaked to the skin because it had started snowing again when he had left the station and his overcoat had been designed for looks rather than durability.

'Why didn't you telephone from the station? Or take a taxi?' she asked, peeling off his coat with her own hands while the servant stood pointedly staring at the spots he was making on the hall floor.

'Stony broke,' Basil said, through clenched teeth, starting to shiver now he was standing still. The walk had kept him warm. Well, warmish. 'Not even pennies for the phone. And have you ever tried to get a taxi at a provincial railway station on Christmas Eve?'

'Aren't you supposed to be with Mummy and Dad?' she asked, handing the wet coat and hat to the reluctant servant and running a motherly hand over his hair.

'Couldn't face it,' Basil said. 'Mum and Dad, Aunt Molly and Uncle Vivian and their children, and all the flaming punch and plum puddings and jolly carol-singing? Ugh!'

'Well, it's exactly what you'll get here,' she warned. 'We like the traditional Christmas. Oh, Basil, there's not a bit of you that's not wet! I don't think a towel is going to do any good. You'd better have a hot bath before you catch pneumonia.' She turned to the servant. 'Tell Susan to run upstairs and run Mr Compton a bath. And put fresh sheets on in the yellow bedroom – and mind they're aired first. And tell Cook one more for dinner. Come and have a drink by the fire while your bath's running. I hope you've got a dry change of clothes in that bag because you won't fit anything of Freddie's. He's much taller than you.'

In the drawing room the fire was bright, and Freddie was peacefully settled in an armchair with the newspaper and – to Basil's horror – slippers on his feet. But he roused himself politely and came to shake Basil's hand, asked him about the snow, commented on the weather forecast, mixed him a stiffish whisky, and only then asked him how long he was staying. Basil gave him full credit for his forbearance.

'I'm not sure,' Basil said. 'A few days, if that's all right.'

'We have people coming in to dinner tonight,' Freddie mentioned, managing not to sound as if that was a good reason for Basil to leave.

'I'll have a tray in my room,' Basil offered.

'Nonsense,' said Barbara. 'I want to show off my smart London brother – if you can find something fit to wear. Anyway, I've already given the order to Cook, and a tray in your room saves nobody trouble. Much easier to put you in at the table.'

She came into the bathroom later when he was in the bath, and sat on the rim to talk to him, as she had often done in years past when they were both living at home. He noticed that her pregnancy was beginning to show, and tried to avert his eyes from the swelling because it embarrassed him. She seemed to him altogether too young and too much like his Babsy to be pregnant with another man's child.

'So what are you really doing here?' she asked him, when there had been some desultory chat about Christmas and trains.

So he told her about Gloria. 'And now she's gone to The Pines, laden with presents, for horrid old Cedric and the even horrider child, for Christmas, and I can see it's going to be the same every year. Off she goes, leaving me all alone, and I *hate* it!'

Barbara was trying not to look shocked, because he would accuse her of being a provincial if she did, but she couldn't help saying, 'Oh, Basil, it's awful!'

He gave her a grateful look. 'I'm glad you understand! I know I shouldn't be jealous but I can't help it. I hate thinking of her with them. She says she doesn't love Cedric any more, but why doesn't she get rid of him if that's true? She doesn't have to go running off to him every Christmas and Easter. And giving dinner parties with him in London. When she tells me she can't see me at the weekend I know what's happening and I just want to kill him!' He raised wet, clenched fists.

'Sit forward, I'll wash your back for you,' Barbara said. It was a way for him not to see her expression. She soaped the sponge and began to move it over his lean, young-man's back in wide, slow circles, hoping it would soothe his agitation and give her some idea of what to say. She was not so innocent that she didn't know married people sometimes had affairs – particularly fashionable London people – but it was still wrong. And that her own brother should be mixed up in it! Thank Heaven the parents didn't know. He had had the sense not to let it out to them, at least.

But then her affection for him pushed uppermost in her mind. Poor Basil, to be left behind every time there was a special occasion. It must hurt so. Yet she ought not to encourage him. 'Well, really, you know,' she said, trying to find something neutral, 'a married woman has certain obligations.'

He made an explosive but muted comment along the lines of 'married be damned'.

'Does she love you?' she asked next.

'Of course she does. I think so. She says she does.' Basil raised his head from the steam and looked at her with canine melancholy. 'If she loves me, why does she treat me so badly?'

'It doesn't *sound* as if she treats you badly. The flat, and the clothes, and the presents—'

'But I *love* her,' he cried. 'I love her so much. I just want to be with her all the time. And she goes off and sees people and goes to work and to the bloody old Pines as if she doesn't miss me at all, when I miss her *every single moment* I'm not with her.'

Barbara was relieved by these words, which proved he had the right instincts and wasn't just toying with the woman. 'Would you like me to wash your hair?' she asked tenderly. He grunted, and she took it as a yes. His hair, like hers, was thick, dark, glossy, and with just the right amount of natural curl. They were very lucky with their hair, she thought, as she washed it, digging her fingers well in to massage his scalp. He liked the feeling, and began to relax.

'Well, it seems to me,' she said tentatively, 'that there's nothing you can do about it, so you might as well make the best of things and have a nice Christmas here with us. No use kicking against the pricks, Bozzy darling.'

'Darling Babsy, I can't accuse myself of ever having kicked against a prick.' He grinned at last. 'Golly, I'm glad I had you to run to. I'd have gone nuts at Aunt Molly's.'

'Does Aunt Molly know about – about Gloria?' she asked, unwilling to speak the name out loud.

'*Idiot!* Of course she doesn't. She'd tell the Aged Ps if she knew.'

'Don't call me an idiot – *beast*!'

'Half-wit, then, is that better? Ow! Ouch! I've got soap in my eyes!'

'Serves you right!'

A certain amount of splashing followed, and a lot of giggling. They looked at each other and smiled affectionately. They really were very alike, so much so that many people had thought they were twins. Each saw his own face looking back, and felt contentment.

'I'm glad you came,' Barbara said.

'Me too,' said Basil.

That evening he joined their dinner party dressed in day clothes, which had to be explained to the dinner-jacketed and evening-dressed guests, who looked put out by such informality. Barbara was nervous, and chirruped rather, trying to keep things going, wishing Freddie, nice as he was, was more of a chatterer. Basil plunged into the breach to rescue his sister, drank too much, and talked loudly and rather too outrageously about London society; and when his comments didn't elicit the laughter or admiring looks he felt they should have, he grew more outrageous to compensate. The worthy burghers of Petersfield didn't know what to make of him. It was not, all things considered, a successful evening.

CHAPTER TWENTY-TWO

Barbara had put a call through to Aunt Molly's flat as soon as Basil had gone upstairs for his bath, to let her, and therefore their parents, know that Basil was with her. Fortunately the three minutes were up before Molly could suggest calling either Helen or Jack to the telephone, and Barbara made that the excuse for ringing off with a hasty 'Wish everyone a merry Christmas from us all.'

Helen was disappointed not to see her boy, and cross on Barbara's behalf that she had been put-upon, but Molly said Barbara had seemed very happy to have him, and Jack put his arm round her shoulders and said, 'Best to let sleeping Basils lie. Don't let it spoil Christmas for us.' He was privately rather glad Basil would not be there, for there was no doubt the boy drank too much whenever he had the chance, and said things he ought not when he did. Christmas with him in the house would have kept Jack on tenterhooks; it was much more peaceful this way.

He was in a very happy frame of mind, these days. It was grand to be back with the old firm, and to find so many familiar faces still there, including engineer Fred Sigrist, with whom he had developed some of the earliest models. The works at Canbury Road had hardly changed, except that metal presses, millers and lathes were replacing the old wood-working machinery.

Development of the fighter had gone ahead rapidly since

August. Jack had made a valuable contribution, and not only with the retractable landing gear. The design of the aircraft was to give good all-round visibility to the pilot, to which end the cockpit was mounted high on the fuselage, giving the aeroplane a distinctive hump-backed profile. Getting into the cockpit was a problem, which Jack solved by designing a retractable stirrup, mounted below the trailing edge of the port wing. This was linked to a spring-loaded, hinged flap, which covered a handhold on the fuselage, just behind the cockpit. When the flap was shut, the foot-step retracted into the fuselage, leaving a smooth, aerodynamic surface.

The prototype was ready by October, and the parts were transported by road to Brooklands and put together in the Hawker assembly shed on the 23rd, after which there followed two weeks of ground testing and taxi trials. On the 6th of November she was ready for her test flight, with George Bulman, the firm's chief test pilot, taking her up. Jack was delighted to be allowed to take some of the test flights. Tom said his experience would be invaluable in spotting anything that could be improved for the pilot in combat.

'She handles like a dream,' was Jack's verdict. Stability, manoeuvrability and a steady gun platform, together with the ease of production of the simple design, would make the new aircraft a valuable addition to the RAF. It was to be called the Hurricane – a pleasing alliteration with Hawker, Jack thought.

There were still more test flights to carry out and some modification to be made, but Tom had said the Hurricane should be going into production some time in 1936, and that a new factory and airfield might have to be acquired to handle the orders. Already some Hawker production had been moved to Hucclecote, to the Gloster works, which Hawker had taken over. That was where Violet's son Henry worked, of course. Jack had been down there and met the youngster, who seemed to have something like a hero-worship of him – a touch embarrassing, but still rather gratifying. He had spoken to him encouragingly, glad to see him dedicating his talents to aircraft design. They needed all the bright new people they could get in the business.

Already, even before the Hurricane was in production, Hawker were thinking ahead to a larger fighter-bomber that would be needed if there was another war. Sydney Camm, the chief designer, had started sketching ideas on odd pieces of paper, often asking Jack for his opinion. Camm had been too young to fly during the war; sometimes he seemed almost wistful about the fact. 'But having you here is the next best thing,' he said.

Jack and Helen had been invited to spend Christmas with the Sopwiths (Tom had remarried and the couple had had a son, Tommy, in 1933) but they had already accepted the invitation from Molly and Vivian. Jack was sorry not to have the chance of talking aeroplanes non-stop over several days of leisure, but another part of him was glad there was no likelihood of his old friend being exposed to Basil. Tom remembered him only as a very pretty baby: the present reality would be a shock. Even Helen agreed that Basil was more lovable in absence, these days.

'The sooner that boy gets married, the better,' was Jack's final verdict on the matter.

Richard hadn't been able to get to Chelmsford House on Christmas Eve. It was a night when a very large number of chauffeured cars had been ordered, and every driver was needed; he didn't finish work until after three, so he went home and fell into his bed for a few hours, before heading off to Pall Mall in time for a late breakfast.

Christmas Day was full of planned activity, the dinner itself, present-giving, church, carol singing, so he waited until Boxing Day – a more leisurely day in Town, where there was no hunt to attend – to drop his bombshell. People came down to breakfast at different times, as the spirit moved them, and when everyone was at the table, at various stages of ingestion or digestion, he put down his coffee cup and said, 'I've got some news. Mama, this will please you in particular, I know.' All eyes turned to him enquiringly. 'I'm engaged to be married.'

The first reaction was smiling, the first comments congratulations. Charlotte and Milo exchanged a glance: this would take the attention away from them, hers said.

'My dear boy, I'm so happy for you,' Violet said. 'Who is she? I had no idea you were interested in anyone. Do we know her?'

'No, but you've heard me talk about her, I'm sure. It's Cynthia Nevinson.'

Violet looked blank as she tried to tie the name into a memory. 'No, I don't think I remember your talking of her. Do we know her people? How did you meet her?'

'Mother, dear,' Richard said affectionately, 'your memory! Nevinson is the name of my distinguished employer. Samuel Nevinson, proprietor of Mayfair Motors.'

'Well, darling, how was I supposed to know that?' Violet said; and then the import caught up with her. 'This Cynthia Nevinson . . .'

'Is his daughter, yes,' Richard said.

Robert choked on something, and spluttered into his napkin, though whether it was mere chance, or emotion, Richard didn't know.

Violet looked bewildered. 'But – but how?' was all she managed to get out.

Avis took over from her. 'How did this come about?' he asked smoothly. 'We had no idea you were fond of the lady.'

'Oh, it's been a slow development,' Richard said. 'But the thing is, Samuel is not in the best of health, and Hannah – that's Mrs Nevinson – wants him to stop working so hard.

He hinted quite some time ago about taking on a partner to ease the load, and it's all come together quite suddenly. I am to marry Cynthia and become an equal partner with Samuel, and his share is to pass to Cynthia on his death, so that the whole company can go to our son, assuming we have one.'

'Oh, it's just like a fairy tale,' Charlotte said, 'where the king gives the hero who saves them half his kingdom and the princess's hand in marriage.'

Richard smiled at her. 'I'm sure that's exactly what was in Samuel's mind when he said it,' he agreed.

'I don't know much about this business of yours,' Oliver said. 'Is it a big one?'

'It's getting bigger,' Richard said, turning to him gratefully, away from his mother's blank look. 'Samuel and I have been expanding into new ventures, the biggest of which is the accompanied holidays. There's enormous scope there – people are terribly keen to go abroad, and we're building up contacts all over France. Cynthia's handling most of that side of the business, with her mother's help, but Hannah wants to step back and have a few years of peace and quiet with Samuel, so we'll take over from her there as well. It's certainly a big enough concern now to support us all, and I think Nevinson's Holidays is going to be much the larger part of the business in time. It seems to me there's no limit to how far we can expand it.'

'Unless there's another war,' Kit remarked.

But Violet had found her voice. 'Are you serious about this?'

Robert had also recovered from his choking. 'Marrying this girl to get hold of this paltry business? It's preposterous.'

Emma spoke up. 'Now, Robert, Richard didn't say that was why he was marrying her.'

'He's never said a word to any of us about her until now,' Robert said.

Charlotte was hot to her brother's defence. 'He loves her – don't you, Richard? He wouldn't marry someone he didn't love.'

'But who are they,' Violet said, 'these Nevinsons? We don't know them. Where do they come from?'

'From Poland, originally,' Richard said serenely. 'Hannah's maiden name was Abramowicz, and her parents and Samuel's both came over to England last century.'

'You mean to say they're—?' Robert began.

'I'm sure they're very nice people,' Avis said hastily.

'Perhaps they may be,' Violet said, turning to him, 'but one doesn't marry people because they're nice.'

'Well, I think nowadays one does,' Kit said. 'The old rules all got washed away with the war, didn't they?'

'Not all of them,' Violet said. 'Look at you and Emma.'

'I'd have married Emma whoever she was.'

'And I'd have married you, darling, if you were a chimney-sweeper's son,' Emma replied mischievously, for her own father had been just that.

'Well, Mummy dear,' Richard said, with a hint of steel under his always-pleasant voice, 'I had hoped for a little more congratulation when I broke my news, but I'm sure you'll get used to the idea. Cynthia is a splendid girl, and she'll make a splendid wife. And she's very keen to have babies, so she'll present you with the gaggle of grandchildren you've long been wanting.'

'It's *Robert* who has to have children,' Violet corrected him, but it only made him laugh.

'Yes,' Robert said, 'you might think of me. Very pleasant for someone in my position to have in-laws of that sort.'

'Of what sort?' Richard asked dangerously.

Verena gave a meaning cough, and Violet shook herself, sat up straight and stitched a smile onto her face. They had been guilty of quarrelling over the breakfast table in someone else's house – a shocking breach of manners. 'We'll talk about it some other time,' she said. 'Verena, what do you have planned for us today?'

But though Violet would not speak any more about it, and slapped Robert down very sharply when he tried to revive the subject, the atmosphere remained tense. Charlotte felt very sorry for Richard. She wasn't sure if he really loved Cynthia Nevinson or was settling for a comfortable life – she hoped the former – but whichever it was he surely deserved the support of his family. He had brought on himself exactly the storm she had feared would break on her own head when the fact of Milo's existence became known. As it happened, that storm had passed over her, since Milo had turned out not to be a male version of Cynthia Nevinson after all, but someone her mother could approve of.

Finding herself alone with Richard before luncheon, she asked him whether he really loved Cynthia.

He gave her a half-humorous, half-exasperated look. 'What on earth does it matter?'

'It matters to me,' she said. 'I want my brother to be happy.'

'Did you know Robert is courting a very plain girl called Joan Whittington who happens to be the niece of the Earl of Duncrammond, and who has connections to the Guinness family?'

'No, I didn't,' Charlotte said. 'Do you mean he's courting her for his career's sake?'

'I have no idea,' Richard said. 'But if he is, do you suppose our mother would mind? Of course not.'

Charlotte faltered. 'I know it sounds bad. But it isn't quite like that. She said to me that it's important that one marries someone from one's own background, whatever that may be. Because marriage goes more smoothly that way.'

'Well, my background is now Earls Court,' Richard said. 'As a younger son, I was always going to have to make my own way in life and – I'm sorry if Mama doesn't like it – that was always going to mean a change of station.'

Charlotte said, 'But do you *love* her?'

'Persistent little beast, aren't you?' he said with a smile. 'Yes, I love her, does that satisfy you?'

Charlotte examined his face, but could read nothing. She wasn't sure she believed him; but it was best that she accepted it. She gave a brisk little nod. 'In that case, I shall ride to the rescue.'

He looked alarmed. 'What are you going to do?'

'Don't worry, Dicky darling. I'm on your side,' she said, reached up to kiss his cheek, and went away.

And so, over luncheon, she announced to the assembled company that she and Milo were engaged.

'Well, that's something more like!' Robert said.

Milo gave her a surprised look, but did his part, getting up to walk round the table and kiss her, and saying to Avis, 'Perhaps I ought to have asked your permission first, sir, but I was swept away.'

'You don't need my permission,' Avis said, 'but you'd have it if you did.'

'This calls for champagne,' Oliver said. 'I had an idea when I saw you two together what was in the wind.'

Charlotte couldn't help contrasting this reception with that given to Richard, and was hurt and angry on his behalf. But he looked at her across the table and nodded and smiled, pleased to have the attention taken from him and the tense atmosphere dispersed. He really didn't care about parental or family approval. All that had been smashed to smithereens when his father had died bankrupt, leaving them at the mercy of the world. He was his own man now, and he was happy that way.

The champagne came and the glasses were lifted, and Oliver proposed, 'To Charlotte and Milo.'

Charlotte lifted her own, and said firmly, 'And to Richard and Cynthia.'

Emma and Kit joined in immediately, 'Yes, to Richard

and Cynthia,' and after the merest scintilla of hesitation, Violet repeated the toast as well. All drank it, though Robert drank without saying anything, a sort of dishonourable compromise.

Then Avis said, 'I hope you will come down for a Saturday-to-Monday after Christmas, Charlotte and Milo. And that you will come, Richard, and bring Cynthia so that we can meet her.'

Violet felt ashamed of her earlier cool reception. She had had time to think since, and had come to much the same conclusion as Richard: that as he was now middle class, that was where he must look for a wife. 'Yes,' she said, endorsing the invitation, 'and we ought to have a dinner for her parents, too. Would they come down to Tunstead, do you think? Or should it be in Town?'

Charlotte gave her mother a large and grateful smile, and Richard said, as easily as if there had never been any opposition, 'Oh, Tunstead, of course. I'm sure they'd love to see the place. And I know you'll love Cynthia when you meet her.'

'We'll arrange it, then,' Violet said. She added, 'Does Mr Nevinson shoot, do you suppose?'

'Oh, Mummy!' Charlotte said in despair; but Milo couldn't control his laughter, and after a moment everyone else was laughing too, even Violet.

Gloria was back in London by the 3rd of January and Basil hurried round as soon as he received the telephone message from the porter. She seemed as eager for him as he was for her, and they fell together in a passionate embrace that led them straight to her bedroom. Afterwards, as they lay languorously entwined, she asked, perhaps unwisely, 'Did you have a nice time over Christmas?'

'No! It was absolutely bloody. I went to my sister's.'

'I thought you liked your sister.'

'What's that to do with it? I wanted to be with you.'

'Oh, Basil, don't start that again.'

'I can't help it. I want to be with you all the time. Why do you have to go to the bloody old Pines?'

'You know why,' she said, a trifle wearily.

'Well, why can't you divorce him and marry me?'

She laughed. It wasn't much of a laugh, and it was more tired than amused, but it hurt his feelings. He flounced out of bed, reminding her that, despite his prowess as a lover, he was only just twenty, and his dignity was tender. 'If you find that so ridiculous . . .' he began.

'I wasn't laughing at you, darling,' she said, 'just the thought that it would be as easy as that.'

'Why not? I don't see why it shouldn't be.'

'I know you don't. You just have to believe me that it wouldn't be. It would be horrid and painful, like a long-drawn-out motor accident, and we'd both be left wounded. Now do drop the subject, and let's talk about something more pleasant. Come back to bed, Basil darling.'

He resisted a moment longer, but in truth it was cold, standing naked near the window, so he returned, a little sulkily, got under the covers and they both lit cigarettes.

'What do you want to talk about?' he asked, putting her lighter back on top of his cigarette case on the bedside cabinet.

'Your birthday is on the seventeenth,' she said. He brightened. 'Which is a Friday. Now, I'm engaged that weekend, and I'm sure your family will want to see you, but how would you like to go away for a few days the following week? We can go away on Monday the twentieth, and come back on the Friday.'

He decided not to challenge her about the weekend, or ask why they had to come back on the Friday. It might take the shine off the thing. And he was being offered the best part of a week alone with her.

'Where would we go?' he asked.

569

'How about Paris? Have you ever been there?'

'No,' he said. Paris! The very word sounded naughty.

'Then I shall take pleasure in showing it to you. If we had longer, we could go down to the South of France, but it would take too long getting there and back to be worth it. We'll do that another time. At least in Paris the weather doesn't matter much. I have to be back for an important house sale in Derbyshire on the twenty-sixth.'

'Can't one of the others go for you?'

'No, darling. I have to go myself. But you can come with me, if you like.' He was placated. 'And when we're in Paris, I'll buy you some new clothes. That can be my birthday present to you.'

He knew enough about her to know that there would be a present for him on the day, as well: the clothes would be in addition. 'Tell me about Paris,' he said. 'What shall we see?'

She stubbed out her cigarette and nestled herself onto his shoulder, and told him about the Champs-Élysées and Montmartre and the Left Bank and Les Halles and Notre Dame. And after a bit he stubbed out his cigarette, too, and they made love again.

Emma was annoyed to discover that Kit had accepted an invitation for both of them to go to the Fort for a Saturday-to-Monday on the 11th of January. 'I thought you said you were going to get us out of Fort weekends?'

'No, *you* said that,' he retorted. 'I don't mind it as much as you do. And Teddy Oxenford's going to be there.'

'That's no comfort to me. You two just talk to each other.'

'Well, you're Wallis Simpson's new best friend so you can talk to her.'

'How did you get us into this?' Emma sighed.

'I was round at Bryanston Court yesterday,' he said casually, 'and Sir dropped in for cockers. He insisted on Wally going to the Fort this weekend, and I got caught up in the wake.'

'*Why* did you go to Bryanston Court?' Emma asked, exasperated. 'You must have known how it would end.'

'Well, my darling, you were out, and one must have one's cocktail somewhere. I didn't know HRH was going to arrive. And poor Wallis practically begged me to stay – didn't want to be left alone with him. It was quite funny when he asked her to the Fort because I could see she was teetering on the brink of refusing. Apparently, Ernest is furious about the trip to America, so it's a bit much if she's popping off to the Fort as well, instead of staying home and having some uxorious time with him before she goes. But of course she can't refuse the Prince. So then she asked me, and promised me Teddy if I said yes, and Sir beetled off, to make sure he didn't bump into Ernest coming home from work.'

'I shall be glad when they set off for Palm Beach. At least one will get some peace and quiet.'

'I doubt if that will come off. When the King hears about it he'll put his foot down. A trip to America is much more political than a villa in France. It can't be undertaken in that casual way.'

'I'm surprised he hasn't heard about it already,' Emma said.

'Well, apparently he hasn't been well – got a beast of a cold, poor old fellow – so he's keeping to his rooms. I dare say someone will tell him when he's better.'

As it happened, the Fort weekend was cancelled: the King's cold was so bad it prevented him from carrying out his duties, and the Prince of Wales was deputed to take his place. During the following week, Eddie called round at Manchester Square, and said the King was really very poorly.

'I don't think Wales is going to be able to take the trip,' he said, accepting a cigarette from Kit and sitting on the sofa, which he had to share with Eos. 'Frankly, the King's condition is pretty grave. The cold is settling on his chest, and at his age . . .' He shrugged.

'You mean, he might die?' Emma said in alarm.

'He hasn't long, one way or another. If he recovers this time, it will certainly leave him further weakened. The crisis could soon be upon us.'

'You mean – the Wally and David crisis?'

'Just so.' There was a brief silence, informed by the ticking of the clock and the sound of cigarette smoke being exhaled. Eddie resumed. 'I had an interesting chat with Tommy Lascelles at Sandringham over Christmas.' Alan Lascelles, always known as Tommy, was the King's assistant private secretary. 'He told me the Prince said he was keeping on his Canadian ranch as a place he could retire to. Tommy asked, "You mean for a holiday, sir?" and the Prince said, "No, I mean for good." Tommy's convinced he's planning to give up the succession, and retire into private life with Mrs Simpson. Alec Hardinge said the same – he's had hints from HRH as well, along the same lines.'

'And what do you think?' Kit asked. 'I'd have thought a Canadian ranch would be anathema to him. And I can't see Mrs S punching cows, or whatever they do on ranches.'

'I'm not sure he's desperate enough for that yet,' Eddie said thoughtfully, 'though the time may come. At the moment, I think he still believes that when the time comes he can be king in name and enjoy the riches and the power, but without doing any of the work or taking any of the responsibility. I'm pretty sure Mrs Simpson encourages him in the belief. Being American she doesn't understand the monarchy – all she knows are American millionaires, who do exactly as they like and take no denial from anyone. She thinks a king has the same freedom.'

'You may be right,' Kit said. 'It'll be a shock to their systems when they find out otherwise.'

'I hope they find out sooner rather than later,' Eddie sighed. 'It would be no bad thing if he did go to Canada and marry Mrs Simpson.'

'Aren't you forgetting *Mr* Simpson?' Emma said.

'Oh, he's a decent cove – he'd do the right thing and go to Brighton with a girl. But he'd have to get on with it before the King dies. After that, it'll be too late.'

'Once he's king, he may settle down,' Emma said.

'What – marry a princess, get an heir?' Eddie said. 'I'm not sure he's capable.'

'Oh, I say!' Kit protested, shocked not by the idea but by hearing Eddie say it. He had never discussed his theory with anyone but Emma.

'I'm sorry,' Eddie said, 'but one hears things – from more than one source.' He caught Emma and Kit exchanging a glance, and misinterpreted it. 'I'm sorry,' he said again, but to Emma this time. 'Not a subject for the drawing room.'

'Surely if he becomes king he has to marry?' she asked.

'There's no reason he shouldn't be a bachelor king. It's unusual, but there's nothing in the rule book about it. It might be the best thing – let him see out his time, with Mrs Simpson discreetly in the background. Let the country ride it out, wait for the next generation. Bertie York may not outlive him, but he has those two sweet girls. The elder one is very sensible and level-headed – the Queen adores her. I'd settle for that. The last thing we need is a constitutional crisis, with things as they are, troubles abroad, the world in turmoil – perhaps another war coming. An abdication could fatally weaken the Crown. Enough thrones fell during the last packet.'

'That's true,' said Kit. 'Do you think the country would see it that way, though? The people do so love there to be family life at the palace.'

'Oh, the people still adore him. They wouldn't want him to go. And I hope the Establishment would see sense, and agree to leave well alone.' He looked more cheerful. 'If he doesn't pass over the succession to Bertie York in the next few months, which would be my hope, I really think that would be the answer. Let him have his Mrs Simpson. After all, Edward VII had Mrs Keppel and no-one minded that.'

When Eddie had left, Emma said doubtfully, '*Would* Wallis remain in the background? Would David leave her there?'

'Oh, I think it might work out,' Kit said, ever the optimist. 'He'll be a lot busier, and without the King to disapprove of everything he does, he may calm down and let his private life settle into a routine. Wallis is right about one thing,' he added. 'Upsetting him only makes things worse. I think she could manage him all right as long as the Establishment left him alone. The power behind the throne, don't you know? It could work out very well.'

'Poor Ernest,' was Emma's comment. And then, 'Darling, *look* at the time! We have to dress for the Mountbattens. You know what Dickie's like if anyone's late.'

The Fort weekend was rescheduled for the 18th of January, but on the 16th the King's condition suddenly worsened. Mrs Simpson called on Emma at Manchester Square to tell her that the weekend was cancelled again.

'David was shooting in Windsor Great Park with Duff Cooper when a message came from the Queen,' she said, puffing nervously on a cigarette, her 'charm' bracelet rattling every time she lifted her hand. 'Apparently the King can't catch his breath, and he's sleepy and lethargic. She said David ought to propose himself for the weekend at Sandringham. He came back to Town and called in to tell me, asked me to tell everyone. He's going down first thing tomorrow morning.'

'I'm afraid he'll have a bad drive of it,' Emma said. 'It's looking like snow. Is the King in danger?'

'I don't know. I imagine the Queen would have said something if he was. If she thought it could wait until the weekend . . .' She met Emma's eyes reluctantly.

'But this could be it,' Emma suggested. She wondered how many of the difficulties ahead Mrs Simpson really foresaw.

'He has a cold. People don't die of colds,' she said stubbornly.

'But they do die eventually,' Emma said.

'We'll cross that bridge when we come to it. Anyway, it won't change anything for David and me, except to make things easier.'

The news from Sandringham was not good. Kit called in at Oliver's consulting rooms the next day, knowing he would have the latest from the royal doctors. 'The bronchial catarrh is constricting his breathing and affecting his heart, which as you know is already damaged,' Oliver said. 'He's very weak. Dawson says he's sinking and there's little chance he will rally. You have to consider his age.'

'Does the Prince know?' Kit wondered.

'I think he must,' Oliver said. 'The Kents and the Princess Royal have gone down and a Council of State is to be set up to deal with the backlog of papers waiting for the King's attention. They only ever set up a Council of State *in extremis*.'

On Sunday the 19th, the Prince drove back to London, and straight to Bryanston Court. Wallis telephoned Emma afterwards, invited herself to tea, and arrived with the news that the Prince had been on his way to see the Prime Minister. 'He's gone to tell him that the King only has a few days to live, but he had to let me know first.' There was the faintest hint of pride, Emma thought, in the last remark. 'He said the King is so weak and confused he hardly recognises anyone, and that it can't be long now. The Queen is amazingly calm, he says. It's more than I can say for him.'

'He's bound to be upset,' Emma suggested.

'It's worse than that – he's in a funk. He doesn't want to be king, Emma.' She stared through her smoke at the fire. 'You'd think after forty years he would be used to the idea, but I don't think he ever truly thought the day would come. Now it looks as though it's coming, and he's in a terrible flap. *He doesn't want to be king.*'

575

'It must be daunting. The throne is a high and lonely place.'

'I know he feels that,' Wallis said. 'He told me last night, "You are all and everything I have in life." He said we must hold tight to each other.' She sighed. 'It isn't going to be easy. I'm terribly afraid he'll go to pieces.'

'How is Ernest taking it?' Emma asked.

'He's an absolute angel,' said Wallis, 'being so kind and affectionate to me.'

Emma wondered if perhaps Mr Simpson thought he could be on the brink of having his wife back to himself. Whatever the material benefits, it must have been harder and harder for him to cope with the situation over the past year.

The following evening, the 20th of January, huge crowds gathered in front of Buckingham Palace, waiting in silence for news. Wireless bulletins were given out every quarter-hour. At nine thirty the bulletin said, 'The King's life is moving peacefully towards its close.' And at a quarter to midnight, Sir John Reith himself made the announcement on the BBC that the King had died. There was no further broadcasting, except for solemn and melancholy music. The next morning, the newspapers were black-bordered, and contained no other news. 'A Peaceful Ending at Midnight,' said the headline.

It had snowed again during the night and the streets were suitably muffled. The roofs looked startlingly white with their burden against a gunmetal sky. The guns were sounding from Hyde Park, and several churches were ringing muffled peals, a strangely gloomy sound on the flat air. Nothing stirred in the streets, not even a sparrow. Only on the pond in St James's Park a few ducks paddled, with the eternal imperviousness of ducks to all cataclysms. The ripples of their passage met the ripples caused by the guns' concussion, blended, and died away.

Both Houses of Parliament were summoned early in the

morning, before seven o'clock, to swear allegiance to the new King. Oliver called in at Manchester Square on his way there, and Kit received him in his dressing-gown.

'I'm sorry to get you up, but I had to speak to you.'

'That's all right. I wasn't asleep,' Kit said. 'I'm dressed under here, all but my jacket. I have to go to the House as well, you know. I've sent for some coffee. You look as though you need some.' Oliver was looking round the drawing room, with an air of shock, and he added, 'It's a thing, isn't it, when the King dies, even if you were expecting it? Takes you all aback.'

'That's what I came to talk to you about. I have to tell someone. But it must be an absolute secret. You must promise me not even to tell Emma.'

'If you insist,' Kit said, in surprise. 'But what is it, old man?'

'You and I, we were both doctors during the war. We saw a lot of things.' He shook his head. 'I keep thinking, what would my mother say? I'm remembering her here, in this room; I can almost hear her voice. She'd be shocked beyond anything.'

'Shocked about what? You're not making any sense,' Kit said kindly.

'The King,' Oliver said. His eyes came back to Kit with a look of raw pain. 'He didn't die naturally. That's what I have to tell you. It's burning a hole in me, Kit. I had it from Keppner, Dawson's assistant. Dawson injected him with a fatal dose of morphine and cocaine at eleven last night so that he would die before midnight. He thought the notice would look better coming first in the quality morning papers, rather than the evening tabloids.'

'But – good God, man, do you know what you're saying?' Kit was aghast. 'What about the Queen? And the princes? Surely they would have said something?'

'I understand he told them it was a mission of mercy not to artificially extend the King's life when he was clearly dying.

577

Whether they understood what he meant to do I can't tell you. But there's a difference between not artificially extending a life and actively ending it. You know what it is, don't you?'

'He shortened the King's life by a few hours,' Kit said awkwardly. 'Perhaps it isn't so terrible.'

'You know it is,' Oliver said. 'It's murder.' The word was out, ugly on the quiet air. Kit felt the hair stand up on his scalp. Oliver went on, 'And worse than that, it's regicide. He was the Lord's Anointed. It's for God to determine when a king dies, not for any man. To kill a king is the worst crime of all.'

'Oliver, old man,' Kit said, laying a hand on his arm. 'I think you're making too much of it.' It was not that he didn't feel it, but that he couldn't bear it.

Oliver pushed the hand off and gave him a bitter look. 'My God, you've changed,' he said. 'I know you're not prac- tising any more, but you're still a doctor. You took the oath. How can you take such a thing lightly?'

'I don't, but we don't really know the truth of it, do we? You only have Keppner's word. He may have been mistaken.'

Oliver shook his head and turned away. 'I must go.'

'Don't you want some coffee? We can go together.'

'No,' he said. 'I have to walk. I need the movement.' He turned back to say, 'It's a terrible way to begin a new reign. There can be no luck to it now.'

The moment the King died, Queen Mary, with the rigid sense of duty that had sustained her all her public life, took the Prince of Wales's hand and kissed it, and the Duke of Kent, who was standing beside her, followed suit. It was that – Wallis later told Emma – that had overset him. It had made him realise at last that the instant his father drew his last breath, he, David, was king. There was no process, no transitional period, no if and no but. He could not get out of it. He was king, and the realisation drove him into a frenzy of grief and fear. He became hysterical, cried loudly, kept clutching the

Queen as though she might save him. Alec Hardinge said afterwards to Eddie that his emotion was 'frantic and unreasonable'.

He rang Mrs Simpson several times through the night, and she talked soothingly to him, promising to stand by him and take care of him. The next day the new King – he was taking the name of Edward, and so would be Edward VIII – flew up to London with the Duke of York, the first time a British monarch had travelled in an aeroplane, for the Accession Privy Council and the proclamation. By the time he arrived, Mrs Simpson was already installed in St James's Palace, to be where he needed her. He had a speech to make to the Council, and he practised it by walking up and down in her room and saying it to her until he – and she – had it off by heart.

On the following day, the proclamation took place of the new King, by Garter King of Arms in Friary Court, and Emma watched from a window in company with Duff and Diana Cooper. Kit was elsewhere in the palace with the lords. The trumpeters in scarlet and gold came out onto the Proclamation Gallery, the fanfare sounded, and a twenty-five-gun salute began on Horse Guards' Parade as the herald began to read the words, many of them drowned by the percussion.

Diana Cooper nudged Emma and said, 'I knew it! I knew he'd sneak her in somehow. Look across there, at that window. It's Mrs Simpson.'

It was a prominent window in the main façade, and in full view of the world's press, gathered below with their newsreel cameras.

'He was bound to want her to watch,' Emma said.

'It's unseemly,' Diana said. 'And look at her – smirking like that. She's not taking it seriously at all. It's just a game to her. "English customs, my, how quaint!"'

Mrs Simpson, in a black fur coat and a close black hat, was chatting away to someone unseen by them, with a smile on her face. She laughed, looking over her shoulder, gesturing, evidently being vivacious for someone's benefit.

Then Diana drew a breath and clutched Emma's arm. 'Oh, my God, look at that! Duff, do you see?'

One of the shadowy forms behind Mrs Simpson had moved forward, stood beside her, looking out, and in doing so became solid, recognisable. It was the King. Against all custom and precedent, he was attending his own proclamation. Mrs Simpson said something to him and laughed again, and he smiled in response.

'This is just the kind of thing I hoped so much he wouldn't do,' Duff groaned. 'It causes so much criticism, and does so much harm. Already people are talking about her, and criticising him. What if it gets into the papers? It'll cause a frightful stink.'

Emma was as disapproving, but not surprised. It was a childish thing to do, not to be able to resist the urge to see yourself proclaimed, and a tactless beginning to a new reign, to break with precedent so blatantly; but if Mrs Simpson was there at the window, of course he would want to be too.

Afterwards, going out towards the Mall to look for a taxi, Emma bumped into Wallis, standing in the doorway adjusting her gloves. 'Did you see it?' she greeted Emma cheerfully. 'So picturesque! It's the kind of thing only this country does. Those heralds looked exactly like a pack of cards! It brought it home to me how very different the King's life is going to be from now on.'

'I hope the King understands that as well,' Emma couldn't help saying.

Wallis gave her a sharp look, but decided against quarrelling. 'Are you going home?'

'Yes. I shall look for a taxi.'

'Oh, don't bother. David's sending the car round for me to take me to Bryanston Court. He's got to go back to

Sandringham. We go practically past your door – we can drop you off.'

No, Emma thought, whatever she says, I don't believe she does think it will be different. To her he's not the King of the United Kingdom of Great Britain and Ireland, its Colonies and Dependencies, Emperor of India and Defender of the Faith. He's just David.

Polly received a letter from Lennie in January, to say that his mother-in-law had died quietly in her sleep on the 30th of December.

Her life was painful to her after Beth died. She had nothing to live for, and one cannot wish her back. It was a gentle release to one who has suffered so much. We had the funeral on the 4th of January and her coffin was placed next to Beth's in the Hollywood Memorial Park Cemetery.

I feel now that a chapter of my life is closed. Beth seemed close to me as long as Marion was alive, but now she has gone, and I find it difficult to remember things about her – the colour of her hair, the sound of her voice, how she walked. Everything changes, I know, and it's wrong to surrender to memories instead of getting on with life, but I feel a little resentful that my mind should let her go so easily. Yet I know it's what she would have wanted. She wouldn't have wanted me to mourn her for ever.

So I feel that a change of scene would be the best thing possible for me. I want to get away from Hollywood for a while, and of course the one place that I really want to be is at Morland Place, and near you. May I come, Polly? Does your generous offer still stand? It was made in the heat of the moment and you may have regretted it in the cold light of day. If so, you have only to drop me a hint. But if you still want to see me, I can promise I will come with a heart full of gratitude and affection. It will take me some weeks to wind things up here, in order to allow me an absence of several months. It needn't all be at Morland Place, I hasten to add! I expect you have a busy life and I must fit in with that. But I feel it's not worth coming so far for a short time, so I shall plan on being away at least three months, perhaps more. Perhaps I shall never go back.

There are great things afoot in the world of radio and – my hobby, now don't laugh! – television. I should like to explore the advances made in these fields in Europe, and hope also to expand my business into England. Why shouldn't every English person have the same right to buy a Manning's radio as we Yankees? And, needless to say, to increase my fortune by a little bit!

Write to me as soon as possible, dear Polly, to say if a visit would be welcome. If I may come, I would plan to leave here around the beginning of March and, the journey taking ten days or two weeks, would be with you by the middle of the month.

God bless you, dear.

Ever your loving cousin,

Lennie

Polly read the letter several times, with a painful squeezed feeling in her heart. To see him again, dear Lennie, who had always loved and understood her, the one person to whom she could always tell everything! She wondered if he had changed a lot since she had last seen him. She supposed he must have – marriage and widowing would leave their marks; but her mind conjured him up as she had last seen him in New York, when Alec was a new baby, when she had got the letter from Jessie begging her to come home. He had parted from her bravely, not allowing his unhappiness to

582

show, but she had known how he hurt. Of course, there had been no Beth then. At that time he had never loved anyone but her.

She wanted so badly to see him. She saw, in retrospect, that the two unfortunate mistakes of the heart she had suffered since she came home, John Burton and Charles Eastlake, fell into a pattern. She had loved them because they reminded her just a little of Lennie: they had seemed to have some of his qualities, had seemed to promise her the security and understanding she had always had from him. She had been wrong about them – shamingly wrong – but it was only now that she understood why.

She wrote back immediately, telling him to come as soon as he could and for as long as he liked; and then went to find James – still at home and waiting for a summons from Charles Bedaux – to tell him the good news. On the way, looking for him, she came across the butler, Barlow, and said, 'We must have the North Bedroom redecorated. That paper is terribly shabby. And the drapes are such a gloomy colour. See to it, will you?'

'Yes, madam,' Barlow said, with discernible surprise.

'Have someone send for the decorator to come, and bring wallpaper samples and colour swatches. Right away, please. I want the work started without delay. I'm expecting an important visitor in March.'

'Yes, madam.'

In March, she thought. *I shall see him in March.* She strode across the great hall, a pack of dogs at her heels and a smile on her face.